Charles V. Bassi

KOSHU - KAIDO ROAD

TOKAIDŌ ROAD

HONSHU

KWANTO
(THE EIGHT PROVINCES)

Kozuke   Shimozuke

Hidachi

SHINANO

Kigahara

Musashi   MUSASHI

TOKAIDŌ ROAD

Sagami   Yedo (Tokyo)

Anjiro   Yokohama   Shimosa

KAI

Kazusa
Awa

IZU   MT FUJI   SAGAMI

SURUGA

Mishima   Odawara

Numazu

Atami

OCEAN

Yokose

IZU   Anjiro

SCALE

0   10   20   30   40

SHŌGUN

SHŌGUN

A NOVEL OF JAPAN

BY

JAMES CLAVELL

VOLUME 1

ATHENEUM   NEW YORK

For two seafarers, Captains, Royal Navy,

who loved their ships more than their women

—as was expected of them.

AUTHOR'S NOTE

I would like to thank all those here, in Asia, and in Europe—the living and the dead—who helped to make this novel possible.

Lookout Mountain, California

SHŌGUN

PROLOGUE

THE gale tore at him and he felt its bite deep within and he knew that if they did not make landfall in three days they would all be dead. Too many deaths on this voyage, he thought, I'm Pilot-Major of a dead fleet. One ship left out of five—eight and twenty men from a crew of one hundred and seven and now only ten can walk and the rest near death and our Captain-General one of them. No food, almost no water and what there is, brackish and foul.

His name was John Blackthorne and he was alone on deck but for the bowsprit lookout—Salamon the mute—who huddled in the lee, searching the sea ahead.

The ship heeled in a sudden squall and Blackthorne held on to the arm of the seachair that was lashed near the wheel on the quarterdeck until she righted, timbers squealing. She was the *Erasmus,* two hundred and sixty tons, a three-masted trader-warship out of Rotterdam, armed with twenty cannon and sole survivor of the first expeditionary force sent from the Netherlands to ravage the enemy in the New World. The first Dutch ships ever to breach the secrets of the Strait of Magellan. Four hundred and ninety-six men, all volunteers. All Dutch except for three Englishmen—two pilots, one officer. Their orders: to plunder Spanish and Portuguese possessions in the New World and put them to the torch; to open up permanent trading concessions; to discover new islands in the Pacific Ocean that could serve as permanent bases and to claim the territory for the Netherlands; and, within three years, to come home again.

Protestant Netherlands had been at war with Catholic Spain for more than four decades, struggling to throw off the yoke of their hated Spanish masters. The Netherlands, sometimes called Holland, Dutchland, or the Low Countries, were still legally part of the Spanish Empire. England, their only allies, the first country in Christendom to break with the Papal Court at Rome and become Protestant some seventy-odd years ago, had also been warring on Spain for the last twenty years, and openly allied with the Dutch for a decade.

The wind freshened even more and the ship lurched. She was riding under bare poles but for storm tops'ls. Even so the tide and the storm bore her strongly toward the darkening horizon.

There's more storm there, Blackthorne told himself, and more reefs and more shoals. And unknown sea. Good. I've set myself against the sea all my life and I've always won. I always will.

First English pilot ever to get through Magellan's Pass. Yes, the first —and first pilot ever to sail these Asian waters, apart from a few bastard Portuguese or motherless Spaniards who still think they own the world. First Englishman in these seas. . . .

So many firsts. Yes. And so many deaths to win them.

Again he tasted the wind and smelled it, but there was no hint of land. He searched the ocean but it was dull gray and angry. Not a fleck of seaweed or splash of color to give a hint of a sanding shelf. He saw the spire of another reef far on the starboard quarter but that told him nothing. For a month now outcrops had threatened them, but never a sight of land. This ocean's endless, he thought. Good. That's what you were trained for—to sail the unknown sea, to chart it and come home again. How many days from home? One year and eleven months and two days. The last landfall Chile, one hundred and thirty-three days aft, across the ocean Magellan had first sailed eighty years ago called Pacific.

Blackthorne was famished and his mouth and body ached from the scurvy. He forced his eyes to check the compass course and his brain to calculate an approximate position. Once the plot was written down in his rutter—his sea manual—he would be safe in this speck of the ocean. And if he was safe, his ship was safe and then together they might find the Japans, or even the Christian King Prester John and his Golden Empire that legend said lay to the north of Cathay, wherever Cathay was.

And with my share of the riches I'll sail on again, westward for home, first English pilot ever to circumnavigate the globe, and I'll never leave home again. Never. By the head of my son!

The cut of the wind stopped his mind from wandering and kept him awake. To sleep now would be foolish. You'll never wake from that sleep, he thought, and stretched his arms to ease the cramped muscles in his back and pulled his cloak tighter around him. He saw that the sails were trimmed and the wheel lashed secure. The bow lookout was awake. So patiently he settled back and prayed for land.

"Go below, Pilot. I take this watch if it pleases you." The third mate, Hendrik Specz, was pulling himself up the gangway, his face gray with fatigue, eyes sunken, skin blotched and sallow. He leaned heavily against the binnacle to steady himself, retching a little. "Blessed Lord Jesus, piss on the day I left Holland."

"Where's the mate, Hendrik?"

"In his bunk. He can't get out of his *scheit voll* bunk. And he won't —not this side of Judgment Day."

"And the Captain-General?"

"Moaning for food and water." Hendrik spat. "I tell him I roast him a capon and bring it on a silver platter with a bottle of brandy to wash it down. *Scheit-huis! Coot!*"

"Hold your tongue!"

"I will, Pilot. But he's a maggot-eaten fool and we'll be dead because of him." The young man retched and brought up mottled phlegm. "Blessed Lord Jesus help me!"

"Go below. Come back at dawn."

Hendrik lowered himself painfully into the other seachair. "There's the reek of death below. I take the watch if it pleases you. What's the course?"

"Wherever the wind takes us."

"Where's the landfall you promised us? Where's the Japans—where is it, I ask?"

"Ahead."

"Always ahead! *Gottimhimmel,* it wasn't in our orders to sail into the unknown. We should be back home by now, safe, with our bellies full, not chasing St. Elmo's fire."

"Go below or hold your tongue."

Sullenly Hendrik looked away from the tall bearded man. Where are we now? he wanted to ask. Why can't I see the secret rutter? But he knew you don't ask those questions of a pilot, particularly this one. Even so, he thought, I wish I was as strong and healthy as when I left Holland. Then I wouldn't wait. I'd smash your gray-blue eyes now and stamp that maddening half-smile off your face and send you to the hell you deserve. Then I'd be Captain-Pilot and we'd have a Netherlander running the ship—not a foreigner—and the secrets would be safe for us. Because soon we'll be at war with you English. We want the same thing: to command the sea, to control all trade routes, to dominate the New World, and to strangle Spain.

"Perhaps there is no Japans," Hendrik muttered suddenly. "It's *Gottbewonden* legend."

"It exists. Between latitudes thirty and forty north. Now hold your tongue or go below."

"There's death below, Pilot," Hendrik muttered and put his eyes ahead, letting himself drift.

Blackthorne shifted in his seachair, his body hurting worse today. You're luckier than most, he thought, luckier than Hendrik. No, not luckier. More careful. You conserved your fruit while the others consumed theirs carelessly. Against your warnings. So now your scurvy is still mild whereas the others are constantly hemorrhaging, their bowels diarrhetic, their eyes sore and rheumy, and their teeth lost or loose in their heads. Why is it men never learn?

He knew they were all afraid of him, even the Captain-General, and that most hated him. But that was normal, for it was the pilot who commanded at sea; it was he who set the course and ran the ship, he who brought them from port to port.

Any voyage today was dangerous because the few navigational charts that existed were so vague as to be useless. And there was absolutely no way to fix longitude.

"Find how to fix longitude and you're the richest man in the world," his old teacher, Alban Caradoc, had said. "The Queen, God bless her 'll give you ten thousand pound and a dukedom for the answer to the riddle. The dung-eating Portuguese'll give you more—a golden galleon. And the motherless Spaniards'll give you twenty! Out of sight of land you're always lost, lad." Caradoc had paused and shaken his head sadly at him as always. "You're lost, lad. Unless . . ."

"Unless you have a rutter!" Blackthorne had shouted happily, knowing that he had learned his lessons well. He was thirteen then and had already been apprenticed a year to Alban Caradoc, pilot and shipwright, who had become the father he had lost, who had never beaten him but taught him and the other boys the secrets of shipbuilding and the intimate way of the sea.

A rutter was a small book containing the detailed observation of a pilot *who had been there before.* It recorded magnetic compass courses between ports and capes, headlands and channels. It noted the sounding and depths and color of the water and the nature of the seabed. It set down the *how we got there and how we got back:* how many days on a special tack, the pattern of the wind, when it blew and from where, what currents to expect and from where; the time of storms and the time of fair winds; where to careen the ship and where to water; where there were friends and where foes; shoals, reefs, tides, havens; at best, *everything* necessary for a safe voyage.

The English, Dutch, and French had rutters for their own waters, but the waters of the rest of the world had been sailed only by captains from Portugal and Spain, and these two countries considered all rutters secret. Rutters that revealed the seaways to the New World or unraveled the mysteries of the Pass of Magellan and the Cape of Good Hope—both Portuguese discoveries—and thence the seaways to Asia were guarded as national treasures by the Portuguese and Spanish, and sought after with equal ferocity by their Dutch and English enemies.

But a rutter was only as good as the pilot who wrote it, the scribe who hand-copied it, the very rare printer who printed it, or the scholar who translated it. A rutter could therefore contain errors. Even deliberate ones. A pilot never knew for certain *until he had been there himself*. At least once.

At sea the pilot was leader, sole guide, and final arbiter of the ship and her crew. Alone he commanded from the quarterdeck.

That's heady wine, Blackthorne told himself. And once sipped, never to be forgotten, always to be sought, and always necessary. That's one of the things that keep you alive when others die.

He got up and relieved himself in the scuppers. Later the sand ran out of the hourglass by the binnacle and he turned it and rang the ship's bell.

"Can you stay awake, Hendrik?"

"Yes. Yes, I believe so."

"I'll send someone to replace the bow lookout. See he stands in the wind and not in the lee. That'll keep him sharp and awake." For a moment he wondered if he should turn the ship into the wind and heave to for the night but he decided against it, went down the companionway, and opened the fo'c'sle door. The companionway led into the crew's quarters. The cabin ran the width of the ship and had bunks and hammock space for a hundred and twenty men. The warmth surrounded him and he was grateful for it and ignored the ever present stench from the bilges below. None of the twenty-odd men moved from his bunk.

"Get aloft, Maetsukker," he said in Dutch, the lingua franca of the Low Countries which he spoke perfectly, along with Portuguese and Spanish and Latin.

"I'm near death," the small, sharp-featured man said, cringing deeper into the bunk. "I'm sick. Look, the scurvy's taken all my teeth. Lord Jesus help us, we'll all perish! If it wasn't for you we'd all be home by now, safe! I'm a merchant. I'm not a seaman. I'm not part of the crew. . . . Take someone else. Johann there's—" He screamed as Blackthorne jerked him out of the bunk and hurled him against the door. Blood flecked his mouth and he was stunned. A brutal kick in his side brought him out of his stupor.

"You get your face aloft and stay there till you're dead or we make landfall."

The man pulled the door open and fled in agony.

Blackthorne looked at the others. They stared back at him. "How are you feeling, Johann?"

"Good enough, Pilot. Perhaps I'll live."

Johann Vinck was forty-three, the chief gunner and bosun's mate, the oldest man aboard. He was hairless and toothless, the color of aged oak and just as strong. Six years ago he had sailed with Blackthorne on the ill-fated search for the Northeast Passage, and each man knew the measure of the other.

"At your age most men are already dead, so you're ahead of us all." Blackthorne was thirty-six.

Vinck smiled mirthlessly. "It's the brandy, Pilot, that an' fornication an' the saintly life I've led."

No one laughed. Then someone pointed at a bunk. "Pilot, the bosun's dead."

"Then get the body aloft! Wash it and close his eyes! You, you, and you!"

The men were quickly out of their bunks this time and together they half dragged, half carried the corpse from the cabin.

"Take the dawn watch, Vinck. And Ginsel, you're bow lookout."

"Yes sir."

Blackthorne went back on deck.

He saw that Hendrik was still awake, that the ship was in order. The relieved lookout, Salamon, stumbled past him, more dead than alive, his eyes puffed and red from the cut of the wind. Blackthorne crossed to the other door and went below. The passageway led to the great cabin aft, which was the Captain-General's quarters and magazine. His own cabin was starboard and the other, to port, was usually for the three mates. Now Baccus van Nekk, the chief merchant, Hendrik the third mate, and the boy, Croocq, shared it. They were all very sick.

He went into the great cabin. The Captain-General, Paulus Spillbergen, was lying half conscious in his bunk. He was a short, florid man, normally very fat, now very thin, the skin of his paunch hanging slackly in folds. Blackthorne took a water flagon out of a secret drawer and helped him drink a little.

"Thanks," Spillbergen said weakly. "Where's land—where's land?"

"Ahead," he replied, no longer believing it, then put the flagon away, closed his ears to the whines and left, hating him anew.

Almost exactly a year ago they had reached Tierra del Fuego, the winds favorable for the stab into the unknown of Magellan's Pass. But the Captain-General had ordered a landing to search for gold and treasure.

"Christ Jesus, look ashore, Captain-General! There's no treasure in those wastes."

"Legend says it's rich with gold and we can claim the land for the glorious Netherlands."

"The Spaniards have been here in strength for fifty years."

"Perhaps—but perhaps not this far south, Pilot-Major."

"This far south the seasons're reversed. May, June, July, August're dead winter here. The rutter says the timing's critical to get through the Straits—the winds turn in a few weeks, then we'll have to stay here, winter here for months."

"How many weeks, Pilot?"

"The rutter says eight. But seasons don't stay the same—"

"Then we'll explore for a couple of weeks. That gives us plenty of time and then, if necessary, we'll go north again and sack a few more towns, eh, gentlemen?"

"We've got to try now, Captain-General. The Spanish have very few warships in the Pacific. Here the seas are teeming with them and they're looking for us. I say we've got to go on now."

But the Captain-General had overridden him and put it to a vote of the other captains—not to the other pilots, one English and three Dutch —and had led the useless forays ashore.

The winds had changed early that year and they had had to winter there, the Captain-General afraid to go north because of Spanish fleets. It was four months before they could sail. By then one hundred and fifty-six men in the fleet had died of starvation, cold, and the flux and they were eating the calfskin that covered the ropes. The terrible storms within the Strait had scattered the fleet. *Erasmus* was the only ship that made the rendezvous off Chile. They had waited a month for the others and then, the Spaniards closing in, had set sail into the unknown. The secret rutter stopped at Chile.

Blackthorne walked back along the corridor and unlocked his own cabin door, relocking it behind him. The cabin was low-beamed, small, and orderly, and he had to stoop as he crossed to sit at his desk. He unlocked a drawer and carefully unwrapped the last of the apples he had hoarded so carefully all the way from Santa Maria Island, off Chile. It was bruised and tiny, with mold on the rotting section. He cut off a quarter. There were a few maggots inside. He ate them with the flesh, heeding the old sea legend that the apple maggots were just as effective against scurvy as the fruit and that, rubbed into the gums, they helped prevent your teeth from falling out. He chewed the fruit gently because his teeth were aching and his gums sore and tender, then sipped water from the wine skin. It tasted brackish. Then he wrapped the remainder of the apple and locked it away.

A rat scurried in the shadows cast by the hanging oil lantern over his head. Timbers creaked pleasantly. Cockroaches swarmed on the floor.

I'm tired. I'm so tired.

He glanced at his bunk. Long, narrow, the straw palliasse inviting.

I'm so tired.

Go to sleep for this hour, the devil half of him said. Even for ten minutes—and you'll be fresh for a week. You've had only a few hours for days now, and most of that aloft in the cold. You must sleep. Sleep. They rely on you. . . .

"I won't, I'll sleep tomorrow," he said aloud, and forced his hand to unlock his chest and take out his rutter. He saw that the other one, the Portuguese one, was safe and untouched and that pleased him. He took a clean quill and began to write: "April 21 1600. Fifth hour. Dusk. 133d day from Santa Maria Island, Chile, on the 32 degree North line of latitude. Sea still high and wind strong and the ship rigged as before. The color of the sea dull gray-green and bottomless. We are still running before the wind along a course of 270 degrees, veering to North North West, making way briskly, about two leagues, each of three miles this hour. Large reefs shaped like a triangle were sighted at half the hour bearing North East by North half a league distant.

"Three men died in the night of the scurvy—Joris sailmaker, Reiss gunner, 2d mate de Haan. After commending their souls to God, the Captain-General still being sick, I cast them into the sea without shrouds, for there was no one to make them. Today Bosun Rijckloff died.

"I could not take the declension of the sun at noon today, again due to overcast. But I estimate we are still on course and that landfall in the Japans should be soon. . . ."

"But how soon?" he asked the sea lantern that hung above his head, swaying with the pitch of the ship. How to make a chart? There must be a way, he told himself for the millionth time. How to set longitude? There must be a way. How to keep vegetables fresh? What *is* scurvy . . . ?

"They say it's a flux from the sea, boy," Alban Caradoc had said. He was a huge-bellied, great-hearted man with a tangled gray beard.

"But could you boil the vegetables and keep the broth?"

"It sickens, lad. No one's ever discovered a way to store it."

"They say that Francis Drake sails soon."

"No. You can't go, boy."

"I'm almost fourteen. You let Tim and Watt sign on with him and he needs apprentice pilots."

"They're sixteen. You're just thirteen."

"They say he's going to try for Magellan's Pass, then up the coast to the unexplored region—to the Californias—to find the Straits of Anian that join Pacific with Atlantic. From the Californias all the way to Newfoundland, the Northwest Passage at long last . . ."

"The *supposed* Northwest Passage, lad. No one's proved that legend yet."

"He will. He's Admiral now and we'll be the first English ship through Magellan's Pass, the first in the Pacific, the first— I'll never get another chance like this."

"Oh, yes, you will, and he'll never breach Magellan's secret way 'less he can steal a rutter or capture a Portuguese pilot to guide him through. How many times must I tell you—a pilot must have patience. Learn patience, boy. You've plen—"

"Please!"

"No."

"Why?"

"Because he'll be gone two, three years, perhaps more. The weak and the young will get the worst of the food and the least of the water. And of the five ships that go, only his will come back. You'll never survive, boy."

"Then I'll sign for his ship only. I'm strong. He'll take me!"

"Listen, boy, I was with Drake in *Judith,* his fifty tonner, at San Juan de Ulua when we and Admiral Hawkins—he was in *Minion*—when we fought our way out of harbor through the dung-eating Spaniards. We'd been trading slaves from Guinea to the Spanish Main, but we had no Spanish license for the trade and they tricked Hawkins and trapped our fleet. They'd thirteen great ships, we six. We sank three of theirs, and they sank our *Swallow, Angel, Caravelle,* and the *Jesus of Lubeck.* Oh, yes, Drake fought us out of the trap and brought us home. With eleven men aboard to tell the tale. Hawkins had fifteen. Out of four hundred and eight jolly Jack Tars. Drake is merciless, boy. He wants glory and gold, but only for Drake, and too many men are dead proving it."

"But I won't die. I'll be one of—"

"No. You're apprenticed for twelve years. You've ten more to go and then you're free. But until that time, until 1588, you'll learn how to build ships and how to command them—you'll obey Alban Caradoc, Master Shipwright and Pilot and Member of Trinity House, or you'll never have a license. And if you don't have a license, you'll never pilot *any* ship in English waters, you'll never command the quarterdeck of *any* English ship in *any* waters because that was good King Harry's law, God rest his soul. It was the great whore Mary Tudor's law, may her soul burn in hell, it's the Queen's law, may she reign forever, it's England's law, and the best sea law that's ever been."

Blackthorne remembered how he had hated his master then, and hated Trinity House, the monopoly created by Henry VIII in 1514 for the training and licensing of all English pilots and masters, and hated his twelve years of semibondage, without which he knew he could never get the one thing in the world he wanted. And he had hated Alban Caradoc even more when, to everlasting glory, Drake and his hundred-ton sloop, the *Golden Hind* had miraculously come back to England after disappearing for three years, the first English ship to circumnavigate the globe, bringing with her the richest haul of plunder aboard ever brought back to those shores: an incredible million and a half sterling in gold, silver, spices, and plate.

That four of the five ships were lost and eight out of every ten men were lost and Tim and Watt were lost and a captured Portuguese pilot had led the expedition for Drake through the Magellan into the Pacific did not assuage his hatred; that Drake had hanged one officer, excommunicated the chaplain Fletcher, and failed to find the Northwest Passage did not detract from national admiration. The Queen took fifty percent of the treasure and knighted him. The gentry and merchants who had put up the money for the expedition received three hundred percent profit and pleaded to underwrite his next corsair voyage. And all seamen begged to sail with him, because he did get plunder, he did come home, and, with their share of the booty, the lucky few who survived were rich for life.

I would have survived, Blackthorne told himself. I would. And my share of the treasure then would have been enough to—

"*Rotz vooruiiiiiiiit!*" Reef ahead!

He felt the cry at first more than he heard it. Then, mixed with the gale, he heard the wailing scream again.

He was out of the cabin and up the companionway onto the quarterdeck, his heart pounding, his throat parched. It was dark night now and pouring, and he was momentarily exulted for he knew that the canvas raintraps, made so many weeks ago, would soon be full to overflowing. He opened his mouth to the near horizontal rain and tasted its sweetness, then turned his back on the squall.

He saw that Hendrik was paralyzed with terror. The bow lookout, Maetsukker, cowered near the prow, shouting incoherently, pointing ahead. Then he too looked beyond the ship.

The reef was barely two hundred yards ahead, great black claws of rocks pounded by the hungry sea. The foaming line of surf stretched port and starboard, broken intermittently. The gale was lifting huge swathes of spume and hurling them at the night blackness. A forepeak halliard snapped and the highest top gallant spar was carried away. The mast shuddered in its bed but held, and the sea bore the ship inexorably to its death.

"All hands on deck!" Blackthorne shouted, and rang the bell violently.

The noise brought Hendrik out of his stupor. "We're lost!" he screamed in Dutch. "Oh, Lord Jesus help us!"

"Get the crew on deck, you bastard! You've been asleep! You've both been asleep!" Blackthorne shoved him toward the companionway, held onto the wheel, slipped the protecting lashing from the spokes, braced himself, and swung the wheel hard aport.

He exerted all his strength as the rudder bit into the torrent. The whole ship shuddered. Then the prow began to swing with increasing velocity as the wind bore down and soon they were broadside to the sea and the wind. The storm tops'ls bellied and gamely tried to carry the weight of the ship and all the ropes took the strain, howling. The following sea towered above them and they were making way, parallel to the reef, when he saw the great wave. He shouted a warning at the men who were coming from the fo'c'sle, and hung on for his life.

The sea fell on the ship and she heeled and he thought they'd floundered but she shook herself like a wet terrier and swung out of the trough. Water cascaded away through the scuppers and he gasped for air. He saw that the corpse of the bosun that had been put on deck for burial tomorrow was gone and that the following wave was coming in even stronger. It caught Hendrik and lifted him, gasping and struggling, over the side and out to sea. Another wave roared across the deck and Blackthorne locked one arm through the wheel and the water passed him by. Now Hendrik was fifty yards to port. The wash sucked him back alongside, then a giant comber threw him high above the ship, held him there for a moment shrieking, then took him away and pulped him against a rock spine and consumed him.

The ship nosed into the sea trying to make way. Another halliard gave and the block and tackle swung wildly until it tangled with the rigging.

Vinck and another man pulled themselves onto the quarterdeck and leaned on the wheel to help. Blackthorne could see the encroaching reef to starboard, nearer now. Ahead and to port were more outcrops, but he saw gaps here and there.

"Get aloft, Vinck. Fores'ls ho!" Foot by foot Vinck and two seamen hauled themselves into the shrouds of the foremast rigging as others, below, leaned on the ropes to give them a hand.

"Watch out for'ard," Blackthorne shouted.

The sea foamed along the deck and took another man with it and brought the corpse of the bosun aboard again. The bow soared out of the water and smashed down once more bringing more water aboard. Vinck and the other men cursed the sail out of its ropes. Abruptly it fell open, cracked like a cannonade as the wind filled it, and the ship lurched.

Vinck and his helpers hung there, swaying over the sea, then began their descent.

"Reef—reef ahead!" Vinck screamed.

Blackthorne and the other man swung the wheel to starboard. The ship hesitated then turned and cried out as the rocks, barely awash, found the side of the ship. But it was an oblique blow and the rock nose crumbled. The timbers held safe and the men aboard began to breathe once more.

Blackthorne saw a break in the reef ahead and committed the ship to it. The wind was harder now, the sea more furious. The ship swerved with a gust and the wheel spun out of their hands. Together they grabbed it and set her course again, but she bobbed and twisted drunkenly. Sea flooded aboard and burst into the fo'c'sle, smashing one man against the bulkhead, the whole deck awash like the one above.

"Man the pumps!" Blackthorne shouted. He saw two men go below. The rain was slashing his face and he squinted against the pain. The binnacle light and aft riding light had long since been extinguished. Then as another gust shoved the ship further off course, the seaman slipped and again the wheel spun out of their grasp. The man shrieked as a spoke smashed the side of his head and he lay there at the mercy of the sea. Blackthorne pulled him up and held him until the frothing comber had passed. Then he saw that the man was dead so he let him slump into the seachair and the next sea cleaned the quarterdeck of him.

The gulch through the reef was three points to windward and, try as he could, Blackthorne could not gain way. He searched desperately for another channel but knew there was none, so he let her fall off from the wind momentarily to gain speed, then swung her hard to windward again. She gained way a fraction and held course.

There was a wailing, tormented shudder as the keel scraped the razor spines below and all aboard imagined they saw the oak timbers burst apart and the sea flood in. The ship reeled forward out of control now.

Blackthorne shouted for help but no one heard him so he fought the wheel alone against the sea. Once he was flung aside but he groped back and held on again, wondering in his thickening mind how the rudder had survived so long.

In the neck of the pass the sea became a maelstrom, driven by the tempest and hemmed in by the rocks. Huge waves smashed at the reef, then reeled back to fight the incomer until the waves fought among themselves and attacked on all quarters of the compass. The ship was sucked into the vortex, broadside and helpless.

"Piss on you, storm!" Blackthorne raged. "Get your dung-eating hands off my ship!"

The wheel spun again and threw him away and the deck heeled sickeningly. The bowsprit caught a rock and tore loose, part of the rigging with it, and she righted herself. The foremast was bending like a bow and it snapped. The men on deck fell on the rigging with axes to cut it adrift as the ship floundered down the raging channel. They hacked the mast free and it went over the side and one man went with it, caught in the tangled mess. The man cried out, trapped, but there was nothing they could do and they watched as he and the mast appeared and disappeared alongside, then came back no more.

Vinck and the others who were left looked back at the quarterdeck and saw Blackthorne defying the storm like a madman. They crossed themselves and doubled their prayers, some weeping with fear, and hung on for life.

The strait broadened for an instant and the ship slowed, but ahead it narrowed ominously again and the rocks seemed to grow, to tower over them. The current ricocheted off one side, taking the ship with it, turned her abeam again and flung her to her doom.

Blackthorne stopped cursing the storm and fought the wheel to port and hung there, his muscles knotted against the strain. But the ship knew not her rudder and neither did the sea.

"Turn, you whore from hell," he gasped, his strength ebbing fast. "Help me!"

The sea race quickened and he felt his heart near bursting but still he strained against the press of the sea. He tried to keep his eyes focused but his vision reeled, the colors wrong and fading. The ship was (in the neck and) dead but just then the keel scraped a mud shoal. The shock turned her head. The rudder bit into the sea. And then the wind and the sea joined to help and together they spun her before the wind and she sped through the pass to safety. Into the bay beyond.

BOOK ONE

BOOK ONE

CHAPTER 1

BLACKTHORNE was suddenly awake. For a moment he thought he was dreaming because he was ashore and the room unbelievable. It was small and very clean and covered with soft mats. He was lying on a thick quilt and another was thrown over him. The ceiling was polished cedar and the walls were lathes of cedar, in squares, covered with an opaque paper that muted the light pleasantly. Beside him was a scarlet tray bearing small bowls. One contained cold cooked vegetables and he wolfed them, hardly noticing the piquant taste. Another contained a fish soup and he drained that. Another was filled with a thick porridge of wheat or barley and he finished it quickly, eating with his fingers. The water in an odd-shaped gourd was warm and tasted curious—slightly bitter but savory.

Then he noticed the crucifix in its niche.

This house is Spanish or Portuguese, he thought aghast. Is this the Japans? or Cathay?

A panel of the wall slid open. A middle-aged, heavy-set, round-faced woman was on her knees beside the door and she bowed and smiled. Her skin was golden and her eyes black and narrow and her long black hair was piled neatly on her head. She wore a gray silk robe and short white socks with a thick sole and a wide purple band around her waist.

"*Goshujinsama, gokibun wa ikaga desu ka?*" she said. She waited as he stared at her blankly, then said it again.

"Is this the Japans?" he asked. "Japans? Or Cathay?"

She stared at him uncomprehendingly and said something else he could not understand. Then he realized that he was naked. His clothes were nowhere in sight. With sign language he showed her that he wanted to get dressed. Then he pointed at the food bowls and she knew that he was still hungry.

She smiled and bowed and slid the door shut.

He lay back exhausted, the untoward, nauseating nonmotion of the floor making his head spin. With an effort he tried to collect himself. I remember getting the anchor out, he thought. With Vinck. I think it was Vinck. We were in a bay and the ship had nosed a shoal and stopped. We could hear waves breaking on the beach but everything was safe. There were lights ashore and then I was in my cabin and blackness. I don't remember anything. Then there were lights through the blackness and strange voices. I was talking English, then Portuguese. One of the natives talked a little Portuguese. Or was he Portuguese? No, I think he was a native. Did I ask him where we were? I don't remember. Then we were back in the reef again and the big wave came once more and I was carried out to sea and drowning—it was freezing—no, the sea was warm and like a silk bed a fathom thick. They must have carried me ashore and put me here.

"It must have been this bed that felt so soft and warm," he said aloud. "I've never slept on silk before." His weakness overcame him and he slept dreamlessly.

When he awoke there was more food in earthenware bowls and his clothes were beside him in a neat pile. They had been washed and pressed and mended with tiny, exquisite stitching.

But his knife was gone, and so were his keys.

I'd better get a knife and quickly, he thought. Or a pistol.

His eyes went to the crucifix. In spite of his dread, his excitement quickened. All his life he had heard legends told among pilots and sailormen about the incredible riches of Portugal's secret empire in the East, how they had by now converted the heathens to Catholicism and so held them in bondage, where gold was as cheap as pig iron, and emeralds, rubies, diamonds, and sapphires as plentiful as pebbles on a beach.

If the Catholic part's true, he told himself, perhaps the rest is too. About the riches. Yes. But the sooner I'm armed and back aboard *Erasmus* and behind her cannon, the better.

He consumed the food, dressed, and stood shakily, feeling out of his element as he always did ashore. His boots were missing. He went to the door, reeling slightly, and put out a hand to steady himself but the light, square lathes could not bear his weight and they shattered, the paper ripping apart. He righted himself. The shocked woman in the corridor was staring up at him.

"I'm sorry," he said, strangely ill at ease with his clumsiness. The purity of the room was somehow defiled.

"Where are my boots?"

The woman stared at him blankly. So, patiently, he asked her again with sign language and she hurried down a passage, knelt and opened another lathe door, and beckoned him. Voices were nearby, and the sound of running water. He went through the doorway and found himself in another room, also almost bare. This opened onto a veranda with steps leading to a small garden surrounded by a high wall. Beside this main entrance were two old women, three children dressed in scarlet robes, and an old man, obviously a gardener, with a rake in his hand. At once they all bowed gravely and kept their heads low.

To his astonishment Blackthorne saw that the old man was naked but for a brief, narrow loincloth, hardly covering his organs.

"Morning," he said to them, not knowing what to say.

They stayed motionless, still bowing.

Nonplussed, he stared at them, then, awkwardly he bowed back to them. They all straightened and smiled at him. The old man bowed once more and went back to work in the garden. The children stared at him, then, laughing, dashed away. The old women disappeared into the depths of the house. But he could feel their eyes on him.

He saw his boots at the bottom of the steps. Before he could pick them up, the middle-aged woman was there on her knees, to his embarrassment, and she helped him to put them on.

"Thank you," he said. He thought a moment and then pointed at himself. "Blackthorne," he said deliberately. "Blackthorne." Then he pointed at her. "What's your name?"

She stared at him uncomprehendingly.

"*Black-thorne,*" he repeated carefully, pointing at himself, and again pointed at her. "What's your name?"

She frowned, then with a flood of understanding pointed at herself and said, "*Onna! Onna!*"

"*Onna!*" he repeated, very proud of himself as she was with herself. "*Onna.*"

She nodded happily. "*Onna!*"

The garden was unlike anything he had ever seen: a little waterfall and stream and small bridge and manicured pebbled paths and rocks and flowers and shrubs. It's so clean, he thought. So neat.

"Incredible," he said.

" 'Nkerriberr?" she repeated helpfully.

"Nothing," he said. Then not knowing what else to do, he waved her away. Obediently she bowed politely and left.

Blackthorne sat in the warm sun, leaning against a post. Feeling very frail, he watched the old man weeding an already weedless garden. I wonder where the others are. Is the Captain-General still alive? How many days have I been asleep? I can remember waking and eating and sleeping again, the eating unsatisfactory like the dreams.

The children flurried past, chasing one another, and he was embarrassed for them at the gardener's nakedness, for when the man bent over or stooped you could see everything and he was astounded that the children appeared not to notice. He saw tiled and thatched roofs of other buildings over the wall and, far off, high mountains. A crisp wind broomed the sky and kept the cumulus advancing. Bees were foraging and it was a lovely spring day. His body begged for more sleep but he pushed himself erect and went to the garden door. The gardener smiled and bowed and ran to open the door and bowed and closed it after him.

The village was set around the crescent harbor that faced east, perhaps two hundred houses unlike any he'd ever seen nestling at the beginning of the mountain which spilled down to the shore. Above were terraced fields and dirt roads that led north and south. Below, the waterfront was cobbled and a stone launching ramp went from the shore into the sea. A good safe harbor and a stone jetty, and men and women cleaning fish and making nets, a uniquely designed boat being built at the northern side. There were islands far out to sea, to the east and to the south. The reefs would be there or beyond the horizon.

In the harbor were many other quaintly shaped boats, mostly fishing craft, some with one large sail, several being sculled—the oarsmen standing and pushing against the sea, not sitting and pulling as he would have done. A few of the boats were heading out to sea, others were nosing at the wooden dock, and *Erasmus* was anchored neatly, fifty yards from shore, in good water, with three bow cables. Who did that? he asked himself. There were boats alongside her and he could see native men aboard. But none of his. Where could they be?

He looked around the village and became conscious of the many people watching him. When they saw that he had noticed them they all bowed and, still uncomfortable, he bowed back. Once more there was happy activity and they passed to and fro, stopping, bargaining, bowing to each other, seemingly oblivious of him, like so many multicolored butterflies. But he felt eyes studying him from every window and doorway as he walked toward the shore.

What is it about them that's so weird? he asked himself. It's not just their clothes and behavior. It's—*they've no weapons,* he thought, astounded. No swords or guns! Why is that?

Open shops filled with odd goods and bales lined the small street. The floors of the shops were raised and the sellers and the buyers knelt or squatted on the clean wooden floors. He saw that most had clogs or rush sandals, some with the same white socks with the thick sole that were split between the big toe and the next to hold the thongs, but they left the clogs and sandals outside in the dirt. Those who were barefoot cleansed their feet and slipped on clean, indoor sandals that were waiting for them. That's very sensible if you think about it, he told himself, awed.

Then he saw the tonsured man approaching and fear swept sickeningly from his testicles into his stomach. The priest was obviously Portuguese or Spanish, and, though his flowing robe was orange, there was no mistaking the rosary and crucifix at his belt, or the cold hostility on his face.

His robe was travel stained and his European-style boots besmirched with mud. He was looking out into the harbor at *Erasmus,* and Blackthorne knew that he must recognize her as Dutch or English, new to most seas, leaner, faster, a merchant fighting ship, patterned and improved on the English privateers that had wreaked so much havoc on the Spanish Main. With the priest were ten natives, black-haired and black-eyed, one dressed like him except that he had thong slippers. The others wore varicolored robes or loose trousers, or simply loincloths. But none was armed.

Blackthorne wanted to run while there was time but he knew he did not have the strength and there was nowhere to hide. His height and size and the color of his eyes made him alien in this world. He put his back against the wall.

"Who are you?" the priest said in Portuguese. He was a thick, dark, well-fed man in his middle twenties, with a long beard.

"Who are you?" Blackthorne stared back at him.

"That's a Netherlander privateer. You're a heretic Dutchman. You're pirates. God have mercy on you!"

"We're not pirates. We're peaceful merchants, except to our enemies. I'm pilot of that ship. Who are you?"

"Father Sebastio. How did you get here? How?"

"We were blown ashore. What is this place? Is it the Japans?"

"Yes. Japan. Nippon," the priest said impatiently. He turned to one of the men, older than the rest, small and lean with strong arms and calloused hands, his pate shaved and his hair drawn into a thin queue as gray as his eyebrows. The priest spoke haltingly to him in Japanese, pointing at Blackthorne. All of them were shocked and one made the sign of the cross protectively.

"Dutchmen are heretics, rebels, and pirates. What's your name?"

"Is this a Portuguese settlement?"

The priest's eyes were hard and bloodshot. "The village headman says he's told the authorities about you. Your sins have caught up with you. Where's the rest of your crew?"

"We were blown off course. We just need food and water and time to repair our ship. Then we'll be off. We can pay for every—"

"Where's the rest of your crew?"

"I don't know. Aboard. I suppose they're aboard."

Again the priest questioned the headman who replied and motioned to the other end of the village, explaining at length. The priest turned back to Blackthorne. "They crucify criminals here, Pilot. You're going to die. The *daimyo's* coming with his samurai. God have mercy on you."

"What's a *daimyo?*"

"A feudal lord. He owns this whole province. How did you get here?"

"And *samurai?*"

"Warriors—soldiers—members of the warrior caste," the priest said with growing irritation. "Where did you come from and who are you?"

"I don't recognize your accent," Blackthorne said, to throw him off balance. "You're a Spaniard?"

"I'm Portuguese," the priest flared, taking the bait. "I told you, I'm Father Sebastio from Portugal. Where did you learn such good Portuguese. Eh?"

"But Portugal and Spain are the same country now," Blackthorne said, taunting. "You've the same king."

"We're a separate country. We're a different people. We have been forever. We fly our own flag. Our overseas possessions are separate, yes, separate. King Philip agreed when he stole my country." Father Sebastio controlled his temper with an effort, his fingers trembling. "He took my country by force of arms twenty years ago! His soldiers and that devil-spawned Spaniard tyrant, the Duke of Alva, they crushed our real king. *Que va!* Now Philip's son rules but he's not our real king either. Soon we'll have our own king back again." Then he added with venom, "You know it's the truth. What devil Alva did to your country he did to mine."

"That's a lie. Alva was a plague in the Netherlands, but he never conquered them. They're still free. Always will be. But in Portugal he smashed one small army and the whole country gave in. No courage. You could throw the Spaniard out if you wanted to, but you'll never do it. No honor. No *cojones.* Except to burn innocents in the name of God."

"May God burn you in hellfire for all eternity," the priest flared. "Satan walks abroad and will be stamped out. Heretics will be stamped out. You're cursed before God!"

In spite of himself Blackthorne felt the religious terror begin to rise within him. "Priests don't have the ear of God, or speak with His voice. We're free of your stinking yoke and we're going to stay free!"

It was only forty years ago that Bloody Mary Tudor was Queen of England and the Spaniard Philip II, Philip the Cruel, her husband. This deeply religious daughter of Henry VIII had brought back Catholic priests and inquisitors and heresy trials and the dominance of the foreign Pope again to England and had reversed her father's curbs and historic changes to the Church of Rome in England, against the will of the majority. She had ruled for five years and the realm was torn asunder with hatred and fear and bloodshed. But she had died and Elizabeth became queen at twenty-four.

Blackthorne was filled with wonder, and deep filial love, when he thought of Elizabeth. For forty years she's battled with the world. She's outfoxed and outfought Popes, the Holy Roman Empire, France and Spain combined. Excommunicated, spat on, reviled abroad, she's led us into harbor—safe, strong, separate.

"We're free," Blackthorne said to the priest. "You're broken. We've our own schools now, our own books, our own bible, our own Church. You Spaniards are all the same. Offal! You monks are all the same. Idol worshipers!"

The priest lifted his crucifix and held it between Blackthorne and himself as a shield. "Oh, God, protect us from this evil! I'm not Spanish, I tell you! I'm Portuguese. And I'm not a monk. I'm a brother of the Society of Jesus!"

"Ah, one of them. A Jesuit!"

"Yes. May God have mercy on your soul!" Father Sebastio snapped something in Japanese and the men surged toward Blackthorne. He backed against the wall and hit one man hard but the others swarmed over him and he felt himself choking.

"*Nanigoto da?*"

Abruptly the melee ceased.

The young man was ten paces away. He wore breeches and clogs and a light kimono and two scabbarded swords were stuck into his belt. One was daggerlike. The other, a two-handed killing sword, was long and slightly curved. His right hand was casually on the hilt.

"*Nanigoto da?*" he asked harshly and when no one answered instantly, "*NANIGOTO DA?*"

The Japanese fell to their knees, their heads bowed into the dirt. Only the priest stayed on his feet. He bowed and began to explain haltingly, but the man contemptuously cut him short and pointed at the headman. "Mura!"

Mura, the headman, kept his head bowed and began explaining rapidly. Several times he pointed at Blackthorne, once at the ship, and twice at the priest. Now there was no movement on the street. All who were visible were on their knees and bowing low. The headman finished. The armed man arrogantly questioned him for a moment and he was answered deferentially and quickly. Then the soldier said something to the headman and waved with open contempt at the priest, then at Blackthorne, and the gray-haired man put it more simply to the priest, who flushed.

The man, who was a head shorter and much younger than Blackthorne, his handsome face slightly pock-marked, stared at the stranger. "*Onushi ittai doko kara kitanoda? Doko no kuni no monoda?*"

The priest said nervously, "Kasigi Omi-san says, 'Where do you come from and what's your nationality?'"

"Is Mr. Omisan the *daimyo?*" Blackthorne asked, afraid of the swords in spite of himself.

"No. He's a samurai, the samurai in charge of the village. His surname's Kasigi, Omi's his given name. Here they always put their surnames first. 'San' means 'honorable,' and you add it to all names as a politeness. You'd better learn to be polite—and find some manners quickly. Here they don't tolerate lack of manners." His voice edged. "Hurry up and answer!"

"Amsterdam. I'm English."

Father Sebastio's shock was open. He said, "English. England," to the samurai and began an explanation but Omi impatiently cut him short and rapped out a flurry of words.

"Omi-san asks if you're the leader. The headman says there are only a few of you heretics alive and most are sick. Is there a Captain-General?"

"I'm the leader," Blackthorne answered even though, truly, now that they were ashore, the Captain-General was in command. "I'm in command," he added, knowing that Captain-General Spillbergen could command nothing, ashore or afloat, even when he was fit and well.

Another spate of words from the samurai. "Omi-san says, because you are the leader you are allowed to walk around the village freely, wherever you want, until his master comes. His master, the *daimyo*, will decide your fate. Until then, you are permitted to live as a guest in the headman's house and come and go as you please. But you are not to leave the village. Your crew are confined to their house and are not allowed to leave it. Do you understand?"

"Yes. Where are my crew?"

Father Sebastio pointed vaguely at a cluster of houses near a wharf, obviously distressed by Omi's decision and impatience. "There! Enjoy your freedom, pirate. Your evil's caught up with—"

"*Wakarimasu ka?*" Omi said directly to Blackthorne.

"He says, 'Do you understand?'"

"What's 'yes' in Japanese?"

Father Sebastio said to the samurai, "*Wakarimasu.*"

Omi disdainfully waved them away. They all bowed low. Except one man who rose deliberately, without bowing.

With blinding speed the killing sword made a hissing silver arc and the man's head toppled off his shoulders and a fountain of blood sprayed the earth. The body rippled a few times and was still. Involuntarily, the priest had backed off a pace. No one else in the street had moved a muscle. Their heads remained low and motionless. Blackthorne was rigid, in shock.

Omi put his foot carelessly on the corpse.

"*Ikinasai!*" he said, motioning them away.

The men in front of him bowed again, to the earth. Then they got up and went away impassively. The street began to empty. And the shops.

Father Sebastio looked down at the body. Gravely he made the sign of the cross over him and said, "*In nomine Patris et Filii et Spiritus Sancti.*" He stared back at the samurai without fear now.

"*Ikinasai!*" The tip of the gleaming sword rested on the body.

After a long moment the priest turned and walked away. With dignity. Omi watched him narrowly, then glanced at Blackthorne. Blackthorne backed away and then, when safely distant, he quickly turned a corner and vanished.

Omi began to laugh uproariously. The street was empty now. When his laughter was exhausted, he grasped his sword with both hands and began to hack the body methodically into small pieces.

Blackthorne was in a small boat, the boatman sculling happily toward *Erasmus.* He had had no trouble in getting the boat and he could see men on the main deck. All were samurai. Some had steel breastplates but most wore simple kimonos, as the robes were called, and the two swords. All wore their hair the same way: the top of the head shaved and the hair at the back and sides gathered into a queue, oiled, then doubled over the crown and tied neatly. Only samurai were allowed this style and, for them, it was obligatory. Only samurai could wear the two swords—always the long, two-handed killing sword and the short, daggerlike one—and, for them, the swords were obligatory.

The samurai lined the gunwales of his ship watching him.

Filled with disquiet, he climbed up the gangway and came on deck. One samurai, more elaborately dressed than the others, came over to him and bowed. Blackthorne had learned well and he bowed back equally and everyone on the deck beamed genially. He still felt the horror of the sudden killing in the street, and their smiles did not allay his foreboding. He went toward the companionway and stopped abruptly. Across the doorway was pasted a wide band of red silk and, beside it, a small sign with queer, squiggled writing. He hesitated, checked the other door, but that too was sealed up with a similar band, and a similar sign was nailed to the bulkhead.

He reached out to remove the silk.

"*Hotté oké!*" To make the point quite clear the samurai on guard shook his head. He was no longer smiling.

"But this is my ship and I want . . ." Blackthorne bottled his anxiety, eyes on the swords. I've got to get below, he thought. I've got to get the rutters, mine and the secret one. Christ Jesus, if they're found and given to the priests or to the Japaners we're finished. Any court in the world —outside of England and the Netherlands—would convict us as pirates with that evidence. My rutter gives dates, places, and amounts of plunder taken, the number of dead at our three landings in the Americas and the one in Spanish Africa, the number of churches sacked, and how we burned the towns and the shipping. And the Portuguese rutter? That's our death warrant, for of course it's stolen. At least it was bought from a Portuguese traitor, and by their law any foreigner caught in possession of any rutter of theirs, let alone one that unlocks the Magellan, is to be put to death at once. And if the rutter is found aboard an enemy ship, the ship is to be burned and all aboard executed without mercy.

"*Nan no yoda?*" one of the samurai said.

"Do you speak Portuguese?" Blackthorne asked in that language.

The man shrugged. "*Wakarimasen.*"

Another came forward and deferentially spoke to the leader, who nodded in agreement.

"Portugeezu friend," this samurai said in heavily accented Portuguese. He opened the top of his kimono and showed the small wooden crucifix that hung from his neck.

"Christ'an!" He pointed at himself and smiled. "Christ'an." He pointed at Blackthorne. "Christ'an *ka?*"

Blackthorne hesitated, nodded. "Christian."

"Portugeezu?"

"English."

The man chattered with the leader, then both shrugged and looked back at him. "Portugeezu?"

Blackthorne shook his head, not liking to disagree with them on anything. "My friends? Where?"

The samurai pointed to the east end of the village. "Friends."

"This is my ship. I want to go below." Blackthorne said it in several ways and with signs and they understood.

"*Ah, so desu! Kinjiru,*" they said emphatically, indicating the notice, and beamed.

It was quite clear that he was not allowed to go below. *Kinjiru* must mean forbidden, Blackthorne thought irritably. Well, to hell with that! He snapped the handle of the door down and opened it a fraction.

"*KINJIRU!*"

He was jerked around to face the samurai. Their swords were half out of the scabbards. Motionlessly the two men waited for him to make up his mind. Others on deck watched impassively.

Blackthorne knew he had no option but to back down, so he shrugged and walked away and checked the hawsers and the ship as best he could. The tattered sails were down and tied in place. But the lashings were different from any he'd ever seen, so he presumed that the Japaners had made the vessel secure. He started down the gangway, and stopped. He felt the cold sweat as he saw them all staring at him malevolently and he thought, Christ Jesus, how could I be so stupid. He bowed politely and at once the hostility vanished and they all bowed and were smiling again. But he could still feel the sweat trickling down his spine and he hated everything about the Japans and wished himself and his crew back aboard, armed, and out to sea.

"By the Lord Jesus, I think you're wrong, Pilot," Vinck said. His toothless grin was wide and obscene. "If you can put up with the swill they call food, it's the best place I've been. Ever. I've had two women in three days and they're like rabbits. They'll do anything if you show 'em how."

"That's right. But you can't do nothing without meat or brandy. Nor for long. I'm tired out, and I could only do it once," Maetsukker said, his narrow face twitching. "The yellow bastards won't understand that we need meat and beer and bread. And brandy or wine."

"That's the worst! Lord Jesus, my kingdom for some grog!" Baccus van Nekk was filled with gloom. He walked over and stood close to Blackthorne and peered up at him. He was very nearsighted and had lost his last pair of spectacles in the storm. But even with them he would always stand as close as possible. He was chief merchant, treasurer, and representative of the Dutch East India Company that had put up the money for the voyage. "We're ashore and safe and I haven't had a drink yet. Not a beautiful drop! Terrible. Did you get any, Pilot?"

"No." Blackthorne disliked having anyone near him, but Baccus was a friend and almost blind so he did not move away. "Just hot water with herbs in it."

"They simply won't understand grog. Nothing to drink but hot water and herbs—the good Lord help us! Suppose there's no liquor in the whole country!" His eyebrows soared. "Do me a huge favor, Pilot. Ask for some liquor, will you?"

Blackthorne had found the house that they had been assigned on the eastern edge of the village. The samurai guard had let him pass, but his men had confirmed that they themselves could not go out of the garden gate. The house was many-roomed like his, but bigger and staffed with many servants of various ages, both men and women.

There were eleven of his men alive. The dead had been taken away by the Japanese. Lavish portions of fresh vegetables had begun to banish the scurvy and all but two of the men were healing rapidly. These two had blood in their bowels and their insides were fluxed. Vinck had bled them but this had not helped. By nightfall he expected them to die. The Captain-General was in another room, still very sick.

Sonk, the cook, a stocky little man, was saying with a laugh, "It's good here, like Johann says, Pilot, excepting the food and no grog. And it's all right with the natives so long as you don't wear your shoes in the house. It sends the little yellow bastards mad if you don't take off your shoes."

"Listen," Blackthorne said. "There's a priest here. A Jesuit."

"Christ Jesus!" All banter left them as he told them about the priest and about the beheading.

"Why'd he chop the man's head off, Pilot?"

"I don't know."

"We better get back aboard. If Papists catch us ashore . . ."

There was great fear in the room now. Salamon, the mute, watched Blackthorne. His mouth worked, a bubble of phlegm appearing at the corners.

"No, Salamon, there's no mistake," Blackthorne said kindly, answering the silent question. "He said he was Jesuit."

"Christ, Jesuit or Dominican or what-the-hell-ever makes no muck-eating difference," Vinck said. "We'd better get back aboard. Pilot, you ask that samurai, eh?"

"We're in God's hands," Jan Roper said. He was one of the merchant adventurers, a narrow-eyed young man with a high forehead and thin nose. "He will protect us from the Satan worshipers."

Vinck looked back at Blackthorne. "What about Portuguese, Pilot? Did you see any around?"

"No. There were no signs of them in the village."

"They'll swarm here soon as they know about us." Maetsukker said it for all of them and the boy Croocq let out a moan.

"Yes, and if there's one priest, there's got to be others." Ginsel licked dry lips. "And then their God-cursed conquistadores are never far away."

"That's right," Vinck added uneasily. "They're like lice."

"Christ Jesus! Papists!" someone muttered. "And conquistadores!"

"But we're in the Japans, Pilot?" van Nekk asked. "He told you that?"

"Yes. Why?"

Van Nekk moved closer and dropped his voice. "If priests are here, and some of the natives are Catholic, perhaps the other part's true—about the riches, the gold and silver and precious stones." A hush fell on them. "Did you see any, Pilot? Any gold? Any gems on the natives, or gold?"

"No. None." Blackthorne thought a moment. "I don't remember seeing any. No necklaces or beads or bracelets. Listen, there's something else to tell you. I went aboard *Erasmus* but she's sealed up." He related what had happened and their anxiety increased.

"Jesus, if we can't go back aboard and there are priests ashore and Papists. . . . We've got to get away from here." Maetsukker's voice began to tremble. "Pilot, what are we going to do? They'll burn us! Conquistadores—those bastards'll shove their swords . . ."

"We're in God's hands," Jan Roper called out confidently. "He will protect us from the anti-Christ. That's His promise. There's nothing to be afraid of."

Blackthorne said, "The way the samurai Omi-san snarled at the priest—I'm sure he hated him. That's good, eh? What I'd like to know is why the priest wasn't wearing their usual robes. Why the orange one? I've never seen that before."

"Yes, that's curious," van Nekk said.

Blackthorne looked up at him. "Maybe their hold here isn't strong. That could help us greatly."

"What should we do, Pilot?" Ginsel asked.

"Be patient and wait till their chief, this *daimyo,* comes. He'll let us go. Why shouldn't he? We've done them no harm. We've goods to trade. We're not pirates, we've nothing to fear."

"Very true, and don't forget the Pilot said the savages aren't all Papists," van Nekk said, more to encourage himself than the others. "Yes. It's good the samurai hated the priest. And it's only the samurai who are armed. That's not so bad, eh? Just watch out for the samurai and get our weapons back—that's the idea. We'll be aboard before you know it."

"What happens if this *daimyo's* Papist?" Jan Roper asked.

No one answered him. Then Ginsel said, "Pilot, the man with the sword? He cut the other wog into pieces, after chopping his head off?"

"Yes."

"Christ! They're barbarians! Lunatics!" Ginsel was tall, a goodlooking youth with short arms and very bowed legs. The scurvy had taken all his teeth. "After he chopped his head off, the others just walked away? Without saying anything?"

"Yes."

"Christ Jesus, an unarmed man, murdered, just like that? Why'd he do it? Why'd he kill him?"

"I don't know, Ginsel. But you've never seen such speed. One moment the sword was sheathed, the next the man's head was rolling."

"God protect us!"

"Dear Lord Jesus," van Nekk murmured. "If we can't get back to the ship. . . . God damn that storm, I feel so helpless without my spectacles!"

"How many samurai were aboard, Pilot?" Ginsel asked.

"Twenty-two were on deck. But there were more ashore."

"The wrath of God will be upon the heathen and on sinners and they'll burn in hell for all eternity."

"I'd like to be sure of that, Jan Roper," Blackthorne said, an edge to his voice, as he felt the fear of God's vengeance sweep through the room. He was very tired and wanted to sleep.

"You can be sure, Pilot, oh yes, I am. I pray that your eyes are opened to God's truth. That you come to realize we're here only because of you —what's left of us."

"What?" Blackthorne said dangerously.

"Why did you really persuade the Captain-General to try for the Japans? It wasn't in our orders. We were to pillage the New World, to carry the war into the enemy's belly, then go home."

"There were Spanish ships south and north of us and nowhere else to run. Has your memory gone along with your wits? We had to sail west— it was our only chance."

"I never saw enemy ships, Pilot. None of us did."

"Come now, Jan," van Nekk said wearily. "The Pilot did what he thought best. Of course the Spaniards were there."

"Aye, that's the truth, and we was a thousand leagues from friends and in enemy waters, by God!" Vinck spat. "That's the God's truth—and the God's truth was we put it to a vote. We all said yes."

"I didn't."

Sonk said, "No one asked me."

"Oh, Christ Jesus!"

"Calm down, Johann," van Nekk said, trying to ease the tension. "We're the first ones to reach Japans. Remember all the stories, eh? We're rich if we keep our wits. We have trade goods and there's gold here—there must be. Where else could we sell our cargo? Not there in the New World, hunted and harried! They were hunting us and the Spaniards knew we were off Santa Maria. We had to quit Chile and there was no escape back through the Strait—of course they'd be lying in wait for us, of course they would! No, here was our only chance and a good idea. Our cargo exchanged for spices and gold and silver, eh? Think of the profit—a thousandfold, that's usual. We're in the Spice Islands. You know the riches of the Japans and Cathay, you've heard about them forever. We all have. Why else did we all sign on? We'll be rich, you'll see!"

"We're dead men, like all the others. We're in the land of Satan."

Vinck said angrily, "Shut your mouth, Roper! The Pilot did right. Not his fault the others died—not his fault. Men always die on these voyages."

Jan Roper's eyes were flecked, the pupils tiny. "Yes, God rest their souls. My brother was one."

Blackthorne looked into the fanatic eyes, hating Jan Roper. Inside he was asking himself if he had really sailed west to elude the enemy ships. Or was it because he was the first English pilot through the Strait, first in position, ready and able to stab west and therefore first with the chance of circumnavigating?

Jan Roper hissed, "Didn't the others die through your ambition, Pilot? God will punish you!"

"Now hold your tongue." Blackthorne's words were soft and final.

Jan Roper stared back with the same frozen hatchet face, but he kept his mouth shut.

"Good." Blackthorne sat tiredly on the floor and rested against one of the uprights.

"What should we do, Pilot?"

"Wait and get fit. Their chief is coming soon—then we'll get everything settled."

Vinck was looking out into the garden at the samurai who sat motionless on his heels beside the gateway. "Look at that bastard. Been there for hours, never moves, never says anything, doesn't even pick his nose."

"He's been no trouble though, Johann. None at all," van Nekk said.

"Yes, but all we've been doing is sleeping and fornicating and eating the swill."

"Pilot, he's only one man. We're ten," Ginsel said quietly.

"I've thought of that. But we're not fit enough yet. It'll take a week for the scurvy to go," Blackthorne replied, disquieted. "There are too many of them aboard ship. I wouldn't like to take on even one without a spear or gun. Are you guarded at night?"

"Yes. They change guard three or four times. Has anyone seen a sentry asleep?" van Nekk asked.

They shook their heads.

"We could be aboard tonight," Jan Roper said. "With the help of God we'll overpower the heathen and take the ship."

"Clear the shit out of your ears! The Pilot's just got through telling you! Don't you listen?" Vinck spat disgustedly.

"That's right," Pieterzoon, a gunner, agreed. "Stop hacking at old Vinck!"

Jan Roper's eyes narrowed even more. "Look to your soul, Johann Vinck. And yours, Hans Pieterzoon. The Day of Judgment approaches." He walked away and sat on the veranda.

Van Nekk broke the silence. "Everything is going to be all right. You'll see."

"Roper's right. It's greed that put us here," the boy Croocq said, his voice quavering. "It's God's punishment that—"

"Stop it!"

The boy jerked. "Yes, Pilot. Sorry, but—well . . ." Maximilian Croocq was the youngest of them, just sixteen, and he had signed on for the voyage because his father had been captain of one of the ships and they were going to make their fortune. But he had seen his father die badly when they had sacked the Spanish town of Santa Magdellana in the Argentine. The plunder had been good and he had seen what rape was and he had tried it, hating himself, glutted by the blood smell and the killing. Later he had seen more of his friends die and the five ships became one and now he felt he was the oldest among them. "Sorry. I'm sorry."

"How long have we been ashore, Baccus?" Blackthorne asked.

"This is the third day." Van Nekk moved close again, squatting on his haunches. "Don't remember the arrival too clearly, but when I woke up the savages were all over the ship. Very polite and kind though. Gave us food and hot water. They took the dead away and put the anchors out. Don't remember much but I think they towed us to a safe mooring. You were delirious when they carried you ashore. We wanted to keep you with us but they wouldn't let us. One of them spoke a few words of Portuguese. He seemed to be the headman, he had gray hair. He didn't understand 'Pilot-Major' but knew 'Captain.' It was quite clear he wanted our 'Captain' to have different quarters from us, but he said we shouldn't worry because you'd be well looked after. Us too. Then he guided us here, they carried us mostly, and said we were to stay inside until *his* captain came. We didn't want to let them take you but there was nothing we could do. Will you ask the headman about wine or brandy, Pilot?" Van Nekk licked his lips thirstily, then added, "Now that I think of it, he mentioned '*daimyo*' too. What's going to happen when the *daimyo* arrives?"

"Has anyone got a knife or a pistol?"

"No," van Nekk said, scratching absently at the lice in his hair. "They took all our clothes away to clean them and kept the weapons. I didn't think anything about it at the time. They took my keys too, as well as my pistol. I had all my keys on a ring. The strong room, the strongbox, and the magazine."

"Everything's locked tight aboard. No need to worry about that."

"I don't like not having my keys. Makes me very nervous. Damn my eyes, I could use a brandy right now. Even a flagon of ale."

"Lord Jesus! The sameree cut him into pieces, did he?" Sonk said to no one in particular.

"For the love of God, shut your mouth. It's 'samurai.' You're enough to make a man shit himself," Ginsel said.

"I hope that bastard priest doesn't come here," Vinck said.

"We're safe in the good Lord's hands." Van Nekk was still trying to sound confident. "When the *daimyo* comes we'll be released. We'll get our ship back and our guns. You'll see. We'll sell all our goods and we'll get back to Holland rich and safe having gone round the world—the first Dutchmen ever. The Catholics'll go to hell and that's the end of it."

"No, it isn't," Vinck said. "Papists make my skin crawl. I can't help it. That and the thought of the conquistadores. You think they'll be here in strength, Pilot?"

"I don't know. I'd think yes! I wish we had all our squadron here."

"Poor bastards," Vinck said. "At least we're alive."

Maetsukker said, "Maybe they're back home. Maybe they turned back at the Magellan when the storms scattered us."

"I hope you're right," Blackthorne said. "But I think they're lost with all hands."

Ginsel shuddered. "At least we're alive."

"With Papists here, and these heathens with their stinking tempers, I wouldn't give an old whore's crack for our lives."

"Goddamn the day I left Holland," Pieterzoon said. "Goddamn all grog! If I hadn't been drunker than a fiddler's bitch I'd still be heads down in Amsterdam with my old woman."

"Damn what you like, Pieterzoon. But don't damn liquor. It's the stuff of life!"

"I'd say we're in the sewer, up to our chins, and the tide's coming in fast." Vinck rolled his eyes. "Yes, very fast."

"I never thought we'd reach land," Maetsukker said. He looked like a ferret, except he had no teeth. "Never. Least of all the Japans. Lousy stinking Papists! We'll never leave here alive! I wish we had some guns. What a rotten landfall! I didn't mean anything, Pilot," he said quickly as Blackthorne looked at him. "Just bad luck, that's all."

Later servants brought them food again. Always the same: vegetables —cooked and raw—with a little vinegar, fish soup, and the wheat or barley porridge. They all spurned the small pieces of raw fish and asked for meat and liquor. But they were not understood and then, near sunset, Blackthorne left. He had wearied of their fears and hates and obscenities. He told them that he would return after dawn.

The shops were busy on the narrow streets. He found his street and the gate of his house. The stains on the earth had been swept away and the body had vanished. It's almost as though I dreamed the whole thing, he thought. The garden gate opened before he could put a hand on it.

The old gardener, still loinclothed although there was a chill on the wind, beamed and bowed. *"Konbanwa."*

"Hello," Blackthorne said without thinking. He walked up the steps, stopped, remembering his boots. He took them off and went barefoot onto the veranda and into the room. He crossed it into a corridor but could not find his room.

"Onna!" he called out.

An old woman appeared. *"Hai?"*

"Where's Onna?"

The old woman frowned and pointed to herself. "Onna!"

"Oh, for the love of God," Blackthorne said irritably. "Where's my room? Where's Onna?" He slid open another latticed door. Four Japanese were seated on the floor around a low table, eating. He recognized one of them as the gray-haired man, the village headman, who had been with the priest. They all bowed. "Oh, sorry," he said, and pulled the door to.

"Onna!" he called out.

The old woman thought a moment, then beckoned. He followed her into another corridor. She slid a door aside. He recognized his room from the crucifix. The quilts were already laid out neatly.

"Thank you," he said, relieved. "Now fetch Onna!"

The old woman padded away. He sat down, his head and body aching, and wished there was a chair, wondering where they were kept. How to get aboard? How to get some guns? There must be a way. Feet padded back and there were three women now, the old woman, a young round-faced girl, and the middle-aged lady.

The old woman pointed at the girl, who seemed a little frightened. "Onna."

"No." Blackthorne got up ill-temperedly and jerked a finger at the middle-aged woman. "This is Onna, for God's sake! Don't you know your name? Onna! I'm hungry. Could I have some food?" He rubbed his stomach parodying hunger. They looked at each other. Then the middle-aged woman shrugged, said something that made the others laugh, went over to the bed, and began to undress. The other two squatted, wide-eyed and expectant.

Blackthorne was appalled. "What are you doing?"

"*Ishimasho!*" she said, setting aside her wide waistband and opening her kimono. Her breasts were flat and dried up and her belly huge.

It was quite clear that she was going to get into the bed. He shook his head and told her to get dressed and took her arm and they all began chattering and gesticulating and the woman was becoming quite angry. She stepped out of her long underskirt and, naked, tried to get back into bed.

Their chattering stopped and they all bowed as the headman came quietly down the corridor. "*Nanda? Nanda?*" he asked.

The old woman explained what was the matter. "You want this woman?" he asked incredulously in heavily accented, barely understandable Portuguese, motioning at the naked woman.

"No. No, of course not. I just wanted Onna to get me some food." Blackthorne pointed impatiently at her. "Onna!"

"*Onna* mean 'woman.'" The Japanese motioned at all of them. "*Onna—onna—onna*. You want *onna?*"

Blackthorne wearily shook his head. "No. No, thank you. I made a mistake. Sorry. What's her name?"

"Please?"

"What's her name?"

"Ah! Namu is Haku. Haku," he said.

"Haku?"

"*Hai.* Haku!"

"I'm sorry, Haku-san. Thought *onna* your name."

The man explained to Haku and she was not at all pleased. But he said something and they all looked at Blackthorne and tittered behind their hands and left. Haku walked off naked, her kimono over her arm, with a vast amount of dignity.

"Thank you," Blackthorne said, enraged at his own stupidity.

"This my house. My namu Mura."

"Mura-san. Mine's Blackthorne."

"Please?"

"My namu. Blackthorne."

"Ah! Berr—rakk—fon" Mura tried to say it several times but could not. Eventually he gave up and continued to study the colossus in front of him. This was the first barbarian he had ever seen except for Father Sebastio, and the other priest, so many years ago. But anyway, he thought, the priests are dark-haired and dark-eyed and of normal height. But this man: tall and golden-haired and golden-bearded with blue eyes and a weird pallor to his skin where it is covered and redness where it is exposed. Astonishing! I thought *all* men had black hair and dark eyes. *We* all do. The Chinese do, and isn't China the whole world, except for the land of the southern Portugee barbarians? Astonishing! And why does Father Sebastio hate this man so much? Because he's a Satan worshiper? I wouldn't think so, because Father Sebastio could cast out the devil if he wanted. Eeee, I've never seen the good Father so angry. Never. Astonishing!

Are blue eyes and golden hair the mark of Satan?

Mura looked up at Blackthorne and remembered how he had tried to question him aboard the ship and then, when this Captain had become unconscious, he had decided to bring him to his own house because he was the leader and should have special consideration. They had laid him on the quilt and undressed him, more than just a little curious.

"His Peerless Parts are certainly impressive, *neh?*" Mura's mother, Saiko, had said. "I wonder how large he would be when erect?"

"Large," he had answered and they had all laughed, his mother and wife and friends and servants, and the doctor.

"I expect their women must be—must be as well endowed," his wife, Niji, said.

"Nonsense, girl," said his mother. "Any number of our courtesans could happily make the necessary accommodation." She shook her head in wonder. "I've never seen anything like him in my whole life. Very odd indeed, *neh?*"

They had washed him and he had not come out of his coma. The doctor had thought it unwise to immerse him in a proper bath until he was awake. "Perhaps we should remember, Mura-san, we don't know how the barbarian really is," he had said with careful wisdom. "So sorry, but we might kill him by mistake. Obviously he's at the limit of his strength. We should exercise patience."

"But what about the lice in his hair?" Mura had asked.

"They will have to stay for the time being. I understand all barbarians have them. So sorry, I'd advise patience."

"Don't you think we could at least shampoo his head?" his wife had said. "We'd be very careful. I'm sure the Mistress would supervise our poor efforts. That should help the barbarian and keep our house clean."

"I agree. You can shampoo him," his mother had said with finality. "But I'd certainly like to know how large he is when erect."

Now Mura glanced down at Blackthorne involuntarily. Then he remembered what the priest had told them about these Satanists and pirates. God the Father protect us from this evil, he thought. If I'd known that he was so terrible I would never have brought him into my house. No, he told himself. You are obliged to treat him as a special guest until Omi-san says otherwise. But you were wise to send word to the priest and send word to Omi-san instantly. Very wise. You're headman, you've protected the village and you, alone, are responsible.

Yes. And Omi-san will hold you responsible for the death this morning and the dead man's impertinence, and quite rightly.

"Don't be stupid, Tamazaki! You risk the good name of the village, *neh?*" he had warned his friend the fisherman a dozen times. "Stop your intolerance. Omi-san has no option but to sneer at Christians. Doesn't our *daimyo* detest Christians? What else can Omi-san do?"

"Nothing, I agree, Mura-san, please excuse me." Tamazaki had always replied as formally. "But Buddhists should have more tolerance, *neh?* Aren't they both Zen Buddhists?" Zen Buddhism was self-disciplining; it relied heavily on self-help and meditation to find Enlightenment. Most samurai belonged to the Zen Buddhist sect, since it suited, seemed almost to be designed for, a proud, death-seeking warrior.

"Yes, Buddhism teaches tolerance. But how many times must you be reminded they're samurai, and this is Izu and not Kyushu, and even if it were Kyushu, you're still the one that's wrong. Always. *Neh?*"

"Yes. Please excuse me, I know I'm wrong. But sometimes I feel I cannot live with my inner shame when Omi-san is so insulting about the True Faith."

And now, Tamazaki, you are dead of your own choosing because you insulted Omi-san by not bowing simply because he said, ". . . this smelly priest of the foreign religion." Even though the priest does smell and the Truth Faith is foreign. My poor friend. That truth will not feed your family now or remove the stain from my village.

Oh, Madonna, bless my old friend and give him the joy of thy Heaven.

Expect a lot of trouble from Omi-san, Mura told himself. And if that isn't bad enough, now our *daimyo* is coming.

A pervading anxiety always filled him whenever he thought of his feudal lord, Kasigi Yabu, *daimyo* of Izu, Omi's uncle—the man's cruelty and lack of honor, the way he cheated all the villages of their rightful share of their catch and their crops, and the grinding weight of his rule. When war comes, Mura asked himself, which side will Yabu declare for, Lord Ishido or Lord Toranaga? We're trapped between the giants and in pawn to both.

Northwards, Toranaga, the greatest general alive, Lord of the Kwanto, the Eight Provinces, the most important *daimyo* in the land, Chief General of the Armies of the East; to the west the domains of Ishido, Lord of Osaka Castle, conqueror of Korea, Protector of the Heir, Chief General of the Armies of the West. And to the north, the Tokaido, the Great Coastal Road that links Yedo, Toranaga's capital city, to Osaka, Ishido's capital city—three hundred miles westward over which their legions must march.

Who will win the war?

Neither.

Because their war will envelop the empire again, alliances will fall apart, provinces will fight provinces until it is village against village as it ever was. Except for the last ten years. For the last ten years, incredibly, there had been a warlessness called peace throughout the empire, for the first time in history.

I was beginning to like peace, Mura thought.

But the man who made the peace is dead. The peasant soldier who became a samurai and then a general and then the greatest general and finally the Taikō, the absolute Lord Protector of Japan, is dead a year and his seven-year-old son is far too young to inherit supreme power. So the boy, like us, is in pawn. Between the giants. And war inevitable. Now not even the Taikō himself can protect his beloved son, his dynasty, his inheritance, or his empire.

Perhaps this is as it should be. The Taikō subdued the land, made the peace, forced all the *daimyos* in the land to grovel like peasants before him, rearranged fiefs to suit his whim—promoting some, deposing others —and then he died. He was a giant among pygmies. But perhaps it's right that all his work and greatness should die with him. Isn't man but a blossom taken by the wind, and only the mountains and the sea and the stars and this Land of the Gods real and everlasting?

We're all trapped and that is a fact; war will come soon and that is a fact; Yabu alone will decide which side we are on and that is a fact; the village will always be a village because the paddy fields are rich and the sea abundant and that is a last fact.

Mura brought his mind back firmly to the barbarian pirate in front of him. You're a devil sent to plague us, he thought, and you've caused us nothing but trouble since you arrived. Why couldn't you have picked another village?

"Captain-san want *onna?*" he asked helpfully. At his suggestion the village council made physical arrangements for the other barbarians, both as a politeness and as a simple means of keeping them occupied until the authorities came. That the village was entertained by the subsequent stories of the liaisons more than compensated for the money which had had to be invested.

"*Onna?*" he repeated, naturally presuming that as the pirate was on his feet, he would be equally content to be on his belly, his Heavenly Spear warmly encased before sleeping, and anyway, all the preparations had been made.

"No!" Blackthorne wanted only to sleep. But because he knew that he needed this man on his side he forced a smile, indicated the crucifix. "You're a Christian?"

Mura nodded. "Christian."

"I'm Christian."

"Father say not. Not Christian."

"I'm a Christian. Not a Catholic. But I'm still Christian."

But Mura could not understand. Neither was there any way Blackthorne could explain, however much he tried.

"Want *onna?*"

"The—the dimyo—when come?"

"Dimyo? No understand."

"Dimyo—ah, I mean *daimyo.*"

"Ah, *daimyo. Hai. Daimyo!*" Mura shrugged. "*Daimyo* come when come. Sleep. First clean. Please."

"What?"

"Clean. Bath, please."

"I don't understand."

Mura came closer and crinkled his nose distastefully.

"Stinku. Bad. Like all Portugeezu. Bath. This clean house."

"I'll bath when I want and I don't stink!" Blackthorne fumed. "Everyone knows baths are dangerous. You want me to catch the flux? You think I'm God-cursed stupid? You get the hell out of here and let me sleep!"

"Bath!" Mura ordered, shocked at the barbarian's open anger—the height of bad manners. And it was not just that the barbarian stank, as indeed he did, but he had not bathed correctly for three days to his knowledge, and the courtesan quite rightly would refuse to pillow with him, however much the fee. These awful foreigners, he thought. Astonishing! How astoundingly filthy their habits are! Never mind. I'm responsible for you. You will be taught manners. You will bath like a human being, and Mother will know that which she wants to know. "Bath!"

"Now get out before I snap you into pieces!" Blackthorne glowered at him, motioning him away.

There was a moment's pause and the other three Japanese appeared along with three of the women. Mura explained curtly what was the matter, then said with finality to Blackthorne, "Bath. Please."

"Out!"

Mura came forward alone into the room. Blackthorne shoved out his arm, not wanting to hurt the man, just to push him away. Suddenly Blackthorne let out a bellow of pain. Somehow Mura had chopped his elbow with the side of his hand and now Blackthorne's arm hung down, momentarily paralyzed. Enraged, he charged. But the room spun and he was flat on his face and there was another stabbing, paralyzing pain in his back and he could not move. "By God . . ."

He tried to get up but his legs buckled under him. Then Mura calmly put out his small but iron-hard finger and touched a nerve center in Blackthorne's neck. There was a blinding pain.

"Good sweet Jesus . . ."

"Bath? Please?"

"Yes—yes," Blackthorne gasped through his agony, astounded that he had been overcome so easily by such a tiny man and now lay helpless as any child, ready to have his throat cut.

Years ago Mura had learned the arts of judo and karate as well as how to fight with sword and spear. This was when he was a warrior and fought for Nakamura, the peasant general, the Taikō—long before the Taikō had become the Taikō—when peasants could be samurai and samurai could be peasants, or craftsmen or even lowly merchants, and warriors again. Strange, Mura thought absently, looking down at the fallen giant, that almost the first thing the Taikō did when he became all powerful was to order all peasants to cease being soldiers and at once give up all weapons. The Taikō had forbidden them weapons forever and set up the immutable caste system that now controlled all the lives in all the empire: samurai above all, below them the peasants, next craftsmen, then the merchants followed by actors, outcasts, and bandits, and finally at the bottom of the scale, the *eta,* the nonhumans, those who dealt with dead bodies, the curing of leather and handling of dead animals, who were also the public executioners, branders, and mutilators. Of course, any barbarian was beneath consideration in this scale.

"Please excuse me, Captain-san," Mura said, bowing low, ashamed for the barbarian's loss of face as he lay groaning like a baby still at suck. Yes, I'm very sorry, he thought, but it had to be done. You provoked me beyond all reasonableness, even for a barbarian. You shout like a lunatic, upset my mother, interrupt my house's tranquillity, disturb the servants, and my wife's already had to replace one shoji door. I could not possibly permit your obvious lack of manners to go unopposed. Or allow you to go against my wishes in my own house. It's really for your own good. Then, too, it's not so bad because you barbarians really have no face to lose. Except the priests—they're different. They still smell horrible, but they're the anointed of God the Father so they have great face. But you—you're a liar as well as a pirate. No honor. How astonishing! Claiming to be a Christian! Unfortunately that won't help you at all. Our *daimyo* hates the True Faith and barbarians and tolerates them only because he has to. But you're not a Portuguese or a Christian, therefore not protected by law, *neh*? So even though you are a dead man—or at least a mutilated one—it is my duty to see that you go to your fate clean. "Bath very good!"

He helped the other men carry the still dazed Blackthorne through the house, out into the garden, along a roofed-in walk of which he was very proud, and into the bath house. The women followed.

It became one of the great experiences of his life. He knew at the time that he would tell and retell the tale to his incredulous friends over barrels of hot saké, as the national wine of Japan was called; to his fellow elders, fishermen, villagers, to his children who also would not at first believe him. But they, in their turn, would regale their children and the name of Mura the fisherman would live forever in the village of Anjiro which was in the province of Izu on the southeastern coast of the main island of Honshu. All because he, Mura the fisherman, had the good fortune to be headman in the first year after the death of the Taikō and therefore temporarily responsible for the leader of the strange barbarians who came out of the eastern sea.

CHAPTER 2

THE *daimyo*, Kasigi Yabu, Lord of Izu, wants to know who you are, where you come from, how you got here, and what acts of piracy you have committed," Father Sebastio said.

"I keep telling you we're not pirates." The morning was clear and warm and Blackthorne was kneeling in front of the platform in the village square, his head still aching from the blow. Keep calm and get your brain working, he told himself. You're on trial for your lives. You're the spokesman and that's all there is to it. The Jesuit's hostile and the only interpreter available and you'll have no way of knowing what he's saying except you can be sure he'll not help you. . . . 'Get your wits about you boy,' he could almost hear old Alban Caradoc saying. 'When the storm's the worst and the sea the most dreadful, that's when you need your special wits. That's what keeps you alive and your ship alive—if you're the pilot. Get your wits about you and take the juice out of every day, however bad. . . .'

The juice of today is bile, Blackthorne thought grimly. Why do I hear Alban's voice so clearly?

"First tell the *daimyo* that we're at war, that we're enemies," he said. "Tell him England and the Netherlands are at war with Spain and Portugal."

"I caution you again to speak simply and not to twist the facts. The Netherlands—or Holland, Zeeland, the United Provinces, whatever you filthy Dutch rebels call it—is a small, rebellious province of the Spanish Empire. You're leader of traitors who are in a state of insurrection against their lawful king."

"England's at war and the Netherlands have been sepa—" Blackthorne did not continue because the priest was no longer listening but interpreting.

The *daimyo* was on the platform, short, squat, and dominating. He knelt comfortably, his heels tucked neatly under him, flanked by four lieutenants, one of whom was Kasigi Omi, his nephew and vassal. They all wore silk kimonos and, over them, ornate surcoats with wide belts nipping them in at the waist and huge, starched shoulders. And the inevitable swords.

Mura knelt in the dirt of the square. He was the only villager present and the only other onlookers were the fifty samurai who came with the *daimyo*. They sat in disciplined, silent rows. The rabble of the ship's crew were behind Blackthorne and, like him, were on their knees, guards nearby. They had had to carry the Captain-General with them when they were sent for, even though he was ailing badly. He had been allowed to lie down in the dirt, still in semicoma. Blackthorne had bowed with all of them when they had come in front of the *daimyo,* but this was not enough. Samurai had slammed all of them on their knees and pushed their heads into the dust in the manner of peasants. He had tried to resist and shouted to the priest to explain that it was not their custom, that he was the leader and an emissary of their country and should be treated as such. But the haft of a spear had sent him reeling. His men gathered themselves for an impulsive charge, but he shouted at them to stop and to kneel. Fortunately they obeyed. The *daimyo* had uttered something guttural and the priest interpreted this as a caution to him to tell the truth and tell it quickly. Blackthorne had asked for a chair but the priest said the Japanese did not use chairs and there were none in Japan.

Blackthorne was concentrating on the priest as he spoke to the *daimyo,* seeking a clue, a way through this reef.

There's arrogance and cruelty in the *daimyo's* face, he thought. I'll bet he's a real bastard. The priest's Japanese isn't fluent. Ah, see that? Irritation and impatience. Did the *daimyo* ask for another word, a clearer word? I think so. Why's the Jesuit wearing orange robes? Is the *daimyo* a Catholic? Look, the Jesuit's very deferential and sweating a lot. I'll bet the *daimyo's* not a Catholic. Be accurate! *Perhaps* he's not a Catholic. Either way you'll get no quarter from him. How can you use the evil bastard? How do you talk direct to him? How're you going to work the priest? How discredit him? What's the bait? Come on, think! You know enough about Jesuits—

"The *daimyo* says hurry up and answer his questions."

"Yes. Of course, I'm sorry. My name's John Blackthorne. I'm English, Pilot-Major of a Netherlands fleet. Our home port's Amsterdam."

"Fleet? What fleet? You're lying. There's no fleet. Why is an Englishman pilot of a Dutch ship?"

"All in good time. First please translate what I said."

"Why are you the pilot of a Dutch privateer? Hurry up!"

Blackthorne decided to gamble. His voice abruptly hardened and it cut through the morning warmth. *"Que va!* First translate what I said, *Spaniard!* Now!"

The priest flushed. "I'm Portuguese. I've told you before. Answer the question."

"I'm here to talk to the *daimyo,* not to you. Translate what I said, you motherless offal!" Blackthorne saw the priest redden even more and felt that this had not gone unnoticed by the *daimyo*. Be cautious, he warned himself. That yellow bastard will carve you into pieces quicker than a school of sharks if you overreach yourself. "Tell the lord *daimyo!*" Blackthorne deliberately bowed low to the platform and felt the chill sweat beginning to pearl as he committed himself irrevocably to his course of action.

Father Sebastio knew that his training should make him impervious to the pirate's insults and the obvious plan to discredit him in front of the *daimyo*. But, for the first time, it did not and he felt lost. When Mura's messenger had brought news of the ship to his mission in the neighboring province, he had been rocked by the implications. It can't be Dutch or English! he had thought. There had never been a heretic ship in the Pacific except those of the archdevil corsair Drake, and never one here in Asia. The routes were secret and guarded. At once he had prepared to leave and had sent an urgent carrier pigeon message to his superior in Osaka, wishing that he could first have consulted with him, knowing that he was young, almost untried and new to Japan, barely two years here, not yet ordained, and not competent to deal with this emergency. He had rushed to Anjiro, hoping and praying that the news was untrue. But the ship was Dutch and the pilot English, and all of his loathing for the satanic heresies of Luther, Calvin, Henry VIII, and the archfiend Elizabeth, his bastard daughter, had overwhelmed him. And still swamped his judgment.

"Priest, translate what the pirate said," he heard the *daimyo* say.

O Blessed Mother of God, help me to do thy will. Help me to be strong in front of the *daimyo* and give me the gift of tongues, and let me convert him to the True Faith.

Father Sebastio gathered his wits and began to speak more confidently.

Blackthorne listened carefully, trying to pick out the words and meanings. The Father used "England" and "Blackthorne" and pointed at the ship which lay nicely at anchor in the harbor.

"How did you get here?" Father Sebastio said.

"By Magellan's Pass. This is the one hundred and thirty-sixth day from there. Tell the *daimyo*—"

"You're lying. Magellan's Pass is secret. You came via Africa and India. You'll have to tell the truth eventually. They use torture here."

"The Pass *was* secret. A Portuguese sold us a rutter. One of your own people sold you out for a little Judas gold. You're all manure! Now all English warships—and Dutch warships—know the way through to the Pacific. There's a fleet—twenty English ships-of-the-line, sixty-cannon warships—attacking Manila right now. Your empire's finished."

"You're lying!"

Yes, Blackthorne thought, knowing there was no way to prove the lie except to go to Manila. "That fleet will harry your sea lanes and stamp out your colonies. There's another Dutch fleet due here any week now. The Spanish-Portuguese pig is back in his pigsty and your Jesuit General's penis is in his anus—where it belongs!" He turned away and bowed low to the *daimyo*.

"God curse you and your filthy mouth!"

"*Ano mono wa nani o moshité oru?*" the *daimyo* snapped impatiently.

The priest spoke more quickly, harder, and said "Magellan" and "Manila" but Blackthorne thought that the *daimyo* and his lieutenants did not seem to understand too clearly.

Yabu was wearying of this trial. He looked out into the harbor, to the ship that had obsessed him ever since he had received Omi's secret message, and he wondered again if it was the gift from the gods that he hoped.

"Have you inspected the cargo yet, Omi-san?" he had asked this morning as soon as he had arrived, mud-spattered and very weary.

"No, Lord. I thought it best to seal up the ship until you came personally, but the holds are filled with crates and bales. I hope I did it correctly. Here are all their keys. I confiscated them."

"Good." Yabu had come from Yedo, Toranaga's capital city, more than a hundred miles away, post haste, furtively and at great personal risk, and it was vital that he return as quickly. The journey had taken almost two days over foul roads and spring-filled streams, partly on horseback and partly by palanquin. "I'll go to the ship at once."

"You should see the strangers, Lord," Omi had said with a laugh. "They're incredible. Most of them have blue eyes—like Siamese cats—and golden hair. But the best news of all is that they're pirates. . . ."

Omi had told him about the priest and what the priest had related about these corsairs and what the pirate had said and what had happened, and his excitement had tripled. Yabu had conquered his impatience to go aboard the ship and break the seals. Instead he had bathed and changed and ordered the barbarians brought in front of him.

"You, priest," he said, his voice sharp, hardly able to understand the priest's bad Japanese. "Why is he so angry with you?"

"He's evil. Pirate. He worship devil."

Yabu leaned over to Omi, the man on his left. "Can you understand what he's saying, nephew? Is he lying? What do you think?"

"I don't know, Lord. Who knows what barbarians really believe? I imagine the priest *thinks* the pirate is a devil worshiper. Of course, that's all nonsense."

Yabu turned back to the priest, detesting him. He wished that he could crucify him today and obliterate Christianity from his domain once and for all. But he could not. Though he and all other *daimyos* had total power in their own domains, they were still subject to the overriding authority of the Council of Regents, the military ruling junta to whom the Taikō had legally willed his power during his son's minority, and subject, too, to edicts the Taikō had issued in his lifetime, which were all still legally in force. One of these, promulgated years ago, dealt with the Portuguese barbarians and ordered that they were all protected persons and, within reason, their religion was to be tolerated and their priests allowed, within reason, to proselytize and convert. "You, priest! What else did the pirate say? What was he saying to you? Hurry up! Have you lost your tongue?"

"Pirate says bad things. Bad. About more pirate war boatings—many."

"What do you mean, 'war boatings'?"

"Sorry, Lord, I don't understand."

"'War boatings' doesn't make sense, *neh?*"

"Ah! Pirate says other ships war are in Manila, in Philippines."

"Omi-san, do you understand what he's talking about?"

"No, Lord. His accent's appalling, it's almost gibberish. Is he saying that more pirate ships are east of Japan?"

"You, priest! Are these pirate ships off our coast? East? Eh?"

"Yes, Lord. But I think he's lying. He says at Manila."

"I don't understand you. Where's Manila?"

"East. Many days' journey."

"If any pirate ships come here, we'll give them a pleasant welcome, wherever Manila is."

"Please excuse me, I don't understand."

"Never mind," Yabu said, his patience at an end. He had already decided the strangers were to die and he relished the prospect. Obviously these men did not come within the Taikō's edict that specified "Portuguese barbarians," and anyway they were pirates. As long as he could remember he had hated barbarians, their stench and filthiness and disgusting meat-eating habits, their stupid religion and arrogance and detestable manners. More than that, he was shamed, as was every *daimyo,* by their stranglehold over this Land of the Gods. A state of war had existed between China and Japan for centuries. China would allow no trade. Chinese silk cloth was vital to make the long, hot, humid Japanese summer bearable. For generations only a minuscule amount of contraband cloth had slipped through the net and was available, at huge cost, in Japan. Then, sixty-odd years ago, the barbarians had first arrived. The Chinese Emperor in Peking gave them a tiny permanent base at Macao in southern China and agreed to trade silks for silver. Japan had silver in abundance. Soon trade was flourishing. Both countries prospered. The middlemen, the Portuguese, grew rich, and their priests— Jesuits mostly—soon became vital to the trade. Only the priests managed to learn to speak Chinese and Japanese and therefore could act as negotiators and interpreters. As trade blossomed, the priests became more essential. Now the yearly trade was huge and touched the life of every samurai. So the priests had to be tolerated and the spread of their religion tolerated or the barbarians would sail away and trade would cease.

By now there were a number of very important Christian *daimyos* and many hundreds of thousands of converts, most of whom were in Kyushu, the southern island that was nearest to China and contained the Portuguese port of Nagasaki. Yes, Yabu thought, we must tolerate the priests and the Portuguese, but not these barbarians, the new ones, the unbelievable golden-haired, blue-eyed ones. His excitement filled him. Now at last he could satisfy his curiosity as to how well a barbarian would die when put to torment. And he had eleven men, eleven different tests, to experiment with. He never questioned why the agony of others pleasured him. He only knew that it did and therefore it was something to be sought and enjoyed.

Yabu said, "This ship, alien, non-Portuguese, and pirate, is confiscated with all it contains. All pirates are sentenced to immediate—" His mouth dropped open as he saw the pirate leader suddenly leap at the priest and rip the wooden crucifix from his belt, snap it into pieces and hurl the pieces on the ground, then shout something very loudly. The pirate immediately knelt and bowed low to him as the guards jumped forward, swords raised.

"Stop! Don't kill him!" Yabu was astounded that anyone could have the impertinence to act with such lack of manners in front of him. "These barbarians are beyond belief!"

"Yes," Omi said, his mind flooding with the questions that such an action implied.

The priest was still kneeling, staring fixedly at the pieces of the cross. They watched as his hand reached out shakily and picked up the violated wood. He said something to the pirate, his voice low, almost gentle. His eyes closed, he steepled his fingers, and his lips began to move slowly. The pirate leader was looking up at them motionlessly, pale blue eyes unblinking, catlike, in front of his rabble crew.

Yabu said, "Omi-san. First I want to go on the ship. Then we'll begin." His voice thickened as he contemplated the pleasure he had promised himself. "I want to begin with that red-haired one on the end of the line, the small man."

Omi leaned closer and lowered his excited voice. "Please excuse me, but this has never happened before, Sire. Not since the Portuguese barbarians came here. Isn't the crucifix their sacred symbol? Aren't they *always* deferential to their priests? Don't they always kneel to them openly? Just like our Christians? Haven't the priests absolute control over them?"

"Come to your point."

"We all detest the Portuguese, Sire. Except the Christians among us, *neh*? Perhaps these barbarians are worth more to you alive than dead."

"How?"

"Because they're unique. They're anti-Christian! Perhaps a wise man could find a way to use their hatred—or irreligiousness—to our advantage. They're your property, to do with as you wish. *Neh?*"

Yes. And I want them in torment, Yabu thought. Yes, but you can enjoy that at any time. Listen to Omi. He's a good counselor. But is he to be trusted now? Does he have a secret reason for saying this? Think.

"Ikawa Jikkyu is Christian," he heard his nephew say, naming his hated enemy—one of Ishido's kinsmen and allies—who sat on his western borders. "Doesn't this filthy priest have his home there? Perhaps these barbarians could give you the key to unlock Ikawa's whole province. Perhaps Ishido's. Perhaps even Lord Toranaga's," Omi added delicately.

Yabu studied Omi's face, trying to reach what was behind it. Then his eyes went to the ship. He had no doubt now that it had been sent by the gods. Yes. But was it as a gift or a plague?

He put away his own pleasure for the security of his clan. "I agree. But first break these pirates. Teach them manners. Particularly *him*."

"Good sweet Jesus' death!" Vinck muttered.

"We should say a prayer," van Nekk said.

"We've just said one."

"Perhaps we'd better say another. Lord God in Heaven, I could use a pint of brandy."

They were crammed into a deep cellar, one of the many that the fishermen used to store sun-dried fish. Samurai had herded them across the square, down a ladder, and now they were locked underground. The cellar was five paces long and five wide and four deep, with an earthen floor and walls. The ceiling was made of planks with a foot of earth above and a single trapdoor set into it.

"Get off my foot, you God-cursed ape!"

"Shut your face, shit picker!" Pieterzoon said genially. "Hey! Vinck, move up a little, you toothless old fart, you've got more room than anyone! By God, I could use a cold beer! Move up."

"I can't, Pieterzoon. We're tighter than a virgin's arse here."

"It's the Captain-General. He's got all the space. Give him a shove. Wake him up!" Maetsukker said.

"Eh? What's the matter? Leave me alone. What's going on? I'm sick. I've got to lie down. Where are we?"

"Leave him alone. He's sick. Come on, Maetsukker, get up, for the love of God." Vinck angrily pulled Maetsukker up and shoved him against the wall. There was not room enough for them all to lie down, or even to sit comfortably, at the same time. The Captain-General, Paulus Spillbergen, was lying full length under the trapdoor where there was the best air, his head propped on his bundled cloak. Blackthorne was leaning against a corner, staring up at the trapdoor. The crew had left him alone and stayed clear of him uneasily, as best they could, recognizing from long experience his mood, and the brooding, explosive violence that always lurked just below his quiet exterior.

Maetsukker lost his temper and smashed his fist into Vinck's groin. "Leave me alone or I'll kill you, you bastard."

Vinck flew at him, but Blackthorne grabbed both of them and rammed their heads against the wall.

"Shut up, all of you," he said softly. They did as they were ordered. "We'll split into watches. One watch sleeps, one sits, and one stands. Spillbergen lies down until he's fit. That corner's the latrine." He divided them up. When they had rearranged themselves it was more bearable.

We'll have to break out of here within a day or we'll be too weak, Blackthorne thought. When they bring the ladder back to give us food or water. It will have to be tonight or tomorrow night. Why did they put us here? We're no threat. We could help the *daimyo*. Will he understand? It was my only way to show him that the priest's our real enemy. Will he understand? The priest had.

"Perhaps God may forgive your sacrilege but I won't," Father Sebastio had said, very quietly. "I will never rest until you and your evil are obliterated."

The sweat was dribbling down his cheeks and chin. He wiped it away absently, ears tuned to the cellar as they would be when he was aboard and sleeping, or off watch and drifting; just enough to try to hear the danger before it happened.

We'll have to break out and take the ship. I wonder what Felicity's doing. And the children. Let's see, Tudor's seven years old now and

Lisbeth is. . . . We're one year and eleven months and six days from Amsterdam, add thirty-seven days provisioning and coming from Chatham to there, add lastly, the eleven days that she was alive before the embarkation at Chatham. That's her age exactly—if all's well. All should be well. Felicity will be cooking and guarding and cleaning and chattering as the kids grow up, as strong and fearless as their mother. It will be fine to be home again, to walk together along the shore and in the forests and glades and beauty that is England.

Over the years he had trained himself to think about them as characters in a play, people that you loved and bled for, the play never ending. Otherwise the hurt of being away would be too much. He could almost count his days at home in the eleven years of marriage. They're few, he thought, too few. "It's a hard life for a woman, Felicity," he had said before. And she had said, "Any life is hard for a woman." She was seventeen then and tall and her hair was long and sensu—

His ears told him to beware.

The men were sitting or leaning or trying to sleep. Vinck and Pieterzoon, good friends, were talking quietly. Van Nekk was staring into space with the others. Spillbergen was half awake, and Blackthorne thought the man was stronger than he let everyone believe.

There was a sudden silence as they heard the footsteps overhead. The footsteps stopped. Muted voices in the harsh, strange-sounding language. Blackthorne thought he recognized the samurai's voice—Omisan? Yes, that was his name—but he could not be certain. In a moment the voices stopped and the footsteps went away.

"You think they'll feed us, Pilot?" Sonk said.

"Yes."

"I could use a drink. Cold beer, by God," Pieterzoon said.

"Shut up," Vinck said. "You're enough to make a man sweat."

Blackthorne was conscious of his soaking shirt. And the stench. By the Lord God I could use a bath, he thought and abruptly he smiled, remembering.

Mura and the others had carried him into the warm room that day and laid him on a stone bench, his limbs still numb and slow moving. The three women, led by the old crone, had begun to undress him and he had tried to stop them but every time he moved, one of the men would stab a nerve and hold him powerless, and however much he raved and cursed they continued to undress him until he was naked. It was not that he was ashamed of being naked in front of a woman, it was just that undressing was always done in private and that was the custom. And he did not like being undressed by anyone, let alone these uncivilized natives. But to be undressed publicly like a helpless baby and to be washed everywhere like a baby with warm, soapy, scented water while they chattered and smiled as he lay on his back was too much. Then he had become erect and as much as he tried to stop it from happening, the worse it became—at least he thought so, but the women did not. Their eyes became bigger and he began to blush. Jesus Lord God the One and Only, I can't be blushing, but he was and this seemed to increase his size and the old woman clapped her hands in wonder and said something to which they all nodded and she shook her head awed and said something else to which they nodded even more.

Mura had said with enormous gravity, "Captain-san, Mother-san thank you, the best her life, now die happy!" and he and they had all bowed as one and then he, Blackthorne, had seen how funny it was and he had begun to laugh. They were startled, then they were laughing too, and his laughter took his strength away and the crone was a little sad and said so and this made him laugh more and them also. Then they had laid him gently into the vast heat of the deep water and soon he could bear it no longer, and they laid him gasping on the bench once more. The women had dried him and then an old blind man had come. Blackthorne had never known massage. At first he had tried to resist the probing fingers but then their magic seduced him and soon he was almost purring like a cat as the fingers found the knots and unlocked the blood or elixir that lurked beneath skin and muscle and sinew.

Then he had been helped to bed, strangely weak, half in dream, and the girl was there. She was patient with him, and after sleeping, when he had strength, he took her with care even though it had been so long.

He had not asked her name, and in the morning when Mura, tense and very frightened, had pulled him out of sleep, she was gone.

Blackthorne sighed. Life is marvelous, he thought.

In the cellar, Spillbergen was querulous again, Maetsukker was nursing his head and moaning, not from pain but from fear, the boy Croocq near breaking, and Jan Roper said, "What's there to smile about, Pilot?"

"Go to hell."

"With respect, Pilot," van Nekk said carefully, bringing into the open what was foremost in their minds, "you were most unwise to attack the priest in front of the rotten yellow bastard."

There was general though carefully expressed agreement.

"If you hadn't, I don't think we'd be in this filthy mess."

Van Nekk did not go near Blackthorne. "All you've got to do is put your head in the dust when the Lord Bastard's around and they're as meek as lambs."

He waited for a reply but Blackthorne made none, just turned back to the trapdoor. It was as though nothing had been said. Their unease increased.

Paulus Spillbergen lifted himself on one elbow with difficulty. "What are you talking about, Baccus?"

Van Nekk went over to him and explained about the priest and the cross and what had happened and why they were here, his eyes hurting today worse than ever.

"Yes, that was dangerous, Pilot-Major," Spillbergen said. "Yes, I'd say quite wrong—pass me some water. Now the Jesuits'll give us no peace at áll."

"You should have broken his neck, Pilot. Jesuits'll give us no peace anyway," Jan Roper said. "They're filthy lice and we're here in this stink hole as God's punishment."

"That's nonsense, Roper," Spillbergen said. "We're here becau—"

"It is God's punishment! We should have burned all the churches in Santa Magdellana—not just two. We should have. Cesspits of Satan!"

Spillbergen slapped weakly at a fly. "The Spanish troops were regrouping and we were outnumbered fifteen to one. Give me some water! We'd sacked the town and got the plunder and rubbed their noses in the dust. If we'd stayed we would have been killed. For God's sake, give me some water, someone. We'd've all been killed if we hadn't retrea—"

"What does it matter if you're doing the work of God? We failed Him."

"Perhaps we're here to do God's work," van Nekk said, placatingly, for Roper was a good though zealous man, a clever merchant and his partner's son. "Perhaps we can show the natives here the error of their Papist ways. Perhaps we could convert them to the True Faith."

"Quite right," Spillbergen said. He still felt weak, but his strength was returning. "I think you should have consulted Baccus, Pilot-Major. After all, he's chief merchant. He's very good at parleying with savages. Pass the water, I said!"

"There isn't any, Paulus." Van Nekk's gloom increased. "They've given us no food or water. We haven't even got a pot to piss in."

"Well, ask for one! And some water! God in heaven, I'm thirsty. Ask for water! You!"

"Me?" Vinck asked.

"Yes. You!"

Vinck looked at Blackthorne but Blackthorne just watched the trapdoor obliviously, so Vinck stood under the opening and shouted, "Hey! You up there! Give us God-cursed water! We want food and water!"

There was no answer. He shouted again. No answer. The others gradually took up the shouts. All except Blackthorne. Soon their panic and the nausea of their close confinement crept into their voices and they were howling like wolves.

The trapdoor opened. Omi looked down at them. Beside him was Mura. And the priest.

"Water! And food, by God! Let us out of here!" Soon they were all screaming again.

Omi motioned to Mura, who nodded and left. A moment later Mura returned with another fisherman, carrying a large barrel between them. They emptied the contents, rotting fish offal and seawater, onto the heads of the prisoners.

The men in the cellar scattered and tried to escape, but all of them could not. Spillbergen was choking, almost drowned. Some of the men slipped and were trampled on. Blackthorne had not moved from the corner. He just stared up at Omi, hating him.

Then Omi began talking. There was a cowed silence now, broken only by coughing and Spillbergen's retching. When Omi had finished, the priest nervously came to the opening.

"These are Kasigi Omi's orders: You will begin to act like decent human beings. You will make no more noise. If you do, next time five barrels will be poured into the cellar. Then ten, then twenty. You will be given food and water twice a day. When you have learned to behave, you will be allowed up into the world of men. Lord Yabu has graciously spared all your lives, providing you serve him loyally. All except one. One of you is to die. At dusk. You are to choose who it will be. But you"—he pointed at Blackthorne—"you are not to be the one chosen." Ill at ease, the priest took a deep breath, half bowed to the samurai, and stepped back.

Omi peered down into the pit. He could see Blackthorne's eyes and he felt the hatred. It will take much to break that man's spirit, he thought. No matter. There's time enough.

The trapdoor slammed into place.

CHAPTER 3

YABU lay in the hot bath, more content, more confident than he had ever been in his life. The ship had revealed its wealth and this wealth gave him a power that he had never dreamed possible.

"I want everything taken ashore tomorrow," he had said. "Repack the muskets in their crates. Camouflage everything with nets or sacking."

Five hundred muskets, he thought exultantly. With more gunpowder and shot than Toranaga has in all the Eight Provinces. And twenty cannon, five thousand cannon balls with an abundance of ammunition. Fire arrows by the crate. All of the best European quality. "Mura, you will provide porters. Igurashi-san, I want all this armament, including the cannon, in my castle at Mishima forthwith, in secret. You will be responsible."

"Yes, Lord." They had been in the main hold of the ship and everyone had gaped at him: Igurashi, a tall, lithe, one-eyed man, his chief retainer, Zukimoto his quartermaster, together with ten sweat-stained villagers who had opened the crates under Mura's supervision, and his personal bodyguard of four samurai. He knew they did not understand his exhilaration or the need to be clandestine. Good, he thought.

When the Portuguese had first discovered Japan in 1542, they had introduced muskets and gunpowder. Within eighteen months the Japanese were manufacturing them. The quality was not nearly as good as the European equivalent but that did not matter because guns were considered merely a novelty and, for a long time, used only for hunting —and even for that bows were far more accurate. Also, more important, Japanese warfare was almost ritual; hand-to-hand individual combat, the sword being the most honorable weapon. The use of guns was considered cowardly and dishonorable and completely against the samurai code, *bushido,* the Way of the Warrior, which bound samurai to fight with honor, to live with honor, and to die with honor; to have undying, unquestioning loyalty to one's feudal lord; to be fearless of death—even to seek it in his service; and to be proud of one's own name and keep it unsullied.

For years Yabu had had a secret theory. At long last, he thought exultantly, you can expand it and put it into effect: Five hundred chosen samurai, armed with muskets *but trained as a unit,* spearheading your twelve thousand conventional troops, supported by twenty cannon used in a special way by special men, also trained *as a unit*. A new strategy for a new era! In the coming war, guns could be decisive!

What about *bushido?* the ghosts of his ancestors had always asked him.

What about *bushido?* he had always asked them back.

They had never answered.

Never in his wildest dreams had he thought he'd ever be able to afford five hundred guns. But now he had them for nothing and he alone knew how to use them. But whose side to use them for? Toranaga's or Ishido's? Or should he wait—and perhaps be the eventual victor?

"Igurashi-san. You'll travel by night and maintain strict security."

"Yes, Lord."

"This is to remain secret, Mura, or the village will be obliterated."

"Nothing will be said, Lord. I can speak for my village. I cannot speak for the journey, or for other villages. Who knows where there are spies? But nothing will be said by us."

Next Yabu had gone to the strong room. It contained what he presumed to be pirate plunder: silver and gold plate, cups, candelabra and ornaments, some religious paintings in ornate frames. A chest contained women's clothes, elaborately embroidered with gold thread and colored stones.

"I'll have the silver and gold melted into ingots and put in the treasury," Zukimoto had said. He was a neat, pedantic man in his forties who was not a samurai. Years ago he had been a Buddhist warrior-priest, but the Taikō, the Lord Protector, had stamped out his monastery in a campaign to purge the land of certain Buddhist militant warrior monasteries and sects that would not acknowledge his absolute suzerainty. Zukimoto had bribed his way out of that early death and become a peddler, at length a minor merchant in rice. Ten years ago he had joined Yabu's commissariat and now he was indispensable. "As to the clothes, perhaps the gold thread and gems have value. With your permission, I'll have them packed and sent to Nagasaki with anything else I can salvage." The port of Nagasaki, on the southernmost coast of the south island of Kyushu, was the legal entrepôt and trading market of the Portuguese. "The barbarians might pay well for these odds and ends."

"Good. What about the bales in the other hold?"

"They all contain a heavy cloth. Quite useless to us, Sire, with no market value at all. But this should please you." Zukimoto had opened the strongbox.

The box contained twenty thousand minted silver pieces. Spanish doubloons. The best quality.

Yabu stirred in his bath. He wiped the sweat from his face and neck with the small white towel and sank deeper into the hot scented water. If, three days ago, he told himself, a soothsayer had forecast that all this would happen, you would have fed him his tongue for telling impossible lies.

Three days ago he had been in Yedo, Toranaga's capital. Omi's message had arrived at dusk. Obviously the ship had to be investigated at once but Toranaga was still away in Osaka for the final confrontation with General Lord Ishido and, in his absence, had invited Yabu and all friendly neighboring *daimyos* to wait until his return. Such an invitation could not be refused without dire results. Yabu knew that he and the other independent *daimyos* and their families were merely added protection for Toranaga's safety and, though of course the word would never be used, they were hostages against Toranaga's safe return from the impregnable enemy fortress at Osaka where the meeting was being held. Toranaga was President of the Council of Regents which the Taikō had appointed on his deathbed to rule the empire during the minority of his son Yaemon, now seven years old. There were five Regents, all eminent *daimyos,* but only Toranaga and Ishido had real power.

Yabu had carefully considered all the reasons for going to Anjiro, the risks involved, and the reasons for staying. Then he had sent for his wife and his favorite consort. A consort was a formal, legal mistress. A man could have as many consorts as he wished, but only one wife at one time.

"My nephew Omi has just sent secret word that a barbarian ship came ashore at Anjiro."

"One of the Black Ships?" his wife had asked excitedly. These were the huge, incredibly rich trading ships that plied annually with the monsoon winds between Nagasaki and the Portuguese colony of Macao that lay almost a thousand miles south on the China mainland.

"No. But it might be rich. I'm leaving immediately. You're to say that I've been taken sick and cannot be disturbed for any reason. I'll be back in five days."

"That's incredibly dangerous," his wife warned. "Lord Toranaga gave specific orders for us to stay. I'm sure he'll make another compromise with Ishido and he's too powerful to offend. Sire, we could never guarantee that someone won't suspect the truth—there are spies everywhere. If Toranaga returned and found you'd gone, your absence would be misinterpreted. Your enemies would poison his mind against you."

"Yes," his consort added. "Please excuse me, but you must listen to the Lady, your wife. She's right. Lord Toranaga would never believe that you'd disobeyed just to look at a barbarian ship. Please send someone else."

"But this isn't an ordinary barbarian ship. It's *not* Portuguese. Listen to me. Omi says it's from a different country. These men talk a different-sounding language among themselves and they have *blue eyes* and *golden hair*."

"Omi-san's gone mad. Or he's drunk too much saké," his wife said.

"This is much too important to joke about, for him and for you."

His wife had bowed and apologized and said that he was quite right to correct her, but that the remark was not meant in jest. She was a small, thin woman, ten years older than he, who had given him a child a year for eight years until her womb had dried up, and of these, five had been sons Three had become warriors and died bravely in the war against China. Another had become a Buddhist priest and the last, now nineteen, he despised.

His wife, the Lady Yuriko, was the only woman he had ever been afraid of, the only woman he had ever valued—except his mother, now dead—and she ruled his house with a silken lash.

"Again, please excuse me," she said. "Does Omi-san detail the cargo?"

"No. He didn't examine it, Yuriko-san. He says he sealed the ship at once because it was so unusual. There's never been a non-Portuguese ship before, *neh*? He says also it's a fighting ship. With twenty cannon on its decks."

"Ah! Then someone must go immediately."

"I'm going myself."

"Please reconsider. Send Mizuno. Your brother's clever and wise. I implore you not to go."

"Mizuno's weak and not to be trusted."

"Then order him to commit seppuku and have done with him," she said harshly. Seppuku, sometimes called hara-kiri, the ritual suicide by disembowelment, was the only way a samurai could expiate a shame, a sin, or a fault with honor, and was the sole prerogative of the samurai caste. All samurai—women as well as men—were prepared from infancy, either for the act itself or to take part in the ceremony as a second. Women committed seppuku only with a knife in the throat.

"Later, not now," Yabu told his wife.

"Then send Zukimoto. He's certainly to be trusted."

"If Toranaga hadn't ordered all wives and consorts to stay here too, I'd send you. But that would be too risky. I have to go. I have no option. Yuriko-san, you tell me my treasury's empty. You say I've no more credit with the filthy moneylenders. Zukimoto says we're getting the maximum tax out of my peasants. I have to have more horses, armaments, weapons, and more samurai. Perhaps the ship will supply the means."

"Lord Toranaga's orders were quite clear, Sire. If he comes back and finds—"

"Yes. *If* he comes back, Lady. I still think he's put himself into a trap. The Lord Ishido has eighty thousand samurai in and around Osaka Castle alone. For Toranaga to go there with a few hundred men was the act of a madman."

"He's much too shrewd to risk himself unnecessarily," she said confidently.

"If I were Ishido and I had him in my grasp I would kill him at once."

"Yes," Yuriko said. "But the mother of the Heir is still hostage in Yedo until Toranaga returns. General Lord Ishido dare not touch Toranaga until she's safely back at Osaka."

"I'd kill him. If the Lady Ochiba lives or dies, it doesn't matter. The Heir's safe in Osaka. With Toranaga dead, the succession is certain. Toranaga's the only real threat to the Heir, the only one with a chance at using the Council of Regents, usurping the Taikō's power, and killing the boy."

"Please excuse me, Sire, but perhaps General Lord Ishido can carry the other three Regents with him and impeach Toranaga, and that's the end of Toranaga, *neh?*" his consort said.

"Yes, Lady, if Ishido could he would, but I don't think he can—yet— nor can Toranaga. The Taikō picked the five Regents too cleverly. They despise each other so much it's almost impossible for them to agree on anything." Before taking power, the five great *daimyos* had publicly sworn eternal allegiance to the dying Taikō and to his son and his line forever. And they had taken public, sacred oaths agreeing to unanimous rule in the Council, and vowed to pass over the realm intact to Yaemon when he came of age on his fifteenth birthday. "Unanimous rule means nothing really can be changed until Yaemon inherits."

"But some day, Sire, four Regents will join against one—through jealousy, fear or ambition—*neh?* The four will bend the Taikō's orders just enough for war, *neh?*"

"Yes. But it will be a small war, Lady, and the *one* will always be smashed and his lands divided up by the victors, who will then have to appoint a fifth Regent and, in time, it will be four against one and again the one will be smashed and his lands forfeit—all as the Taikō planned. My only problem is to decide who will be the one this time—Ishido or Toranaga."

"Toranaga will be the one isolated."

"Why?"

"The others fear him too much because they all *know* he secretly wants to be Shōgun, however much he protests he doesn't."

Shōgun was the ultimate rank a mortal could achieve in Japan. Shōgun meant Supreme Military Dictator. Only one *daimyo* at a time could possess the title. And only His Imperial Highness, the reigning Emperor, the Divine Son of Heaven, who lived in seclusion with the Imperial Families at Kyoto, could grant the title.

With the appointment of Shōgun went absolute power: the Emperor's seal and mandate. The Shōgun ruled in the Emperor's name. All power was derived from the Emperor because he was directly descended from the gods. Therefore any *daimyo* who opposed the Shōgun was automatically in rebellion against the throne, and at once outcast and all his lands forfeit.

The reigning Emperor was worshiped as a divinity because he was descended in an unbroken line from the Sun Goddess, Amaterasu Omikami, one of the children of the gods Izanagi and Izanami, who had formed the islands of Japan from the firmament. By divine right the ruling Emperor owned all the land and ruled and was obeyed without question. But in practice, for more than six centuries real power had rested behind the throne.

Six centuries ago there had been a schism when two of the three great rival, semiregal samurai families, the Minowara, Fujimoto and Takashima, backed rival claimants to the throne and plunged the realm into civil war. After sixty years the Minowara prevailed over the Takashuma, and the Fujimoto, the family that had stayed neutral, bided its time.

From then on, jealously guarding their rule, the Minowara Shōguns dominated the realm, decreed their Shōgunate hereditary and began to intermarry some of their daughters with the Imperial line. The Emperor and the entire Imperial Court were kept completely isolated in walled palaces and gardens in the small enclave at Kyoto, most times in penury, and their activities perpetually confined to observing the rituals of Shinto, the ancient animistic religion of Japan, and to intellectual pursuits such as calligraphy, painting, philosophy, and poetry.

The Court of the Son of Heaven was easy to dominate because, though it possessed all the land, it had no revenue. Only *daimyos,* samurai, possessed revenue and the right to tax. And so it was that although all members of the Imperial Court were above all samurai in rank, they still existed on a stipend granted the Court at the whim of the Shōgun, the Kwampaku—the civil Chief Adviser—or the ruling military junta of the day. Few were generous. Some Emperors had even had to barter their signatures for food. Many times there was not enough money for a coronation.

At length the Minowara Shōguns lost their power to others, to Takashima or Fujimoto descendants. And as the civil wars continued unabated over the centuries, the Emperor became more and more the creature of the *daimyo* who was strong enough to obtain physical possession of Kyoto. The moment the new conqueror of Kyoto had slaughtered the ruling Shōgun and his line, he would—providing he was Minowara, Takashima, or Fujimoto—with humility, swear allegiance to the throne and humbly invite the powerless Emperor to grant him the now vacant rank of Shōgun. Then, like his predecessors, he would try to extend his rule outward from Kyoto until he in his turn was swallowed by another. Emperors married, abdicated, or ascended the throne at the whim of the Shōgunate. But always the reigning Emperor's bloodline was inviolate and unbroken.

So the Shōgun was all powerful. Until he was overthrown.

Many were unseated over the centuries as the realm splintered into ever smaller factions. For the last hundred years no single *daimyo* had ever had enough power to become Shōgun. Twelve years ago the peasant General Nakamura had had the power and he had obtained the mandate from the present Emperor, Go-Nijo. But Nakamura could not be granted Shōgun rank however much he desired it, because he was born a peasant. He had to be content with the much lesser civilian title of Kwampaku, Chief Adviser, and later, when he resigned that title to his infant son, Yaemon—though keeping all power, as was quite customary—he had to be content with Taikō. By historic custom only the descendants of the sprawling, ancient, semidivine families of the Minowara, Takashima, and Fujimoto were entitled to the rank of Shōgun.

Toranaga was descended from the Minowara. Yabu could trace his lineage to a vague and minor branch of the Takashima, enough of a connection if ever he could become supreme.

"Eeeee, Lady," Yabu said, "of course Toranaga wants to be Shōgun, but he'll never achieve it. The other Regents despise and fear him. They neutralize him, as the Taikō planned." He leaned forward and studied his wife intently. "You say Toranaga's going to lose to Ishido?"

"He will be isolated, yes. But in the end I don't think he'll lose, Sire. I beg you not to disobey Lord Toranaga, and not to leave Yedo just to examine the barbarian ship, no matter how unusual Omi-san says it is. Please send Zukimoto to Anjiro."

"What if the ship contains bullion? Silver or gold? Would you trust Zukimoto or any of our officers with it?"

"No," his wife had said.

So that night he had slipped out of Yedo secretly, with only fifty men, and now he had wealth and power beyond his dreams and unique captives, one of whom was going to die tonight. He had arranged for a courtesan and a boy to be ready later. At dawn tomorrow he would return to Yedo. By sunset tomorrow the guns and the bullion would begin their secret journey.

Eeeee, the guns! he thought exultantly. The guns and the plan together will give me the power to make Ishido win, or Toranaga—whomever I chose. Then I'll become a Regent in the loser's place, *neh?* Then the most powerful Regent. Why not even Shōgun? Yes. It's all possible *now*.

He let himself drift pleasantly. How to use the twenty thousand pieces of silver? I can rebuild the castle keep. And buy special horses for the cannon. And expand our espionage web. What about Ikawa Jikkyu? Would a thousand pieces be enough to bribe Ikawa Jikkyu's cooks to poison him? More than enough! Five hundred, even one hundred in the right hands would be plenty. Whose?

The afternoon sun was slanting through the small window set into the stone walls. The bath water was very hot and heated by a wood fire built into the outside wall. This was Omi's house and it stood on a small hill overlooking the village and the harbor. The garden within its walls was neat and serene and worthy.

The bathroom door opened. The blind man bowed. "Kasigi Omi-san sent me, Sire. I am Suwo, his masseur." He was tall and very thin and old, his face wrinkled.

"Good." Yabu had always had a terror of being blinded. As long as he could remember he had had dreams of waking in blackness, knowing it was sunlight, feeling the warmth but not seeing, opening his mouth to scream, knowing that it was dishonorable to scream, but screaming even so. Then the real awakening and the sweat streaming.

But this horror of blindness seemed to increase his pleasure at being massaged by the sightless.

He could see the jagged scar on the man's right temple and the deep cleft in the skull below it. That's a sword cut, he told himself. Did that cause his blindness? Was he a samurai once? For whom? Is he a spy?

Yabu knew that the man would have been searched very carefully by his guards before being allowed to enter, so he had no fear of a concealed weapon. His own prized long sword was within reach, an ancient

blade made by the master swordsmith Murasama. He watched the old
man take off his cotton kimono and hang it up without seeking the peg.
There were more sword scars on his chest. His loincloth was very clean.
He knelt, waiting patiently.

Yabu got out of the bath when he was ready and lay on
the stone bench. The old man dried Yabu carefully, put fragrant oil on
his hands, and began to knead the muscles in the *daimyo's* neck and back.

Tension began to vanish as the very strong fingers moved over Yabu,
probing deeply with surprising skill. "That's good. Very good," he said
after a while.

"Thank you, Yabu-sama," Suwo said. *Sama,* meaning "Lord," was
an obligatory politeness when addressing a superior.

"Have you served Omi-san long?"

"Three years, Sire. He is very kind to an old man."

"And before that?"

"I wandered from village to village. A few days here, half a year there,
like a butterfly on the summer's breath." Suwo's voice was as soothing
as his hands. He had decided that the *daimyo* wanted him to talk and he
waited patiently for the next question and then he would begin. Part of
his art was to know what was required and when. Sometimes his ears
told him this, but mostly it was his fingers that seemed to unlock the secret of the man or woman's mind. His fingers were telling him to beware
of this man, that he was dangerous and volatile, his age about forty, a
good horseman and excellent sword fighter. Also that his liver was bad
and that he would die within two years. Saké, and probably aphro-
disiacs, would kill him. "You are strong for your age, Yabu-sama."

"So are you. How old are you, Suwo?"

The old man laughed but his fingers never ceased. "I'm the oldest man
in the world—my world. Everyone I've ever known is dead long since.
It must be more than eighty years—I'm not sure. I served Lord Yoshi
Chikitada, Lord Toranaga's grandfather, when the clan's fief was no bigger than this village. I was even at the camp the day he was assassinated."

Yabu deliberately kept his body relaxed with an effort of will but his
mind sharpened and he began to listen intently.

"That was a grim day, Yabu-sama. I don't know how old I was—but
my voice hadn't broken yet. The assassin was Obata Hiro, a son of his
most powerful ally. Perhaps you know the story, how the youth struck
Lord Chikitada's head off with a single blow of his sword. It was a Murasama blade and that's what started the superstition that all Murasama
blades are filled with unluck for the Yoshi clan."

Is he telling me that because of my own Murasama sword? Yabu asked himself. Many people know I possess one. Or is he just an old man who remembers a special day in a long life? "What was Toranaga's grandfather like?" he asked, feigning lack of interest, testing Suwo.

"Tall, Yabu-sama. Taller than you and much thinner when I knew him. He was twenty-five the day he died." Suwo's voice warmed. "Eeee, Yabu-sama, he was a warrior at twelve and our liege lord at fifteen when his own father was killed in a skirmish. At that time, Lord Chikitada was married and had already sired a son. It was a pity that he had to die. Obata Hiro was his friend as well as vassal, seventeen then, but someone had poisoned young Obata's mind, saying that Chikitada had planned to kill his father treacherously. Of course it was all lies but that didn't bring Chikitada back to lead us. Young Obata knelt in front of the body and bowed three times. He said that he had done the deed out of filial respect for his father and now wished to atone for his insult to us and our clan by committing seppuku. He was given permission. First he washed Chikitada's head with his own hands and set it in a place of reverence. Then he cut himself open and died manfully, with great ceremony, one of our men acting as his second and removing his head with a single stroke. Later his father came to collect his son's head and the Murasama sword. Things became bad for us. Lord Chikitada's only son was taken hostage somewhere and our part of the clan fell on evil times. That was—"

"You're lying, old man. You were never there." Yabu had turned around and he was staring up at the man, who had frozen instantly. "The sword was broken and destroyed after Obata's death."

"No, Yabu-sama. That is the legend. I saw the father come and collect the head and the sword. Who would want to destroy such a piece of art? That would have been sacrilege. His father collected it."

"What did he do with it?"

"No one knows. Some said he threw it into the sea because he liked and honored our Lord Chikitada as a brother. Others said that he buried it and that it lurks in wait for the grandson, Yoshi Toranaga."

"What do *you* think he did with it?"

"Threw it into the sea."

"Did you see him?"

"No."

Yabu lay back again and the fingers began their work. The thought that someone else knew that the sword had not been broken thrilled him strangely. You should kill Suwo, he told himself. Why? How could a blind man recognize the blade? It is like any Murasama blade and the handle and scabbard have been changed many times over the years. No one can know that your sword is *the* sword that has gone from hand to hand with increasing secrecy as the power of Toranaga increased. Why kill Suwo? The fact that he's alive has added a zest. You're stimulated. Leave him alive—you can kill him at any time. With the sword.

That thought pleased Yabu as he let himself drift once more, greatly at ease. One day soon, he promised himself, I will be powerful enough to wear my Murasama blade in Toranaga's presence. One day, perhaps, I will tell him the story of my sword.

"What happened next?" he asked, wishing to be lulled by the old man's voice.

"We just fell on evil times. That was the year of the great famine, and, now that my master was dead, I became *ronin*." *Ronin* were landless or masterless peasant-soldiers or samurai who, through dishonor or the loss of their masters, were forced to wander the land until some other lord would accept their services. It was difficult for *ronin* to find new employment. Food was scarce, almost every man was a soldier, and strangers were rarely trusted. Most of the robber bands and corsairs who infested the land and the coast were *ronin*. "That year was very bad and the next. I fought for anyone—a battle here, a skirmish there. Food was my pay. Then I heard that there was food in plenty in Kyushu so I started to make my way west. That winter I found a sanctuary. I managed to become hired by a Buddhist monastery as a guard. I fought for them for half a year, protecting the monastery and their rice fields from bandits. The monastery was near Osaka and, at that time—long before the Taikō obliterated most of them—the bandits were as plentiful as swamp mosquitoes. One day, we were ambushed and I was left for dead. Some monks found me and healed my wound. But they could not give me back my sight."

His fingers probed deeper and ever deeper. "They put me with a blind monk who taught me how to massage and to see again with my fingers. Now my fingers tell me more than my eyes used to, I think.

"The last thing I can remember seeing with my eyes was the bandit's widespread mouth and rotting teeth, the sword a glittering arc and beyond, after the blow, the scent of flowers. I saw perfume in all its colors, Yabu-sama. That was all long ago, long before the barbarians came to our land—fifty, sixty years ago—but I saw the perfume's colors. I saw nirvana, I think, and for the merest moment, the face of Buddha. Blindness is a small price to pay for such a gift, *neh?*"

There was no answer. Suwo had expected none. Yabu was sleeping, as was planned. Did you like my story, Yabu-sama? Suwo asked silently, amused as an old man would be. It was all true but for one thing. The monastery was not near Osaka but across your western border. The name of the monk? Su, uncle of your enemy, Ikawa Jikkyu.

I could snap your neck so easily, he thought. It would be a favor to Omi-san. It would be a blessing to the village. And it would repay, in tiny measure, my patron's gift. Should I do it now? Or later?

Spillbergen held up the bundled stalks of rice straw, his face stretched. "Who wants to pick first?"

No one answered. Blackthorne seemed to be dozing, leaning against the corner from which he had not moved. It was near sunset.

"Someone's got to pick first," Spillbergen rasped. "Come on, there's not much time."

They had been given food and a barrel of water and another barrel as a latrine. But nothing with which to wash away the stinking offal or to clean themselves. And the flies had come. The air was fetid, the earth mud-mucous. Most of the men were stripped to the waist, sweating from the heat. And from fear.

Spillbergen looked from face to face. He came back to Blackthorne. "Why—why are you eliminated? Eh? Why?"

The eyes opened and they were icy. "For the last time: I—don't—know."

"It's not fair. Not fair."

Blackthorne returned to his reverie. There must be a way to break out of here. There must be a way to get the ship. That bastard will kill us all eventually, as certain as there's a north star. There's not much time, and I was eliminated because they've some particular rotten plan for me.

When the trapdoor had closed they had all looked at him, and someone had said, "What're we going to do?"

"I don't know," he had answered.

"Why aren't you to be picked?"

"I don't know."

"Lord Jesus help us," someone whimpered.

"Get the mess cleared up," he ordered. "Pile the filth over there!"

"We've no mops or—"

"Use *your hands!*"

They did as he ordered and he helped them and cleaned off the Captain-General as best he could. "You'll be all right now."

"How—how are we to choose someone?" Spillbergen asked.

"We don't. We fight them."

"With what?"

"You'll go like a sheep to the butcher? *You* will?"

"Don't be ridiculous—they don't want me—it wouldn't be right for me to be the one."

"Why?" Vinck asked.

"I'm the Captain-General."

"With respect, sir," Vinck said ironically, "maybe you should volunteer. It's your place to volunteer."

"A very good suggestion," Pieterzoon said. "I'll second the motion, by God."

There was general assent and everyone thought, Lord Jesus, anyone but me.

Spillbergen had begun to bluster and order but he saw the pitiless eyes. So he stopped and stared at the ground, filled with nausea. Then he said, "No. It—it wouldn't be right for someone to volunteer. It—we'll —we'll draw lots. Straws, one shorter than the rest. We'll put our hands —we'll put ourselves into the hands of God. Pilot, you'll hold the straws."

"I won't. I'll have nothing to do with it. I say we fight."

"They'll kill us all. You heard what the samurai said: our lives are spared—except one." Spillbergen wiped the sweat off his face and a cloud of flies rose and then settled again. "Give me some water. It's better for one to die than all of us."

Van Nekk dunked the gourd in the barrel and gave it to Spillbergen. "We're ten. Including you, Paulus," he said. "The odds are good."

"Very good—unless you're the one." Vinck glanced at Blackthorne. "Can we fight those swords?"

"Can you go meekly to the torturer if you're the one picked?"

"I don't know."

Van Nekk said, "We'll draw lots. We'll let God decide."

"Poor God," Blackthorne said. "The stupidities He gets blamed for!"

"How else do we choose?" someone shouted.

"We don't!"

"We'll do as Paulus says. He's Captain-General," said van Nekk. "We'll draw straws. It's best for the majority. Let's vote. Are we all in favor?"

They had all said yes. Except Vinck. "I'm with the Pilot. To hell with sewer-sitting pissmaking witch-festering straws!"

Eventually Vinck had been persuaded. Jan Roper, the Calvinist, had led the prayers. Spillbergen broke the ten pieces of straw with exactitude. Then he halved one of them.

Van Nekk, Pieterzoon, Sonk, Maetsukker, Ginsel, Jan Roper, Salamon, Maximilian Croocq, and Vinck.

Again he said, "Who wants to pick first?"

"How do we know that—that the one who picks the wrong, the short straw'll go? How do we know that?" Maetsukker's voice was raw with terror.

"We don't. Not for certain. We should know for certain," Croocq, the boy, said.

"That's easy," Jan Roper said. "Let's swear we will do it in the name of God. In His name. To—to die for the others in His name. Then there's no worry. The anointed Lamb of God will go straight to Everlasting Glory."

They all agreed.

"Go on, Vinck. Do as Roper says."

"All right." Vinck's lips were parched. "If—if it's me—I swear by the Lord God that I'll go with them if—if I pick the wrong straw. In God's name."

They all followed. Maetsukker was so frightened he had to be prompted before he sank back into the quagmire of his living nightmare.

Sonk chose first. Pieterzoon was next. Then Jan Roper, and after him Salamon and Croocq. Spillbergen felt himself dying fast because they had agreed he would not choose but his would be the last straw and now the odds were becoming terrible.

Ginsel was safe. Four left.

Maetsukker was weeping openly, but he pushed Vinck aside and took a straw and could not believe that it was not the one.

Spillbergen's fist was shaking and Croocq helped him steady his arm. Feces ran unnoticed down his legs.

Which one do I take? van Nekk was asking himself desperately. Oh, God help me! He could barely see the straws through the fog of his myopia. If only I could see, perhaps I'd have a clue which to pick. Which one?

He picked and brought the straw close to his eyes to see his sentence clearly. But the straw was not short.

Vinck watched his fingers select the next to last straw and it fell to the ground but everyone saw that it was the shortest thus far. Spillbergen unclenched his knotted hand and everyone saw that the last straw was long. Spillbergen fainted.

They were all staring at Vinck. Helplessly he looked at them, not seeing them. He half shrugged and half smiled and waved absently at the flies. Then he slumped down. They made room for him, kept away from him as though he were a leper.

Blackthorne knelt in the ooze beside Spillbergen.

"Is he dead?" van Nekk asked, his voice almost inaudible.

Vinck shrieked with laughter, which unnerved them all, and ceased as violently as he had begun. "I'm the—the one that's dead," he said. "I'm dead!"

"Don't be afraid. You're the anointed of God. You're in God's hands," Jan Roper said, his voice confident.

"Yes," van Nekk said. "Don't be afraid."

"That's easy now, isn't it?" Vinck's eyes went from face to face but none could hold his gaze. Only Blackthorne did not look away.

"Get me some water, Vinck," he said quietly. "Go over to the barrel and get some water. Go on."

Vinck stared at him. Then he got the gourd and filled it with water and gave it to him. "Lord Jesus God, Pilot," he muttered, "what am I going to do?"

"First help me with Paulus. Vinck! Do what I say! Is he going to be all right?"

Vinck pushed his agony away, helped by Blackthorne's calm. Spillbergen's pulse was weak. Vinck listened to his heart, pulled the eyelids away, and watched for a moment. "I don't know, Pilot. Lord Jesus, I can't think properly. His heart's all right, I think. He needs bleeding but —but I've no way—I—I can't concentrate. . . . Give me . . ." He stopped exhaustedly, sat back against the wall. Shudders began to rack him.

The trapdoor opened.

Omi stood etched against the sky, his kimono blooded by the dying sun.

CHAPTER 4

V INCK tried to make his legs move but he could not. He had faced death many times in his life but never like this, meekly. It had been decreed by the straws. Why me? his brain screamed. I'm no worse than the others and better than most. Dear God in Heaven, why me?

A ladder had been lowered. Omi motioned for the one man to come up, and quickly. *"Isogi!"* Hurry up!

Van Nekk and Jan Roper were praying silently, their eyes closed. Pieterzoon could not watch. Blackthorne was staring up at Omi and his men.

"Isogi!" Omi barked out again.

Once more Vinck tried to stand. "Help me, someone. Help me to get up!"

Pieterzoon, who was nearest, bent down and put his hand under Vinck's arm and helped him to his feet, then Blackthorne was at the foot of the ladder, both feet planted firmly in the slime.

"Kinjiru!" he shouted, using the word from the ship. A gasp rushed through the cellar. Omi's hand tightened on his sword and he moved to the ladder. Immediately Blackthorne twisted it, daring Omi to put a foot there.

"Kinjiru!" he said again.

Omi stopped.

"What's going on?" Spillbergen asked, frightened, as were all of them.

"I told him it's forbidden! None of my crew is walking to death without a fight."

"But—but we agreed!"

"I didn't."

"Have you gone mad!"

"It's all right, Pilot," Vinck whispered. "I—we did agree and it was fair. It's God's will. I'm going—it's . . ." He groped to the foot of the ladder but Blackthorne stood implacably in the way, facing Omi.

"You're not going without a fight. No one is."

"Get away from the ladder, Pilot! You're ordered away!" Spillbergen shakily kept to his corner, as far from the opening as possible. His voice shrilled, "Pilot!"

But Blackthorne was not listening. "Get ready!"

Omi stepped back a pace and snarled orders to his men. At once a samurai, closely followed by two others, started down the steps, swords unsheathed. Blackthorne twisted the ladder and grappled with the lead man, swerving from his violent sword blow, trying to choke the man to death.

"Help me! Come on! For your *lives!*"

Blackthorne changed his grip to pull the man off the rungs, braced sickeningly as the second man stabbed downward. Vinck came out of his cataleptic state and threw himself at the samurai, berserk. He intercepted the blow that would have sliced Blackthorne's wrist off, held the shuddering sword arm at bay, and smashed his other fist into the man's groin. The samurai gasped and kicked viciously. Vinck hardly seemed to notice the blow. He climbed the rungs and tore at the man for possession of the sword, his nails ripping at the man's eyes. The other two samurai were hampered by the confined space and Blackthorne, but a kick from one of them caught Vinck in the face and he reeled away. The samurai on the ladder hacked at Blackthorne, missed, then the entire crew hurled themselves at the ladder.

Croocq hammered his fist onto the samurai's instep and felt a small bone give. The man managed to throw his sword out of the pit—not wishing the enemy armed—and tumbled heavily to the mud. Vinck and Pieterzoon fell on him. He fought back ferociously as others rushed for the encroaching samurai. Blackthorne picked up the cornered Japanese's dagger and started up the ladder, Croocq, Jan Roper, and Salamon following. Both samurai retreated and stood at the entrance, their killing swords viciously ready. Blackthorne knew his dagger was useless against the swords. Even so he charged, the others in close support. The moment his head was above ground one of the swords swung at him, missing him by a fraction of an inch. A violent kick from an unseen samurai drove him underground again.

He turned and jumped back, avoiding the writhing mass of fighting men who tried to subdue the samurai in the stinking ooze. Vinck kicked the man in the back of the neck and he went limp. Vinck pounded him again and again until Blackthorne pulled him off.

"Don't kill him—we can use him as a hostage!" he shouted and wrenched desperately at the ladder, trying to pull it down into the cellar. But it was too long. Above, Omi's other samurai waited impassively at the trapdoor's entrance.

"For God's sake, Pilot, stop it!" Spillbergen wheezed. "They'll kill us all—you'll kill us all! Stop him, someone!"

Omi was shouting more orders and strong hands aloft prevented Blackthorne from jamming the entrance with the ladder.

"Look out!" he shouted.

Three more samurai, carrying knives and wearing only loincloths, leapt nimbly into the cellar. The first two crashed deliberately onto Blackthorne, carrying him helpless to the floor, oblivious of their own danger, then attacked ferociously.

Blackthorne was crushed beneath the strength of the men. He could not use the knife and felt his will to fight subsiding and he wished he had Mura the headman's skill at unarmed combat. He knew, helplessly, that he could not survive much longer but he made a final effort and jerked one arm free. A cruel blow from a rock-hard hand rattled his head and another exploded colors in his brain but still he fought back.

Vinck was gouging at one of the samurai when the third dropped on him from the sky door, and Maetsukker screamed as a dagger slashed his arm. Van Nekk was blindly striking out and Pieterzoon was saying, "For Christ's sake, hit them not me," but the merchant did not hear for he was consumed with terror.

Blackthorne caught one of the samurai by the throat, his grip slipping from the sweat and slime, and he was almost on his feet like a mad bull, trying to shake them off when there was a last blow and he fell into blankness. The three samurai hacked their way up and the crew, now leaderless, retreated from the circling slash of their three daggers, the samurai dominating the cellar now with their whirling daggers, not trying to kill or to maim, but only to force the panting, frightened men to the walls, away from the ladder where Blackthorne and the first samurai lay inert.

Omi came down arrogantly into the pit and grabbed the nearest man, who was Pieterzoon. He jerked him toward the ladder.

Pieterzoon screamed and tried to struggle out of Omi's grasp, but a knife sliced his wrist and another opened his arm. Relentlessly the shrieking seaman was backed against the ladder.

"Christ help me, it's not me that's to go, it's not me it's not me—" Pieterzoon had both feet on the rung and he was retreating up and away from the agony of the knives and then, "Help me, for God's sake," he screamed a last time, turned, and fled raving into the air.

Omi followed without hurrying.

A samurai retreated. Then another. The third picked up the knife that Blackthorne had used. He turned his back contemptuously, stepped over the prostrate body of his unconscious comrade, and climbed away.

The ladder was jerked aloft. Air and sky and light vanished. Bolts crashed into place. Now there was only gloom, and in it heaving chests and rending heartbeats and running sweat and the stench. The flies returned.

For a moment no one moved. Jan Roper had a small cut on his cheek, Maetsukker was bleeding badly, the others were mostly in shock. Except Salamon. He groped his way over to Blackthorne, pulled him off the unconscious samurai. He mouthed gutturally and pointed at the water. Croocq fetched some in a gourd, helped him to prop Blackthorne, still lifeless, against the wall. Together they began to clean the muck off his face.

"When those bastards—when they dropped on him I thought I heard his neck or shoulder go," the boy said, his chest heaving. "He looks like a corpse, Lord Jesus!"

Sonk forced himself to his feet and picked his way over to them. Carefully he moved Blackthorne's head from side to side, felt his shoulders. "Seems all right. Have to wait till he comes round to tell."

"Oh, Jesus God," Vinck began whimpering. "Poor Pieterzoon—I'm damned—I'm damned . . ."

"You were going. The Pilot stopped you. You were going like you promised, I saw you, by God." Sonk shook Vinck but he paid no attention. "I saw you, Vinck." He turned to Spillbergen, waving the flies away. "Wasn't that right?"

"Yes, he was going. Vinck, stop moaning! It was the Pilot's fault. Give me some water."

Jan Roper dipped some water with the gourd and drank and daubed the cut on his cheek. "Vinck should have gone. He was the lamb of God. He was ordained. And now his soul's forfeit. Oh, Lord God have mercy on him, he'll burn for all eternity."

"Give me some water," the Captain-General whimpered.

Van Nekk took the gourd from Jan Roper and passed it to Spillbergen. "It wasn't Vinck's fault," van Nekk said tiredly. "He couldn't get up, don't you remember? He asked someone to help him up. I was so frightened I couldn't move either, and I didn't have to go."

"It wasn't Vinck's fault," Spillbergen said. "No. It was him." They all looked at Blackthorne. "He's mad."

"All the English are mad," Sonk said. "Have you ever known one that wasn't? Scratch one of 'em and you find a maniac—and a pirate."

"Bastards, all of them!" Ginsel said.

"No, not all of them," van Nekk said. "The Pilot was only doing what he felt was right. He's protected us and brought us ten thousand leagues."

"Protected us, piss! We were five hundred when we started and five ships. Now there's nine of us!"

"Wasn't his fault the fleet split up. Wasn't his fault that the storms blew us all—"

"Weren't for him we'd have stayed in the New World, by God. It was him who said we could get to the Japans. And for Jesus Christ's sweet sake, look where we are now."

"We agreed to try for the Japans. We all agreed," van Nekk said wearily. "We all voted."

"Yes. But it was him that persuaded us."

"Look out!" Ginsel pointed at the samurai who was stirring and moaning. Sonk quickly slid over to him, crashed his fist into his jaw. The man went out again.

"Christ's death! What'd the bastards leave him here for? They could've carried him out with them, easy. Nothing we could've done."

"You think they thought he was dead?"

"Don't know! They must've seen him. By the Lord Jesus, I could use a cold beer," Sonk said.

"Don't hit him again, Sonk, don't kill him. He's a hostage." Croocq looked at Vinck, who sat huddled against a wall, locked into his whimpering self-hatred. "God help us all. What'll they do to Pieterzoon? What'll they do to us?"

"It's the Pilot's fault," Jan Roper said. "Only him."

Van Nekk peered compassionately at Blackthorne. "It doesn't matter now. Does it? Whose fault it is or was."

Maetsukker reeled to his feet, the blood still flowing down his forearm. "I'm hurt, help me someone."

Salamon made a tourniquet from a piece of shirt and staunched the blood. The slice in Maetsukker's bicep was deep but no vein or artery had been cut. The flies began to worry the wound.

"God-cursed flies! And God curse the Pilot to hell," Maetsukker said. "It was agreed. But, oh no! He had to save Vinck! Now Pieterzoon's blood's on his hands and we'll all suffer because of him."

"Shut your face! He said none of his crew—"

There were footsteps above. The trapdoor opened. Villagers began pouring barrels of fish offal and seawater into the cellar. When the floor was six inches awash, they stopped.

The screams began when the moon was high.

Yabu was kneeling in the inner garden of Omi's house. Motionless. He watched the moonlight in the blossom tree, the branches jet against the lighter sky, the clustered blooms now barely tinted. A petal spiraled and he thought,

> *Beauty*
> *Is not less*
> *For falling*
> *In the breeze.*

Another petal settled. The wind sighed and took another. The tree was scarcely as tall as a man, kneaded between moss rocks that seemed to have grown from the earth, so cleverly had they been placed.

It took all of Yabu's will to concentrate on the tree and blossoms and sky and night, to feel the gentle touch of the wind, to smell its sea-sweetness, to think of poems, and yet to keep his ears reaching for the agony. His spine felt limp. Only his will made him graven as the rocks. This awareness gave him a level of sensuality beyond articulation. And tonight it was stronger and more violent than it had ever been.

"Omi-san, how long will our Master stay there?" Omi's mother asked in a frightened whisper from inside the house.

"I don't know."

"The screams are terrible. When will they stop?"

"I don't know," Omi said.

They were sitting behind a screen in the second best room. The best room, his mother's, had been given to Yabu, and both these rooms faced onto the garden that he had constructed with so much effort. They could see Yabu through the lattice, the tree casting stark patterns on his face, moonlight sparking on the handles of his swords. He wore a dark haori, or outer jacket, over his somber kimono.

"I want to go to sleep," the woman said, trembling. "But I can't sleep with all this noise. When will it stop?"

"I don't know. Be patient, Mother," Omi said softly. "The noise will stop soon. Tomorrow Lord Yabu will go back to Yedo. Please be patient." But Omi knew that the torture would continue to the dawn. It had been planned that way.

He tried to concentrate. Because his feudal lord meditated within the screams, he tried again to follow his example. But the next shriek brought him back and he thought, I can't. I can't, not yet. I don't have his control or power.

Or is it power? he asked himself.

He could see Yabu's face clearly. He tried to read the strange expression on his *daimyo's* face: the slight twisting of the slack full lips, a fleck of saliva at the corners, eyes set into dark slits that moved only with the petals. It's almost as though he's just climaxed—was almost climaxing—without touching himself. Is that possible?

This was the first time that Omi had been in close contact with his uncle, for he was a very minor link in the clan chain, and his fief of Anjiro and the surrounding area poor and unimportant. Omi was the youngest of three sons and his father, Mizuno, had six brothers. Yabu was the eldest brother and leader of the Kasigi clan, his father second eldest. Omi was twenty-one and had an infant son of his own.

"Where's your miserable wife," the old woman whimpered querulously. "I want her to rub my back and shoulders."

"She had to go to visit her father, don't you remember? He's very sick, Mother. Let me do it for you."

"No. You can send for a maid in a moment. Your wife's most inconsiderate. She could have waited a few days. I come all the way from Yedo to visit you. It took two weeks of terrible journeying and what happens? I've only been here a week and she leaves. She should have waited! Good for nothing, that's her. Your father made a very bad mistake arranging your marriage to her. You should tell her to stay away permanently—divorce the good-for-nothing once and for all. She can't even massage my back properly. At the very least you should give her a good beating. Those dreadful screams! Why won't they stop?"

"They will. Very soon."

"You should give her a good beating."

"Yes." Omi thought about his wife Midori and his heart leapt. She was so beautiful and fine and gentle and clever, her voice so clear, and her music as good as that of any courtesan in Izu.

"Midori-san, you must go at once," he had said to her privately.

"Omi-san, my father is not so sick and my place is here, serving your mother, neh?" she had responded. "If our lord daimyo arrives, this house has to be prepared. Oh, Omi-san, this is so important, the most important time of your whole service, neh? If the Lord Yabu is impressed, perhaps he'll give you a better fief, you deserve so much better! If anything happened while I was away, I'd never forgive myself and this is the first time you've had an opportunity to excell and it must succeed. He must come. Please, there's so much to do."

"Yes, but I would like you to go at once, Midori-san. Stay just two days, then hurry home again."

She had pleaded but he had insisted and she had gone. He had wanted her away from Anjiro before Yabu arrived and while the man was a guest in his house. Not that the daimyo would dare to touch her without permission—that was unthinkable because he, Omi, would then have the right, the honor, and the duty by law, to obliterate the daimyo.

But he had noticed Yabu watching her just after they had been married in Yedo and he had wanted to remove a possible source of irritation, anything that could upset or embarrass his lord while he was here. It was so important that he impress Yabu-sama with his filial loyalty, his foresight, and with his counsel. And so far everything had succeeded beyond possibility. The ship had been a treasure trove, the crew another. Everything was perfect.

"I've asked our house *kami* to watch over you," Midori had said just before she left, referring to the particular Shinto spirit that had their house in his care, "and I've sent an offering to the Buddhist temple for prayers. I've told Suwo to be his most perfect, and sent a message to Kiku-san. Oh, Omi-san, please let me stay."

He had smiled and sent her on her way, the tears spoiling her makeup.

Omi was sad to be without her, but glad that she had gone. The screams would have pained her very much.

His mother winced under the torment on the wind, moved slightly to ease the ache in her shoulders, her joints bad tonight. It's the west sea breeze, she thought. Still, it's better here than in Yedo. Too marshy there and too many mosquitoes.

She could just see the soft outline of Yabu in the garden. Secretly she hated him and wanted him dead. Once Yabu was dead, Mizuno, her husband, would be *daimyo* of Izu and would lead the clan. That would be very nice, she thought. Then all the rest of the brothers and their wives and children would be subservient to her and, of course, Mizuno-san would make Omi heir when Yabu was dead and gone.

Another pain in her neck made her move slightly.

"I'll call Kiku-san," Omi said, referring to the courtesan who waited patiently for Yabu in the next room, with the boy. "She's very, very deft."

"I'm all right, just tired, *neh?* Oh, very well. She can massage me."

Omi went into the next room. The bed was ready. It consisted of over- and under-coverlets called futons that were placed on the floor matting. Kiku bowed and tried to smile and murmured she would be honored to try to use her modest skill on the most honorable mother of the household. She was even paler than usual and Omi could see the screams were taking their toll on her too. The boy was trying not to show his fear.

When the screams had begun Omi had had to use all his skill to persuade her to stay. "Oh, Omi-san, I cannot bear it—it's terrible. So sorry, please let me go—I want to close my ears but the sound comes through my hands. Poor man—it's terrible," she had said.

"Please, Kiku-san, please be patient. Yabu-sama has ordered this, *neh?* There is nothing to be done. It will stop soon."

"It's too much, Omi-san. I can't bear it."

By inviolate custom, money of itself could not buy a girl if she, or her employer, wished to refuse the client, whoever he was. Kiku was a courtesan of the First Class, the most famous in Izu, and though Omi was convinced she would not compare even to a courtesan of the Second Class of Yedo, Osaka, or Kyoto, here she was at the pinnacle and correctly prideful and exclusive. And even though he had agreed with her employer, the mama-san Gyoko, to pay five times the usual price, he was still not sure that Kiku would stay.

Now he was watching her nimble fingers on his mother's neck. She was beautiful, tiny, her skin almost translucent and so soft. Usually she would bubble with zest for life. But how could such a plaything be happy under the weight of the screams, he asked himself. He enjoyed watching her, enjoyed the knowledge of her body and her warmth—

Abruptly the screams stopped.

Omi listened, his mouth half-open, straining to catch the slightest noise, waiting. He noticed Kiku's fingers had stopped, his mother uncomplaining, listening as intently. He looked through the lattice at Yabu. The *daimyo* remained statuelike.

"Omi-san!" Yabu called at last.

Omi got up and went onto the polished veranda and bowed. "Yes, Lord."

"Go and see what has happened."

Omi bowed again and went through the garden, out onto the tidily pebbled roadway that led down the hill to the village and on to the shore. Far below he could see the fire near one of the wharfs and the men beside it. And, in the square that fronted the sea, the trapdoor to the pit and the four guards.

As he walked toward the village he saw that the barbarian ship was safe at anchor, oil lamps on the decks and on the nestling boats. Villagers—men and women and children—were still unloading the cargo, and fishing boats and dinghies were going back and forth like so many fireflies. Neat mounds of bales and crates were piling up on the beach. Seven cannon were already there and another was being hauled by ropes from a boat onto a ramp, thence onto the sand.

He shuddered though there was no chill on the wind. Normally the villagers would be singing at their labors, as much from happiness as to help them pull in unison. But tonight the village was unusually quiet though every house was awake and every hand employed, even the sickest. People hurried back and forth, bowed and hurried on again. Silent. Even the dogs were hushed.

It's never been like this before, he thought, his hand unnecessarily tight on his sword. It's almost as though our village *kami* have deserted us.

Mura came up from the shore to intercept him, forewarned the moment Omi had opened the garden door. He bowed. "Good evening, Omi-sama. The ship will be unloaded by midday."

"Is the barbarian dead?"

"I don't know, Omi-sama. I'll go and find out at once."

"You can come with me."

Obediently Mura followed, half a pace behind. Omi was curiously glad of his company.

"By midday, you said?" Omi asked, not liking the quiet.

"Yes. Everything is going well."

"What about the camouflage?"

Mura pointed to groups of old women and children near one of the net houses who were platting rough mats, Suwo with them.

"We can dismantle the cannon from their carriages and wrap them up. We'll need at least ten men to carry one. Igurashi-san has sent for more porters from the next village."

"Good."

"I'm concerned that secrecy should be maintained, Sire."

"Igurashi-san will impress on them the need, *neh?*"

"Omi-sama, we'll have to expend all our rice sacks, all our twine, all our nets, all our matting straw."

"So?"

"How then can we catch fish or bale our harvest?"

"You will find a way." Omi's voice sharpened. "Your tax is increased by half again this season. Yabu-san has tonight ordered it."

"We have already paid this year's tax and next."

"That's a peasant's privilege, Mura. To fish and to till and to harvest and to pay tax. Isn't it?"

Mura said calmly, "Yes, Omi-sama."

"A headman who cannot control his village is a useless object, *neh?*"

"Yes, Omi-sama."

"That villager, he was a fool as well as insulting. Are there others like him?"

"None, Omi-sama."

"I hope so. Bad manners are unforgivable. His family is fined the value of one koku of rice—in fish, rice, grain, or whatever. To be paid within three moons."

"Yes, Omi-sama."

Both Mura and Omi the samurai knew that this sum was totally beyond the family's means. There was only the fishing boat and the single half-hectare rice paddy which the three Tamazaki brothers—now two—shared with their wives, four sons and three daughters, and Tamazaki's widow and three children. A koku of rice was a measure that approximated the amount of rice it took to keep one family alive for one year. About five bushels. Perhaps three hundred and fifty pounds of rice. All income in the realm was measured by koku. And all taxes.

"Where would this Land of the Gods be if we forgot manners?" Omi asked. "Both to those beneath us and to those above us?"

"Yes, Omi-sama." Mura was estimating where to gain that one koku of value, because the village would have to pay if the family could not. And where to obtain more rice sacks, twine, and nets. Some could be salvaged from the journey. Money would have to be borrowed. The headman of the next village owed him a favor. Ah! Isn't Tamazaki's eldest daughter a beauty at six, and isn't six the perfect age for a girl to be sold? And isn't the best child broker in all Izu my mother's sister's third cousin?—the money-hungry, hair-rending, detestable old hag. Mura sighed, knowing that he now had a series of furious bargaining sessions ahead. Never mind, he thought. Perhaps the child'll bring even two koku. She's certainly worth much more.

"I apologize for Tamazaki's misconduct and ask your pardon," he said.

"It was his misconduct—not yours," Omi replied as politely.

But both knew that it was Mura's responsibility and there had better be no more Tamazakis. Yet both were satisfied. An apology had been offered and it had been accepted but refused. Thus the honor of both men was satisfied.

They turned the corner of the wharf and stopped. Omi hesitated, then motioned Mura away. The headman bowed, left thankfully.

"Is he dead, Zukimoto?"

"No, Omi-san. He's just fainted again."

Omi went to the great iron cauldron that the village used for rendering blubber from the whales they sometimes caught far out to sea in the winter months, or for the rendering of glue from fish, a village industry.

The barbarian was immersed to his shoulders in the steaming water. His face was purple, his lips torn back from his mildewed teeth.

At sunset Omi watched Zukimoto, puffed with vanity, supervising while the barbarian was trussed like a chicken, his arms around his knees, his hands loosely to his feet, and put into cold water. All the time, the little red-headed barbarian that Yabu had wanted to begin with had babbled and laughed and wept, the Christian priest there at first droning his cursed prayers.

Then the stoking of the fire had begun. Yabu had not been at the shore, but his orders had been specific and had been followed diligently. The barbarian had begun shouting and raving, then tried to beat his head to pulp on the iron lip until he was restrained. Then came more praying, weeping, fainting, waking, shrieking in panic before the pain truly began. Omi had tried to watch as you would watch the immolation of a fly, trying not to see the man. But he could not and had gone away as soon as possible. He had discovered that he did not relish torture. There was no dignity in it, he had decided, glad for the opportunity to know the truth, never having seen it before. There was no dignity for either the sufferer or the torturer. It removed the dignity from death, and without that dignity, what was the ultimate point of life? he asked himself.

Zukimoto calmly poked the parboiled flesh of the man's legs with a stick as one would a simmered fish to see if it was ready. "He'll come to life again soon. Extraordinary how long he's lasted. I don't think they're made like us. Very interesting, eh?" Zukimoto said.

"No," Omi said, detesting him.

Zukimoto was instantly on his guard and his unctuousness returned. "I mean nothing, Omi-san," he said with a deep bow. "Nothing at all."

"Of course. Lord Yabu is pleased that you have done so well. It must require great skill not to give too much fire, yet to give enough."

"You're too kind, Omi-san."

"You've done it before?"

"Not like this. But Lord Yabu honors me with his favors. I just try to please him."

"He wants to know how long the man will live."

"Until dawn. With care."

Omi studied the cauldron thoughtfully. Then he walked up the beach into the square. All the samurai got up and bowed.

"Everything's quiet down there, Omi-san," one of them said with a laugh, jerking a thumb at the trapdoor. "At first there was some talk—it sounded angry—and some blows. Later, two of them, perhaps more, were whimpering like frightened children. But there's been quiet for a long time."

Omi listened. He could hear water sloshing and distant muttering. An occasional moan. "And Masijiro?" he asked, naming the samurai who, on his orders, had been left below.

"We don't know, Omi-san. Certainly he hasn't called out. He's probably dead."

How dare Masijiro be so useless, Omi thought. To be overpowered by defenseless men, most of whom are sick! Disgusting! Better he is dead. "No food or water tomorrow. At midday remove any bodies, *neh?* And I want the leader brought up then. Alone."

"Yes, Omi-san."

Omi went back to the fire and waited until the barbarian opened his eyes. Then he returned to the garden and reported what Zukimoto had said, the torment once more keening on the wind.

"You looked into the barbarian's eyes?"

"Yes, Yabu-sama."

Omi was kneeling now behind the *daimyo,* ten paces away. Yabu had remained immobile. Moonlight shadowed his kimono and made a phallus of his sword handle.

"What—what did you see?"

"Madness. The essence of madness. I've never seen eyes like that. And limitless terror."

Three petals fell gently.

"Make up a poem about him."

Omi tried to force his brain to work. Then, wishing he were more adequate, he said:

> "His eyes
> Were just the end
> Of Hell—
> All pain,
> Articulate."

Shrieks came wafting up, fainter now, the distance seeming to make their cut more cruel.

Yabu said, after a moment:

> "If you allow
> Their chill to reach
> Into the great, great deep,
> You become one with them,
> Inarticulate."

Omi thought about that a long time in the beauty of the night.

CHAPTER 5

JUST before first light, the cries had ceased.

Now Omi's mother slept. And Yabu.

The village was still restless in the dawn. Four cannon had yet to be brought ashore, fifty more kegs of powder, a thousand more cannon shot.

Kiku was lying under the coverlet watching the shadows on the shoji wall. She had not slept even though she was more exhausted than she had ever been. Wheezing snores from the old woman in the next room drowned the soft deep breathing of the *daimyo* beside her. The boy slept soundlessly on the other coverlets, one arm thrown over his eyes to shut out the light.

A slight tremor went through Yabu and Kiku held her breath. But he remained in sleep and this pleased her for she knew that very soon she would be able to leave without disturbing him. As she waited patiently, she forced herself to think of pleasant things. 'Always remember, child,' her first teacher had impressed on her, 'that to think bad thoughts is really the easiest thing in the world. If you leave your mind to itself it will spiral you down into ever-increasing unhappiness. To think good thoughts, however, requires effort. This is one of the things that discipline—training—is about. So train your mind to dwell on sweet perfumes, the touch of this silk, tender raindrops against the shoji, the curve of this flower arrangement, the tranquillity of dawn. Then, at length, you won't have to make such a great effort and you will be of value to yourself, a value to our profession—and bring honor to our world, the Willow World. . . .'

She thought about the sensuous glory of the bath she soon would have that would banish this night, and afterwards the soothing caress of Suwo's hands. She thought of the laughter she would have with the other girls and with Gyoko-san, the mama-san, as they swapped gossip and rumors and stories, and of the clean, oh so clean, kimono that she would wear tonight, the golden one with yellow and green flowers and the hair ribbons that matched. After the bath she would have her hair dressed and from the money of last night there would be very much to pay off her debt to her employer, Gyoko-san, some to send to her father who was a peasant farmer, through the money exchanger, and still some for herself. Soon she would see her lover and it would be a perfect evening.

Life is very good, she thought.

Yes. But it's very difficult to put away the screams. Impossible. The other girls will be just as unhappy, and poor Gyoko-san! But never mind. Tomorrow we will all leave Anjiro and go home to our lovely tea house in Mishima, the biggest city in Izu, which surrounds the *daimyo's* greatest castle in Izu, where life begins and is.

I'm sorry the Lady Midori sent for me.

Be serious, Kiku, she told herself sharply. You shouldn't be sorry. You are not sorry, *neh?* It was an honor to serve our Lord. Now that you have been honored, your value to Gyoko-san is greater than ever, *neh?* It was an experience, and now you will be known as the Lady of the Night of the Screams and, if you are lucky, someone will write a ballad about you and perhaps the ballad will even be sung in Yedo itself. Oh, that would be very good! Then certainly your lover will buy your contract and you will be safe and content and bear sons.

She smiled to herself. Ah, what stories the troubadours will make up about tonight that will be told in every tea house throughout Izu. About the lord *daimyo,* who sat motionless in the screams, his sweat streaming. What did he do in the bed? they will all want to know. And why the boy? How was the pillowing? What did the Lady Kiku do and say and what did Lord Yabu do and say? Was his Peerless Pestle insignificant or full? Was it once or twice or never? Did nothing happen?

A thousand questions. But none ever directly asked or ever answered. That's wise, Kiku thought. The first and last rule of the Willow World was absolute secrecy, never to tell about a client or his habits or what was paid, and thus to be completely trustworthy. If someone else told, well, that was his affair, but with walls of paper and houses so small and people being what they are, stories always sped from the bed to the ballad—never the truth, always exaggerated, because people are people, *neh?* But nothing from *the* Lady. An arched eyebrow perhaps or hesitant shrug, a delicate smoothing of a perfect coiffure or fold of the kimono was all that was allowed. And always enough, if the girl had wit.

When the screams stopped, Yabu had remained statuelike in the moonlight for what had seemed a further eternity and then he had got up. At once she had hurried back into the other room, her silk kimono sighing like a midnight sea. The boy was frightened, trying not to show it, and wiped away the tears that the torment had brought. She had smiled at him reassuringly, forcing a calm that she did not feel.

Then Yabu was at the door. He was bathed in sweat, his face taut and his eyes half-closed. Kiku helped him take off his swords, then his soaking kimono and loincloth. She dried him, helped him into a sun-fresh kimono and tied its silken belt. Once she had begun to greet him but he had put a gentle finger on her lips.

Then he had gone over to the window and looked up at the waning moon, trancelike, swaying slightly on his feet. She remained quiescent, without fear, for what was there now to fear? He was a man and she a woman, trained to be a woman, to give pleasure, in whatever way. But not to give or to receive pain. There were other courtesans who specialized in that form of sensuality. A bruise here or there, perhaps a bite, well, that was part of the pleasure-pain of giving and receiving, but always within reason, for honor was involved and she was a Lady of the Willow World of the First Class Rank, never to be treated lightly, always to be honored. But part of her training was to know how to keep a man tamed, within limits. Sometimes a man became untamed and then it became terrible. For the Lady was alone. With no rights.

Her coiffure was impeccable but for the tiny locks of hair so carefully loosed over her ears to suggest erotic disarray, yet, at the same time, to enhance the purity of the whole. The red- and black-checkered outer kimono, bordered with the purest green that increased the whiteness of her skin, was drawn tight to her tiny waist by a wide stiff sash, an obi, of iridescent green. She could hear the surf on the shore now and a light wind rustled the garden.

Finally Yabu had turned and looked at her, then at the boy.

The boy was fifteen, the son of a local fisherman, apprenticed at the nearby monastery to a Buddhist monk who was an artist, a painter and illustrator of books. The boy was one of those who was pleased to earn money from those who enjoyed sex with boys and not with women.

Yabu motioned to him. Obediently the boy, now also over his fear, loosed the sash of his kimono with a studied elegance. He wore no loincloth but a woman's wrapped underskirt that reached the ground. His body was smooth and curved and almost hairless.

Kiku remembered how still the room had been, the three of them locked together by the stillness and the vanished screams, she and the boy waiting for Yabu to indicate that which was required, Yabu standing there between them, swaying slightly, glancing from one to another.

At length he had signed to her. Gracefully she unknotted the ribbon of her obi, unwound it gently and let it rest. The folds of her three gossamer kimonos sighed open and revealed the misted underskirt that enhanced her loins. He lay on the bedding and at his bidding they lay on either side of him. He put their hands on him and held them equally. He warmed quickly, showing them how to use their nails in his flanks, hurrying, his face a mask, faster, faster and then his shuddering violent cry of utter pain. For a moment, he lay there panting, eyes tightly closed, chest heaving, then turned over and, almost instantly, was asleep.

In the quiet they caught their breaths, trying to hide their surprise. It had been over so quickly.

The boy had arched an eyebrow in wonder. "Were we inept, Kiku-san? I mean, everything was so fast," he whispered.

"We did everything he wanted," she said.

"He certainly reached the Clouds and the Rain," the boy said. "I thought the house was going to fall down."

She smiled. "Yes."

"I'm glad. At first I was very frightened. It's very good to please."

Together they dried Yabu gently and covered him with the quilt. Then the boy lay back languorously, half propped on one elbow and stifled a yawn.

"Why don't you sleep, too," she said.

The boy pulled his kimono closer and shifted his position to kneel opposite her. She was sitting beside Yabu, her right hand gently stroking the *daimyo's* arm, gentling his tremored sleep.

"I've never been together with a man and a lady at the same time before, Kiku-san," the boy whispered.

"Neither have I."

The boy frowned. "I've never been with a girl either. I mean I've never pillowed with one."

"Would you like me?" she had asked politely. "If you wait a little, I'm sure our Lord won't wake up."

The boy frowned. Then he said, "Yes please," and afterwards he said, "That was very strange, Lady Kiku."

She smiled within. "Which do you prefer?"

The boy thought a long time as they lay at peace, in each other's arms. "This way is rather hard work."

She buried her head in his shoulder and kissed the nape of his neck to hide her smile. "You are a marvelous lover," she whispered. "Now you must sleep after so much hard work." She caressed him to sleep, then left him and went to the other quilts.

The other bed had been cool. She did not want to move into Yabu's warmth lest she disturb him. Soon her side was warm.

The shadows from the shoji were sharpening. Men are such babies, she thought. So full of foolish pride. All the anguish of this night for something so transitory. For a passion that is in itself but an illusion, *neh?*

The boy stirred in his sleep. Why did you make the offer to him? she asked herself. For his pleasure—for him and not for me, though it amused me and passed the time and gave him the peace he needed. Why don't you sleep a little? Later. I'll sleep later, she told herself.

When it was time she slipped from the soft warmth and stood up. Her kimonos whispered apart and the air chilled her skin. Quickly she folded her robes perfectly and retied her obi. A deft but careful touch to her coiffure. And to her makeup.

She made no sound as she left.

The samurai sentry at the veranda entrance bowed and she bowed back and she was in the dawning sunshine. Her maid was waiting for her.

"Good morning, Kiku-san."

"Good morning."

The sun felt very good and washed away the night. It's very fine to be alive, she thought.

She slipped her feet into her sandals, opened her crimson parasol, and started through the garden, out onto the path that led down to the village, through the square, to the tea house that was her temporary home. Her maid followed.

"Good morning, Kiku-san," Mura called out, bowing. He was resting momentarily on the veranda of his house, drinking cha, the pale green tea of Japan. His mother was serving him. "Good morning, Kiku-san," she echoed.

"Good morning, Mura-san. Good morning, Saiko-san, how well you are looking," Kiku replied.

"How are you?" the mother asked, her old old eyes boring into the girl. "What a terrible night! Please join us for cha. You look pale, child."

"Thank you, but please excuse me, I must go home now. You do me too much honor. Perhaps later."

"Of course, Kiku-san. You honor our village by being here."

Kiku smiled and pretended not to notice their searching stares. To add spice to their day and to hers, she pretended a slight pain in her nether regions.

That will sail around the village, she thought happily as she bowed, winced again, and went off as though stoically covering an intensity of pain, the folds of her kimonos swaying to perfection, and her sunshade tilted to give her just that most marvelous light. She was very glad that she had worn this outer kimono and this parasol. On a dull day the effect would never have been so dramatic.

"Ah, poor, poor child! She's so beautiful, *neh?* What a shame! Terrible!" Mura's mother said with a heart-rending sigh.

"What's terrible, Saiko-san?" Mura's wife asked, coming onto the veranda.

"Didn't you see the poor girl's agony? Didn't you see how bravely she was trying to hide it? Poor child. Only seventeen and to have to go through all that!"

"She's eighteen," Mura said dryly.

"All of what, Mistress?" one of the maids said breathlessly, joining them.

The old woman looked around to ensure that everyone was listening and whispered loudly. "I heard"—she dropped her voice—"I heard that she'll . . . she'll be useless . . . for three months."

"Oh, no! Poor Kiku-san! Oh! But why?"

"He used his teeth. I have it on the best authority."

"Oh!"

"Oh!"

"But why does he have the boy as well, Mistress? Surely he doesn't—"

"Ah! Run along! Back to your work, good-for-nothings! This isn't for your ears! Go on, off with the lot of you. The Master and I have to talk."

She shooed them all off the veranda. Even Mura's wife. And sipped her cha, benign and very content.

Mura broke the silence. "Teeth?"

"Teeth. Rumor has it that the screams make him large because he was frightened by a dragon when he was small," she said in a rush. "He always has a boy there to remind him of himself when he was a boy and petrified, but actually the boy's there only to pillow with, to exhaust himself—otherwise he'd bite everything off, poor girl."

Mura sighed. He went into the small outhouse beside the front gate and farted involuntarily as he began to relieve himself into the bucket. I wonder what really happened, he asked himself, titillated. Why was Kiku-san in pain? Perhaps the *daimyo* really does use his teeth! How extraordinary!

He walked out, shaking himself to ensure that he did not stain his loincloth, and headed across the square deep in thought. Eeeee, how I would like to have one night with the Lady Kiku! What man wouldn't? How much did Omi-san have to pay her mama-san—which we will have to pay eventually? Two koku? They say her mama-san, Gyoko-san, demanded and got ten times the regular fee. Does she get five koku for one night? Kiku-san would certainly be worth it, *neh*? Rumor has it she's as practiced at eighteen as a woman twice her age. She's supposed to be able to prolong. . . . Eeeee, the joy of her! If it was me—how would *I* begin?

Absently he adjusted himself into his loincloth as his feet took him out of the square, up the well-worn path to the funeral ground.

The pyre had been prepared. The deputation of five men from the village was already there.

This was the most delightful place in the village, where the sea breezes were coolest in summer and the view the best. Nearby was the village Shinto shrine, a tiny thatched roof on a pedestal for the *kami,* the spirit, that lived there, or might wish to live there if it pleased him. A gnarled yew that had seeded before the village was born leaned against the wind.

Later Omi walked up the path. With him were Zukimoto and four guards. He stood apart. When he bowed formally to the pyre and to the shroud-covered, almost disjointed body that lay upon it, they all bowed with him, to honor the barbarian who had died that his comrades might live.

At his signal Zukimoto went forward and lit the pyre. Zukimoto had asked Omi for the privilege and the honor had been granted to him. He bowed a last time. And then, when the fire was well alight, they went away.

Blackthorne dipped into the dregs of the barrel and carefully measured a half cup of water and gave it to Sonk. Sonk tried to sip it to make it last, his hand trembling, but he could not. He gulped the tepid liquid, regretting that he had done so the moment it had passed his parched throat, groped exhaustedly to his place by the wall, stepping over those whose turn it was to lie down. The floor was now deep ooze, the stench and the flies hideous. Faint sunlight came into the pit through the slats of the trapdoor.

Vinck was next for water and he took his cup and stared at it, sitting near the barrel, Spillbergen on the other side. "Thanks," he muttered dully.

"Hurry up!" Jan Roper said, the cut on his cheek already festering. He was the last for water and, being so near, his throat was torturing him. "Hurry up, Vinck, for Christ's sweet sake."

"Sorry. Here, you take it," Vinck muttered, handing him the cup, oblivious of the flies that speckled him.

"Drink it, you fool! It's the last you'll get till sunset. Drink it!" Jan Roper shoved the cup back into the man's hands. Vinck did not look up at him but obeyed miserably, and slipped back once more into his private hell.

Jan Roper took his cup of water from Blackthorne. He closed his eyes and said a silent grace. He was one of those standing, his leg muscles aching. The cup gave barely two swallows.

And now that they had all been given their ration, Blackthorne dipped and sipped gratefully. His mouth and tongue were raw and burning and dusty. Flies and sweat and filth covered him. His chest and back were badly bruised.

He watched the samurai who had been left in the cellar. The man was huddled against the wall, between Sonk and Croocq, taking up as little space as possible, and he had not moved for hours. He was staring bleakly into space, naked but for his loincloth, violent bruises all over him, a thick weal around his neck.

When Blackthorne had first come to his senses, the cellar was in complete darkness. The screams were filling the pit and he thought that he was dead and in the choking depths of hell. He felt himself being sucked down into muck that was clammy and flesh-crawling beyond measure, and he had cried out and flailed in panic, unable to breathe, until, after an eternity, he had heard, "It's all right, Pilot, you're not dead, it's all right. Wake up, wake up, for the love of Christ, it's not hell but it might just as well be. Oh, Blessed Lord Jesus, help us all."

When he was fully conscious they had told him about Pieterzoon and the barrels of seawater.

"Oh, Lord Jesus, get us out of here!" someone whimpered.

"What're they doing to poor old Pieterzoon? What're they doing to him? Oh, God help us. I can't stand the screams!"

"Oh, Lord, let the poor man die. Let him die."

"Christ God, stop the screams! Please stop the screams!"

The pit and Pieterzoon's screams had measured them all, had forced them to look within themselves. And no man had liked what he had seen.

The darkness makes it worse, Blackthorne had thought.

It had been an endless night, in the pit.

With the gloaming the cries had vanished. When dawn trickled down to them they had seen the forgotten samurai.

"What're we going to do about him?" van Nekk had asked.

"I don't know. He looks as frightened as we are," Blackthorne said, his heart pumping.

"He'd better not start anything, by God."

"Oh, Lord Jesus, get me out of here—" Croocq's voice started to crescendo. "Helllp!"

Van Nekk, who was near him, shook him and gentled him. "It's all right, lad. We're in God's hands. He's watching over us."

"Look at my arm," Maetsukker moaned. The wound had festered already.

Blackthorne stood shakily. "We'll all be raving lunatics in a day or two if we don't get out of here," he said to no one in particular.

"There's almost no water," van Nekk said.

"We'll ration what there is. Some now—some at noon. With luck, there'll be enough for three turns. God curse all flies!"

So he had found the cup and had given them a ration, and now he was sipping his, trying to make it last.

"What about him—the Japaner?" Spillbergen said. The Captain-General had fared better than most during the night because he had shut his ears to the screams with a little mud, and, being next to the water barrel, had cautiously slaked his thirst. "What are we going to do about him?"

"He should have some water," van Nekk said.

"The pox on that," Sonk said. "I say he gets none."

They all voted on it and it was agreed he got none.

"I don't agree," Blackthorne said.

"You don't agree to anything we say," Jan Roper said. "He's the enemy. He's a heathen devil and he almost killed you."

"You've almost killed me. Half a dozen times. If your musket had fired at Santa Magdellana, you'd have blown my head off."

"I wasn't aiming at you. I was aiming at stinking Satanists."

"They were unarmed priests. And there was plenty of time."

"I wasn't aiming at you."

"You've almost killed me a dozen times, with your God-cursed anger, your God-cursed bigotry, and your God-cursed stupidity."

"Blasphemy's a mortal sin. Taking His name in vain is a sin. We're in His hands, not yours. You're not a king and this isn't a ship. You're not our keep—"

"But you will do what I say!"

Jan Roper looked round the cellar, seeking support in vain. "Do what you want," he said sullenly.

"I will."

The samurai was as parched as they, but he shook his head to the offered cup. Blackthorne hesitated, put the cup to the samurai's swollen lips, but the man smashed the cup away, spilling the water, and said something harshly. Blackthorne readied to parry the following blow. But it never came. The man made no further move, just looked away into space.

"He's mad. They're all mad," Spillbergen said.

"There's more water for us. Good," Jan Roper said. "Let him go to the hell he deserves."

"What's your name? *Namu?*" Blackthorne asked. He said it again in different ways but the samurai appeared not to hear.

They left him alone. But they watched him as if he were a scorpion. He did not watch them back. Blackthorne was certain the man was trying to decide on something, but he had no idea what it could be.

What's on his mind, Blackthorne asked himself. Why should he refuse water? Why was he left here? Was that a mistake by Omi? Unlikely. By plan? Unlikely. Could we use him to get out? Unlikely. The whole world's unlikely except it's likely we're going to stay here until they *let* us out . . . if they let us out. And if they let us out, what next? What happened to Pieterzoon?

The flies swarmed with the heat of the day.

Oh, God, I wish I could lie down—wish I could get into that bath— they wouldn't have to carry me there now. I never realized how important a bath is. That old blind man with the steel fingers! I could use him for an hour or two.

What a waste! All our ships and men and effort for this. A total failure. Well, almost. Some of us are still alive.

"Pilot!" Van Nekk was shaking him. "You were asleep. It's him— he's been bowing to you for a minute or more." He motioned to the samurai who knelt, head bowed in front of him.

Blackthorne rubbed the exhaustion out of his eyes. He made an effort and bowed back.

"*Hai?*" he asked curtly, remembering the Japanese word for "yes."

The samurai took hold of the sash of his shredded kimono and wrapped it around his neck. Still kneeling, he gave one end to Blackthorne and the other to Sonk, bowed his head, and motioned them to pull it tight.

"He's afraid we'll strangle him," Sonk said.

"Christ Jesus, I think that's what he wants us to do." Blackthorne let the sash fall and shook his head. "*Kinjiru,*" he said, thinking how useful that word was. How do you say to a man who doesn't speak your language that it's against your code to commit murder, to kill an unarmed man, that you're not executioners, that suicide is damned before God?

The samurai asked again, clearly begging him, but again Blackthorne shook his head. "*Kinjiru.*" The man looked around wildly. Suddenly he was on his feet and he had shoved his head deep into the latrine bucket to try to drown himself. Jan Roper and Sonk immediately pulled him out, choking and struggling.

"Let him go," Blackthorne ordered. They obeyed. He pointed at the latrine. "Samurai, if that's what you want, go ahead!"

The man was retching, but he understood. He looked at the foul bucket and knew that he did not have the strength to hold his head there long enough. In abject misery the samurai went back to his place by the wall.

"Jesus," someone muttered.

Blackthorne dipped half a cup of water from the barrel, got to his feet, his joints stiff, went over to the Japanese and offered it. The samurai looked past the cup.

"I wonder how long he can hold out," Blackthorne said.

"Forever," Jan Roper said. "They're animals. They're not human."

"For Christ's sake, how much longer will they keep us here?" Ginsel asked.

"As long as they want."

"We'll have to do anything they want," van Nekk said. "We'll have to if we want to stay alive and get out of this hell hole. Won't we, Pilot?"

"Yes." Blackthorne thankfully measured the sun's shadows. "It's high noon, the watch changes."

Spillbergen, Maetsukker, and Sonk began to complain but he cursed them to their feet and when all were rearranged he lay down gratefully. The mud was foul and the flies worse than ever, but the joy of being able to stretch out full length was enormous.

What did they do to Pieterzoon? he asked himself, as he felt his fatigue engulfing him. Oh, God help us to get out of here. I'm so frightened.

There were footsteps above. The trapdoor opened. The priest stood there flanked by samurai.

"Pilot. You are to come up. You are to come up alone," he said.

CHAPTER 6

A LL eyes in the pit went to Blackthorne.

"What do they want with me?"

"I don't know," Father Sebastio said gravely. "But you must come up at once."

Blackthorne knew that he had no option, but he did not leave the protective wall, trying to summon more strength.

"What happened to Pieterzoon?"

The priest told him. Blackthorne translated for those who did not speak Portuguese.

"The Lord have mercy on him," van Nekk whispered over the horrified silence. "Poor man. Poor man."

"I'm sorry. There was nothing I could do," the priest said with a great sadness. "I don't think he knew me or anyone the moment they put him into the water. His mind was gone. I gave him absolution and prayed for him. Perhaps, through God's mercy. . . . *In nomine Patris et Filii et Spiritus Sancti*. Amen." He made the sign of the cross over the cellar. "I beg you all to renounce your heresies and be accepted back into God's faith. Pilot, you must come up."

"Don't leave us, Pilot, for the love of God!" Croocq cried out.

Vinck stumbled to the ladder and started to climb. "They can take me—not the Pilot. Me, not him. Tell him—" He stopped, helplessly, both feet on the rungs. A long spear was an inch away from his heart. He tried to grab the haft but the samurai was ready and if Vinck had not jumped back he would have been impaled.

This samurai pointed at Blackthorne and beckoned him up. Harshly. Still Blackthorne did not move. Another samurai shoved a long barbed staff into the cellar and tried to hook Blackthorne out.

No one moved to help Blackthorne except the samurai in the cellar. He caught the barb fast and said something sharply to the man above, who hesitated; then he looked across at Blackthorne, shrugged and spoke.

"What did he say?"

The priest replied, "It's a Japanese saying: 'A man's fate is a man's fate and life is but an illusion.'"

Blackthorne nodded to the samurai and went to the ladder without looking back and scaled it. When he came into full sunlight, he squinted against the painful brilliance, his knees gave way, and he toppled to the sandy earth.

Omi was to one side. The priest and Mura stood near the four samurai. Some distant villagers watched for a moment and then turned away.

No one helped him.

Oh, God, give me strength, Blackthorne prayed. I've got to get on my feet and pretend to be strong. That's the only thing they respect. Being strong. Showing no fear. Please help me.

He gritted his teeth and pushed against the earth and stood up, swaying slightly. "What the hell do you want with me, you poxy little bastard?" he said directly at Omi, then added to the priest, "Tell the bastard I'm a *daimyo* in my own country and what sort of treatment is this? Tell him we've no quarrel with him. Tell him to let us out or it'll be the worse for him. Tell him I'm a *daimyo,* by God. I'm heir to Sir William of Micklehaven, may the bastard be dead long since. Tell him!"

The night had been terrible for Father Sebastio. But during his vigil he had come to feel God's presence and gained a serenity he had never experienced before. Now he knew that he could be an instrument of God against the heathen, that he was shielded against the heathen, and the pirate's cunning. He knew, somehow, that this night had been a preparation, a crossroads for him.

"Tell him."

The priest said in Japanese, "The pirate says he's a lord in his own country." He listened to Omi's reply. "Omi-san says he does not care if you are a king in your own country. Here you live at Lord Yabu's whim—you and all your men."

"Tell him he's a turd."

"You should beware of insulting him."

Omi began talking again.

"Omi-san says that you will be given a bath. And food and drink. If you behave, you will not be put back into the pit."

"What about my men?"

The priest asked Omi.

"They will stay below."

"Then tell him to go to hell." Blackthorne walked toward the ladder to go below again. Two of the samurai prevented him, and though he struggled against them, they held him easily.

Omi spoke to the priest, then to his men. They released him and Blackthorne almost fell.

"Omi-san says that unless you behave, another of your men will be taken up. There is plenty of firewood and plenty of water."

If I agree now, thought Blackthorne, they've found the means to control me and I'm in their power forever. But what does it matter, I'm in their power now and, in the end, I will have to do what they want. Van Nekk was right. I'll have to do anything.

"What does he want me to do? What does it mean to 'behave'?"

"Omi-san says, it means to obey. To do what you are told. To eat dung if need be."

"Tell him to go to hell. Tell him I piss on him and his whole country —and his *daimyo*."

"I recommend you agree to wh—"

"Tell him what I said, exactly, by God!"

"Very well—but I did warn you, Pilot."

Omi listened to the priest. The knuckles on his sword hand whitened. All of his men shifted uneasily, their eyes knifing into Blackthorne.

Then Omi gave a quiet order.

Instantly two samurai went down into the pit and brought out Croocq, the boy. They dragged him over to the cauldron, trussed him while others brought firewood and water. They put the petrified boy into the brimming cauldron and ignited the wood.

Blackthorne watched the soundless mouthings of Croocq and the terror that was all of him. Life has no value to these people at all, he thought. God curse them to hell, they'll boil Croocq as certain as I'm standing on this God-forsaken earth.

Smoke billowed across the sand. Sea gulls were mewing around the fishing boats. A piece of wood fell out of the fire and was kicked back again by a samurai.

"Tell him to stop," Blackthorne said. "Ask him to stop."

"Omi-san says, you agree to behave?"

"Yes."

"He says, you will obey all orders?"

"As far as I can, yes."

Omi spoke again. Father Sebastio asked a question and Omi nodded.

"He wants you to answer directly to him. The Japanese for 'yes' is 'hai.' He says, you will obey all orders?"

"As far as I can, *hai*."

The fire was beginning to warm the water and a nauseating groan broke from the boy's mouth. Flames from the wooden fire that was set into the bricks below the iron licked the metal. More wood was piled on.

"Omi-san says, lie down. Immediately."

Blackthorne did as he was ordered.

"Omi-san says that he had not insulted you personally, neither was there any cause for you to insult him. Because you are a barbarian and know no better yet, you will not be killed. But you will be taught manners. Do you understand?"

"Yes."

"He wants you to answer direct to him."

There was a wailing cry from the boy. It went on and on and then the boy fainted. One of the samurai held his head out of the water.

Blackthorne looked up at Omi. Remember, he ordered himself, remember that the boy is in your hands alone, the lives of all your crew are in your hands. Yes, the devil half of him began, but there's no guarantee that the bastard'll honor a bargain.

"Do you understand?"

"*Hai.*"

He saw Omi hitch up his kimono and ease his penis out of his loincloth. He had expected the man to piss in his face. But Omi did not. He pissed on his back. By the Lord God, Blackthorne swore to himself, I will remember this day and somehow, somewhere, Omi will pay.

"Omi-san says, it is bad manners to say that you will piss on anyone. Very bad. It is bad manners and very stupid to say you will piss on anyone when you are unarmed. It is very bad manners and even more stupid to say you will piss on anyone when you are unarmed, powerless, and not prepared to allow your friends or family or whomever to perish first."

Blackthorne said nothing. He did not take his eyes off Omi.

"*Wakarimasu ka?*" Omi said.

"He says, do you understand?"

"*Hai.*"

"*Okiro.*"

"He says you will get up."

Blackthorne got up, pain hammering in his head. His eyes were on Omi and Omi stared back at him.

"You will go with Mura and obey his orders."

Blackthorne made no reply.

"*Wakarimasu ka?*" Omi said sharply.

"*Hai.*" Blackthorne was measuring the distance between himself and Omi. He could feel his fingers on the man's neck and face already, and he prayed he could be quick and strong enough to take Omi's eyes out before they tore him off the man. "What about the boy?" he said.

The priest spoke to Omi haltingly.

Omi glanced at the cauldron. The water was hardly tepid yet. The boy had fainted but was unharmed. "Take him out of there," he ordered. "Get a doctor if he needs one."

His men obeyed. He saw Blackthorne go over to the boy and listen to his heart.

Omi motioned to the priest. "Tell the leader that the youth can also stay out of the pit today. If the leader behaves and the youth behaves, another of the barbarians *may* come out of the pit tomorrow. Then another. Perhaps. Or more than one. Perhaps. It depends on how the ones above behave. But you—" he looked directly at Blackthorne—"you are responsible for the smallest infraction of any rule or order. Do you understand?"

After the priest had translated this, Omi heard the barbarian say, "Yes," and saw part of the blood-chilling anger go out of his eyes. But the hatred remained. How foolish, Omi thought, and how naïve to be so open. I wonder what he would have done if I had played with him further—pretended to go back on what I had promised, or implied that I had promised.

"Priest, what's his name again? Say it slowly."

He heard the priest say the name several times but it still sounded like gibberish.

"Can you say it?" he asked one of his men.

"No, Omi-san."

"Priest, tell him from now on his name is Anjin—Pilot—*neh?* When he merits it, he will be called Anjin-san. Explain to him that there are no sounds in our tongue for us to say his real name as it is." Omi added dryly, "Impress upon him that this is not meant to be insulting. Good-by, Anjin, for the moment."

They all bowed to him. He returned the salutation politely and walked away. When he was well clear of the square and certain that no one was watching, he allowed himself to smile broadly. To have tamed the chief of the barbarians so quickly! To have discerned at once how to dominate him, and them!

How extraordinary those barbarians are, he thought. Eeee, the sooner the Anjin speaks our language the better. Then we'll know how to smash the Christian barbarians once and for all!

"Why didn't you piss in his face?" Yabu asked.

"At first I'd intended to, Lord. But the Pilot's still an untamed animal, totally dangerous. To do it in his face—well, with us, to touch a man's face is the worst of insults, *neh?* So I reasoned that I might have insulted him so deeply he would lose control. So I pissed on his back—which I think will be sufficient."

They were seated on the veranda of his house, on silk cushions.

Omi's mother was serving them cha—tea—with all the ceremony she could command, and she had been well trained in her youth. She offered the cup with a bow to Yabu. He bowed and politely offered it to Omi, who of course refused with a deeper bow; then he accepted it and sipped with enjoyment, feeling complete.

"I'm very impressed with you, Omi-san," he said. "Your reasoning is exceptional. Your planning and handling of this whole business has been splendid."

"You are too kind, Sire. My efforts could have been much better, much better."

"Where did you learn so much about the barbarian mind?"

"When I was fourteen, for a year I had a teacher who was the monk called Jiro. Once he'd been a Christian priest, at least he was an apprentice priest, but fortunately he learned the errors of his stupidity. I've always remembered one thing he told me. He said that the Christian religion was vulnerable because they taught that their chief deity, Jesu, said that all people should 'love' one another—he taught nothing about honor or duty, only love. And also that life was sacred—'Thou shalt not kill,' *neh*? And other stupidities. These new barbarians claim to be Christian also, even though the priest denies it, so I reasoned that perhaps they're just a different sect, and that's the cause of their enmity, just as some of the Buddhist sects hate each other. I thought if they 'love one another,' perhaps we could control the leader by taking the life or even threatening to take the life of one of his men." Omi knew that this conversation was dangerous because of the torture death, the befouled death. He felt his mother's unspoken warning crossing the space between them.

"Will you have more cha, Yabu-sama?" his mother asked.

"Thank you," Yabu said. "It's very, very good."

"Thank you, Sire. But Omi-san, is the barbarian broken for good?" his mother asked, twisting the conversation. "Perhaps you should tell our Lord if you think it's temporary or permanent."

Omi hesitated. "Temporary. But I think he should learn our language as fast as possible. That's very important to you, Sire. You will probably have to destroy one or two of them to keep him and the rest in control, but by that time he will have learned how to behave. Once you can talk directly to him, Yabu-sama, you can use his knowledge. If what the priest said is true—that he piloted the ship ten thousand *ri*—he must be more than just a little clever."

"You're more than just a little clever." Yabu laughed. "You're put in charge of the animals. Omi-san, trainer of men!"

Omi laughed with him. "I'll try, Lord."

"Your fief is increased from five hundred koku to three thousand. You will have control within twenty *ri*." A *ri* was a measure of distance that approximated one mile. "As a further token of my affection, when I return to Yedo I will send you two horses, twenty silk kimonos, one suit of armor, two swords, and enough arms to equip a further hundred samurai which you will recruit. When war comes you will immediately join my personal staff as a hatamoto." Yabu was feeling expansive: a hatamoto was a special personal retainer of a *daimyo* who had the right of access to his lord and could wear swords in the presence of his lord. He was delighted with Omi and felt rested, even reborn. He had slept exquisitely. When he had awoken he was alone, which was to be expected, because he had not asked either the girl or the boy to stay. He had drunk a little tea and eaten sparingly of rice gruel. Then a bath and Suwo's massage.

That was a marvelous experience, he thought. Never have I felt so close to nature, to the trees and mountains and earth, to the inestimable sadness of life and its transience. The screams had perfected everything.

"Omi-san, there's a rock in my garden at Mishima that I'd like you to accept, also to commemorate this happening, and that marvelous night and our good fortune. I'll send it with the other things," he said. "The stone comes from Kyushu. I called it 'The Waiting Stone' because we were waiting for the Lord Taikō to order an attack when I found it. That was, oh, fifteen years ago. I was part of his army which smashed the rebels and subdued the island."

"You do me much honor."

"Why not put it here, in your garden, and rename it? Why not call it 'The Stone of Barbarian Peace,' to commemorate the night and his endless waiting for peace."

"Perhaps I may be allowed to call it 'The Happiness Stone' to remind me and my descendants of the honors you do to me, Uncle?"

"No—better just simply name it 'The Waiting Barbarian.' Yes, I like that. That joins us further together—him and me. He was waiting as I was waiting. I lived, he died." Yabu looked at the garden, musing. "Good, 'The Waiting Barbarian'! I like that. There are curious flecks on one side of the rock that remind me of tears, and veins of blue mixed with a reddish quartz that remind me of flesh—the impermanence of it!" Yabu sighed, enjoying his melancholy. Then he added, "It's good for a man to plant a stone and name a stone. The barbarian took a long time to die, *neh*? Perhaps he will be reborn Japanese, to compensate for his suffering. Wouldn't that be marvelous? Then one day, perhaps, his descendants would see his stone and be content."

Omi poured out his heartfelt thanks, and protested that he did not deserve such bounty. Yabu knew that the bounty was not more than deserved. He could easily have given more, but he had remembered the old adage that you can always increase a fief, but to reduce one causes enmity. And treachery.

"Oku-san," he said to the woman, giving her the title of Honorable Mother, "my brother should have told me sooner about the great qualities of his youngest son. Then Omi-san would have been much further advanced today. My brother's too retiring, too thoughtless."

"My husband's too thoughtful for you, my Lord, to worry you," she replied, aware of the underlying criticism. "I'm glad that my son has had an opportunity of serving you, and that he's pleased you. My son has only done his duty, *neh?* It's our duty—Mizuno-san and all of us—to serve."

Horses clattered up the rise. Igurashi, Yabu's chief retainer, strode through the garden. "Everything's ready, Sire. If you want to get back to Yedo quickly we should leave now."

"Good. Omi-san, you and your men will go with the convoy and assist Igurashi-san to see it safely into the castle." Yabu saw a shadow cross Omi's face. "What?"

"I was just thinking about the barbarians."

"Leave a few guards for them. Compared to the convoy, they're unimportant. Do what you want with them—put them back into the pit, do what you like. When and if you obtain anything useful from them, send me word."

"Yes, Lord," Omi replied. "I'll leave ten samurai and specific instructions with Mura—they'll come to no harm in five or six days. What do you want done with the ship itself?"

"Keep it safe here. You're responsible for it, of course. Zukimoto has sent letters to a dealer at Nagasaki to offer it for sale to the Portuguese. The Portuguese can come and collect it."

Omi hesitated. "Perhaps you should keep the ship, Sire, and get the barbarians to train some of our sailors to handle it."

"What do I need with barbarian ships?" Yabu laughed derisively. "Should I become a filthy merchant?"

"Of course not, Sire," Omi said quickly. "I just thought Zukimoto might have found a use for such a vessel."

"What do I need with a trading ship?"

"The priest said this was a warship, Sire. He seemed afraid of it. When war starts, a warship could—"

"Our war will be fought on land. The sea's for merchants, all of whom are filthy usurers, pirates or fishermen." Yabu got up and began to walk down the steps toward the garden gate where a samurai was holding the bridle of his horse. He stopped and stared out to sea. His knees went weak.

Omi followed his glance.

A ship was rounding the headland. She was a large galley with a multitude of oars, the swiftest of the Japanese coastal vessels because she depended neither upon the wind, nor upon the tide. The flag at the masthead carried the Toranaga crest.

CHAPTER 7

Toda Hiro-matsu, overlord of the provinces of Sagami and Kozuké, Toranaga's most trusted general and adviser, commander-in-chief of all his armies, strode down the gangplank onto the wharf alone. He was tall for a Japanese, just under six feet, a bull-like man with heavy jowls, who carried his sixty-seven years with strength. His military kimono was brown silk, stark but for the five small Toranaga crests—three interlocked bamboo sprays. He wore a burnished breastplate and steel arm protectors. Only the short sword was in his belt. The other, the killing sword, he carried loose in his hand. He was ready to unsheathe it instantly and to kill instantly to protect his liege lord. This had been his custom ever since he was fifteen.

No one, not even the Taikō, had been able to change him.

A year ago, when the Taikō died, Hiro-matsu had become Toranaga's vassal. Toranaga had given him Sagami and Kozuké, two of his eight provinces, to overlord, five hundred thousand koku yearly, and had also left him to his custom. Hiro-matsu was very good at killing.

Now the shore was lined with all the villagers—men, women, children—on their knees, their heads low. The samurai were in neat, formal rows in front of them. Yabu was at their head with his lieutenants.

If Yabu had been a woman or a weaker man, he knew that he would be beating his breast and wailing and tearing his hair out. This was too much of a coincidence. For the famous Toda Hiro-matsu to be here, on this day, meant that Yabu had been betrayed—either in Yedo by one of his household, or here in Anjiro by Omi, one of Omi's men, or one of the villagers. He had been trapped in disobedience. An enemy had taken advantage of his interest in the ship.

He knelt and bowed and all his samurai followed him, and he cursed the ship and all who sailed in it.

"Ah, Yabu-sama," he heard Hiro-matsu say, and saw him kneel on the matting that had been set out for him and return his bow. But the depth of the bow was less than correct and Hiro-matsu did not wait for him to bow again, so he knew, without being told, that he was in vast jeopardy. He saw the general sit back on his heels. "Iron Fist" he was called behind his back. Only Toranaga or one of three counselors would have the privilege of flying the Toranaga flag. Why send so important a general to catch me away from Yedo?

"You honor me by coming to one of my poor villages, Hiro-matsu-sama," he said.

"My Master ordered me here." Hiro-matsu was known for his bluntness. He had neither guile nor cunning, only an absolute trustworthiness to his liege lord.

"I'm honored and very glad," Yabu said. "I rushed here from Yedo because of that barbarian ship."

"Lord Toranaga invited all friendly *daimyos* to wait in Yedo until he returned from Osaka."

"How is our Lord? I hope everything goes well with him?"

"The sooner Lord Toranaga is safe in his own castle at Yedo the better. The sooner the clash with Ishido is open and we marshal our armies and cut a path back to Osaka Castle and burn it to the bricks, the better." The old man's jowls reddened as his anxiety for Toranaga increased; he hated being away from him. The Taikō had built Osaka Castle to be invulnerable. It was the greatest in the Empire, with interlocking keeps and moats, lesser castles, towers, and bridges, and space for eighty thousand soldiers within its walls. And around the walls and the huge city were other armies, equally disciplined and equally well armed, all fanatic supporters of Yaemon, the Heir. "I've told him a dozen times that he was mad to put himself into Ishido's power. Lunatic!"

"Lord Toranaga had to go, *neh?* He had no choice." The Taikō had ordered that the Council of Regents, who ruled in Yaemon's name, were to meet for ten days at least twice a year and always within Osaka's castle keep, bringing with them a maximum of five hundred retainers within the walls. And all other *daimyos* were equally obliged to visit the castle with their families to pay their respects to the Heir, also twice a year. So all were controlled, all defenseless for part of the year, every year. "The meeting was fixed, *neh?* If he didn't go it would be treason, *neh?*"

"Treason against whom?" Hiro-matsu reddened even more. "Ishido's trying to isolate our Master. Listen, if I had Ishido in my power like he has Lord Toranaga, I wouldn't hesitate for a moment—whatever the risks. Ishido's head would have been off his shoulders long since, and his spirit awaiting rebirth." The general was involuntarily twisting the well-used sheath of the sword that he carried in his left hand. His right hand, gnarled and calloused, lay ready in his lap. He studied *Erasmus*. "Where are the cannon?"

"I had them brought ashore. For safety. Will Toranaga-sama make another compromise with Ishido?"

"When I left Osaka, all was quiet. The Council was to meet in three days."

"Will the clash become open?"

"I'd like it open. But my Lord? If he wants to compromise, he will compromise." Hiro-matsu looked back at Yabu. "He ordered all allied *daimyos* to wait for him at Yedo. Until he returned. This is not Yedo."

"Yes. I felt that the ship was important enough to our cause to investigate it immediately."

"There was no need, Yabu-san. You should have more confidence. Nothing happens without our Master's knowledge. He would have sent someone to investigate it. It happens he sent me. How long have you been here?"

"A day and a night."

"Then you were two days coming from Yedo?"

"Yes."

"You came very quickly. You are to be complimented." ·

To gain time Yabu began telling Hiro-matsu about his forced march. But his mind was on more vital matters. Who was the spy? How had Toranaga got the information about the ship as quickly as he himself? And who had told Toranaga about his departure? How could he maneuver now and deal with Hiro-matsu?

Hiro-matsu heard him out, then said pointedly, "Lord Toranaga has confiscated the ship and all its contents."

A shocked silence swamped the shore. This was Izu, Yabu's fief, and Toranaga had no rights here. Neither had Hiro-matsu any rights to order anything. Yabu's hand tightened on his sword.

Hiro-matsu waited with practiced calmness. He had done exactly as Toranaga had ordered and now he was committed. It was implacably kill or be killed.

Yabu knew also that now he must commit himself. There was no more waiting. If he refused to give up the ship he would have to kill Hiro-matsu Iron Fist, because Hiro-matsu Iron Fist would never leave without it. There were perhaps two hundred elite samurai on the galley that was moored to the dock. They would also have to die. He could invite them ashore and beguile them, and within a few hours he could easily have enough samurai in Anjiro to overwhelm them all, for he was a master at ambush. But that would force Toranaga to send armies against Izu. You will be swallowed up, he told himself, unless Ishido comes to your rescue. And why should Ishido rescue you when your enemy Ikawa Jikkyo is Ishido's kinsman and wants Izu for himself? Killing Hiro-matsu will open hostilities, because Toranaga will be honor bound to move against you, which would force Ishido's hand, and Izu would be the first battlefield.

What about my guns? My beautiful guns and my beautiful plan? I'll lose my immortal chance forever if I have to turn them over to Toranaga.

His hand was on the Murasama sword and he could feel the blood in his sword arm and the blinding urge to begin. He had discarded at once the possibility of not mentioning the muskets. If the news of the ship had been betrayed, certainly the identity of its cargo was equally betrayed. But how did Toranaga get the news so quickly? By carrier pigeon! That's the only answer. From Yedo or from here? Who possesses carrier pigeons here? Why haven't I such a service? That's Zukimoto's fault—he should have thought of it, *neh?*

Make up your mind. War or no war?

Yabu called down the ill will of Buddha, of all *kami*, of all gods that had ever been or were yet to be invented, upon the man or men who had betrayed him, upon their parents and upon their descendants for ten thousand generations. And he conceded.

"Lord Toranaga cannot confiscate the ship because it's already a gift to him. I've dictated a letter to that effect. Isn't that so, Zujimoto?"

"Yes, Sire."

"Of course, if Lord Toranaga wishes to consider it confiscated he may. But it was to be a gift." Yabu was pleased to hear that his voice sounded matter-of-fact. "He will be happy with the booty."

"Thank you on behalf of my Master." Hiro-matsu again marveled at Toranaga's foresight. Toranaga had predicted that this would happen and that there would be no fighting. 'I don't believe it,' Hiro-matsu had said. 'No *daimyo* would stand for such usurping of his rights. Yabu won't. I certainly wouldn't. Not even to you, Sire.'

'But you would have obeyed orders and you would have told me about the ship. Yabu must be manipulated, *neh?* I need his violence and cunning—he neutralizes Ikawa Jikkyu and guards my flank.'

Here on the beach under a good sun Hiro-matsu forced himself into a polite bow, hating his own duplicity. "Lord Toranaga will be delighted with your generosity."

Yabu was watching him closely. "It's not a Portuguese ship."

"Yes. So we heard."

"And it's pirate." He saw the general's eyes narrow.

"Eh?"

As he told him what the priest had said, Yabu thought, if that's news to you as it was to me, doesn't that mean that Toranaga had the same original information as I? But if you know the contents of the ship, then the spy is Omi, one of his samurai, or a villager. "There's an abundance of cloth. Some treasure. Muskets, powder, and shot."

Hiro-matsu hesitated. Then he said, "The cloth is Chinese silks?"

"No, Hiro-matsu-san," he said, using the "san." They were *daimyos* equally. But now that he was magnanimously "giving" the ship, he felt safe enough to use the less deferential term. He was pleased to see that the word had not gone unnoticed by the older man. I'm *daimyo* of Izu, by the sun, the moon, and the stars!

"It's very unusual, a thick heavy cloth, totally useless to us," he said. "I've had everything worth salvaging brought ashore."

"Good. Please put all of it aboard my ship."

"What?" Yabu's bowels almost burst.

"All of it. At once."

"Now?"

"Yes. So sorry, but you'll naturally understand that I want to return to Osaka as soon as possible."

"Yes but—but will there be space for everything?"

"Put the cannon back on the barbarian ship and seal it up. Boats will be arriving within three days to tow it to Yedo. As to the muskets, powder, and shot, there's—" Hiro-matsu stopped, avoiding the trap that he suddenly realized had been set for him.

'There's just enough space for the five hundred muskets,' Toranaga had told him. 'And all the powder and the twenty thousand silver doubloons aboard the galley. Leave the cannon on the deck of the ship and the cloth in the holds. Let Yabu do the talking and give him orders, don't let him have time to think. But don't get irritated or impatient with him. I need him, but I want those guns and that ship. Beware of his trying to trap you into revealing that you know the exactness of the cargo, because he must not uncover our spy.'

Hiro-matsu cursed his inability to play these necessary games. "As to the space needed," he said shortly, "perhaps you should tell me. And just exactly what is the cargo? How many muskets and shot and so forth? And is the bullion in bar or coins—is it silver or gold?"

"Zukimoto!"

"Yes, Yabu-sama."

"Get the list of the contents." I'll deal with you later, Yabu thought. Zukimoto hurried away.

"You must be tired, Hiro-matsu-san. Perhaps some cha? Accommodations have been prepared for you, such as they are. The baths are totally inadequate, but perhaps one would refresh you a little."

"Thank you. You're very thoughtful. Some cha and a bath would be excellent. Later. First tell me everything that has happened since the ship arrived here."

Yabu told him the facts, omitting the part about the courtesan and the boy, which was unimportant. On Yabu's orders, Omi told his story, except for his private conversations with Yabu. And Mura told his, excluding the part about the Anjin's erection which, Mura reasoned, though interesting, might have offended Hiro-matsu, whose own, at his age, might be few and far between.

Hiro-matsu looked at the plume of smoke that still rose from the pyre. "How many of the pirates are left?"

"Ten, Sire, including the leader," Omi said.

"Where's the leader now?"

"In Mura's house."

"What did he do? What was the first thing he did there after getting out of the pit?"

"He went straight to the bath house, Sire," Mura said quickly. "Now he's asleep, Sire, like a dead man."

"You didn't have to carry him this time?"

"No, Sire."

"He seems to learn quickly." Hiro-matsu glanced back at Omi. "You think they can be taught to behave?"

"No. Not for certain, Hiro-matsu-sama."

"Could you clean away an enemy's urine from your back?"

"No, Lord."

"Nor could I. Never. Barbarians are very strange." Hiro-matsu turned his mind back to the ship. "Who will be supervising the loading?"

"My nephew, Omi-san."

"Good. Omi-san, I want to leave before dusk. My captain will help you be very quick. Within three sticks." The unit of time was the time it took for a standard stick of incense to smolder away, approximately one hour for one stick.

"Yes, Lord."

"Why not come with me to Osaka, Yabu-san?" Hiro-matsu said as though it was a sudden thought. "Lord Toranaga would be delighted to receive all these things from your hands. Personally. Please, there's room enough." When Yabu began to protest he allowed him to continue for a time, as Toranaga had ordered, and then he said, as Toranaga had ordered, "I insist. In Lord Toranaga's name, I insist. Your generosity needs to be rewarded."

With my head and my lands? Yabu asked himself bitterly, knowing that there was nothing he could do now but accept gratefully. "Thank you. I would be honored."

"Good. Well then, that's all done," Iron Fist said with obvious relief. "Now some cha. And a bath."

Yabu politely led the way up the hill to Omi's house. The old man was washed and scoured and then he lay gratefully in the steaming heat. Later Suwo's hands made him new again. A little rice and raw fish and pickled vegetables taken sparingly in private. Cha sipped from good porcelain. A short dreamless nap.

After three sticks the shoji slid open. The personal bodyguard knew better than to go into the room uninvited; Hiro-matsu was already awake and the sword half unsheathed and ready.

"Yabu-sama is waiting outside, Sire. He says the ship is loaded."

"Excellent."

Hiro-matsu went onto the veranda and relieved himself into the bucket. "Your men are very efficient, Yabu-san."

"Your men helped, Hiro-matsu-san. They are more than efficient."

Yes, and by the sun, they had better be, Hiro-matsu thought, then said genially, "Nothing like a good piss from a full bladder so long as there's plenty of power behind the stream. *Neh?* Makes you feel young again. At my age you need to feel young." He eased his loincloth comfortably, expecting Yabu to make some polite remark in agreement, but none was forthcoming. His irritation began to rise but he curbed it. "Have the pirate leader taken to my ship."

"What?"

"You were generous enough to make a gift of the ship and the contents. The crew are contents. So I'm taking the pirate leader to Osaka. Lord Toranaga wants to see him. Naturally you do what you like with the rest of them. But during your absence, please make certain that your retainers realize the barbarians are my Master's property and that there had better be nine in good health, alive, and here when he wants them."

Yabu hurried away to the jetty where Omi would be.

When, earlier, he had left Hiro-matsu to his bath, he had walked up the track that meandered past the funeral ground. There he had bowed briefly to the pyre and continued on, skirting the terraced fields of wheat and fruit to come out at length on a small plateau high above the village. A tidy *kami* shrine guarded this tender place. An ancient tree bequeathed shade and tranquillity. He had gone there to quell his rage and to think. He had not dared to go near the ship or Omi or his men for he knew that he would have ordered most, if not all of them, to commit seppuku, which would have been a waste, and he would have slaughtered the village, which would have been foolish—peasants alone caught the fish and grew the rice that provided the wealth of the samurai.

While he had sat and fumed alone and tried to sharpen his brain, the sun bent down and drove the sea mists away. The clouds that shrouded the distant mountains to the west had parted for an instant and he had seen the beauty of the snow-capped peaks soaring. The sight had settled him and he had begun to relax and think and plan.

Set your spies to find the spy, he told himself. Nothing that Hiro-matsu said indicated whether the betrayal was from here or from Yedo. In Osaka you've powerful friends, the Lord Ishido himself among them. Perhaps one of them can smell out the fiend. But send a private message at once to your wife in case the informer is there. What about Omi? Make him responsible for finding the informer here? Is he the informer? That's not likely, but not impossible. It's more than probable the betrayal began in Yedo. A matter of timing. If Toranaga in Osaka got the information about the ship when it arrived, then Hiro-matsu would have been here first. You've informers in Yedo. Let them prove their worth.

What about the barbarians? Now they're your only profit from the ship. How can you use them? Wait, didn't Omi give you the answer? You could use their knowledge of the sea and ships to barter with Toranaga for guns. *Neh?*

Another possibility: become Toranaga's *vassal* completely. Give him your plan. Ask him to allow you to lead the Regiment of the Guns—for *his* glory. But a *vassal should never expect his lord to reward his services or even acknowledge them: To serve is duty, duty is samurai, samurai is immortality.* That would be the best way, the very best, Yabu thought. Can I truly be his *vassal?* Or Ishido's?

No, that's unthinkable. Ally yes, vassal no.

Good, so the barbarians are an asset after all. Omi's right again.

He had felt more composed and then, when the time had come and a messenger had brought the information that the ship was loaded, he had gone to Hiro-matsu and discovered that now he had lost even the barbarians.

He was boiling when he reached the jetty.

"Omi-san!"

"Yes, Yabu-sama?"

"Bring the barbarian leader here. I'm taking him to Osaka. As to the others, see that they're well cared for while I'm away. I want them fit, and well behaved. Use the pit if you have to."

Ever since the galley had arrived, Omi's mind had been in a turmoil and he had been filled with anxiety for Yabu's safety. "Let me come with you, Lord. Perhaps I can help."

"No, now I want you to look after the barbarians."

"Please. Perhaps in some small way I can repay your kindness to me."

"There's no need," Yabu said, more kindly than he wanted to. He remembered that he had increased Omi's salary to three thousand koku and extended his fief because of the bullion and the guns. Which now had vanished. But he had seen the concern that filled the youth and had felt an involuntary warmth. With vassals like this, I will carve an empire, he promised himself. Omi will lead one of the units when I get back my guns. "When war comes—well, I'll have a very important job for you, Omi-san. Now go and get the barbarian."

Omi took four guards with him. And Mura to interpret.

Blackthorne was dragged out of sleep. It took him a minute to clear his head. When the fog lifted Omi was staring down at him.

One of the samurai had pulled the quilt off him, another had shaken him awake, the other two carried thin, vicious-looking bamboo canes. Mura had a short coil of rope.

Mura knelt and bowed. "*Konnichi wa*"—Good day.

"*Konnichi wa*." Blackthorne pulled himself onto his knees and, though he was naked, he bowed with equal politeness.

It's only a politeness, Blackthorne told himself. It's their custom and they bow for good manners so there's no shame to it. And nakedness is ignored and is also their custom, and there's no shame to nakedness either.

"Anjin. Please to dress," Mura said.

Anjin? Ah, I remember now. The priest said they can't pronounce my name so they've given me the name "Anjin" which means "pilot" and this is not meant as an insult. And I will be called "Anjin-san"— Mr. Pilot—when I merit it.

Don't look at Omi, he cautioned himself. Not yet. Don't remember the village square and Omi and Croocq and Pieterzoon. One thing at a time. That's what you're going to do. That's what you have sworn before God to do: One thing at a time. Vengeance will be mine, by the Lord God.

Blackthorne saw that his clothes had been cleaned again and he blessed whoever had done it. He had crawled out of his clothes in the bath house as though they had been plague-infested. Three times he had made them scour his back. With the roughest sponge and with pumice. But he could still feel the piss-burn.

He took his eyes off Mura and looked at Omi. He derived a twisted pleasure from the knowledge that his enemy was alive and nearby.

He bowed as he had seen equals bow and he held the bow. "*Konnichi wa*, Omi-san," he said. There's no shame in speaking their language, no shame in saying "good day" or in bowing first as is their custom.

Omi bowed back.

Blackthorne noted that it was not quite equal, but it was enough for the moment.

"*Konnichi wa*, Anjin," Omi said.

The voice was polite, but not enough.

"Anjin-*san!*" Blackthorne looked directly at him.

Their wills locked and Omi was called as a man is called at cards or at dice. Do you have manners?

"*Konnichi wa*, Anjin-*san*," Omi said at length, with a brief smile.

Blackthorne dressed quickly.

He wore loose trousers and a codpiece, socks and shirt and coat, his long hair tied into a neat queue and his beard trimmed with scissors the barber had loaned to him.

"*Hai*, Omi-san?" Blackthorne asked when he was dressed, feeling better but very guarded, wishing he had more words to use.

"Please, hand," Mura said.

Blackthorne did not understand and said so with signs. Mura held out his own hands and parodied tying them together.

"Hand, please."

"No." Blackthorne said it directly to Omi and shook his head. "That's not necessary," he said in English, "not necessary at all. I've given my word." He kept his voice gentle and reasonable, then added harshly, copying Omi, "*Wakarimasu ka*, Omi-san?" Do you understand?

Omi laughed. Then he said, "*Hai*, Anjin-san. *Wakarimasu.*" He turned and left.

Mura and the others stared after him, astounded. Blackthorne followed Omi into the sun. His boots had been cleaned. Before he could slip them on, the maid "Onna" was there on her knees and she helped him.

"Thank you, Haku-san," he said, remembering her real name. What's the word for "thank you"? he wondered.

He walked through the gate, Omi ahead.

I'm after you, you God-cursed bas—Wait a minute! Remember what you promised yourself? And why swear at him, even to yourself? He hasn't sworn at you. Swearing's for the weak, or for fools. Isn't it?

One thing at a time. It is enough that you are after him. You know it clearly and he knows it clearly. Make no mistake, he knows it very clearly.

The four samurai flanked Blackthorne as he walked down the hill, the harbor still hidden from him, Mura discreetly ten paces back, Omi ahead.

Are they going to put me underground again? he wondered. Why did they want to bind my hands? Didn't Omi say yesterday—Christ Jesus, was that only yesterday?—'If you behave you can stay out of the pit. If you behave, tomorrow another man will be taken out of the pit. Perhaps. And more, perhaps.' Isn't that what he said? Have I behaved? I wonder how Croocq is. The lad was alive when they carried him off to the house where the crew first stayed.

Blackthorne felt better today. The bath and the sleep and the fresh food had begun to repair him. He knew that if he was careful and could rest and sleep and eat, within a month he would be able to run a mile and swim a mile and command a fighting ship and take her around the earth.

Don't think about that yet! Just guard your strength this day. A month's not much to hope for, eh?

The walk down the hill and through the village was tiring him. You're weaker than you thought. . . . No, you are stronger than you thought, he ordered himself.

The masts of *Erasmus* jutted over the tiled roofs and his heart quickened. Ahead the street curved with the contour of the hillside, slid down to the square and ended. A curtained palanquin stood in the sun. Four bearers in brief loincloths squatted beside it, absently picking their teeth. The moment they saw Omi they were on their knees, bowing mightily.

Omi barely nodded at them as he strode past, but then a girl came out of the neat gateway to go the palanquin and he stopped.

Blackthorne caught his breath and stopped also.

A young maid ran out to hold a green parasol to shade the girl. Omi bowed and the girl bowed and they talked happily to each other, the strutting arrogance vanishing from Omi.

The girl wore a peach-colored kimono and a wide sash of gold and gold-thonged slippers. Blackthorne saw her glance at him. Clearly she and Omi were discussing him. He did not know how to react, or what to do, so he did nothing but wait patiently, glorying in the sight of her, the cleanliness and the warmth of her presence. He wondered if she and Omi were lovers, or if she was Omi's wife, and he thought, Is she truly real?

Omi asked her something and she answered and fluttered her green fan that shimmered and danced in the sunlight, her laugh musical, the delicacy of her exquisite. Omi was smiling too, then he turned on his heel and strode off, samurai once more.

Blackthorne followed. Her eyes were on him as he passed and he said, "*Konnichi wa.*"

"*Konnichi wa,* Anjin-san," she replied, her voice touching him. She was barely five feet tall and perfect. As she bowed slightly the breeze shook the outer silk and showed the beginnings of the scarlet under-kimono which he found surprisingly erotic.

The girl's perfume still surrounded him as he turned the corner. He saw the trapdoor and *Erasmus*. And the galley. The girl vanished from his mind.

Why are our gun ports empty? Where are our cannon and what in the name of Christ is a slave galley doing here and what's happened in the pit?

One thing at a time.

First *Erasmus*: the stub of the foremast that the storm had carried away jutted nastily. That doesn't matter, he thought. We could get her out to sea easily. We could slip the moorings—the night airflow and the tide would take us out silently and we could careen tomorrow on the far side of that speck of island. Half a day to step the spare mast and then all sails ho and away into the far deep. Maybe it'd be better not to anchor but to flee to safer waters. But who'd crew? You can't take her out by yourself.

Where did that slaver come from? And why is it here?

He could see knots of samurai and sailors down at the wharf. The sixty-oared vessel—thirty oars a side—was neat and trim, the oars stacked with care, ready for instant departure, and he shivered involuntarily. The last time he'd seen a galley was off the Gold Coast two years ago when his fleet was outward bound, all five ships together. She had been a rich coastal trader, a Portuguese, and she was fleeing from him against the wind. *Erasmus* could not catch her, to capture her or sink her.

Blackthorne knew the North African coast well. He had been a pilot and ship's master for ten years for the London Company of Barbary Merchants, the joint stock company that fitted out fighting merchant-men to run the Spanish blockade and trade the Barbary Coast. He had piloted to West and North Africa, south as far as Lagos, north and eastward through the treacherous straits of Gibraltar—ever Spanish patrolled—as far as Salerno in the Kingdom of Naples. The Mediterranean was dangerous to English and Dutch shipping. Spanish and Portuguese enemy were there in strength and, worse, the Ottomans, the infidel Turks, swarmed the seas with slave galleys and with fighting ships.

These voyages had been very profitable for him and he had bought his own ship, a hundred-fifty-ton brig, to trade on his own behalf. But he had had her sunk under him and lost everything. They had been caught a-lee, windless off Sardinia, when the Turk galley had come out of the sun. The fight was cruel and then, toward sunset, the enemy ram caught their stern and they were boarded fast. He had never forgotten the screaming cry 'Allahhhhhhhh!' as the corsairs came over his gunwales. They were armed with swords and with muskets. He had rallied his men and the first attack had been beaten off, but the second overwhelmed them and he ordered the magazine fired. His ship was in flames and he decided that it was better to die than to be put to the oars. He had always had a mortal terror of being taken alive and made a galley slave—not an unusual fate for a captured seaman.

When the magazine blew, the explosion tore the bottom out of his ship and destroyed part of the corsair galley and, in the confusion, he managed to swim to the longboat and escape with four of the crew. Those who could not swim to him he had had to leave and he still remembered their cries for help in God's name. But God had turned His face from those men that day, so they had perished or gone to the oars. And God had kept His face on Blackthorne and the four men that time, and they had managed to reach Cagliari in Sardinia. And from there they had made it home, penniless.

That was eight years ago, the same year that plague had erupted again in London. Plague and famine and riots of the starving unemployed. His younger brother and family had been wiped out. His own first-born son had perished. But in the winter the plague vanished and he had easily got a new ship and gone to sea to repair his fortune. First for the London Company of Barbary Merchants. Then a voyage to the West Indies hunting Spaniards. After that, a little richer, he navigated for Kees Veerman, the Dutchman, on his second voyage to search for the legendary Northeast Passage to Cathay and the Spice Islands of Asia, that was supposed to exist in the Ice Seas, north of tsarist Russia. They searched for two years, then Kees Veerman died in the Arctic wastes with eighty percent of the crew and Blackthorne turned back and led the rest of the men home. Then, three years ago, he'd been approached by the newly formed Dutch East India Company and asked to pilot their first expedition to the New World. They whispered secretly that they had acquired, at huge cost, a contraband Portuguese rutter that supposedly gave away the secrets of Magellan's Strait, and they wanted to prove it. Of course the Dutch merchants would have preferred to use one of their own pilots, but there was none to compare in quality with Englishmen trained by the monopolistic Trinity House, and the awesome value of this rutter forced them to gamble on Blackthorne. But he was the perfect choice: he was the best Protestant pilot alive, his mother had been Dutch, and he spoke Dutch perfectly. Blackthorne had agreed enthusiastically and accepted the fifteen percent of all profit as his fee and, as was custom, had solemnly, before God, sworn allegiance to the Company and vowed to take their fleet out, and to bring it home again.

By God, I am going to bring *Erasmus* home, Blackthorne thought. And with as many of the men as He leaves alive.

They were crossing the square now and he took his eyes off the slaver and saw the three samurai guarding the trapdoor. They were eating deftly from bowls with the wooden sticks that Blackthorne had seen them use many times but could not manage himself.

"Omi-san!" With signs he explained that he wanted to go to the trapdoor, just to shout down to his friends. Only for a moment. But Omi shook his head and said something he did not understand and continued across the square, down the foreshore, past the cauldron, and on to the jetty. Blackthorne followed obediently. One thing at a time, he told himself. Be patient.

Once on the jetty, Omi turned and called back to the guards on the trapdoor. Blackthorne saw them open the trapdoor and peer down. One of them beckoned to villagers who fetched the ladder and a full fresh-water barrel and carried it below. The empty one they brought back aloft. And the latrine barrel.

There! If you're patient and play their game with their rules, you can help your crew, he thought with satisfaction.

Groups of samurai were collected near the galley. A tall old man was standing apart. From the deference that the *daimyo* Yabu showed him, and the way the others jumped at his slightest remark, Blackthorne immediately realized his importance. Is he their king? he wondered.

Omi knelt with humility. The old man half bowed, turned his eyes on him.

Mustering as much grace as he could, Blackthorne knelt and put his hands flat on the sand floor of the jetty, as Omi had done, and bowed as low as Omi.

"*Konnichi wa*, Sama," he said politely.

He saw the old man half bow again.

Now there was a discussion between Yabu and the old man and Omi. Yabu spoke to Mura.

Mura pointed at the galley. "Anjin-san. Please there."

"Why?"

"Go! Now. Go!"

Blackthorne felt his panic rising. "Why?"

"*Isogi!*" Omi commanded, waving him toward the galley.

"No, I'm not going to—"

There was an immediate order from Omi and four samurai fell on Blackthorne and pinioned his arms. Mura produced the rope and began to bind his hands behind him.

"You sons of bitches!" Blackthorne shouted. "I'm not going to go aboard that God-cursed slave ship!"

"Madonna! Leave him alone! Hey, you piss-eating monkeys, let that bastard alone! *Kinjiru, neh?* Is he the Pilot? The Anjin, *ka?*"

Blackthorne could scarcely believe his ears. The boisterous abuse in Portuguese had come from the deck of the galley. Then he saw the man start down the gangway. As tall as he and about his age, but black-haired and dark-eyed and carelessly dressed in seaman's clothes, rapier by his side, pistols in his belt. A jeweled crucifix hung from his neck. He wore a jaunty cap and a smile split his face.

"Are you the Pilot? The Pilot of the Dutchman?"

"Yes," Blackthorne heard himself reply.

"Good. Good. I'm Vasco Rodrigues, Pilot of this galley!" He turned to the old man and spoke a mixture of Japanese and Portuguese, and called him Monkey-sama and sometimes Toda-sama but the way it sounded it came out "Toady-sama." Twice he pulled out his pistol and pointed it emphatically at Blackthorne and stuck it back in his belt, his Japanese heavily laced with sweet vulgarities in gutter Portuguese that only seafarers would understand.

Hiro-matsu spoke briefly and the samurai released Blackthorne and Mura untied him.

"That's better. Listen, Pilot, this man's like a king. I told him I'd be responsible for you, that I'd blow your head off as soon as drink with you!" Rodrigues bowed to Hiro-matsu, then beamed at Blackthorne. "Bow to the Bastard-sama."

Dreamlike, Blackthorne did as he was told.

"You do that like a Japper," Rodrigues said with a grin. "You're really the Pilot?"

"Yes."

"What's the latitude of The Lizard?"

"Forty-nine degrees fifty-six minutes North—and watch out for the reefs that bear sou' by sou'west."

"You're the Pilot, by God!" Rodrigues shook Blackthorne's hand warmly. "Come aboard. There's food and brandy and wine and grog and all pilots should love all pilots who're the sperm of the earth. Amen! Right?"

"Yes," Blackthorne said weakly.

"When I heard we were carrying a pilot back with us, good says I. It's years since I had the pleasure of talking to a real pilot. Come aboard. How did you sneak past Malacca? How did you avoid our Indian Ocean patrols, eh? Whose rutter did you steal?"

"Where are you taking me?"

"Osaka. The Great Lord High Executioner himself wants to see you."

Blackthorne felt his panic returning. "Who?"

"Toranaga! Lord of the Eight Provinces, wherever the hell they are! The chief *daimyo* of Japan—a *daimyo's* like a king or feudal lord but better. They're all despots."

"What's he want with me?"

"I don't know but that's why we're here, and if Toranaga wants to see you, Pilot, he'll see you. They say he's got a million of these slant-eyed fanatics who'll die for the honor of wiping his arse if that's his pleasure! 'Toranaga wants you to bring back the pilot, Vasco,' his interpreter said. 'Bring back the pilot and the ship's cargo. Take old Toda Hiromatsu there to examine the ship and—' Oh yes, Pilot, it's all confiscated, so I hear, your ship, and everything in it!"

"Confiscated?"

"It may be a rumor. Jappers sometimes confiscate things with one hand, give 'em back with the other—or pretend they've never given the order. It's hard to understand the poxy little bastards!"

Blackthorne felt the cold eyes of the Japanese boring into him and he tried to hide his fear. Rodrigues followed his glance. "Yes, they're getting restless. Time enough to talk. Come aboard." He turned but Blackthorne stopped him.

"What about my friends, my crew?"

"Eh?"

Blackthorne told him briefly about the pit. Rodrigues questioned Omi in pidgin Japanese. "He says they'll be all right. Listen, there's nothing you or me can do now. You'll have to wait—you can never tell with a Jappo. They're six-faced and three-hearted." Rodrigues bowed like a European courtier to Hiro-matsu. "This is the way we do it in Japan. Like we're at the court of Fornicating Philip II, God take that

Spaniard to an early grave." He led the way on deck. To Blackthorne's astonishment there were no chains and no slaves.

"What's the matter? You sick?" Rodrigues asked.

"No. I thought this was a slaver."

"They don't have 'em in Japan. Not even in their mines. Lunatic, but there you are. You've never seen such lunatics and I've traveled the world three times. We've samurai rowers. They're soldiers, the old bugger's personal soldiers—and you've never seen slaves row better, or men fight better." Rodrigues laughed. "They put their arses into the oars and I push 'em just to watch the buggers bleed. They never quit. We came all the way from Osaka—three-hundred-odd sea miles in forty hours. Come below. We'll cast off shortly. You sure you're all right?"

"Yes. Yes, I think so." Blackthorne was looking at *Erasmus*. She was moored a hundred yards away. "Pilot, there's no chance of going aboard, is there? They haven't let me back aboard, I've no clothes and they sealed her up the moment we arrived. Please?"

Rodrigues scrutinized the ship.

"When did you lose the foremast?"

"Just before we made landfall here."

"There a spare still aboard?"

"Yes."

"Where's her home port?"

"Rotterdam."

"She was built there?"

"Yes."

"I've been there. Bad shoals but a pisscutter of a harbor. She's got good lines, your ship. New—haven't seen one of her class before. Madonna, she'd be fast, very fast. Very rough to deal with." Rodrigues looked at him. "Can you get your gear quickly?" He turned over the half-hour glass sand timer that was beside the hourglass, both attached to the binnacle.

"Yes." Blackthorne tried to keep his growing hope off his face.

"There'd be a condition, Pilot. No weapons, up your sleeve or anywhere. Your word as a pilot. I've told the monkeys I'd be responsible for you."

"I agree." Blackthorne watched the sand falling silently through the neck of the timer.

"I'll blow your head off, pilot or no, if there's the merest whiff of trickery, or cut your throat. *If* I agree."

"I give you my word, pilot to pilot, by God. And the pox on the Spanish!"

Rodrigues smiled and banged him warmly on the back. "I'm beginning to like you, Ingeles."

"How'd you know I'm English?" Blackthorne asked, knowing his Portuguese was perfect and that nothing he had said could have differentiated him from a Dutchman.

"I'm a soothsayer. Aren't all pilots?" Rodrigues laughed.

"You talked to the priest? Father Sebastio told you?"

"I don't talk to priests if I can help it. Once a week's more than enough for any man." Rodrigues spat deftly into the scuppers and went to the port gangway that overlooked the jetty. "Toady-sama! *Ikimasho ka?*"

"*Ikimasho*, Rodrigu-san. *Ima!*"

"*Ima* it is." Rodrigues looked at Blackthorne thoughtfully. " '*Ima*' means 'now,' 'at once.' We're to leave at once, Ingeles."

The sand had already made a small, neat mound in the bottom of the glass.

"Will you ask him, please? If I can go aboard my ship?"

"No, Ingeles. I won't ask him a poxy thing."

Blackthorne suddenly felt empty. And very old. He watched Rodrigues go to the railing of the quarterdeck and bellow to a small, distinguished seaman who stood on the raised fore-poop deck at the bow. "Hey, Captain-san. *Ikimasho?* Get samurai aboard-u, *ima! Ima, wakarimasu ka?*"

"*Hai*, Anjin-san."

Immediately Rodrigues rang the ship's bell loudly six times and the Captain-san began shouting orders to the seamen and samurai ashore and aboard. Seamen hurried up on deck from below to prepare for departure and, in the disciplined, controlled confusion, Rodrigues quietly took Blackthorne's arm and shoved him toward the starboard gangway, away from the shore.

"There's a dinghy below, Ingeles. Don't move fast, don't look around, and don't pay attention to anyone but me. If I tell you to come back, do it quickly."

Blackthorne walked across the deck, down the gangway, toward the small Japanese skiff. He heard angry voices behind him and he felt the hairs on his neck rising for there were many samurai all over the ship, some armed with bows and arrows, a few with muskets.

"You don't have to worry about him, Captain-san, I'm responsible. Me, Rodrigu-san, *ichi ban* Anjin-san, by the Virgin! *Wakarimasu ka?*" was dominating the other voices, but they were getting angrier every moment.

Blackthorne was almost in the dinghy now and he saw that there were no rowlocks. I can't scull like they do, he told himself. I can't use the boat! It's too far to swim. Or is it?

He hesitated, checking the distance. If he had had his full strength he would not have waited a moment. But now?

Feet clattered down the gangway behind him and he fought the impulse to turn.

"Sit in the stern," he heard Rodrigues say urgently. "Hurry up!"

He did as he was told and Rodrigues jumped in nimbly, grabbed the oars and, still standing, shoved off with great skill.

A samurai was at the head of the gangway, very perturbed, and two other samurai were beside him, bows ready. The captain samurai called out, unmistakably beckoning them to come back.

A few yards from the vessel Rodrigues turned. "Just go there," he shouted up at him, pointing at *Erasmus*. "Get samurai aboard!" He set his back firmly to his ship and continued sculling, pushing against the oars in Japanese fashion, standing amidships. "Tell me if they put arrows in their bows, Ingeles! Watch 'em carefully! What're they doing now?"

"The captain's very angry. You won't get into trouble, will you?"

"If we don't sail at the turn, Old Toady might have cause for complaint. What're those bowmen doing?"

"Nothing. They're listening to him. He seems undecided. No. Now one of them's drawing out an arrow."

Rodrigues prepared to stop. "Madonna, they're too God-cursed accurate to risk anything. Is it in the bow yet?"

"Yes—but wait a moment! The captain's—someone's come up to him, a seaman I think. Looks like he's asking him something about the ship. The captain's looking at us. He said something to the man with the arrow. Now the man's putting it away. The seaman's pointing at something on deck."

Rodrigues sneaked a quick look to make sure and breathed easier. "That's one of the mates. It'll take him all of the half hour to get his oarsmen settled."

Blackthorne waited, the distance increased. "The captain's looking at us again. No, we're all right. He's gone away. But one of the samurai's watching us."

"Let him." Rodrigues relaxed but he did not slacken the pace of his sculling or look back. "Don't like my back to samurai, not when they've weapons in their hands. Not that I've ever seen one of the bastards unarmed. They're all bastards!"

"Why?"

"They love to kill, Ingeles. It's their custom even to sleep with their swords. This is a great country, but samurai're dangerous as vipers and a sight more mean."

"Why?"

"I don't know why, Ingeles, but they are," Rodrigues replied, glad to talk to one of his own kind. "Of course, all Jappos are different from us—they don't feel pain or cold like us—but samurai are even worse. They fear nothing, least of all death. Why? Only God knows, but it's the truth. If their superiors say 'kill,' they kill, 'die' and they'll fall on their swords or slit their own bellies open. They kill and die as easily as we piss. Women're samurai too, Ingeles. They'll kill to protect their masters, that's what they call their husbands here, or they'll kill themselves if they're ordered to. They do it by slitting their throats. Here a samurai can order his wife to kill herself and that's what she's got to do, by law. Jesu Madonna, the women are something else though, a different species, Ingeles, nothing on earth like them, but the men. . . . Samurai're reptiles and the safest thing to do is treat them like poisonous snakes. You all right now?"

"Yes, thank you. A bit weak but all right."

"How was your voyage?"

"Rough. About them—the samurai—how do they get to be one? Do they just pick up the two swords and get that haircut?"

"You've got to be born one. Of course, there are all ranks of samurai from *daimyos* at the top of the muckheap to what we'd call a foot soldier at the bottom. It's hereditary mostly, like with us. In the olden days, so I was told, it was the same as in Europe today—peasants could be soldiers and soldiers peasants, with hereditary knights and nobles up to kings. Some peasant soldiers rose to the highest rank. The Taikō was one."

"Who's he?"

"The Great Despot, the ruler of all Japan, the Great Murderer of all times—I'll tell you about him one day. He died a year ago and now he's burning in hell." Rodrigues spat overboard. "Nowadays you've got to be born samurai to be one. It's all hereditary, Ingeles. Madonna, you've no idea how much store they put on heritage, on family, rank, and the like—you saw how Omi bows to that devil Yabu and they both grovel to old Toady-sama. 'Samurai' comes from a Jappo word meaning 'to serve.' But while they'll all bow and scrape to the man above, they're all samurai equally, with a samurai's special privileges. What's happening aboard?"

"The captain's jabbering away at another samurai and pointing at us. What's special about them?"

"Here samurai rule everything, own everything. They've their own code of honor and sets of rules. Arrogant? Madonna, you've no idea! The lowest of them can legally kill any non-samurai, *any* man, woman, or child, for any reason or for no reason. They can kill, legally, just to test the edge of their piss-cutting swords—I've seen 'em do it—and they have the best swords in the world. Better'n Damascus steel. What's that fornicator doing now?"

"Just watching us. His bow's on his back now." Blackthorne shuddered. "I hate those bastards more than Spaniards."

Again Rodrigues laughed as he sculled. "If the truth's known, they curdle my piss too! But if you want to get rich quick you've got to work with them because they own everything. You sure you're all right?"

"Yes. Thanks. You were saying? Samurai own everything?"

"Yes. Whole country's split up into castes, like in India. Samurai at the top, peasants next important." Rodrigues spat overboard. "Only peasants can *own* land. Understand? But samurai own all the produce. They own all the rice and that's the only important crop, and they give back part to the peasants. Only samurai're allowed to carry arms. For anyone except a samurai to attack a samurai is rebellion, punishable by instant death. And anyone who sees such an attack and doesn't report it at once is equally liable, and so are their wives, and even their kids. The whole family's put to death if one doesn't report it. By the Madonna, they're Satan's whelps, samurai! I've seen kids chopped into mincemeat." Rodrigues hawked and spat. "Even so, if you know a thing or two this place is heaven on earth." He glanced back at the galley to reassure himself, then he grinned. "Well, Ingeles, nothing like a boat ride around the harbor, eh?"

Blackthorne laughed. The years dropped off him as he reveled in the familiar dip of the waves, the smell of the sea salt, gulls calling and playing overhead, the sense of freedom, the sense of arriving after so very long. "I thought you weren't going to help me get to *Erasmus!*"

"That's the trouble with all Ingeles. No patience. Listen, here you don't *ask* Japmen anything—samurai or others, they're all the same. If you do, they'll hesitate, then ask the man above for the decision. Here you have to *act*. Of course"—his hearty laugh ran across the waves—"sometimes you get killed if you act wrong."

"You scull very well. I was wondering how to use the oars when you came."

"You don't think I'd let you go alone, do you? What's your name?"

"Blackthorne. John Blackthorne."

"Have you ever been north, Ingeles? Into the far north?"

"I was with Kees Veerman in *Der Lifle*. Eight years ago. It was his second voyage to find the Northeast Passage. Why?"

"I'd like to hear about that—and all the places you've been. Do you think they'll ever find the way? The northern way to Asia, east or west?"

"Yes. You and the Spanish block both southern routes, so we'll have to. Yes, we will. Or the Dutch. Why?"

"And you've piloted the Barbary Coast, eh?"

"Yes. Why?"

"And you know Tripoli?"

"Most pilots have been there. Why?"

"I thought I'd seen you once. Yes, it was Tripoli. You were pointed out to me. The famous Ingeles pilot. Who went with the Dutch explorer, Kees Veerman, into the Ice Seas—and was once a captain with Drake, eh? At the Armada? How old were you then?"

"Twenty-four. What were you doing in Tripoli?"

"I was piloting an Ingeles privateer. My ship'd got taken in the Indies by this pirate, Morrow—Henry Morrow was his name. He burned my ship to the waterline after he'd sacked her and offered me the pilot's job—his man was useless, so he said—you know how it is. He wanted to go from there—we were watering off Hispaniola when he caught us— south along the Main, then back across the Atlantic to try to intercept the annual Spanish gold ship near the Canaries, then on through the Straits to Tripoli if we missed her to try for other prizes, then north again to England. He made the usual offer to free my comrades, give them food and boats in return if I joined them. I said, 'Sure, why not? Providing we don't take any Portuguese shipping and you put me ashore near Lisbon and don't steal my rutters.' We argued back and forth as usual—you know how it is. Then I swore by the Madonna and we both swore on the Cross and that was that. We had a good voyage and some fat Spanish merchantmen fell into our wake. When we were off Lisbon he asked me to stay aboard, gave me the usual message from Good Queen Bess, how she'd pay a princely bounty to any Portuguese pilot who'd join her and teach others the skill at Trinity House, and give five thousand guineas for the rutter of Magellan's Pass, or the Cape of Good Hope." His smile was broad, his teeth white and strong, and his dark mustache and beard well groomed. "I didn't have them. At least that's what I told him. Morrow kept his word, like all pirates should. He put me ashore with my rutters—of course he'd had them copied though he himself couldn't read or write, and he even gave me my share of the prize money. You ever sail with him, Ingeles?"

"No. The Queen knighted him a few years ago. I've never served on one of his ships. I'm glad he was fair with you."

They were nearing *Erasmus*. Samurai were peering down at them quizzically.

"That was the second time I'd piloted for heretics. The first time I wasn't so lucky."

"Oh?"

Rodrigues shipped his oars and the boat swerved neatly to the side and he hung onto the boarding ropes. "Go aloft but leave the talking to me."

Blackthorne began to climb while the other pilot tied the boat safely. Rodrigues was the first on deck. He bowed like a courtier. *"Konnichi wa* to all sod-eating samas!"

There were four samurai on deck. Blackthorne recognized one of them as a guard of the trapdoor. Nonplussed, they bowed stiffly to the Portuguese. Blackthorne aped him, feeling awkward, and would have preferred to bow correctly.

Rodrigues walked straight for the companionway. The seals were neatly in place. One of the samurai intercepted him.

"Kinjiru, gomen nasai." It's forbidden, so sorry.

"Kinjiru, eh?" the Portuguese said, openly unimpressed. "I'm Rodrigu-san, anjin for Toda Hiro-matsu-sama. This seal," he said, pointing to the red stamp with the odd writing on it, "Toda Hiro-matsu-sama, *ka?"*

"Iyé," the samurai said, shaking his head. "Kasigi Yabu-sama!"

"IYÉ?" Rodrigues said. "Kasigi Yabu-sama? I'm from Toda Hiro-matsu-sama, who's a bigger king than your bugger and Toady-sama's from Toranaga-sama, who's the biggest bugger-sama in this whole world. *Neh?"* He ripped the seal off the door, dropped a hand to one of his pistols. The swords were half out of their scabbards and he said quietly to Blackthorne, "Get ready to abandon ship," and to the samurai he said gruffly, "Toranaga-sama!" He pointed with his left hand at the flag which fluttered at his own masthead. *"Wakarimasu ka?"*

The samurai hesitated, their swords ready. Blackthorne prepared to dive over the side.

"Toranaga-sama!" Rodrigues crashed his foot against the door, the latch snapped and the door burst open. *"WAKARIMASU KA?"*

"Wakarimasu, Anjin-san." The samurai quickly put their swords away and bowed and apologized and bowed again and Rodrigues said hoarsely, "That's better," and led the way below.

"Christ Jesus, Rodrigues," Blackthorne said when they were on the lower deck. "Do you do this all the time and get away with it?"

"I do it very seldom," the Portuguese said, wiping the sweat from his brow, "and even then I wish I'd never started it."

Blackthorne leaned against the bulkhead. "I feel as if someone's kicked me in the stomach."

"It's the only way. You've got to act like a king. Even so, you can never tell with a samurai. They're as dangerous as a pissed priest with a candle in his arse sitting on a half-full powder keg."

"What did you say to them?"

"Toda Hiro-matsu is Toranaga's chief adviser—he's a bigger *daimyo* than this local one. That's why they gave in."

"What's he like, Toranaga?"

"Long story, Ingeles." Rodrigues sat on the step, pulled his boot off, and rubbed his ankle. "I nearly broke my foot on your lice-eaten door."

"It wasn't locked. You could have just opened it."

"I know. But that wouldn't have been as effective. By the Blessed Virgin, you've got a lot to learn!"

"Will you teach me?"

Rodrigues pulled his boot back on. "That depends," he said.

"On what?"

"We'll have to see, won't we? I've done all the talking so far, which is fair—I'm fit, you're not. Soon it'll be your turn. Which is your cabin?"

Blackthorne studied him for a moment. The smell below decks was stiff and weathered. "Thanks for helping me come aboard."

He led the way aft. His door was unlocked. The cabin had been ransacked and everything removable had been taken. There were no books or clothes or instruments or quills. His sea chest too was unlocked. And empty.

White with rage, he walked into the Great Cabin, Rodrigues watching intently. Even the secret compartment had been found and looted.

"They've taken everything. The sons of plague-infested lice!"

"What did you expect?"

"I don't know. I thought—with the seals—" Blackthorne went to the strong room. It was bare. So was the magazine. The holds contained only the bales of woolen cloth. "God curse all Jappers!" He went back to his cabin and slammed his sea chest closed.

"Where are they?" Rodrigues asked.

"What?"

"Your rutters. Where are your rutters?"

Blackthorne looked at him sharply.

"No pilot'd worry about clothes. You came for the rutters. Didn't you?"

"Yes."

"Why're you so surprised, Ingeles? Why do you think I came aboard? To help you get more rags? They're threadbare as it is and you'll need others. I've plenty for you. But where are the rutters?"

"They've gone. They were in my sea chest."

"I'm not going to steal them, Ingeles. I just want to read them. And copy them, if need be. I'll cherish them like my own, so you've no need to worry." His voice hardened. "Please get them, Ingeles, we've little time left."

"I can't. They've gone. They were in my sea chest."

"You wouldn't have left them there—not coming into a foreign port. You wouldn't forget a pilot's first rule—to hide them carefully, and leave only false ones unprotected. Hurry up!"

"They're stolen!"

"I don't believe you. But I'll admit you've hidden them very well. I searched for two hours and didn't get a fornicating whiff."

"What?"

"Why are you so surprised, Ingeles? Is your head up your arse? Naturally I came here from Osaka to investigate your rutters!"

"You've already been aboard?"

"Madonna!" Rodrigues said impatiently. "Yes, of course, two or three hours ago with Hiro-matsu, who wanted to look around. He broke the seals and then, when we left, this local *daimyo* sealed her up again. Hurry up, by God," he added. "The sand's running out."

"*They're stolen!*" Blackthorne told him how they had arrived and how he had awakened ashore. Then he kicked his sea chest across the room, infuriated at the men who had looted his ship. "They're stolen! All my charts! All my rutters! I've copies of some in England, but my rutter of this voyage's gone and the—" He stopped.

"And the Portuguese rutter? Come on, Ingeles, it had to be Portuguese."

"Yes, and the Portuguese one, it's gone too." Get hold of yourself, he thought. They're gone and that's the end. Who has them? The Japanese? Or did they give them to the priest? Without the rutters and the charts you can't pilot your way home. You'll never get home. . . . That's not true. You can pilot your way home, with care, and enormous luck. . . . Don't be ridiculous! You're half-way around the earth, in enemy land, in enemy hands, and you've neither rutter nor charts. "Oh, Lord Jesus, give me strength!"

Rodrigues was watching him intently. At length he said, "I'm sorry for you, Ingeles. I know how you feel—it happened to me once. He was an Ingeles too, the thief, may his ship drown and he burn in hell forever. Come on, let's go back aboard."

Omi and the others waited on the jetty until the galley rounded the headland and vanished. To the west layers of night already etched the crimson sky. To the east, night joined the sky and the sea together, horizonless.

"Mura, how long will it take to get all the cannon back on the ship?"

"If we work through the night, by midday tomorrow, Omi-san. If we begin at dawn, we'll be finished well before sunset. It would be safer to work during the day."

"Work through the night. Bring the priest to the pit at once."

Omi glanced at Igurashi, Yabu's chief lieutenant, who was still looking out toward the headland, his face stretched, the livid scar tissue over his empty eye socket eerily shadowed. "You'd be welcome to stay, Igurashi-san. My house is poor but perhaps we could make you comfortable."

"Thank you," the older man said, turning back to him, "but our Master said to return to Yedo at once, so I will return at once." More of his concern showed. "I wish I was on that galley."

"Yes."

"I hate the thought of Yabu-sama being aboard with only two men. I hate it."

"Yes."

He pointed at *Erasmus*. "A devil ship, that's what it is! So much wealth, then nothing."

"Surely everything? Won't Lord Toranaga be pleased, enormously pleased with Lord Yabu's gift?"

"That money-infected province grabber is so filled with his own importance, he won't even notice the amount of silver he'll have stolen from our Master. Where are your brains?"

"I presume only your anxiety over the possible danger to our Lord prompted you to make such a remark."

"You're right, Omi-san. No insult was intended. You've been very clever and helpful to our Master. Perhaps you're right about Toranaga too," Igurashi said, but he was thinking, Enjoy your newfound wealth, you poor fool. I know my Master better than you, and your increased fief will do you no good at all. Your advancement would have been a fair return for the ship, the bullion, and the arms. But now they've vanished. And because of you, my Master's in jeopardy. You sent the message and you said, 'See the barbarians first,' tempting him. We should have left yesterday. Yes, then my Master would have been safely away by now, with the money and arms. Are you a traitor? Are you acting for yourself, or your stupid father, or for an enemy? For Toranaga, perhaps? It doesn't matter. You can believe me, Omi, you dung-eating young fool, you and your branch of the Kasigi clan are not long for this earth. I'd tell you to your face but then I'd have to kill you and I would have spurned my Master's trust. He's the one to say when, not me.

"Thank you for your hospitality, Omi-san," he said. "I'll look forward to seeing you soon, but I'll be on my way now."

"Would you do something for me, please? Give my respects to my father. I'd appreciate it very much."

"I'd be happy to. He's a fine man. And I haven't congratulated you yet on your new fief."

"You're too kind."

"Thank you again, Omi-san." He raised his hand in friendly salutation, motioned to his men, and led the phalanx of horsemen out of the village.

Omi went to the pit. The priest was there. Omi could see the man was angry and he hoped that he would do something overt, publicly, so he could have him thrashed.

"Priest, tell the barbarians they are to come up, one by one. Tell them Lord Yabu has said they may live again in the world of men." Omi kept his language deliberately simple. "But the smallest breaking of a rule, and two will be put back into the pit. They are to behave and obey all orders. Is that clear?"

"Yes."

Omi made the priest repeat it to him as before. When he was sure the man had it all correctly, he made him speak it down into the pit.

The men came up, one by one. All were afraid. Some had to be helped. One man was in great pain and screamed every time someone touched his arm.

"There should be nine."

"One is dead. His body is down there, in the pit," the priest said.

Omi thought for a moment. "Mura, burn the corpse and keep the ashes with those of the other barbarian. Put these men in the same house as before. Give them plenty of vegetables and fish. And barley soup and fruit. Have them washed. They stink. Priest, tell them that if they behave and obey, the food will continue."

Omi watched and listened carefully. He saw them all react gratefully and he thought with contempt, how stupid! I deprive them for only two days, then give back a pittance and now they'll eat dung, they really will. "Mura, make them bow properly and take them away."

Then he turned to the priest. "Well?"

"I go now. Go my home. Leave Anjiro."

"Better you leave and stay away forever, you and every priest like you. Perhaps the next time one of you comes into *my* fief it is because some of *my* Christian peasants or vassals are considering treason," he said, using the veiled threat and classic ploy that anti-Christian samurai used to control the indiscriminate spread of the foreign dogma in their fiefs, for though foreign priests were protected, their Japanese converts were not.

"Christians good Japanese. Always. Only good vassals. Never had bad thoughts. No."

"I'm glad to hear it. Don't forget my fief stretches twenty *ri* in every direction. Do you understand?"

"I understand. Yes. I understand very well."

He watched the man bow stiffly—even barbarian priests had to have manners—and walk away.

"Omi-san?" one of his samurai said. He was young and very handsome.

"Yes?"

"Please excuse me, I know you haven't forgotten but Masijiro-san is still in the pit." Omi went to the trapdoor and stared down at the samurai. Instantly the man was on his knees, bowing deferentially.

The two days had aged him. Omi weighed his past service and his future worth. Then he took the young samurai's dagger from his sash and dropped it into the pit.

At the bottom of the ladder Masijiro stared at the knife in disbelief. Tears began coursing his cheeks. "I don't deserve this honor, Omi-san," he said abjectly.

"Yes."

"Thank you."

The young samurai beside Omi said, "May I please ask that he be allowed to commit seppuku here, on the beach?"

"He failed in the pit. He stays in the pit. Order the villagers to fill it in. Obliterate all traces of it. The barbarians have defiled it."

Kiku laughed and shook her head. "No, Omi-san, so sorry, please no more saké for me or my hair will fall down, I'll fall down, and then where would we be?"

"I'd fall down with you and we'd pillow and be in nirvana, outside ourselves," Omi said happily, his head swimming from the wine.

"Ah, but I'd be snoring and you can't pillow a snoring, horrid drunken girl and get much pleasure. Certainly not, so sorry. Oh no, Omi-sama of the Huge New Fief, you deserve better than that!" She poured another thimble of the warm wine into the tiny porcelain cup and offered it with both hands, her left forefinger and thumb delicately holding the cup, the forefinger of her right hand touching the underside. "Here, because you are wonderful!"

He accepted it and sipped, enjoying its warmth and mellow tang. "I'm so glad I was able to persuade you to stay an extra day, *neh?* You are so beautiful, Kiku-san."

"You are beautiful, and it is my pleasure." Her eyes were dancing in the light of a candle encased in a paper and bamboo flower that hung from the cedar rafter. This was the best suite of rooms in the tea house near the square. She leaned over to help him to some more rice from the simple wooden bowl that was on the low black lacquered table in front of him, but he shook his head.

"No, no, thank you."

"You should eat more, a strong man like you."

"I'm full, really."

He did not offer her any because she had barely touched her small salad—thinly sliced cucumbers and tiny sculptured radishes pickled in sweet vinegar—which was all she would accept of the whole meal. There had been slivers of raw fish on balls of tacky rice, soup, the salad, and some fresh vegetables served with a piquant sauce of soya and ginger. And rice.

She clapped her hands softly and the shoji was opened instantly by her personal maid.

"Yes, Mistress?"

"Suisen, take all these things away and bring more saké and a fresh pot of cha. And fruit. The saké should be warmer than last time. Hurry up, good-for-nothing!" She tried to sound imperious.

Suisen was fourteen, sweet, anxious to please, and an apprentice courtesan. She had been with Kiku for two years and Kiku was responsible for her training.

With an effort, Kiku took her eyes off the pure white rice that she would have loved to have eaten and dismissed her own hunger. You ate before you arrived and you will eat later, she reminded herself. Yes, but even then it was so little. 'Ah, but ladies have tiny appetites, very tiny appetites,' her teacher used to say. 'Guests eat and drink—the more the better. Ladies don't, and certainly never with guests. How can ladies talk or entertain or play the samisen or dance if they're stuffing their mouths? You will eat later, be patient. Concentrate on your guest.'

While she watched Suisen critically, gauging her skill, she told Omi stories to make him laugh and forget the world outside. The young girl knelt beside Omi, tidied the small bowls and chopsticks on the lacquer tray into a pleasing pattern as she had been taught. Then she picked up the empty saké flask, poured to make sure it was empty—it would have been very bad manners to have shaken the flask—then got up with the tray, noiselessly carried it to the shoji door, knelt, put the tray down, opened the shoji, got up, stepped through the door, knelt again, lifted the tray out, put it down again as noiselessly, and closed the door completely.

"I'll really have to get another maid," Kiku said, not displeased. That color suits her, she was thinking. I must send to Yedo for some more of that silk. What a shame it's so expensive! Never mind, with all the money Gyoko-san was given for last night and tonight, there will be more than enough from my share to buy little Suisen twenty kimonos. She's such a sweet child, and really very graceful. "She makes so much noise—it disturbs the whole room—so sorry."

"I didn't notice her. Only you," Omi said, finishing his wine.

Kiku fluttered her fan, her smile lighting her face. "You make me feel very good, Omi-san. Yes. And beloved."

Suisen brought the saké quickly. And the cha. Her mistress poured Omi some wine and gave it to him. The young girl unobtrusively filled the cups. She did not spill a drop and she thought the sound that the liquid made going into the cup had the right quiet kind of ring to it, so she sighed inwardly with vast relief, sat back on her heels, and waited.

Kiku was telling an amusing story that she had heard from one of her friends in Mishima and Omi was laughing. As she did so, she took one of the small oranges and, using her long fingernails, opened it as though it were a flower, the sections of the fruit the petals, the divisions of the skin its leaves. She removed a fleck of pith and offered it with both hands as if this were the usual way a lady would serve the fruit to her guest.

"Would you like an orange, Omi-san?"

Omi's first reaction was to say, I can't destroy such beauty. But that would be inept, he thought, dazzled by her artistry. How can I compliment her, and her unnamed teacher? How can I return the happiness that she has given me, letting me watch her fingers create something so precious yet so ephemeral?

He held the flower in his hands for a moment then nimbly removed four sections, equidistant from each other, and ate them with enjoyment. This left a new flower. He removed four more sections, creating a third floral design. Next he took one section, and moved a second so that the remaining three made still another blossom.

Then he took two sections and replaced the last in the orange cradle, in the center on its side, as though a crescent moon within a sun.

He ate one very slowly. When he had finished, he put the other in the center of his hand and offered it. "This you must have because it is the second to last. This is my gift to you."

Suisen could hardly breathe. What was the last one for?

Kiku took the fruit and ate it. It was the best she had ever tasted.

"This, the last one," Omi said, putting the whole flower gravely into the palm of his right hand, "this is my gift to the gods, whoever they are, wherever they are. I will never eat this fruit again, unless it is from your hands."

"That is too much, Omi-sama," Kiku said. "I release you from your vow! That was said under the influence of the *kami* who lives in all saké bottles!"

"I refuse to be released."

They were very happy together.

"Suisen," she said. "Now leave us. And please, child, please try to do it with grace."

"Yes, Mistress." The young girl went into the next room and checked that the futons were meticulous, the love instruments and pleasure beads near at hand, and the flowers perfect. An imperceptible crease was smoothed from the already smooth cover. Then, satisfied, Suisen sat down, sighed with relief, fanned the heat out of her face with her lilac fan, and contentedly waited.

In the next room, which was the finest of all the rooms in the tea house, the only one with a garden of its own, Kiku picked up the long-handled samisen. It was three-stringed, guitarlike, and Kiku's first soaring chord filled the room. Then she began to sing. At first soft, then trilling, soft again then louder, softer and sighing sweetly, ever sweetly, she sang of love and unrequited love and happiness and sadness.

"Mistress?" The whisper would not have awakened the lightest sleeper but Suisen knew that her mistress preferred not to sleep after the Clouds and the Rain, however strong. She preferred to rest, half awake, in tranquillity.

"Yes, Sui-chan?" Kiku whispered as quietly, using "chan" as one would to a favorite child.

"Omi-san's wife has returned. Her palanquin has just gone up the path to his house."

Kiku glanced at Omi. His neck rested comfortably on the padded wooden pillow, arms interlocked. His body was strong and unmarked, his skin firm and golden, a sheen there. She caressed him gently, enough to make the touch enter his dream but not enough to awaken him. Then she slid from under the quilt, gathering her kimonos around herself.

It took Kiku very little time to renew her makeup as Suisen combed and brushed her hair and retied it into the shimoda style. Then mistress and maid walked noiselessly along the corridor, out onto the veranda, through the garden to the square. Boats, like fireflies, plied from the barbarian ship to the jetty where seven of the cannon still remained to be loaded. It was still deep night, long before dawn.

The two women slipped along the narrow alley between a cluster of houses and began to climb the path.

Sweat-stained and exhausted bearers were collecting their strength around the palanquin on the hilltop outside Omi's house. Kiku did not knock on the garden door. Candles were lit in the house and servants were hurrying to and fro. She motioned to Suisen, who immediately went to the veranda near the front door, knocked, and waited. In a moment the door opened. The maid nodded and vanished. Another moment and the maid returned and beckoned Kiku and bowed low as she swept past. Another maid scurried ahead and opened the shoji of the best room.

Omi's mother's bed was unslept in. She was sitting, rigidly erect, near the small alcove that held the flower arrangement. A small window shoji was open to the garden. Midori, Omi's wife, was opposite her.

Kiku knelt. Is it only a night ago that I was here and terrified on the Night of the Screams? She bowed, first to Omi's mother, then to his wife, feeling the tension between the two women and she asked herself, Why is it there is always such violence between mother-in-law and daughter-in-law? Doesn't daughter-in-law, in time, become mother-in-law? Why does she then always treat her own daughter-in-law to a lashing tongue and make her life a misery, and why does that girl do the same in her turn? Doesn't anyone learn?

"I'm sorry to disturb you, Mistress-san."

"You're very welcome, Kiku-san," the old woman replied. "There's no trouble, I hope?"

"Oh, no, but I didn't know whether or not you'd want me to awaken your son," she said to her, already knowing the answer. "I thought I'd better ask you, as you, Midori-san"—she turned and smiled and bowed slightly to Midori, liking her greatly—"as you had returned."

The old woman said, "You're very kind, Kiku-san, and very thoughtful. No, leave him in peace."

"Very well. Please excuse me, disturbing you like this, but I thought it best to ask. Midori-san, I hope your journey was not too bad."

"So sorry, it was awful," Midori said. "I'm glad to be back and hated being away. Is my husband well?"

"Yes, very well. He laughed a lot this evening and seemed to be happy. He ate and drank sparingly and he's sleeping soundly."

"The Mistress-san was beginning to tell me some of the terrible things that happened while I was away and—"

"You shouldn't have gone. You were needed here," the old woman interrupted, venom in her voice. "Or perhaps not. Perhaps you should have stayed away permanently. Perhaps you brought a bad *kami* into our house along with your bed linen."

"I'd never do that, Mistress-san," Midori said patiently. "Please believe I would rather kill myself than bring the slightest stain to your good name. Please forgive my being away and my faults. I'm sorry."

"Since that devil ship came here we've had nothing but trouble. That's bad *kami*. Very bad. And where were you when you were needed? Gossiping in Mishima, stuffing yourself and drinking saké."

"My father died, Mistress-san. The day before I arrived."

"Huh, you haven't even got the courtesy or the foresight to be at your own father's deathbed. The sooner you permanently leave our house, the better for all of us. I want some cha. We have a guest here and you haven't even remembered your manners enough to offer her refreshment!"

"It was ordered, instantly, the moment she—"

"It hasn't arrived instantly!"

The shoji opened. A maid nervously brought cha and some sweet cakes. First Midori served the old woman, who cursed the maid roundly and chomped toothlessly on a cake, slurping her drink. "You must excuse the maid, Kiku-san," the old woman said. "The cha's tasteless. Tasteless! And scalding. I suppose that's only to be expected in this house."

"Here, please have mine." Midori blew gently on the tea to cool it.

The old woman took it grudgingly. "Why can't it be correct the first time?" She lapsed into sullen silence.

"What do you think about all this?" Midori asked Kiku. "The ship and Yabu-sama and Toda Hiro-matsu-sama?"

"I don't know what to think. As to the barbarians, who knows? They're certainly an extraordinary collection of men. And the great *daimyo*, Iron Fist? It's very curious that he arrived almost the same time

as Lord Yabu, *neh?* Well, you must excuse me, no, please, I can see myself out."

"Oh, no, Kiku-san, I wouldn't hear of it."

"There, you see, Midori-san," the old woman interrupted impatiently.
"Our guest's uncomfortable and the cha awful."

"Oh, the cha was sufficient for me, Mistress-san, really. No, if you'll
excuse me, I am a little tired. Perhaps before I go tomorrow, I may be
allowed to come to see you. It's always such a pleasure to talk with you."

The old woman allowed herself to be cajoled and Kiku followed
Midori onto the veranda and into the garden.

"Kiku-san, you're so thoughtful," Midori said, holding her arm,
warmed by her beauty. "It was very kind of you, thank you."

Kiku glanced back at the house momentarily, and shivered. "Is she
always like that?"

"Tonight she was polite, compared to some times. If it wasn't for
Omi and my son I swear I'd shake her dust off my feet, shave my head,
and become a nun. But I have Omi and my son and that makes up for
everything. I only thank all *kami* for that. Fortunately Mistress-san pre-
fers Yedo and can't stay away from there for very long." Midori smiled
sadly. "You train yourself not to listen, you know how it is." She sighed,
so beautiful in the moonlight. "But that's unimportant. Tell me what's
happened since I left."

This was why Kiku had come to the house so urgently, for obviously
neither the mother nor the wife would wish Omi's sleep disturbed. She
came to tell the lovely Lady Midori everything, so she could help to
guard Kasigi Omi as she herself would try to guard him. She told her all
that she knew except what had happened in the room with Yabu. She
added the rumors she had heard and the stories the other girls had
passed on to her or invented. And everything that Omi had told her—
his hopes and fears and plans—everything about him, except what had
happened in the room tonight. She knew that this was not important to
his wife.

"I'm afraid, Kiku-san, afraid for my husband."

"Everything he advised was wise, Lady. I think everything he did was
correct. Lord Yabu doesn't reward anyone lightly and three thousand
koku is a worthy increase."

"But the ship's Lord Toranaga's now, and all that money."

"Yes, but for Yabu-sama to offer the ship as a gift was an idea of
genius. Omi-san gave the idea to Yabu—surely this itself is payment
enough, *neh?* Omi-san must be recognized as a preeminent vassal." Kiku
twisted the truth just a trifle, knowing that Omi was in great danger, and

all his house. What is to be will be, she reminded herself. But it does no harm to ease the brow of a nice woman.

"Yes, I can see that," Midori said. Let it be the truth, she prayed. Please let it be the truth. She embraced the girl, her eyes filling with tears. "Thank you. You're so kind, Kiku-san, so kind." She was seventeen.

CHAPTER 8

WHAT do you think, Ingeles?"
"I think there'll be a storm."
"When?"
"Before sunset."

It was near noon and they were standing on the quarterdeck of the galley under a gray overcast. This was the second day out to sea.

"If this was your ship, what would you do?"

"How far is it to our landfall?" Blackthorne asked.

"After sunset."

"How far to the nearest land?"

"Four or five hours, Ingeles. But to run for cover will cost us half a day and I can't afford that. What would you do?"

Blackthorne thought a moment. During the first night the galley had sped southward down the east coast of the Izu peninsula, helped by the large sail on the midships mast. When they had come abreast of the southmost cape, Cape Ito, Rodrigues had set the course West South West and had left the safety of the coast for the open sea, heading for a landfall at Cape Shinto two hundred miles away.

"Normally in one of these galleys we'd hug the coast—for safety," Rodrigues had said, "but that'd take too much time and time is important. Toranaga asked me to pilot Toady to Anjiro and back. Quickly. There's a bonus for me if we're very quick. One of their pilots'd be just as good on a short haul like this, but the poor son of a whore'd be frightened to death carrying so important a *daimyo* as Toady, particularly out of sight of land. They're not oceaners, Japmen. Great pirates and fighters and coastal sailors. But the deep frightens them. The old Taikō even made a law that the few ocean ships Japmen possess were always to have Portuguese pilots aboard. It's still the law of their land today."

"Why did he do that?"

Rodrigues shrugged. "Perhaps someone suggested it to him."

"Who?"

"Your stolen rutter, Ingeles, the Portuguese one. Whose was it?"

"I don't know. There was no name on it, no signature."

"Where'd you get it?"

"From the chief merchant of the Dutch East India Company."

"Where'd he get it from?"

Blackthorne shrugged.

Rodrigues' laugh had no humor in it. "Well, I never expected you to tell me—but whoever stole it and sold it, I hope he burns in hellfire forever!"

"You're employed by this Toranaga, Rodrigues?"

"No. I was just visiting Osaka, my Captain and I. This was just a favor to Toranaga. My Captain volunteered me. I'm pilot of the—" Rodrigues had stopped. "I keep forgetting you're the enemy, Ingeles."

"Portugal and England have been allies for centuries."

"But we're not now. Go below, Ingeles. You're tired and so am I and tired men make mistakes. Come on deck when you're rested."

So Blackthorne had gone below to the pilot's cabin and had lain on the bunk. Rodrigues' rutter of the voyage was on the sea desk which was pinned to the bulkhead like the pilot's chair on the quarterdeck. The book was leather-covered and used but Blackthorne did not open it.

"Why leave it there?" he had asked previously.

"If I didn't, you'd search for it. But you won't touch it there—or even look at it—uninvited. You're a pilot—not a pig-bellied whoring thieving merchant or soldier."

"I'll read it. You would."

"Not uninvited, Ingeles. No pilot'd do that. Even I wouldn't!"

Blackthorne had watched the book for a moment and then he closed his eyes. He slept deeply, all of that day and part of the night. It was just before dawn when he awoke as always. It took time to adjust to the untoward motion of the galley and the throb of the drum that kept the oars moving as one. He lay comfortably on his back in the dark, his arms under his head. He thought about his own ship and put away his worry of what would happen when they reached shore and Osaka. One thing at a time. Think about Felicity and Tudor and home. No, not now. Think that if other Portuguese are like Rodrigues, you've a good chance now. You'll get a ship home. Pilots are not enemies and the pox on other things! But you can't say that, lad. You're English, the hated heretic and anti-Christ. Catholics own this world. They *owned* it. Now we and the Dutch're going to smash them.

What nonsense it all is! Catholic and Protestant and Calvinist and Lutherist and every other shitist. You should have been born Catholic. It was only fate that took your father to Holland where he met a woman, Anneke van Droste, who became his wife and he saw Spanish Catholics and Spanish priests and the Inquisition for the first time. I'm glad he had his eyes opened, Blackthorne thought. I'm glad mine are open.

Then he had gone on deck. Rodrigues was in his chair, his eyes red-rimmed with sleeplessness, two Japanese sailors on the helm as before.

"Can I take this watch for you?"

"How do you feel, Ingeles?"

"Rested. Can I take the watch for you?" Blackthorne saw Rodrigues measuring him. "I'll wake you if the wind changes—anything."

"Thank you, Ingeles. Yes, I'll sleep a little. Maintain this course. At the turn, go four degrees more westerly and at the next, six more westerly. You'll have to point the new course on the compass for the helmsman. *Wakarimasu ka?*"

"*Hai!*" Blackthorne laughed. "Four points westerly it is. Go below, Pilot, your bunk's comfortable."

But Vasco Rodrigues did not go below. He merely pulled his sea cloak closer and settled deeper into the seachair. Just before the turn of the hourglass he awoke momentarily and checked the course change without moving and immediately went back to sleep again. Once when the wind veered he awoke and then, when he had seen there was no danger, again he slept.

Hiro-matsu and Yabu came on deck during the morning. Blackthorne noticed their surprise that he was conning the ship and Rodrigues sleeping. They did not talk to him, but returned to their conversation and, later, they went below again.

Near midday Rodrigues had risen from the seachair to stare northeast, sniffing the wind, all his senses concentrated. Both men studied the sea and the sky and the encroaching clouds.

"What would you do, Ingeles, if this was your ship?" Rodrigues said again.

"I'd run for the coast if I knew where it was—the nearest point. This craft won't take much water and there's a storm there all right. About four hours away."

"Can't be *tai-fun*," Rodrigues muttered.

"What?"

"*Tai-fun*. They're huge winds—the worst storms you've ever seen. But we're not in *tai-fun* season."

"When's that?"

"It's not now, enemy." Rodrigues laughed. "No, not now. But it could be rotten enough so I'll take your piss-cutting advice. Steer North by West."

As Blackthorne pointed the new course and the helmsman turned the ship neatly, Rodrigues went to the rail and shouted at the captain, "*Isogi!* Captain-san. *Wakarimasu ka?*"

"*Isogi, hai!*"

"What's that? Hurry up?"

The corners of Rodrigues' eyes crinkled with amusement. "No harm in you knowing a little Japman talk, eh? Sure, Ingeles, '*isogi*' means to hurry. All you need here's about ten words and then you can make the buggers shit if you want to. If they're the right words, of course, and if they're in the mood. I'll go below now and get some food."

"You cook too?"

"In Japland, every civilized man has to cook, or personally has to train one of the monkeys to cook, or you starve to death. All they eat's raw fish, raw vegetables in sweet pickled vinegar. But life here can be a pisscutter if you know how."

"Is 'pisscutter' good or bad?"

"It's mostly very good but sometimes terribly bad. It all depends how you feel and you ask too many questions."

Rodrigues went below. He barred his cabin door and carefully checked the lock on his sea chest. The hair that he had placed so delicately was still there. And a similar hair, equally invisible to anyone but him, that he had put on the cover of his rutter was also untouched.

You can't be too careful in this world, Rodrigues thought. Is there any harm in his knowing that you're pilot of the *Nao del Trato,* this year's great Black Ship from Macao? Perhaps. Because then you'd have to explain that she's a leviathan, one of the richest, biggest ships in the world, more than sixteen hundred tons. You might be tempted to tell him about her cargo, about trade and about Macao and all sorts of illuminating things that are very, very private and very, very secret. But we are at war, us against the English and Dutch.

He opened the well-oiled lock and took out his private rutter to check some bearings for the nearest haven and his eyes saw the sealed packet the priest, Father Sebastio, had given him just before they had left Anjiro.

Does it contain the Englishman's rutters? he asked himself again.

He weighed the package and looked at the Jesuit seals, sorely tempted to break them and see for himself. Blackthorne had told him that the Dutch squadron had come by way of Magellan's Pass and little else. The Ingeles asks lots of questions and volunteers nothing, Rodrigues thought. He's shrewd, clever, and dangerous.

Are they his rutters or aren't they? If they are, what good are they to the Holy Fathers?

He shuddered, thinking of Jesuits and Franciscans and Dominicans and all monks and all priests and the Inquisition. There are good priests and bad priests and they're mostly bad, but they're still priests. The Church has to have priests and without them to intercede for us we're lost sheep in a Satanic world. Oh, Madonna, protect me from all evil and bad priests!

Rodrigues had been in his cabin with Blackthorne in Anjiro harbor when the door had opened and Father Sebastio had come in uninvited. They had been eating and drinking and the remains of their food was in the wooden bowls.

"You break bread with heretics?" the priest had asked. "It's dangerous to eat with them. They're infectious. Did he tell you he's a pirate?"

"It's only Christian to be chivalrous to your enemies, Father. When I was in their hands they were fair to me. I only return their charity." He had knelt and kissed the priest's cross. Then he had got up and, offering wine, he said, "How can I help you?"

"I want to go to Osaka. With the ship."

"I'll ask them at once." He had gone and had asked the captain and the request had gradually gone up to Toda Hiro-matsu, who replied that Toranaga had said nothing about bringing a foreign priest from Anjiro so he regretted he could not bring the foreign priest from Anjiro.

Father Sebastio had wanted to talk privately so he had sent the Englishman on deck and then, in the privacy of the cabin, the priest had brought out the sealed package.

"I would like you to deliver this to the Father-Visitor."

"I don't know if his Eminence'll still be at Osaka when I get there." Rodrigues did not like being a carrier of Jesuit secrets. "I might have to go back to Nagasaki. My Captain-General may have left orders for me."

"Then give it to Father Alvito. Make absolutely sure you put it only in his hands."

"Very well," he had said.

"When were you last at Confession, my son?"

"On Sunday, Father."

"Would you like me to confess you now?"

"Yes, thank you." He was grateful that the priest had asked, for you never knew if your life depended on the sea, and, afterwards, he had felt much better as always.

Now in the cabin, Rodrigues put back the package, greatly tempted. Why Father Alvito? Father Martin Alvito was chief trade negotiator and had been personal interpreter for the Taikō for many years and therefore an intimate of most of the influential *daimyos*. Father Alvito plied between Nagasaki and Osaka and was one of the very few men, and the only European, who had had access to the Taikō at any time—an enormously clever man who spoke perfect Japanese and knew more about them and their way of life than any man in Asia. Now he was the Portuguese's most influential mediator to the Council of Regents, and to Ishido and Toranaga in particular.

Trust the Jesuits to get one of their men into such a vital position,

Rodrigues thought with awe. Certainly if it hadn't been for the Society of Jesus the flood of heresy would never have been stopped, Portugal and Spain might have gone Protestant, and we'd have lost our immortal souls forever. Madonna!

"Why do you think about priests all the time?" Rodrigues asked himself aloud. "You know it makes you nervous!" Yes. Even so, why Father Alvito? If the package contains the rutters, is the package meant for one of the Christian *daimyos,* or Ishido or Toranaga, or just for his Eminence, the Father-Visitor himself? Or for my Captain-General? Or will the rutters be sent to Rome, for the Spaniards? Why Father Alvito? Father Sebastio could have easily said to give it to one of the other Jesuits.

And why does Toranaga want the Ingeles?

In my heart I know I should kill Blackthorne. He's the enemy, he's a heretic. But there's something else. I've a feeling this Ingeles is a danger to all of us. Why should I think that? He's a pilot—a great one. Strong. Intelligent. A good man. Nothing there to worry about. So why am I afraid? Is he evil? I like him very much but I feel I should kill him quickly and the sooner the better. Not in anger. Just to protect ourselves. Why?

I am afraid of him.

What to do? Leave it to the hand of God? The storm's coming and it'll be a bad one.

"God curse me and my lack of wits! Why don't I know what to do easily?"

The storm came before sunset and caught them out to sea. Land was ten miles away. The bay they raced for was haven enough and dead ahead when they had crested the horizon. There were no shoals or reefs to navigate between them and safety, but ten miles was ten miles and the sea was rising fast, driven by the rain-soaked wind.

The gale blew from the northeast, on the starboard quarter, and veered badly as gusts swirled easterly or northerly without pattern, the sea grim. Their course was northwest so they were mostly broadside to the swell, rolling badly, now in the trough, now sickeningly on the crest. The galley was shallow draft and built for speed and kind waters, and though the rowers were game and very disciplined, it was hard to keep their oars in the sea and their pull clean.

"You'll have to ship the oars and run before the wind," Blackthorne shouted.

"Maybe, but not yet! Where are your *cojones,* Ingeles?"

"Where they should be, by God, and where I want 'em to stay!"

Both men knew that if they turned into the wind they could never make way against the storm, so the tide and the wind would take them away from sanctuary and out to sea. And if they ran before the wind, the tide and the wind would take them away from sanctuary and out to sea as before, only faster. Southward was the Great Deep. There was no land southward for a thousand miles, or, if you were unlucky, for a thousand leagues.

They wore lifelines that were lashed to the binnacle and they were glad of them as the deck pitched and rolled. They hung on to the gunwales as well, riding her.

As yet, no water had come aboard. She was heavily ladened and rode lower in the water than either would have liked. Rodrigues had prepared properly in the hours of waiting. Everything had been battened down, the men forewarned. Hiro-matsu and Yabu had said that they would stay below for a time and then come on deck. Rodrigues had shrugged and told them clearly that it would be very dangerous. He was sure they did not understand.

"What'll they do?" Blackthorne had asked.

"Who knows, Ingeles? But they won't be weeping with fear, you can be sure."

In the well of the main deck the oarsmen were working hard. Normally there would be two men on each oar but Rodrigues had ordered three for strength and safety and speed. Others were waiting below decks to spell these rowers when he gave the order. On the foredeck the captain oar-master was experienced and his beat was slow, timed to the waves. The galley was still making way, though every moment the roll seemed more pronounced and the recovery slower. Then the squalls became erratic and threw the captain oar-master off stroke.

"Watch out for'ard!" Blackthorne and Rodrigues shouted almost in the same breath. The galley rolled sickeningly, twenty oars pulled at air instead of sea and there was chaos aboard. The first comber had struck and the port gunwale was awash. They were floundering.

"Go for'ard," Rodrigues ordered. "Get 'em to ship half the oars each side! Madonna, hurry, hurry!"

Blackthorne knew that without his lifeline he could easily be carried overboard. But the oars had to be shipped or they were lost.

He slipped the knot and fought along the heaving, greasy deck, down the short gangway to the main deck. Abruptly the galley swerved and he was carried to the down side, his legs taken away by some of the rowers who had also slipped their safety lines to try to fight order into their oars. The gunwale was under water and one man went overboard. Blackthorne felt himself going too. His hand caught the gunwale, his tendons stretched but his grip held, then his other hand reached the rail and, choking, he pulled himself back. His feet found the deck and he shook himself, thanking God, and thought, there's your seventh life gone. Alban Caradoc had always said a good pilot had to be like a cat, except that the pilot had to have at least ten lives whereas a cat is satisfied with nine.

A man was at his feet and he dragged him from the grip of the sea, held him until he was safe, then helped him to his place. He looked back at the quarterdeck to curse Rodrigues for letting the helm get away from him. Rodrigues waved and pointed and shouted, the shout swallowed by a squall. Blackthorne saw their course had changed. Now they were almost into the wind, and he knew the swerve had been planned. Wise, he thought. That'll give us a respite to get organized, but the bastard could have warned me. I don't like losing lives unnecessarily.

He waved back and hurled himself into the work of resorting the rowers. All rowing had stopped except for the two oars most for'ard, which kept them tidily into the wind. With signs and yelling, Blackthorne got the oars shipped, doubled up the men on the working ones, and went aft again. The men were stoic and though some were very sick they stayed and waited for the next order.

The bay was closer but it still seemed a million leagues away. To the northeast the sky was dark. Rain whipped them and the gusts strengthened. In *Erasmus* Blackthorne would not have been worried. They could have made harbor easily or could have turned back carelessly onto their real course, heading for their proper landfall. His ship was built and rigged for weather. This galley was not.

"What do you think, Ingeles?"

"You'll do what you want, whatever I think," he shouted against the wind. "But she won't take much water and we'll go down like a stone, and the next time I go for'ard, tell me you're putting her into wind. Better still, put her to windward while I've my line on and then we'll both reach port."

"That was the hand of God, Ingeles. A wave slammed her rump around."

"That nearly put me overboard."

"I saw."

Blackthorne was measuring their drift. "If we stay on this course we'll never make the bay. We'll be swept past the headland by a mile or more."

"I'm going to stay into the wind. Then, when the time's ripe, we'll stab for the shore. Can you swim?"

"Yes."

"Good. I never learned. Too dangerous. Better to drown quickly than slow, eh?" Rodrigues shuddered involuntarily. "Blessed Madonna, protect me from a water grave! This sow-bellied whore of a ship's going to get to harbor tonight. Has to. My nose says if we turn and run we'll flounder. We're too heavily laden."

"Lighten her. Throw the cargo overboard."

"King Toady'd never agree. He has to arrive with it or he might as well not arrive."

"Ask him."

"Madonna, are you deaf? I've told you! I know he won't agree!" Rodrigues went closer to the helmsmen and made sure they understood they were to keep heading into the wind without fail.

"Watch them, Ingeles! You have the con." He untied his lifeline and went down the gangway, sure-footed. The rowers watched him intently as he walked to the captain-san on the forepoop deck to explain with signs and with words the plan he had in mind. Hiro-matsu and Yabu came on deck. The captain-san explained the plan to them. Both men were pale but they remained impassive and neither vomited. They looked shoreward through the rain, shrugged and went below again.

Blackthorne stared at the bay to port. He knew the plan was dangerous. They would have to wait until they were just past the near headland, then they would have to fall off from the wind, turn northwest again and pull for their lives. The sail wouldn't help them. It would have to be their strength alone. The southern side of the bay was rock-fanged and reefed. If they misjudged the timing they would be driven ashore there and wrecked.

"Ingeles, lay for'ard!"

The Portuguese was beckoning him.

He went forward.

"What about the sail?" Rodrigues shouted.

"No. That'll hurt more than help."

"You stay here then. If the captain fails with the beat, or we lose him, you take it up. All right?"

"I've never sailed one of these before—I've never mastered oars. But I'll try."

Rodrigues looked landward. The headland appeared and disappeared in the driving rain. Soon he would have to make the stab. The seas were growing and already whitecaps fled from the crests. The race between the headlands looked evil. This one's going to be filthy, he thought. Then he spat and decided.

"Go aft, Ingeles. Take the helm. When I signal, go West North West for that point. You see it?"

"Yes."

"Don't hesitate and hold that course. Watch me closely. This sign means hard aport, this hard astarboard, this steady as she goes."

"Very well."

"By the Virgin, you'll wait for my orders and you'll obey my orders?"

"You want me to take the helm or not?"

Rodrigues knew he was trapped. "I have to trust you, Ingeles, and I hate trusting you. Go aft," he said. He saw Blackthorne read what was behind his eyes and walk away. Then he changed his mind and called after him, "Hey, you arrogant pirate! Go with God!"

Blackthorne turned back gratefully. "And you, Spaniard!"

"Piss on all Spaniards and long live Portugal!"

"Steady as she goes!"

They made harbor but without Rodrigues. He was washed overboard when his lifeline snapped.

The ship had been on the brink of safety when the great wave came out of the north and, though they had taken much water previously and had already lost the Japanese captain, now they were awash and driven backward toward the rock-infested shore.

Blackthorne saw Rodrigues go and he watched him, gasping and struggling in the churning sea. The storm and the tide had taken them far to the south side of the bay and they were almost on the rocks, all aboard knowing that the ship was lost.

As Rodrigues was swept alongside Blackthorne threw him a wooden life ring. The Portuguese flailed for the life ring but the sea swept it out of his reach. An oar crashed into him and he grabbed for it. The rain slashed down and the last Blackthorne saw of Rodrigues was an arm and the broken oar and, just ahead, the surf raging against the tormented shore. He could have dived overboard and swum to him and survived, perhaps, there was time, perhaps, but his first duty was to his ship and his last duty was to his ship and *his* ship was in danger.

So he turned his back on Rodrigues.

The wave had taken some rowers with it and others were struggling to fill the empty places. A mate had bravely slipped his safety line. He jumped onto the foredeck, secured himself, and restarted the beat. The chant leader also began again, the rowers tried to get order out of chaos.

"*Isogiiiii!*" Blackthorne shouted, remembering the word. He bent his weight on the helm to help get the bow more into wind, then went to the rail and beat time, called out One-Two-One-Two, trying to encourage the crew.

"Come on, you bastards, *puuull!*"

The galley was on the rocks, at least the rocks were just astern and to port and to starboard. The oars dipped and pulled, but still the ship made no way, the wind and the tide winning, dragging her backward perceptibly.

"Come on, pull, you bastards!" Blackthorne shouted again, his hand beating time.

The rowers took strength from him.

First they held their own with the sea. Then they conquered her.

The ship moved away from the rocks. Blackthorne held the course for the lee shore. Soon they were in calmer waters. There was still gale but it was overhead. There was still tempest but it was out to sea.

"Let go the starboard anchor!"

No one understood the words but all seamen knew what was wanted. They rushed to do his bidding. The anchor splashed over the side. He let the ship fall off slightly to test the firmness of the seabed, the mate and rowers understanding his maneuver.

"Let go the port anchor!"

When his ship was safe, he looked aft.

The cruel shore line could hardly be seen through the rain. He gauged the sea and considered possibilities.

The Portuguese's rutter is below, he thought, drained. I can con the ship to Osaka. I could con it back to Anjiro. But were you right to disobey him? I didn't disobey Rodrigues. I was on the quarterdeck. Alone.

'Steer south,' Rodrigues had screamed when the wind and the tide carried them perilously near the rocks. 'Turn and run before the wind!'

'No!' he had shouted back, believing their only chance was to try for the harbor and that in the open sea they'd flounder. 'We can make it!'

'God curse you, you'll kill us all!'

But I didn't kill anyone, Blackthorne thought. Rodrigues, you knew and I knew that it was my responsibility to decide—if there was a time of decision. I was right. The ship's safe. Nothing else matters.

He beckoned to the mate, who hurried from the foredeck. Both helmsmen had collapsed, their arms and legs almost torn from their sockets. The rowers were like corpses, fallen helplessly over their oars. Others weakly came from below to help. Hiro-matsu and Yabu, both badly shaken, were assisted onto the deck, but once on deck both *daimyos* stood erect.

"*Hai*, Anjin-san?" the mate asked. He was a middle-aged man with strong white teeth and a broad, weatherbeaten face. A livid bruise marked his cheek where the sea had battered him against the gunwale.

"You did very well," Blackthorne said, not caring that his words would not be understood. He knew his tone would be clear and his smile. "Yes, very well. You're Captain-san now. *Wakarimasu?* You! Captain-san!"

The man stared at him open-mouthed, then he bowed to hide both his astonishment and his pleasure. "*Wakarimasu,* Anjin-san. *Hai. Arigato goziemashita.*"

"Listen, Captain-san," Blackthorne said. "Get the men food and drink. Hot food. We'll stay here tonight." With signs Blackthorne made him comprehend.

Immediately the new captain turned and shouted with new authority. Instantly seamen ran to obey him. Filled with pride, the new captain looked back at the quarterdeck. I wish I could speak your barbarian language, he thought happily. Then I could thank you, Anjin-san, for saving the ship and with the ship the life of our Lord Hiro-matsu. Your magic gave us all new strength. Without your magic we would have floundered. You may be a pirate but you are a great seaman, and while you are pilot I will obey you with my life. I'm not worthy to be captain, but I will try to deserve your trust. "What do you want me to do next?" he asked.

Blackthorne was looking over the side. The seabed was obscured. He took mental bearings and when he was sure that the anchors had not slipped and the sea was safe, he said, "Launch the skiff. And get a good sculler."

Again with signs and with words Blackthorne made himself understood.

The skiff was launched and manned instantly.

Blackthorne went to the gunwale and would have scaled down the side but a harsh voice stopped him. He looked around. Hiro-matsu was there, Yabu beside him.

The old man was badly bruised about the neck and shoulders but he still carried the long sword. Yabu was bleeding from his nose, his face bruised, his kimono blotched, and he tried to staunch the flow with a small piece of material. Both men were impassive, seemingly unaware of their hurts or the chill of the wind.

Blackthorne bowed politely. "*Hai,* Toda-sama?"

Again the harsh words and the old man pointed with his sword at the skiff and shook his head.

"Rodrigu-san there!" Blackthorne pointed to the south shore in answer. "I go look!"

"*Iyé!*" Hiro-matsu shook his head again, and spoke at length, clearly refusing him permission because of the danger.

"I'm Anjin-san of this whore-bitch ship and if I want to go ashore I'm going ashore." Blackthorne kept his voice very polite but strong and it was equally obvious what he meant. "I know that skiff won't live in that sea. *Hai!* But I'm going ashore there—by that point. You see that point, Toda Hiro-matsu-sama? By that small rock. I'm going to work my way around the headland, there. I'm in no hurry to die and I've nowhere to run. I want to get Rodrigu-san's body." He cocked a leg over the side. The scabbarded sword moved a fraction. So he froze. But his gaze was level, his face set.

Hiro-matsu was in a dilemma. He could understand the pirate wanting to find Rodrigu-san's body but it was dangerous to go there, even by foot, and Lord Toranaga had said to bring the barbarian back safely, so he was going to be brought safely. It was equally clear that the man intended to go.

He had seen him during the storm, standing on the pitching deck like an evil sea *kami,* unafraid, in his element and part of the storm, and he had thought grimly at the time, better to get this man and all barbarians like him on the land where we can deal with them. At sea we're in their power.

He could see the pirate was impatient. How insulting they are, he told himself. Even so I should thank you. Everyone says you alone are responsible for bringing the ship to harbor, that the Rodrigu anjin lost his nerve and waved us away from land, but you held our course. Yes. If we'd gone out to sea we'd have sunk certainly and then I would have failed my Master. Oh, Buddha, protect me from that!

All his joints were aching and his piles inflamed. He was exhausted by the effort it took to remain stoic in front of his men, Yabu, the crew, even this barbarian. Oh, Buddha, I'm so tired. I wish I could lie in a bath and soak and soak and have one day of rest from pain. Just one day. Stop your stupid womanish thoughts! You've been in pain for almost sixty years. What is pain to a man? A privilege! Masking pain is the measure of a man. Thank Buddha you are still alive to protect your Master when you should have been dead a hundred times. I do thank Buddha.

But I hate the sea. I hate the cold. And I hate pain.

"Stay where you are, Anjin-san," he said, pointing with his scabbard for clarity, bleakly amused by the ice-blue fire in the man's eyes. When he was sure the man understood he glanced at the mate. "Where are we? Whose fief is this?"

"I don't know, Sire. I think we're somewhere in Ise Province. We could send someone ashore to the nearest village."

"Can you pilot us to Osaka?"

"Providing we stay very close to shore, Sire, and go slowly, with great caution. I don't know these waters and I could never guarantee your safety. I don't have enough knowledge and there's no one aboard, Sire, who has. Except this Pilot. If it was left to me I would advise you to go by land. We could get you horses or palanquins."

Hiro-matsu shook his head irascibly. To go overland was out of the question. It would take far too long—the way was mountainous and there were few roads—and they would have to go through many territories controlled by allies of Ishido, the enemy. Added to this danger were also the multitudinous bandit groups that infested the passes. This would mean he would have to take all his men. Certainly he could fight his way through the bandits, but he could never force a passage if Ishido or his allies decided to inhibit him. All this would delay him further, and his orders were to deliver the cargo, the barbarian, and Yabu, quickly and safely.

"If we follow the coast, how long would it take us?"

"I don't know, Sire. Four or five days, perhaps more. I would feel very unsure of myself—I'm not a captain, so sorry."

Which means, Hiro-matsu thought, that I have to have the cooperation of this barbarian. To prevent him going ashore I'll have to tie him up. And who knows if he'll be cooperative tied up?

"How long will we have to stay here?"

"The Pilot said overnight."

"Will the storm be gone by then?"

"It should, Sire, but one never knows."

Hiro-matsu studied the mountain coast, then the Pilot, hesitating.

"May I offer a suggestion, Hiro-matsu-san?" Yabu said.

"Yes, yes, of course," he said testily.

"As we seem to need the pirate's cooperation to get us to Osaka, why not let him go ashore but send men with him to protect him, and order them back before dark. As to going overland, I agree it would be too dangerous for you—I would never forgive myself if anything happened to you. Once the storm has blown itself out you'll be safer with the ship and you'll get to Osaka much quicker, *neh?* Surely by sunset tomorrow."

Reluctantly Hiro-matsu nodded. "Very well." He beckoned a samurai. "Takatashi-san! You will take six men and go with the Pilot. Bring the Portuguese's body back if you can find it. But if even one of this barbarian's eyelashes is damaged, you and your men will commit seppuku instantly."

"Yes, Lord."

"And send two men to the nearest village and find out exactly where we are and in whose fief we are."

"Yes, Lord."

"With your permission, Hiro-matsu-san, I will lead the party ashore," Yabu said. "If we arrived in Osaka without the pirate, I'd be so ashamed that I'd feel obliged to kill myself anyway. I'd like the honor of carrying out your orders."

Hiro-matsu nodded, inwardly surprised that Yabu would put himself in such jeopardy. He went below.

When Blackthorne realized that Yabu was going ashore with him, his pulse quickened. I haven't forgotten Pieterzoon or my crew or the pit—or the screams or Omi or any part of it. Look to your life, bastard.

CHAPTER 9

THEY were quickly on land. Blackthorne intended to lead but Yabu usurped that position and set a strong pace, which he was hard put to keep up with. The other six samurai were watching him carefully. I've nowhere to run, you fools, he thought, misunderstanding their concern, as his eyes automatically quartered the bay, looking for shoals or hidden reefs, measuring bearings, his mind docketing the important things for future transcription.

Their way led first along the pebbled shore, then a short climb over sea-smoothed rocks up onto a path that skirted the cliff and crept precariously around the headland southward. The rain had stopped but the gale had not. The closer they came to the exposed tongue of land, the higher the surf—hurled against the rocks below—sprayed into the air. Soon they were soaked.

Although Blackthorne felt chilled, Yabu and the others, who had their light kimonos carelessly tucked into their belts, did not seem to be affected by the wet or the cold. It must be as Rodrigues had said, he thought, his fear returning. Japmen just aren't built like us. They don't *feel* cold or hunger or privations or wounds as we do. They are more like animals, their nerves dulled, compared to us.

Above them the cliff soared two hundred feet. The shore was fifty feet below. Beyond and all around were mountains and not a house or hut in the whole bay area. This was not surprising for there was no room for fields, the shore pebbles quickly becoming foreshore rocks and then granite mountain with trees on the upper slopes.

The path dipped and rose along the cliff face, very unsafe, the surface loose. Blackthorne plodded along, leaning against the wind, and noticed that Yabu's legs were strong and muscular. Slip, you whore-bastard, he thought. Slip—splatter yourself on the rocks below. Would that make you scream? What would make you scream?

With an effort he took his eyes off Yabu and went back to searching the foreshore. Each crevice and cleft and gulley. The spume wind was gusting and tore the tears from him. Sea spilled back and forth, swirled and eddied. He knew there was a minimal hope of finding Rodrigues, there would be too many caves and hidden places that could never be investigated. But he had had to come ashore to try. He owed Rodrigues the try. All pilots prayed helplessly for death ashore and burial ashore.

All had seen too many sea-bloated corpses and half-eaten corpses and crab-mutilated corpses.

They rounded the headland and stopped gratefully in the lee. There was no need to go further. If the body wasn't to windward then it was hidden or swallowed up or already carried out to sea, into the deep. Half a mile away a small fishing village nestled on the white-frothed shore. Yabu motioned to two of the samurai. Immediately they bowed and loped off toward it. A last look, then Yabu wiped the rain out of his face, glanced up at Blackthorne, motioning their return. Blackthorne nodded and they set off again, Yabu leading, the other samurai still watching him so carefully, and again he thought how stupid they were.

Then, when they were halfway back, they saw Rodrigues.

The body was caught in a cleft between two great rocks, above the surf but washed by part of it. One arm was sprawled in front. The other was still locked to the broken oar which moved slightly with the ebb and flow. It was this movement that had attracted Blackthorne's attention as he bent into the wind, trudging in Yabu's wake.

The only way down was over the short cliff. The climb would only be fifty or sixty feet but it was a sheer drop and there were almost no footholds.

What about the tide? Blackthorne asked himself. It's flowing, not ebbing. That'll take him out to sea again. Jesus, it looks foul down there. What's it to be?

He went closer to the edge and immediately Yabu moved in his way, shaking his head, and the other samurai surrounded him.

"I'm only trying to get a better look, for the love of Christ," he said. "I'm not trying to escape! Where the hell can I run to?"

He backed off a little and peered down. They followed his look and chatted among themselves, Yabu doing most of the talking.

There's no chance, he decided. It's too dangerous. We'll come back at dawn with ropes. If he's here, he's here, and I'll bury him ashore. Reluctantly he turned and, as he did, the edge of the cliff crumbled and he began to slip. Immediately Yabu and the others grabbed him and pulled him back, and all at once he realized that they were concerned only for his safety. They're only trying to protect me!

Why should they want me safe? Because of Tora— What was his name? Toranaga? Because of him? Yes, but also perhaps because there's no one else aboard to pilot us. Is that why they let me come ashore, gave me my way? Yes, it must be. So now I have power over the ship, over the old *daimyo,* and over this bastard. How can I use it?

He relaxed and thanked them and let his eyes roam below. "We've got to get him, Yabu-san. *Hai!* The only way's that way. Over the cliff.

I'll bring him up, me, Anjin-san!" Again he moved forward as though he was going to climb down and again they restrained him and he said with feigned anxiety, "We've got to get Rodrigu-san. Look! There's not much time, light's going."

"*Iyé*, Anjin-san," Yabu said.

He stood towering over Yabu. "If you won't let me go, Yabu-san, then send one of your men. Or go yourself. You!"

The wind tore around them, whining off the cliff face. He saw Yabu look down, weighing the climb and the falling light, and he knew Yabu was hooked. You're trapped, bastard, your vanity's trapped you. If you start down there you'll get hurt. But don't kill yourself, please, just shatter your legs or ankles. Then drown.

A samurai began to climb down but Yabu ordered him back.

"Return to the ship. Fetch some ropes immediately," Yabu said. The man ran off.

Yabu kicked off his thong slippers. He took his swords out of his belt and put them safely under cover. "Watch them and watch the barbarian. If anything happens to either, I'll sit you on your own swords."

"Please let me go down there, Yabu-sama," Takatashi said. "If you're hurt or lost I'll—"

"You think that you can succeed where I will fail?"

"No, Sire, of course not."

"Good."

"Please wait for the ropes then. I'll never forgive myself if anything happens to you." Takatashi was short and stocky with a heavy beard.

Why not wait for the ropes? Yabu asked himself. It would be sensible, yes. But not clever. He glanced up at the barbarian and nodded briefly. He knew that he had been challenged. He had expected it. And hoped for it. That's why I volunteered for this mission, Anjin-san, he said to himself, silently amused. You're really very simple. Omi was right.

Yabu took off his soaking kimono and, clad only in his loincloth, went to the cliff edge and tested it through the soles of his cotton tabi—his sock-shoes. Better to keep them on, he thought, his will and his body, forged by a lifetime of training all samurai had to undergo, dominating the cold that cut into him. The tabi will give you a firmer grip—for a time. You'll need all your strength and skill to get down there alive. Is it worth it?

During the storm and the stab for the bay he had come on deck and, unnoticed by Blackthorne, had taken a place at the oars. Gladly he had used his strength with the rowers, detesting the miasma below and the sickness he had felt. He had decided that it was better to die in the air than suffocate below.

As he worked with the others in the driving cold, he began watching the pilots. He saw very clearly that, at sea, the ship and all aboard were in the power of these two men. The pilots were in their element, riding the pitching decks as carelessly as he himself rode a galloping horse. No Japanese aboard could match them. For skill or courage or knowledge. And gradually this awareness had spawned a majestic concept: modern barbarian ships filled with samurai, piloted by samurai, captained by samurai, sailed by samurai. *His* samurai.

If I had three barbarian ships initially, I could easily control the sea lanes between Yedo and Osaka. Based in Izu, I could strangle all shipping or let it pass. So nearly all the rice and all the silk. Wouldn't I then be arbiter between Toranaga and Ishido? At the very least, a balance between them?

No *daimyo* has ever yet taken to the sea.

No *daimyo* has ships or pilots.

Except me.

I have a ship—had a ship—and now I *might* have my ship back—if I'm clever. I have a pilot and therefore a trainer of pilots, if I can get him away from Toranaga. If I can dominate him.

Once he is my vassal of his own accord, he will train my men. And build ships.

But how to make him a true vassal? The pit did not break his spirit.

First get him alone and keep him alone—isn't that what Omi said? Then this pilot could be persuaded to manners and taught to speak Japanese. Yes. Omi's very clever. Too clever perhaps—I'll think about Omi later. Concentrate on the pilot. How to dominate a barbarian—a Christian filth eater?

What was it Omi said? 'They value life. Their chief deity, Jesus the Christ, teaches them to love one another and to value life.' Could I give him back his life? Save it, yes, that would be very good. How to bend him?

Yabu had been so swept by his excitement he had hardly noticed the motion of the ship or the seas. A wave cascaded over him. He saw it envelop the Pilot. But there was no fear in the man at all. Yabu was astounded. How could someone who had meekly allowed an enemy to piss on his back to save the life of an insignificant vassal, how could this man have the strength to forget such eternal dishonor and stand there on the quarterdeck calling the gods of the sea to battle like any legendary hero—to save the same enemies? And then, when the great wave had taken the Portuguese away and they were floundering, the Anjin-san had miraculously laughed at death and given them the strength to pull away from the rocks.

I'll never understand them, he thought.

On the cliff edge, Yabu looked back a last time. Ah, Anjin-san, I know you think I go to my death, that you've trapped me. I know you wouldn't go down there yourself. I was watching you closely. But I grew up in the mountains and here in Japan we climb for pride and for pleasure. So I pit myself now on *my* terms, not on yours. I will try, and if I die it is nothing. But if I succeed then you, as a man, you'll know I'm better than you, on *your* terms. You'll be in my debt, too, if I bring the body back.

You will be my vassal, Anjin-san!

He went down the side of the cliff with great skill. When he was half-way down he slipped. His left hand held onto an outcrop. This stopped his fall, and he swung between life and death. His fingers dug deeply as he felt his grip failing and he ground his toes into a crevice, fighting for another hold. As his left hand ripped away, his toes found a cleft and they held and he hugged the cliff desperately, still off-balance, pressing against it, seeking holds. Then his toehold gave way. Though he managed to catch another outcrop with both hands, ten feet below, and hang on momentarily, this outcrop gave way too. He fell the last twenty feet.

He had prepared as best he could and landed on his feet like a cat, tumbled the sloping rock face to break the shock, and came to rest in a wheezing ball. He clutched his lacerated arms around his head, protecting himself against the stone avalanche that could follow. But none did. He shook his head to clear it and got up. One ankle was twisted. A searing pain shot up his leg into his bowels and the sweat started. His toes and fingernails were bleeding but that was to be expected.

There's no pain. You will not feel pain. Stand upright. The barbarian is watching.

A column of spray doused him and the cold helped to ease the hurt. With care, he slid over the seaweeded boulders, and eased himself across the crevices and then he was at the body.

Abruptly Yabu realized that the man was still alive. He made sure, then sat back for a moment. Do I want him alive or dead? Which is better?

A crab scuttled from under a rock and plopped into the sea. Waves rushed in. He felt the salt rip his wounds. Which is better, alive or dead?

He got up precariously and shouted, "Takatashi-san! This pilot's still alive! Go to the ship, bring a stretcher and a doctor, if there's one on the ship!"

Takatashi's words came back faintly against the wind, "Yes, Lord," and to his men as he ran off, "Watch the barbarian, don't let anything happen to him!"

Yabu peered at the galley, riding her anchors gently. The other samurai he had sent back for ropes was already beside the skiffs. He watched while the man jumped into one and it was launched. He smiled to himself, glanced back. Blackthorne had come to the edge of the cliff and was shouting urgently at him.

What is he trying to say? Yabu asked himself. He saw the pilot pointing to the sea but that didn't mean anything to him. The sea was rough and strong but it was no different from before.

Eventually Yabu gave up trying to understand and turned his attention to Rodrigues. With difficulty he eased the man up onto the rocks, out of the surf. The Portuguese's breathing was halting, but his heart seemed strong. There were many bruises. A splintered bone jutted through the skin of the left calf. His right shoulder seemed dislocated. Yabu looked for blood seepage from any openings but there was none. If he's not hurt inside, then perhaps he will live, he thought.

The *daimyo* had been wounded too many times and had seen too many dying and wounded not to have gained some measure of diagnostic skill. If Rodrigu can be kept warm, he decided, given saké and strong herbs, plenty of warm baths, he'll live. He may not walk again but he'll live. Yes. I want this man to live. If he can't walk, no matter. Perhaps that would be better. I'll have a spare pilot—this man certainly owes me his life. If the pirate won't cooperate, perhaps I can use this man. Would it be worthwhile to pretend to become a Christian? Would that bring them both around to me?

What would Omi do?

That one's clever—Omi. Yes. Too clever? Omi sees too much too fast. If he can see that far, he must perceive that his father would lead the clan if I vanish—my son's too inexperienced yet to survive by himself— and after the father, Omi himself. *Neh?*

What to do about Omi?

Say I gave Omi to the barbarian? As a toy.

What about that?

There were anxious shouts from above. Then he realized what the barbarian had been pointing at. The tide! The tide was coming in fast. Already it was encroaching on this rock. He scrambled up and winced at a shaft of pain from his ankle. All other escape along the shore was blocked by the sea. He saw that the tide mark on the cliff was over a man's full height above the base.

He looked at the skiff. It was near the ship now. On the foreshore Takatashi was still running well. The ropes won't arrive in time, he told himself.

His eyes searched the area diligently. There was no way up the cliff. No rocks offered sanctuary. No caves. Out to sea there were outcrops but he could never reach them. He could not swim and there was nothing to use as a raft.

The men above were watching him. The barbarian pointed to the outcrops seaward and made motions of swimming, but he shook his head. He searched carefully again. Nothing.

There's no escape, he thought. Now you are committed to death. Prepare yourself.

Karma, he told himself, and turned away from them, settling himself more comfortably, enjoying the vast clarity that had come to him. Last day, last sea, last light, last joy, last everything. How beautiful the sea and the sky and the cold and salt. He began to think of the final poem-song that he should now, by custom, compose. He felt fortunate. He had time to think clearly.

Blackthorne was shouting, "Listen, you whore-bastard! Find a ledge—there's got to be a ledge somewhere!"

The samurai were standing in his way, gazing at him as though he were a madman. It was clear to them there was no escape and that Yabu was simply preparing for a sweet death, as they would be doing if they had been he. And they resented these ravings as they knew Yabu would.

"Look down there, all of you. Maybe there's a ledge!"

One of them went to the edge and peered down, shrugged, and talked to his comrades and they shrugged too. Each time Blackthorne tried to go closer to the edge to search for an escape they stopped him. He could have easily shoved one of them to his death and he was tempted to. But he understood them and their problems. Think of a way to help that bastard. You've got to save him to save Rodrigues.

"Hey, you rotten, no good, piss-cutting, shit-tailed Japman! Hey, Kasigi Yabu! Where are your cojones? Don't give up! Only cowards give up! Are you a man or a sheep!" But Yabu paid no attention. He was as still as the rock upon which he sat.

Blackthorne picked up a stone and hurled it at him. It fell unnoticed into the water and the samurai shouted at Blackthorne angrily. He knew that at any moment they were going to fall on him and bind him up. But how could they? They've no rope—

Rope! Get some rope! Can you make some?

His eyes fell on Yabu's kimono. He started tearing it into strips, testing them for strength. The silk was very strong. "Come on!" he ordered the samurai, taking off his own shirt. "Make a rope. *Hai?*"

They understood. Rapidly they untied their sashes, took off their kimonos, and copied him. He began knotting the ends, sashes as well.

While they completed the rope, Blackthorne carefully lay down and inched for the edge, making two of them hold onto his ankles for safety. He didn't need their help but he wanted to reassure them.

He stuck his head out as far as he dared, conscious of their anxiety. Then he began to search as you would search at sea. Quarter by quarter. Using every part of his vision but mostly the sides.

A complete sweep. Nothing.

Once more.

Nothing.

Again.

What's that? Just above the tide line? Is it a crack in the cliff? Or a shadow?

Blackthorne shifted position, keenly aware that the sea had almost covered the rock that Yabu sat on, and almost all of the rocks between him and the base of the cliff. Now he could see better and he pointed.

"There! What's that?"

One of the samurai was on his hands and knees and he followed Blackthorne's outstretched finger but saw nothing.

"There! Isn't that a ledge?"

With his hands he formed the ledge and with two fingers made a man and stood the man on the ledge and, with another finger, made a long bundle over the shoulder of the man, so now a man stood on a ledge—*that ledge*—with another over his shoulder.

"Quick! *Isogi!* Make him understand—Kasigi Yabu-sama! *Wakarimasu ka?*"

The man scrambled up and talked rapidly to the others and they looked too. Now they all saw the ledge. And they began to shout. Still no movement from Yabu. He seemed like a stone. They went on and Blackthorne added his shouts but it was as if they made no sound at all.

One of them spoke to the others briefly and they all nodded and bowed. He bowed back. Then, with a sudden screaming shout of "*Bansaiiiiiii!*" he cast himself off the cliff and fell to his death. Yabu came violently out of his trance, whirled around and scrambled up.

The other samurai shouted and pointed but Blackthorne heard nothing and saw nothing but the broken corpse that lay below, already being taken by the sea. What kind of men are these? he thought helplessly. Was that courage or just insanity? That man deliberately committed suicide on the off-chance he'd attract the attention of another man who had given up. It doesn't make sense! They don't make sense.

He saw Yabu stagger up. He expected him to scramble for safety, leaving Rodrigues. That's what I would have done. Is it? I don't know. But Yabu half crawled, half slid, dragging the unconscious man with him through the surf-disturbed shallows to the bottom of the cliff. He found the ledge. It was barely a foot wide. Painfully he shoved Rodrigues onto it, almost losing him once, then hauled himself up.

The rope was twenty feet short. Quickly the samurai added their loincloths. Now, if Yabu stood, he could just reach the end.

They shouted encouragement and began to wait.

In spite of Blackthorne's hatred he had to admire Yabu's courage. Half a dozen times waves almost engulfed him. Twice Rodrigues was lost but each time Yabu dragged him back, and held his head out of the grasping sea, long after Blackthorne knew that he himself would have given up. Where do you get the courage, Yabu? Are you just devil-born? All of you?

To climb down in the first place had taken courage. At first Blackthorne had thought that Yabu had acted out of bravado. But soon he had seen that the man was pitting his skill against the cliff and almost winning. Then he had broken his fall as deftly as any tumbler. And he had given up with dignity.

Christ Jesus, I admire that bastard, and detest him.

For almost an hour Yabu set himself against the sea and against his failing body, and then, in the dusk, Takatashi came back with the ropes. They made a cradle and shinned down the cliff with a skill that Blackthorne had never seen ashore.

Quickly Rodrigues was brought aloft. Blackthorne would have tried to succor him but a Japanese with close-cropped hair was already on his knees beside him. He watched as this man, obviously a doctor, examined the broken leg. Then a samurai held Rodrigues' shoulders as the doctor leaned his weight on the foot and the bone slid back under the flesh. His fingers probed and shoved and reset it and tied it to the splint. He began to wrap noxious-looking herbs around the angry wound and then Yabu was brought up.

The *daimyo* shook off any help, waved the doctor back to Rodrigues, sat down and began to wait.

Blackthorne looked at him. Yabu felt his eyes. The two men stared at each other.

"Thank you," Blackthorne said finally, pointing at Rodrigues. "Thank you for saving his life. Thank you, Yabu-san." Deliberately he bowed. That's for your courage, you black-eyed son of a shit-festered whore.

Yabu bowed back as stiffly. But inside, he smiled.

BOOK TWO

CHAPTER 10

THEIR journey from the bay to Osaka was uneventful. Rodrigues' rutters were explicit and very accurate. During the first night Rodrigues regained consciousness. In the beginning he thought he was dead but the pain soon reminded him differently.

"They've set your leg and dressed it," Blackthorne said. "And your shoulder's strapped up. It was dislocated. They wouldn't bleed you, much as I tried to make them."

"When I get to Osaka the Jesuits can do that." Rodrigues' tormented eyes bored into him. "How did I get here, Ingeles? I remember going overboard but nothing else."

Blackthorne told him.

"So now I owe you a life. God curse you."

"From the quarterdeck it looked as though we could make the bay. From the bow, your angle of sight would be a few degrees different. The wave was bad luck."

"That doesn't worry me, Ingeles. You had the quarterdeck, you had the helm. We both knew it. No, I curse you to hell because I owe you a life now— Madonna, my leg!" Tears welled because of the pain and Blackthorne gave him a mug of grog and watched him during the night, the storm abating. The Japanese doctor came several times and forced Rodrigues to drink hot medicine and put hot towels on his forehead and opened the portholes. And every time the doctor went away Blackthorne closed the portholes, for everyone knew that disease was airborne, that the tighter closed the cabin the safer and more healthy, when a man was as bad as Rodrigues.

At length the doctor shouted at him and posted a samurai on the portholes so they remained open.

At dawn Blackthorne went on deck. Hiro-matsu and Yabu were both there. He bowed like a courtier. *"Konnichi wa"* Osaka?"

They bowed in return. "Osaka. *Hai,* Anjin-san," Hiro-matsu said.

"Hai! Isogi, Hiro-matsu-sama. Captain-san! Weigh anchor!"

"Hai, Anjin-san!"

He smiled involuntarily at Yabu. Yabu smiled back, then limped away and thought, that's one hell of a man, although he is a devil and a murderer. Aren't *you* a murderer, too? Yes—but not that way, he told himself.

Blackthorne conned the ship to Osaka with ease. The journey took that day and the night and just after dawn the next day they were near the Osaka roads. A Japanese pilot came aboard to take the ship to her wharf so, relieved of his responsibility, he gladly went below to sleep.

Later the captain shook him awake, bowed, and pantomimed that Blackthorne should be ready to go with Hiro-matsu as soon as they docked.

"*Wakarimasu ka,* Anjin-san?"

"*Hai.*"

The seaman went away. Blackthorne stretched his back, aching, then saw Rodrigues watching him.

"How do you feel?"

"Good, Ingeles. Considering my leg's on fire, my head's bursting, I want to piss, and my tongue tastes like a barrel of pig shit looks."

Blackthorne gave him the chamber pot, then emptied it out the porthole. He refilled the tankard with grog.

"You make a foul nurse, Ingeles. It's your black heart." Rodrigues laughed and it was good to hear him laugh again. His eyes went to the rutter that was open on the desk, and to his sea chest. He saw that it had been unlocked. "Did I give you the key?"

"No. I searched you. I had to have the true rutter. I told you when you woke the first night."

"That's fair. I don't remember, but that's fair. Listen, Ingeles, ask any Jesuit where Vasco Rodrigues is in Osaka and they'll guide you to me. Come to see me—then you can make a copy of my rutter, if you wish."

"Thanks. I've already taken one. At least, I copied what I could, and I've read the rest very carefully."

"Thy mother!" Rodrigues said in Spanish.

"And thine."

Rodrigues turned to Portuguese again. "Speaking Spanish makes me want to retch, even though you can swear better in it than any language. There's a package in my sea chest. Give it to me, please."

"The one with the Jesuit seals?"

"Yes."

He gave it to him. Rodrigues studied it, fingering the unbroken seals, then seemed to change his mind and put the package on the rough blanket under which he lay, leaning his head back again. "Ah, Ingeles, life is so strange."

"Why?"

"If I live, it is because of God's grace, helped by a heretic and a Japman. Send the sod-eater below so I can thank him, eh?"

"Now?"

"Later."

"All right."

"This fleet of yours, the one you claim's attacking Manila, the one you told the Father about—what's the truth, Ingeles?"

"A fleet of our warships'll wreck your Empire in Asia, won't it?"

"Is there a fleet?"

"Of course."

"How many ships were in your fleet?"

"Five. The rest are out to sea, a week or so. I came ahead to probe Japan and got caught in the storm."

"More lies, Ingeles. But I don't mind—I've told my captors as many. There are no more ships or fleets."

"Wait and see."

"I will." Rodrigues drank heavily.

Blackthorne stretched and went to the porthole, wanting to stop this conversation, and looked out at the shore and the city. "I thought London was the biggest city on earth, but compared to Osaka it's a small town."

"They've dozens of cities like this one," Rodrigues said, also glad to stop the cat-and-mouse game that would never bear fruit without the rack. "Miyako, the capital, or Kyoto as it's sometimes called, is the biggest city in the Empire, more than twice the size of Osaka, so they say. Next comes Yedo, Toranaga's capital. I've never been there, nor any priest or Portuguese—Toranaga keeps his capital locked away—a forbidden city. Still," Rodrigues added, lying back in his bunk and closing his eyes, his face stretched with pain, "still, that's no different to everywhere. All Japan's officially forbidden to us, except the ports of Nagasaki and Hirado. Our priests rightly don't pay much attention to the orders and go where they please. But we seamen can't or traders, unless it's on a special pass from the Regents, or a great *daimyo,* like Toranaga. Any *daimyo* can seize one of our ships—like Toranaga's got yours—outside of Nagasaki or Hirado. That's their law."

"Do you want to rest now?"

"No, Ingeles. Talking's better. Talking helps to take the pain away. Madonna, my head hurts! I can't think clearly. Let's talk until you go ashore. Come back and see me—there's lots I want to ask you. Give me some more grog. Thank you, thank you, Ingeles."

"Why're you forbidden to go where you please?"

"What? Oh, here in Japan? It was the Taikō—he started all the trouble. Ever since we first came here in 1542 to begin God's work and to bring them civilization, we and our priests could move freely, but when the

Taikō got all power he started the prohibitions. Many believe . . . could you shift my leg, take the blanket off my foot, it's burning . . . yes—oh, Madonna, be careful—there, thank you, Ingeles. Yes, where was I? Oh yes . . . many believe the Taikō was Satan's penis. Ten years ago he issued Edicts against the Holy Fathers, Ingeles, and all who wanted to spread the word of God. And he banished everyone, except traders, ten, twelve-odd years ago. It was before I came to these waters—I've been here seven years, off and on. The Holy Fathers say it was because of the heathen priests—the Buddhists—the stinking, jealous idol worshipers, these heathens, they turned the Taikō against our Holy Fathers, filled him with lies, when they'd almost converted him. Yes, the Great Murderer himself almost had his soul saved. But he missed his chance for salvation. Yes. Anyway, he ordered all of our priests to leave Japan. . . . Did I tell you this was ten-odd years ago?"

Blackthorne nodded, glad to let him ramble and glad to listen, desperate to learn.

"The Taikō had all the Fathers collected at Nagasaki, ready to ship them out to Macao with written orders never to return on pain of death. Then, as suddenly, he left them all alone and did no more. I told you Japmen are upside-downers. Yes, he left them alone and soon it was as before, except that most of the Fathers stayed in Kyushu where we're welcome. Did I tell you Japan's made up of three big islands, Kyushu, Shikoku, and Honshu? And thousands of little ones. There's another island far to the north—some say it's the mainland—called Hokkaido, but only hairy natives live there.

"Japan's an upside-down world, Ingeles. Father Alvito told me it became again as though nothing had ever happened. The Taikō was as friendly as before, though he never converted. He hardly shut down a church and only banished two or three of the Christian *daimyos*—but that was just to get their lands—and never enforced his Expulsion Edicts. Then, three years ago, he went mad again and martyred twenty-six Fathers. He crucified them at Nagasaki. For no reason. He was a maniac, Ingeles. But after murdering the twenty-six he did nothing more. He died soon after. It was the Hand of God, Ingeles. The curse of God was on him and is on his seed. I'm sure of it."

"Do you have many converts here?"

But Rodrigues did not seem to hear, lost in his own half-consciousness. "They're animals, the Japaners. Did I tell you about Father Alvito? He's the interpreter—Tsukku-san they call him, Mr. Interpreter. He was the Taikō's interpreter, Ingeles, now he's the official interpreter for the Council of Regents and he speaks Japanese better'n most Japanese and knows more about them than any man alive. He told me there's a mound of earth fifty feet high in Miyako—that's the capital, Ingeles. The Taikō had the noses and ears of all the Koreans killed in the war collected and buried there—Korea's part of the mainland, west of Kyushu. It's the truth! By the Blessed Virgin, there was never a killer like him—and they're all as bad." Rodrigues' eyes were closed and his forehead flushed.

"Do you have many converts?" Blackthorne carefully asked again, wanting desperately to know how many enemies were here.

To his shock, Rodrigues said, "Hundreds of thousands, and more every year. Since the Taikō's death we have more than ever before, and those who were secretly Christian now go to the church openly. Most of the island of Kyushu's Catholic now. Most of the Kyushu *daimyos* are converts. Nagasaki's a Catholic city, Jesuits own it and run it and control all trade. All trade goes through Nagasaki. We have a cathedral, a dozen churches, and dozens more spread through Kyushu, but only a few yet here in the main island, Honshu, and . . ." Pain stopped him again. After a moment he continued, "There are three or four million people in Kyushu alone—they'll all be Catholic soon. There's another twenty-odd million Japmen in the islands and soon—"

"That's not possible!" Blackthorne immediately cursed himself for interrupting the flow of information.

"Why should I lie? There was a census ten years ago. Father Alvito said the Taikō ordered it and he should know, he was there. Why should he lie?" Rodrigues' eyes were feverish and now his mouth was running away with him. "That's more than the population of all Portugal, all Spain, all France, the Spanish Netherlands, and England added together and you could almost throw in the whole Holy Roman Empire as well to equal it!"

Lord Jesus, Blackthorne thought, the whole of England hasn't got more than three million people. And that includes Wales as well.

If there are that many Japanese, how can we deal with them? If there's twenty million, that'd mean they could easily press an army of more men than we've got in our entire population if they wanted. And if they're all as ferocious as the ones I've seen—and why shouldn't they be—by God's wounds, they'd be unbeatable. And if they're already partially Catholic, and if the Jesuits are here in strength, their numbers will increase, and there's no fanatic like a converted fanatic, so what chance have we and the Dutch got in Asia?

None at all.

"If you think that's a lot," Rodrigues was saying, "wait till you go to China. They're all yellow men there, all with black hair and eyes. Oh,

Ingeles, I tell you you've so much new to learn. I was in Canton last year, at the silk sales. Canton's a walled city in south China, on the Pearl River, north of our City of the Name of God at Macao. There's a million of the heathen dog-eaters within those walls alone. China's got more people than all the rest of the world put together. Must have. Think of that!" A spasm of pain went through Rodrigues and his good hand held onto his stomach. "Was there any blood seeping out of me? Anywhere?"

"No. I made sure. It's just your leg and shoulder. You're not hurt inside, Rodrigues—at least, I don't think so."

"How bad is the leg?"

"It was washed by the sea and cleaned by the sea. The break was clean and the skin's clean, at the moment."

"Did you pour brandy over it and fire it?"

"No. They wouldn't let me—they ordered me off. But the doctor seemed to know what he's doing. Will your own people come aboard quickly?"

"Yes. Soon as we dock. That's more than likely."

"Good. You were saying? About China and Canton?"

"I was saying too much, perhaps. Time enough to talk about them."

Blackthorne watched the Portuguese's good hand toy with the sealed package and he wondered again what significance it had. "Your leg will be all right. You'll know within the week."

"Yes, Ingeles."

"I don't think it'll rot—there's no pus—you're thinking clearly so your brain's all right. You'll be fine, Rodrigues."

"I still owe you a life." A shiver ran through the Portuguese. "When I was drowning, all I could think of was the crabs climbing in through my eyes. I could feel them churning inside me, Ingeles. That's the third time I've been overboard and each time it's worse."

"I've been sunk at sea four times. Three times by Spaniards."

The cabin door opened and the captain bowed and beckoned Blackthorne aloft.

"*Hai!*" Blackthorne got up. "You owe me nothing, Rodrigues," he said kindly. "You gave me life and succor when I was desperate, and I thank you for that. We're even."

"Perhaps, but listen, Ingeles, here's some truth for you, in part payment: Never forget Japmen're six-faced and have three hearts. It's a saying they have, that a man has a false heart in his mouth for all the world to see, another in his breast to show his very special friends and his family, and the real one, the true one, the secret one, which is never known to anyone except himself alone, hidden only God knows where. They're treacherous beyond belief, vice-ridden beyond redemption."

"Why does Toranaga want to see me?"

"I don't know. By the Blessed Virgin! I don't know. Come back to see me, if you can."

"Yes. Good luck, Spaniard!"

"Thy sperm! Even so, go with God."

Blackthorne smiled back, unguarded, and then he was on deck and his mind whirled from the impact of Osaka, its immensity, the teeming ant-hills of people, and the enormous castle that dominated the city. From within the castle's vastness came the soaring beauty of the donjon—the central keep—seven or eight stories high, pointed gables with curved roofs at each level, the tiles all gilded and the walls blue.

That's where Toranaga will be, he thought, an ice barb suddenly in his bowels.

A closed palanquin took him to a large house. There he was bathed and he ate, inevitably, fish soup, raw and steamed fish, a few pickled vegetables, and the hot herbed water. Instead of wheat gruel, this house provided him with a bowl of rice. He had seen rice once in Naples. It was white and wholesome, but to him tasteless. His stomach cried for meat and bread, new-baked crusty bread heavy with butter, and a haunch of beef and pies and chickens and beer and eggs.

The next day a maid came for him. The clothes that Rodrigues had given him were laundered. She watched while he dressed, and helped him into new tabi sock-shoes. Outside was a new pair of thongs. His boots were missing. She shook her head and pointed at the thongs and then at the curtained palanquin. A phalanx of samurai surrounded it. The leader motioned him to hurry up and get in.

They moved off immediately. The curtains were tight closed. After an age, the palanquin stopped.

"You will not be afraid," he said aloud, and got out.

The gigantic stone gate of the castle was in front of him. It was set into a thirty-foot wall with interlocking battlements, bastions, and out-works. The door was huge and iron plated and open, the forged iron portcullis up. Beyond was a wooden bridge, twenty paces wide and two hundred long, that spanned the moat and ended at an enormous draw-bridge, and another gate that was set into the second wall, equally vast.

Hundreds of samurai were everywhere. All wore the same somber gray uniform—belted kimonos, each with five small circular insignias, one on each arm, on each breast, and one in the center of the back. The insignia was blue, seemingly a flower or flowers.

"Anjin-san!"

Hiro-matsu was seated stiffly on an open palanquin carried by four liveried bearers. His kimono was brown and stark, his belt black, the same as the fifty samurai that surrounded him. Their kimonos, too, had five insignias, but these were scarlet, the same that had fluttered at the masthead, Toranaga's cipher. These samurai carried long gleaming spears with tiny flags at their heads.

Blackthorne bowed without thinking, taken by Hiro-matsu's majesty. The old man bowed back formally, his long sword loose in his lap, and signed for him to follow.

The officer at the gate came forward. There was a ceremonial reading of the paper that Hiro-matsu offered and many bows and looks toward Blackthorne and then they were passed on to the bridge, an escort of the Grays falling in beside them.

The surface of the deep moat was fifty feet below and stretched about three hundred paces on either side, then followed the walls as they turned north and Blackthorne thought, Lord God, I'd hate to have to try to mount an attack here. The defenders could let the outer-wall garrison perish and burn the bridge, then they're safe inside. Jesus God, the outer wall must be nearly a mile square and look, it must be twenty, thirty feet thick—the inner one, too. And it's made out of huge blocks of stone. Each one must be ten feet by ten feet! At least! And cut perfectly and set into place without mortar. They must weigh fifty tons at least. Better than any we could make. Siege guns? Certainly they could batter the outer walls, but the guns defending would give as good as they got. It'd be hard to get them up here, and there's no higher point from which to lob fireballs into the castle. If the outer wall was taken, the defenders could still blast the attackers off the battlements. But even if siege guns could be mounted there and they were turned on the next wall and battered it, they wouldn't hurt it. They could damage the far gate, but what would that accomplish? How could the moat be crossed? It's too vast for the normal methods. The castle must be impregnable— with enough soldiers. How many soldiers are here? How many towns-people would have sanctuary inside?

It makes the Tower of London like a pigsty. And the whole of Hampton Court would fit into one corner!

At the next gate there was another ceremonial checking of papers and the road turned left immediately, down a vast avenue lined with heavily fortified houses behind easily defended greater walls and lesser walls, then doubled on itself into a labyrinth of steps and roads. Then there was another gate and more checking, another portcullis and another vast moat and new twistings and turnings until Blackthorne, who was an acute observer with an extraordinary memory and sense of direction, was lost in the deliberate maze. And all the time numberless Grays stared down at them from escarpments and ramparts and battlements and parapets and bastions. And there were more on foot, guarding, marching, training or tending horses in open stables. Soldiers everywhere, by the thousand. All well armed and meticulously clothed.

He cursed himself for not being clever enough to get more out of Rodrigues. Apart from the information about the Taikō and the converts, which was staggering enough, Rodrigues had been as close-mouthed as a man should be—as you were, avoiding his questions.

Concentrate. Look for clues. What's special about this castle? It's the biggest. No, something's different. What?

Are the Grays hostile to the Browns? I can't tell, they're all so serious.

Blackthorne watched them carefully and focused on details. To the left was a carefully tended, multicolored garden, with little bridges and a tiny stream. The walls were now spaced closer together, the roads narrower. They were nearing the donjon. There were no townspeople inside but hundreds of servants and— *There are no cannon!* That's what's different!

You haven't seen any cannon. Not one.

Lord God in Heaven, no cannon—therefore no siege guns!

If you had modern weapons and the defenders none, could you blow the walls down, the doors down, rain fireballs on the castle, set it afire and take it?

You couldn't get across the first moat.

With siege guns you could make it difficult for the defenders but they could hold out forever—if the garrison was determined, if there were enough of them, with enough food, water, and ammunition.

How to cross the moats? By boat? Rafts with towers?

His mind was trying to devise a plan when the palanquin stopped. Hiro-matsu got down. They were in a narrow cul-de-sac. A huge iron-fortified timber gate was let into the twenty-foot wall which melted into the outworks of the fortified strongpoint above, still distant from the donjon, which from here was mostly obscured. Unlike all other gateways this was guarded by Browns, the only ones Blackthorne had seen within the castle. It was clear that they were more than a little pleased to see Hiro-matsu.

The Grays turned and left. Blackthorne noted the hostile looks they had received from the Browns.

So they're enemies!

The gate swung open and he followed the old man inside. Alone. The other samurai stayed outside.

The inner courtyard was guarded by more Browns and so was the garden beyond. They crossed the garden and entered the fort. Hiro-matsu kicked off his thongs and Blackthorne did likewise.

The corridor inside was richly carpeted with tatamis, the same rush mats, clean and kind to the feet, that were set into the floors of all but the poorest houses. Blackthorne had noticed before that they were all the same size, about six feet by three feet. Come to think of it, he told himself, I've never seen any mats shaped or cut to size. And there's never been an odd-shaped room! Haven't all the rooms been exactly square or rectangular? Of course! That means that all houses—or rooms —must be constructed to fit an exact number of mats. So they're all standard! How very odd!

They climbed winding, defendable stairs, and went along additional corridors and more stairs. There were many guards, always Browns. Shafts of sunlight from the wall embrasures cast intricate patterns. Black-thorne could see that now they were high over the three encircling main walls. The city and the harbor were a patterned quilt below.

The corridor turned a sharp corner and ended fifty paces away.

Blackthorne tasted bile in his mouth. Don't worry, he told himself, you've decided what to do. You're committed.

Massed samurai, their young officer in front of them, protected the last door—each with right hand on the sword hilt, left on the scabbard, motionless and ready, staring toward the two men who approached.

Hiro-matsu was reassured by their readiness. He had personally se-lected these guards. He hated the castle and thought again how danger-ous it had been for Toranaga to put himself into the enemy's power. Directly he had landed yesterday he had rushed to Toranaga, to tell him what had happened and to find out if anything untoward had occurred in his absence. But all was still quiet though their spies whispered about dangerous enemy buildups to the north and east, and that their main allies, the Regents, Onoshi and Kiyama, the greatest of the Christian *daimyos,* were going to defect to Ishido. He had changed the guard and the passwords and had again begged Toranaga to leave, to no avail.

Ten paces from the officer he stopped.

CHAPTER 11

Y OSHI NAGA, officer of the watch, was a mean-tempered, dangerous youth of seventeen. "Good morning, Sire. Welcome back."
"Thank you. Lord Toranaga's expecting me."
"Yes." Even if Hiro-matsu had not been expected, Naga would still
have admitted him. Toda Hiro-matsu was one of only three persons in
the world who were to be allowed into Toranaga's presence by day or by
night, without appointment.

"Search the barbarian," Naga said. He was Toranaga's fifth son by
one of his consorts, and he worshiped his father.

Blackthorne submitted quietly, realizing what they were doing. The
two samurai were very expert. Nothing would have escaped them.

Naga motioned to the rest of his men. They moved aside. He opened
the thick door himself.

Hiro-matsu entered the immense audience room. Just beyond the
doorway he knelt, put his swords on the floor in front of him, placed
his hands flat on the floor beside them and bowed his head low, waiting
in that abject position.

Naga, ever watchful, indicated to Blackthorne to do the same.

Blackthorne walked in. The room was forty paces square and ten
high, the tatami mats the best quality, four fingers thick and impeccable.
There were two doors in the far wall. Near the dais, in a niche, was a
small earthenware vase with a single spray of cherry blossom and this
filled the room with color and fragrance.

Both doors were guarded. Ten paces from the dais, circling it, were
twenty more samurai, seated cross-legged and facing outward.

Toranaga sat on a single cushion on the dais. He was repairing a
broken wing feather of a hooded falcon as delicately as any ivory carver.

Neither he nor anyone in the room had acknowledged Hiro-matsu or
paid any attention to Blackthorne as he walked in and stopped beside the
old man. But unlike Hiro-matsu, Blackthorne bowed as Rodrigues had
shown him, then, taking a deep breath, he sat cross-legged and stared at
Toranaga.

All eyes flashed to Blackthorne.

In the doorway Naga's hand was on his sword. Hiro-matsu had already grasped his, though his head was still bent.

Blackthorne felt naked but he had committed himself and now he could only wait. Rodrigues had said, 'With Japmen you've got to act like a king,' and though this wasn't acting like a king, it was more than enough.

Toranaga looked up slowly.

A bead of sweat started at Blackthorne's temple as everything Rodrigues had told him about samurai seemed to crystallize in this one man. He felt the sweat trickle down his cheek to his chin. He willed his blue eyes firm and unblinking, his face calm.

Toranaga's gaze was equally steady.

Blackthorne felt the almost overwhelming power of the man reach out to him. He forced himself to count slowly to six, and then he inclined his head and bowed slightly again and formed a small, calm smile.

Toranaga watched him briefly, his face impassive, then looked down and concentrated on his work again. Tension subsided in the room.

The falcon was a peregrine and she was in her prime. The handler, a gnarled old samurai, knelt in front of Toranaga and held her as though she were spun glass. Toranaga cut the broken quill, dipped the tiny bamboo imping needle into the glue and inserted it into the haft of the feather, then delicately slipped the new cut feather over the other end. He adjusted the angle until it was perfect and bound it with a silken thread. The tiny bells on her feet jingled, and he gentled the fear out of her.

Yoshi Toranaga, Lord of the Kwanto—the Eight Provinces—head of the clan Yoshi, Chief General of the Armies of the East, President of the Council of Regents, was a short man with a big belly and large nose. His eyebrows were thick and dark and his mustache and beard gray-flecked and sparse. Eyes dominated his face. He was fifty-eight and strong for his age. His kimono was simple, an ordinary Brown uniform, his sash belt cotton. But his swords were the best in the world.

"There, my beauty," he said with a lover's tenderness. "Now you are whole again." He caressed the bird with a feather as she sat hooded on the handler's gauntleted fist. She shivered and preened herself contentedly. "We'll fly her within the week."

The handler bowed and left.

Toranaga turned his eyes on the two men at the door. "Welcome, Iron Fist, I'm pleased to see you," he said. "So this is your famous barbarian?"

"Yes, Lord." Hiro-matsu came closer, leaving his swords at the doorway as was custom, but Toranaga insisted he bring them with him.

"I would feel uncomfortable if you didn't have them in your hands," he said.

Hiro-matsu thanked him. Even so, he sat five paces away. By custom, no one armed could safely come closer to Toranaga. In the front rank of the guards was Usagi, Hiro-matsu's favorite grandson-in-law, and he nodded to him briefly. The youth bowed deeply, honored and pleased to be noticed. Perhaps I should adopt him formally, Hiro-matsu told himself happily, warmed by the thought of his favorite granddaughter and his first great-grandson that they had presented him with last year.

"How is your back?" Toranaga asked solicitously.

"All right, thank you, Lord. But I must tell you I'm glad to be off that ship and on land again."

"I hear you've a new toy here to idle away the hours with, *neh?*"

The old man guffawed. "I can only tell you, Lord, the hours weren't idle. I haven't been so hard in years."

Toranaga laughed with him. "Then we should reward her. Your health is important to me. May I send her a token of my thanks?"

"Ah, Toranaga-sama, you're so kind." Hiro-matsu became serious. "You could reward all of us, Sire, by leaving this hornet's nest at once, and going back to your castle at Yedo where your vassals can protect you. Here we're naked. Any moment Ishido could—"

"I will. As soon as the Council of Regents meeting is concluded." Toranaga turned and beckoned the lean-faced Portuguese who was sitting patiently in his shadow. "Will you interpret for me now, my friend?"

"Certainly, Sire." The tonsured priest came forward, with practiced grace kneeled in Japanese style close to the dais, his body as spare as his face, his eyes dark and liquid, an air of serene concentration about him. He wore tabi socks and a flowing kimono that seemed, on him, to belong. A rosary and a carved golden cross hung at his belt. He greeted Hiro-matsu as an equal, then glanced pleasantly at Blackthorne.

"My name is Martin Alvito of the Society of Jesus, Captain-Pilot. Lord Toranaga has asked me to interpret for him."

"First tell him that we're enemies and that—"

"All in good time," Father Alvito interrupted smoothly. Then he added, "We can speak Portuguese, Spanish, or, of course, Latin—whichever you prefer."

Blackthorne had not seen the priest until the man came forward. The dais had hidden him, and the other samurai. But he had been expecting him, forewarned by Rodrigues, and loathed what he saw: the easy elegance, the aura of strength and natural power of the Jesuits. He had assumed the priest would be much older, considering his influential position and the way Rodrigues had talked about him. But they were practically of an age, he and the Jesuit. Perhaps the priest was a few years older.

"Portuguese," he said, grimly hoping that this might give him a slight advantage. "You're Portuguese?"

"I have that privilege."

"You're younger than I expected."

"Senhor Rodrigues is very kind. He gives me more credit than I deserve. He described you perfectly. Also your bravery."

Blackthorne saw him turn and talk fluently and affably to Toranaga for a while, and this further perturbed him. Hiro-matsu alone, of all the men in the room, listened and watched attentively. The rest stared stonily into space.

"Now, Captain-Pilot, we will begin. You will please listen to everything that Lord Toranaga says, without interruption," Father Alvito began. "Then you will answer. From now on I will be translating what you say almost simultaneously, so please answer with great care."

"What's the point? I don't trust you!"

Immediately Father Alvito was translating what he had said to Toranaga, who darkened perceptibly.

Be careful, thought Blackthorne, he's playing you like a fish! Three golden guineas to a chewed farthing he can land you whenever he wants. Whether or not he translates accurately, you've got to create the correct impression on Toranaga. This may be the only chance you'll ever have.

"You can trust me to translate exactly what you say as best I can." The priest's voice was gentle, in complete command. "This is the court of Lord Toranaga. I am the official interpreter to the Council of Regents, to General Lord Toranaga and to General Lord Ishido. Lord Toranaga has favored me with his confidence for many years. I suggest you answer truthfully because I can assure you he is a most discerning man. Also I should point out that I am not Father Sebastio, who is, perhaps, overzealous and does not, unfortunately, speak Japanese very well, or, unfortunately, have much experience in Japan. Your sudden presence took away God's grace from him and, regrettably, he allowed his personal past to overwhelm him—his parents and brothers and sisters were massacred in the most horrible way in the Netherlands by your—by forces of the Prince of Orange. I ask your indulgence for him and your compassion." He smiled benignly. "The Japanese word for 'enemy' is 'teki.' You may use it if you wish. If you point at me and use the word, Lord Toranaga will understand clearly what you mean. Yes, I am your enemy, Captain-Pilot John Blackthorne. Completely. But not your assassin. That you will do yourself."

Blackthorne saw him explain to Toranaga what he had said and heard the word "teki" used several times and he wondered if it truly meant "enemy." Of course it does, he told himself. This man's not like the other one.

"Please, for a moment, forget that I exist," Father Alvito said. "I'm merely an instrument for making your answers known to Lord Toranaga, exactly as I will put *his* questions to you." Father Alvito settled himself, turned to Toranaga, bowed politely.

Toranaga spoke curtly. The priest began translating simultaneously, a few words or so later, his voice an uncanny mirror of inflection and inner meaning.

"Why are you an enemy of Tsukku-san, my friend and interpreter, who's an enemy of no one?" Father Alvito added by way of explanation, "Tsukku-san's my nickname as Japanese cannot pronounce my name either. They have no 'l' or 'th' sounds in their language. Tsukku's a pun on the Japanese word '*tsuyaku*'—to interpret. Please answer the question."

"We're enemies because our countries are at war."

"Oh? What is your country?"

"England."

"Where's that?"

"It's an island kingdom, a thousand miles north of Portugal. Portugal's part of a peninsula in Europe."

"How long have you been at war with Portugal?"

"Ever since Portugal became a *vassal* state of Spain. That was in 1580, twenty years ago. Spain conquered Portugal. We're really at war with Spain. We've been at war with Spain for almost thirty years."

Blackthorne noticed Toranaga's surprise and his searching glance at Father Alvito, who stared serenely into the distance.

"You say Portugal's part of Spain?"

"Yes, Lord Toranaga. A vassal state. Spain conquered Portugal and now they're in effect the same country with the same king. But the Portuguese are subservient to Spain in most parts of the world and their leaders treated as unimportant in the Spanish Empire."

There was a long silence. Then Toranaga spoke directly to the Jesuit, who smiled and answered at length.

"What did he say?" Blackthorne asked sharply.

Father Alvito did not answer but translated as before, almost simultaneously, aping his inflection, continuing a virtuoso performance of interpreting.

Toranaga answered Blackthorne directly, his voice flinty and cruel. "What I said is no concern of yours. When I wish you to know something I will tell you."

"I'm sorry, Lord Toranaga, I did not mean to be rude. May I tell you that we come in peace—"

"You may not tell me anything at the moment. You will hold your tongue until I require an answer. Do you understand?"

"Yes."

Mistake number one. Watch yourself. You can't make mistakes, he told himself.

"Why are you at war with Spain? And Portugal?"

"Partially because Spain is bent on conquering the world and we English, and our allies the Netherlands, refuse to be conquered. And partially because of our religions."

"Ah! A religious war? What is your religion?"

"I'm a Christian. Our Church—"

"The Portuguese and Spanish are Christians! You said your religion was different. What is your religion?"

"It's Christian. It's difficult to explain simply and quickly, Lord Toranaga. They're both—"

"There's no need to be quick, Mr. Pilot, just accurate. I have plenty of time. I'm very patient. You're a cultured man—obviously no peasant —so you can be simple or complicated as you wish, just so long as you're clear. If you stray from the point I will bring you back. You were saying?"

"My religion is Christian. There are two main Christian religions, Protestant and Catholic. Most English are Protestant."

"You worship the same God, the Madonna and Child?"

"No, Sire. Not the way the Catholics do." What does he want to know? Blackthorne was asking himself. Is he a Catholic? Should you answer what you think he wants to know, or what you think is the truth? Is he anti-Christian? Didn't he call the Jesuit "my friend"? Is Toranaga a Catholic sympathizer, or is he going to become a Catholic?

"Do you believe the Jesus is God?"

"I believe in God," he said carefully.

"Do not evade a direct question! Do you believe the Jesus is God? Yes or no?"

Blackthorne knew that in any Catholic court in the world he would have been damned long since for heresy. And in most, if not all, Protestant courts. Even to hesitate before answering such a question was an admission of doubt. Doubt was heresy. "You can't answer questions about God with a simple 'yes' or 'no.' There have to be shades of 'yes' or 'no.' You don't know for certain about God until you're dead. Yes, I believe Jesus was God, but no, I don't know for certain until I'm dead."

"Why did you smash the priest's cross when you first arrived in Japan?"

Blackthorne had not been expecting this question. Does Toranaga know everything that's happened since I arrived? "I—I wanted to show the *daimyo* Yabu that the Jesuit, Father Sebastio—the only interpreter there—that he was my enemy, that he wasn't to be trusted, at least, in my opinion. Because I was sure he wouldn't necessarily translate accurately, not as Father Alvito is doing now. He accused us of being pirates, for instance. We're not pirates, we come in peace."

"Ah yes! Pirates. I'll come back to piracy in a moment. You say both your sects are Christian, both venerate Jesus the Christ? Isn't the essence of his teaching 'to love one another'?"

"Yes."

"Then how can you be enemies?"

"Their faith—their version of Christianity is a false interpretation of the Scriptures."

"Ah! At last we're getting somewhere. So you're at war through a difference of opinion about what is God or not God?"

"Yes."

"That's a very stupid reason to go to war."

Blackthorne said, "I agree." He looked at the priest. "I agree with all my heart."

"How many ships are in your fleet?"

"Five."

"And you were the senior pilot?"

"Yes."

"Where are the others?"

"Out to sea," Blackthorne said carefully, continuing his lie, presuming that Toranaga had been primed to ask certain questions by Alvito. "We were split up in a storm and scattered. Where exactly I don't know, Sire."

"Your ships were English?"

"No, Sire. Dutch. From Holland."

"Why is an Englishman in charge of Dutch ships?"

"That's not unusual, Sire. We're allies—Portuguese pilots sometimes lead Spanish ships and fleets. I understand Portuguese pilots con some of your ocean-going ships by law."

"There are no Dutch pilots?"

"Many, Sire. But for such a long voyage English are more experienced."

"But why you? Why did they want *you* to lead their ships?"

"Probably because my mother was Dutch and I speak the language fluently and I'm experienced. I was glad of the opportunity."

"Why?"

"This was my first opportunity to sail into these waters. No English ships were planning to come so far. This was a chance to circumnavigate."

"You yourself, Pilot, you joined the fleet because of your religion and to war against your enemies Spain and Portugal?"

"I'm a pilot, Sire, first and foremost. No one English or Dutch has been in these seas before. We're primarily a trading fleet, though we've letters of marque to attack the enemy in the New World. We came to Japan to trade."

"What are letters of marque?"

"Legal licenses issued by the Crown—or government—giving authority to war on the enemy."

"Ah, and your enemies are here. Do you plan to war on them here?"

"We did not know what to expect when we got here, Sire. We came here only to trade. Your country's almost unknown—it's legend. The Portuguese and Spanish are very closemouthed about this area."

"Answer the question: Your enemies are here. Do you plan to war on them here?"

"If they war on me. Yes."

Toranaga shifted irritably. "What you do at sea or in your own countries is your own affair. But here there is one law for all and foreigners are in our land by permission only. *Any* public mischief or quarrel is dealt with immediately by death. Our laws are clear and will be obeyed. Do you understand?"

"Yes, Sire. But we come in peace. We came here to trade. Could we discuss trade, Sire? I need to careen my ship and make repairs—we can pay for everything. Then there's the ques—"

"When I wish to discuss trade or anything else I will tell you. Meanwhile please confine yourself to answering the questions. So you joined the expedition to trade, for profit, not because of duty or loyalty? For money?"

"Yes. It's our custom, Sire. To be paid and to have a share of all plun—of all trade and all enemy goods captured."

"So you're a mercenary?"

"I was hired as senior pilot to lead the expedition. Yes." Blackthorne could feel Toranaga's hostility but he did not understand why. What did I say that was wrong? Didn't the priest say I'd assassinate myself?

"It's a normal custom with us, Toranaga-sama," he said again.

Toranaga started conversing with Hiro-matsu and they exchanged views in obvious agreement. Blackthorne thought he could see disgust in their faces. Why? Obviously it has something to do with "mercenary," he thought. What's wrong with that? Isn't everyone paid? How else do you make enough money to live on? Even if you've inherited land, you still—

"You said earlier you came here to trade peacefully," Toranaga was saying. "Why then do you carry so many guns and so much powder, muskets and shot?"

"Our Spanish and Portuguese enemies are very powerful and strong, Lord Toranaga. We have to protect ourselves and—"

"You're saying your arms are merely defensive?"

"No. We use them not only to protect ourselves but to attack our enemies. And we produce them in abundance for trade, the best quality arms in the world. Perhaps we could trade with you in these, or in the other goods we carried."

"What is a pirate?"

"An outlaw. A man who rapes, kills, or plunders for personal profit."

"Isn't that the same as mercenary? Isn't that what you are? A pirate and the leader of pirates?"

"No. The truth is my ships have letters of marque from the legal rulers of Holland authorizing us to carry the war into all seas and places dominated up to now by our enemies. And to find markets for our goods. To the Spanish—and most Portuguese—yes, we're pirates, and religious heretics, but I repeat, the truth is we're not."

Father Alvito finished translating, then began to talk quietly but firmly, direct to Toranaga.

I wish to God I could talk as directly, Blackthorne thought, cursing. Toranaga glanced at Hiro-matsu and the old man put some questions to the Jesuit, who answered lengthily. Then Toranaga returned to Blackthorne and his voice became even more severe.

"Tsukku-san says that these 'Dutchlands'—the Netherlands—were vassals of the Spanish king up to a few years ago. Is that true?"

"Yes."

"Therefore the Netherlands—your allies—are in a state of rebellion against their lawful king?"

"They're fighting against the Spaniard, yes. But—"

"Isn't that rebellion? Yes or no?"

"Yes. But there are mitigating circumstances. Serious miti—"

"There are no 'mitigating circumstances' when it comes to rebellion against a sovereign lord."

"Unless you win."

Toranaga looked intently at him. Then laughed uproariously. He said something to Hiro-matsu through his laughter and Hiro-matsu nodded.

"Yes, Mister Foreigner with the impossible name, yes. You named *the one* mitigating factor." Another chuckle, then the humor vanished as suddenly as it had begun. "Will you win?"

"*Hai.*"

Toranaga spoke again but the priest didn't translate at once. He was smiling peculiarly, his eyes fixed on Blackthorne. He sighed and said, "You're very sure?"

"Is that what he said or what you're saying?"

"Lord Toranaga said that. My—he said that."

"Yes. Tell him yes, I'm very sure. May I please explain why?"

Father Alvito talked to Toranaga, for much longer than it took to translate that simple question. Are you as calm as you make out? Blackthorne wanted to ask him. What's the key that'll unlock you? How do I destroy you?

Toranaga spoke and took a fan out of his sleeve.

Father Alvito began translating again with the same eerie unfriendliness, heavy with irony. "Yes, Pilot, you may tell me why you think you will win this war."

Blackthorne tried to remain confident, aware that the priest was dominating him. "We presently rule the seas in Europe—most of the seas in Europe," he said, correcting himself. Don't get carried away. Tell the truth. Twist it a little, just as the Jesuit's sure to be doing, but tell the truth. "We English smashed two huge Spanish and Portuguese war armadas—invasions—and they're unlikely to be able to mount any others. Our small island's a fortress and we're safe now. Our navy dominates the sea. Our ships are faster, more modern, and better armed. The Spanish haven't beaten the Dutch after more than fifty years of terror, Inquisition, and bloodshed. Our allies are safe and strong and something more—they're bleeding the Spanish Empire to death. We'll win because we own the seas and because the Spanish king, in his vain arrogance, won't let an alien people free."

"You own the seas? Our seas too? The ones around our coasts?"

"No, of course not, Toranaga-sama. I didn't mean to sound arrogant. I meant, of course, European seas, though—"

"Good, I'm glad that's clear. You were saying? Though . . . ?"

"Though on *all* the high seas, we will soon be sweeping the enemy away," Blackthorne said clearly.

"You said 'the enemy.' Perhaps we're your enemies too? What then? Will you try to sink our ships and lay waste our shores?"

"I cannot conceive of being enemy to you."

"I can, very easily. What then?"

"If you came against my land I would attack you and try to beat you," Blackthorne said.

"And if your ruler orders you to attack us here?"

"I would advise against it. Strongly. Our Queen would listen. She's—"

"You're ruled by a queen and not a king?"

"Yes, Lord Toranaga. Our Queen is wise. She wouldn't—couldn't make such an unwise order."

"And if she did? Or if your legal ruler did?"

"Then I would commend my soul to God for I would surely die. One way or another."

"Yes. You would. You and all your legions." Toranaga paused for a moment. Then: "How long did it take you to come here?"

"Almost two years. Accurately one year, eleven months, and two days. An approximate sea distance of four thousand leagues, each of three miles."

Father Alvito translated, then added a brief elaboration. Toranaga and Hiro-matsu questioned the priest, and he nodded and replied. Toranaga used his fan thoughtfully.

"I converted the time and distance, Captain-Pilot Blackthorne, into their measures," the priest said politely.

"Thank you."

Toranaga spoke directly again. "How did you get here? By what route?"

"By the Pass of Magellan. If I had my maps and rutters I could show you clearly, but they were stolen—they were removed from my ship with my letters of marque and all my papers. If you—"

Blackthorne stopped as Toranaga spoke brusquely with Hiro-matsu, who was equally perturbed.

"You claim all your papers were removed—stolen?"

"Yes."

"That's terrible, if true. We abhor theft in Nippon—Japan. The punishment for theft is death. The matter will be investigated instantly. It seems incredible that any Japanese would do such a thing, though there are foul bandits and pirates, here and there."

"Perhaps they were misplaced," Blackthorne said. "And put in safekeeping somewhere. But they are valuable, Lord Toranaga. Without my sea charts I would be like a blind man in a maze. Would you like me to explain my route?"

"Yes, but later. First tell me *why* you came all that distance."

"We came to trade, peacefully," Blackthorne repeated, holding on to his impatience. "To trade and go home again. To make you richer and us richer. And to try—"

"You richer and us richer? Which of those is most important?"

"Both partners must profit, of course, and trade must be fair. We're seeking long-term trade; we'll offer better terms than you get from the Portuguese and Spanish and give better service. Our merchants—" Blackthorne stopped at the sound of loud voices outside the room. Hiromatsu and half the guards were instantly at the doorway and the others moved into a tight knot screening the dais. The samurai on the inner doors readied as well.

Toranaga had not moved. He spoke to Father Alvito.

"You are to come over here, Captain Blackthorne, away from the door," Father Alvito said with carefully contained urgency. "If you value your life, don't move suddenly or say anything." He moved slowly to the left inner door and sat down near it.

Blackthorne bowed uneasily to Toranaga, who ignored him, and walked toward the priest cautiously, deeply conscious that from his point of view the interview was a disaster. "What's going on?" he whispered as he sat.

The nearby guards stiffened menacingly and the priest said something quickly to reassure them. "You'll be a dead man the next time you speak," he said to Blackthorne, and thought, the sooner the better. With measured slowness, he took a handkerchief from his sleeve and wiped the sweat off his hands. It had taken all his training and fortitude to remain calm and genial during the heretic's interview, which had been worse than even he and the Father-Visitor had expected.

"You'll have to be present?" the Father-Visitor had asked last night.

"Toranaga has asked me specifically."

"I think it's very dangerous for you and for all of us. Perhaps you could plead sickness. If you're there you'll have to translate what the pirate says—and from what Father Sebastio writes he's a devil on earth, as cunning as a Jew."

"It's much better I should be there, Eminence. At least I'll be able to intercept Blackthorne's less obvious lies."

"Why has he come here? Why now, when everything was becoming perfect again? Do they really have other ships in the Pacific? Is it possible they've sent a fleet against Spanish Manila? Not that I care one whit for that pestilential city or any of the Spanish colonies in the Philippines, but an enemy fleet in the Pacific! That would have terrible implications for us here in Asia. And if he could get Toranaga's ear, or Ishido's, or any of the more powerful *daimyos*—well, it would be enormously difficult, to say the least."

"Blackthorne's a fact. Fortunately we're in a position to deal with him."

"As God is my judge, if I didn't know better I'd almost believe the Spaniards—or more probably their misguided lackeys, the Franciscans and Benedictines—deliberately guided him here just to plague us."

"Perhaps they did, Eminence. There's nothing the monks won't do to destroy us. But that's only jealousy because we're succeeding where they're failing. Surely God will show them the error of their ways! Perhaps the Englishman will 'remove' himself before he does any harm. His rutters prove him to be what he is. A pirate and leader of pirates!"

"Read them to Toranaga, Martin. The parts where he describes the sacking of the defenseless settlements from Africa to Chile, and the lists of plunder and all the killings."

"Perhaps we should wait, Eminence. We can always produce the rutters. Let's hope he'll damn himself without them."

Father Alvito wiped the palms of his hands again. He could feel Blackthorne's eyes on him. God have mercy on you, he thought. For what you've said today to Toranaga, your life's not worth a counterfeit mite, and worse, your soul's beyond redemption. You're crucified, even without the evidence in your rutters. Should we send them back to Father Sebastio so he can return them to Mura? What would Toranaga do if the papers were never discovered? No, that'd be too dangerous for Mura.

The door at the far end shivered open.

"Lord Ishido wishes to see you, Sire," Naga announced. "He's—he's here in the corridor and he wishes to see you. At once, he says."

"All of you, go back to your places," Toranaga said to his men. He was instantly obeyed. But all samurai sat facing the door, Hiro-matsu at their head, swords eased in their scabbards. "Naga-san, tell Lord Ishido he is always welcome. Ask him to come in."

The tall man strode into the room. Ten of his samurai—Grays—followed, but they remained at the doorway and, at his signal, sat cross-legged.

Toranaga bowed with precise formality and the bow was returned with equal exactitude.

Father Alvito blessed his luck that he was present. The impending clash between the two rival leaders would completely affect the course of the Empire and the future of Mother Church in Japan, so any clue or direct information that might help the Jesuits to decide where to throw their influence would be of immeasurable importance. Ishido was Zen Buddhist and fanatically anti-Christian, Toranaga was Zen Buddhist and openly sympathetic. But most Christian *daimyos* supported Ishido, fearing—with justification, Father Alvito believed—the ascendence of Toranaga. The Christian *daimyos* felt that if Toranaga eliminated Ishido's influence from the Council of Regents, Toranaga would usurp all power for himself. And once he had power, they believed he would implement the Taikō's Expulsion Edicts and stamp out the True Faith. If, however, Toranaga was eliminated, the succession, a weak succession, would be assured and the Mother Church would prosper.

As the allegiance of the Christian *daimyos* wavered, so it was with all the other *daimyos* in the land, and the balance of power between the two leaders fluctuated constantly, so no one knew for certain which side was, in reality, the most powerful. Even he, Father Alvito, the most informed European in the Empire, could not say for certain which side even the Christian *daimyos* would actually support when the clash became open, or which faction would prevail.

He watched Toranaga walk off the dais, through the encircling safety of his men.

"Welcome, Lord Ishido. Please sit there." Toranaga gestured at the single cushion on the dais. "I'd like you to be comfortable."

"Thank you, no, Lord Toranaga." Ishido Kazunari was lean and swarthy and very tough, a year younger than Toranaga. They were ancient enemies. Eighty thousand samurai in and around Osaka Castle did his bidding, for he was Commander of the garrison—and therefore Commander of the Heir's Bodyguard—Chief General of the Armies of the West, Conqueror of Korea, member of the Council of Regents, and formally Inspector General of all the late Taikō's armies, which were legally all the armies of all *daimyos* throughout the realm.

"Thank you, no," he repeated. "I'd be embarrassed to be comfortable while you were not, *neh?* One day I will take your cushion, but not today."

A current of anger went through the Browns at Ishido's implied threat, but Toranaga replied amiably, "You came at a most opportune moment. I was just finishing interviewing the new barbarian. Tsukku-san, please tell him to stand up."

The priest did as he was bidden. He felt Ishido's hostility from across the room. Apart from being anti-Christian, Ishido had always been vigorous in his condemnation of all Europeans and wanted the Empire totally closed to them.

Ishido looked at Blackthorne with pronounced distaste. "I heard he was ugly but I didn't realize how ugly. Rumor has it that he's a pirate. Is he?"

"Can you doubt it? And he's also a liar."

"Then before you crucify him, please let me have him for half a day.

The Heir might be amused to see him with his head on first." Ishido laughed roughly. "Or perhaps he should be taught to dance like a bear, then you could exhibit him throughout the Empire: 'The Freak from the East.'"

Though it was true that Blackthorne had, uniquely, come out of the eastern seas—unlike the Portuguese, who always came from the south and hence were called Southern Barbarians—Ishido was blatantly implying that Toranaga, who dominated the eastern provinces, was the true freak.

But Toranaga merely smiled as though he did not understand. "You're a man of vast humor, Lord Ishido," he said. "But I agree the sooner the barbarian's removed the better. He's long-winded, arrogant, loud-mouthed, an oddity, yes, but one of little value, and with no manners whatsoever. Naga-san, send some men and put him with the common criminals. Tsukku-san, tell him to follow them."

"Captain-Pilot, you are to follow those men."

"Where am I going?"

Father Alvito hesitated. He was glad that he had won, but his opponent was brave and had an immortal soul which could yet be saved. "You are to be detained," he said.

"For how long?"

"I don't know, my son. Until Lord Toranaga decides."

CHAPTER 12

As Toranaga watched the barbarian leave the room, he took his mind regretfully off the startling interview and came to grips with the more immediate problem of Ishido.

Toranaga had decided not to dismiss the priest, knowing it would further infuriate Ishido, even though he was equally certain the continued presence of the priest might be dangerous. The less foreigners know, the better. The less anyone knows the better, he thought. Will Tsukku-san's influence on the Christian *daimyos* be for me or against me? Until today I would have trusted him implicitly. But there were some strange moments with the barbarian that I don't yet understand.

Ishido deliberately did not follow the usual courtesies but came instantly to the point. "Again I must ask, what is your answer to the Council of Regents?"

"Again I repeat: As President of the Council of Regents I do not believe any answer is necessary. I've made a few minor family relationships that are unimportant. No answer is required."

"You betroth your son, Naga-san, to the daughter of Lord Masamune—marry one of your granddaughters to Lord Zataki's son and heir —another granddaughter to Lord Kiyama's son. All the marriages are to feudal lords or their close relations and therefore not minor and absolutely contrary to our Master's orders."

"Our late Master, the Taikō, has been dead a year. Unfortunately. Yes. I regret my brother-in-law's death and would have preferred him alive and still guiding the destiny of the Empire." Toranaga added pleasantly, turning a knife in a constant wound, "If my brother-in-law were alive there's no doubt he would approve these family connections. His instructions applied to marriages that threatened the succession of *his* house. I don't threaten his house or my nephew Yaemon, the Heir. I'm content as Lord of the Kwanto. I seek no more territory. I'm at peace with my neighbors and wish his peace to continue. By the Lord Buddha, I'll not be the first to break the peace."

For six centuries the realm had been seared by constant civil war. Thirty-five years ago, a minor *daimyo* called Goroda had taken possession of Kyoto, abetted mainly by Toranaga. Over the next two decades this warrior had miraculously subdued half of Japan, made a mountain of skulls and declared himself Dictator—still not yet powerful enough to petition the reigning Emperor to grant him the title Shōgun though he was vaguely descended from a branch of the Fujimotos. Then, sixteen years ago, Goroda was assassinated by one of his generals and his power fell into the hands of his chief vassal and most brilliant general, the peasant Nakamura.

In four short years, General Nakamura, helped by Toranaga, Ishido, and others, obliterated Goroda's descendants and brought the whole of Japan under his absolute, sole control, the first time in history that one man had subjugated all the realm. In triumph, he went to Kyoto to bow before Go-Nijo, the Son of Heaven. There, because he was born peasant, Nakamura had had to accept the lesser title of Kwampaku, Chief Adviser, which later he renounced in favor of his son, taking for himself the title Taikō. But every *daimyo* bowed before him, even Toranaga. Incredibly, there had been complete peace for twelve years. Last year the Taikō had died.

"By the Lord Buddha," Toranaga said again. "I'll not be the first to break the peace."

"But you will go to war?"

"A wise man prepares for treachery, *neh?* There are evil men in every province. Some are in high places. We both know the limitless extent of treachery in the hearts of men." Toranaga stiffened. "Where the Taikō left a legacy of unity, now we are split into my East and your West. The Council of Regents is divided. The *daimyos* are at odds. A Council cannot rule a maggot-infested hamlet, let alone an Empire. The sooner the Taikō's son is of age, the better. The sooner there's another Kwampaku the better."

"Or perhaps Shōgun?" Ishido said insinuatingly.

"Kwampaku or Shōgun or Taikō, the power is the same," Toranaga said. "Of what real value is a title? The *power* is the only important thing. Goroda never became Shōgun. Nakamura was more than content as Kwampaku and later Taikō. He *ruled* and that is the important thing. What does it matter that my brother-in-law was once a peasant? What does it matter that my family is ancient? What does it matter that you're low born? You're a general, a liege lord, even one of the Council of Regents."

It matters very much, Ishido thought. You know it. I know it. Every *daimyo* knows it. Even the Taikō knew it. "Yaemon is seven. In seven years he becomes Kwampaku. Until that time—"

"In *eight* years, General Ishido. That's our historic law. When my nephew is fifteen he becomes adult and inherits. Until that time we five Regents rule in his name. That's what our late Master willed."

"Yes. And he also ordered that no hostages were to be taken by Regents against one another. Lady Ochiba, the mother of the Heir, is hostage in your castle at Yedo, against your safety here, and that also violates his will. You formally agreed to obey his covenants as did all the Regents. You even signed the document in your own blood."

Toranaga sighed. "The Lady Ochiba is visiting Yedo where her only sister is in labor. Her sister is married to my son and heir. My son's place is in Yedo while I am here. What's more natural than for a sister to visit a sister at such a time? Isn't she honored? Perhaps I'll have a first grandson, *neh?*"

"The mother of the Heir is the most important lady in the Empire. She should not be in—" Ishido was going to say "enemy hands" but he thought better of it—"in an unusual city." He paused, then added clearly, "The Council would like you to order her home today."

Toranaga avoided the trap. "I repeat, the Lady Ochiba's no hostage and therefore is not under my orders and never was."

"Then let me put it differently. The Council requests her presence in Osaka instantly."

"Who requests this?"

"I do. Lord Sugiyama. Lord Onoshi and Lord Kiyama. Further, we're all agreed we wait here until she's back in Osaka. Here are their signatures."

Toranaga was livid. Thus far he had manipulated the Council so that voting was always split two to three. He had never been able to win a four-to-one against Ishido, but neither had Ishido against him. Four to one meant isolation and disaster. Why had Onoshi defected? And Kiyama? Both implacable enemies even before they had converted to the foreign religion. And what hold had Ishido now over them?

Ishido knew that he had shattered his enemy. But one move remained to make victory complete. So he implemented the plan that he and Onoshi had agreed upon. "We Regents are all agreed that the time has come to finish with those who are planning to usurp my Master's power and kill the Heir. Traitors will be condemned. They will be exhibited in the streets as common criminals, with all their generations, and then they will be executed like common criminals, with all their generations. Fujimoto, Takashima, low born, high born—no matter who. Even Minowara!"

A gasp of rage broke from every Toranaga samurai, for such sacrilege against the semi-regal families was unthinkable; then the young samurai, Usagi, Hiro-matsu's grandson-in-law, was on his feet, flushed with anger. He ripped out his killing sword and leapt at Ishido, the naked blade readied for the two-handed slash.

Ishido was prepared for the death blow and made no move to defend himself. This was what he had planned for, hoped for, and his men had been ordered not to interfere until he was dead. If he, Ishido, were killed here, now, by a Toranaga samurai, the whole Osaka garrison could fall on Toranaga legitimately and slay him, irrespective of the hostage. Then the Lady Ochiba would be eliminated in retaliation by Toranaga's sons and the remaining Regents would be forced to move jointly against the Yoshi clan, who, now isolated, would be stamped out. Only then would the Heir's succession be guaranteed and he, Ishido, would have done his duty to the Taikō.

But the blow did not come. At the last moment Usagi came to his senses and tremulously sheathed the sword.

"Your pardon, Lord Toranaga," he said, kneeling abjectly. "I could not bear the shame of—of having you hear such—such insults. I ask permission—I apologize and—I ask permission to commit seppuku immediately for I cannot live with this shame."

Though Toranaga had remained still, he had been ready to intercept the blow and he knew Hiro-matsu was ready and that others would have been ready also, and that probably Ishido would only have been wounded. He understood, too, why Ishido had been so insulting and inflammatory. I will repay you with an enormity of interest, Ishido, he promised silently.

Toranaga gave his attention to the kneeling youth. "How dare you imply that anything Lord Ishido said was meant in any way as an insult to *me*. Of course he would never be so impolite. How dare you listen to conversations that do not concern you. No, you will not be allowed to commit seppuku. That's an honor. You have no honor and no self-discipline. You will be crucified like a common criminal today. Your swords will be broken and buried in the *eta* village. Your son will be buried in the *eta* village. Your head will be put on a spike for all the population to jeer at with a sign on it: 'This man was born samurai by mistake. His name has ceased to be!' "

With a supreme effort Usagi controlled his breathing but the sweat dripped and the shame of it tortured him. He bowed to Toranaga, accepting his fate with outward calm.

Hiro-matsu walked forward and tore both swords from his grandson-in-law's belt.

"Lord Toranaga," he said gravely, "with your permission I will personally see that your orders are carried out."

Toranaga nodded.

The youth bowed a last time then began to get up, but Hiro-matsu pushed him back on the floor. "Samurai walk," he said. "So do men. But you're neither. You will crawl to your death."

Silently Usagi obeyed.

And all in the room were warmed by the strength of the youth's self-discipline now, and the measure of his courage. He will be reborn samurai, they told themselves contentedly.

CHAPTER 13

THAT night Toranaga could not sleep. This was rare for him because normally he could defer the most pressing problem until the next day, knowing that if he was alive the next day he would solve it to the best of his ability. He had long since discovered that peaceful sleep could provide the answer to most puzzles, and if not, what did it really matter? Wasn't life just a dewdrop within a dewdrop?

But tonight, there were too many perplexing questions to ponder.

What will I do about Ishido?

Why has Onoshi defected to the enemy?

How will I deal with the Council?

Have the Christian priests meddled again?

Where will the next assassination attempt come from?

When should Yabu be dealt with?

And what must I do about the barbarian?

Was he telling the truth?

Curious how the barbarian came out of the eastern seas just at this time. Is that an omen? Is it his *karma* to be the spark that will light the powder keg?

Karma was an Indian word adopted by Japanese, part of Buddhist philosophy that referred to a person's fate in this life, his fate immutably fixed because of deeds done in a previous life, good deeds giving a better position in this life's strata, bad deeds the reverse. Just as the deeds of this life would completely affect the next rebirth. A person was ever being reborn into this world of tears until, after enduring and suffering and learning through many lifetimes, he became perfect at long last, going to *nirvana*, the Place of Perfect Peace, never having to suffer rebirth again.

Strange that Buddha or some other god or perhaps just *karma* brought the Anjin-san to Yabu's fief. Strange that he landed at the exact village where Mura, the secret head of the Izu spy system, had been settled so many years ago under the very nose of the Taikō and Yabu's pox-diseased father. Strange that Tsukku-san was here in Osaka to interpret and not in Nagasaki where he'd normally be. That also the chief priest of the Christians is here in Osaka, and also the Captain-General of the Portuguese. Strange that the pilot, Rodrigues, was also available to take Hiro-matsu to Anjiro in time to capture the barbarian alive and take possession of the guns. Then there's Kasigi Omi, son of the man who will give me Yabu's head if I but crook my little finger.

How beautiful life is and how sad! How fleeting, with no past and no future, only a limitless *now*.

Toranaga sighed. One thing is certain: the barbarian will never leave. Neither alive nor dead. He is part of the realm forever.

His ears heard almost imperceptible approaching footsteps and his sword was ready. Each night he changed his sleeping room, his guards, and the password haphazardly, against the assassins that were always waiting. The footsteps stopped outside the shoji. Then he heard Hiro-matsu's voice and the beginning of the password: " 'If the Truth is already clear, what is the use of meditation?' "

" 'And if the Truth is hidden?' " Toranaga said.

" 'It's already clear,' " Hiro-matsu answered correctly. The quotation was from the ancient Tantric Buddhist teacher, Saraha.

"Come in."

Only when Toranaga saw that it was, in truth, his counselor, did his sword relax. "Sit down."

"I heard you weren't sleeping. I thought you might need something."

"No. Thank you." Toranaga observed the deepened lines around the old man's eyes. "I'm glad you're here, old friend," he said.

"You're sure you're all right?"

"Oh, yes."

"Then I'll leave you. Sorry to disturb you, Lord."

"No, please, come in, I'm glad you're here. Sit down."

The old man sat down beside the door, his back straight. "I've doubled the guards."

"Good."

After a while Hiro-matsu said, "About that madman, everything was done as you ordered. Everything."

"Thank you."

"His wife—as soon as she heard the sentence, my granddaughter asked my permission to kill herself, to accompany her husband and her son into the Great Void. I refused and ordered her to wait, pending your approval." Hiro-matsu was bleeding inside. How terrible life is!

"You did correctly."

"I formally ask permission to end my life. What he did put you in mortal danger, but it was my fault. I should have detected his flaw. I failed you."

"You may not commit seppuku."

"Please. I formally ask permission."

"No. You're needed alive."

"I will obey you. But please accept my apologies."

"Your apologies are accepted."

After a time, Toranaga said, "What about the barbarian?"

"Many things, Sire. One: If you hadn't been waiting for the barbarian today you would have been hawking since first light, and Ishido would never have enmeshed you in such a disgusting meeting. You have no choice now but to declare war on him—if you can get out of this castle and back to Yedo."

"Second?"

"And third and forty-third and a hundred and forty-third? I'm no-where near as clever as you, Lord Toranaga, but even I could see that everything we've been led to believe by the Southern Barbarians is not true." Hiro-matsu was glad to talk. It helped ease the hurt. "But if there are *two* Christian religions which hate each other, and if the Portuguese are part of the bigger Spanish nation and if this new barbarian's country —whatever it was called—wars on both and beats them, and if this same country's an island nation like ours, and the great 'if' of all, if he's telling the truth and if the priest's saying accurately what the barbarian was say-ing. . . . Well, you can put all these 'ifs' together and make sense out of them, and a plan. I can't, so sorry. I only know what I saw at Anjiro, and aboard the ship. That the Anjiro-san is very strong in his head— weak in his body presently, though that would be because of the long voyage—and dominating at sea. I don't understand anything about him. How could he be all of these things yet allow a man to piss on his back? Why did he save Yabu's life after what the man did to him, and also the life of his self-admitted enemy, the Portuguese Rodrigu? My head spins from so many questions as though I'm sodden with saké." Hiro-matsu paused. He was very weary. "But I think we should keep him on land and all like him, if others follow, and kill them all very quickly."

"What about Yabu?"

"Order him to commit seppuku tonight."

"Why?"

"He's got no manners. You foretold what he'd do when I arrived at Anjiro. He was going to steal your property. And he's a liar. Don't bother to see him tomorrow as you've arranged. Instead, let me take him your order now. You'll have to kill him sooner or later. Better now when he's accessible, with none of his own vassals surrounding him. I advise no delay."

There was a soft knock on the inner door. "Tora-chan?"

Toranaga smiled as he always did at that very special voice, with that special diminutive. "Yes, Kiri-san?"

"I've taken the liberty, Lord, of bringing cha for you and your guest. May I please come in?"

"Yes."

Both men returned her bow. Kiri closed the door and busied herself with the pouring. She was fifty-three and substantial, Matron of Toranaga's ladies-in-waiting, Kiritsubo-noh-Toshiko, nicknamed Kiri, the oldest of the ladies of his court. Her hair was gray-flecked, her waist thick, but her face sparkled with an eternal joy. "You shouldn't be awake, no, not at this time of night, Tora-chan! It will be dawn soon and I suppose then you'll be out in the hills with your hawks, *neh?* You need sleep!"

"Yes, Kiri-chan!" Toranaga patted her vast rump affectionately.

"Please don't Kiri-chan me!" Kiri laughed. "I'm an old woman and I need lots of respect. Your other ladies give me enough trouble as it is. Kiritsubo-Toshiko-san, if you please, my Lord Yoshi Toranaga-noh-Chikitada!"

"There, you see, Hiro-matsu. After twenty years she still tries to dominate me."

"So sorry, it's more than thirty years, Tora-sama," she said proudly. "And you were as manageable then as you are now!"

When Toranaga was in his twenties he had been a hostage, too, then of the despotic Ikawa Tadazaki, Lord of Suruga and Totomi, father of the present Ikawa Jikkyu, who was Yabu's enemy. The samurai responsible for Toranaga's good conduct had just taken Kiritsubo as his second wife. She was seventeen then. Together this samurai and Kiri, his wife, had treated Toranaga honorably, given him wise counsel, and then, when Toranaga had rebelled against Tadazuki and joined Goroda, had followed him with many warriors and had fought bravely at his side. Later, in the fighting for the capital, Kiri's husband had been killed. Toranaga had asked her if she would become one of his consorts and she had accepted gladly. In those days she was not fat. But she was equally protective and equally wise. That was her nineteenth year, his twenty-fourth, and she had been a focus of his household ever since. Kiri was very shrewd and very capable. For years now, she had run his household and kept it free of trouble.

As free of trouble as any household with women could ever be, Toranaga thought.

"You're getting fat," he said, not minding that she was fat.

"Lord Toranaga! In front of Lord Toda! Oh, so sorry, I shall have to commit seppuku—or at least, I'll have to shave my head and become a nun, and I thought I was so young and slender!" She burst out laughing. "Actually I agree I have a fat rump but what can I do? I just like to eat and that's Buddha's problem and my *karma, neh?*" She offered the cha. "There. Now I'll be off. Would you like me to send the Lady Sazuko?"

"No, my thoughtful Kiri-san, no, thank you. We'll talk for a little, then I'll sleep."

"Good night, Tora-sama. Sweet dreamlessness." She bowed to him and to Hiro-matsu and then she was gone.

They sipped their tea appreciatively.

Toranaga said, "I'm always sorry we never had a son, Kiri-san and I. Once she conceived but she miscarried. That was when we were at the battle of Nagakudé."

"Ah, that one."

"Yes."

This was just after the Dictator Goroda had been assassinated when General Nakamura—the Taikō-to-be—was trying to consolidate all power into his own hands. At that time the issue was in doubt, as Toranaga supported one of Goroda's sons, the legal heir. Nakamura came against Toranaga near the little village of Nagakudé and his force was mauled and routed and he lost that battle. Toranaga retreated cleverly, pursued by a new army, now commanded for Nakamura by Hiro-matsu. But Toranaga avoided the trap and escaped to his home provinces, his whole army intact, ready to battle again. Fifty thousand men died at Nagakudé, very few of them Toranaga's. In his wisdom, the Taikō-to-be called off the civil war against Toranaga, though he would have won. Nagakudé was the only battle the Taikō had ever lost and Toranaga the only general who had ever beaten him.

"I'm glad we never joined battle, Sire," Hiro-matsu said.

"Yes."

"You would have won."

"No. The Taikō was the greatest general and the wisest, cleverest man that has ever been."

Hiro-matsu smiled. "Yes. Except you."

"No. You're wrong. That's why I became *his* vassal."

"I'm sorry he's dead."

"Yes."

"And Goroda—he was a fine man, *neh?* So many good men dead." Hiro-matsu unconsciously turned and twisted the battered scabbard. "You'll have to move against Ishido. That will force every *daimyo* to choose sides, once and for all. We'll win the war eventually. Then you can disband the Council and become Shōgun."

"I don't seek that honor," Toranaga said sharply. "How many times do I have to say it?"

"Your pardon, Sire. I know. But I feel it would be best for Japan."

"That's treason."

"Against whom, Lord? Against the Taikō? He's dead. Against his last will and testament? That's a piece of paper. Against the boy Yaemon? Yaemon's the son of a peasant who usurped the power and heritage of a general whose heirs he stamped out. We were Goroda's allies, then the Taikō's vassals. Yes. But they're both very dead."

"Would you advise that if you were one of the Regents?"

"No. But then I'm not one of the Regents, and I'm very glad. I'm your vassal only. I chose sides a year ago. I did this freely."

"Why?" Toranaga had never asked him before.

"Because you're a man, because you're Minowara and because you'll do the wise thing. What you said to Ishido was right: we're not a people to be ruled by committee. We need a leader. Whom should I have chosen to serve of the five Regents? Lord Onoshi? Yes, he's a very wise man, and a good general. But he's Christian and a cripple and his flesh is so rotten with leprosy that he stinks from fifty paces. Lord Sugiyama? He's the richest *daimyo* in the land, his family's as ancient as yours. But he's a gutless turncoat and we both know him from eternity. Lord Kiyama? Wise, brave, a great general, and an old comrade. But he's Christian too, and I think we have enough gods of our own in this Land of the Gods not to be so arrogant as to worship only one. Ishido? I've detested that treacherous peasant's offal as long as I've known him and the only reason I never killed him was because he was the Taikō's dog." His leathery face cracked into a smile. "So you see, Yoshi Toranaga-noh-Minowara, you gave me no choice."

"And if I go against your advice? If I manipulate the Council of Regents, even Ishido, and put Yaemon into power?"

"Whatever you do is wise. But all the Regents would like you dead. That's the truth. I advocate immediate war. *Immediate.* Before they isolate you. Or more probably murder you."

Toranaga thought about his enemies. They were powerful and abundant.

It would take him all of three weeks to get back to Yedo, traveling the Tokaido Road, the main trunk road that followed the coast between Yedo and Osaka. To go by ship was more dangerous, and perhaps more time consuming, except by galley which could travel against wind and tide.

Toranaga's mind ranged again over the plan he had decided upon. He could find no flaw in it.

"I heard secretly yesterday that Ishido's mother is visiting her grandson in Nagoya," he said and Hiro-matsu was at once attentive. Nagoya was a huge city-state that was, as yet, not committed to either side. "The lady should be 'invited' by the Abbot to visit the Johji Temple. To see the cherry blossoms."

"Immediately," Hiro-matsu said. "By carrier pigeon." The Johji Temple was famous for three things: its avenue of cherry trees, the militancy of its Zen Buddhist monks, and its open, undying fidelity to Toranaga who had, years ago, paid for the building of the temple and maintained its upkeep ever since. "The blossoms will be past their prime but she will be there tomorrow. I don't doubt the venerable lady will want to stay a few days, it's so calming. Her grandson should go too, *neh?*"

"No—just her. That would make the Abbot's 'invitation' too obvious. Next: send a secret cipher to my son, Sudara: 'I leave Osaka the moment the Council concludes this session—in four days.' Send it by runner and confirm it by carrier pigeon tomorrow."

Hiro-matsu's disapproval was apparent. "Then can I order up ten thousand men at once? To Osaka?"

"No. The men here are sufficient. Thank you, old friend. I think I'll sleep now."

Hiro-matsu got up and stretched his shoulders. Then at the doorway, "I may give Fujiko, my granddaughter, permission to kill herself?"

"No."

"But Fujiko's samurai, Lord, and you know how mothers are about their sons. The child was her first."

"Fujiko can have many children. How old is she? Eighteen—barely nineteen? I will find her another husband."

Hiro-matsu shook his head, "She will not accept one. I know her too well. It's her innermost wish to end her life. Please?"

"Tell your granddaughter I do not approve of useless death. Permission is refused."

At length Hiro-matsu bowed, and began to leave.

"How long would the barbarian live in that prison?" Toranaga asked.

Hiro-matsu did not turn back. "It depends how cruel a fighter he is."

"Thank you. Good night, Hiro-matsu." When he was sure that he was alone, he said quietly, "Kiri-san?"

The inner door opened, she entered and knelt.

"Send an immediate message to Sudara: 'All is well.' Send it by racing pigeons. Release three of them at the same time at dawn. At noon do the same again."

"Yes, Lord." She went away.

One will get through, he thought. At least four will fall to arrows, spies, or hawks. But unless Ishido's broken our code, the message will still mean nothing to him.

The code was very private. Four people knew it. His eldest son, Noboru; his second son and heir, Sudara; Kiri; and himself. The message deciphered meant: "Disregard all other messages. Activate Plan Five." By prearrangement, Plan Five contained orders to gather all Yoshi clan leaders and their most trusted inner counselors immediately at his capital, Yedo, and to mobilize for war. The code word that signaled war was "Crimson Sky." His own assassination, or capture, made Crimson Sky inexorable and launched the war—an immediate fanatic assault upon Kyoto led by Sudara, his heir, with *all* the legions, to gain possession of that city and the puppet Emperor. This would be coupled with secret, meticulously planned insurrections in fifty provinces which had been prepared over the years against such eventuality. All targets, passes, cities, castles, bridges, had long since been selected. There were enough arms and men and resolve to carry it through.

It's a good plan, Toranaga thought. But it will fail if I don't lead it. Sudara will fail. Not through want of trying or courage or intelligence, or because of treachery. Merely because Sudara hasn't yet enough knowledge or experience and cannot carry enough of the uncommitted *daimyos* with him. And also because Osaka Castle and the heir, Yaemon, stand inviolate in the path, the rallying point for all the enmity and jealousy that I've earned in fifty-two years of war.

Toranaga's war had begun when he was six and had been ordered as hostage into the enemy camp, then reprieved, then captured by other enemies and pawned again, to be repawned until he was twelve. At twelve, he had led his first patrol and won his first battle.

So many battles. None lost. But so many enemies. And now they're gathering together.

Sudara will fail. You're the only one who could win with Crimson Sky, perhaps. The Taikō could do it, absolutely. But it would be better not to have to implement Crimson Sky.

CHAPTER 14

For Blackthorne it was a hellish dawn. He was locked in a death battle with a fellow convict. The prize was a cup of gruel. Both men were naked. Whenever a convict was put into this vast, single-storied, wooden cell block, his clothes were taken away. A clothed man occupied more space and clothes could hide weapons.

The murky and suffocating room was fifty paces long and ten wide and packed with naked, sweating Japanese. Scarcely any light filtered through the boards and beams that made up the walls and low ceiling.

Blackthorne could barely stand erect. His skin was blotched and scratched from the man's broken nails and the wood burns from the walls. Finally, he butted his head into the man's face, grabbed his throat and hammered the man's head against the beams until he was senseless. Then he threw the body aside and charged through the sweating mass to the place he had claimed in the corner, and he readied himself for another attack.

At dawn it had been feeding time and the guards began passing the cups of gruel and water through the small opening. This was the first food and water that had been given them since he was put inside at dusk the previous day. The lining up for food and water had been unusually calm. Without discipline no one would eat. Then this apelike man—unshaven, filthy, lice-ridden—had chopped him over the kidneys and taken his ration while the others waited to see what would happen. But Blackthorne had been in too many seafaring brawls to be beaten with one treacherous blow, so he feigned helplessness, then kicked out viciously and the fight had been joined. Now, in the corner, Blackthorne saw to his amazement that one of the men was offering the cup of gruel and the water that he had presumed lost. He took it and thanked the man.

The corners were the choicest areas. A beam ran lengthwise, along the earthen floor, partitioning the room into two sections. In each section were three rows of men, two rows facing each other, their backs to the wall or beam, the other row between them. Only the weak and the sick took the center row. When the stronger men in the outer rows wanted to stretch their legs they had to do so over those in the middle.

Blackthorne saw two corpses, swollen and flyblown, in one of the middle rows. But the feeble and dying men nearby seemed to ignore them.

He could not see far in the heating gloom. Sun was baking the wood already. There were latrine buckets but the stench was terrible because the sick had befouled themselves and the places in which they hunched.

From time to time guards opened the iron door and names were called out. The men bowed to their comrades and left, but others were soon brought in and the space occupied again. All the prisoners seemed to have accepted their lot and tried, as best they could, to live unselfishly in peace with their immediate neighbors.

One man against the wall began to vomit. He was quickly shoved into the middle row and collapsed, half suffocated, under the weight of legs.

Blackthorne had to close his eyes and fight to control his terror and claustrophobia. Bastard Toranaga! I pray I get the opportunity of putting you inside here one day.

Bastard guards! Last night when they had ordered him to strip he had fought them with a bitter hopelessness, knowing he was beaten, fighting only because he refused to surrender passively. And then he had been forced through the door.

There were four such cell blocks. They were on the edge of the city, in a paved compound within high stone walls. Outside the walls was a roped-off area of beaten earth beside the river. Five crosses were erected there. Naked men and one woman had been bound straddled to the crosspieces by their wrists and ankles, and while Blackthorne had walked on the perimeter following his samurai guards, he saw executioners with long lances thrust the lances crisscross into the victims' chests while the crowd jeered. Then the five were cut down and five more put up and samurai came forward and hacked the corpses into pieces with their long swords, laughing all the while.

Bloody-gutterfestering-bastards!

Unnoticed, the man Blackthorne had fought was coming to his senses. He lay in the middle row. Blood had congealed on one side of his face and his nose was smashed. Suddenly he leapt at Blackthorne, oblivious of the men in his way.

Blackthorne saw him coming at the last moment, frantically parried the onslaught and knocked him in a heap. The prisoners that the man fell on cursed him and one of them, heavyset and built like a bulldog, chopped him viciously on the neck with the side of his hand. There was a dry snap and the man's head sagged.

The bulldog man lifted the half-shaven head by its scraggy, lice-infected topknot and let it fall. He looked up at Blackthorne, said something gutturally, smiled with bare, toothless gums, and shrugged.

"Thanks," Blackthorne said, struggling for breath, thankful that his assailant had not had Mura's skill at unarmed combat. "My namu Anjin-san," he said, pointing at himself. "You?"

"*Ah, so desu!* Anjin-san!" Bulldog pointed at himself and sucked in his breath. "*Minikui.*"

"Minikui-san?"

"*Hai,*" and he added a spate of Japanese.

Blackthorne shrugged tiredly. "*Wakarimasen.*" I don't understand.

"*Ah, so desu!*" Bulldog chattered briefly with his neighbors. Then he shrugged again and Blackthorne shrugged and together they lifted the dead man and put him with the other corpses. When they came back to the corner no one had taken their places.

Most of the inmates were asleep or fitfully trying to sleep.

Blackthorne felt filthy and horrible and near death. Don't worry, he told himself, you've a long way to go before you die. . . . No, I can't live long in this hell hole. There're too many men. Oh, God, let me out! Why is the room swimming up and down, and is that Rodrigues floating up from the depths with moving pincers for eyes? I can't breathe, I can't breathe. I've got to get out of here, please, please, don't put more wood in the fire and what are you doing here, Croocq lad, I thought they let you go. I thought you were back in the village but now we're here in the village and how did I get here—it's so cool and there's that girl, so pretty, down by the docks but why are they dragging her away to the shore, the naked samurai, Omi there laughing? Why down across the sand, blood marks in the sand, all naked, me naked, hags and villagers and children, and there's the cauldron and we're in the cauldron and no, no more wood no more wood, I'm drowning in liquid filth, Oh God Oh God oh God I'm dying dying dying "*In nomine Patris et Filii et Spiritus Sancti.*" That's the Last Sacrament and you're Catholic we're all Catholic and you'll burn or drown in piss and burn with fire the fire the fire. . . .

He dragged himself out of the nightmare, his ears exploding with the peaceful, earth-shattering finality of the Last Sacrament. For a moment he did not know if he was awake or asleep because his disbelieving ears heard the Latin benediction again and his incredulous eyes were seeing a wrinkled old scarecrow of a European stooped over the middle row, fifteen paces away. The toothless old man had long filthy hair and a matted beard and broken nails and wore a foul, threadbare smock. He raised a hand like a vulture's claw and held up the wooden cross over the half-hidden body. A shaft of sun caught it momentarily. Then he closed the dead man's eyes, and mumbled a prayer and glanced up. He saw Blackthorne staring at him.

"Mother of God, art thou real?" the man croaked in coarse, peasant Spanish, crossing himself.

"Yes," Blackthorne said in Spanish. "Who are you?"

The old man groped his way over, mumbling to himself. The other inmates let him pass or step on them or over them without saying a word. He stared down at Blackthorne through rheumy eyes, his face warted. "Oh, Blessed Virgin, the señor is real. Who art thou? I'm . . . I'm Friar . . . Friar Domingo . . . Domingo . . . Domingo of the Sacred . . . the Sacred Order of St. Francis . . . the Order . . ." and then for a while his words became a jumble of Japanese and Latin and Spanish. His head twitched and he wiped away the ever present spittle that dribbled to his chin. "The señor is real?"

"Yes, I'm real." Blackthorne eased himself up.

The priest muttered another Hail Mary, the tears coursing his cheeks. He kissed the cross repeatedly and would have got down on his knees if there had been space. Bulldog shook his neighbor awake. Both squatted and made just enough room for the priest to sit.

"By the Blessed St. Francis, my prayers have been answered. Thou, thou, thou, I thought that I was seeing another apparition, señor, a ghost. Yes, an evil spirit. I've seen so many—so many—how long is the señor here? It's hard for a body to see in the gloom and my eyes, they're not good. . . . How long?"

"Yesterday. And you?"

"I don't know, señor. A long time. I'm put here in September—it was in the year of our Lord fifteen hundred ninety-eight."

"It's May now. Sixteen hundred."

"Sixteen hundred?"

A moaning cry distracted the monk. He got up and picked his way over the bodies like a spider, encouraging a man here, touching another there, his Japanese fluent. He could not find the dying man so he droned the last rites to that part of the cell and blessed everyone and no one minded.

"Come with me, my son."

Without waiting, the monk hobbled down the cage, through the mass of men, into the gloom. Blackthorne hesitated, not wanting to leave his place. Then he got up and followed. After ten paces he looked back. His place had vanished. It seemed impossible that he had ever been there at all.

He continued down the length of the hut. In the far corner was, incredibly, an open space. Just enough room for a small man to lie down in. It contained a few pots and bowls and an ancient straw mat.

Father Domingo stepped through the men into the space and beckoned him. The surrounding Japanese watched silently, letting Blackthorne pass.

"They are my flock, señor. They are all my sons in the Blessed Lord Jesus. I've converted so many here—this one's John, and here's Mark and Methuselah. . . ." The priest stopped for breath. "I'm so tired. Tired. I . . . must, I must . . ." His words trailed off and he slept.

At dusk more food arrived. When Blackthorne began to get up, one of the nearby Japanese motioned him to stay and brought him a well-filled bowl. Another man gently patted the priest awake, offering the food.

"*Iyé,*" the old man said, shaking his head, a smile on his face, and pushed the bowl back into the man's hands.

"*Iyé, Farddah-sama.*"

The priest allowed himself to be persuaded and ate a little, then got up, his joints creaking, and handed his bowl to one of those in the middle row. This man touched the priest's hand to his forehead and he was blessed.

"I'm so pleased to see another of my own kind," the priest said, sitting beside Blackthorne again, his peasant voice thick and sibilant. He pointed weakly to the other end of the cell block. "One of my flock said the señor used the word 'pilot,' 'anjin'? The señor is a pilot?"

"Yes."

"There are others of the señor's crew here?"

"No, I'm alone. Why are you here?"

"If the señor is alone—the señor came from Manila?"

"No. I've never been to Asia before," Blackthorne said carefully, his Spanish excellent. "This was my first voyage as pilot. I was . . . I was outward bound. Why are you here?"

"Jesuits put me here, my son. Jesuits and their filthy lies. The señor was outward bound? Thou art not Spanish, no—nor Portuguese . . ." The monk peered at him suspiciously and Blackthorne was surrounded by his reeking breath. "Was the ship Portuguese? Tell the truth, before God!"

"No, Father. It was not Portuguese. Before God!"

"Oh, Blessed Virgin, thank you! Please forgive me, señor. I was afraid —I'm old and stupid and diseased. Thy ship was Spanish out of where? I'm so glad—where is the señor from originally? Spanish Flanders? Or the Duchy of Brandenburg perhaps? Some part of our dominions in Germania? Oh, it's so good to talk my blessed mother tongue again! Was the señor shipwrecked like us? Then foully thrown into this jail, falsely accused by those devil Jesuits? May God curse them and show them the error of their treachery!" His eyes glittered fiercely. "The señor said he has never been to Asia before?"

"No."

"If the señor has never been to Asia before, then he will be like a child in the wilderness. Yes, there's so much to tell! Does the señor know that

Jesuits are merely traders, gun runners, and usurers? That they control all the silk trade here, all trade with China? That the annual Black Ship is worth a million in gold? That they've forced His Holiness, the Pope, to grant them total power over Asia—them and their dogs, the Portuguese? That all other religious are forbidden here? That Jesuits deal in gold, buying and selling for profit—for themselves and the heathen—against the direct orders of His Holiness, Pope Clement, of King Philip, and against the laws of this land? That they secretly smuggled guns into Japan for Christian kings here, inciting them to rebellion? That they meddle in politics and pimp for the kings, lie and cheat and bear false witness against us! That their Father Superior himself sent a secret message to our Spanish Viceroy in Luzon asking him for conquistadores to conquer the land—they begged for a Spanish invasion to cover more Portuguese mistakes. All our troubles can be put at their threshold, señor. It's the Jesuits who have lied and cheated and spread poison against Spain and our beloved King Philip! Their lies put me here and caused twenty-six Holy Fathers to be martyred! They think that just because I was a peasant once, I don't understand . . . but I can read and write, señor, I can read and write! I was one of his Excellency's secretaries, the Viceroy. They think we Franciscans don't understand . . ."

At this point he broke into another ranting jumble of Spanish and Latin.

Blackthorne's spirit had been revived, his curiosity agog with what the priest had said. What guns? What gold? What trade? What Black Ship? A million? What invasion? What Christian kings?

Aren't you cheating the poor sick man? he asked himself. He thinks you're friend, not enemy.

I haven't lied to him.

But haven't you implied you're friend?

I answered him directly.

But you volunteered nothing?

No.

Is that fair?

That's the first rule of survival in enemy waters: volunteer nothing.

The monk's tantrum grew apace. The nearby Japanese shifted uneasily. One of them got up and shook the priest gently and spoke to him. Father Domingo gradually came out of his fit, his eyes cleared. He looked at Blackthorne with recognition, replied to the Japanese, and calmed the rest.

"So sorry, señor," he said breathlessly. "They—they thought I was angry against—against the señor. God forgive my foolish rage! It was just—*que va,* Jesuits come from hell, along with heretics and heathens. I can tell you much about them." The monk wiped the spittle off his chin and tried to calm himself. He pressed his chest to ease the pain there. "The señor was saying? Thy ship, it was cast ashore?"

"Yes. In a way. We came aground," Blackthorne replied. He eased his legs carefully. The men who were watching and listening gave him more room. One got up and motioned him to stretch out. "Thanks," he said at once. "Oh, how do you say 'thank you,' Father?"

" 'Domo.' Sometimes you say 'arigato.' A woman has to be very polite, señor. She says 'arigato goziemashita.' "

"Thank you. What's his name?" Blackthorne indicated the man who had got up.

"That's Gonzalez."

"But what's his Japanese name?"

"Ah yes! He's Akabo. But that just means 'porter,' señor. They don't have names. Only samurai have names."

"What?"

"Only samurai have names, first names and surnames. It's their law, señor. Everyone else has to make do with what they are—porter, fisherman, cook, executioner, farmer, and so on. Sons and daughters are mostly just First Daughter, Second Daughter, First Son, and so on. Sometimes they'd call a man 'fisherman who lives near the elm tree' or 'fisherman with bad eyes.' " The monk shrugged and stifled a yawn. "Ordinary Japanese aren't allowed names. Whores give themselves names like Carp or Moon or Petal or Eel or Star. It's strange, señor, but it's their law. We give them Christian names, real names, when we baptize them, bringing them salvation and the word of God . . ." His words trailed off and he slept.

"Domo, Akabo-san," Blackthorne said to the porter.

The man smiled shyly and bowed and sucked in his breath.

Later the monk awakened and said a brief prayer and scratched. "Only yesterday, the señor said? He came here only yesterday? What occurred with the señor?"

"When we landed there was a Jesuit there," Blackthorne said. "But you, Father. You were saying they accused you? What happened to you and your ship?"

"Our ship? Did the señor ask about our ship? Was the señor coming from Manila like us? Or—oh, how foolish of me! I remember now, the señor was outward bound from home and never in Asia before. By the Blessed Body of Christ, it's so good to talk to a civilized man again, in my blessed mother's tongue! Que va, it's been so long. My head aches, aches, señor. Our ship? We were going home at long last. Home from Manila to Acapulco, in the land of Cortes, in Mexico, thence overland to Vera Cruz. And thence another ship and across the Atlantic, and at long, long last, to *home*. My village is outside Madrid, señor, in the mountains. It is called Santa Veronica. Forty years I've been away, señor. In the New World, in Mexico and in the Philippines. Always with our glorious conquistadores, may the Virgin watch over them! I was in Luzon when we destroyed the heathen native king, Lumalon, and conquered Luzon, and so brought the word of God to the Philippines. Many of our Japan converts fought with us even then, señor. Such fighters! That was in 1575. Mother Church is well planted there, my son, and never a filthy Jesuit or Portuguese to be seen. I came to the Japans for almost two years, then had to leave for Manila again when the Jesuits betrayed us."

The monk stopped and closed his eyes, drifting off. Later he came back again, and, as old people will sometimes do, he continued as though he had never slept. "My ship was the great galleon *San Felipe*. We carried a cargo of spices, gold and silver, and specie to the value of a million and a half silver pesos. One of the great storms took us and cast us onto the shores of Shikoku. Our ship broke her back on the sand bar—on the third day—by that time we had landed our bullion and most of our cargo. Then word came that everything was confiscated, confiscated by the Taikō himself, that we were pirates and . . ." He stopped at the sudden silence.

The iron door of the cell cage had swung open.

Guards began to call names from the list. Bulldog, the man who had befriended Blackthorne, was one of those called. He walked out and did not look back. One of the men in the circle also was chosen. Akabo. Akabo knelt to the monk, who blessed him and made the sign of the cross over him and quickly gave him the Last Sacrament. The man kissed the cross and walked away.

The door closed again.

"They're going to execute him?" Blackthorne asked.

"Yes, his Calvary is outside the door. May the Holy Madonna take his soul swiftly and give him his everlasting reward."

"What did that man do?"

"He broke the law—their law, señor. The Japanese are a simple people. And very severe. They truly have only one punishment—death. By the cross, by strangulation, or by decapitation. For the crime of arson, it is death by burning. They have almost no other punishment—banishment sometimes, cutting the hair from women sometimes. But"—the old man sighed—"but most always it is death."

"You forgot imprisonment."

The monk's nails picked absently at the scabs on his arm. "It's not one of their punishments, my son. To them, prison is just a temporary place to keep the man until they decide his sentence. Only the guilty come here. For just a little while."

"That's nonsense. What about you? You've been here a year, almost two years."

"One day they will come for me, like all the others. This is but a resting place between the hell of earth and the glory of Everlasting Life."

"I don't believe you."

"Have no fear, my son. It is the will of God. I am here and can hear the señor's confession and give him absolution and make him perfect—the glory of Everlasting Life is barely a hundred steps and moments away from that door. Would the señor like me to hear his confession now?"

"No—no, thank you. Not now." Blackthorne looked at the iron door. "Has anyone ever tried to break out of here?"

"Why should they do that? There is nowhere to run—nowhere to hide. The authorities are very strict. Anyone helping an escaped convict or even a man who commits a crime—" He pointed vaguely at the door of the hut. "Gonzalez—Akabo—the man who has—has left us. He's a kaga-man. He told me—"

"What's a kaga-man?"

"Oh, those are the porters, señor, the men that carry the palanquins, or the smaller two-man kaga that's like a hammock swung on a pole. He told us his partner stole a silken scarf from a customer, poor fellow, and because he himself did not report the theft, his life is forfeit also. The señor may believe me, to try to escape or even to help someone to escape, the man would lose his life and all his family. They are very severe, señor."

"So everyone goes to execution like sheep then?"

"There is no other choice. It is the will of God."

Don't get angry, or panic, Blackthorne warned himself. Be patient. You can think of a way. Not everything the priest says is true. He's deranged. Who wouldn't be after so much time?

"These prisons are new to them, señor," the monk was saying. "The Taikō instituted prisons here a few years ago, so they say. Before him there were none. In previous days when a man was caught, he confessed his crime and he was executed."

"And if he didn't confess?"

"Everyone confesses—sooner is better, señor. It is the same in our world, if you are caught."

The monk slept a little, scratching in his sleep and muttering. When he woke up, Blackthorne said, "Please tell me, Father, how the cursed Jesuits put a man of God in this pest hole."

"There is not much to tell, and everything. After the Taikō's men came and took all our bullion and goods, our Captain-General insisted on going to the capital to protest. There was no cause for the confiscation. Were we not servants of His Most Imperial Catholic Majesty, King Philip of Spain, ruler of the greatest and richest empire in the world? The most powerful monarch in the world? Were we not friends? Was not the Taikō asking Spanish Manila to trade direct with Japan, to break the filthy monopoly of the Portuguese? It was all a mistake, the confiscation. It had to be.

"I went with our Captain-General because I could speak a little Japanese—not much in those days. Señor, the *San Felipe* had floundered and come ashore in October of 1597. The Jesuits—one was of the name Father Martin Alvito—they dared to offer to mediate for us, there in Kyoto, the capital. The impertinence! Our Franciscan Father Superior, Friar Braganza, he was in the capital, and he was an ambassador—a real ambassador from Spain to the court of the Taikō! The Blessed Friar Braganza, he had been there in the capital, in Kyoto, for five years, señor. The Taikō himself, personally, had asked our Viceroy in Manila to send Franciscan monks and an ambassador to Japan. So the Blessed Friar Braganza had come. And we, señor, we of the *San Felipe,* we knew that he was to be trusted, not like the Jesuits.

"After many, many days of waiting, we had one interview with the Taikō—he was a tiny, ugly little man, señor—and we asked for our goods back and another ship, or passage on another ship, which our Captain-General offered to pay for handsomely. The interview went well, we thought, and the Taikō dismissed us. We went to our monastery in Kyoto and waited and then, over the next months while we waited for his decision, we continued to bring the word of God to the heathen. We held our services openly, not like thieves in the night as the Jesuits do." Friar Domingo's voice was edged with contempt. "We wore our habits and vestments—we didn't go disguised, like native priests, as they do. We brought the Word to the people, the halt and sick and poor, not like the Jesuits, who consort with princes only. Our congregations increased. We had a hospital for lepers, our own church, and our flock prospered, señor. Greatly. We were about to convert many of their kings and then one day we were betrayed.

"One day in January, we Franciscans, we were all brought before the magistrate and accused under the Taikō's personal seal, señor, accused as violators of their law, as disturbers of their peace, and sentenced to death by crucifixion. There were forty-three of us. Our churches throughout the land were to be destroyed, all our congregations to be torn apart—Franciscan—not Jesuit, señor. Just us, señor. We had been falsely accused. The Jesuits had poured poison in the Taikō's ear that we were conquistadores, that we wanted to invade these shores, when it was Jesuits who begged his Excellency, our Viceroy, to send an army from Manila. I saw the letter myself! From their Father Superior! They're devils who pretend to serve the Church and Christ, but they serve only themselves. They lust for power, power at any cost. They hide behind a net of poverty and piousness, but underneath, they feed like kings and amass fortunes. *Que va,* señor, the truth is that they were jealous of our congregations, jealous of our church, jealous of our truth and way of life. The *daimyo* of Hizen, Dom Francisco—his Japanese name is Harima Tadao but he has been baptized Dom Francisco—he interceded for us. He is just like a king, all *daimyos* are like kings, and he's a Franciscan and he interceded for us, but to no avail.

"In the end, twenty-six were martyred. Six Spaniards, seventeen of our Japanese neophytes, and three others. The Blessed Braganza was one, and there were three boys among the neophytes. Oh, señor, the faithful were there in their thousands that day. Fifty, a hundred thousand people watched the Blessed Martyrdom at Nagasaki, so I was told. It was a bitter cold February day and a bitter year. That was the year of the earthquakes and typhoons and flood and storm and fire, when the Hand of God lay heavy on the Great Murderer and even smashed down his great castle, Fushimi, when He shuddered the earth. It was terrifying but marvelous to behold, the Finger of God, punishing the heathen and the sinners.

"So they were martyred, señor, six good Spaniards. Our flock and our church were laid waste and the hospital closed up." The old man's face drained. "I—I was one of those chosen for martyrdom, but—but it was not to be my honor. They set us marching from Kyoto and when we came to Osaka they put some of us in one of our missions here and the rest—the rest had one of their ears cut off, then they were paraded like common criminals in the streets. Then the Blessed Brethren were set walking westward. For a month. Their blessed journey ended at the hill called Nishizaki, overlooking the great harbor of Nagasaki. I begged the samurai to let me go with them but, señor, he ordered me back to the mission here in Osaka. For no reason. And then, months later, we were put in this cell. There were three of us—I think it was three, but I was the only Spaniard. The others were neophytes, our lay brothers, Japaners. A few days later the guards called out their names. But they never called out mine. Perhaps it is the will of God, señor, or perhaps those filthy Jesuits leave me alive just to torture me—they who took away my chance at martyrdom among my own. It's hard, señor, to be patient. So very hard . . ."

The old monk closed his eyes, prayed, and cried himself to sleep.

Much as he wished it, Blackthorne could not sleep though night had come. His flesh crawled from the lice bites. His head swarmed with terror.

He knew, with terrible clarity, there was no way to break out. He was overwhelmed with futility and sensed he was on the brink of death. In the darkest part of the night terror swamped him, and, for the first time in his life, he gave up and wept.

"Yes, my son?" the monk murmured. "What is it?"

"Nothing, nothing," Blackthorne said, his heart thundering. "Go back to sleep."

"There's no need to fear. We are all in God's hands," the monk said and slept again.

The great terror left Blackthorne. In its place was a terror that could be lived with. I'll get out of here somehow, he told himself, trying to believe the lie.

At dawn came food and water. Blackthorne was stronger now. Stupid to let go like that, he cautioned himself. Stupid and weak and danger-ous. Don't do that again or you'll break and go mad and surely die. They'll put you in the third row and you'll die. Be careful and be patient and guard yourself.

"How are you today, señor?"

"Fine, thank you, Father. And you?"

"Quite well, thank you."

"How do I say that in Japanese?"

"*Domo, genki desu.*"

"*Domo, genki desu.* You were saying yesterday, Father, about the Portuguese Black Ships—what are they like? Have you seen one?"

"Oh, yes, señor. They're the greatest ships in the world, almost two thousand tons. As many as two hundred men and boys are necessary to sail one, señor, and with crew and passengers her complement would be almost a thousand souls. I'm told these carracks sail well before the wind but lumber when the wind's abeam."

"How many guns do they carry?"

"Sometimes twenty or thirty on three decks."

Father Domingo was glad to answer questions and talk and teach, and Blackthorne was equally glad to listen and learn. The monk's ram-bling knowledge was priceless and far reaching.

"No, señor," he was saying now. "*Domo* is thank you and *dozo* is please. Water is *mizu*. Always remember that Japaners put a great price on manners and courtesy. Once when I was in Nagasaki— Oh, if I only had ink and a quill and paper! Ah, I know—here, trace the words in the dirt, that will help you to remember them . . ."

"*Domo*," Blackthorne said. Then, after memorizing a few more words, he asked, "How long've Portuguese been here?"

"Oh, the land was discovered in 1542, señor, the year I was born. There were three men, da Mota, Peixoto, and I can't remember the other name. They were all Portuguese traders, trading the China coasts in a China junk from a port in Siam. Has the señor been to Siam?"

"No."

"Ah, there is much to see in Asia. These three men were trading but they were caught in a great storm, a typhoon, and blown off their course to land safely at Tanegashima at Kyushu. That was the first time a European set foot on Japan's soil, and at once trade began. A few years later, Francis Xavier, one of the founding members of the Jesuits, arrived here. That was in 1549 . . . a bad year for Japan, señor. One of our Brethren should have been first, then we would have inherited this realm, not the Portuguese. Francis Xavier died three years later in China, alone and forsaken. . . . Did I tell the señor there's a Jesuit already at the court of the Emperor of China, in a place called Peking? . . . Oh, you should see Manila, señor, and the Philippines! We have four cathedrals and almost three thousand conquistadores and nearly six thousand Japaner soldiers spread through the islands and three hundred Brethren. . . ."

Blackthorne's mind filled with facts and Japanese words and phrases. He asked about life in Japan and *daimyos* and samurai and trade and Nagasaki and war and peace and Jesuits and Franciscans and Portuguese in Asia and about Spanish Manila, and always more about the Black Ship that plied annually from Macao. For three days and three nights Blackthorne sat with Father Domingo and questioned and listened and learned and slept in nightmare, to awaken and ask more questions and gain more knowledge.

Then, on the fourth day, they called out his name.

"Anjin-san!"

CHAPTER 15

IN the utter silence, Blackthorne got to his feet.

"Thy confession, my son, say it quickly."

"I—I don't think—I—" Blackthorne realized through his dulled mind that he was speaking English, so he pressed his lips together and began to walk away. The monk scrambled up, presuming his words to be Dutch or German, and grabbed his wrist and hobbled with him.

"Quickly, señor. I will give the absolution. Be quick, for thine immortal soul. Say it quickly, just that the señor confesses before God all things past and present—"

They were nearing the iron gate now, the monk holding on to Blackthorne with surprising strength.

"Say it now! The Blessed Virgin will watch over you!"

Blackthorne tore his arm away, and said hoarsely in Spanish, "Go with God, Father."

The door slammed behind him.

The day was incredibly cool and sweet, the clouds meandering before a fine southeasterly wind.

He inhaled deep draughts of the clean, glorious air and blood surged through his veins. The joy of life possessed him.

Several naked prisoners were in the courtyard along with an official, jailers with spears, *eta,* and a group of samurai. The official was dressed in a somber kimono and an overmantle with starched, winglike shoulders and he wore a small dark hat. This man stood in front of the first prisoner and read from a delicate scroll and, as he finished, each man began to plod after his party of jailers toward the great doors of the courtyard. Blackthorne was last. Unlike the others he was given a loincloth, cotton kimono, and thonged clogs for his feet. And his guards were samurai.

He had decided to run for it the moment he had passed the gate, but as he approached the threshold, the samurai surrounded him more closely and locked him in. They reached the gateway together. A large crowd looked on, clean and spruce, with crimson and yellow and golden sunshades. One man was already roped to his cross and the cross was lifted into the sky. And beside each cross two *eta* waited, their long lances sparkling in the sun.

Blackthorne's pace slowed. The samurai jostled closer, hurrying him. He thought numbly that it would be the better to die now, quickly, so he steadied his hand to lunge for the nearest sword. But he never took the opportunity because the samurai turned away from the arena and walked toward the perimeter, heading for the streets that led to the city and toward the castle.

Blackthorne waited, scarcely breathing, wanting to be sure. They walked through the crowd, who backed away and bowed, and then they were in a street and now there was no mistake.

Blackthorne felt reborn.

When he could speak, he said, "Where are we going?" not caring that the words would not be understood or that they were in English. Blackthorne was quite light-headed. His step hardly touched the ground, the thongs of his clogs were not uncomfortable, the untoward touch of the kimono was not unpleasing. Actually, it feels quite good, he thought. A little draughty perhaps, but on a fine day like this—just the sort of thing to wear on the quarterdeck!

"By God, it's wonderful to speak English again," he said to the samurai. "Christ Jesus, I thought I was a dead man. That's my eighth life gone. Do you know that, old friends? Now I've only one to go. Well, never mind! Pilots have ten lives, at least, that's what Alban Caradoc used to say." The samurai seemed to be growing irritated by his incomprehensible talk.

Get hold of yourself, he told himself. Don't make them touchier than they are.

He noticed now that the samurai were all Grays. Ishido's men. He had asked Father Alvito the name of the man who opposed Toranaga. Alvito had said "Ishido." That was just before he had been ordered to stand up and had been taken away. Are all Grays Ishido's men? As all Browns are Toranaga's?

"Where are we going? There?" He pointed at the castle which brooded above the town. "There, hai?"

"Hai." The leader nodded a cannonball head, his beard grizzled.

What does Ishido want with me? Blackthorne asked himself.

The leader turned into another street, always going away from the harbor. Then he saw her—a small Portuguese brig, her blue and white flag waving in the breeze. Ten cannon on the main deck, with bow and stern twenty-pounders. Erasmus could take her easily, Blackthorne told himself. What about my crew? What are they doing back there at the village? By the Blood of Christ, I'd like to see them. I was so glad to leave them that day and go back to my own house where Onna—Haku—was, the house of . . . what was his name? Ah yes, Mura-san. And what about that girl, the one in my floor-bed, and the other one, the angel beauty who talked that day to Omi-san? The one in the dream who was in the cauldron too.

But why remember that nonsense? It weakens the mind. 'You've got to be very strong in the head to live with the sea,' Alban Caradoc had said. Poor Alban.

Alban Caradoc had always appeared so huge and godlike, all seeing, all knowing, for so many years. But he had died in terror. It had been on the seventh day of the Armada. Blackthorne was commanding a hundred-ton gaff-rigged ketch out of Portsmouth, running arms and powder and shot and food to Drake's war galleons off Dover as they harried and tore into the enemy fleet which was beating up the channel toward Dunkirk where the Spanish legions lay, waiting to transship to conquer England.

The great Spanish fleet had been ripped by storms and by the more vicious, more sleek, more maneuverable warships that Drake and Howard had built.

Blackthorne had been in a swirling attack near Admiral Howard's flagship *Renown* when the wind had changed, freshened to gale force, the squalls monstrous, and he had had to decide whether to try to beat to windward to escape the broadside that would burst from the great galleon *Santa Cruz* just ahead, or to run before the wind alone, through the enemy squadron, the rest of Howard's ships having already turned about, hacking more northerly.

"Go north to windward!" Alban Caradoc had shouted. He had shipped as second in command. Blackthorne was Captain-Pilot and responsible, and this his first command. Alban Caradoc had insisted on coming to the fight, even though he had no right to be aboard except that he was an Englishman and all Englishmen had the right to be aboard in this darkest time in history.

"Belay there!" Blackthorne had ordered and had swung the tiller southward, heading into the maw of the enemy fleet, knowing the other way would leave them doomed by the guns of the galleon that now towered above them.

So they had gone southerly, racing before the wind, through the galleons. The three-deck cannonade of the *Santa Cruz* passed safely overhead and he got off two broadsides into her, flea bites to so huge a vessel, and then they were scudding through the center of the enemy. The galleons on either side did not wish to fire at this lone ship, for their broadsides might have damaged each other, so the guns stayed silent. Then his ship was through and escaping when a three-deck cannonade from the *Madre de Dios* straddled them. Both their masts careened away like arrows, men enmeshed in the rigging. Half the starboard main deck had vanished, the dead and the dying everywhere.

He had seen Alban Caradoc lying against a shattered gun carriage, so incredibly tiny without legs. He cradled the old seaman whose eyes were almost starting out of his head, his screams hideous. "Oh Christ I don't want to die don't want to die, help help me, help me help me, oh Jesus Christ it's the pain, *helllp!*" Blackthorne knew there was only one thing he could do for Alban Caradoc. He picked up a belaying pin and smashed down with all his force.

Then, weeks later, he had to tell Felicity that her father was dead. He told her no more than that Alban Caradoc had been killed instantly. He did not tell her he had blood on his hands that would never come off. . . .

Blackthorne and the samurai were walking through a wide winding street now. There were no shops, only houses side by side, each within its own land and high fences, the houses and fences and the road itself all staggeringly clean.

This cleanliness was incredible to Blackthorne because in London and the cities and towns of England—and Europe—offal and night soil and urine were cast into the streets, to be scavenged or allowed to pile up until pedestrians and carts and horses could not pass. Only then would most townships perhaps cleanse themselves. The scavengers of London were great herds of swine that were driven through the main thoroughfares nightly. Mostly the rats and the packs of wild dogs and cats and fires did the cleansing of London. And the flies.

But Osaka was so different. How do they do it? he asked himself. No pot holes, no piles of horse dung, no wheel ruts, no filth or refuse of any sort. Just hard-packed earth, swept and clean. Walls of wood and houses of wood, sparkling and neat. And where are the packs of beggars and cripples that fester every township in Christendom? And the gangs of footpads and wild youths that would inevitably be skulking in the shadows?

The people they passed bowed politely, some knelt. Kaga-men hurried along with palanquins or the one-passenger kagas. Parties of samurai—Grays, never Browns—walked the streets carelessly.

They were walking a shop-lined street when his legs gave out. He toppled heavily and landed on his hands and knees.

The samurai helped him up but, for the moment, his strength had gone and he could walk no further.

"*Gomen nasai, dozo ga matsu,*"—I'm sorry, please wait—he said, his legs cramped. He rubbed his knotted calf muscles and blessed Friar Domingo for the priceless things that the man had taught him.

The samurai leader looked down at him and spoke at length.

"*Gomen nasai, nihon go ga hanase-masen,*"—I'm sorry, I don't speak Japanese, Blackthorne replied, slowly but clearly. "*Dozo, ga matsu.*"

"*Ah! So desu,* Anjin-san. *Wakarimasu,*" the man said, understanding him. He gave a short sharp command and one of the samurai hurried away. After a while Blackthorne got up, tried to hobble along, but the leader of the samurai said "*Iyé*" and motioned him to wait.

Soon the samurai came back with four semi-naked kaga-men and their kaga. Samurai showed Blackthorne how to recline in it and to hold on to the strap that hung from the central pole.

The party set off again. Soon Blackthorne recovered his strength and preferred walking again, but he knew he was still weak. I've got to get some rest, he thought. I've no reserve. I must get a bath and some food. Real food.

Now they were climbing wide steps that joined one street to another and entered a new residential section that skirted a substantial wood with tall trees and paths through it. Blackthorne found it vastly enjoyable to be out of the streets, the well-tended sward soft underfoot, the track wandering through the trees.

When they were deep in the wood, another party of thirty-odd Grays approached from around a curve ahead. As they came alongside, they stopped, and after the usual ceremonial of their captains greeting each other, all their eyes turned on Blackthorne. There was a volley of questions and answers and then, as these men began to reassemble to leave, their leader calmly pulled out his sword and impaled the leader of Blackthorne's samurai. Simultaneously the new group fell on the rest of Blackthorne's samurai. The ambush was so sudden and so well planned that all ten Grays were dead almost at the same instant. Not one had even had time to draw his sword.

The kaga-men were on their knees, horrified, their foreheads pressed into the grass. Blackthorne stood beside them. The captain-samurai, a heavyset man with a large paunch, sent sentries to either end of the track. Others were collecting the swords of the dead men. During all of this, the men paid Blackthorne no attention at all, until he began to back away. Immediately there was a hissing command from the captain which clearly meant to stay where he was.

At another command all these new Grays stripped off their uniform kimonos. Underneath they wore a motley collection of rags and ancient kimonos. All pulled on masks that were already tied around their necks. One man collected the gray uniforms and vanished with them into the woods.

They must be bandits, Blackthorne thought. Why else the masks? What do they want with me?

The bandits chattered quietly among themselves, watching him as they cleaned their swords on the clothes of the dead samurai.

"Anjin-san? *Hai?*" The captain's eyes above the cloth mask were round and jet and piercing.

"*Hai,*" Blackthorne replied, his skin crawling.

The man pointed at the ground, clearly telling him not to move. "*Wakarimasu ka?*"

"*Hai.*"

They looked him up and down. Then one of their outpost sentries— no longer gray-uniformed but masked, like all of them—came out of the bushes for an instant, a hundred paces away. He waved and vanished again.

Immediately the men surrounded Blackthorne, preparing to leave. The bandit captain put his eyes on the kaga-men, who shivered like dogs of a cruel master and put their heads deeper into the grass.

Then the bandit leader barked an order. The four slowly raised their heads with disbelief. Again the same command and they bowed and groveled and backed away; then as one, they took to their heels and vanished into the undergrowth.

The bandit smiled contemptuously and motioned Blackthorne to begin walking back toward the city.

He went with them, helplessly. There was no running away.

They were almost to the edge of the wood when they stopped. There were noises ahead and another party of thirty samurai rounded the bend. Browns and Grays, the Browns the vanguard, their leader in a palanquin, a few pack horses following. They stopped immediately. Both groups moved into skirmish positions, eyeing each other hostilely, seventy paces between them. The bandit leader walked into the space between, his movements jerky, and shouted angrily at the other samurai, pointing at Blackthorne and then further back to where the ambush had taken place. He tore out his sword, held it threateningly on high, obviously telling the other party to get out of the way.

All the swords of his men sang out of their scabbards. At his order one of the bandits stationed himself behind Blackthorne, his sword raised and readied, and again the leader harangued the opposition.

Nothing happened for a moment, then Blackthorne saw the man in the palanquin get down and he instantly recognized him. It was Kasigi Yabu. Yabu shouted back at the bandit leader but this man shook his sword furiously, ordering them out of the way. His tirade stopped with finality. Then Yabu gave a curt order, and charged with a screaming battle cry, limping slightly, sword high, his men rushing with him, Grays not far behind.

Blackthorne dropped to escape the sword blow that would have cut him in half, but the blow was ill-timed and the bandit leader turned and fled into the undergrowth, his men following.

The Browns and the Grays were quickly alongside Blackthorne, who scrambled to his feet. Some of the samurai charged after the bandits into the bushes, others ran up the track, and the rest scattered protectively. Yabu stopped at the edge of the brush, shouted orders imperiously, then came back slowly, his limp more pronounced.

"*So desu,* Anjin-san," he said, panting from his exertion.

"*So desu,* Kasigi Yabu-san," Blackthorne replied, using the same phrase which meant something like "well" or "oh really" or "is that the truth." He pointed in the direction that the bandits had run away. "*Domo.*" He bowed politely, equal to equal, and said another blessing for Friar Domingo. "*Gomen nasai, nihon go ga hanase-masen*"—I'm sorry, I can't speak Japanese.

"*Hai,*" Yabu said, not a little impressed, and added something that Blackthorne did not understand.

"*Tsuyaku ga imasu ka?*" Blackthorne asked. Do you have an interpreter?

"*Iyé,* Anjin-san. *Gomen nasai.*"

Blackthorne felt a little easier. Now he could communicate directly. His vocabulary was sparse, but it was a beginning.

Eeeee, I wish I did have an interpreter, Yabu was thinking fervently. By the Lord Buddha!

I'd like to know what happened when you met Toranaga, Anjin-san, what questions he asked and what you answered, what you told him about the village and guns and cargo and ship and galley and about Rodrigu. I'd like to know everything that was said, and how it was said, and where you've been and why you're here. Then I'd have an idea of what was in Toranaga's mind, the way he's thinking. Then I could plan what I'm going to tell him today. As it is now, I'm helpless.

Why did Toranaga see *you* immediately when we arrived, and not *me*? Why no word or orders from him since we docked until today, other than the obligatory, polite greeting and "I look forward with pleasure to seeing you shortly"? Why has he sent for me today? Why has our meeting been postponed twice? Was it because of something you said? Or Hiro-matsu? Or is it just a normal delay caused by all his other worries?

Oh, yes, Toranaga, you've got almost insurmountable problems. Ishido's influence is spreading like fire. And do you know about Lord

Onoshi's treachery yet? Do you know that Ishido has offered me Ikawa Jikkyu's head and province if I secretly join him now?

Why did you pick today to send for me? Which good *kami* put me here to save the Anjin-san's life, only to taunt me because I can't talk directly to him, or even through someone else, to find the key to your secret lock? Why did you put him into prison for execution? Why did Ishido want him out of prison? Why did the bandits try to capture him for ransom? Ransom from whom? And why is the Anjin-san still alive? That bandit should have easily cut him in half.

Yabu noticed the deeply etched lines that had not been in Blackthorne's face the first time he had seen him. He looks starved, thought Yabu. He's like a wild dog. But not one of the pack, the leader of the pack, *neh?*

Oh yes, Pilot, I'd give a thousand koku for a trustworthy interpreter right now.

I'm going to be your master. You're going to build my ships and train my men. I have to manipulate Toranaga somehow. If I can't, it doesn't matter. In my next life I'll be better prepared.

"Good dog!" Yabu said aloud to Blackthorne and smiled slightly. "All you need is a firm hand, a few bones, and a few whippings. First I'll deliver you to Lord Toranaga—after you've been bathed. You stink, Lord Pilot!"

Blackthorne did not understand the words, but he sensed friendliness in them and saw Yabu's smile. He smiled back. *"Wakarimasen"*—I don't understand.

"Hai, Anjin-san."

The *daimyo* turned away and glanced after the bandits. He cupped his hands around his mouth and shouted. Instantly all the Browns returned to him. The chief samurai of the Grays was standing in the center of the track and he too called off the chase. None of the bandits were brought back.

When this captain of the Grays came up to Yabu there was much argument and pointing to the city and to the castle, and obvious disagreement between them.

At length Yabu overrode him, his hand on his sword, and motioned Blackthorne to get into the palanquin.

"Iyé," the captain said.

The two men were beginning to square up to one another and the Grays and the Browns shifted nervously.

"Anjin-san desu shunjin Toranaga-sama . . ."

Blackthorne caught a word here, another there. *Watakushi* meant "I," *hitachi* added meant "we," *shunjin* meant "prisoner." And then he remembered what Rodrigues had said, so he shook his head and interrupted sharply. *"Shunjin, iyé! Watakushi wa* Anjin-san!"

Both men stared at him.

Blackthorne broke the silence and added in halting Japanese, knowing the words to be ungrammatical and childishly spoken, but hoping they would be understood, "I friend. Not prisoner. Understand please. Friend. So sorry, friend want bath. Bath, understand? Tired. Hungry. Bath." He pointed to the castle donjon. "Go there! Now, please. Lord Toranaga one, Lord Ishido two. Go *now.*"

And with added imperiousness on the last *"ima"* he got awkwardly into the palanquin and lay down on the cushions, his feet sticking far out.

Then Yabu laughed, and everyone joined in.

"Ah so, Anjin-sama!" Yabu said with a mocking bow.

"Iyé, Yabu-sama. Anjin-*san."* Blackthorne corrected him contentedly. Yes, you bastard. I know a thing or two now. But I haven't forgotten about you. And soon I'll be walking on your grave.

CHAPTER 16

Perhaps it would have been better to consult me before removing *my* prisoner from *my* jurisdiction, Lord Ishido," Toranaga was saying.

"The barbarian was in the common prison with common people. Naturally I presumed you'd no further interest in him, otherwise I wouldn't have had him taken out of there. Of course, I never meant to interfere with your private affairs." Ishido was outwardly calm and deferential but inside he was seething. He knew that he had been trapped into an indiscretion. It was true that he should have asked Toranaga first. Ordinary politeness demanded it. Even that would not have mattered at all if he still had the barbarian in his power, in his quarters; he would simply have handed over the foreigner at his leisure, if and when Toranaga had asked for him. But for some of his men to have been intercepted and ignominiously killed, and then for the *daimyo* Yabu and some of Toranaga's men to have taken physical possession of the barbarian from more of his men changed the position completely. He had lost face, whereas his whole strategy for Toranaga's public destruction was to put Toranaga into precisely that position. "Again I apologize."

Toranaga glanced at Hiro-matsu, the apology music to their ears. Both men knew how much inner bleeding it had cost Ishido. They were in the great audience room. By prior agreement, the two antagonists had only five guards present, men of guaranteed reliability. The rest were waiting outside. Yabu was also waiting outside. And the barbarian was being cleaned. Good, Toranaga thought, feeling very pleased with himself. He put his mind on Yabu briefly and decided not to see him today after all, but to continue to play him like a fish. So he asked Hiro-matsu to send him away and turned again to Ishido. "Of course your apology is accepted. Fortunately no harm was done."

"Then I may take the barbarian to the Heir—as soon as he's presentable?"

"I'll send him as soon as I've finished with him."

"May I ask when that will be? The Heir was expecting him this morning."

"We shouldn't be too concerned about that, you and I, *neh?* Yaemon's only seven. I'm sure a seven-year-old boy can possess himself with patience. *Neh?* Patience is a form of discipline and requires practice.

Doesn't it? I'll explain the misunderstanding myself. I'm giving him another swimming lesson this morning."

"Oh?"

"Yes. You should learn to swim too, Lord Ishido. It's excellent exercise and could come in very useful during war. All my samurai can swim. I insist that all learn that art."

"Mine spend their time practicing archery, swordsmanship, riding, and shooting."

"Mine add poetry, penmanship, flower arranging, the *cha-no-yu* ceremony. Samurai should be well versed in the arts of peace to be strong for the arts of war."

"Most of my men are already more than proficient in those arts," Ishido said, conscious that his own writing was poor and his learning limited. "Samurai are birthed for war. I understand war very well. That is enough at the moment. That and obedience to our Master's will."

"Yaemon's swimming lesson is at the Hour of the Horse." The day and the night were each split into six equal parts. The day began with the Hour of the Hare, from 5 A.M. to 7 A.M., then the Dragon, from 7 A.M. to 9 A.M. The hours of the Snake, Horse, Goat, Monkey, Cock, Dog, Boar, Rat and Ox followed, and the cycle ended with the Hour of the Tiger between 3 A.M. and 5 A.M. "Would you like to join the lesson?"

"Thank you, no. I'm too old to change my ways," Ishido said thinly.

"I hear the captain of your men was ordered to commit seppuku."

"Naturally. The bandits should have been caught. At least one of them should have been caught. Then we would have found the others."

"I'm astounded that such carrion could operate so close to the castle."

"I agree. Perhaps the barbarian could describe them."

"What would a barbarian know?" Toranaga laughed. "As to the bandits, they were *ronin,* weren't they? *Ronin* are plentiful among your men. Inquiries there might prove fruitful. *Neh?*"

"Inquiries are being pressed. In many directions." Ishido passed over the veiled sneer about *ronin,* the masterless, almost outcast mercenary samurai who had, in their thousands, flocked to the Heir's banner when Ishido had whispered it abroad that he, on behalf of the Heir and the mother of the Heir, would accept their fidelity, would—incredibly—forgive and forget their indiscretions or past, and would, in the course of time, repay their loyalty with a Taikō's lavishness. Ishido knew that it had been a brilliant move. It gave him an enormous pool of trained samurai to draw upon; it guaranteed loyalty, for *ronin* knew they would never get another such chance; it brought into his camp all the angry ones, many of whom had been made *ronin* by Toranaga's conquests and those of his allies. And lastly, it removed a danger to the realm—an increase in the bandit population—for almost the only supportable way of life open to a samurai unlucky enough to become *ronin* was to become a monk or bandit.

"There are many things I don't understand about this ambush," Ishido said, his voice tinged with venom. "Yes. Why, for instance, should bandits try to capture this barbarian for ransom? There are plenty of others in the city, vastly more important. Isn't that what the bandit said? It was ransom he wanted. Ransom from whom? What's the barbarian's value? None. And how did they know where he would be? It was only yesterday that I gave the order to bring him to the Heir, thinking it would amuse the boy. Very curious."

"Very," Toranaga said.

"Then there's the coincidence of Lord Yabu being in the vicinity with some of your men and some of mine at that exact time. Very curious."

"Very. Of course he was there because I had sent for him, and your men were there because we agreed—at your suggestion—that it was good policy and a way to begin to heal the breach between us, that your men accompany mine wherever they go while I'm on this official visit."

"It is also strange that the bandits who were sufficiently brave and well organized to slay the first ten without a fight acted like Koreans when our men arrived. The two sides were equally matched. Why didn't the bandits fight, or take the barbarian into the hills immediately, and not stupidly stay on a main path to the castle? Very curious."

"Very. I'll certainly be taking double guards with me tomorrow when I go hawking. Just in case. It's disconcerting to know bandits are so close to the castle. Yes. Perhaps you'd like to hunt, too? Fly one of your hawks against mine? I'll be hunting the hills to the north."

"Thank you, no. I'll be busy tomorrow. Perhaps the day after? I've ordered twenty thousand men to sweep all the forests, woods, and glades around Osaka. There won't be a bandit within twenty *ri* in ten days. That I can promise you."

Toranaga knew that Ishido was using the bandits as an excuse to increase the number of his troops in the vicinity. If he says twenty, he means fifty. The neck of the trap is closing, he told himself. Why so soon? What new treachery has happened? Why is Ishido so confident? "Good. Then the day after tomorrow, Lord Ishido. You'll keep your men away from my hunting area? I wouldn't want my game disturbed," he added thinly.

"Of course. And the barbarian?"

"He is and always was my property. And his ship. But you can have him when I've finished with him. And afterwards you can send him to the execution ground if you wish."

"Thank you. Yes, I'll do that." Ishido closed his fan and slipped it into his sleeve. "He's unimportant. What is important and the reason for my coming to see you is that—oh, by the way, I heard that the lady, my mother, is visiting the Johji monastery."

"Oh? I would have thought the season's a little late for looking at cherry blossoms. Surely they'd be well past their prime now?"

"I agree. But then if she wishes to see them, why not? You can never tell with the elderly, they have minds of their own and see things differently, *neh?* But her health isn't good. I worry about her. She has to be very careful—she takes a chill very easily."

"It's the same with my mother. You have to watch the health of the old." Toranaga made a mental note to send an immediate message to remind the abbot to watch over the old woman's health very carefully. If she were to die in the monastery the repercussions would be terrible. He would be shamed before the Empire. All *daimyos* would realize that in the chess game for power he had used a helpless old woman, the mother of his enemy, as a pawn, and failed in his responsibility to her. Taking a hostage was, in truth, a dangerous ploy.

Ishido had become almost blind with rage when he had heard that his revered mother was in the Toranaga stronghold at Nagoya. Heads had fallen. He had immediately brought forward plans for Toranaga's destruction, and had taken a solemn resolve to invest Nagoya and obliterate the *daimyo,* Kazamaki—in whose charge she had ostensibly been—the moment hostilities began. Last, a private message had been sent to the abbot through intermediaries, that unless she was brought safely out of the monastery within twenty-four hours, Naga, the only son of Toranaga within reach and any of his women that could be caught, would, unhappily, wake up in the leper village, having been fed by them, watered by them, and serviced by one of their whores. Ishido knew that while his mother was in Toranaga's power he had to tread lightly. But he had made it clear that if she was not let go, he would set the Empire to the torch. "How is the lady, your mother, Lord Toranaga," he asked politely.

"She's very well, thank you." Toranaga allowed his happiness to show, both at the thought of his mother and at the knowledge of Ishido's impotent fury. "She's remarkably fit for seventy-four. I only hope I'm as strong as she is when I'm her age."

You're fifty-eight, Toranaga, but you'll never reach fifty-nine, Ishido promised himself. "Please give her my best wishes for a continued happy life. Thank you again and I'm sorry that you were inconvenienced." He bowed with great politeness, and then, holding in his soaring pleasure with difficulty, he added, "Oh, yes, the important matter I wanted to see you about was that the last formal meeting of the Regents has been post-poned. We do not meet tonight at sunset."

Toranaga kept the smile on his face but inside he was rocked. "Oh? Why?"

"Lord Kiyama's sick. Lord Sugiyama and Lord Onoshi have agreed to the delay. So did I. A few days are unimportant, aren't they, on such important matters?"

"We can have the meeting without Lord Kiyama."

"We have agreed that we should not." Ishido's eyes were taunting.

"Formally?"

"Here are our four seals."

Toranaga was seething. Any delay jeopardized him immeasurably. Could he barter Ishido's mother for an immediate meeting? No, because it would take too much time for the orders to go back and forth and he would have conceded a very great advantage for nothing. "When will the meeting be?"

"I understand Lord Kiyama should be well tomorrow, or perhaps the next day."

"Good. I'll send my personal physician to see him."

"I'm sure he'd appreciate that. But his own has forbidden any visitors. The disease might be contagious, *neh?*"

"What disease?"

"I don't know, my Lord. That's what I was told."

"Is the doctor a barbarian?"

"Yes. I understand the chief doctor of the Christians. A Christian doctor-priest for a Christian *daimyo.* Ours are not good enough for so—so important a *daimyo,*" Ishido said with a sneer.

Toranaga's concern increased. If the doctor were Japanese, there were many things he could do. But with a Christian doctor—inevitably a Jesuit priest—well, to go against one of them, or even to interfere with one of them, might alienate all Christian *daimyos,* which he could not afford to risk. He knew his friendship with Tsukku-san would not help him against the Christian *daimyos* Onoshi or Kiyama. It was in Christian interests to present a united front. Soon he would have to approach them, the barbarian priests, to make an arrangement, to find out the price of their cooperation. If Ishido truly has Onoshi and Kiyama with him—and all the Christian *daimyos* would follow these two if they acted jointly—then I'm isolated, he thought. Then my only way left is Crimson Sky.

"I'll visit Lord Kiyama the day after tomorrow," he said, naming a deadline.

"But the contagion? I'd never forgive myself if anything happened to you while you're here in Osaka, my Lord. You are our guest, in my care. I must insist you do not."

"You may rest comfortably, my Lord Ishido, the contagion that will topple me has not yet been born, *neh?* You forget the soothsayer's prediction." When the Chinese embassy had come to the Taikō six years ago to try to settle the Japanese-Korean-Chinese war, a famous astrologer had been among them. This Chinese had forecast many things that had since come true. At one of the Taikō's incredibly lavish ceremonial dinners, the Taikō had asked the soothsayer to predict the deaths of certain of his counselors. The astrologer had said that Toranaga would die by the sword when he was middle-aged. Ishido, the famous conqueror of Korea—or Chosen as Chinese called that land—would die undiseased, an old man, his feet firm in the earth, the most famous man of his day. But the Taikō himself would die in his bed, respected, revered, of old age, leaving a healthy son to follow him. This had so pleased the Taikō, who was still childless, that he had decided to let the embassy return to China and not kill them as he had planned for their previous insolences. Instead of negotiating for peace as he had expected, the Chinese Emperor, through this embassy, had merely offered to "invest him as King of the Country of Wa," as the Chinese called Japan. So he had sent them home alive and not in the very small boxes that had already been prepared for them, and renewed the war against Korea and China.

"No, Lord Toranaga, I haven't forgotten," Ishido said, remembering very well. "But contagion can be uncomfortable. Why be uncomfortable? You could catch the pox like your son Noboru, so sorry—or become a leper like Lord Onoshi. He's still young, but he suffers. Oh, yes, he suffers."

Momentarily Toranaga was thrown off balance. He knew the ravages of both diseases too well. Noboru, his eldest living son, had caught the Chinese pox when he was seventeen—ten years ago—and all the cures of the doctors, Japanese, Chinese, Korean, and Christian, had not managed to allay the disease which had already defaced him but would not kill him. If I become all powerful, Toranaga promised himself, perhaps I can stamp out that disease. Does it really come from women? How do women get it? How can it be cured? Poor Noboru, Toranaga thought. Except for the pox you'd be my heir, because you're a brilliant soldier, a better administrator than Sudara, and very cunning. You must have done many bad things in a previous life to have had to carry so many burdens in this one.

"By the Lord Buddha, I'd not wish either of those on anyone," he said.

"I agree," Ishido said, believing Toranaga would wish them both on him if he could. He bowed again and left.

Toranaga broke the silence. "Well?"

Hiro-matsu said, "If you stay or leave now, it's the same—disaster, because now you've been betrayed and you are isolated, Sire. If you stay for the meeting—you won't get a meeting for a week—Ishido will have mobilized his legions around Osaka and you'll never escape, whatever happens to the Lady Ochiba in Yedo, and clearly Ishido's decided to risk her to get you. It's obvious you're betrayed and the four Regents will make a decision against you. A four against one vote in Council impeaches you. If you leave, they'll still issue whatever orders Ishido wishes. You're bound to uphold a four-to-one decision. You swore to do it. You cannot go against your solemn word as a Regent."

"I agree."

The silence held.

Hiro-matsu waited, with growing anxiety. "What are you going to do?"

"First I'm going to have my swim," Toranaga said with surprising joviality. "Then I'll see the barbarian."

The woman walked quietly through Toranaga's private garden in the castle toward the little thatched hut that was set so prettily in a glade of maples. Her silk kimono and obi were the most simple yet the most elegant that the most famous craftsmen in China could make. She wore her hair in the latest Kyoto fashion, piled high and held in place with long silver pins. A colorful sunshade protected her very fair skin. She was tiny, just five feet, but perfectly proportioned. Around her neck was a thin golden chain, and hanging from it, a small golden crucifix.

Kiri was waiting on the veranda of the hut. She sat heavily in the shade, her buttocks overflowing her cushion, and she watched the woman approach along the steppingstones which had been set so carefully into the moss that they seemed to have grown there.

"You're more beautiful than ever, younger than ever, Toda Mariko-san," Kiri said without jealousy, returning her bow.

"I wish that were true, Kiritsubo-san," Mariko replied, smiling. She knelt on a cushion, unconsciously arranging her skirts into a delicate pattern.

"It's true. When did we last meet? Two—three years ago? You haven't changed a hair's breadth in twenty years. It must be almost twenty years since we first met. Do you remember? It was at a feast Lord Goroda gave. You were fourteen, just married and rare."

"And frightened."

"No, not you. Not frightened."

"It was sixteen years ago, Kiritsubo-san, not twenty. Yes, I remember it very well." Too well, she thought, heartsick. That was the day my brother whispered that he believed our revered father was going to be revenged on his liege Lord, the Dictator Goroda, that he was going to assassinate him. *His liege Lord!*

Oh, yes, Kiri-san, I remember that day and that year and that hour. It was the beginning of all the horror. I've never admitted to anyone that I knew what was going to happen before it happened. I never warned my husband, or Hiro-matsu, his father—both faithful vassals of the Dictator—that treachery was planned by one of his greatest generals. Worse, I never warned Goroda my liege Lord. So I failed in my duty to my liege Lord, to my husband, to his family, which because of my marriage is my only family. Oh, Madonna, forgive me my sin, help me to cleanse myself. I kept silent to protect my beloved father, who desecrated the honor of a thousand years. O my God, O Lord Jesus of Nazareth, save this sinner from eternal damnation. . . .

"It was sixteen years ago," Mariko said serenely.

"I was carrying Lord Toranaga's child that year," Kiri said, and she thought, if Lord Goroda had not been foully betrayed and murdered by your father, my Lord Toranaga would never have had to fight the battle of Nagakudé, I would never have caught a chill there and my child would never have miscarried. Perhaps, she told herself. And perhaps not. It was just *karma,* my *karma,* whatever happened, *neh?* "Ah, Mariko-san," she said, no malice in her, "that's so long ago, it almost seems like another lifetime. But you're ageless. Why can't I have your figure and beautiful hair, and walk so daintily?" Kiri laughed. "The answer's simple: Because I eat too much!"

"What does it matter? You bask in Lord Toranaga's favor, *neh?* So you're fulfilled. You're wise and warm and whole and happy in yourself."

"I'd rather be thin and still able to eat and be in favor," Kiri said. "But you? You're not happy in yourself?"

"I'm only an instrument for my Lord Buntaro to play upon. If the Lord, my husband, is happy, then of course I'm happy. His pleasure's my pleasure. It's the same with you," Mariko said.

"Yes. But not the same." Kiri moved her fan, the golden silk catching the afternoon sun. I'm so glad I'm not you, Mariko, with all your beauty and brilliance and courage and learning. No! I couldn't bear being married to that hateful, ugly, arrogant, violent man for a day, let alone seventeen years. He's so opposite to his father, Lord Hiro-matsu. Now, there's a wonderful man. But Buntaro? How do fathers have such terrible sons? I wish I had a son, oh, how I wish! But you, Mariko, how have you borne such ill treatment all these years? How have you endured your tragedies? It seems impossible that there's no shadow of them on your face or in your soul. "You're an amazing woman, Toda Buntaro Mariko-san."

"Thank you, Kiritsubo Toshiko-san. Oh Kiri-san, it's so good to see you."

"And you. How is your son?"

"Beautiful—beautiful—beautiful. Saruji's fifteen now, can you imagine it? Tall and strong and just like his father, and Lord Hiro-matsu has given Saruji his own fief and he's—did you know that he's going to be married?"

"No, to whom?"

"She's a granddaughter of Lord Kiyama's. Lord Toranaga's arranged it so well. A very fine match for our family. I only wish the girl herself was—was more attentive to my son, more worthy. Do you know she . . ." Mariko laughed, a little shyly. "There, I sound like every mother-in-law that's ever been. But I think you'd agree, she isn't really trained yet."

"You'll have time to do that."

"Oh, I hope so. Yes. I'm lucky I don't have a mother-in-law. I don't know what I'd do."

"You'd enchant her and train her as you train all your household, *neh?*"

"Eeeee, I wish that was also true." Mariko's hands were motionless in her lap. She watched a dragonfly settle, then dart away. "My husband ordered me here. Lord Toranaga wishes to see me?"

"Yes. He wants you to interpret for him."

Mariko was startled. "With whom?"

"The new barbarian."

"Oh! But what about Father Tsukku-san? Is he sick?"

"No." Kiri played with her fan. "I suppose it's left to us to wonder why Lord Toranaga wants you here and not the priest, as in the first interview. Why is it, Mariko-san, that we have to guard all the monies, pay all the bills, train all the servants, buy all the food and household goods—even most times the clothes of our Lords—but they don't really *tell* us anything, do they?"

"Perhaps that's what our intuition's for."

"Probably." Kiri's gaze was level and friendly. "But I'd imagine that this would all be a very private matter. So you would swear by your Christian God not to divulge anything about this meeting. To anyone."

The day seemed to lose its warmth.

"Of course," Mariko said uneasily. She understood very clearly that Kiri meant she was to say nothing to her husband or to his father or to her confessor. As her husband had ordered her here, obviously at Lord Toranaga's request, her duty to her liege Lord Toranaga overcame her duty to her husband, so she could withhold information freely from him. But to her confessor? Could she say nothing to him? And why was she the interpreter and not Father Tsukku-san? She knew that once more, against her will, she was involved in the kind of political intrigue that had bedeviled her life, and wished again that her family was not ancient and Fujimoto, that she had never been born with the gift of tongues that had allowed her to learn the almost incomprehensible Portuguese and Latin languages, and that she had never been born at all. But then, she thought, I would never have seen my son, nor learned about the Christ Child or His Truth, or about the Life Everlasting.

It is your *karma*, Mariko, she told herself sadly, just *karma*. "Very well, Kiri-san." Then she added with foreboding, "I swear by the Lord my God, that I will not divulge anything said here today, or at any time I am interpreting for my liege Lord."

"I would also imagine that you might have to exclude part of your own feelings to translate exactly what is said. This new barbarian is strange and says peculiar things. I'm sure my Lord picked you above all possibilities for special reasons."

"I am Lord Toranaga's to do with as he wishes. He need never have any fear for my loyalty."

"That was never in question, Lady. I meant no harm."

A spring rain came and speckled the petals and the mosses and the leaves, and disappeared leaving ever more beauty in its wake.

"I would ask a favor, Mariko-san. Would you please put your crucifix under your kimono?"

Mariko's fingers darted for it defensively. "Why? Lord Toranaga has never objected to my conversion, nor has Lord Hiro-matsu, the head of my clan! My husband has—my husband allows me to keep it and wear it."

"Yes. But crucifixes send *this* barbarian mad and my Lord Toranaga doesn't want him mad, he wants him soothed."

Blackthorne had never seen anyone so petite. "*Konnichi wa*," he said. "*Konnichi wa,* Toranaga-sama." He bowed as a courtier, nodded to the boy who knelt, wide-eyed, beside Toranaga, and to the fat woman who was behind him. They were all on the veranda that encircled the small hut. The hut contained a single small room with rustic screens and hewn beams and thatched roof, and a kitchen area behind. It was set on pilings of wood and raised a foot or so above a carpet of pure white sand.

This was a ceremonial tea house for the *cha-no-yu* ceremony and built at vast expense with rare materials for that purpose alone, though some times, because these houses were isolated, in glades, they were used for trysts and private conversations.

Blackthorne gathered his kimono around him and sat on the cushion that had been placed on the sand below and in front of them. *"Gomen nasai,* Toranaga-sama, *nihon go ga hanase-masen. Tsuyaku go imasu ka?"*

"I am your interpreter, senhor," Mariko said at once, in almost flaw-less Portuguese. "But you speak Japanese?"

"No, senhorita, just a few words or phrases," Blackthorne replied, taken aback. He had been expecting Father Alvito to be the interpreter, and Toranaga to be accompanied by samurai and perhaps the *daimyo* Yabu. But no samurai were near, though many ringed the garden.

"My Lord Toranaga asks where—First, perhaps I should ask if you prefer to speak Latin?"

"Whichever you wish, senhorita." Like any educated man, Blackthorne could read, write, and speak Latin, because Latin was the only language of learning throughout the civilized world.

Who is this woman? Where did she learn such perfect Portuguese? And Latin? Where else but from the Jesuits, he thought. In one of their schools. Oh, they're so clever! The first thing they do is build a school.

It was only seventy years ago that Ignatius Loyola had formed the So-ciety of Jesus and now their schools, the finest in Christendom, were spread across the world and their influence bolstered or destroyed kings. They had the ear of the Pope. They had halted the tide of the Reforma-tion and were now winning back huge territories for their Church.

"We will speak Portuguese then," she was saying. "My Master wishes to know where you learned your 'few words and phrases'?"

"There was a monk in the prison, senhorita, a Franciscan monk, and he taught me. Things like, 'food, friend, bath, go, come, true, false, here, there, I, you, please, thank you, want, don't want, prisoner, yes, no,' and so on. It's only a beginning, unfortunately. Would you please tell Lord Toranaga that I'm better prepared now to answer his questions, to help, and more than a little pleased to be out of prison. For which I thank him."

Blackthorne watched as she turned and spoke to Toranaga. He knew that he would have to speak simply, preferably in short sentences, and be careful because, unlike the priest who interpreted simultaneously, this woman waited till he had finished, then gave a synopsis, or a version of what was said—the usual problem of all except the finest interpreters, though even they, as with the Jesuit, allowed their own personalities to influence what was said, voluntarily or involuntarily. The bath and massage and food and two hours of sleep had immeasurably refreshed him. The bath attendants, all women of girth and strength, had pummeled him and shampooed his hair, braiding it in a neat queue, and the barber had trimmed his beard. He had been given a clean loincloth and kimono and sash, and tabi and thongs for his feet. The futons on which he had slept had been so clean, like the room. It had all seemed dreamlike and, waking from dreamlessness, he had wondered momentarily which was the dream, this or the prison.

He had waited impatiently, hoping that he would be guided again to Toranaga, planning what to say and what to reveal, how to outwit Father Alvito and how to gain ascendance over him. And over Toranaga. For he knew, beyond all doubt, because of what Friar Domingo had told him about the Portuguese, and Japanese politics and trade, that he could now help Toranaga, who, in return, could easily give him the riches he desired.

And now, with no priest to fight, he felt even more confident. I need just a little luck and patience.

Toranaga was listening intently to the doll-like interpreter.

Blackthorne thought, I could pick her up with one hand and if I put both hands around her waist, my fingers would touch. How old would she be? Perfect! Married? No wedding ring. Ah, that's interesting. She's wearing no jewelry of any kind. Except the silver pins in her hair. Neither is the other woman, the fat one.

He searched his memory. The other two women in the village had worn no jewelry either, and he had not seen any on any of Mura's household. Why?

And who's the fat woman? Toranaga's wife? Or the boy's nursemaid? Would the lad be Toranaga's son? Or grandson, perhaps? Friar Domingo had said that Japanese had only one wife at one time but as many consorts—legal mistresses—as they wished.

Was the interpreter Toranaga's consort?

What would it be like to have such a woman in bed? I'd be afraid of crushing her. No, she wouldn't break. There are women in England almost as small. But not like her.

The boy was small and straight and round-eyed, his full black hair tied into a short queue, his pate unshaven. His curiosity seemed enormous.

Without thinking, Blackthorne winked. The boy jumped, then laughed and interrupted Mariko and pointed and spoke out, and they listened indulgently and no one hushed him. When he had finished, Toranaga spoke briefly to Blackthorne.

"Lord Toranaga asks why did you do that, senhor?"

"Oh, just to amuse the lad. He's a child like any, and children in my country would usually laugh if you did that. My son must be about his age now. My son's seven."

"The Heir is seven," Mariko said after a pause, then translated what he had said.

"Heir? Does that mean the boy's Lord Toranaga's only son?" Blackthorne asked.

"Lord Toranaga has instructed me to say that you will please confine yourself to answering questions only, for the moment." Then she added, "I'm sure, if you are patient, Pilot-Captain B'ackthon, that you'll be given an opportunity to ask anything you wish later."

"Very well."

"As your name is very hard to say, senhor, for we do not have the sounds to pronounce it—may I, for Lord Toranaga, use your Japanese name, Anjin-san?"

"Of course." Blackthorne was going to ask hers but he remembered what she had said and reminded himself to be patient.

"Thank you. My Lord asks, do you have any other children?"

"A daughter. She was born just before I left my home in England. So she's about two now."

"You have one wife or many?"

"One. That's our custom. Like the Portuguese and Spanish. We don't have consorts—formal consorts."

"Is this your first wife, senhor?"

"Yes."

"Please, how old are you?"

"Thirty-six."

"Where in England do you live?"

"On the outskirts of Chatham. That's a small port near London."

"London is your chief city?"

"Yes."

"He asks, what languages do you speak?"

"English, Portuguese, Spanish, Dutch, and of course, Latin."

"What is 'Dutch?'"

"It's a language spoken in Europe, in the Netherlands. It's very similar to German."

She frowned. "Dutch is a heathen language? German too?"

"Both are non-Catholic countries," he said carefully.

"Excuse me, isn't that the same as heathen?"

"No, senhorita. Christianity is split in two distinct and very separate religions. Catholicism and Protestantism. There are two versions of

Christianity. The sect in Japan is Catholic. At the moment both sects are very hostile to each other." He marked her astonishment and felt Toranaga's growing impatience at being left out of the conversation. Be careful, he cautioned himself. She's certainly Catholic. Lead up to things. And be simple. "Perhaps Lord Toranaga doesn't wish to discuss religion, senhorita, as it was partially covered in our first meeting."

"You are a Protestant Christian?"

"Yes."

"And Catholic Christians are your enemies?"

"Most would consider me heretic and their enemy, yes."

She hesitated, turned to Toranaga and spoke at length.

There were many guards around the perimeter of the garden. All well away, all Browns. Then Blackthorne noticed ten Grays sitting in a neat group in the shade, all eyes on the boy. What significance has that? he wondered.

Toranaga was cross-questioning Mariko, then spoke directly at Blackthorne.

"My Lord wishes to know about you and your family," Mariko began. "About your country, its queen and previous rulers, habits, customs, and history. Similarly about all other countries, particularly Portugal and Spain. All about the world you live in. About your ships, weapons, foods, trade. About your wars and battles and how to navigate a ship, how you guided your ship and what happened on the voyage. He wants to understand— Excuse me, why do you laugh?"

"Only because, senhorita, that seems to be just about everything I know."

"That is precisely what my Master wishes. 'Precisely' is the correct word?"

"Yes, senhorita. May I compliment you on your Portuguese, which is flawless."

Her fan fluttered a little. "Thank you, senhor. Yes, my Master wants to learn the *truth* about everything, what is fact and what would be your opinion."

"I'd be glad to tell him. It might take a little time."

"My Master has the time, he says."

Blackthorne looked at Toranaga. "*Wakarimasu.*"

"If you will excuse me, senhor, my Master orders me to say your accent is a little wrong." Mariko showed him how to say it and he repeated it and thanked her. "I am Senhora Mariko Buntaro, not senhorita."

"Yes, senhora." Blackthorne glanced at Toranaga. "Where would he like me to begin?"

She asked him. A fleeting smile sped across Toranaga's strong face. "He says, at the beginning."

Blackthorne knew that this was another trial. What, out of all the limitless possibilities, should he start with? Whom should he talk to? To Toranaga, the boy, or the woman? Obviously, if only men had been present, to Toranaga. But now? Why were the women and the boy present? That must have significance.

He decided to concentrate on the boy and the women. "In ancient times my country was ruled by a great king who had a magic sword called Excalibur and his queen was the most beautiful woman in the land. His chief counselor was a wizard, Merlin, and the king's name was Arthur," he began confidently, telling the legend that his father used to tell so well in the mists of his youth. "King Arthur's capital was called Camelot and it was a happy time of no wars and good harvests and . . ." Suddenly he realized the enormity of his mistake. The kernel of the story was about Guinevere and Lancelot, an adulterous queen and a faithless vassal, about Mordred, Arthur's illegitimate son, who treacherously goes to war against his father, and about a father who kills this son in battle, only to be mortally wounded by him. Oh, Jesus God, how could I be so stupid? Isn't Toranaga like a great king? Aren't these his ladies? Isn't that his son?

"Are you sick, senhor?"

"No—no, I'm sorry—it was just . . ."

"You were saying, senhor, about this king and the good harvest?"

"Yes. It . . . like most countries, our past is clouded with myths and legends, most of which are unimportant," he said lamely, trying to gain time.

She stared at him perplexed. Toranaga's eyes became more piercing and the boy yawned.

"You were saying, senhor?"

"I—well—" Then he had a flash of inspiration. "Perhaps the best thing I could do is draw a map of the world, senhora, as we know it," he said in a rush. "Would you like me to do that?"

She translated this and he saw a glimmer of interest from Toranaga, nothing from the boy or the women. How to involve them?

"My Master says yes. I will send for paper—"

"Thank you. But this will do for the moment. Later, if you'll give me some writing materials I can draw an accurate one."

Blackthorne got off his cushion and knelt. With his finger he began to draw a crude map in the sand, upside down so that they could see better. "The earth's round, like an orange, but this map is like its skin, cut off in ovals, north to south, laid flat and stretched a bit at the top and bottom.

A Dutchman called Mercator invented the way to do this accurately twenty years ago. It's the first accurate world map. We can even navigate with it—or his globes." He had sketched the continents boldly. "This is north and this south, east and west. Japan is here, my country's on the other side of the world—there. This is all unknown and unexplored . . ." His hand eliminated everything in North America north of a line from Mexico to Newfoundland, everything in South America apart from Peru and a narrow strip of coast land around that continent, then everything north and east of Norway, everything east of Muscovy, all Asia, all inland Africa, everything south of Java and the tip of South America. "We know the coastlines, but little else. The interiors of Africa, the Americas, and Asia are almost entirely mysteries." He stopped to let her catch up.

She was translating more easily now and he felt their interest growing. The boy stirred and moved a little closer.

"The Heir wishes to know where we are on the map."

"Here. This is Cathay, China, I think. I don't know how far we are off the coast. It took me two years to sail from here to here." Toranaga and the fat woman craned to see better.

"The Heir says but why are we so small on your map?"

"It's just a scale, senhora. On this continent, from Newfoundland here, to Mexico here, is almost a thousand leagues, each of three miles. From here to Yedo is about a hundred leagues."

There was a silence, then they talked amongst themselves.

"Lord Toranaga wishes you to show him on the map how you came to Japan."

"This way. This is Magellan's Pass—or Strait—here, at the tip of South America. It's called that after the Portuguese navigator who discovered it, eighty years ago. Since then the Portuguese and Spanish have kept the way secret, for their exclusive use. We were the first outsiders through the Pass. I had one of their secret rutters, a type of map, but even so, I still had to wait six months to get through because the winds were against us."

She translated what he had said. Toranaga looked up, disbelieving.

"My Master says you are mistaken. All bar—all Portuguese come from the south. That is their route, the only route."

"Yes. It's true the Portuguese favor that way—the Cape of Good Hope, we call it—because they have dozens of forts all along these coasts —Africa and India and the Spice Islands—to provision in and winter in. And their galleon-warships patrol and monopolize the sea lanes. However, the Spanish use Magellan's Pass to get to their Pacific American colonies, and to the Philippines, or they cross here, at the narrow isthmus of Panama, going overland to avoid months of travel. For us it was safer to sail via Magellan's Strait, otherwise we'd have had to run the gauntlet of all those enemy Portuguese forts. Please tell Lord Toranaga I know the position of many of them now. Most employ Japanese troops, by the way," he added with emphasis. "The friar who gave me the information in the prison was Spanish and hostile to the Portuguese and hostile to all Jesuits."

Blackthorne saw an immediate reaction on her face, and when she translated, on Toranaga's face. Give her time, and keep it simple, he warned himself.

"Japanese troops? You mean samurai?"

"*Ronin* would describe them, I imagine."

"You said a 'secret' map? My Lord wishes to know how you obtained it."

"A man named Pieter Suyderhof, from Holland, was the private secretary to the Primate of Goa—that's the title of the chief Catholic priest and Goa's the capital of Portuguese India. You know, of course, that the Portuguese are trying to take over that continent by force. As private secretary to this archbishop, who was also the Portuguese Viceroy at the time, all sorts of documents passed through his hands. After many years he obtained some of their rutters—maps—and copied them. These gave the secrets of the way through Magellan's Pass and also how to get around the Cape of Good Hope, and the shoals and reefs from Goa to Japan via Macao. My rutter was the Magellan one. It was with my papers that I lost from my ship. They are vital to me, and could be of immense value to Lord Toranaga."

"My Master says that he has sent orders to seek them. Continue please."

"When Suyderhof returned to Holland, he sold them to the Company of East India Merchants, which was given the monopoly for Far Eastern exploration."

She was looking at him coldly. "This man was a paid spy?"

"He was paid for his maps, yes. That's their custom, that's how they reward a man. Not with a title or land, only money. Holland's a republic. Of course, senhora, my country and our allies, Holland, are at war with Spain and Portugal and have been for years. You'll understand, senhora, in war it's vital to find out your enemies' secrets."

Mariko turned and spoke at length.

"My Lord says, why would this archbishop employ an enemy?"

"The story Pieter Suyderhof told was that this archbishop, who was a Jesuit, was interested only in trade. Suyderhof doubled their revenue, so he was 'cherished.' He was an extremely clever merchant—Hollanders are usually superior to Portuguese in this—so his credentials weren't checked very closely. Also many men with blue eyes and fair hair, Germans and other Europeans, are Catholic." Blackthorne waited till that was translated, then added carefully, "He was chief spy for Holland in Asia, a soldier of the country, and he put some of his people on Portuguese ships. Please tell Lord Toranaga that without Japan's trade, Portuguese India cannot live for long."

Toranaga kept his eyes on the map while Mariko talked. There was no reaction to what she had said. Blackthorne wondered if she had translated everything.

Then: "My Master would like a detailed world map, on paper, as soon as possible, with all the Portuguese bases marked, and the numbers of *ronin* at each. He says please continue."

Blackthorne knew he had made a giant step forward. But the boy yawned so he decided to change course, still heading for the same harbor. "Our world is not always as it seems. For instance, south of this line, we call it the Equator, the seasons are reversed. When we have summer, they have winter; when we have summer, they're freezing."

"Why is that?"

"I don't know, but it's true. Now, the way to Japan is through either of these two southern straits. We English, we're trying to find a northern route, either northeast over the Siberias, or northwest over the Americas. I've been as far north as this. The whole land's perpetual ice and snow here and it's so cold most of the year that if you don't wear fur mittens, your fingers'll freeze in moments. The people who live there are called Laplanders. Their clothes are made out of fur pelts. The men hunt and the women do all the work. Part of the women's work is to make all the clothes. To do this, most times they have to chew the pelts to soften them before they can stitch them."

Mariko laughed out loud.

Blackthorne smiled with her, feeling more confident now. "It's true, senhora. It's *honto*."

"*Sorewa honto desu ka?*" Toranaga asked impatiently. What's true?

Through more laughter, she told him what had been said. They also began to laugh.

"I lived among them for almost a year. We were trapped in the ice and had to wait for the thaw. Their food is fish, seals, occasionally polar bears, and whales, which they eat raw. Their greatest delicacy is to eat raw whale blubber."

"Oh, come now, Anjin-san!"

"It's true. And they live in small round houses made entirely out of snow and they never bathe."

"What, never?" she burst out.

He shook his head, and decided not to tell her baths were rare in England, rarer even than in Portugal and Spain, which were warm countries.

She translated this. Toranaga shook his head in disbelief.

"My Master says this is too much of an exaggeration. No one could live without baths. Even uncivilized people."

"That's the truth—*honto*," he said calmly and raised his hand. "I swear by Jesus of Nazareth and by my soul, I swear it is the truth."

She watched him in silence. "Everything?"

"Yes. Lord Toranaga wanted the truth. Why should I lie? My life is in his hands. It is easy to prove the truth—no, to be honest, it would be very hard to prove what I've said—you'd have to go there and see for yourself. Certainly the Portuguese and Spanish, who are my enemies, won't support me. But Lord Toranaga asked for the truth. He can trust me to tell it to him."

Mariko thought a moment. Then she scrupulously translated what he had said. At length:

"Lord Toranaga says, it is unbelievable that any human could live without bathing."

"Yes. But those are the cold lands. Their habits are different from yours, and mine. For instance, in my country, everyone believes baths are dangerous for your health. My grandmother, Granny Jacoba, used to say, 'A bath when you're birthed and another when laid out'll see thee through the Pearly Gates.'"

"That's very hard to believe."

"Some of your customs are very hard to believe. But it is true that I've had more baths in the short time I've been in your country than in as many years before. I admit freely I feel better for them." He grinned. "I no longer believe baths are dangerous. So I've gained by coming here, no?"

After a pause Mariko said, "Yes," and translated.

Kiri said, "He's astonishing—astonishing, *neh?*"

"What's your judgment of him, Mariko-san?" Toranaga asked.

"I'm convinced he's telling the truth, or believes he's telling it. Clearly it would seem that he could, perhaps, have a great value to you, my Lord. We have such a tiny knowledge of the outside world. Is that valuable to you? I don't know. But it's almost as though he's come down from the stars, or up from under the sea. If he's enemy to the Portuguese and the Spanish, then his information, if it can be trusted, could perhaps be vital to your interests, *neh?*"

"I agree," Kiri said.

"What do you think, Yaemon-sama?"

"Me, Uncle? Oh, I think he's ugly and I don't like his golden hair and cat's eyes and he doesn't look human at all," the boy said breathlessly. "I'm glad I wasn't born barbarian like him but samurai like my father, can we go for another swim, please?"

"Tomorrow, Yaemon," Toranaga said, vexed at not being able to talk directly to the pilot.

While they talked among themselves Blackthorne decided that the time had come. Then Mariko turned to him again.

"My Master asks why were you in the north?"

"I was pilot of a ship. We were trying to find a northeast passage, senhora. Many things I can tell you will sound laughable, I know," he began. "For instance, seventy years ago the kings of Spain and Portugal signed a solemn treaty that split ownership of the New World, the undiscovered world, between them. As your country falls in the Portuguese half, officially your country belongs to Portugal—Lord Toranaga, you, everyone, this castle and everything in it were given to Portugal."

"Oh, please, Anjin-san. Pardon me, that's nonsense!"

"I agree their arrogance is unbelievable. But it's true." Immediately she began to translate and Toranaga laughed derisively.

"Lord Toranaga says he could equally well split the heavens between himself and the Emperor of China, *neh?*"

"Please tell Lord Toranaga, I'm sorry, but that's not the same," Blackthorne said, aware that he was on dangerous ground. "This is written into legal documents which give each king the right to claim any non-Catholic land discovered by their subjects and to stamp out the existing government and replace it with Catholic rule." On the map, his finger traced a line north to south that bisected Brazil. "Everything east of this line is Portugal's, everything west is Spain's. Pedro Cabral discovered Brazil in 1500, so now Portugal owns Brazil, has stamped out the native culture and legal rulers, and has become rich from the gold and silver taken out of mines and plundered from native temples. All the rest of the Americas so far discovered is Spanish-owned now—Mexico, Peru, almost this whole south continent. They've wiped out the Inca nations, obliterated their culture, and enslaved hundreds of thousands of them. The conquistadores have modern guns—the natives none. With the conquistadores come the priests. Soon a few princes are converted, and enmities used. Then prince is turned against prince and realm swallowed up piecemeal. Now Spain is the richest nation in our world from the Inca and Mexican gold and silver they've plundered and sent back to Spain."

Mariko was solemn now. She had quickly grasped the significance of Blackthorne's lesson. And so had Toranaga.

"My Master says this is a worthless conversation. How could they give themselves such rights?"

"They didn't," Blackthorne said gravely. "The Pope gave them the rights, the Vicar of Christ on earth himself. In return for spreading the word of God."

"I don't believe it," she exclaimed.

"Please translate what I said, senhora. It is *honto*."

She obeyed and spoke at length, obviously unsettled. Then:

"My Master—my Master says you are—you are just trying to poison him against your enemies. What is the truth? On your own life, senhor."

"Pope Alexander VI set the first line of demarcation in 1493," Blackthorne commenced, blessing Alban Caradoc who had hammered so many facts into him when he was young, and Father Domingo for informing him about Japanese pride and giving him clues to Japanese minds. "In 1506 Pope Julius II sanctioned changes to the Treaty of Tordesillas, signed by Spain and Portugal in 1494, which altered the line a little. Pope Clement VII sanctioned the Treaty of Saragossa in 1529, barely seventy years ago, which drew a second line here"—his finger traced a line of longitude in the sand which cut through the tip of southern Japan. "This gives Portugal the exclusive right to your country, all these countries—from Japan, China to Africa—in the way I have said. To exploit exclusively—*by any means*—in return for spreading Catholicism." Again he waited and the woman hesitated, in turmoil, and he could feel Toranaga's growing irritation at having to wait for her to translate.

Mariko forced her lips to speak and repeated what he had said. Then she listened to Blackthorne again, detesting what she heard. Is this really possible? she asked herself. How could His Holiness say such things? Give our country to the Portuguese? It must be a lie. But the pilot swore by the Lord Jesus.

"The pilot says, Lord," she began, "in—in the days that these decisions were made by His Holiness the Pope, all their world, even the Anjin-san's country was Catholic Christian. The schism had not—not yet occurred. So, so these—these papal decisions would, of course, be binding on—on all nations. Even so, he adds that though the Portuguese have exclusivity to *exploit* Japan, Spain and Portugal are quarreling incessantly about the *ownership* because of the richness of our trade with China."

"What's your opinion, Kiri-san?" Toranaga said, as shocked as the others. Only the boy toyed with his fan uninterestedly.

"He believes he's telling the truth," Kiri said. "Yes, I think that. But how to prove it—or part of it?"

"How would you prove it, Mariko-san?" Toranaga asked, most perturbed by Mariko's reaction to what had been said, but very glad that he had agreed to use her as interpreter.

"I would ask Father Tsukku-san," she said. "Then, too, I would send someone—a trusted vassal—out into the world to see. Perhaps with the Anjin-san."

Kiri said, "If the priest does not support these statements, it may not necessarily mean this Anjin-san is lying, *neh?*" Kiri was pleased that she had suggested using Mariko as an interpreter when Toranaga was seeking an alternative to Tsukku-san. She knew Mariko was to be trusted and that, once Mariko had sworn by her alien God, she would ever be silent under rigorous questioning by any Christian priest. The less those devils know, the better, Kiri thought. And what a treasure of knowledge this barbarian has!

Kiri saw the boy yawn again and was glad of it. The less the child understands the better, she told herself. Then she said, "Why not send for the leader of the Christian priests and ask about these facts? See what he says. Their faces are open, mostly, and they have almost no subtlety."

Toranaga nodded, his eyes on Mariko. "From what you know about the Southern Barbarians, Mariko-san, would you say that a Pope's orders would be obeyed?"

"Without doubt."

"His orders would be considered as though the voice of the Christian God was speaking?"

"Yes."

"Would all Catholic Christians obey his orders?"

"Yes."

"Even our Christians here?"

"I would think, yes."

"Even you?"

"Yes, Sire. If it was a direct order from His Holiness to me personally. Yes, for my soul's salvation." Her gaze was firm. "But until that time I will obey no man but my liege lord, the head of my family, or my husband. I am Japanese, a Christian yes, but first I am samurai."

"I think it would be good then, that this Holiness stays away from our shores." Toranaga thought for a moment. Then he decided what to do with the barbarian, Anjin-san. "Tell him . . ." He stopped. All their eyes went to the path and to the elderly woman who approached. She wore the cowled habit of a Buddhist nun. Four Grays were with her. The Grays stopped and she came on alone.

CHAPTER 17

THEY all bowed low. Toranaga noticed that the barbarian copied him and did not get up or stare, which all barbarians except Tsukku-san would have done, according to their own custom. The pilot learns quickly, he thought, his mind still blazing from what he had heard. Ten thousand questions were crowding him, but, according to his discipline, he channeled them away temporarily to concentrate on the present danger.

Kiri had scurried to give the old woman her cushion and helped her to sit, then knelt behind her, in motionless attendance.

"Thank you, Kiritsubo-san," the woman said, returning their bow. Her name was Yodoko. She was the widow of the Taikō and now, since his death, a Buddhist nun. "I'm sorry to come uninvited and to interrupt you, Lord Toranaga."

"You're never unwelcome or uninvited, Yodoko-sama."

"Thank you, yes, thank you." She glanced at Blackthorne and squinted to try to see better. "But I think I did interrupt. I can't see who— Is he a barbarian? My eyes are getting worse and worse. It's not Tsukku-san, is it?"

"No, he's the new barbarian," Toranaga said.

"Oh, him!" Yodoko peered closer. "Please tell him I can't see very well, hence my impoliteness."

Mariko did as she was told. "He says many people in his country are short-sighted, Yodoko-sama, but they wear spectacles. He asked if we have them. I told him yes, some of us—from the Southern Barbarians. That you used to wear them but don't anymore."

"Yes. I prefer the mist that surrounds me. Yes, I don't like a lot of what I see nowadays." Yodoko turned back and looked at the boy, pretending to have just seen him. "Oh! My son! So there you are. I was looking for you. How good it is to see the Kwampaku!" She bowed deferentially.

"Thank you, First Mother," Yaemon beamed and bowed back. "Oh, you should have heard the barbarian. He's been drawing us a map of the world and telling us funny things about people who don't bathe at all! Never in their whole lives and they live in snow houses and wear skins like evil *kami*."

The old lady snorted. "The less they come here the better, I think, my son. I could never understand them and they always smell so horrible. I could never understand how the Lord Taikō, your father, could tolerate them. But then he was a man and you're a man, and you've more patience than a lowly woman. You've a good teacher, Yaemon-sama." Her old eyes flicked back to Toranaga. "Lord Toranaga's got more patience than anyone in the Empire."

"Patience is important for a man, vital for a leader," Toranaga said. "And a thirst for knowledge is a good quality too, eh, Yaemon-sama? And knowledge comes from strange places."

"Yes, Uncle. Oh yes," Yaemon said. "He's right, isn't he, First Mother?"

"Yes, yes. I agree. But I'm glad I'm a woman and don't have to worry about these things, *neh?*" Yodoko hugged the boy, who had come to sit beside her. "So, my son. Why am I here? To fetch the Kwampaku. Why? Because the Kwampaku is late for his food and late for his writing lessons."

"I hate writing lessons and I'm going swimming!"

Toranaga said with mock gravity, "When I was your age I used to hate writing too. But then, when I was twenty, I had to stop fighting battles and go back to school. I hated that worse."

"Go back to school, Uncle? After leaving it forever? Oh, how terrible!"

"A leader has to write well, Yaemon-sama. Not only clearly but beautifully, and the Kwampaku better than anyone else. How else can he write to His Imperial Highness or to the great *daimyos?* A leader has to be better than his vassals in everything, in every way. A leader has to do many things that are difficult."

"Yes, Uncle. It's very difficult to be Kwampaku." Yaemon frowned importantly. "I think I'll do my lessons now and not when I'm twenty because then I'll have important matters of state."

They were all very proud of him. "You're very wise, my son," said Yodoko.

"Yes, First Mother. I'm wise like my father, as my mother says. When's Mother coming home?"

Yodoko peered up at Toranaga. "Soon."

"I hope very soon," Toranaga said. He knew Yodoko had been sent to fetch the boy by Ishido. Toranaga had brought the boy and the guards directly to the garden to further irritate his enemy. Also to show the boy the strange pilot and so deprive Ishido of the pleasure of providing that experience for him.

"It's very wearisome being responsible for my son," Yodoko was saying. "It would be very good to have the Lady Ochiba here in Osaka, home again, then I can get back to the temple, *neh?* How is she, and how is the Lady Genjiko?"

"They're both in excellent health," Toranaga told her, chortling to himself. Nine years ago, in an unusual show of friendship, the Taikō had privately invited him to marry Lady Genjiko, the younger sister of Lady Ochiba, his favorite consort. 'Then our houses will be joined together forever, *neh?*' the Taikō had said.

'Yes, Sire. I will obey though I do not deserve the honor,' Toranaga had replied deferentially, desiring the link with the Taikō. But he knew that though Yodoko, the Taikō's wife, might approve, his consort Ochiba hated him and would use her great influence over the Taikō to prevent the marriage. And, too, it was wiser to avoid having Ochiba's sister as his wife, for that would give her enormous powers over him, not the least of which was the keys to his treasury. But, if she were to marry his son, Sudara, then Toranaga as supreme head of the family would have complete domination. It had taken all his skill to maneuver the marriage between Sudara and Genjiko but it had happened and now Genjiko was priceless to him as a defense against Ochiba, because Ochiba adored her sister.

"My daughter-in-law isn't in labor yet—it was expected to begin yesterday—but I would imagine the Lady Ochiba will leave immediately there's no danger."

"After three girls, it's time Genjiko gave you a grandson, *neh?* I will say prayers for his birth."

"Thank you," Toranaga said, liking her as always, knowing that she meant it, even though he represented nothing but danger to her house.

"I hear your Lady Sazuko's with child?"

"Yes. I'm very fortunate." Toranaga basked in the thought of his newest consort, the youth of her, the strength of her, and the warmth. I hope we have a son, he told himself. Yes, that would be very good. Seventeen's a good age to have a first child, if you've perfect health as she has. "Yes, I'm very fortunate."

"Buddha has blessed you." Yodoko felt a twinge of envy. It seemed so unfair that Toranaga had five sons living and four daughters and five granddaughters already, and, with this child of Sazuko's soon to arrive, and still many strong years left in him and many consorts in his house, he could sire many more sons. But all her hopes were centered on this one seven-year-old child, her child as much as Ochiba's. Yes, he's as much my son, she thought. How I hated Ochiba in the beginning. . . .

She saw them all staring at her and she was startled. "Yes?"

Yaemon frowned. "I said, can we go and have my lessons, First Mother? I said it two times."

"I'm sorry, my son, I was drifting away. That's what happens when you get old. Yes, come along then." Kiri helped her up. Yaemon ran off ahead. The Grays were already on their feet and one of them caught him and affectionately swung him onto his shoulders. The four samurai who had escorted her waited separately.

"Walk with me a little, Lord Toranaga, would you please? I need a strong arm to lean on."

Toranaga was on his feet with surprising agility. She took his arm but did not use his strength. "Yes. I need a strong arm. Yaemon does. And so does the realm."

"I'm always ready to serve you," Toranaga said.

When they were away from the others, she said quietly, "Become sole Regent. Take the power and rule yourself. Until Yaemon becomes of age."

"The Taikō's testament forbids this—even if I wished it, which I don't. The curbs he made preclude one Regent's taking power. I don't seek sole power. I never have."

"Tora-chan," she said, using the nickname the Taikō had given him so long ago, "we have few secrets, you and I. You could do it, if you wished. I will answer for the Lady Ochiba. Take the power for your own lifetime. Become Shōgun and make—"

"Lady, what you say is treason. I-do-not-seek-to-be-Shōgun."

"Of course, but please listen to me a last time. Become Shōgun, make Yaemon your *sole* heir—your sole heir. He could be Shōgun, after you. Isn't his bloodline Fujimoto—through Lady Ochiba back to her grandfather Goroda and through him back to antiquity? Fujimoto!"

Toranaga stared at her. "You think the *daimyos* would agree to such a claim, or that His Highness, the Son of Heaven, could approve the appointment?"

"No. Not for Yaemon by himself. But if you were Shōgun first, and you adopted him, you could persuade them, all of them. We will support you, the Lady Ochiba and I."

"She has agreed to this?" asked Toranaga, astounded.

"No. We've never discussed it. It's my idea. But she will agree. I will answer for her. In advance."

"This is an impossible conversation, Lady."

"You can manage Ishido, and all of them. You always have. I'm afraid of what I hear, Tora-chan, rumors of war, the taking of sides, and the Dark Centuries beginning again. When war begins it will go on forever and eat Yaemon up."

"Yes. I believe that, too. Yes, if it begins it will last forever."

"Then take the power! Do what you wish, to whomever you wish, however you wish. Yaemon's a worthy boy. I know you like him. He has his father's mind and with your guidance, we would all benefit. He should have his heritage."

"I'm not opposing him, or his succession. How many times need I say it?"

"The Heir will be destroyed unless you actively support him."

"I do support him!" Toranaga said. "In every way. That's what I agreed with the Taikō, your late husband."

Yodoko sighed and pulled her habit closer. "These old bones are chilled. So many secrets and battles, treacheries and deaths and victories, Tora-chan. I'm only a woman, and very much alone. I'm glad that I'm dedicated to Buddha now, and that most of my thoughts are toward Buddha and my next life. But in this one I have to protect my son and to say these things to you. I hope you will forgive my impertinence."

"I always seek and enjoy your counsel."

"Thank you." Her back straightened a little. "Listen, while I'm alive neither the Heir nor the Lady Ochiba will ever go against you."

"Yes."

"Will you consider what I proposed?"

"My late Master's will forbids it. I cannot go against the will or my sacred promise as a Regent."

They walked in silence. Then Yodoko sighed. "Why not take her to wife?"

Toranaga stopped in his tracks. "Ochiba?"

"Why not? She's totally worthy as a political choice. A perfect choice for you. She's beautiful, young, strong, her bloodline's the best, part Fujimoto, part Minowara, the sun dances in her, and she has an immense joy of life. You've no official wife now—so why not? This would solve the problem of the succession and stop the realm from being torn apart. You would have other sons by her surely. Yaemon would succeed you, then his sons or her other sons. You could become Shōgun. You would have the power of the realm and the power of a father so you could train Yaemon to your way. You would adopt him formally and he would be as much your son as any you have. Why not marry Lady Ochiba?"

Because she's a wildcat, a treacherous tigress with the face and body of a goddess, who thinks she's an empress and acts like one, Toranaga told himself. You could never trust her in your bed. She'd be just as likely to thread a needle through your eyes when you're asleep as she'd be to caress you. Oh no, not her! Even if I married her in name only—which she'd never agree to—oh no! It's impossible! For all sorts of reasons, not the least of which is that she's hated me and plotted my downfall, and that of my house, ever since she whelped for the first time, eleven years ago.

Even then, even at seventeen, she had committed herself to my destruction. Ah, so soft outwardly, like the first ripe peach of summer, and as fragrant. But inwardly sword steel with a mind to match, weaving her spells, soon making the Taikō mad over her to the exclusion of all others. Yes, she had the Taikō cowed since she was fifteen when he first took her formally. Yes, and don't forget, truly, she pillowed him, even then, not he her, however much he believed it. Yes, even at fifteen, Ochiba knew what she sought and the way to obtain it. Then the miracle happening, giving the Taikō a son at long last, she alone of all the women he had in his life. How many pillow ladies? A hundred at least, him a stoat who sprayed more Joyful Juice into more Heavenly Chambers than ten ordinary men! Yes. And these women of all ages and all castes, casual or consort, from a Fujimoto princess to Fourth Class courtesans. But none ever even became pregnant, though later, many of those that the Taikō dismissed or divorced or married off had children by other men. None, except the Lady Ochiba.

But she gave him his first son at fifty-three, poor little thing, sickly and dying so soon, the Taikō rending his clothes, almost crazy with grief, blaming himself and not her. Then, four years later, miraculously she whelped again, miraculously another son, miraculously healthy this time, she twenty-one now. Ochiba the Peerless, the Taikō had called her.

Did the Taikō father Yaemon or not? Eeeee, I'd give a lot to know the truth. Will we ever know the truth? Probably not, but what would I not give for proof, one way or another.

Strange that the Taikō, so clever about everything else, was not clever about Ochiba, doting on her and Yaemon to insanity. Strange that of all the women she should have been the mother of his heir, she whose father and stepfather and mother were dead because of the Taikō.

Would she have the cleverness to pillow with another man, to take his seed, then obliterate this same man to safeguard herself? Not once but twice?

Could she be so treacherous? Oh, yes.

Marry Ochiba? Never.

"I'm honored that you would make such a suggestion," Toranaga said.

"You're a *man,* Tora-chan. You could handle such a woman easily. You're the only man in the Empire who could, *neh?* She would make a marvelous match for you. Look how she fights to protect her son's interests now, and she's only a defenseless woman. She'd be a worthy wife for you."

"I don't think she would ever consider it."

"And if she did?"

"I would like to know. Privately. Yes, that would be an inestimable honor."

"Many people believe that only you stand between Yaemon and the succession."

"Many people are fools."

"Yes. But you're not, Toranaga-sama. Neither is the Lady Ochiba."

Nor are you, my Lady, he thought.

CHAPTER 18

IN the darkest part of the night the assassin came over the wall into the garden. He was almost invisible. He wore close-fitting black clothes and his tabi were black, and a black cowl and mask covered his head. He was a small man and he ran noiselessly for the front of the stone inner fortress and stopped just short of the soaring walls. Fifty yards away two Browns guarded the main door. Deftly he threw a cloth-covered hook with a very thin silk rope attached to it. The hook caught on the stone ledge of the embrasure. He shinned up the rope, squeezed through the slit, and disappeared inside.

The corridor was quiet and candle-lit. He hurried down it silently, opened an outside door, and went out onto the battlements. Another deft throw and a short climb and he was into the corridor above. The sentries that were on the corners of the battlements did not hear him though they were alert.

He pressed into an alcove of stone as other Browns walked by quietly, on patrol. When they had passed, he slipped along the length of this passageway. At the corner he stopped. Silently he peered around it. A samurai was guarding the far door. Candles danced in the quiet. The guard was sitting cross-legged and he yawned and leaned back against the wall and stretched. His eyes closed momentarily. Instantly, the assassin darted forward. Soundlessly. He formed a noose with the silk rope in his hands, dropped it over the guard's neck and jerked tight. The guard's fingers tried to claw the garrote away but he was already dying. A short stab with the knife between the vertebrae as deft as a surgeon's and the guard was motionless.

The man eased the door open. The audience room was empty, the inner doors unguarded. He pulled the corpse inside and closed the door again. Unhesitatingly he crossed the space and chose the inner left door. It was wood and heavily reinforced. The curved knife slid into his right hand. He knocked softly.

"'In the days of the Emperor Shirakawa . . .'" he said, giving the first part of the password.

From the other side of the door there was a sibilance of steel leaving a scabbard and the reply, "'. . . there lived a wise man called Enraku-ji . . .'"

"'. . . who wrote the thirty-first sutra.' I have urgent dispatches for Lord Toranaga."

The door swung open and the assassin lunged forward. The knife went upward into the first samurai's throat just below the chin and came out as fast and buried itself identically into the second of the guards. A slight twist and out again. Both men were dead on their feet. He caught one and let him slump gently; the other fell, but noiselessly. Blood ran out of them onto the floor and their bodies twitched in the throes of death.

The man hurried down this inner corridor. It was poorly lit. Then a shoji opened. He froze, slowly looked around.

Kiri was gaping at him, ten paces away. A tray was in her hands.

He saw that the two cups on the tray were unused, the food untouched. A thread of steam came from the teapot. Beside it, a candle spluttered. Then the tray was falling and her hands went into her obi and emerged with a dagger, her mouth worked but made no sound, and he was already racing for the corner. At the far end a door opened and a startled, sleep-drenched samurai peered out.

The assassin rushed toward him and tore open a shoji on his right that he sought. Kiri was screaming and the alarm had sounded, and he ran, sure-footed in the darkness, across this anteroom, over the waking women and their maids, into the innermost corridor at the far side.

Here it was pitch dark but he groped along unerringly to find the right door in the gathering furor. He slid the door open and jumped for the figure that lay on the futon. But his knife arm was caught by a viselike grip and now he was thrashing in combat on the floor. He fought with cunning, broke free, and slashed again but missed, entangled with the quilt. He hurled it off and threw himself at the figure, knife poised for the death thrust. But the man twisted with unexpected agility and a hardened foot dug into his groin. Pain exploded in him as his victim darted for safety.

Then samurai were crowding the doorway, some with lanterns, and Naga, wearing only a loincloth, his hair tousled, leapt between him and Blackthorne, sword on high.

"Surrender!"

The assassin feinted once, shouted, *"Namu Amida Butsu—"* In the Name of the Buddha Amida—turned the knife on himself and with both hands thrust it up under the base of his chin. Blood spurted and he slumped to his knees. Naga slashed once, his sword a whirling arc, and the head rolled free.

In the silence Naga picked the head up and ripped off the mask. The face was ordinary, the eyes still fluttering. He held the head, hair dressed like a samurai, by its topknot.

"Does anyone know him?"

No one answered. Naga spat in the face, threw the head angrily to one of his men, tore open the black clothes and lifted the man's right arm, and found what he was looking for. The small tattoo—the Chinese character for Amida, the special Buddha—was etched in the armpit.

"Who is officer of the watch?"

"I am, Lord." The man was white with shock.

Naga leaped at him and the others scattered. The officer made no attempt to avoid the ferocious sword blow which took off his head and part of his shoulder and one arm.

"Hayabusa-san, order all samurai from this watch into the court-yard," Naga said to an officer. "Double guards for the new watch. Get the body out of here. The rest of you are—" He stopped as Kiri came to the doorway, the dagger still in her hand. She looked at the corpse, then at Blackthorne.

"The Anjin-san's not hurt?" she asked.

Naga glanced at the man who towered over him, breathing with diffi-culty. He could see no wounds or blood. Just a sleep-tousled man who had almost been killed. White-faced but no outward fear. "Are you hurt, Pilot?"

"I don't understand."

Naga went over and pulled the sleeping kimono away to see if the pilot had been wounded.

"Ah, understand now. No. No hurt," he heard the giant say and he saw him shake his head.

"Good," he said. "He seems unhurt, Kiritsubo-san."

He saw the Anjin-san point at the body and say something. "I don't understand you," Naga replied. "Anjin-san, you stay here," and to one of the men he said, "Bring him some food and drink if he wants it."

"The assassin, he was Amida-tattooed, *neh?*" Kiri asked.

"Yes, Lady Kiritsubo."

"Devils—devils."

"Yes."

Naga bowed to her then looked at one of the appalled samurai. "You follow me. Bring the head!" He strode off, wondering how he was going to tell his father. Oh, Buddha, thank you for guarding my father.

"He was a *ronin*," Toranaga said curtly. "You'll never trace him, Hiro-matsu-san."

"Yes. But Ishido's responsible. He had no honor to do this, *neh?* None. To use these dung-offal assassins. Please, I beg you, let me call up our legions now. I'll stop this once and for all time."

"No." Toranaga looked back at Naga. "You're sure the Anjin-san's not hurt?"

"No, Sire."

"Hiro-matsu-san. You will demote all guards of this watch for failing in their duty. They are forbidden to commit seppuku. They're ordered to live with their shame in front of all my men as soldiers of the lowest class. Have the dead guards dragged by their feet through the castle and city to the execution ground. The dogs can feed off them."

Now he looked at his son, Naga. Earlier that evening, urgent word had arrived from Johji Monastery in Nagoya about Ishido's threat against Naga. Toranaga had at once ordered his son confined to close quarters and surrounded by guards, and the other members of the family in Osaka—Kiri and the Lady Sazuko—equally guarded. The message from the abbot had added that he had considered it wise to release Ishido's mother at once and send her back to the city with her maids. "I dare not risk the life of one of your illustrious sons foolishly. Worse, her health is not good. She has a chill. It's best she should die in her own house and not here."

"Naga-san, you are equally responsible the assassin got in," Toranaga said, his voice cold and bitter. "Every samurai is responsible, whether on watch or off watch, asleep or awake. You are fined half your yearly revenue."

"Yes, Lord," the youth said, surprised that he was allowed to keep anything, including his head. "Please demote me also," he said. "I cannot live with the shame. I deserve nothing but contempt for my own failure, Lord."

"If I wanted to demote you I would have done so. You are ordered to Yedo at once. You will leave with twenty men tonight and report to your brother. You will get there in record time! Go!" Naga bowed and went away, white-faced. To Hiro-matsu he said equally roughly, "Quadruple my guards. Cancel my hunting today, and tomorrow. The day after the meeting of Regents I leave Osaka. You'll make all the preparations, and until that time, I will stay here. I will see no one uninvited. No one."

He waved his hand in angry dismissal. "All of you can go. Hiro-matsu, you stay."

The room emptied. Hiro-matsu was glad that his humiliation was to be private, for, of all of them, as Commander of the Bodyguard, he was the most responsible. "I have no excuse, Lord. None."

Toranaga was lost in thought. No anger was visible now. "If you wanted to hire the services of the secret Amida Tong, how would you find them? How would you approach them?"

"I don't know, Lord."

"Who would know?"

"Kasigi Yabu."

Toranaga looked out of the embrasure. Threads of dawn were mixed with the eastern dark. "Bring him here at dawn."

"You think he's responsible?"

Toranaga did not answer, but returned to his musings.

At length the old soldier could not bear the silence. "Please Lord, let me get out of your sight. I'm so ashamed with our failure—"

"It's almost impossible to prevent such an attempt," Toranaga said.

"Yes. But we should have caught him outside, nowhere near you."

"I agree. But I don't hold you responsible."

"I hold myself responsible. There's something I must say, Lord, for I *am* responsible for your safety until you're back in Yedo. There will be more attempts on you, and all our spies report increased troop movement. Ishido is mobilizing."

"Yes," Toranaga said casually. "After Yabu, I want to see Tsukku-san, then Mariko-san. Double the guards on the Anjin-san."

"Despatches came tonight that Lord Onoshi has a hundred thousand men improving his fortifications in Kyushu," Hiro-matsu said, beset by his anxiety for Toranaga's safety.

"I will ask him about it, when we meet."

Hiro-matsu's temper broke. "I don't understand you at all. I must tell you that you risk everything stupidly. Yes, stupidly. I don't care if you take my head for telling you, but it's the truth. If Kiyama and Onoshi vote with Ishido you will be impeached! You're a dead man—you've risked everything by coming here and you've lost! Escape while you can. At least you'll have your head on your shoulders!"

"I'm in no danger yet."

"Doesn't this attack tonight mean anything to you? If you hadn't changed your room again you'd be dead now."

"Yes, I might, but probably not," Toranaga said. "There were multiple guards outside *my* doors tonight and also last night. And you were on guard tonight as well. No assassin could get near me. Even this one who was so well prepared. He knew the way, even the password, *neh?* Kiri-san said she heard him use it. So I think he knew which room I was in. I wasn't his prey. It was the Anjin-san."

"The barbarian?"

"Yes."

Toranaga had anticipated that there would be further danger to the barbarian after the extraordinary revelations of this morning. Clearly the Anjin-san was too dangerous to some to leave alive. But Toranaga had never presumed that an attack would be mounted within his private quarters or so fast. Who's betraying me? He discounted a leakage of information from Kiri, or Mariko. But castles and gardens always have secret places to eavesdrop, he thought. I'm in the center of the enemy stronghold, and where I have one spy, Ishido—and others—will have twenty. Perhaps it was just a spy.

"Double the guards on the Anjin-san. He's worth ten thousand men to me."

After Lady Yodoko had left this morning, he had returned to the garden tea house and had noticed at once the Anjin-san's inner frailty, the overbright eyes and grinding fatigue. So he had controlled his own excitement and almost overpowering need to probe deeper, and had dismissed him, saying that they would continue tomorrow. The Anjin-san had been given into Kiri's care with instructions to get him a doctor, to harbor his strength, to give him barbarian food if he wished it, and even to let him have the sleeping room that Toranaga himself used most nights. "Give him anything you feel necessary, Kiri-san," he had told her privately. "I need him very fit, very quickly, in mind and body."

Then the Anjin-san had asked that he release the monk from prison today, for the man was old and sick. He had replied that he would consider it and sent the barbarian away with thanks, not telling him that he had already ordered samurai to go to the prison at once and fetch this monk, who was perhaps equally valuable, both to him and to Ishido.

Toranaga had known about this priest for a long time, that he was Spanish and hostile to the Portuguese. But the man had been ordered there by the Taikō so he was the Taikō's prisoner, and he, Toranaga, had no jurisdiction over anyone in Osaka. He had sent the Anjin-san deliberately into that prison not only to pretend to Ishido that the stranger was worthless, but also in the hope that the impressive pilot would be able to draw out the monk's knowledge.

The first clumsy attempt on the Anjin-san's life in the cell had been foiled, and at once a protective screen had been put around him. Toranaga had rewarded his vassal spy, Minikui, a kaga-man, by extracting him safely and giving him four kagas of his own and the hereditary right to use the stretch of the Tokaido Road—the great trunk road that joined Yedo and Osaka—between the Second and Third Stages, which were in his domains near Yedo, and had sent him secretly out of Osaka the first day. During the following days his other spies had sent reports that the two men were friends now, the monk talking and the Anjin-san asking questions and listening. The fact that Ishido probably had spies in the cell too did not bother him. The Anjin-san was protected and safe. Then Ishido had unexpectedly tried to spirit him out, into alien influence.

Toranaga remembered the amusement he and Hiro-matsu had had in planning the immediate "ambush"—the "ronin bandits" being one of the small, isolated groups of his own elite samurai who were secreted in and around Osaka—and in arranging the delicate timing of Yabu who, unsuspecting, had effected the "rescue." They had chuckled together, knowing that once more they had used Yabu as a puppet to rub Ishido's nose in his own dung.

Everything had succeeded beautifully. Until today.

Today the samurai he had sent to fetch the monk had returned empty-handed. "The priest is dead," the man had reported. "When his name was called, he didn't come out, Lord Toranaga. I went in to fetch him, but he was dead. The criminals around him said when the jailers called his name, he just collapsed. He was dead when I turned him over. Please excuse me, you sent me for him and I've failed to do what you ordered. I didn't know if you wanted his head, or his head on his body seeing he was a barbarian, so I brought the body with the head still on. Some of the criminals around him said they were his converts. They wanted to keep the corpse and they tried to keep it so I killed a few and brought the corpse. It's stinking and verminous but it's in the courtyard, Sire."

Why did the monk die? Toranaga asked himself again. Then he saw Hiro-matsu looking at him questioningly. "Yes?"

"I just asked who would want the pilot dead?"

"Christians."

Kasigi Yabu followed Hiro-matsu along the corridor, feeling grand in the dawn. There was a nice salt tang to the breeze, and it reminded him of Mishima, his home city. He was glad that at long last he was to see Toranaga and the waiting was over. He had bathed and dressed with care. Last letters had been written to his wife and to his mother and his final will sealed in case the interview went against him. Today he was wearing the Murasama blade within its battle-honored scabbard.

They turned another corner, then unexpectedly Hiro-matsu opened an iron-bound reinforced door and led the way up the stone steps into the inner central keep of this part of the fortifications. There were many guards on duty and Yabu sensed danger.

The stairs curled upward and ended at an easily defendable redoubt. Guards opened the iron door. He went out onto the battlements. Has Hiro-matsu been told to throw me off, or will I be ordered to jump? he asked himself unafraid.

To his surprise Toranaga was there and, incredibly, Toranaga got up to greet him with a jovial deference he had no right to expect. After all, Toranaga was Lord of the Eight Provinces, whereas he was only Lord of Izu. Cushions had been placed carefully. A teapot was cradled in a sheath of silk. A richly dressed, square-faced girl of little beauty was bowing low. Her name was Sazuko and she was the seventh of Toranaga's official consorts, the youngest, and very pregnant.

"How nice to see you, Kasigi Yabu-san. I'm so sorry to have kept you waiting."

Now Yabu was certain that Toranaga had decided to remove his head, one way or another, for, by universal custom, your enemy is never more polite than when he is planning or has planned your destruction. He took out both his swords and placed them carefully on the stone flags, allowed himself to be led away from them and seated in the place of honor.

"I thought it would be interesting to watch the dawning, Yabu-san. I think the view here is exquisite—even better than from the Heir's donjon. *Neh?*"

"Yes, it is beautiful," Yabu said without reservation, never having been so high in the castle before, sure now that Toranaga's remark about "the Heir" implied that his secret negotiations with Ishido were known. "I'm honored to be allowed to share it with you."

Below them were the sleeping city and harbor and islands, Awaji to the west, the coastline falling off to the east, the growing light in the eastern sky slashing the clouds with flecks of crimson.

"This is my Lady Sazuko. Sazuko, this is my ally, the famous Lord Kasigi Yabu of Izu, the *daimyo* who brought us the barbarian and the treasure ship!" She bowed and complimented him and he bowed and she returned his bow again. She offered Yabu the first cup of tea but he politely declined the honor, beginning the ritual, and asked her to give it to Toranaga, who refused, and pressed him to accept it. Eventually, continuing the ritual, as the honored guest he allowed himself to be persuaded. Hiro-matsu accepted the second cup, his gnarled fingers holding the porcelain with difficulty, the other hand wrapped around the haft of his sword, loose in his lap. Toranaga accepted a third cup and sipped his cha, then together they gave themselves to nature and watched the sunrise. In the silence of the sky.

Gulls mewed. The city sounds began. The day was born.

Lady Sazuko sighed, her eyes wet with tears. "It makes me feel like a goddess being so high, watching so much beauty, *neh?* It's so sad that it's gone forever, Sire. So very sad, *neh?*"

"Yes," Toranaga said.

When the sun was halfway above the horizon, she bowed and left. To Yabu's surprise, the guards left also. Now they were alone. The three of them.

"I was pleased to receive your gift, Yabu-san. It was most generous, the whole ship and everything in it," Toranaga said.

"Whatever I have is yours," Yabu said, still deeply affected by the dawning. I wish I had more time, he thought. How elegant of Toranaga to do this! To give me a lastness of such immensity. "Thank you for this dawn."

"Yes," Toranaga said. "It was mine to give. I'm pleased that you enjoyed my gift, as I enjoyed yours."

There was a silence.

"Yabu-san. What do you know about the Amida Tong?"

"Only what most people know: that it's a secret society of ten—units of ten—a leader and never more than nine acolytes in any one area, women and men. They are sworn by the most sacred and secret oaths of the Lord Buddha Amida, the Dispenser of Eternal Love, to obedience, chastity, and death; to spend their lives training to become a perfect weapon for one kill; to kill only at the order of the leader, and if they fail to kill the person chosen, be it a man, woman, or child, to take their own life at once. They're religious fanatics who are certain they'll go directly from this life to Buddhahood. Not one of them has ever been caught alive." Yabu knew about the attempt on Toranaga's life. All Osaka knew by now and knew also that the Lord of the Kwanto, the Eight Provinces, had locked himself safely inside hoops of steel. "They kill rarely, their secrecy is complete. There's no chance of revenge on them because no one knows who they are, where they live, or where they train."

"If you wanted to employ them, how would you go about it?"

"I would whisper it in three places—in the Heinan Monastery, at the gates of the Amida shrine, and in the Johji Monastery. Within ten days, if you are considered an acceptable employer, you will be approached through intermediaries. It is all so secret and devious that, even if you wished to betray them or catch them, it would never be possible. On the tenth day they ask for a sum of money, in silver, the amount depending on the person to be assassinated. There is no bargaining, you pay what they ask beforehand. They guarantee only that one of their members will attempt the kill within ten days. Legend has it that if the kill is successful, the assassin goes back to their temple and then, with great ceremony, commits ritual suicide."

"Then you think we could never find out who paid for the attack today?"

"No."

"Do you think there will be another?"

"Perhaps. Perhaps not. They contract for one attempt at one time, *neh?* But you'd be wise to improve your security—among your samurai, and also among your women. The Amida women are trained in poison, as well as knife and garrote, so they say."

"Have you ever employed them?"

"No."

"But your father did?"

"I don't know, not for certain. I was told that the Taikō asked him to contact them once."

"Was the attack successful?"

"Anything the Taikō did was successful. One way or another."

Yabu felt someone behind him and presumed it to be the guards coming back secretly. He was measuring the distance to his swords. Do I try to kill Toranaga? he asked himself again. I had decided to and now I don't know. I've changed. Why?

"What would you have to pay them for my head?" Toranaga asked him.

"There is not enough silver in all Asia to tempt me to employ them to do this."

"What would another have to pay?"

"Twenty thousand koku—fifty thousand—a hundred—perhaps more, I don't know."

"Would you pay a hundred thousand koku to become Shōgun? Your bloodline goes back to the Takashimas, *neh?*"

Yabu said proudly, "I would pay nothing. Money's filth—a toy for women to play with or for dung-filled merchants. But if that were possible, which it isn't, I would give my life and the life of my wife and mother and all my kin except my one son, and all my samurai in Izu and all their women and children to be Shōgun one day."

"And what would you give for the Eight Provinces?"

"Everything as before, except the life of my wife and mother and son."

"And for Suruga Province?"

"Nothing," Yabu said with contempt. "Ikawa Jikkyu's worth nothing. If I don't take his head and all his generation in this life I'll do it in another. I piss on him and his seed for ten thousand lifetimes."

"And if I were to give him to you? And all Suruga—and perhaps the next province, Totomi, as well?"

Yabu suddenly tired of the cat-and-mouse game and the talk about the Amida. "You've decided to take my head, Lord Toranaga—very well. I'm ready. I thank you for the dawn. But I've no wish to spoil such elegance with further talk, so let's be done."

"But I haven't decided to take your head, Yabu-san," Toranaga said. "Whatever gave you the thought? Has an enemy poured poison in your ears? Ishido perhaps? Aren't you my favored ally? Do you think that I'd entertain you here, without guards, if I thought you hostile?"

Yabu turned slowly. He had expected to find samurai behind him, swords poised. There was no one there. He looked back at Toranaga. "I don't understand."

"I brought you here so we could talk privately. And to see the dawn. Would you like to rule the provinces of Izu, Suruga, and Totomi—if I do not lose this war?"

"Yes. Very much," Yabu said, his hopes soaring.

"You would become my vassal? Accept me as your liege lord?"

Yabu did not hesitate. "Never," he said. "As ally, yes. As my leader, yes. Lesser than you always, yes. My life and all I possess thrown onto your side, yes. But Izu is mine. I am *daimyo* of Izu and I will never give power over Izu to anyone. I swore that oath to my father, and the Taikō who reaffirmed our hereditary fief, first to my father and then to me. The Taikō confirmed Izu to me and my successors forever. He was our liege lord and I swore never to have another until his heir became of age."

Hiro-matsu twisted his sword slightly in his hand. Why doesn't Toranaga let me get it over with once and for all? It's been agreed. Why all the wearing talk? I ache and I want to piss and I need to lie down.

Toranaga scratched his groin. "What did Ishido offer you?"

"Jikkyu's head—the moment that yours is off. And his province."

"In return for what?"

"Support when war begins. To attack your southern flank."

"Did you accept?"

"You know me better than that."

Toranaga's spies in Ishido's household had whispered that the bargain had been struck, and that it included responsibility for the assassination of his three sons, Noboru, Sudara, and Naga. "Nothing more? Just support?"

"By every means at my disposal," Yabu said delicately.

"Including assassination?"

"I intend to wage the war, when it begins, with all my force. For my ally. In any way I can to guarantee his success. We need a sole Regent in Yaemon's minority. War between you and Ishido is inevitable. It's the only way."

Yabu was trying to read Toranaga's mind. He was scornful of Toranaga's indecision, knowing that he himself was the better man, that Toranaga needed his support, that at length he would vanquish him. But meanwhile what to do? he asked himself and wished Yuriko, his wife, were here to guide him. She would know the wisest course. "I can be very valuable to you. I can help you become sole Regent," he said, deciding to gamble.

"Why should I wish to be sole Regent?"

"When Ishido attacks I can help you to conquer him. When he breaks the peace," Yabu said.

"How?"

He told them his plan with the guns.

"A regiment of five hundred gun-samurai?" Hiro-matsu erupted.

"Yes. Think of the fire power. All elite men, trained to act as one man. The twenty cannon equally together."

"It's a bad plan. Disgusting," Hiro-matsu said. "You could never keep it secret. If we start, the enemy would start also. There would never be an end to such horror. There's no honor in it and no future."

"Isn't this coming war the only one we're concerned with, Lord Hiromatsu?" Yabu replied. "Aren't we concerned only with Lord Toranaga's safety? Isn't that the duty of his allies and vassals?"

"Yes."

"All Lord Toranaga has to do is win the one great battle. That will give him the heads of all his enemies—and power. I say this strategy will give him victory."

"I say it won't. It's a disgusting plan with no honor."

Yabu turned to Toranaga. "A new era requires clear thinking about the meaning of honor."

A sea gull soared overhead mewing.

"What did Ishido say to your plan?" Toranaga asked.

"I did not discuss it with him."

"Why? If you think your plan's valuable to me, it would be equally valuable to him. Perhaps more so."

"You gave me a dawn. You're not a peasant like Ishido. You're the wisest, most experienced leader in the Empire."

What's the real reason? Toranaga was asking himself. Or have you told Ishido too? "If this plan were to be followed, the men would be half yours and half mine?"

"Agreed. I would command them."

"My appointee would be second-in-command?"

"Agreed. I would need the Anjin-san to train my men as gunners, cannoneers."

"But he would be my property permanently, you would cherish him as you do the Heir? You'd be totally responsible for him and do with him precisely as I say?"

"Agreed."

Toranaga watched the crimson clouds for a moment. This planning is all nonsense, he thought. I will have to declare Crimson Sky myself and lunge for Kyoto at the head of all my legions. One hundred thousand against ten times that number. "Who will be interpreter? I can't detach Toda Mariko-san forever."

"For a few weeks, Sire? I will see that the barbarian learns our language."

"That'd take years. The only barbarians who've ever mastered it are Christian priests, *neh?* They spend years. Tsukku-san's been here almost thirty years, *neh?* He won't learn fast enough, anymore than we can learn their foul languages."

"Yes. But I promise you, this Anjin-san'll learn very quickly." Yabu told them the plan Omi had suggested to him as if it were his own idea.

"That might be too dangerous."

"It would make him learn quickly, *neh?* And then he's tamed."

After a pause, Toranaga said, "How would you maintain secrecy during the training?"

"Izu is a peninsula, security is excellent there. I'll base near Anjiro, well south and away from Mishima and the border for more safety."

"Good. We'll set up carrier pigeon links from Anjiro to Osaka and Yedo at once."

"Excellent. I need only five or six months and—"

"We'll be lucky to have six days!" Hiro-matsu snorted. "Are you saying that your famous espionage net has been swept away, Yabu-san? Surely you've been getting reports? Isn't Ishido mobilizing? Isn't Onoshi mobilizing? Aren't we locked in here?"

Yabu did not answer.

"Well?" Toranaga said.

Yabu said, "Reports indicate all that is happening and more. If it's six days then it's six days and that's *karma*. But I believe you're much too clever to be trapped here. Or provoked into an early war."

"If I agreed to your plan, you would accept me as your leader?"

"Yes. And when you win, I would be honored to accept Suruga and Totomi as part of my fief forever."

"Totomi would depend on the success of your plan."

"Agreed."

"You will obey me? With all your honor?"

"Yes. By *bushido,* by the Lord Buddha, by the life of my mother, my wife, and my future posterity."

"Good," Toranaga said. "Let's piss on the bargain."

He went to the edge of the battlements. He stepped up on the ledge of the embrasure, then onto the parapet itself. Seventy feet below was the inner garden. Hiro-matsu held his breath, aghast at his master's bravado. He saw him turn and beckon Yabu to stand beside him. Yabu obeyed. The slightest touch could have sent them tumbling to their deaths.

Toranaga eased his kimono and loincloth aside, as did Yabu. Together they urinated and mixed their urine and watched it dew the garden below.

"The last bargain I sealed this way was with the Taikō himself," Toranaga said, greatly relieved at being able to empty his bladder. "That was when he decided to give me the Kwanto, the Eight Provinces, as my fief. Of course, at that time the enemy Hojo still owned them, so first I had to conquer them. They were our last remaining opposition. Of course, too, I had to give up my hereditary fiefs of Imagawa, Owari, and Ise at once for the honor. Even so, I agreed and we pissed on the bargain." He straddled the parapet easily, settling his loincloth comfortably as though he stood in the garden itself, not perched like an eagle so far above. "It was a good bargain for both of us. We conquered the Hojo and took over five thousand heads within the year. Stamped him out and all his tribe. Perhaps you're right, Kasigi Yabu-san. Perhaps you can help me as I helped the Taikō. Without me, the Taikō would never have become Taikō."

"I can help to make you sole Regent, Toranaga-sama. But not Shōgun."

"Of course. That's the one honor I don't seek, as much as my enemies say I do." Toranaga jumped down to the safety of the stone flags. He looked back at Yabu who still stood on the narrow parapet adjusting his sash. He was sorely tempted to give him a quick shove for his insolence. Instead he sat down and broke wind loudly. "That's better. How's your bladder, Iron Fist?"

"Tired, Lord, very tired." The old man went to the side and emptied himself thankfully over the battlements too, but he did not stand where Toranaga and Yabu had stood. He was very glad that he did not also have to seal the bargain with Yabu. That's one bargain I will never honor. Never.

"Yabu-san. This must all be kept secret. I think you should leave within the next two or three days," Toranaga said.

"Yes. With the guns and the barbarian, Toranaga-sama?"

"Yes. You will go by ship." Toranaga looked at Hiro-matsu. "Prepare the galley."

"The ship is ready. The guns and powder are still in the holds," Hiro-matsu replied, his face mirroring his disapproval.

"Good."

You've done it, Yabu wanted to shout. You've got the guns, the Anjin-san, everything. You've got your six months. Toranaga'll never go to war quickly. Even if Ishido assassinates him in the next few days, you've still got everything. Oh, Buddha, protect Toranaga until I'm at sea! "Thank you," he said, his sincerity openly vast. "You'll never have a more faithful ally."

When Yabu was gone, Hiro-matsu wheeled on Toranaga. "That was a bad thing to do. I'm ashamed of that bargain. I'm ashamed that my advice counts for so little. I've obviously outlived my usefulness to you and I'm very tired. That little snot-dung *daimyo* knows he's manipulated you like a puppet. Why, he even had the effrontery to wear his Mura-sama sword in your presence."

"I noticed," Toranaga said.

"I think the gods have bewitched you, Lord. You openly dismiss such an insult and allow him to gloat in front of you. You openly allow Ishido to shame you in front of all of us. You prevent me and all of us from protecting you. You refuse my granddaughter, a samurai lady, the honor and peace of death. You've lost control of the Council, your enemy has outmaneuvered you, and now you piss on a solemn bargain that is as disgusting a plan as I've ever heard, and you do this with a man who deals in filth, poison, and treachery like his father before him." He was shaking with rage. Toranaga did not answer, just stared calmly at him as though he had said nothing. "By all *kami,* living and dead, you are bewitched." Hiro-matsu burst out, "I question you—and shout and insult you and you only stare at me! You've gone mad or I have. I ask permission to commit seppuku or if you won't allow me that peace I'll shave my head and become a monk—anything, anything, but let me be gone."

"You will do neither. But you will send for the barbarian priest, Tsukku-san."

And then Toranaga laughed.

CHAPTER 19

ATHER ALVITO rode down the hill from the castle at the head of his usual company of Jesuit outriders. All were dressed as Buddhist priests except for the rosary and crucifix they wore at their waists. There were forty outriders, Japanese, all well-born sons of Christian samurai, students from the seminary at Nagasaki who had accompanied him to Osaka. All were well mounted and caparisoned and as disciplined as the entourage of any *daimyo*.

He hurried along in a brisk trot, oblivious of the warm sunshine, through the woods and the city streets toward the Jesuit Mission, a large stone European-style house that stood near the wharves and soared from its clustered outbuildings, treasure rooms, and warehouses, where all of Osaka's silks were bartered and paid for.

The cortege clattered through the tall iron gates set in the high stone walls and into the paved central courtyard and stopped near the main door. Servants were already waiting to help Father Alvito dismount. He slid out of the saddle and threw them the reins. His spurs jingled on the stone as he strode up the cloistered walk of the main building, turned the corner, passed the small chapel, and went through some arches into the innermost courtyard which contained a fountain and a peaceful garden. The antechamber door was open. He threw off his anxiety, composed himself, and walked in.

"Is he alone?" he asked.

"No, no, he isn't, Martin," Father Soldi said. He was a small, benign, pock-marked man from Naples who had been the Father-Visitor's secretary for almost thirty years, twenty-five of them in Asia. "Captain-General Ferriera's with his Eminence. Yes, the peacock's with him. But his Eminence said you were to go in at once. What's gone wrong, Martin?"

"Nothing."

Soldi grunted and went back to sharpening his quill. " 'Nothing,' the wise Father said. Well, I'll know soon enough."

"Yes," Alvito said, liking the older man. He walked for the far door. A wood fire was burning in a grate, illuminating the fine heavy furniture, dark with age and rich with polish and care. A small Tintoretto of a Madonna and Child that the Father-Visitor had brought with him from Rome, which always pleased Alvito, hung over the fireplace.

"You saw the Ingeles again?" Father Soldi called after him.

Alvito did not answer. He knocked at the door.

"Come in."

Carlo dell'Aqua, Father-Visitor of Asia, personal representative of the General of the Jesuits, the most senior Jesuit and thus the most powerful man in Asia, was also the tallest. He stood six feet three inches, with a physique to match. His robe was orange, his cross exquisite. He was tonsured, white-haired, sixty-one years old, and by birth a Neapolitan.

"Ah, Martin, come in, come in. Some wine?" he said, speaking Portuguese with a marvelous Italian liquidity. "You saw the Ingeles?"

"No, your Eminence. Just Toranaga."

"Bad?"

"Yes."

"Some wine?"

"Thank you."

"How bad?" Ferriera asked. The soldier sat beside the fire in the high-backed leather chair as proudly as a falcon and as colorful—the *fidaglio*, the Captain-General of the *Nao del Trato,* this year's Black Ship. He was in his middle thirties, lean, slight, and formidable.

"I think very bad, Captain-General. For instance, Toranaga said the matter of this year's trade could wait."

"Obviously trade can't wait, nor can I," Ferriera said. "I'm sailing on the tide."

"You don't have your port clearances. I'm afraid you'll have to wait."

"I thought everything was arranged months ago." Again Ferriera cursed the Japanese regulations that required all shipping, even their own, to have incoming and outgoing licenses. "We shouldn't be bound by stupid native regulations. You said this meeting was just a formality —to collect the documents."

"It should have been, but I was wrong. Perhaps I'd better explain—"

"I must return to Macao immediately to prepare the Black Ship. We've already purchased a million ducats' worth of the best silks at February's Canton Fair and we'll be carrying at least a hundred thousand ounces of Chinese gold. I thought I'd made it clear that every penny of cash in Macao, Malacca, and Goa, and every penny the Macao traders and city fathers can borrow is invested in this year's venture. And every penny of yours."

"We're just as aware as you are of its importance," dell'Aqua said pointedly.

"I'm sorry, Captain-General, but Toranaga's President of the Regents and it's the custom to go to him," Alvito said. "He wouldn't discuss this year's trade or your clearances. He said, initially, he did not approve of assassination."

"Who does, Father?" Ferriera said.

"What's Toranaga talking about, Martin?" dell'Aqua asked. "Is this some sort of ruse? Assassination? What has that to do with us?"

"He said: 'Why would you Christians want to assassinate my prisoner, the Pilot?'"

"What?"

"Toranaga believes the attempt last night was on the Ingeles, not him. Also he says there was another attempt in prison." Alvito kept his eyes fixed on the soldier.

"What do you accuse me of, Father?" Ferriera said. "An assassination attempt? Me? In Osaka Castle? This is the first time I've ever been in Japan!"

"You deny any knowledge of it?"

"I do not deny that the sooner the heretic's dead the better," Ferriera said coldly. "If the Dutch and English start spreading their filth in Asia we're in for trouble. All of us."

"We're already in trouble," Alvito said. "Toranaga began by saying that he understands from the Ingeles that incredible profits are being made from the Portuguese *monopoly* of the China trade, that the Portuguese are extravagantly overpricing the silks that only the Portuguese can buy in China, paying for them with the sole commodity the Chinese will accept in exchange, Japanese silver—which again the Portuguese are equally ludicrously underpricing. Toranaga said: 'Because hostility exists between China and Japan and all direct trade between us is forbidden and the Portuguese alone have their permission to carry the trade, the Pilot's charge of "usury" should be formally replied to—*in writing*—by the Portuguese.' He 'invites' you, Eminence, to provide the Regents with a report on rates of exchange—silver to silk, silk to silver, gold to silver. He added that he does not, of course, object to our making a large profit, providing it comes from the Chinese."

"You will, of course, refuse such an arrogant request," Ferriera said.

"That is very difficult."

"Then provide a false report."

"That would endanger our whole position, which is based on trust," dell'Aqua said.

"Can you trust a Jappo? Of course not. Our profits must remain secret. That God-cursed heretic!"

"I'm sorry to tell you Blackthorne seems to be particularly well informed." Alvito looked involuntarily at dell'Aqua, his guard dropping momentarily.

The Father-Visitor said nothing.

"What else did the Jappo say?" Ferriera asked, pretending that he had not seen the look between them, wishing he knew the full extent of their knowledge.

"Toranaga asks me to provide him, by tomorrow noon, with a map of the world showing the lines of demarcation between Portugal and Spain, the names of the Popes who approved the treaties, and their dates. Within three days he 'requests' a written explanation of our 'conquests' in the New World, and 'purely for my own interest' were his exact words, the amount of gold and silver taken back—he actually used Blackthorne's word 'plundered'—taken back to Spain and Portugal from the New World. And he also requests another map showing the extent of the Empires of Spain and Portugal a hundred years ago, fifty years ago, and to-day, together with exact positions of our bases from Malacca to Goa—he named them all accurately by the way; they were written on a piece of paper—and also the numbers of Japanese mercenaries employed by us at each of our bases."

Dell'Aqua and Ferriera were appalled. "This must absolutely be refused," the soldier boomed.

"You can't refuse Toranaga," dell'Aqua said.

"I think, your Eminence, you put too much reliance on his importance," Ferriera said. "It seems to me that this Toranaga's just another despot king among many, just another murdering heathen, certainly not to be feared. Refuse him. Without our Black Ship their whole economy collapses. They're begging for our Chinese silks. Without silks there'd be no kimonos. They must have our trade. I say the pox on Toranaga. We can trade with the Christian kings—what were their names? Onoshi and Kiyama—and the other Christian kings of Kyushu. After all, Nagasaki's there, we're there in strength, all trade's done there."

"We can't, Captain," dell'Aqua said. "This is your first visit to Japan so you've no idea of our problems here. Yes, they need us, but we need them more. Without Toranaga's favor—and Ishido's—we'll lose influence over the Christian kings. We'll lose Nagasaki and everything we've built over fifty years. Did you precipitate the attempt on this heretic pilot?"

"I said openly to Rodrigues, and to anyone else who would listen from the very first, that the Ingeles was a dangerous pirate who would infect anyone he came into contact with, and who therefore should be removed in any way possible. You said the same in different words, your Eminence. So did you, Father Alvito. Didn't the matter come up at our conference with Onoshi and Kiyama two days ago? Didn't you say this pirate was dangerous?"

"Yes. But—"

"Father, you will forgive me, but sometimes it is necessary for soldiers to do God's work in the best way they can. I must tell you I was furious with Rodrigues for not creating an 'accident' during the storm. He, of all people, should have known better! By the Body of Christ, look what that devil Ingeles has already done to Rodrigues himself. The poor fool's grateful to him for saving his life when it's the most obvious trick in the world to gain his confidence. Wasn't Rodrigues fooled into allowing the heretic pilot to usurp his own quarterdeck, certainly almost causing his death? As to the castle attempt, who knows what happened? That has to have been ordered by a native, that's a Jappo trick. I'm not sad they tried, only disgusted that they failed. When *I* arrange for his removal, you may rest assured he will be removed."

Alvito sipped his wine. "Toranaga said that he was sending Black-thorne to Izu."

"The peninsula to the east?" Ferriera asked.

"Yes."

"By land or by ship?"

"By ship."

"Good. Then I regret to tell you that all hands may be lost at sea in a regrettable storm."

Alvito said coldly, "And I regret to tell you, Captain-General, that Toranaga said—I'll give you his exact words: 'I am putting a personal guard around the pilot, Tsukku-san, and if any accident befalls him it will be investigated to the limit of my power and the power of the Regents, and if, by chance, a Christian is responsible, or anyone remotely associated with Christians, it's quite possible the Expulsion Edicts would be reexamined and very possible that all Christian churches, schools, places of rest, will be immediately closed.'"

Dell'Aqua said, "God forbid that should happen."

"Bluff," Ferriera sneered.

"No, you're wrong, Captain-General. Toranaga's as clever as a Machiavelli and as ruthless as Attila the Hun." Alvito looked back at dell'-Aqua. "It would be easy to blame us if anything happened to the Ingeles."

"Yes."

"Perhaps you should go to the source of your problem," Ferriera said bluntly. "Remove Toranaga."

"This is no time for jokes," the Father-Visitor said.

"What has worked brilliantly in India and Malaya, Brazil, Peru, Mexico, Africa, the Main and elsewhere will work here. I've done it myself in Malacca and Goa a dozen times with the help of Jappo mercenaries, and I've nowhere near your influence and knowledge. We use the Christian kings. We'll help one of them to remove Toranaga if he's the problem. A few hundred conquistadores would be enough. Divide and rule. I'll approach Kiyama. Father Alvito, if you'll interpret—"

"You cannot equate Japanese with Indians or with illiterate savages like the Incas. You cannot divide and rule here. Japan is not like any other nation. Not at all," dell'Aqua said wearily. "I must ask you formally, Captain-General, not to interfere in the internal politics of this country."

"I agree. Please forget what I said. It was indelicate and naïve to be so open. Fortunately storms are normal at this time of the year."

"If a storm occurs, that is in the Hand of God. But you will *not* attack the pilot."

"Oh?"

"No. Nor will you order anyone to do it."

"I am bound by *my* king to destroy the enemies of my king. The Ingeles is an enemy national. A parasite, a pirate, a heretic. If I choose to eliminate him, that is my affair. I am Captain-General of the Black Ship this year, therefore Governor of Macao this year, with viceregal powers over these waters this year, and if I want to eliminate him, or Toranaga or whomever, I will."

"Then you do so over my direct orders to the contrary and thereby risk immediate excommunication."

"This is beyond your jurisdiction. It is a temporal matter, not a spiritual one."

"The position of the Church here is, regrettably, so intermixed with politics and with the silk trade, that everything touches the safety of the Church. And while I live, by my hope of salvation, no one will jeopardize the future of the Mother Church here!"

"Thank you for being so explicit, your Eminence. I will make it my business to become more knowledgeable about Jappo affairs."

"I suggest you do, for all our sakes. Christianity is tolerated here only because all *daimyos* believe absolutely that if they expel us and stamp out the Faith, the Black Ships will never come back. We Jesuits are sought after and have some measure of influence only because we alone can speak Japanese and Portuguese and can interpret and intercede for them on matters of trade. *Unfortunately* for the Faith, what they believe is not true. I'm certain trade would continue, irrespective of our position and the position of the Church, because Portuguese traders are more concerned with their own selfish interests than with the service of our Lord."

"Perhaps the selfish interests of the clerics who wish to force us—even to the extent of asking His Holiness for the legal powers—to force us to sail into whatever port they decide and trade with whatever *daimyo* they prefer, irrespective of the hazards, is equally evident!"

"You forget yourself, Captain-General!"

"I do not forget that the Black Ship of last year was lost between here and Malacca with all hands, with over two hundred tons of gold aboard and five hundred thousand crusados worth of silver bullion, after being delayed unnecessarily into the bad weather season because of your personal requests. Or that this catastrophe almost ruined everyone from here to Goa."

"It was necessary because of the Taikō's death and the internal politics of the succession."

"I do not forget you asked the Viceroy of Goa to cancel the Black Ship three years ago, to send it only when you said, to which port you decided, or that he overruled this as an arrogant interference."

"That was to curb the Taikō, to bring him an economic crisis in the midst of his stupid war on Korea and China, because of the Nagasaki martyrdoms he had ordered, because of his insane attack on the Church and the Expulsion Edicts he had just published expelling us all from Japan. If you cooperate with us, follow our advice, all Japan would be Christian in a single generation! What is more important—trade or the salvation of souls?"

"My answer is souls. But since you've enlightened me on Jappo affairs let me put Jappo affairs in their correct perspective. Jappo silver alone unlocks Chinese silks and Chinese gold. The immense profits we make and export to Malacca and Goa and thence to Lisbon support our whole Asian Empire, all forts, all missions, all expeditions, all missionaries, all discoveries, and pays for most, if not all of our European commitments, prevents the heretics from overrunning us and keeps them out of Asia, which would provide them with all the wealth they need to destroy us and the Faith at home. What's more important, Father—Spanish, Portuguese, and Italian Christendom, or Jappo Christendom?"

Dell'Aqua glared down at the soldier. "Once and for all, you-will-not-involve-yourself-with-the-internal-politics-here!"

A coal fell from the fire and spluttered on the rug. Ferriera, the nearest, kicked it to safety. "And if I'm to be—to be curbed, what do you propose to do about the heretic? Or Toranaga?"

Dell'Aqua sat down, believing that he had won. "I don't know, at the moment. But even to think of removing Toranaga is ludicrous. He's very sympathetic to us, and very sympathetic to increasing trade"—his voice became more withering—"and therefore to increasing your profits."

"And your profits," Ferriera said, taking the bit again.

"Our profits are committed to the work of Our Lord. As you well know." Dell'Aqua tiredly poured some wine, offered it, placating him. "Come now, Ferriera, let's not quarrel in this fashion. This business of the heretic—terrible, yes. But quarreling avails nothing. We need your counsel and your brains and your strength. You can believe me, Toranaga is vital to us. Without him to restrain the other Regents, this whole country will go back to anarchy again."

"Yes, it's true, Captain-General," Alvito said. "But I don't understand why he's still in the castle and has agreed to a delay in the meeting. It's incredible that he seems to have been outmaneuvered. He must surely know that Osaka's locked tighter than a jealous crusader's chastity belt. He should have left days ago."

Ferriera said, "If he's vital, why support Onoshi and Kiyama? Haven't those two sided with Ishido against him? Why don't you advise them against it? It was discussed only two days ago."

"They told us of their decision, Captain. We did not discuss it."

"Then perhaps you should have, Eminence. If it's so important, why not order them against it? With a threat of excommunication."

Dell'Aqua sighed. "I wish it were so simple. You don't do things like that in Japan. They abhor outside interference in their internal affairs. Even a suggestion on our part has to be offered with extreme delicacy."

Ferriera drained his silver goblet and poured some more wine and calmed himself, knowing that he needed the Jesuits on his side, that without them as interpreters he was helpless. You've got to make this voyage successful, he told himself. You've soldiered and sweated eleven years in the service of the King to earn, rightfully—twenty times over—the richest prize in his power to give, the Captain-Generalship of the annual Black Ship for one year and the tenth part that goes with the honor, a tenth of all silk, of all gold, of all silver, and of all profit from each transaction. You're rich for life now, for thirty lifetimes if you had them, all from this one single voyage. If you accomplish it.

Ferriera's hand went to the haft of his rapier, to the silver cross that formed part of the silver filigree. "By the Blood of Christ, my Black Ship will sail on time from Macao to Nagasaki and then, the richest treasure ship in history, she'll head south with the monsoon in November for Goa and thence home! As Christ is my judge, that's what's going to happen." And he added silently, if I have to burn all Japan and all Macao and all China to do it, by the Madonna!

"Our prayers are with you, of course they are," dell'Aqua replied, meaning it. "We know the importance of your voyage."

"Then what do you suggest? Without port clearances and safe conducts to trade, I'm hamstrung. Can't we avoid the Regents? Perhaps there's another way?"

Dell'Aqua shook his head. "Martin? You're our trade expert."

"I'm sorry, but it's not possible," Alvito said. He had listened to the heated exchange with simmering indignation. Foul-mannered, arrogant, motherless cretin, he had thought, then immediately, oh, God, give me patience, for without this man and others like him, the Church dies here. "I'm sure within a day or two, Captain-General, everything will be sealed. A week at the most. Toranaga has very special problems at the moment. It will be all right, I'm sure."

"I'll wait a week. No more." The undercurrent of menace in Ferriera's tone was frightening. "I'd like to get my hands on that heretic. I'd rack the truth out of him. Did Toranaga say anything about the supposed fleet? An enemy fleet?"

"No."

"I'd like to know that truth, because inbound, my ship will be wallowing like a fat pig, her holds bulging with more silks than have ever been sent at one time. We're one of the biggest ships in the world but I've no escort, so if a single enemy frigate were to catch us at sea—or that Dutch whore, the *Erasmus*—we'd be at her mercy. She'd make me haul down the Imperial flag of Portugal with no trouble at all. The Ingeles had better not get his ship to sea, with gunners and cannon and shot aboard."

"*E vero, è solamente vero,*" dell'Aqua muttered.

Ferriera finished his wine. "When's Blackthorne being sent to Izu?"

"Toranaga didn't say," Alvito replied. "I got the impression it would be soon."

"Today?"

"I don't know. Now the Regents meet in four days. I would imagine it would be after that."

Dell'Aqua said heavily, "Blackthorne must not be interfered with. Neither he nor Toranaga."

Ferriera stood up. "I'll be getting back to my ship. You'll dine with us? Both of you? At dusk? There's a fine capon, a joint of beef and Madeira wine, even some new bread."

"Thank you, you're very kind." Dell'Aqua brightened slightly. "Yes, some good food again would be wonderful. You're very kind."

"You'll be informed the instant I have word from Toranaga, Captain-General," Alvito said.

"Thank you."

When Ferriera had gone and the Visitor was sure that he and Alvito could not be overheard, he said anxiously, "Martin, what else did Toranaga say?"

"He wants an explanation, in writing, of the gun-running incident, and the request for conquistadores."

"*Mamma mia . . .*"

"Toranaga was friendly, even gentle, but—well, I've never seen him like this before."

"What exactly did he say?"

" 'I understand, Tsukku-san, that the previous head of your order of Christians, Father da Cunha, wrote to the governors of Macao, Goa, and the Spanish Viceroy in Manila, Don Sisco y Vivera, in July of 1588 of your counting, asking for an invasion of hundreds of Spanish soldiers with guns to support some Christian *daimyos* in a rebellion which the chief Christian priest was trying to incite against their lawful liege lord, my late master, the Taikō. What were the names of these *daimyos?* Is it true that no soldiers were sent but vast numbers of guns were smuggled into Nagasaki under your Christian seal from Macao? Is it true that the Father-Giant secretly seized these guns when he returned to Japan for the second time, as Ambassador from Goa, in March or April 1590, by your counting, and secretly smuggled them out of Nagasaki on the Portuguese ship, the *Santa Cruz,* back to Macao?' " Alvito wiped the sweat off his hands.

"Did he say anything more?"

"Not of importance, Eminence. I had no chance to explain—he dismissed me at once. The dismissal was polite but it was still a dismissal."

"Where is that cursed Englishman getting his information from?"

"I wish I knew."

"Those dates and names. You're not mistaken? He said them exactly like that?"

"No, Eminence. The names were written on a piece of paper. He showed it to me."

"Blackthorne's writing?"

"No. The names were written phonetically in Japanese, in *hiragana.*"

"We've got to find out who's interpreting for Toranaga. He must be astonishingly good. Surely not one of ours? It can't be Brother Manuel, can it?" he asked bitterly, using Masamanu Jiro's baptismal name. Jiro was the son of a Christian samurai who had been educated by the Jesuits since childhood and, being intelligent and devout, had been selected to enter the seminary to be trained to be a full priest of the four vows, of which there were none from the Japanese yet. Jiro had been with the Society for twenty years, then, incredibly, he left before being ordained and he was now a violent antagonist of the Church.

"No. Manuel's still in Kyushu, may he burn in hell forever. He's still a violent enemy of Toranaga's, he'd never help him. Fortunately, he was never party to any political secrets. The interpreter was the Lady Maria," Alvito said, using Toda Mariko's baptismal name.

"Toranaga told you that?"

"No, your Eminence. But I happen to know that she's been visiting the castle, and she was seen with the Ingeles."

"You're sure?"

"Our information is completely accurate."

"Good," dell'Aqua said. "Perhaps God is helping us in His inscrutable fashion. Send for her at once."

"I've already seen her. I made it my business to meet her by chance. She was delightful as always, deferential, pious as always, but she said pointedly before I had an opportunity to question her, 'Of course, the Empire is a very private land, Father, and some things, by custom, have to stay very private. Is it the same in Portugal, and within the Society of Jesus?'"

"You're her confessor."

"Yes. But she won't say anything."

"Why?"

"Clearly she's been forewarned and forbidden to discuss what happened and what was said. I know them too well. In this, Toranaga's influence would be greater than ours."

"Is her faith so small? Has our training of her been so inept? Surely not. She's as devout and as good a Christian as any woman I've ever met. One day she'll become a nun—perhaps even the first Japanese abbess."

"Yes. But she will say nothing now."

"The Church is in jeopardy. This is important, perhaps too important," dell'Aqua said. "She would understand that. She's far too intelligent not to realize it."

"I beg you, do not put her faith to the test in this. We must lose. She warned me. That's what she was saying as clearly as if it were written down."

"Perhaps it would be good to put her to the test. For her own salvation."

"That's up to you to order or not to order. But I'm afraid that she must obey Toranaga, Eminence, and not us."

"I will think about Maria. Yes," dell'Aqua said. He let his eyes drift to the fire, the weight of his office crushing him. Poor Maria. That cursed heretic! How do we avoid the trap? How do we conceal the truth about the guns? How could a Father Superior and Vice-Provincial like da Cunha, who was so well trained, so experienced, with seven years' practical knowledge in Macao and Japan—how could he make such a hideous mistake?

"How?" he asked the flames.

I can answer, he told himself. It's too easy. You panic or you forget the glory of God or become pride-filled or arrogant or petrified. Who wouldn't have, perhaps, under the same circumstances? To be received by the Taikō at sunset with favor, a triumphal meeting with pomp and ceremony—almost like an act of contrition by the Taikō, who was seemingly on the point of converting. And then to be awakened in the middle of the same night with the Taikō's Expulsion Edicts decreeing that all religious orders were to be out of Japan within twenty days on pain of death, never to return, and worse, that all Japanese converts throughout the land were ordered to recant at once or they would immediately be exiled or put to death.

Driven to despair, the Superior had wildly advised the Kyushu Christian *daimyos*—Onoshi, Misaki, Kiyama and Harima of Nagasaki among them—to rebel to save the Church and had written frantically for conquistadores to stiffen the revolt.

The fire spluttered and danced in the iron grate. Yes, all true, dell'-Aqua thought. If only I'd known, if only da Cunha had consulted me first. But how could he? It takes six months to send a letter to Goa and perhaps another six months for one to return and da Cunha did write immediately but he was the Superior and on his own and had to cope at once with the disaster.

Though dell'Aqua had sailed immediately on receiving the letter, with hastily arranged credentials as Ambassador from the Viceroy of Goa, it had taken months to arrive at Macao, only to learn that da Cunha was dead, and that he and all Fathers were forbidden to enter Japan on pain of death.

But the guns had already gone.

Then, after ten weeks, came the news that the Church was not obliterated in Japan, that the Taikō was not enforcing his new laws. Only half a hundred churches had been burned. Only Takayama had been smashed. And word seeped back that though the Edicts would remain officially in force, the Taikō was now prepared to allow things to be as they were, provided that the Fathers were much more discreet in their conversions, their converts more discreet and well behaved, and that there were no more blatant public worship or demonstrations and no burning of Buddhist churches by zealots.

Then, when the ordeal seemed at an end, dell'Aqua had remembered that the guns had gone weeks before, under Father Superior da Cunha's seal, that they still lay in the Jesuit Nagasaki warehouses.

More weeks of agony ensued until the guns were secretly smuggled back to Macao—yes, under my seal this time, dell'Aqua reminded himself, hopefully the secret buried forever. But those secrets never leave you in peace, however much you wish or pray.

How much does the heretic know?

For more than an hour his Eminence sat motionless in his high-backed leather chair, staring sightlessly at the fire. Alvito waited patiently near the bookcase, his hands in his lap. Shafted sunlight danced off the silver crucifix on the wall behind the Father-Visitor. On one side wall was a small oil by the Venetian painter Titian that dell'Aqua had bought in his youth in Padua, where he had been sent by his father to study law. The other wall was lined with his Bibles and his books, in Latin, Portuguese, Italian, and Spanish. And, from the Society's own movable-type press at Nagasaki that he had ordered and brought at so much cost from Goa ten years ago, two shelves of Japanese books and pamphlets: devotional books and catechisms of all sorts, translated with painstaking labor into Japanese by Jesuits; works adapted from Japanese into Latin to try to help Japanese acolytes learn that language; and last, two small books that were beyond price, the first Portuguese-Japanese grammar, Father Sancho Alvarez's life's work, printed six years ago, and its companion, the incredible Portuguese-Latin-Japanese dictionary printed last year in Roman letters as well as *hiragana* script. It had been begun at his order twenty years ago, the first dictionary of Japanese words ever compiled.

Father Alvito picked up the book and caressed it lovingly. He knew that it was a unique work of art. For eighteen years he himself had been compiling such a work and it was still nowhere near finished. But his was to be a dictionary with explanatory supplements and far more detailed—almost an introduction to Japan and the Japanese, and he knew without vanity that if he managed to finish it, it would be a masterpiece compared to Father Alvarez's work, that if his name was ever to be remembered, it would be because of his book and the Father-Visitor, who was the only father he had ever known.

"You want to leave Portugal, my son, and join the service of God?" the giant Jesuit had said the first day he had met him.

"Oh, yes, please, Father," he had replied, craning up at him with desperate longing.

"How old are you, my son?"

"I don't know, Father, perhaps ten, perhaps eleven, but I can read and write, the priest taught me, and I'm alone, I've no one of my own, I belong to no one. . . ."

Dell'Aqua had taken him to Goa and thence to Nagasaki, where he had joined the seminary of the Society of Jesus, the youngest European in Asia, at long last belonging. Then came the miracle of the gift of tongues and the positions of trust as interpreter and trade adviser, first to Harima Tadao, *daimyo* of the fief of Hizen in Kyushu where Nagasaki lay, and then in time to the Taikō himself. He was ordained, and later even attained the privilege of the fourth vow. This was the special vow over and above the normal vows of poverty, chastity, and obedience, given only to the elite of Jesuits, the vow of obedience to the Pope personally—to be his personal tool for the work of God, to go where the Pope personally ordered and do what he personally wanted; to become as the founder of the Society, the Basque soldier Loyola, designed, one of the Regimini Militantis Ecclesiae, one of the professed, the special private soldiers of God for His elected general on earth, the Vicar of Christ.

I've been so very lucky, Alvito thought. Oh, God, help me to help.

At last dell'Aqua got up and stretched and went to the window. Sun sparkled off the gilded tiles of the soaring central castle donjon, the sheer elegance of the structure belying its massive strength. Tower of evil, he thought. How long will it stand there to remind each one of us? Is it only fifteen—no, it was seventeen years ago that the Taikō put four hundred thousand men to building and excavating, and bled the country to pay for this, his monument, and then, in two short years, Osaka Castle was finished. Incredible man! Incredible people! Yes. And there it stands, indestructible. Except to the Finger of God. He can humble it in an instant, if He wishes. Oh, God, help me to do Thy will.

"Well, Martin, it seems we have work to do." Dell'Aqua began to walk up and down, his voice now as firm as his step. "About the English pilot: If we don't protect him he'll be killed and we risk Toranaga's disfavor. If we manage to protect him he'll soon hang himself. But dare we wait? His presence is a threat to us and there is no telling how much further damage he can do before that happy date. Or we can help Toranaga to remove him. Or, last, we can convert him."

Alvito blinked. "What?"

"He's intelligent, very knowledgeable about Catholicism. Aren't most Englishmen really Catholic at heart? The answer is yes if their king or queen is Catholic, and no if he or she is Protestant. The English are careless about religion. They're fanatic against us at the moment, but isn't that because of the Armada? Perhaps Blackthorne can be converted. That would be the perfect solution—to the Glory of God, and save his heretic soul from a damnation he's certainly going to.

"Next, Toranaga: We'll give him the maps he wants. Explain about 'spheres of influence.' Isn't that really what the lines of demarcation were for, to separate the influence of the Portuguese and our Spanish friends? *Sì, è vero!* Tell him that on the other important matters I will personally be honored to prepare them for him and will give them to him as soon as possible. Because I'll have to check the facts in Macao, could he please grant a reasonable delay? And in the same breath say that you are delighted to inform him that the Black Ship will sail three weeks early, with the biggest cargo of silks and gold ever, that all our assignments of goods and our portion of the cargo and . . ." he thought a moment—"and at least thirty percent of the whole cargo will be sold through Toranaga's personally appointed broker."

"Eminence, the Captain-General won't like sailing early and won't like—"

"It will be your responsibility to get Toranaga's immediate sailing clearance for Ferriera. Go and see him at once with my reply. Let him be impressed with our efficiency, isn't that one of the things he admires? With immediate clearances, Ferriera will concede the minor point of arriving early in the season, and as to the broker, what's the difference to the Captain-General between one native or another? He will still get his percentage."

"But Lords Onoshi and Kiyama and Harima usually split the brokerage of the cargo between them. I don't know if they'd agree."

"Then solve the problem. Toranaga will agree to the delay for a concession. The only concessions he needs are power, influence, and money. What can we give him? We cannot deliver the Christian *daimyos* to him. We—"

"Yet," Alvito said.

"Even if we could, I don't know yet if we should or if we will. Onoshi and Kiyama are bitter enemies, but they've joined against Toranaga because they're sure he'd obliterate the Church—and them—if he ever got control of the Council."

"Toranaga will support the Church. Ishido's our real enemy."

"I don't share your confidence, Martin. We mustn't forget that because Onoshi and Kiyama are Christians, all their followers are Christians in their tens of thousands. We cannot offend them. The only concession we can give to Toranaga is something to do with trade. He's fanatic about trade but has never managed to participate personally. So the concession I suggest might tempt him to grant a delay which perhaps we can extend into a permanent one. You know how the Japanese like this form of solution—the big stick poised, which both sides pretend does not exist, eh?"

"In my opinion it's politically unwise for Lord Onoshi and Lord Kiyama to turn against Toranaga at this time. They should follow the old proverb about keeping a line of retreat open, no? I could suggest to them that an offer to Toranaga of twenty-five percent—so each has an equal share, Onoshi, Kiyama, Harima, and Toranaga—would be a small consideration to soften the impact of their 'temporary' siding with Ishido against him."

"Then Ishido will distrust them and hate us even more when he finds out."

"Ishido hates us immeasurably now. Ishido doesn't trust them any more than they trust him and we don't know yet why they've taken his side. With Onoshi and Kiyama's agreement, we would formally put the proposal as though it was merely *our* idea to maintain impartiality between Ishido and Toranaga. Privately we can inform Toranaga of their generosity."

Dell'Aqua considered the virtues and defects of the plan. "Excellent," he said at length. "Put it into effect. Now, about the heretic. Give his rutters to Toranaga today. Go back to Toranaga at once. Tell him that the rutters were sent to us secretly."

"How do I explain the delay in giving them to him?"

"You don't. Just tell the truth: they were brought by Rodrigues but that neither of us realized the sealed package contained the missing rutters. Indeed, we did not open them for two days. They were in truth forgotten in the excitement about the heretic. The rutters prove Blackthorne to be pirate, thief, and traitor. His own words will dispose of him once and for all, which is surely divine justice. Tell Toranaga the truth—that Mura gave them to Father Sebastio, as indeed happened, who sent them to us knowing we would know what to do with them. That clears Mura, Father Sebastio, everyone. We should tell Mura by carrier pigeon what has been done. I'm sure Toranaga will realize that we have had his interests at heart over Yabu's. Does he know that Yabu's made an arrangement with Ishido?"

"I would say certainly, Eminence. But rumor has it that Toranaga and Yabu are friends now."

"I wouldn't trust that satan's whelp."

"I'm sure Toranaga doesn't. Any more than Yabu has really made any commitment to him."

Suddenly they were distracted by an altercation outside. The door opened and a cowled monk came bare-footed into the room, shaking off Father Soldi. "The blessings of Jesus Christ upon you," he said, his voice rasping with hostility. "May He forgive you your sins."

"Friar Perez—what are you doing here?" dell'Aqua burst out.

"I've come back to this cesspit of a land to proclaim the word of God to the heathen again."

"But you're under Edict never to return on pain of immediate death for inciting to riot. You escaped the Nagasaki martyrdom by a miracle and you were ordered—"

"That was God's will, and a filthy heathen Edict of a dead maniac has nothing to do with me," the monk said. He was a short, lean Spaniard with a long unkempt beard. "I'm here to continue God's work." He glanced at Father Alvito. "How's trade, Father?"

"Fortunately for Spain, very good," Alvito replied icily.

"I don't spend time in the counting house, Father. I spend it with my flock."

"That's commendable," dell'Aqua said sharply. "But spend it where the Pope ordered—outside of Japan. This is *our* exclusive province. And it's also Portuguese territory, not Spanish. Do I have to remind you that three Popes have ordered all denominations out of Japan except us? King Philip also ordered the same."

"Save your breath, Eminence. The work of God surpasses earthly orders. I'm back and I'll throw open the doors of the churches and beseech the multitudes to rise up against the ungodly."

"How many times must you be warned? You can't treat Japan like an Inca protectorate peopled with jungle savages who have neither history nor culture. I forbid you to preach and insist you obey Holy orders."

"We will convert the heathen. Listen, Eminence, there's another hundred of my brothers in Manila waiting for ships here, good Spaniards all, and lots of our glorious conquistadores to protect us if need be. We'll preach openly and we'll wear our robes openly, not skulk about in idolatrous silken shirts like Jesuits!"

"You must not agitate the authorities or you'll reduce Mother Church to ashes!"

"I tell you to your face we're coming back to Japan and we'll stay in Japan. We'll preach the Word in spite of you—in spite of any prelate, bishop, king, or even any pope, for the glory of God!" The monk slammed the door behind him.

Flushed with rage, dell'Aqua poured a glass of Madeira. A little of the wine slopped onto the polished surface of his desk. "Those Spaniards will destroy us all." Dell'Aqua drank slowly, trying to calm himself. At length he said, "Martin, send some of our people to watch him. And you'd better warn Kiyama and Onoshi at once. There's no telling what'll happen if that fool flaunts himself in public."

"Yes, Eminence." At the door Alvito hesitated. "First Blackthorne and now Perez. It's almost too much of a coincidence. Perhaps the Spaniards in Manila knew about Blackthorne and let him come here just to bedevil us."

"Perhaps, but probably not." Dell'Aqua finished his glass and set it down carefully. "In any event, with the help of God and due diligence, neither of them will be permitted to harm the Holy Mother Church—whatever the cost."

CHAPTER 20

I'LL be a God-cursed Spaniard if this isn't the life!"

Blackthorne lay seraphically on his stomach on thick futons, wrapped partially in a cotton kimono, his head propped on his arms. The girl was running her hands over his back, probing his muscles occasionally, soothing his skin and his spirit, making him almost want to purr with pleasure. Another girl was pouring saké into a tiny porcelain cup. A third waited in reserve, holding a lacquer tray with a heaping bamboo basket of deep-fried fish in Portuguese style, another flask of saké, and some chopsticks.

"*Nan desu ka,* Anjin-san?" What is it, Honorable Pilot—what did you say?

"I can't say that in *Nihon-go,* Rako-san." He smiled at the girl who offered the saké. Instead he pointed at the cup. "What's this called? *Namae ka?*"

"*Sabazuki.*" She said it three times and he repeated it and then the other girl, Asa, offered the fish and he shook his head. "*Iyé, domo.*" He did not know how to say "I'm full now" so he tried instead "not hungry now."

"*Ah! Ima hara hette wa oranu,*" Asa explained, correcting him. He said the phrase several times and they all laughed at his pronunciation, but eventually he made it sound right.

I'll never learn this language, he thought. There's nothing to relate the sounds to in English, or even Latin or Portuguese.

"Anjin-san?" Asa offered the tray again.

He shook his head and put his hand on his stomach gravely. But he accepted the saké and drank it down. Sono, the girl who was massaging his back, had stopped, so he took her hand and put it on his neck and pretended to groan with pleasure. She understood at once and continued to massage him.

Each time he finished the little cup it was immediately refilled. Better go easy, he thought, this is the third flask and I can feel the warmth into my toes.

The three girls, Asa, Sono, and Rako, had arrived with the dawn, bringing cha, which Friar Domingo had told him the Chinese sometimes called *t'ee,* and which was the national drink of China and Japan. His sleep had been fitful after the encounter with the assassin but the hot piquant drink had begun to restore him. They had brought small rolled hot towels, slightly scented. When he did not know what they were used for, Rako, the chief of the girls, showed him how to use them on his face and hands.

Then they had escorted him with his four samurai guards to the steaming baths at the far side of this section of the castle and handed him over to the bath attendants. The four guards sweated stoically while he was bathed, his beard trimmed, his hair shampooed and massaged.

Afterwards, he felt miraculously renewed. They gave him another fresh, knee-length cotton kimono and more fresh tabi and the girls were waiting for him again. They led him to another room where Kiri and Mariko were. Mariko said that Lord Toranaga had decided to send the Anjin-san to one of his provinces in the next few days to recuperate and that Lord Toranaga was very pleased with him and there was no need for him to worry about anything for he was in Lord Toranaga's personal care now. Would Anjin-san please also begin to prepare the maps with material that she would provide. There would be other meetings with the Master soon, and the Master had promised that she would be made available soon to answer any questions the Anjin-san might have. Lord Toranaga was very anxious that Blackthorne should learn about the Japanese as he himself was anxious to learn about the outside world, and about navigation and ways of the sea. Then Blackthorne had been led to the doctor. Unlike samurai, doctors wore their hair close-cropped without a queue.

Blackthorne hated doctors and feared them. But this doctor was different. This doctor was gentle and unbelievably clean. European doctors were barbers mostly and uncouth, and as louse-ridden and filthy as everyone else. This doctor touched carefully and peered politely and held Blackthorne's wrist to feel his pulse, looked into his eyes and mouth and ears, and softly tapped his back and his knees and the soles of his feet, his touch and manner soothing. All a European doctor wanted was to look at your tongue and say "where is the pain?" and bleed you to release the foulnesses from your blood and give you a violent emetic to clean away the foulnesses from your entrails.

Blackthorne hated being bled and purged and every time was worse than before. But this doctor had no scalpels or bleeding bowl nor the foul chemic smell that normally surrounded them, so his heart had begun to slow and he relaxed a little.

The doctor's fingers touched the scars on his thigh interrogatively. Blackthorne made the sound of a gun because a musket ball had passed through his flesh there many years ago. The doctor said *"Ah so desu"* and nodded. More probes, deep but not painful, over his loins and stomach. At length, the doctor spoke to Rako, and she nodded and bowed and thanked him.

"*Ichi ban?*" Blackthorne had asked, wanting to know if he was all right.

"*Hai,* Anjin-san."

"*Honto ka?*"

"*Honto.*"

What a useful word, *honto*—'Is it the truth?' 'Yes, the truth,' Blackthorne thought. "*Domo,* Doctor-san."

"*Do itashimashité,*" the doctor said, bowing. You're welcome—think nothing of it.

Blackthorne bowed back. The girls had led him away and it was not until he was lying on the futons, his cotton kimono loosed, the girl Sono gentling his back, that he remembered he had been naked at the doctor's, in front of the girls and the samurai, and that he had not noticed or felt shame.

"*Nan desu ka,* Anjin-san?" Rako asked. What is it, Honorable Pilot? Why do you laugh? Her white teeth sparkled and her eyebrows were plucked and painted in a crescent. She wore her dark hair piled high and a pink flowered kimono with a gray-green obi.

"Because I'm happy, Rako-san. But how to tell you? How do I tell you I laughed because I'm happy and the weight's off my head for the first time since I left home. Because my back feels marvelous—all of me feels marvelous. Because I've Toranaga-sama's ear and I've put three fat broadsides into the God-cursed Jesuits and another six into the poxy Portuguese!" Then he jumped up, tied his kimono tight, and began dancing a careless hornpipe, singing a sea shanty to keep time.

Rako and the others were agog. The shoji had slid open instantly and now the samurai guards were equally popeyed. Blackthorne danced and sang mightily until he could contain himself no longer, then he burst out laughing and collapsed. The girls clapped and Rako tried to imitate him, failing miserably, her trailing kimono inhibiting her. The others got up and persuaded him to show them how to do it, and he tried, the three girls standing in a line watching his feet, holding up their kimonos. But they could not, and soon they were all chattering and giggling and fanning themselves.

Abruptly the guards were solemn and bowing low. Toranaga stood in the doorway flanked by Mariko and Kiri and his ever present samurai guards. The girls all knelt, put their hands flat on the floor and bowed, but the laughter did not leave their faces, nor was there any fear in them. Blackthorne bowed politely also, not as low as the women.

"*Konnichi wa,* Toranaga-sama," Blackthorne said.

"*Konnichi wa,* Anjin-san," Toranaga replied. Then he asked a question.

"My Master says, what were you doing, senhor?" Mariko said.

"It was just a dance, Mariko-san," Blackthorne said, feeling foolish. "It's called a hornpipe. It's a sailors' dance and we sing shanties—songs—at the same time. I was just happy—perhaps it was the saké. I'm sorry, I hope I didn't disturb Toranaga-sama."

She translated.

"My Master says he would like to see the dance and hear the song."

"Now?"

"Of course now."

At once Toranaga sat cross-legged and his small court spread themselves around the room and they looked at Blackthorne expectantly.

There, you fool, Blackthorne told himself. That's what comes of letting your guard down. Now you've got to perform and you know your voice is off and your dancing clumsy.

Even so, he tied his kimono tight and launched himself with gusto, pivoting, kicking, twirling, bouncing, his voice roaring lustily.

More silence.

"My Master says that he's never seen anything like that in his whole life."

"*Arigato goziemashita!*" Blackthorne said, sweating partially from his effort and partially from his embarrassment. Then Toranaga put his swords aside, tucked his kimono high into his belt, and stood beside him. "Lord Toranaga will dance your dance," Mariko said.

"Eh?"

"Please teach him, he says."

So Blackthorne began. He demonstrated the basic step, then repeated it again and again. Toranaga mastered it quickly. Blackthorne was not a little impressed with the agility of the large-bellied, amply-buttocked older man.

Then Blackthorne began to sing and to dance and Toranaga joined in, tentatively at first, to the cheers of the onlookers. Then Toranaga threw off his kimono and folded his arms and began to dance with equal verve alongside Blackthorne, who threw off his kimono and sang louder and picked up the tempo, almost overcome by the grotesqueness of what they were doing, but swept along now by the humor of it. Finally Blackthorne did a sort of hop, skip, and jump and stopped. He clapped and bowed to Toranaga and they all clapped for their master, who was very happy.

Toranaga sat down in the center of the room, breathing easily. Immediately Rako sped forward to fan him and the others ran for his kimono. But Toranaga pushed his own kimono toward Blackthorne and took the simple kimono instead.

Mariko said, "My Master says that he would be pleased for you to accept this as a gift." She added, "Here it would be considered a great honor to be given even a very old kimono by one's liege lord."

"*Arigato goziemashita*, Toranaga-sama." Blackthorne bowed low, then said to Mariko, "Yes, I understand the honor he does to me, Mariko-san. Please thank Lord Toranaga with the correct formal words that I unfortunately do not yet know, and tell him I will treasure it and, even more, the honor that he did me in dancing my dance with me."

Toranaga was even more pleased.

With reverence, Kiri and the servant girls helped Blackthorne into their master's kimono and showed Blackthorne how to tie the sash. The kimono was brown silk with the five scarlet crests, the sash white silk.

"Lord Toranaga says he enjoyed the dance. One day he will perhaps show you some of ours. He would like you to learn to speak Japanese as quickly as possible."

"I'd like that too." But even more, Blackthorne thought, I'd like to be in my own clothes, eating my own food in my own cabin in my own ship with my cannon primed, pistols in my belt, and the quarterdeck tilted under a press of sails. "Would you ask Lord Toranaga when I can have my ship back?"

"Senhor?"

"My ship, senhora. Please ask him when I can get my ship back. My crew, too. All her cargo's been removed—there were twenty thousand pieces of eight in the strongbox. I'm sure he'll understand that we're merchants, and though we appreciate his hospitality, we'd like to trade —with the goods we brought with us—and move on homeward. It'll take us almost eighteen months to get home."

"My Master says you have no need to be concerned. Everything will be done as soon as possible. You must first become strong and healthy. You're leaving at dusk."

"Senhora?"

"Lord Toranaga said you were to leave at dusk, senhor. Did I say it wrongly?"

"No, no, not at all, Mariko-san. But an hour or so ago you told me I'd be leaving in a few days."

"Yes, but now he says you will leave tonight." She translated all this to Toranaga, who replied again.

"My Master says it's better and more convenient for you to go tonight. There is no need to worry, Anjin-san, you are in his personal care. He is sending the Lady Kiritsubo to Yedo to prepare for his return. You will go with her."

"Please thank him for me. Is it possible—may I ask if it would be possible to release Friar Domingo? The man has a great deal of knowledge."

She translated this.

"My Master says, so sorry, the man is dead. He sent for him immediately you asked yesterday but he was already dead."

Blackthorne was dismayed. "How did he die?"

"My Master says he died when his name was called out."

"Oh! Poor man."

"My Master says, death and life are the same thing. The priest's soul will wait until the fortieth day and then it will be reborn again. Why be sad? This is the immutable law of nature." She began to say something but changed her mind, adding only, "Buddhists believe that we have many births or rebirths, Anjin-san. Until at length we become perfect and reach nirvana—heaven."

Blackthorne put off his sadness for the moment and concentrated on Toranaga and the present. "May I please ask him if my crew—" He stopped as Toranaga glanced away. A young samurai came hurriedly into the room, bowed to Toranaga, and waited.

Toranaga said, *"Nan ja?"*

Blackthorne understood none of what was said except he thought he caught Father Alvito's nickname "Tsukku." He saw Toranaga's eyes flick across to him and noted the glimmer of a smile, and he wondered if Toranaga had sent for the priest because of what he had told him. I hope so, he thought, and I hope Alvito's in the muck up to his nostrils. Is he or isn't he? Blackthorne decided not to ask Toranaga though he was tempted greatly.

"Kare ni matsu yoni," Toranaga said curtly.

"Gyoi." The samurai bowed and hurried away. Toranaga turned back to Blackthorne. *"Nan ja,* Anjin-san?"

"You were saying, Captain?" Mariko said. "About your crew?"

"Yes. Can Toranaga-sama take them under his protection too? See that they're well cared for? Will they be sent to Yedo too?"

She asked him. Toranaga stuck his swords in the belt of the short kimono. "My Master says of course their arrangements have already been made. You need have no concern over them. Or over your ship."

"My ship is all right? She's taken care of?"

"Yes. He says the ship is already at Yedo."

Toranaga got up. Everyone began to bow but Blackthorne broke in unexpectedly. "One last thing—" He stopped and cursed himself, realizing that he was being discourteous. Toranaga had clearly terminated the interview and they had all begun to bow but had been stopped by Blackthorne's words and now they were all nonplussed, not knowing whether to complete their bows or to wait, or to start again.

"*Nan ja,* Anjin-san?" Toranaga's voice was brittle and unfriendly, for he too had been momentarily thrown off balance.

"*Gomen nasai,* I'm sorry, Toranaga-sama. I didn't wish to be impolite. I just wanted to ask if the Lady Mariko would be allowed to talk with me for a few moments before I go? It would help me."

She asked him.

Toranaga merely grunted an imperious affirmative and walked out, followed by Kiri and his personal guards.

Touchy bastards, all of you, Blackthorne said to himself. Jesus God, you've got to be so careful here. He wiped his forehead with his sleeve, and saw the immediate distress on Mariko's face. Rako hurriedly proffered a small kerchief that they always seemed to have ready from a seemingly inexhaustible supply, tucked secretly somewhere into the back of their obis. Then he realized that he was wearing "the Master's" kimono and that you don't, obviously, wipe your sweaty forehead with "the Master's" sleeve, by God, so you've committed another blasphemy! I'll never learn, never—Jesus God in Heaven—never!

"Anjin-san?" Rako was offering some saké.

He thanked her and drank it down. Immediately she refilled it. He noticed a sheen of perspiration on all their foreheads.

"*Gomen nasai,*" he said to all of them, apologizing, and he took the cup and offered it to Mariko with good humor. "I don't know if it's a polite custom or not, but would you like some saké? Is that allowed? Or do I have to bang my head on the floor?"

She laughed. "Oh yes, it is quite polite and no, please don't hurt your head. There's no need to apologize to me, Captain. Men don't apologize to ladies. Whatever they do is correct. At least, that is what we ladies believe." She explained what she had said to the girls and they nodded as gravely but their eyes were dancing. "You had no way of knowing, Anjin-san," Mariko continued, then took a tiny sip of the saké and gave him back the cup. "Thank you, but no, I won't have any more saké, thank you. Saké goes straight to my head and to my knees. But you learn quickly—it must be very hard for you. Don't worry, Anjin-san, Lord Toranaga told me that he found your aptitude exceptional. He would never have given you his kimono if he wasn't most pleased."

"Did he send for Tsukku-san?"

"Father Alvito?"

"Yes."

"You should have asked him, Captain. He did not tell me. In that he would be quite wise, for women don't have wisdom or knowledge in political things."

"*Ah, so desu ka?* I wish all our women were equally—wise."

Mariko fanned herself, kneeling comfortably, her legs curled under her. "Your dance was very excellent, Anjin-san. Do your ladies dance the same way?"

"No. Just the men. That was a man's dance, a sailor's dance."

"Since you wish to ask me questions, may I ask you some first?"

"Certainly."

"What is the lady, your wife, like?"

"She's twenty-nine. Tall compared with you. By our measurements, I'm six feet two inches, she's about five feet eight inches, you're about five feet, so she'd be a head taller than you and equally bigger—equally proportioned. Her hair's the color of . . ." He pointed at the unstained polished cedar beams and all their eyes went there, then came back to him again. "About that color. Fair with a touch of red. Her eyes are blue, much bluer than mine, blue-green. She wears her hair long and flowing most of the time."

Mariko interpreted this for the others and they all sucked in their breaths, looked at the cedar beams, back to him once more, the samurai guards also listening intently. A question from Rako.

"Rako-san asks if she is the same as us in her body?"

"Yes. But her hips would be larger and more curved, her waist more pronounced and—well, generally our women are more rounded and have much heavier breasts."

"Are all your women—and men—so much taller than us?"

"Generally yes. But some of our people are as small as you. I think your smallness delightful. Very pleasing."

Asa asked something and all their interests quickened.

"Asa asks, in matters of the pillow, how would you compare your women with ours?"

"Sorry, I don't understand."

"Oh, please excuse me. The pillow—in intimate matters. Pillowing's our way of referring to the physical joining of man and woman. It's more polite than fornication, *neh?*"

Blackthorne squelched his embarrassment and said, "I've, er, I've only had one, er, pillow experience here—that was, er, in the village—and I don't remember it too clearly because, er, I was so exhausted by our voyage that I was half dreaming and half awake. But it, er, seemed to me to be very satisfactory."

Mariko frowned. "You've pillowed only once since you arrived?"

"Yes."

"You must be feeling very constricted, *neh?* One of these ladies would be delighted to pillow with you, Anjin-san. Or all of them, if you wish."

"Eh?"

"Certainly. If you don't want one of them, there's no need to worry, they'd certainly not be offended. Just tell me the sort of lady you'd like and we'll make all the arrangements."

"Thank you," Blackthorne said. "But not now."

"Are you sure? Please excuse me, but Kiritsubo-san has given specific instructions that your health is to be protected and improved. How can you be healthy without pillowing? It's very important for a man, *neh?* Oh, very yes."

"Thank you, but I'm—perhaps later."

"You'd have plenty of time. I would be glad to come back later. There will be plenty of time to talk, if you wish. You'd have at least four sticks of time," she said helpfully. "You don't have to leave until sunset."

"Thanks. But not now," Blackthorne said, flattened by the bluntness and lack of delicacy of the suggestion.

"They'd really like to accommodate you, Anjin-san. Oh! Perhaps—perhaps you would prefer a boy?"

"Eh?"

"A boy. It's just as simple if that's what you wish." Her smile was guileless, her voice matter-of-fact.

"Eh?"

"What's the matter?"

"Are you seriously offering me a boy?"

"Why, yes, Anjin-san. What's the matter? I only said we'd send a boy here if *you* wished it."

"I don't wish it!" Blackthorne felt the blood in his face. "Do I look like a God-cursed sodomite?"

His words slashed around the room. They all stared at him transfixed. Mariko bowed abjectly, kept her head to the floor. "Please forgive me, I've made a terrible error. Oh, I've offended where I was only trying to please. I've never talked to a—to a foreigner other than one of the Holy Fathers before, so I've no way of knowing your—your intimate customs. I was never taught about them, Anjin-san—the Fathers did not discuss them. Here some men want boys sometimes—priests have boys from time to time, ours and some of yours—I foolishly presumed that your customs were the same as ours."

"I'm not a priest and it's not our general custom."

The samurai leader, Kazu Oan, was watching angrily. He was

charged with the barbarian's safety and with the barbarian's health and he had seen, with his own eyes, the incredible favor that Lord Toranaga had shown to the Anjin-san, and now the Anjin-san was furious. "What's the matter with him?" he asked challengingly, for obviously the stupid woman had said something to offend his very important prisoner.

Mariko explained what had been said and what the Anjin-san had replied. "I really don't understand what he's irritated about, Oan-san," she told him.

Oan scratched his head in disbelief. "He's like a mad ox just because you offered him a boy?"

"Yes."

"So sorry, but were you polite? Did you use a wrong word, perhaps?"

"Oh, no, Oan-san, I'm quite sure. I feel terrible. I'm obviously responsible."

"It must be something else. What?"

"No, Oan-san. It was just that."

"I'll never understand these barbarians," Oan said exasperatedly. "For all our sakes, please calm him down, Mariko-san. It must be because he hasn't pillowed for such a long time. You," he ordered Sono, "you get more saké, hot saké, and hot towels! You, Rako, rub the devil's neck." The maids fled to obey. A sudden thought: "I wonder if it's because he's impotent. His story about pillowing in the village was vague enough, *neh?* Perhaps the poor fellow's enraged because he can't pillow at all and you brought the subject up?"

"So sorry, I don't think so. The doctor said he's very well endowed."

"If he was impotent—that would explain it, *neh?* It'd be enough to make me shout too. Yes! Ask him."

Mariko immediately did as she was ordered, and Oan was horrified as the blood rushed into the barbarian's face again and a spate of foul-sounding barbarian filled the room.

"He—he said 'no.'" Mariko's voice was barely a whisper.

"All that just meant 'no'?"

"They—they use many descriptive curse words when they get excited."

Oan was beginning to sweat with anxiety for he was responsible. "Calm him down!"

One of the other samurai, an older soldier, said helpfully, "Oan-san, perhaps he's one of those that likes dogs, *neh?* We heard some strange stories in Korea about the Garlic Eaters. Yes, they like dogs and . . . I remember now, yes, dogs and ducks. Perhaps these golden heads are like the Garlic Eaters, they stink like them, hey? Maybe he wants a duck."

Oan said, "Mariko-san, ask him! No, perhaps you'd better not. Just calm—" He stopped short. Hiro-matsu was approaching from the far corner. "Salute," he said crisply, trying to keep his voice from quaking because old Iron Fist, in the best of circumstances a disciplinarian, had been like a tiger with boils on his arse for the last week and today he had been even worse. Ten men had been demoted for untidiness, the entire night watch paraded in ignominy throughout the castle, two samurai ordered to commit seppuku because they were late for their watch, and four night-soil collectors thrown off the battlements for spilling part of a container in the castle garden.

"Is he behaving himself, Mariko-san?" Oan heard Iron Fist ask irritably. He was certain the stupid woman who had caused all this trouble was going to blurt out the truth, which would have surely lifted their heads, rightfully, off their shoulders.

To his relief he heard her say, "Yes, Lord. Everything is fine, thank you."

"You're ordered to leave with Kiritsubo-san."

"Yes, Lord." As Hiro-matsu continued with his patrol, Mariko brooded over why she was being sent away. Was it merely to interpret for Kiri with the barbarian on the voyage? Surely that's not so important? Were Toranaga's other ladies going? The Lady Sazuko? Isn't it dangerous for Sazuko to go by sea now? Am I to go alone with Kiri, or is my husband going also? If he stays—and it would be his duty to stay with his lord—who will look after his house? Why do we have to go by ship? Surely the Tokaido Road is still safe? Surely Ishido won't harm us? Yes, he would—think of our value as hostages, the Lady Sazuko, Kiritsubo, and the others. Is that why we're to be sent by sea?

Mariko had always hated the sea. Even the sight of it almost made her sick. But if I am to go, I am to go, and there's the end of it. *Karma.* She turned her mind off the inevitable to the immediate problem of the baffling foreign barbarian who was causing her nothing but grief.

When Iron Fist had vanished around the corner, Oan raised his head and all of them sighed. Asa came scurrying down the corridor with the saké, Sono close behind with the hot towels.

They watched while the barbarian was ministered to. They saw the taut mask of his face, and the way he accepted the saké without pleasure and the hot towels with cold thanks.

"Oan-san, why not let one of the women send for the duck?" the old samurai whispered agreeably. "We just put it down. If he wants it everything's fine, if not he'll pretend he hasn't seen it."

Mariko shook her head. "Perhaps we shouldn't take this risk. It seems, Oan-san, his type of barbarian has some aversion to talking about pillowing, *neh?* He *is* the first of his kind to come here, so we'll have to feel our way."

"I agree," Oan said. "He was quite gentle until that was mentioned." He glowered at Asa.

"I'm sorry, Oan-san. You're quite right, it was entirely my fault," Asa said at once, bowing, her head almost to the floor.

"Yes. I shall report the matter to Kiritsubo-san."

"Oh!"

"I really think the Mistress should also be told to take care about discussing pillowing with this man," Mariko said diplomatically. "You're very wise, Oan-san. Yes. But perhaps in a way Asa was a fortunate instrument to save the Lady Kiritsubo and even Lord Toranaga from an awful embarrassment! Just think what would have happened if Kiritsubo-san herself had asked that question in front of Lord Toranaga yesterday! If the barbarian had acted like that in front of him . . ."

Oan winced. "Blood would have flowed! You're quite right, Mariko-san, Asa should be thanked. I will explain to Kiritsubo-san that she was fortunate."

Mariko offered Blackthorne more saké.

"No, thank you."

"Again I apologize for my stupidity. You wanted to ask me some questions?"

Blackthorne had watched them talking among themselves, annoyed at not being able to understand, furious that he couldn't curse them roundly for their insults or bang the guards' heads together. "Yes. You said that sodomy is normal here?"

"Oh, forgive me, may we please discuss other things?"

"Certainly, senhora. But first, so I can understand you, let's finish this subject. Sodomy's normal here, you said?"

"Everything to do with pillowing is normal," she said defiantly, prodded by his lack of manners and obvious imbecility, remembering that Toranaga had told her to be informative about nonpolitical things but to recount to him later all questions asked. Also, she was not to take any nonsense from him, for the Anjin was still a barbarian, a probable pirate, and under a formal death sentence which was presently held in abeyance at Toranaga's pleasure. "Pillowing is quite normal. And as to a man going with another man or boy, what has this got to do with anyone but them? What harm does it do them, or others—or me or you? None!" What am I, she thought, an illiterate outcast without brains? A stupid tradesman to be intimidated by a mere barbarian? No. I'm samurai! Yes, you are, Mariko, but you're also very foolish! You're a woman and you must treat him like any man if he is to be controlled:

flatter him and agree with him and honey him. You forget your weapons. Why does he make you act like a twelve-year-old child?

Deliberately she softened her tone. "But if you think—"

"Sodomy's a foul sin, an evil, God-cursed abomination, and those bastards who practice it are the dregs of the world!" Blackthorne overrode her, still smarting under the insult that she had believed he could be one of those. Christ's blood, how could she? Get hold of yourself, he told himself. You're sounding like a pox-ridden fanatic puritan or a Calvinist! And why are you so fanatic against them? Isn't it because they're ever present at sea, that most sailors have tried it that way, for how else can they stay sane with so many months at sea? Isn't it because you've been tempted and you've hated yourself for being tempted? Isn't it because when you were young you had to fight to protect yourself and once you were held down and almost raped, but you broke away and killed one of the bastards, the knife snapped in his throat, you twelve, and this the first death on your long list of deaths? "It's a God-cursed sin—and absolutely against the laws of God and man!"

"Surely those are Christian words which apply to other things?" she retorted acidly, in spite of herself, nettled by his complete uncouthness. "Sin? Where is the sin in that?"

"You should know. You're Catholic, aren't you? You were brought up by Jesuits, weren't you?"

"A Holy Father educated me to speak Latin and Portuguese and to write Latin and Portuguese. I don't understand the meaning *you* attach to Catholic but I am a Christian, and have been a Christian for almost ten years now, and no, they did not talk to us about pillowing. I've never read your pillow books—only religious books. Pillowing a sin? How could it be? How can anything that gives a human pleasure be sinful?"

"Ask Father Alvito!"

I wish I could, she thought in turmoil. But I am ordered not to discuss anything that is said with anyone but Kiri and my Lord Toranaga. I've asked God and the Madonna to help me but they haven't spoken to me. I only know that ever since you came here, there has been nothing but trouble. I've had nothing but trouble. . . . "If it's a sin as you say, why is it so many of our priests do it and always have? Some Buddhist sects even recommend it as a form of worship. Isn't the moment of the Clouds and the Rain as near to heaven as mortals can get? Priests are not evil men, not all of them. And some of the Holy Fathers have been known to enjoy pillowing this way also. Are they evil? Of course not! Why should they be deprived of an ordinary pleasure if they're forbidden women? It's nonsense to say that anything to do with pillowing is a sin and God-cursed!"

"Sodomy's an abomination, against all law! Ask your confessor!"

You're the one who's the abomination—you, Captain-Pilot, Mariko wanted to shout. How dare you be so rude and how can you be so moronic! Against God, you said? What absurdity! Against your evil god, perhaps. You claim to be a Christian but you're obviously not, you're obviously a liar and a cheat. Perhaps you do know extraordinary things and have been to strange places, but you're no Christian and you blaspheme. Are you sent by Satan? Sin? How grotesque!

You rant over normal things and act like a madman. You upset the Holy Fathers, upset Lord Toranaga, cause strife between us, unsettle our beliefs, and torment us with insinuations about what is true and what isn't—knowing that we can't prove the truth immediately.

I want to tell you that I despise you and all barbarians. Yes, barbarians have beset me all my life. Didn't they hate my father because he distrusted them and openly begged the Dictator Goroda to throw them all out of our land? Didn't barbarians pour poison into the Dictator's mind so he began to hate my father, his most loyal general, the man who had helped him even more than General Nakamura or Lord Toranaga? Didn't barbarians cause the Dictator to insult my father, sending my poor father insane, forcing him to do the unthinkable and thus cause all my agonies?

Yes, they did all that and more. But also they brought the peerless Word of God, and in the dark hours of my need when I was brought back from hideous exile to even more hideous life, the Father-Visitor showed me the Path, opened my eyes and my soul and baptized me. And the Path gave me strength to endure, filled my heart with limitless peace, released me from perpetual torment, and blessed me with the promise of Eternal Salvation.

Whatever happens I am in the Hand of God. Oh, Madonna, give me thy peace and help this poor sinner to overcome thine enemy.

"I apologize for my rudeness," she said. "You're right to be angry. I'm just a foolish woman. Please be patient and forgive my stupidity, Anjin-san."

At once Blackthorne's anger began to fade. How can any man be angry for long with a woman if she openly admits she was wrong and he right? "I apologize too, Mariko-san," he said, a little mollified, "but with us, to suggest a man is a bugger, a sodomite, is the worst kind of insult."

Then you're all childish and foolish as well as vile, uncouth, and without manners, but what can one expect from a barbarian, she told herself, and said, outwardly penitent, "Of course you're right. I meant no harm, Anjin-sama, please accept my apologies. Oh yes," she sighed, her voice so delicately honeyed that even her husband in one of his most foul moods would have been soothed, "oh yes, it was my fault entirely. So sorry."

The sun had touched the horizon and still Father Alvito waited in the audience room, the rutters heavy in his hands.

God damn Blackthorne, he thought.

This was the first time that Toranaga had ever kept him waiting, the first time in years that he had waited for any *daimyo,* even the Taikō. During the last eight years of the Taikō's rule, he had been given the incredible privilege of immediate access, just as with Toranaga. But with the Taikō the privilege had been earned because of his fluency in Japanese and because of his business acumen. His knowledge of the inner workings of international trade had actively helped to increase the Taikō's incredible fortune. Though the Taikō was almost illiterate, his grasp of language was vast and his political knowledge immense. So Alvito had happily sat at the foot of the Despot to teach and to learn, and, if it was the will of God, to convert. This was the specific job he had been meticulously trained for by dell'Aqua, who had provided the best practical teachers among all the Jesuits and among the Portuguese traders in Asia. Alvito had become the Taikō's confidant, one of the four persons —and the only foreigner—ever to see all the Taikō's personal treasure rooms.

Within a few hundred paces was the castle donjon, the keep. It towered seven stories, protected by a further multiplicity of walls and doors and fortifications. On the fourth story were seven rooms with iron doors. Each was crammed with gold bullion and chests of golden coins. In the story above were the rooms of silver, bursting with ingots and chests of coins. And in the one above that were the rare silks and potteries and swords and armor—the treasure of the Empire.

At our present reckoning, Alvito thought, the value must be at least fifty million ducats, more than one year's worth of revenue from the entire Spanish Empire, the Portuguese Empire, and Europe together. The greatest personal fortune of cash on earth.

Isn't this the great prize? he reasoned. Doesn't whoever controls Osaka Castle control this unbelievable wealth? And doesn't this wealth therefore give him power over the land? Wasn't Osaka made impregnable just to protect the wealth? Wasn't the land bled to build Osaka Castle, to make it inviolate to protect the gold, to hold it in trust against the coming of age of Yaemon?

With a hundredth part we could build a cathedral in every city, a church in every town, a mission in every village throughout the land. If only we could get it, to use it for the glory of God!

The Taikō had loved power. And he had loved gold for the power it gave over men. The treasure was the gleaning of sixteen years of undisputed power, from the immense, obligatory gifts that all *daimyos,* by custom, were expected to offer yearly, and from his own fiefs. By right of conquest, the Taikō personally owned one fourth of all the land. His personal annual income was in excess of five million koku. And because he was Lord of all Japan with the Emperor's mandate, in theory he owned all revenue of all fiefs. He taxed no one. But all *daimyos,* all samurai, all peasants, all artisans, all merchants, all robbers, all outcasts, all barbarians, even *eta,* contributed voluntarily, in great measure. For their own safety.

So long as the fortune is intact and Osaka is intact and Yaemon the *de facto* custodian, Alvito told himself, Yaemon will rule when he is of age in spite of Toranaga, Ishido, or anyone.

A pity the Taikō's dead. With all his faults, we knew the devil we had to deal with. Pity, in fact, that Goroda was murdered, for he was a real friend to us. But he's dead, and so is the Taikō, and now we have new pagans to bend—Toranaga and Ishido.

Alvito remembered the night that the Taikō had died. He had been invited by the Taikō to keep vigil—he, together with Yodoko-sama, the Taikō's wife, and the Lady Ochiba, his consort and mother of the Heir. They had watched and waited long in the balm of that endless summer's night.

Then the dying began, and came to pass.

"His spirit's gone. He's in the hands of God now," he had said gently when he was sure. He had made the sign of the cross and blessed the body.

"May Buddha take my Lord into his keeping and rebirth him quickly so that he will take back the Empire into his hands once more," Yodoko had said in silent tears. She was a nice woman, a patrician samurai who had been a faithful wife and counselor for forty-four of her fifty-nine years of life. She had closed the eyes and made the corpse dignified, which was her privilege. Sadly she had made an obeisance three times and then she had left him and the Lady Ochiba.

The dying had been easy. For months the Taikō had been sick and tonight the end was expected. A few hours ago he had opened his eyes and smiled at Ochiba and at Yodoko, and had whispered, his voice like a thread: "Listen, this is my death poem:

"Like dew I was born
Like dew I vanish
Osaka Castle and all that I have ever done
Is but a dream
Within a dream."

A last smile, so tender, from the Despot to them and to him. "Guard my son, all of you." And then the eyes had opaqued forever.

Father Alvito remembered how moved he had been by the last poem, so typical of the Taikō. He had hoped because he had been invited that, on the threshold, the Lord of Japan would have relented and would have accepted the Faith and the Sacrament that he had toyed with so many times. But it was not to be. "You've lost the Kingdom of God forever, poor man," he had muttered sadly, for he had admired the Taikō as a military and political genius.

"What if your Kingdom of God's up a barbarian's back passage?" Lady Ochiba had said.

"What?" He was not certain he had heard correctly, revolted by her unexpected hissing malevolence. He had known Lady Ochiba for almost twelve years, since she was fifteen, when the Taikō had first taken her to consort, and she had ever been docile and subservient, hardly saying a word, always smiling sweetly and happy. But now . . .

"I said, 'What if your God's kingdom's in a barbarian's back passage?' "

"May God forgive you! Your Master's dead only a few moments—"

"The Lord my Master's dead, so your influence over him is dead. *Neh?* He wanted you here, very good, that was his right. But now he's in the Great Void and commands no more. Now I command. Priest, you stink, you always have, and your foulness pollutes the air. Now get out of my castle and leave us to our grief!"

The stark candlelight had flickered across her face. She was one of the most beautiful women in the land. Involuntarily he had made the sign of the cross against her evil.

Her laugh was chilling. "Go away, priest, and never come back. Your days are numbered!"

"No more than yours. I am in the hands of God, Lady. Better you take heed of Him, Eternal Salvation can be yours if you believe."

"Eh? You're in the hands of God? The Christian God, *neh?* Perhaps you are. Perhaps not. What will you do, priest, if when you're dead you discover there is no God, that there's no hell and your Eternal Salvation just a dream within a dream?"

"I believe! I believe in God and in the Resurrection and in the Holy

Ghost!" he said aloud. "The Christian promises are true. They're true, they're true—I believe!"

"*Nan ja,* Tsukku-san?"

For a moment he only heard the Japanese and it had no meaning for him.

Toranaga was standing in the doorway surrounded by his guards.

Father Alvito bowed, collecting himself, sweat on his back and face. "I am sorry to have come uninvited. I—I was just daydreaming. I was remembering that I've had the good fortune to witness so many things here in Japan. My whole life seems to have been here and nowhere else."

"That's been our gain, Tsukku-san."

Toranaga walked tiredly to the dais and sat on the simple cushion. Silently the guards arranged themselves in a protective screen.

"You arrived here in the third year of Tenshō, didn't you?"

"No, Sire, it was the fourth. The Year of the Rat," he replied, using their counting, which had taken him months to understand. All the years were measured from a particular year that was chosen by the ruling Emperor. A catastrophe or a godsend might end an era or begin one, at his whim. Scholars were ordered to select a name of particularly good omen from the ancient books of China for the new era which might last a year or fifty years. Tenshō meant "Heaven Righteousness." The previous year had been the time of the great tidal wave when two hundred thousand had died. And each year was given a number as well as a name—one of the same succession as the hours of the day: Hare, Dragon, Snake, Horse, Goat, Monkey, Cock, Dog, Boar, Rat, Ox and Tiger. The first year of Tenshō had fallen in the Year of the Cock, so it followed that 1576 was the Year of the Rat in the Fourth Year of Tenshō.

"Much has happened in those twenty-four years, *neh,* old friend?"

"Yes, Sire."

"Yes. The rise of Goroda and his death. The rise of the Taikō and his death. And now?" The words ricocheted off the walls.

"That is in the hands of the Infinite." Alvito used a word that could mean God, and also could mean Buddha.

"Neither the Lord Goroda nor the Lord Taikō believed in any gods, or any Infinite."

"Didn't the Lord Buddha say there are many paths to nirvana, Sire?"

"Ah, Tsukku-san, you're a wise man. How is someone so young so wise?"

"I wish sincerely I was, Sire. Then I could be of more help."

"You wanted to see me?"

"Yes. I thought it important enough to come uninvited."

Alvito took out Blackthorne's rutters and placed them on the floor in front of him, giving the explanations dell'Aqua had suggested. He saw Toranaga's face harden and he was glad of it.

"Proof of his *piracy?*"

"Yes, Sire. The rutters even contain the exact words of their orders, which include: 'if necessary to land in force and claim any territory reached or discovered.' If you wish I can make an exact translation of all the pertinent passages."

"Make a translation of everything. Quickly," Toranaga said.

"There's something else the Father-Visitor thought you should know." Alvito told Toranaga everything about the maps and reports and the Black Ship as had been arranged, and he was delighted to see the pleased reaction.

"Excellent," Toranaga said. "Are you sure the Black Ship will be early? Absolutely sure?"

"Yes," Alvito answered firmly. Oh, God, let it happen as we hope!

"Good. Tell your liege lord that I look forward to reading his reports. Yes. I imagine it will take some months for him to obtain the correct facts?"

"He said he would prepare the reports as soon as possible. We will be sending you the maps as you wanted. Would it be possible for the Captain-General to have his clearances soon? That would help enormously if the Black Ship is to come early, Lord Toranaga."

"You guarantee the ship will arrive early?"

"No man can guarantee the wind and storm and sea. But the ship will leave Macao early."

"You will have them before sunset. Is there anything else? I won't be available for three days, until after the conclusion of the meeting of the Regents."

"No, Sire. Thank you. I pray that the Infinite will keep you safe, as always." Alvito bowed and waited for his dismissal, but instead, Toranaga dismissed his guards.

This was the first time Alvito had ever seen a *daimyo* unattended.

"Come and sit here, Tsukku-san." Toranaga pointed beside him, on the dais.

Alvito had never been invited onto the dais before. Is this a vote of confidence—or a sentence?

"War is coming," Toranaga said.

"Yes," he replied, and he thought, this war will never end.

"The Christian Lords Onoshi and Kiyama are strangely opposed to my wishes."

"I cannot answer for any *daimyo*, Sire."

"There are bad rumors, *neh*? About them, and about the other Christian *daimyos*."

"Wise men will always have the interests of the Empire at heart."

"Yes. But in the meantime, against my will, the Empire is being split into two camps. Mine and Ishido's. So all interests in the Empire lie on one side or another. There is no middle course. Where do the interests of the Christians lie?"

"On the side of peace. Christianity is a religion, Sire, not a political ideology."

"Your Father-Giant is head of your Church here. I hear you speak —you can speak in this Pope's name."

"We are forbidden to involve ourselves in your politics, Sire."

"You think Ishido will favor you?" Toranaga's voice hardened. "He's totally opposed to your religion. I've always shown you favor. Ishido wants to implement the Taikō's Expulsion Edicts at once and close the land totally to all barbarians. I want an expanding trade."

"We do not control any of the Christian *daimyos*."

"How do I influence them, then?"

"I don't know enough to attempt to counsel you."

"You know enough, old friend, to understand that if Kiyama and Onoshi stand against me alongside Ishido and the rest of his rabble, all other Christian *daimyos* will soon follow them—then twenty men stand against me for every one of mine."

"If war comes, I will pray you win."

"I'll need more than prayers if twenty men oppose one of mine."

"Is there no way to avoid war? It will never end once it starts."

"I believe that too. Then everyone loses—we and the barbarian and the Christian Church. But if all Christian *daimyos* sided with me now— openly—there would be no war. Ishido's ambitions would be permanently curbed. Even if he raised his standard and revolted, the Regents could stamp him out like a rice maggot."

Alvito felt the noose tightening around his throat. "We are here only to spread the Word of God. Not to interfere in your politics, Sire."

"Your previous leader offered the services of the Christian *daimyos* of Kyushu to the Taikō before we had subdued that part of the Empire."

"He was mistaken to do so. He had no authority from the Church or from the *daimyos* themselves."

"He offered to give the Taikō ships, Portuguese ships, to transport our troops to Kyushu, offered Portuguese soldiers with guns to help us. Even against Korea and against China."

"Again, Sire, he did it mistakenly, without authority from anyone."

"Soon everyone will have to choose sides, Tsukku-san. Yes. Very soon."

Alvito felt the threat physically. "I am always ready to serve you."

"If I lose, will you die with me? Will you commit *jenshi*—will you follow me, or come with me into death, like a loyal retainer?"

"My life is in the hands of God. So is my death."

"Ah, yes. Your Christian God!" Toranaga moved his swords slightly. Then he leaned forward. "Onoshi and Kiyama committed to me, within forty days, and the Council of Regents will repeal the Taikō's Edicts."

How far dare I go? Alvito asked himself helplessly. How far? "We cannot influence them as you believe."

"Perhaps your leader should order them. *Order them!* Ishido will betray you and them. I know him for what he is. So will the Lady Ochiba. Isn't she already influencing the Heir against you?"

Yes, Alvito wanted to shout. But Onoshi and Kiyama have secretly obtained Ishido's sworn commitment in writing to let them appoint all of the Heir's tutors, one of whom will be a Christian. And Onoshi and Kiyama have sworn a Holy Oath that they're convinced you will betray the Church, once you have eliminated Ishido. "The Father-Visitor cannot order them, Lord. It would be an unforgivable interference with your politics."

"Onoshi and Kiyama in forty days, the Taikō's Edicts repealed—and no more of the foul priests. The Regents will forbid them to come to Japan."

"What?"

"You and your priests only. None of the others—the stenching, begging Black Clothes—the barefoot hairies! The ones who shout stupid threats and create nothing but open trouble. Them. You can have all their heads if you want them—the ones who are here."

Alvito's whole being cried caution. Never had Toranaga been so open. One slip now and you'll offend him and make him the Church's enemy forever.

Think what Toranaga's offering! Exclusivity throughout the Empire! The one thing that would guarantee the purity of the Church and her safety while she is growing strong. The one thing beyond price. The one thing no one can provide—not even the Pope! No one—except Toranaga. With Kiyama and Onoshi supporting him openly, Toranaga could smash Ishido and dominate the Council.

Father Alvito would never have believed that Toranaga would be so blunt. Or offer so much. Could Onoshi and Kiyama be made to reverse themselves? Those two hate each other. For reasons only they know they have joined to oppose Toranaga. Why? What would make them betray Ishido?

"I'm not qualified to answer you, Sire, or to speak on such a matter, *neh*? I only tell you our purpose is to save souls," he said.

"I hear my son Naga's interested in your Christian Faith."

Is Toranaga threatening or is he offering? Alvito asked himself. Is he offering to allow Naga to accept the Faith—what a gigantic coup that would be—or is he saying, "Unless you cooperate I will order him to cease"? "The Lord, your son, is one of many nobles who have open minds about religion, Sire."

Alvito suddenly realized the enormity of the dilemma that Toranaga faced. He's trapped—he has to make an arrangement with us, he thought exultantly. He has to try! Whatever we want, he has to give us—if *we* want to make an arrangement with *him*. At long last he openly admits the Christian *daimyos* hold the balance of power! Whatever we want! What else could we have? Nothing at all. Except . . .

Deliberately he dropped his eyes to the rutters that he had laid before Toranaga. He watched his hand reach out and put the rutters safely in the sleeve of his kimono.

"Ah, yes, Tsukku-san," Toranaga said, his voice eerie and exhausted. "Then there's the new barbarian—the pirate. The enemy of your country. They will be coming here soon, in numbers, won't they? They can be discouraged—or encouraged. Like this one pirate. *Neh?*"

Father Alvito knew that now they had everything. Should I ask for Blackthorne's head on a silver platter like the head of St. John the Baptist to seal this bargain? Should I ask for permission to build a cathedral at Yedo, or one within the walls of Osaka Castle? For the first time in his life he felt himself floundering, rudderless in the reach for power.

We want no more than is offered! I wish I could settle the bargain now! If it were up to me alone, I would gamble. I know Toranaga and I would gamble on him. I would agree to try and I'd swear a Holy Oath. Yes, I would excommunicate Onoshi or Kiyama if they would not agree, to gain those concessions for Mother Church. Two souls for tens of thousands, for hundreds of thousands, for millions. That's fair! I would say, Yes, yes, yes, for the Glory of God. But I can settle nothing, as you well know. I'm only a messenger, and part of my message . . .

"I need help, Tsukku-san. I need it now."

"All that I can do, I will do, Toranaga-sama. You have my promise."

Then Toranaga said with finality, "I will wait forty days. Yes. Forty days."

Alvito bowed. He noticed that Toranaga returned the bow lower and more formally than he had ever done before, almost as though he were bowing to the Taikō himself. The priest got up shakily. Then he was outside the room, walking up the corridor. His step quickened. He began to hurry.

Toranaga watched the Jesuit from the embrasure as he crossed the garden, far below. The shoji edged open again but he cursed his guards away and ordered them, on pain of death, to leave him alone. His eyes followed Alvito intently, through the fortified gate, out into the forecourt, until the priest was lost in the maze of innerworks.

And then, in the lonely silence, Toranaga began to smile. And he tucked up his kimono and began to dance. It was a hornpipe.

CHAPTER 21

Just after dusk Kiri waddled nervously down the steps, two maids in attendance. She headed for her curtained litter that stood beside the garden hut. A voluminous cloak covered her traveling kimono and made her appear even more bulky, and a vast, wide-brimmed hat was tied under her jowls.

The Lady Sazuko was waiting patiently for her on the veranda, heavily pregnant, Mariko nearby. Blackthorne was leaning against the wall near the fortified gate. He wore a belted kimono of the Browns and tabi socks and military thongs. In the forecourt, outside the gate, the escort of sixty heavily armed samurai was drawn up in neat lines, every third man carrying a flare. At the head of these soldiers Yabu talked with Buntaro—Mariko's husband—a short, thickset, almost neckless man. Both were attired in chain mail with bows and quivers over their shoulders, and Buntaro wore a horned steel war helmet. Porters and kagamen squatted patiently in well-disciplined silence near the multitudinous baggage.

The promise of summer floated on the slight breeze, but no one noticed it except Blackthorne, and even he was conscious of the tension that surrounded them all. And too, he was intensely aware that he alone was unarmed.

Kiri plodded over to the veranda. "You shouldn't be waiting in the cold, Sazuko-san. You'll catch a chill! You must remember the child now. These spring nights are still filled with damp."

"I'm not cold, Kiri-san. It's a lovely night and it's my pleasure."

"Is everything all right?"

"Oh, yes. Everything's perfect."

"I wish I weren't going. Yes. I hate going."

"There's no need to worry," Mariko said reassuringly, joining them. She wore a similar wide-brimmed hat, but hers was bright where Kiri's was somber. "You'll enjoy getting back to Yedo. Our Master will be following in a few days."

"Who knows what tomorrow will bring, Mariko-san?"

"Tomorrow is in the hands of God."

"Tomorrow will be a lovely day, and if it isn't, it isn't!" Sazuko said. "Who cares about tomorrow? *Now* is good. You're beautiful and we'll all miss you, Kiri-san, and you, Mariko-san!" She glanced at the gateway, distracted, as Buntaro shouted angrily at one of the samurai who had dropped a flare.

Yabu, senior to Buntaro, was nominally in charge of the party. He had seen Kiri arrive and strutted back through the gate. Buntaro followed.

"Oh, Lord Yabu—Lord Buntaro," Kiri said with a flustered bow. "I'm so sorry to have kept you waiting. Lord Toranaga was going to come down, but in the end, decided not to. You are to leave now, he said. Please accept my apologies."

"None are necessary." Yabu wanted to be quit of the castle as soon as possible, and quit of Osaka, and back in Izu. He still could hardly believe that he was leaving with his head, with the barbarian, with the guns, with everything. He had sent urgent messages by carrier pigeon to his wife in Yedo to make sure that all was prepared at Mishima, his capital, and to Omi at the village of Anjiro. "Are you ready?"

Tears glittered in Kiri's eyes. "Just let me catch my breath and then I'll get into the litter. Oh, I wish I didn't have to go!" She looked around, seeking Blackthorne, finally catching sight of him in the shadows. "Who is responsible for the Anjin-san? Until we get to the ship?"

Buntaro said testily, "I've ordered him to walk beside my wife's litter. If she can't keep him in control, I will."

"Perhaps, Lord Yabu, you'd escort the Lady Sazuko—"

"*Guards!*"

The warning shout came from the forecourt. Buntaro and Yabu hurried through the fortified door as all the men swirled after them and others poured from the innerworks.

Ishido was approaching down the avenue between the castle walls at the head of two hundred Grays. He stopped in the forecourt outside the gate and, though no man seemed hostile on either side and no man had his hand on his sword or an arrow in his bow, all were ready.

Ishido bowed elaborately. "A fine evening, Lord Yabu."

"Yes, yes indeed."

Ishido nodded perfunctorily to Buntaro, who was equally offhand, returning the minimum politeness allowable. Both had been favorite generals of the Taikō. Buntaro had led one of the regiments in Korea when Ishido had been in overall command. Each had accused the other of treachery. Only the personal intervention and a direct order of the Taikō had prevented bloodshed and a vendetta.

Ishido studied the Browns. Then his eyes found Blackthorne. He saw the man half bow and nodded in return. Through the gateway he could see the three women and the other litter. His eyes came to rest on Yabu again. "You'd think you were all going into battle, Yabu-san, instead of just being a ceremonial escort for the Lady Kiritsubo."

"Hiro-matsu-san issued orders, because of the Amida assassin. . . ."

Yabu stopped as Buntaro stomped pugnaciously forward and planted his huge legs in the center of the gateway. "We're always ready for battle. With or without armor. We can take on ten men for each one of ours, and fifty of the Garlic Eaters. We never turn our backs and run like snot-nosed cowards, leaving our comrades to be overwhelmed!"

Ishido's smile was filled with contempt, his voice a goad. "Oh? Perhaps you'll get an opportunity soon—to stand against real men, not Garlic Eaters!"

"How soon? Why not tonight? Why not here?"

Yabu moved carefully between them. He also had been in Korea and he knew that there was truth on both sides and that neither was to be trusted, Buntaro less than Ishido. "Not tonight because we're among friends, Buntaro-san," he said placatingly, wanting desperately to avoid a clash that would lock them forever within the castle. "We're among friends, Buntaro-san."

"What friends? I know friends—and I know enemies!" Buntaro whirled back to Ishido. "Where's this man—this real man you talked of, Ishido-san? Eh? Or men? Let him—let them all crawl out of their holes and stand in front of me—Toda Buntaro, Lord of Sakura—if any one of them's got the juice!"

Everyone readied.

Ishido stared back malevolently.

Yabu said, "This is not the time, Buntaro-san. Friends or ene—"

"Friends? Where? In this manure pile?" Buntaro spat into the dust.

One of the Gray's hands flashed for his sword hilt, ten Browns followed, fifty Grays were a split second behind, and now all were waiting for Ishido's sword to come out to signal the attack.

Then Hiro-matsu walked out of the garden shadows, through the gateway into the forecourt, his killing sword loose in his hands and half out of its scabbard.

"You can find friends in manure, sometimes, my son," he said calmly. Hands eased off sword hilts. Samurai on the opposing battlements—Grays and Browns—slackened the tension of their arrow-armed bowstrings. "We have friends all over the castle. All over Osaka. Yes. Our Lord Toranaga keeps telling us so." He stood like a rock in front of his only living son, seeing the blood lust in his eyes. The moment Ishido had been seen approaching, Hiro-matsu had taken up his battle station at the inner doorway. Then, when the first danger had passed, he had moved with catlike quiet into the shadows. He stared down into Buntaro's eyes. "Isn't that so, my son?"

With an enormous effort, Buntaro nodded and stepped back a pace. But he still blocked the way to the garden.

Hiro-matsu turned his attention to Ishido. "We did not expect you tonight, Ishido-san."

"I came to pay my respects to the Lady Kiritsubo. I was not informed until a few moments ago that anyone was leaving."

"Is my son right? We should worry we're not among friends? Are we hostages who should beg favors?"

"No. But Lord Toranaga and I agreed on protocol during his visit. A day's notice of the arrival or departure of high personages was to be given so I could pay the proper respects."

"It was a sudden decision of Lord Toranaga's. He did not consider the matter of sending one of his ladies back to Yedo important enough to disturb you," Hiro-matsu told him. "Yes, Lord Toranaga is merely preparing for his own departure."

"Has that been decided upon?"

"Yes. The day the meeting of the Regents concludes. You'll be informed at the correct time, according to protocol."

"Good. Of course, the meeting may be delayed again. The Lord Kiyama is even sicker."

"Is it delayed? Or isn't it?"

"I merely mentioned that it might be. We hope to have the pleasure of Lord Toranaga's presence for a long time to come, *neh?* He will hunt with me tomorrow?"

"I have requested him to cancel all hunting until the meeting. I don't consider it safe. I don't consider any of this area safe any longer. If filthy assassins can get through your sentries so easily, how much more easy would treachery be outside the walls?"

Ishido let the insult pass. He knew this and the affronts would further inflame his men but it did not suit him to light the fuse yet. He had been glad that Hiro-matsu had interceded for he had almost lost control. The thought of Buntaro's head in the dust, the teeth chattering, had consumed him. "All commanders of the guards on that night have already been ordered into the Great Void as you well know. The Amidas are laws unto themselves, unfortunately. But they will be stamped out very soon. The Regents will be asked to deal with them once and for all. Now, perhaps I may pay my respects to Kiritsubo-san."

Ishido walked forward. His personal bodyguard of Grays stepped after him. They all shuddered to a stop. Buntaro had an arrow in his bow and, though the arrow pointed at the ground, the bow was already bent to its limit. "Grays are forbidden through this gate. That's agreed by protocol!"

"I'm Governor of Osaka Castle and Commander of the Heir's Bodyguard! I have the right to go anywhere!"

Once more Hiro-matsu took control of the situation. "True, you are Commander of the Heir's Bodyguard and you do have the right to go anywhere. But only five men may accompany you through that gate. Wasn't that agreed by you and my Master while he is here?"

"Five or fifty, it makes no difference! This insult is intol—"

"Insult? My son means no insult. He's following orders agreed by his liege Lord and by you. Five men. Five!" The word was an order and Hiro-matsu turned his back on Ishido and looked at his son. "The Lord Ishido does us honor by wishing to pay respect to the Lady Kiritsubo."

The old man's sword was two inches out of its scabbard and no one was sure if it was to slash at Ishido if the fight began or to hack off his son's head if he pointed the arrow. All knew that there was no affection between father and son, only a mutual respect for the other's viciousness. "Well, my son, what do you say to the Commander of the Heir's Bodyguard?"

The sweat was running down Buntaro's face. After a moment he stepped aside and eased the tension off the bow. But he kept the arrow poised.

Many times Ishido had seen Buntaro in the competition lists firing arrows at two hundred paces, six arrows launched before the first hit the target, all equally accurate. He would happily have ordered the attack now and obliterated these two, the father and son, and all the rest. But he knew it would be the act of a fool to start with them and not with Toranaga, and, in any event, perhaps when the real war came Hiro-matsu would be tempted to leave Toranaga and fight with him. The Lady Ochiba had said she would approach old Iron Fist when the time came. She had sworn that he would never forsake the Heir, that she would weld Iron Fist to her, away from Toranaga, perhaps even get him to assassinate his master and so avoid any conflict. What hold, what secret, what knowledge does she have over him? Ishido asked himself again. He had ordered Lady Ochiba to be spirited out of Yedo, if it was possible, before the Regents' meeting. Her life would not be worth a grain of rice after Toranaga's impeachment—which all the other Regents had agreed upon. Impeachment and immediate seppuku, forced if need be. If she escapes, good. If not, never mind. The Heir will rule in eight years.

He strode through the gateway into the garden, Hiro-matsu and Yabu accompanying him. Five guards followed. He bowed politely and wished Kiritsubo well. Then, satisfied that all was as it should be, he turned and left with all his men.

Hiro-matsu exhaled and scratched his piles. "You'd better leave now, Yabu-san. That rice maggot'll give you no more trouble."

"Yes. At once."

Kiri kerchiefed the sweat off her brow. "He's a devil *kami!* I'm afraid for our Master." The tears began to flow. "I don't want to leave!"

"No harm will come to Lord Toranaga, I promise you, Lady," Hiro-matsu said. "You must go. Now!"

Kiri tried to stifle her sobs and unloosed the thick veil that hung from the brim of her wide hat. "Oh, Yabu-sama, would you escort Lady Sazuko inside? Please?"

"Of course."

Lady Sazuko bowed and hurried off, Yabu following. The girl ran up the steps. As she neared the top she slipped and fell.

"The baby!" Kiri shrieked. "Is she hurt?"

All their eyes flashed to the prostrate girl. Mariko ran for her but Yabu reached her first. He picked her up. Sazuko was more startled than hurt. "I'm all right," she said, a little breathlessly. "Don't worry, I'm perfectly all right. It was foolish of me."

When he was sure, Yabu walked back to the forecourt preparing for instant departure.

Mariko came back to the gateway, greatly relieved. Blackthorne was gaping at the garden.

"What is it?" she asked.

"Nothing," he said after a pause. "What did Lady Kiritsubo shout out?"

"'The baby! Is she hurt?' The Lady Sazuko's with child," she explained. "We were all afraid the fall might have hurt her."

"Toranaga-sama's child?"

"Yes," Mariko said, looking back at the litter.

Kiri was inside the closed translucent curtains now, the veil loosed. Poor woman, Mariko thought, knowing she was only trying to hide the tears. I would be equally terrified to leave my Lord, if I were she.

Her eyes went to Sazuko, who waved once more from the top of the steps, then went inside. The iron door clanged after her. That sounded like a death knell, Mariko thought. Will we ever see them again?

"What did Ishido want?" Blackthorne asked.

"He was—I don't know the correct word. He was investigating—making a tour of inspection without warning."

"Why?"

"He's Commander of the castle," she said, not wishing to tell the real reason.

Yabu was shouting orders at the head of the column and set off. Mariko got into her litter, leaving the curtains partially open. Buntaro motioned Blackthorne to move aside. He obeyed.

They waited for Kiri's litter to pass. Blackthorne stared at the half-seen, shrouded figure, hearing the muffled sobs. The two frightened maids, Asa and Sono, walked alongside. Then he glanced back a last time. Hiro-matsu was standing alone beside the little hut, leaning on his sword. Now the garden was shut from his view as samurai closed the huge fortified door. The great wooden bar fell into place. There were no guards in the forecourt now. They were all on the battlements.

"What's going on?" Blackthorne asked.

"Please, Anjin-san?"

"It looks like they're under siege. Browns against the Grays. Are they expecting trouble? More trouble?"

"Oh, so sorry. It's normal to close the doors at night," Mariko said.

He began to walk beside her as her litter moved off, Buntaro and the remainder of the rear guard taking up their station behind him. Blackthorne was watching the litter ahead, the swaying gait of the bearers and the misted figure inside the curtains. He was greatly unsettled though he tried to hide it. When Kiritsubo had suddenly shrieked, he had looked at her instantly. Everyone else was looking at the prostrate girl on the staircase. His impulse was to look over there as well but he saw Kiritsubo suddenly scuttle with surprising speed inside the little hut. For a moment he thought his eyes were playing him tricks because in the night her dark cloak and dark kimono and dark hat and dark veil made her almost invisible. He watched as the figure vanished for a moment, then reappeared, darted into the litter, and jerked the curtains closed. For an instant their eyes met. It was Toranaga.

CHAPTER 22

THE little cortege surrounding the two litters went slowly through the maze of the castle and through the continual checkpoints. Each time there were formal bows, the documents were meticulously examined afresh, a new captain and group of escorting Grays took over, and then they were passed. At each checkpoint Blackthorne watched with ever increasing misgivings as the captain of the guard came close to scrutinize the drawn curtains of Kiritsubo's litter. Each time the man bowed politely to the half-seen figure, hearing the muffled sobs, and in the course of time, waved them on again.

Who else knows, Blackthorne was asking himself desperately. The maids must know—that would explain why they're so frightened. Hiromatsu certainly must have known, and Lady Sazuko, the decoy, absolutely. Mariko? I don't think so. Yabu? Would Toranaga trust him? That neckless maniac Buntaro? Probably not.

Obviously this is a highly secret escape attempt. But why should Toranaga risk his life outside the castle? Isn't he safer inside? Why the secrecy? Who's he escaping from? Ishido? The assassins? Or someone else in the castle? Probably all of them, Blackthorne thought, wishing they were safely in the galley and out to sea. If Toranaga's discovered it's going to rain dung, the fight's going to be to the death and no quarter asked or given. I'm unarmed and even if I had a brace of pistols or a twenty pounder and a hundred bully boys, the Grays'd swamp us. I've nowhere to run and nowhere to hide. It's a turd-stuffed fornicator whichever way you count it!

"Are you tiring, Anjin-san?" Mariko asked daintily. "If you like, I'll walk and you can ride."

"Thanks," he replied sourly, missing his boots, the thonged slippers still awkward. "My legs are fine. I was just wishing we were safe at sea, that's all."

"Is the sea ever safe?"

"Sometimes, senhora. Not often." Blackthorne hardly heard her. He was thinking, by the Lord Jesus, I hope I don't give Toranaga away. That would be terrible! It'd be so much simpler if I hadn't seen him. That was just bad luck, one of those accidents that can disrupt a perfectly planned and executed scheme. The old girl, Kiritsubo, she's a great actress, and the young one too. It was only because I couldn't understand what she'd shouted out that I didn't fall for the ruse. Just bad luck I saw Toranaga clearly—bewigged, made up, kimonoed, and cloaked, just like Kiritsubo, but still Toranaga.

At the next checkpoint the new captain of Grays came closer than ever before, the maids tearfully bowing and standing in the way without trying to appear as though they were standing in the way. The captain peered across at Blackthorne and walked over. After an incredulous scrutiny he talked with Mariko, who shook her head and answered him. The man grunted and strolled back to Yabu, returned the documents and waved the procession onward again.

"What did he say?" Blackthorne asked.

"He wondered where you were from—where your home was."

"But you shook your head. How was that an answer?"

"Oh, so sorry, he said—he wondered if the far-distant ancestors of your people were related to the *kami*—the spirit—that lives to the north, on the outskirts of China. Till quite recently we thought China was the only other civilized place on earth—except for Japan, *neh?* China is so immense it is like the world itself," she said, and closed the subject. The captain had actually asked if she thought this barbarian was descended from Harimwakairi, the *kami* that looked after cats, adding this one certainly stank like a polecat in rut, as the *kami* was supposed to do.

She had replied that she didn't think so, inwardly ashamed of the captain's rudeness, for the Anjin-san did not have a stench like Tsukku-san or the Father-Visitor or usual barbarians. His aroma was almost imperceptible now.

Blackthorne knew she wasn't telling him the truth. I wish I could speak their gibberish, he thought. I wish more I could get off this cursed island, back aboard *Erasmus,* the crew fit and plenty of grub, grog, powder, and shot, our goods traded and away home again. When will that be? Toranaga said soon. Can he be trusted? How did he get the ship to Yedo? Tow it? Did the Portuguese sail her? I wonder how Rodrigues is. Did his leg rot? He should know by now if he's going to live with two legs or one—if the amputation doesn't kill him—or if he's going to die. Jesus God in Heaven, protect me from wounds and all doctors. And priests.

Another checkpoint. For the life of him, Blackthorne could not understand how everyone could remain so polite and patient, always bowing and allowing the documents to be handed over and handed back, always smiling and no sign of irritation whatsoever on either side. They're so different from us.

He glanced at Mariko's face, which was partially obscured by her veil and wide hat. He thought she looked very pretty and he was glad that he had had it out with her over her mistake. At least I won't have any more of that nonsense, he told himself. Bastard queers, they're all blood-mucked bastards!

After he had accepted her apology this morning he had begun to ask about Yedo and Japanese customs and Ishido and about the castle. He had avoided the topic of sex. She had answered at length, but had avoided any political explanations and her replies were informative but innocuous. Soon she and the maids had left to prepare for her departure, and he had been alone with the samurai guards.

Being so closely hemmed in all the time was making him edgy. There's always someone around, he thought. There are too many of them. They're like ants. I'd like the peace of a bolted oak door for a change, the bolt my side and not theirs. I can't wait to get aboard again, out into the air, out to sea. Even in that sow-bellied gut-churner of a galley.

Now as he walked through Osaka Castle, he realized that he would have Toranaga in his own element, at sea, where he himself was king. We'll have time enough to talk, Mariko'll interpret and I'll get everything settled. Trade agreements, the ship, the return of our silver, and payment if he wants to trade for the muskets and powder. I'll make arrangements to come back next year with a full cargo of silk. Terrible about Friar Domingo, but I'll put his information to good use. I'm going to take *Erasmus* and sail her up the Pearl River to Canton and I'll break the Portuguese and China blockade. Give me my ship back and I'm rich. Richer than Drake! When I get home I'll call up all the seadogs from Plymouth to the Zuider Zee and we'll take over the trade of all Asia. Where Drake singed Philip's beard, I'm going to cut off his testicles. Without silk, Macao dies, without Macao, Malacca dies, then Goa! We can roll up the Portuguese Empire like a carpet. 'You want the trade of India, Your Majesty? Afrique? Asia? The Japans? Here's how you can take it in five years!'

'Arise, Sir John!'

Yes, knighthood was within easy reach, at long last. And perhaps more. Captains and navigators became admirals, knights, lords, even earls. The only way for an Englishman, a commoner, to safety, the true safety of position within the realm, was through the Queen's favor, bless her. And the way to her favor was to bring her treasure, to help her pay for the war against stinking Spain, and that bastard the Pope.

Three years'll give me three trips, Blackthorne gloated. Oh, I know about the monsoon winds and the great storms, but *Erasmus*'ll be close-hauled and we'll ship in smaller amounts. Wait a minute—why not do the job properly and forget the small amounts? Why not take this year's Black Ship? Then you have everything!

How?

Easily—if she has no escort and we catch her unawares. But I've not enough men. Wait, there're men at Nagasaki! Isn't that where all the Portuguese are? Didn't Domingo say it was almost like a Portuguese seaport? Rodrigues said the same! Aren't there always seamen in their ships who've been pressed aboard or forced aboard, always some who're ready to jump ship for quick profit on their own, whoever the captain and whatever the flag? With *Erasmus* and our silver I could hire a crew. I know I could. I don't need three years. Two will be enough. Two more years with my ship and a crew, then home. I'll be rich and famous. And we'll part company, the sea and I, at long last. Forever.

Toranaga's the key. How are you going to handle him?

They passed another checkpoint, and turned a corner. Ahead was the last portcullis and last gateway of the castle proper, and beyond it, the final drawbridge and final moat. At the far side was the ultimate strongpoint. A multitude of flares made the night into crimson day.

Then Ishido stepped out of the shadows.

The Browns saw him almost at the same instant. Hostility whipped through them. Buntaro almost leaped past Blackthorne to get nearer the head of the column.

"That bastard's spoiling for a fight," Blackthorne said.

"Senhor? I'm sorry, senhor, what did you say?"

"Just—I said your husband seems—Ishido seems to get your husband very angry, very quickly."

She made no reply.

Yabu halted. Unconcerned he handed the safe conduct to the captain of the gate and wandered over to Ishido. "I didn't expect to see you again. Your guards are very efficient."

"Thank you." Ishido was watching Buntaro and the closed litter behind him.

"Once should be enough to check our pass," Buntaro said, his weapons rattling ominously. "Twice at the most. What are we—a war party? It's insulting."

"No insult is intended, Buntaro-san. Because of the assassin, I ordered tighter security." Ishido eyed Blackthorne briefly and wondered again if he should let him go or hold him as Onoshi and Kiyama wanted. Then he looked at Buntaro again. Offal, he thought. Your head will be on a spike soon. How could such exquisiteness as Mariko stay married to an ape like you?

The new captain was meticulously checking everyone, ensuring that they matched the list. "Everything's in order, Yabu-sama," he said as he returned to the head of the column. "You don't need the pass any-more. We keep it here."

"Good." Yabu turned to Ishido. "We meet soon."

Ishido took a roll of parchment out of his sleeve. "I wanted to ask Lady Kiritsubo if she'd take this with her to Yedo. For my niece. It's unlikely I'll go to Yedo for some time."

"Certainly." Yabu put out his hand.

"Don't trouble yourself, Yabu-san. I'll ask her." Ishido walked toward the litter.

The maids obsequiously intercepted him. Asa held out her hand. "May I take the message, Lord. My Mis—"

"No."

To the surprise of Ishido and everyone nearby, the maids did not move out of the way.

"But my Mis—"

"Move!" Buntaro snarled.

Both maids backed off with abject humility, frightened now.

Ishido bowed to the curtain. "Kiritsubo-san, I wonder if you'd be kind enough to take this message for me to Yedo? To my niece?"

There was a slight hesitation between the sobs and the figure bowed an assent.

"Thank you." Ishido offered up the slim roll of parchment an inch from the curtains.

The sobs stopped. Blackthorne realized Toranaga was trapped. Politeness demanded that Toranaga take the scroll and his hand would give him away.

Everyone waited for the hand to appear.

"Kiritsubo-san?"

Still no movement. Then Ishido took a quick pace forward, jerked the curtains apart and at the same instant Blackthorne let out a bellow and began dancing up and down like a maniac. Ishido and the others whirled on him dumbfounded.

For an instant Toranaga was in full view behind Ishido. Blackthorne thought that perhaps Toranaga could pass for Kiritsubo at twenty paces but here at five, impossible, even though the veil covered his face. And in the never-ending second before Toranaga had tugged the curtains closed again, Blackthorne knew that Yabu had recognized him, Mariko certainly, Buntaro probably, and some of the samurai possibly. He lunged forward, grabbed the roll of parchment and thrust it through a crack in the curtains and turned, babbling, "It's bad luck in my country for a prince to give a message himself like a common bastard . . . bad luck . . ."

It had all happened so unexpectedly and so fast that Ishido's sword was not out until Blackthorne was bowing and raving in front of him like an insane jack-in-the-box, then his reflexes took over and sent the sword slashing for the throat.

Blackthorne's desperate eyes found Mariko. "For Christ's sake, help —bad luck—*bad luck!*"

She cried out. The blade stopped a hair's breadth from his neck. Mariko poured out an explanation of what Blackthorne had said. Ishido lowered his sword, listened for a moment, overrode her with a furious harangue, then shouted with increasing vehemence and hit Blackthorne in the face with the back of his hand.

Blackthorne went berserk. He bunched his great fists and hurled himself at Ishido.

If Yabu hadn't been quick enough to catch Ishido's sword arm Blackthorne's head would have rolled in the dust. Buntaro, a split second later, grabbed Blackthorne, who already had his hands around Ishido's throat. It took four Browns to haul him off Ishido, then Buntaro smashed him hard on the back of the neck, stunning him. Grays leaped to their master's defense, but Browns surrounded Blackthorne and the litters and for a moment it was a standoff, Mariko and the maids deliberately wailing and crying, helping to create further chaos and diversions.

Yabu began placating Ishido, Mariko tearfully repeated over and over in forced semihysteria that the mad barbarian believed he was only trying to save Ishido, the Great Commander—whom he thought was a prince—from a bad *kami.* "And it's the worst insult to touch their faces, just like with us, that's what sent him momentarily mad. He's a senseless barbarian but a *daimyo* in his own land and he was only trying to help you, Lord!"

Ishido ranted and kicked Blackthorne, who was just coming to. Blackthorne heard the tumult with great peace. His eyes cleared. Grays were surrounding them twenty to one, swords drawn, but so far no one was dead and everyone waited in discipline.

Blackthorne saw that all attention was focused on him. But now he knew he had allies.

Ishido spun on him again and came closer, shouting. He felt the grip of the Browns tighten and knew the blow was coming, but this time, instead of trying to fight out of their grasp, which they expected, he started to collapse, then immediately straightened and broke away, laughing insanely, and began a jibbering hornpipe. Friar Domingo had told him that everyone in Japan believed madness was caused only by a *kami* and thus madmen, like all young children and very old men, were not responsible and had special privileges, sometimes. So he capered in a frenzy, singing in time to Mariko, "Help . . . I need help for God's sake . . . can't keep this up much longer . . . help . . ." desperately acting the lunatic, knowing it was the only thing that might save them.

"He's mad—he's possessed," Mariko cried out, at once realizing Blackthorne's ploy.

"Yes," Yabu said, still trying to recover from the shock of seeing Toranaga, not knowing yet if the Anjin-san was acting or if he had really gone mad.

Mariko was beside herself. She didn't know what to do. The Anjin-san saved Lord Toranaga but how did he know? she kept repeating to herself senselessly.

Blackthorne's face was bloodless except for the scarlet weal from the blows. He danced on and on, frantically waiting for help but none came. Then, silently damning Yabu and Buntaro as motherless cowards and Mariko for the stupid bitch she was, he stopped the dance suddenly, bowed to Ishido like a spastic puppet and half walked, half danced for the gateway. "Follow me, follow me!" he shouted, his voice almost strangling him, trying to lead the way like a Pied Piper.

The Grays barred his way. He roared with feigned rage and imperiously ordered them out of the way, immediately switching to hysterical laughter.

Ishido grabbed a bow and arrow. The Grays scattered. Blackthorne was almost through the gateway. He turned at bay, knowing there was no point in running. Helplessly he began his rabid dance again.

"He's mad, a mad dog! Mad dogs have to be dealt with!" Ishido's voice was raw. He armed the bow and aimed.

At once Mariko leapt forward from her protective position near Toranaga's litter and began to walk toward Blackthorne. "Don't worry, Lord Ishido," she cried out. "There's no need to worry—it's a momentary madness—may I be permitted . . ." As she came closer she could see Blackthorne's exhaustion, the set maniacal smile, and she was frightened in spite of herself. "I can help now, Anjin-san," she said hurriedly. "We have to try to—to walk out. I will follow you. Don't worry, he won't shoot us. Please stop dancing now."

Blackthorne stopped instantly, turned and walked quietly onto the bridge. She followed a pace behind him as was custom, expecting the arrows, hearing them.

A thousand eyes watched the giant madman and the tiny woman on the bridge, walking away.

Yabu came to life. "If you want him killed, let me do it, Ishido-sama. It's unseemly for you to take his life. A general doesn't kill with his own hands. Others should do his killing for him." He came very close and he dropped his voice. "Leave him alive. The madness came from your blow. He's a *daimyo* in his own land and the blow—it was as Mariko-san said, *neh?* Trust me, he's valuable to us alive."

"What?"

"He's more valuable alive. Trust me. You can have him dead any time. We need him alive."

Ishido read desperation in Yabu's face, and truth. He put the bow down. "Very well. But one day I'll want him alive. I'll hang him by his heels over the pit."

Yabu swallowed and half bowed. He nervously waved the cortege onward, fearful that Ishido would remember the litter and "Kiritsubo."

Buntaro, pretending deference, took the initiative and started the Browns on their way. He did not question the fact that Toranaga had magically appeared like a *kami* in their midst, only that his master was in danger and almost defenseless. He saw that Ishido had not taken his eyes off Mariko and the Anjin-san, but even so, be bowed politely to him and set himself behind Toranaga's litter to protect his master from any arrows if the fight began here.

The column was approaching the gate now. Yabu fell into place as a lonely rearguard. Any moment he expected the cortege to be halted. Surely some of the Grays must have seen Toranaga, he thought. How soon before they tell Ishido? Won't he think I was part of the escape attempt? Won't this ruin me forever?

Halfway over the bridge Mariko looked back for an instant. "They're following, Anjin-san, both litters are through the gate and they're on the bridge now!"

Blackthorne did not reply or turn back. It required all of his remaining will to stay erect. He had lost his sandals, his face burned from the blow, and his head pounded with pain. The last guards let him through the portcullis and beyond. They also let Mariko pass without stopping. And then the litters.

Blackthorne led the way down the slight hill, past the open ground and across the far bridge. Only when he was in the wooded area totally out of sight of the castle did he collapse.

CHAPTER 23

ANJIN-SAN—Anjin-san!

Semiconscious, he allowed Mariko to help him drink some saké. The column had halted, the Browns arranged tightly around the curtained litter, their escorting Grays ahead and behind. Buntaro had shouted at one of the maids, who had immediately produced the flask from one of the baggage kagas, told his personal guards to keep everyone away from "Kiritsubo-san's" litter, then hurried to Mariko. "Is the Anjin-san all right?"

"Yes, yes, I think so," Mariko replied. Yabu joined them.

To try to throw off the captain of the Grays, Yabu said carelessly, "We can go on, Captain. We'll leave a few men and Mariko-san. When the barbarian's recovered, she and the men can follow."

"With great deference, Yabu-san, we will wait. I'm charged to deliver you all safely to the galley. As one party," the captain told him.

They all looked down as Blackthorne choked slightly on the wine. "Thanks," he croaked. "Are we safe now? Who else knows that—"

"You're safe now!" she interrupted deliberately. She had her back to the captain and she cautioned him with her eyes. "Anjin-san, you're safe now and there's no need to worry. Do you understand? You had some kind of fit. Just look around—you're safe now!"

Blackthorne did as she ordered. He saw the captain and the Grays and understood. His strength was returning quickly now, helped by the wine. "Sorry, senhora. It was just panic, I think. I must be getting old. I go mad often and can never remember afterwards what happened. Speaking Portuguese is exhausting, isn't it?" He switched to Latin. "Canst thou understand?"

"Assuredly."

"Is this tongue 'easier'?"

"Perhaps," she said, relieved that he understood the need for caution, even using Latin, which was to Japanese an almost incomprehensible and unlearnable language except to a handful of men in the Empire, all of whom would be Jesuit trained and most committed to the priesthood. She was the only woman in all their world who could speak and read and write Latin and Portuguese. "Both languages are difficult, each hath dangers."

"Who else knoweth the 'dangers'?"

"My husband and he who leads us."

"Art thou sure?"

"Both indicated thusly."

The captain of Grays shifted restlessly and said something to Mariko.

"He asks if thou art yet dangerous, if thy hands and feet should be restrained. I said no. Thou art cured of thy palsy now."

"Yes," he said, lapsing back into Portuguese. "I have fits often. If someone hits me in the face it sends me mad. I'm sorry. Never can remember what happens during them. It's the Finger of God." He saw that the captain was concentrating on his lips and he thought, caught you, you bastard, I'll bet you understand Portuguese.

Sono the maid had her head bent close to the litter curtains. She listened, and came back to Mariko.

"So sorry, Mariko-sama, but my Mistress asks if the madman is well enough to continue? She asks if you would give him your litter because my Mistress feels we should hurry for the tide. All the trouble that the madman has caused has made her even more upset. But, knowing that the mad are only afflicted by the gods, she will say prayers for his return to health, and will personally give him medicines to cure him once we are aboard."

Mariko translated.

"Yes. I'm all right now." Blackthorne got up and swayed on his feet. Yabu barked a command.

"Yabu-san says you will ride in the litter, Anjin-san." Mariko smiled when he began to protest. "I'm really very strong and you needn't worry, I'll walk beside you so you can talk if you wish."

He allowed himself to be helped into the litter. At once they started again. The rolling gait was soothing and he lay back depleted. He waited until the captain of the Grays had strode away to the head of the column, then whispered in Latin, warning her, "That centurion understandeth the other tongue."

"Aye. And I believe some Latin also," she whispered back as quietly. She walked for a moment. "In seriousness, thou art a brave man. I thank thee for saving him."

"Thou hadst stronger bravery."

"No, the Lord God hath placed my feet onto the path, and rendered me a little useful. Again I thank thee."

The city by night was a fairyland. The rich houses had many colored lanterns, oil-lit and candle-lit, hanging over their gateways and in their gardens, the shoji screens giving off a delightful translucence. Even the poor houses were mellowed by the shojis. Lanterns lit the way of pedestrians and kagas, and of samurai who rode horseback.

"We burn oil for lamps in the houses as well as candles, but with the coming of night, most people go to bed," Mariko explained as they continued through the city streets, winding and curling, the pedestrians bowing and the very poor on their knees until they had passed, the sea glittering in the moonlight.

"It's the same with us. How do you cook? Over a wood stove?" Blackthorne's strength had returned quickly and his legs no longer felt like jelly. She had refused to take the litter back, so he lay there, enjoying the air and the conversation.

"We use a charcoal brazier. We don't eat foods like you do, so our cooking is more simple. Just rice and a little fish, raw mostly, or cooked over charcoal with a sharp sauce and pickled vegetables, a little soup perhaps. No meat—never meat. We're a frugal people—we have to be, only so little of our land, perhaps a fifth of our soil, can be cultivated—and we're many. With us it's a virtue to be frugal, even in the amount of food we eat."

"Thou art brave. I thank thee. The arrows flew not, because of the shield of thy back."

"No, Captain of Ships. It cometh from the will of God."

"Thou art brave and thou art beautiful."

She walked in silence for a moment. No one has ever called me beautiful before—no one, she thought. "I am not brave and I am not beautiful. Swords are beautiful. Honor is beautiful."

"Courage is beautiful and thou hast it in abundance."

Mariko did not answer. She was remembering this morning and all the evil words and evil thoughts. How can a man be so brave and so stupid, so gentle and so cruel, so warming and so detestable—all at the same time? The Anjin-san was limitlessly brave to take Ishido's attention off the litter, and completely clever to feign madness and so lead Toranaga out of the trap. How wise of Toranaga to escape this way! But be cautious, Mariko, she warned herself. Think about Toranaga and not about this stranger. Remember his evil and stop the moist warmth in your loins that you have never had before, the warmth courtesans talk about and storybooks and pillowbooks describe.

"Aye," she said. "Courage is beautiful and thou hast it in abundance." Then she turned to Portuguese once more. "Latin is such a tiring language."

"You learned it in school?"

"No, Anjin-san, it was later. After I was married I lived in the far north for quite a long time. I was alone, except for servants and villagers, and the only books I had were Portuguese and Latin—some grammars and religious books, and a Bible. Learning the languages passed the time very well, and occupied my mind. I was very fortunate."

"Where was your husband?"

"At war."

"How long were you alone?"

"We have a saying that time has no single measure, that time can be like frost or lightning or a tear or siege or storm or sunset, or even like a rock."

"That's a wise saying," he told her. Then added, "Your Portuguese is very good, senhora. And your Latin. Better than mine."

"You have a honeyed tongue, Anjin-san!"

"It's *honto!*"

"*Honto* is a good word. The *honto* is that one day a Christian Father came to the village. We were like two lost souls. He stayed for four years and helped me immensely. I'm glad I can speak well," she said, without vanity. "My father wanted me to learn the languages."

"Why?"

"He thought we should know the devil with which we had to deal."

"He was a wise man."

"No. Not wise."

"Why?"

"One day I will tell you the story. It's a sadness."

"Why were you alone for a rock of time?"

"Why don't you rest? We have a long way to go yet."

"Do you want to ride?" Again he began to get up but she shook her head.

"No, thank you. Please stay where you are. I enjoy walking."

"All right. But you don't want to talk anymore?"

"If it pleases you we can talk. What do you want to know?"

"Why were you alone for a rock of time?"

"My husband sent me away. My presence had offended him. He was perfectly correct to do this. He honored me by not divorcing me. Then he honored me even more by accepting me and our son back again." Mariko looked at him. "My son is fifteen now. I'm really an old lady."

"I don't believe you, senhora."

"It's *honto.*"

"How old were you when you were married?"

"Old, Anjin-san. Very old."

"We have a saying: Age is like frost or siege or sunset, even sometimes like a rock." She laughed. Everything about her is so graceful, he thought, mesmerized by her. "On you, Venerable Lady, old age sits prettily."

"For a woman, Anjin-san, old age is never pretty."

"Thou art wise as thou art beautiful." The Latin came too easily and though it sounded more formal and more regal, it was more intimate. Watch yourself, he thought.

No one has ever called me beautiful before, she repeated to herself. I wish it were true. "Here it is not wise to notice another man's woman," she said. "Our customs are quite severe. For example, if a married woman is found alone with a man in a room with the door closed—just if they are alone and talking privately—by law her husband or his brother or his father has the right to put her to death instantly. If the girl is unmarried, the father can, of course, always do with her as he pleases."

"That's not fair or civilized." He regretted the slip instantly.

"We find ourselves quite civilized, Anjin-san." Mariko was glad to be insulted again, for it had broken the spell and dispelled the warmth. "Our laws are very wise. There are far too many women, free and un-attached, for a man to take one who belongs elsewhere. It's a protection for women, in truth. A wife's duty is solely to her husband. Be patient. You'll see how civilized, how advanced we are. Women have a place, men have a place. A man may have only one official wife at one time—but of course, many consorts—but women here have much more freedom than Spanish or Portuguese ladies, from what I've been told. We can go freely where we please, when we please. We may leave our hus-bands, if we wish, divorce them. We may refuse to marry in the first place, if we wish. We own our own wealth and property, our bodies and our spirits. We have tremendous powers if we wish. Who looks after all your wealth, your money, in your household?"

"I do, naturally."

"Here the wife looks after everything. Money is nothing to a samurai. It's beneath contempt to a real man. I manage all my husband's affairs. He makes all the decisions. I merely carry out his wishes and pay his bills. This leaves him totally free to do his duty to his lord, which is his sole duty. Oh, yes, Anjin-san, you must be patient before you criticize."

"It wasn't meant as a criticism, senhora. It's just that we believe in the sanctity of life, that no one can lightly be put to death unless a law court —the Queen's law court—agrees."

She refused to allow herself to be soothed. "You say a lot of things I don't understand, Anjin-san. But didn't you say 'not fair and not civilized'?"

"Yes."

"That then is a criticism, *neh?* Lord Toranaga asked me to point out it's unseemly to criticize without knowledge. You must remember our civilization, our culture, is thousands of years old. Three thousand of these are documented. Oh yes, we are an ancient people. As ancient as China. How many years does your culture go back?"

"Not long, senhora."

"Our Emperor, Go-Nijo, is the one hundred and seventh of his unbroken line, right back to Jimmu-tenno, the first earthling, who was descended from the five generations of terrestrial spirits and, before them, the seven generations of celestial spirits who came from Kunitoko-tachi-noh-Mikoto—the first spirit—who appeared when the earth was split from the heavens. Not even China can claim such a history. How many generations have your kings ruled your land?"

"Our Queen's the third of the Tudor line, senhora. But she's old now and childless so she's the last."

"One hundred and seven generations, Anjin-san, back to divinity," she repeated proudly.

"If you believe that, senhora, how can you also say you're Catholic?" He saw her bridle, then shrug.

"I am only a ten-year Christian and therefore a novice, and though I believe in the Christian God, in God the Father and the Son and the Holy Ghost, with all my heart, our Emperor is directly descended from the gods or from God. He is divine. There are a lot of things I cannot explain or understand. But the divinity of my Emperor is without question. Yes, I am Christian, but first I am a Japanese."

Is this the key to all of you? That first you are Japanese? he asked himself. He had watched her, astonished by what she was saying. Their customs are insane! Money means nothing *to a real man?* That explains why Toranaga was so contemptuous when I mentioned money at the first meeting. One hundred and seven generations? Impossible! Instant death just for being innocently in a closed room with a woman? That's barbarism—an open invitation to murder. They advocate and admire murder! Isn't that what Rodrigues said? Isn't that what Omi-san did? Didn't he just murder that peasant? By Christ's blood, I haven't thought of Omi-san for days. Or the village. Or the pit or being on my knees in front of him. Forget him, listen to her, be patient as she says, ask her questions because she'll supply the means to bend Toranaga to your plan. Now Toranaga is absolutely in your debt. You saved him. He knows it, everyone knows it. Didn't she thank you, not for saving her but for saving him?

The column was moving through the city heading for the sea. He saw Yabu keeping the pace up and momentarily Pieterzoon's screams came soaring into his head. "One thing at a time," he muttered, half to himself.

"Yes," Mariko was saying. "It must be very difficult for you. Our world is so very different from yours. Very different but very wise." She could see the dim figure of Toranaga within the litter ahead and she thanked God again for his escape. How to explain to the barbarian about us, to compliment him for his bravery? Toranaga had ordered her to explain, but how? "Let me tell you a story, Anjin-san. When I was young my father was a general for a *daimyo* called Goroda. At that time Lord Goroda was not the great Dictator but a *daimyo* still struggling for power. My father invited this Goroda and his chief vassals to a feast. It never occurred to him that there was no money to buy all the food and saké and lacquerware and tatamis that such a visit, by custom, demanded. Lest you think my mother was a bad manager, she wasn't. Every groat of my father's revenue went to his own vassal samurai and although, officially, he had only enough for four thousand warriors, by scrimping and saving and manipulating my mother saw that he led five thousand three hundred into battle to the glory of his liege lord. We, the family—my mother, my father's consorts, my brothers and sisters— we had barely enough to eat. But what did that matter? My father and his men had the finest weapons and the finest horses, and they gave of their best to their lord.

"Yes, there was not enough money for this feast, so my mother went to the wigmakers in Kyoto and sold them her hair. I remember it was like molten darkness and hung to the pit of her back. But she sold it. The wigmakers cut it off the same day and gave her a cheap wig and she bought everything that was necessary and saved the honor of my father. It was her duty to pay the bills and she paid. She did her duty. For us duty is all important."

"What did he say, your father, when he found out?"

"What should he say, other than to thank her? It was her duty to find the money. To save his honor."

"She must have loved him very much."

"Love is a Christian word, Anjin-san. Love is a Christian thought, a Christian ideal. We have no word for 'love' as I understand you to mean it. Duty, loyalty, honor, respect, desire, those words and thoughts are what we have, all that we need." She looked at him and in spite of herself, she relived the instant when he had saved Toranaga, and through Toranaga, her husband. Never forget they were both trapped there, they would both be dead now, but for this man.

She made sure that no one was near. "Why did you do what you did?"

"I don't know. Perhaps because . . ." He stopped. There were so many things he could say: 'Perhaps because Toranaga was helpless and I didn't want to get chopped. . . . Because if he was discovered we'd all be caught in the mess. . . . Because I knew that no one knew except me and it was up to me to gamble. . . . Because I didn't want to die—there's too much to do to waste my life, and Toranaga's the only one who can give me back my ship and my freedom.' Instead he replied in Latin, "Because He hath said, render to Caesar the things that are Caesar's."

"Aye," she said, and added in the same language, "aye, that is what I was attempting to say. To Caesar those things, and to God those things. It is thusly with us. God is God and our Emperor is from God. And Caesar is Caesar, to be honored as Caesar." Then, touched by his understanding and the tenderness in his voice, she said, "Thou art wise. Sometimes I think thou understandst more than thou sayest."

Aren't you doing what you swore you would never do? Blackthorne asked himself. Aren't you playing the hypocrite? Yes and no. I owe them nothing. I'm a prisoner. They've stolen my ship and my goods and murdered one of my men. They're heathen—well, some of them are heathen and the rest are Catholics. I owe nothing to heathens and Catholics. But you'd like to bed her and you were complimenting her, weren't you?

God curse all consciences!

The sea was nearer now, half a mile away. He could see many ships, and the Portuguese frigate with her riding lights. She'd make quite a prize. With twenty bully boys I could take her. He turned back to Mariko. Strange woman, from a strange family. Why did she offend Buntaro—that baboon? How could she bed with that, or marry that? What is the "sadness"?

"Senhora," he said, keeping his voice gentle, "your mother must have been a rare woman. To do that."

"Yes. But because of what she did, she will live forever. Now she is legend. She was as samurai as—as my father was samurai."

"I thought only men were samurai."

"Oh, no, Anjin-san. Men and women are equally samurai, warriors with responsibilities to their lords. My mother was true samurai, her dutifulness to her husband exceeded everything."

"She's at your home now?"

"No. Neither she nor my father nor any of my brothers or sisters or family. I am the last of my line."

"There was a catastrophe?"

Mariko suddenly felt tired. I'm tired of speaking Latin and foul-sounding Portuguese and tired of being a teacher, she told herself. I'm not a teacher. I'm only a woman who knows her duty and wants to do it in peace. I want none of that warmth again and none of this man who unsettles me so much. I want none of him.

"In a way, Anjin-san, it was a catastrophe. One day I will tell you about it." She quickened her pace slightly and walked away, nearer to the other litter. The two maids smiled nervously.

"Have we far to go, Mariko-san?" Sono asked.

"I hope not too far," she said reassuringly.

The captain of Grays loomed abruptly out of the darkness on the other side of the litter. She wondered how much that she had said to the Anjin-san had been overheard.

"You'd like a kaga, Mariko-san? Are you getting tired?" the captain asked.

"No, no thank you." She slowed deliberately, drawing him away from Toranaga's litter. "I'm not tired at all."

"The barbarian's behaving himself? He's not troubling you?"

"Oh, no. He seems to be quite calm now."

"What were you talking about?"

"All sorts of things. I was trying to explain some of our laws and customs to him." She motioned back to the castle donjon that was etched against the sky above. "Lord Toranaga asked me to try to get some sense into him."

"Ah yes, Lord Toranaga." The captain looked briefly at the castle, then back to Blackthorne. "Why's Lord Toranaga so interested in him, Lady?"

"I don't know. I suppose because he's an oddity."

They turned a corner, into another street, with houses behind garden walls. There were few people about. Beyond were wharves and the sea. Masts sprouted over the buildings and the air was thick with the smell of seaweed. "What else did you talk about?"

"They've some very strange ideas. They think of money all the time."

"Rumor says his whole nation's made up of filthy merchant pirates. Not a samurai among them. What's Lord Toranaga want with him?"

"So sorry, I don't know."

"Rumor says he's Christian, he claims to be Christian. Is he?"

"Not our sort of Christian, Captain. You're Christian, Captain?"

"My Master's Christian so I am Christian. My Master is Lord Kiyama."

"I have the honor to know him well. He honored my husband by betrothing one of his granddaughters to my son."

"Yes, I know, Lady Toda."

"Is Lord Kiyama better now? I understand the doctors won't allow anyone to see him."

"I haven't seen him for a week. None of us has. Perhaps it's the Chinese pox. God protect him from that, and God curse all Chinese!" He glared toward Blackthorne. "Doctors say these barbarians brought the pest to China, to Macao, and thence to our shores."

"Sumus omnes in manu Dei," she said. We are all in the hands of God.

"Ita, Amen," the captain replied without thinking, falling into the trap.

Blackthorne had caught the slip also and he saw a flash of anger on the captain's face and heard him say something through his teeth to Mariko, who flushed and stopped also. He slid out of the litter and walked back to them. "If thou speakest Latin, Centurion, then it would be a kindness if thou wouldst speak a little with me. I am eager to learn about this great country of thine."

"Yes, I can speak thy tongue, foreigner."

"It is not my tongue, Centurion, but that of the Church and of all educated people in my world. Thou speakest it well. How and when did thou learn?"

The cortege was passing them and all the samurai, both Grays and Browns, were watching them. Buntaro, near Toranaga's litter, stopped and turned back. The captain hesitated, then began walking again and Mariko was glad that Blackthorne had joined them. They walked in silence a moment.

"The Centurion speaks the tongue fluidly, splendidly, doesn't he?" Blackthorne said to Mariko.

"Yes, indeed. Didst thou learn it in a seminary, Centurion?"

"And thou, foreigner," the captain said coldly, paying her no attention, loathing the recollection of the seminary at Macao that he had been ordered into as a child by Kiyama to learn the languages. "Now that we speak directly, tell me with simplicity why did thou ask this lady: 'Who else knoweth . . .' Who else knoweth what?"

"I recollect not. My mind was wandering."

"Ah, wandering, eh? Then why didst thou say: 'Things of Caesar render to Caesar'?"

"It was just a pleasantry. I was in discussion with this lady, who tells illuminating stories that are sometimes difficult to understand."

"Yes, there is much to understand. What sent thee mad at the gate? And why didst thou recover so quickly from thy fit?"

"That came through the beneficence of God."

They were walking beside the litter once more, the captain furious that he had been trapped so easily. He had been forewarned by Lord Kiyama, his master, that the woman was filled with boundless cleverness: 'Don't forget she carries the taint of treachery throughout her whole being, and the pirate's spawned by the devil Satan. Watch, listen, and remember. Perhaps she'll impeach herself and become a further witness against Toranaga for the Regents. Kill the pirate the moment the ambush begins.'

The arrows came out of the night and the first impaled the captain through the throat and, as he felt his lungs fill with molten fire and death swallowing him, his last thought was one of wonder because the ambush was not to have been here in this street but further on, down beside the wharves, and the attack was not to be against them but against the pirate.

Another arrow had slammed into the litter post an inch from Blackthorne's head. Two arrows had pierced the closed curtains of Kiritsubo's litter ahead, and another had struck the girl Asa in the waist. As she began screaming, the bearers dropped the litters and took to their heels in the darkness. Blackthorne rolled for cover, taking Mariko with him into the lee of the tumbled litter, Grays and Browns scattering. A shower of arrows straddled both litters. One thudded into the ground where Mariko had been the instant before. Buntaro was covering Toranaga's litter with his body as best he could, an arrow stuck into the back of his leather-chainmail-bamboo armor, and then, when the volley ceased, he rushed forward and ripped the curtains apart. The two arrows were imbedded in Toranaga's chest and side but he was unharmed and he jerked the barbs out of the protective armor he wore beneath the kimono. Then he tore off the wide-brimmed hat and the wig. Buntaro searched the darkness for the enemy, on guard, an arrow ready in his bow, while Toranaga fought out of the curtains and, pulling his sword from under the coverlet, leapt to his feet. Mariko started to scramble to help Toranaga but Blackthorne pulled her back with a shout of warning as again arrows bracketed the litters, killing two Browns and a Gray. Another came so close to Blackthorne that it took the skin off his cheek. Another pinned the skirt of his kimono to the earth. The maid, Sono, was beside the writhing girl who was bravely holding back her screams. Then Yabu shouted and pointed and charged. Dim figures could be seen on one of the tiled roofs. A last volley whooshed out of the darkness, always at the litters. Buntaro and other Browns blocked their path to Toranaga. One man died. A shaft ripped through a joint in Buntaro's shoulder armor and he grunted with pain. Yabu and Browns and Grays were near the wall now in pursuit but the ambushers vanished into the blackness, and though a dozen Browns and Grays raced for the corner to head them off, all knew that it was hopeless. Blackthorne groped to his feet and helped Mariko up. She was shaken but untouched.

"Thank you," she said, and hurried over to Toranaga to help screen him from Grays. Buntaro was shouting to some of his men to douse the flares near the litters. Then one of the Grays said, "Toranaga!" and though it was spoken quietly everyone heard.

In the flickering light of the flares, the sweat-streaked makeup made Toranaga seem grotesque.

One of the officer Grays bowed hastily. Here, incredibly, was the enemy of his master, free, outside the castle walls. "You will wait here, Lord Toranaga. You," he snapped at one of his men, "report to Lord Ishido at once," and the man raced away.

"Stop him," Toranaga said quietly. Buntaro launched two arrows. The man fell dying. The officer whipped out his two-handed sword and leaped for Toranaga with a screaming battle cry but Buntaro was ready and parried the blow. Simultaneously the Browns and the Grays, all intermixed, jerked out their swords and jumped for space. The street erupted into a swirling melee. Buntaro and the officer were well matched, feinting and slashing. Suddenly a Gray broke from the pack and charged for Toranaga but Mariko immediately picked up a flare, ran forward, and shoved it into the officer's face. Buntaro hacked his assailant in two, then whirled and ripped the second man apart, and cut down another who was trying to reach Toranaga as Mariko darted back out of the way, a sword now in her hands, her eyes never leaving Toranaga or Buntaro, his monstrous bodyguard.

Four Grays banded together and hurled themselves at Blackthorne, who was still rooted near his litter. Helplessly he saw them coming. Yabu and a Brown leaped to intercept, fighting demonically. Blackthorne jumped away, grabbed a flare, and using it as a whirling mace, threw the attackers momentarily off balance. Yabu killed one, maimed another, then four Browns rushed back to dispose of the last two Grays. Without hesitation Yabu and the wounded Brown hurled themselves into the attack once more, protecting Toranaga. Blackthorne ran forward and picked up a long half-sword, half-spear and raced nearer to Toranaga. Toranaga alone stood motionless, his sword sheathed, in the screaming fracas.

The Grays fought courageously. Four joined in a suicidal charge at Toranaga. The Browns broke it and pressed their advantage. The Grays regrouped and charged again. Then a senior officer ordered three to retreat for help and the rest to guard the retreat. The three Grays tore off, and though they were pursued and Buntaro shot one, two escaped. The rest died.

CHAPTER 24

THEY were hurrying through deserted back streets, circling for the wharf and the galley. There were ten of them—Toranaga leading, Yabu, Mariko, Blackthorne, and six samurai. The rest, under Buntaro, had been sent with the litters and baggage train by the planned route, with instructions to head leisurely for the galley. The body of Asa the maid was in one of the litters. During a lull in the fighting, Blackthorne had pulled the barbed shaft out of her. Toranaga had seen the dark blood that gushed in its wake and had watched, puzzled, as the pilot had cradled her instead of allowing her to die quietly in private dignity, and then, when the fighting had ceased entirely, how gently the pilot had put her into the litter. The girl was brave and had whimpered not at all, just looked up at him until death had come. Toranaga had left her in the curtained litter as a decoy and one of the wounded had been put in the second litter, also as a decoy.

Of the fifty Browns that had formed the escort, fifteen had been killed and eleven mortally wounded. The eleven had been quickly and honorably committed to the Great Void, three by their own hands, eight assisted by Buntaro at their request. Then Buntaro had assembled the remainder around the closed litters and had left. Forty-eight Grays lay in the dust.

Toranaga knew that he was dangerously unprotected but he was content. Everything has gone well, he thought, considering the vicissitudes of chance. How interesting life is! At first I was sure it was a bad omen that the pilot had seen me change places with Kiri. Then the pilot saved me and acted the madman perfectly, and because of him we escaped Ishido. I hadn't planned for Ishido to be at the main gate, only at the forecourt. That was careless. Why was Ishido there? It isn't like Ishido to be so careful. Who advised him? Kiyama? Onoshi? Or Yodoko? A woman, ever practical would—could suspect such a subterfuge.

It had been a good plan—the secret escape dash—and established for weeks, for it was obvious that Ishido would try to keep him in the castle, would turn the other Regents against him by promising them anything, would willingly sacrifice his hostage at Yedo, the Lady Ochiba, and would use any means to keep him under guard until the final meeting of the Regents, where he would be cornered, impeached, and dispatched.

"But they'll still impeach you!" Hiro-matsu had said when Toranaga had sent for him just after dusk last night to explain what was to be attempted and why he, Toranaga, had been vacillating. "Even if you escape, the Regents will impeach you behind your back as easily as they'll do it to your face. So you're bound to commit seppuku when they order it, as they will order it."

"Yes," Toranaga had said. "As President of the Regents I am bound to do that if the four vote against me. But here"—he had taken a rolled parchment out of his sleeve—"here is my formal resignation from the Council of Regents. You will give it to Ishido when my escape is known."

"What?"

"If I resign I'm no longer bound by my Regent's oath. *Neh?* The Taikō never forbade me to resign, *neh?* Give Ishido this, too." He had handed Hiro-matsu the chop, the official seal of his office as President.

"But now you're totally isolated. You're doomed!"

"You're wrong. Listen, the Taikō's testament implanted a council of *five* Regents on the realm. Now there are four. To be legal, before they can exercise the Emperor's mandate, the four have to elect or appoint a new member, a fifth, *neh?* Ishido, Kiyama, Onoshi, and Sugiyama have to *agree, neh?* Doesn't the new Regent have to be acceptable to all of them? Of course! Now, old comrade, who in all the world will those enemies agree to share ultimate power with? Eh? And while they're arguing, no decisions and—"

"We're preparing for war and you're no longer bound and you can drop a little honey here and bile there and those pile-infested dung-makers will eat themselves up!" Hiro-matsu had said with a rush. "Ah, Yoshi Toranaga-noh-Minowara, you're a man among men. I'll eat my arse if you're not the wisest man in the land!"

Yes, it was a good plan, Toranaga thought, and they all played their parts well: Hiro-matsu, Kiri, and my lovely Sazuko. And now they're locked up tight and they will stay that way or they will be allowed to leave. I think they will never be allowed to leave.

I will be sorry to lose them.

He was leading the party unerringly, his pace fast but measured, the pace he hunted at, the pace he could keep up continuously for two days and one night if need be. He still wore the traveling cloak and Kiri's kimono, but the skirts were hitched up out of the way, his military leggings incongruous.

They crossed another deserted street and headed down an alleyway. He knew the alarm would soon reach Ishido and then the hunt would be on in earnest. There's time enough, he told himself.

Yes, it was a good plan. But I didn't anticipate the ambush. That's cost me three days of safety. Kiri was sure she could keep the deception a secret for at least three days. But the secret's out now and I won't be able to slip aboard and out to sea. Who was the ambush for? Me or the pilot? Of course the pilot. But didn't the arrows bracket both litters? Yes, but the archers were quite far away and it would be hard to see, and it would be wiser and safer to kill both, just in case.

Who ordered the attack, Kiyama or Onoshi? or the Portuguese? or the Christian Fathers?

Toranaga turned around to check the pilot. He saw that he was not flagging, nor was the woman who walked beside him, though both were tired. On the skyline he could see the vast squat bulk of the castle and the phallus of the donjon. Tonight was the second time I've almost died there, he thought. Is that castle really going to be my nemesis? The Taikō told me often enough: 'While Osaka Castle lives my line will never die and you, Toranaga Minowara, your epitaph will be written on its walls. Osaka will cause your death, my faithful vassal!' And always the hissing, baiting laugh that set his soul on edge.

Does the Taikō live within Yaemon? Whether he does or not, Yaemon is his legal heir.

With an effort Toranaga tore his eyes away from the castle and turned another corner and fled into a maze of alleys. At length he stopped outside a battered gate. A fish was etched into its timbers. He knocked in code. The door opened at once. Instantly the ill-kempt samurai bowed. "Sire?"

"Bring your men and follow me," Toranaga said and set off again.

"Gladly." This samurai did not wear the Brown uniform kimono, only motley rags of a *ronin*, but he was one of the special elite secret troops that Toranaga had smuggled into Osaka against such an emergency. Fifteen men, similarly clothed, and equally well armed, followed him and quickly fell into place as advance and rear guard, while another ran off to spread the alarm to other secret cadres. Soon Toranaga had fifty troops with him. Another hundred covered his flanks. Another thousand would be ready at dawn should he need them. He relaxed and slackened his pace, sensing that the pilot and the woman were tiring too fast. He needed them strong.

Toranaga stood in the shadows of the warehouse and studied the galley and the wharf and the foreshore. Yabu and a samurai were beside him. The others had been left in a tight knot a hundred paces back down the alley.

A detachment of a hundred Grays waited near the gangway of the galley a few hundred paces away, across a wide expanse of beaten earth that precluded any surprise attack. The galley itself was alongside, moored to stanchions fixed into the stone wharf that extended a hundred yards out into the sea. The oars were shipped neatly, and he could see indistinctly many seamen and warriors on deck.

"Are they ours or theirs?" he asked quietly.

"It's too far to be sure," Yabu replied.

The tide was high. Beyond the galley, night fishing boats were coming in and going out, lanterns serving as their riding and fishing lights. North, along the shore, were rows of beached fishing craft of many sizes, tended by a few fishermen. Five hundred paces south, alongside another stone wharf, was the Portuguese frigate, the *Santa Theresa*. Under the light of flares, clusters of porters were busily loading barrels and bales. Another large group of Grays lolled nearby. This was usual because all Portuguese and all foreign ships in port were, by law, under perpetual surveillance. It was only at Nagasaki that Portuguese shipping moved in and out freely.

If security could be tightened there, the safer we'd all sleep at night, Toranaga told himself. Yes, but could we lock them up and still have trade with China in ever increasing amounts? That's one trap the Southern Barbarians have us in from which there's no escape, not while the Christian *daimyos* dominate Kyushu and the priests are needed. The best we can do is what the Taikō did. Give the barbarians a little, pretend to take it away, try to bluff, knowing that without the China trade, life would be impossible.

"With your permission, Lord, I will attack at once," the samurai whispered.

"I advise against it," Yabu said. "We don't know if our men are aboard. And there could be a thousand men hidden all around here. Those men"—he pointed at the Grays near the Portuguese ship—"those'll raise the alarm. We could never take the ship and get it out to sea before they'd bottled us up. We need ten times the men we've got now."

"General Lord Ishido will know soon," the samurai said. "Then all Osaka'll be swarming with more hostiles than there are flies on a new battlefield. I've a hundred and fifty men with those on our flanks. That'll be enough."

"Not for safety. Not if our sailors aren't ready on the oars. Better to create a diversion, one that'd draw off the Grays—and any that are in hiding. Those, too," Yabu pointed again at the men near the frigate.

"What kind of diversion?" Toranaga said.

"Fire the street."

"That's impossible!" the samurai protested, aghast. Arson was a crime punishable by the public burning of all the family of the guilty person, of every generation of the family. The penalty was the most severe by law because fire was the greatest hazard to any village or town or city in the Empire. Wood and paper were their only building materials, except for tiles on some roofs. Every home, every warehouse, every hovel, and every palace was a tinderbox. "We can't fire the street!"

"What's more important," Yabu asked him, "the destruction of a few streets, or the death of our Master?"

"The fire'd spread, Yabu-san. We can't burn Osaka. There are a million people here—more."

"Is that your answer to my question?"

Ashen, the samurai turned to Toranaga. "Sire, I'll do anything you ask. Is that what you want me to do?"

Toranaga merely looked at Yabu.

The *daimyo* jerked his thumb contemptuously at the city. "Two years ago half of it burned down and look at it now. Five years ago was the Great Fire. How many hundred thousand were lost then? What does it matter? They're only shopkeepers, merchants, craftsmen, and *eta*. It's not as though Osaka's a village filled with peasants."

Toranaga had long since gauged the wind. It was slight and would not fan the blaze. Perhaps. But a blaze could easily become a holocaust that would eat up all the city. Except the castle. Ah, if it would only consume the castle I wouldn't hesitate for a moment.

He turned on his heel and went back to the others. "Mariko-san, take the pilot and our six samurai and go to the galley. Pretend to be almost in panic. Tell the Grays that there's been an ambush—by bandits or *ronin,* you're not sure which. Tell them where it happened, that you were sent ahead urgently by the captain of our escorting Grays to get the Grays here to help, that the battle's still raging, that you think Kiritsubo's been killed or wounded—to please hurry. If you're convincing, this will draw most of them off."

"I understand perfectly, Sire."

"Then, no matter what the Grays do, go on board with the pilot. If our sailors are there and the ship's safe and secure, come back to the gangway and pretend to faint. That's our signal. Do it exactly at the head of the gangway." Toranaga let his eyes rest on Blackthorne. "Tell him what you're going to do, but not that you're going to faint." He turned away to give orders to the rest of his men and special private instructions to the six samurai.

When Toranaga had finished, Yabu drew him aside. "Why send the barbarian? Wouldn't it be safer to leave him here? Safer for you?"

"Safer for him, Yabu-san, but not for me. He's a useful decoy."

"Firing the street would be even safer."

"Yes." Toranaga thought that it was better to have Yabu on his side than on Ishido's. I'm glad I did not make him jump off the tower yesterday.

"Sire?"

"Yes, Mariko-san?"

"I'm sorry, but the Anjin-san asks what happens if the ship's held by the enemy?"

"Tell him there's no need to go with you if he's not strong enough."

Blackthorne kept his temper when she told him what Toranaga had said. "Tell Lord Toranaga that his plan is no good for you, that you should stay here. If all's well I can signal."

"I can't do that, Anjin-san, that's not what our Master has ordered," Mariko told him firmly. "Any plan he makes is bound to be very wise."

Blackthorne realized there was no point in arguing. God curse their bloody-minded, muleheaded arrogance, he thought. But, by the Lord God, what courage they've got! The men and this woman.

He had watched her, standing at the ambush, in her hands the long killing sword that was almost as tall as herself, ready to fight to the death for Toranaga. He had seen her use the sword once, expertly, and though Buntaro had killed the attacker, she had made it easier by forcing the man to back off. There was still blood on her kimono now and it was torn in places and her face was dirty.

"Where did you learn to use a sword?" he had asked while they rushed for the docks.

"You should know that all samurai ladies are taught very early to use a knife to defend their honor and that of their lords," she had said matter-of-factly, and showed him how the stiletto was kept safe in the obi, ready for instant use. "But some of us, a few, are also taught about sword and spear, Anjin-san. Some fathers feel daughters as well as sons must be prepared to do battle for their lords. Of course, some women are more warlike than others and enjoy going into battle with their husbands or fathers. My mother was one of these. My father and mother decided I should know the sword and the spear."

"If it hadn't been for the captain of the Grays being in the way, the first arrow would have gone right through you," he had said.

"Through you, Anjin-san," she corrected him, very sure. "But you did save my life by pulling me to safety."

Now, looking at her, he knew that he would not like anything to happen to her. "Let me go with the samurai, Mariko-san. You stay here. Please."

"That's not possible, Anjin-san."

"Then I want a knife. Better, give me two."

She passed this request to Toranaga, who agreed. Blackthorne slid one under the sash, inside his kimono. The other he tied, haft downwards, to the inside of his forearm with a strip of silk he tore off the hem of his kimono.

"My Master asks do all Englishmen carry knives secretly in their sleeves like that?"

"No. But most seamen do."

"That's not usual here—or with the Portuguese," she said.

"The best place for a spare knife's in your boot. Then you can do wicked damage, very fast. If need be."

She translated this and Blackthorne noticed the attentive eyes of Toranaga and Yabu, and he sensed that they did not like him armed. Good, he thought. Perhaps I can stay armed.

He wondered again about Toranaga. After the ambush had been beaten off and the Grays killed, Toranaga had, through Mariko, thanked him before all the Browns for his "loyalty." Nothing more, no promises, no agreements, no rewards. But Blackthorne knew that those would come later. The old monk had told him that loyalty was the only thing they rewarded. 'Loyalty and duty, señor,' he had said. 'It is their cult, this *bushido*. Where we give our lives to God and His Blessed Son Jesus, and Mary the Mother of God, these animals give themselves to their masters and die like dogs. Remember, señor, for thy soul's sake, they're animals.'

They're not animals, Blackthorne thought. And much of what you said, Father, is wrong and a fanatic's exaggeration.

He said to Mariko, "We need a signal—if the ship's safe or if it isn't."

Again she translated, innocently this time. "Lord Toranaga says that one of our soldiers will do that."

"I don't consider it brave to send a woman to do a man's job."

"Please be patient with us, Anjin-san. There's no difference between men and women. Women are equal as samurai. In this plan a woman would be so much better than a man."

Toranaga spoke to her shortly.

"Are you ready, Anjin-san? We're to go now."

"The plan's rotten and dangerous and I'm tired of being a goddamned sacrificial plucked duck, but I'm ready."

She laughed, bowed once to Toranaga, and ran off. Blackthorne and the six samurai raced after her.

She was very fleet and he did not catch up with her as they rounded the corner and headed across the open space. He had never felt so naked. The moment they appeared, the Grays spotted them and surged forward. Soon they were surrounded, Mariko jabbering feverishly with the samurai and the Grays. Then he too added to the babel in a panting mixture of Portuguese, English, and Dutch, motioning them to hurry, and groped for the gangway to lean against it, not needing to pretend that he was badly winded. He tried to see inside the ship but could make out nothing distinctly, only many heads appearing at the gunwale. He could see the shaven pates of many samurai and many seamen. He could not discern the color of the kimonos.

From behind, one of the Grays was talking rapidly to him, and he turned around, telling him that he didn't understand—to go there, quickly, back up the street where the God-cursed battle was going on. "*Wakarimasu ka?* Get your scuttle-tailed arse to hell out of here! *Wakarimasu ka?* The fight's there!"

Mariko was frantically haranguing the senior officer of the Grays. The officer came back toward the ship and shouted orders. Immediately more than a hundred samurai, all Grays, began pouring off the ship. He sent a few north along the shore to intercept the wounded and help them if necessary. One was sent scurrying off to get help from the Grays near the Portuguese galley. Leaving ten men behind to guard the gangway, he led the remainder in a rush for the street which curled away from the dock, up to the city proper.

Mariko came up to Blackthorne. "Does the ship seem all right to you?" she asked.

"She's floating." With a great effort Blackthorne grasped the gangway ropes and pulled himself on deck. Mariko followed. Two Browns came after her.

The seamen packing the port gunwale gave way. Four Grays were guarding the quarterdeck and two more were on the forepoop. All were armed with bows and arrows as well as swords.

Mariko questioned one of the sailors. The man answered her obligingly. "They're all sailors hired to take Kiritsubo-san to Yedo," she told Blackthorne.

"Ask him . . ." Blackthorne stopped as he recognized the short, squat mate he had made captain of the galley after the storm. "*Konbanwa,* Captain-san!"—Good evening.

"*Konbanwa*, Anjin-san. *Watashi iyé* Captain-san *ima*," the mate replied with a grin, shaking his head. He pointed at a lithe sailor with an iron-gray stubbly queue who stood alone on the quarterdeck. "*Imasu* Captain-san!"

"*Ah, so desu? Halloa,* Captain-san!" Blackthorne called out and bowed, and lowered his voice. "Mariko-san, find out if there are any Grays below."

Before she could say anything the captain had bowed back and shouted to the mate. The mate nodded and replied at length. Some of the sailors also voiced their agreement. The captain and all aboard were very impressed.

"*Ah, so desu,* Anjin-san!" Then the captain cried out, "*Keirei!*"— Salute! All aboard, except the samurai, bowed to Blackthorne in salute.

Mariko said, "This mate told the captain that you saved the ship during the storm, Anjin-san. You did not tell us about the storm or your voyage."

"There's little to tell. It was just another storm. Please thank the captain and say I'm happy to be aboard again. Ask him if we're ready to leave when the others arrive." And added quietly, "Find out if there are any more Grays below."

She did as she was ordered.

The captain came over and she asked for more information and then, picking up the captain's cue concerning the importance of Blackthorne aboard, she bowed to Blackthorne. "Anjin-san, he thanks you for the life of his ship and says they're ready," adding softly, "About the other, he doesn't know."

Blackthorne glanced ashore. There was no sign of Buntaro or the column to the north. The samurai sent running southward toward the *Santa Theresa* was still a hundred yards from his destination, unnoticed as yet. "What now?" he said, when he could stand the waiting no longer.

She was asking herself, Is the ship safe? Decide.

"That man'll get there any moment," he said, looking at the frigate. "What?"

He pointed. "That one—the samurai!"

"What samurai? I'm sorry, I can't see that far, Anjin-san. I can see everything on the ship, though the Grays to the front of the ship are misted. What man?"

He told her, adding in Latin, "Now he is barely fifty paces away. Now he is seen. We need assistance gravely. Who giveth the sign? With importance it should be given quickly."

"My husband, is there any sign of him?" she asked in Portuguese. He shook his head.

Sixteen Grays stand between my Master and his safety, she told herself. Oh Madonna, protect him!

Then, committing her soul to God, frightened that she was making the wrong decision, she went weakly to the head of the gangway and pretended to faint.

Blackthorne was taken unawares. He saw her head crash nastily against the wooden slats. Seamen began to crowd, Grays converged from the dock and from the decks as he rushed over. He picked her up and carried her back, through the men, toward the quarterdeck.

"Get some water—water, *hai?*"

The seamen stared at him without comprehension. Desperately he searched his mind for the Japanese word. The old monk had told it to him fifty times. Christ God, what is it? "Oh—*mizu, mizu, hai?*"

"*Ah, mizu! Hai,* Anjin-san." A man began to hurry away. There was a sudden cry of alarm.

Ashore, thirty of Toranaga's *ronin*-disguised samurai were loping out of the alleyway. The Grays that had begun to leave the dock spun around on the gangway. Those on the quarterdeck and forepoop craned to see better. Abruptly one shouted orders. The archers armed their bows. All samurai, Browns and Grays below, tore out their swords, and most rushed back to the wharf.

"Bandits!" one of the Browns screamed on cue. At once the two Browns on deck split up, one going forward, one aft. The four on land fanned out, intermingling with the waiting Grays.

"Halt!"

Toranaga's *ronin*-samurai charged. An arrow smashed a man in the chest and he fell heavily. Instantly the Brown on the forepoop killed the Gray archer and tried for the other but this samurai was too quick and they locked swords, the Gray shouting a warning of treachery to the others. The Brown on the aft quarterdeck had maimed one of the Grays but the other three dispatched him quickly and they raced for the head of the gangway, seamen scattering. The samurai on the dock below were fighting to the death, the Grays overwhelming the four Browns, knowing that they had been betrayed and that, at any moment, they too would be engulfed by the attackers. The leader of the Grays on deck, a large tough grizzle-bearded man, confronted Blackthorne and Mariko.

"Kill the traitors!" he bellowed, and with a battle cry, he charged.

Blackthorne had seen them all look down at Mariko, still lying in her faint, murder in their eyes, and he knew that if he did not get help soon they were both dead, and that help would not be forthcoming from the seamen. He remembered that only samurai may fight samurai.

He slid his knife into his hand and hurled it in an arc. It took the sam-

urai in the throat. The other two Grays lunged for Blackthorne, killing
swords high. He held the second knife and stood his ground over
Mariko, knowing that he dare not leave her unprotected. From the corner of his eye he saw the battle for the gangway was almost won. Only
three Grays still held the bridge below, only these three kept help from
flooding aboard. If he could stay alive for less than a minute he was
safe and she was safe. Kill 'em, kill the bastards!

He felt, more than saw, the sword slashing for his throat and leaped
backward out of its way. One Gray stabbed after him, the other halted
over Mariko, sword raised. At that instant Blackthorne saw Mariko
come to life. She threw herself into the unsuspecting samurai's legs,
crashing him to the deck. Then, scrambling across to the dead Gray, she
grabbed the sword out of his still twitching hand and leaped on the guard
with a cry. The Gray had regained his feet, and, howling with rage, he
came at her. She backed and slashed bravely but Blackthorne knew she
was lost, the man too strong. Somehow Blackthorne avoided another
death thrust from his own foe and kicked him away and threw his knife
at Mariko's assailant. It struck the man in the back, causing his blow
to go wild, and then Blackthorne found himself on the quarterdeck,
helplessly at bay, one Gray bounding up the steps after him, the other
who had just won the forepoop fight racing toward him along the deck.
He jumped for the gunwale and the safety of the sea but slipped on the
blood-wet deck.

Mariko was staring up, white-faced, at the huge samurai who still
had her cornered, swaying on his feet, his life ebbing fast but not fast
enough. She hacked at him with all her force but he parried the blow,
held her sword, and tore it out of her grasp. He gathered his ultimate
strength, and lunged as the *ronin*-samurai burst up the gangway, over
the dead Grays. One pounced on Mariko's assailant, another fired an
arrow at the quarterdeck.

The arrow ripped into the Gray's back, smashing him off balance,
and his sword sliced past Blackthorne into the gunwale. Blackthorne
tried to scramble away but the man caught him, brought him crashing
to the deck, and clawed for his eyes. Another arrow hit the second Gray
in the shoulder and he dropped his sword, screaming with pain and
rage, tearing futilely at the shaft. A third arrow twisted him around.
Blood surged out of his mouth, and, choking, his eyes staring, he groped
for Blackthorne and fell on him as the last Gray arrived for the kill, a
short stabbing knife in his hands. He hacked downward, Blackthorne
helpless, but a friendly hand caught the knife arm, then the enemy head
had vanished from the neck, a fountain of blood spraying upwards.
Both corpses were pulled off Blackthorne and he was hauled to his feet.

Wiping the blood off his face, he dimly saw that Mariko was stretched out on the deck, *ronin*-samurai milling around her. He shook off his helpers and stumbled toward her, but his knees gave out and he collapsed.

CHAPTER 25

IT took Blackthorne a good ten minutes to regain enough strength to stand unaided. In that time the *ronin*-samurai had dispatched the badly wounded and had cast all corpses into the sea. The six Browns had perished, and all the Grays. They had cleansed the ship and made her ready for instant departure, sent seamen to their oars and stationed others by the stanchions, waiting to slip the mooring ropes. All flares had been doused. A few samurai had been sent to scout north along the shore to intercept Buntaro. The bulk of Toranaga's men hurried southward to a stone breakwater about two hundred paces away, where they took up a strong defensive position against the hundred Grays from the frigate who, having seen the attack, were approaching fast.

When all aboard had been checked and double-checked, the leader cupped his hands around his lips and hallooed shoreward. At once more *ronin*-disguised samurai under Yabu came out of the night, and fanned into protective shields, north and south. Then Toranaga appeared and began to walk slowly toward the gangway alone. He had discarded the woman's kimono and the dark traveling cloak and removed the makeup. Now he wore his armor, and over it a simple brown kimono, swords in his sash. The gap behind him was closed by the last of his guards and the phalanx moved with measured tread toward the wharf.

Bastard, Blackthorne thought. You're a cruel, cold-gutted, heartless bastard but you've got majesty, no doubt about that.

Earlier, he had seen Mariko carried below, helped by a young woman, and he had presumed that she was wounded but not badly, because all badly wounded samurai are murdered at once if they won't or can't kill themselves, and she's samurai.

His hands were very weak but he grasped the helm and pulled himself upright, helped by the seaman, and felt better, the slight breeze taking away the dregs of nausea. Swaying on his feet, still dulled, he watched Toranaga.

There was a sudden flash from the donjon and the faint echoing of alarm bells. Then, from the castle walls, fires began to reach for the stars. Signal fires.

Christ Jesus, they must've got the news, they must've heard about Toranaga's escape!

In the great silence he saw Toranaga looking back and upward. Lights began to flicker all over the city. Without haste Toranaga turned and came aboard.

From the north distant cries came down on the wind. Buntaro! It must be, with the rest of the column. Blackthorne searched the far darkness but could see nothing. Southward the gap between attacking Grays and defending Browns was closing rapidly. He estimated numbers. About equal at the moment. But for how long?

"*Keirei!*" All aboard knelt and bowed low as Toranaga came on deck. Toranaga motioned to Yabu, who followed him. Instantly Yabu took command, giving orders to cast off. Fifty samurai from the phalanx ran up the gangway to take defensive positions, facing shoreward, arming their bows.

Blackthorne felt someone tugging at his sleeve.

"Anjin-san!"

"*Hai?*" He stared down into the captain's face. The man uttered a spate of words, pointing at the helm. Blackthorne realized that the captain presumed he held the con and was asking permission to cast off.

"*Hai,* Captain-san," he replied. "Cast off! *Isogi!*" Yes, very quick, he told himself, wondering how he remembered the word so easily.

The galley eased away from the jetty, helped by the wind, the oarsmen deft. Then Blackthorne saw the Grays hit the breakwater away up the shore and the tumultuous assault began. At that moment, out of the darkness from behind a nearby line of beached boats charged three men and a girl embroiled in a running fight with nine Grays. Blackthorne recognized Buntaro and the girl Sono.

Buntaro led the hacking retreat to the jetty, his sword bloody, arrows sticking into the armor on his chest and back. The girl was armed with a spear but she was stumbling, her wind gone. One of the Browns stopped courageously to cover the retreat. The Grays swamped him. Buntaro raced up the steps, the girl beside him with the last Brown, then he turned and hit the Grays like a mad bull. The first two went crashing off the ten-foot wharf; one broke his back on the stones below and the other fell howling, his right arm gone. The Grays hesitated momentarily, giving the girl time to aim her spear, but all aboard knew it was only a gesture. The last Brown rushed past his master and flung himself headlong at the enemy. The Grays cut him down, then charged en masse.

Archers from the ship fired volley after volley, killing or maiming all but two of the attacking Grays. A sword ricocheted off Buntaro's helmet onto his shoulder armor. Buntaro smashed the Gray under the chin with his mailed forearm, breaking his neck, and hurled himself at the last. This man died too.

The girl was on her knees now, trying to catch her breath. Buntaro did not waste time making sure the Grays were dead. He simply hacked off their heads with single, perfect blows, and then, when the jetty was completely secure, he turned seaward, waved at Toranaga exhausted but happy. Toranaga called back, equally pleased.

The ship was twenty yards from the jetty, the gap still widening.

"Captain-san," Blackthorne called out, gesturing urgently. "Go back to the wharf! *Isogi!*"

Obediently the captain shouted the orders. All oars ceased and began to back water. At once Yabu came hurtling across to the quarterdeck and spoke heatedly to the captain. The order was clear. The ship was not to return.

"There's plenty of time, for Christ's sake. Look!" Blackthorne pointed at the empty beaten earth and at the breakwater where the *ronin* were holding the Grays at bay.

But Yabu shook his head.

The gap was thirty yards now and Blackthorne's mind was shouting, What's the matter with you, that's Buntaro, her husband.

"You can't let him die, he's one of ours," he shouted at Yabu and at the ship. "Him! Buntaro!" He spun round on the captain. "Back there! *Isogi!*" But this time the seaman shook his head helplessly and held the escape course and the oarsmaster continued the beat on the great drum.

Blackthorne rushed for Toranaga, who had his back to him, studying the shore and wharf. At once four bodyguard samurai stepped in the pilot's way, swords on high. He called out, "Toranaga-sama! *Dozo!* Order the ship back! There! *Dozo*—please! Go back!"

"*Iyé,* Anjin-san." Toranaga pointed once at the castle signal flares and once at the breakwater, and turned his back again with finality.

"Why, you shitless coward . . ." Blackthorne began, but stopped. Then he rushed for the gunwale and leaned over it. "Swiiiiimm!" he hollered, making the motions. "Swim, for Christ's sake!"

Buntaro understood. He raised the girl to her feet and spoke to her and half-shoved her toward the wharf edge but she cried out and fell on her knees in front of him. Obviously she could not swim.

Desperately Blackthorne searched the deck. No time to launch a small boat. Much too far to throw a rope. Not enough strength to swim there and back. No life jackets. As a last resort he ran over to the nearest oarsmen, two to each great sweep, and stopped their pull. All oars on the portside were momentarily thrown off tempo, oar crashing into oar. The galley slewed awkwardly, the beat stopped, and Blackthorne showed the oarsmen what he wanted.

Two samurai went forward to restrain him but Toranaga ordered them away.

Together, Blackthorne and four seamen launched the oar like a dart over the side. It sailed for some way then hit the water cleanly, and its momentum carried it to the wharf.

At that moment there was a victory shout from the breakwater. Reinforcements of Grays were streaming down from the city and, though the *ronin*-samurai were holding off the present attackers, it was only a matter of time before the wall was breached.

"Come on," Blackthorne shouted. "*Isogiiii!*"

Buntaro pulled the girl up, pointed at the oar and then out to the ship. She bowed weakly. He dismissed her and turned his full attention to battle, his vast legs set firm on the jetty.

The girl called out once to the ship. A woman's voice answered and she jumped. Her head broke the surface. She flailed for the oar and grabbed it. It bore her weight easily and she kicked for the ship. A small wave caught her and she rode it safely and came closer to the galley. Then her fear caused her to loosen her grip and the oar slipped away from her. She thrashed for an endless moment, then vanished below the surface.

She never came back.

Buntaro was alone now on the wharf and he stood watching the rise and the fall of the battle. More reinforcement Grays, a few cavalry among them, were coming up from the south to join the others and he knew that soon the breakwater would be engulfed by a sea of men. Carefully he examined the north and west and south. Then he turned his back to the battle and went to the far end of the jetty. The galley was safely seventy yards from its tip, at rest, waiting. All fishing boats had long since fled the area and they waited as far away as possible on both sides of the harbor, their riding lights like so many cats' eyes in the darkness.

When he reached the end of the dock, Buntaro took off his helmet and his bow and quiver and his top body armor and put them beside his scabbards. The naked killing sword and the naked short sword he placed separately. Then, stripped to the waist, he picked up his equipment and cast it into the sea. The killing sword he studied reverently, then tossed it with all his force, far out into the deep. It vanished with hardly a splash.

He bowed formally to the galley, to Toranaga, who went at once to the quarterdeck where he could be seen. He bowed back.

Buntaro knelt and placed the short sword neatly on the stone in front of him, moonlight flashing briefly on the blade, and stayed motionless, almost as though in prayer, facing the galley.

"What the hell's he waiting for?" Blackthorne muttered, the galley eerily quiet without the drumbeat. "Why doesn't he jump and swim?"

"He's preparing to commit seppuku."

Mariko was standing nearby, propped by a young woman.

"Jesus, Mariko, are you all right?"

"All right," she said, hardly listening to him, her face haggard but no less beautiful.

He saw the crude bandage on her left arm near the shoulder where the sleeve had been slashed away, her arm resting in a sling of material torn from a kimono. Blood stained the bandage and a dribble ran down her arm.

"I'm so glad—" Then it dawned on him what she had said. "Seppuku? He's going to kill himself? Why? There's plenty of time for him to get here! If he can't swim, look—there's an oar that'll hold him easily. There, near the jetty, you see it? Can't you see it?"

"Yes, but my husband can swim, Anjin-san," she said. "All of Lord Toranaga's officers must—must learn—he insists. But he has decided not to swim."

"For Christ's sake, why?"

A sudden frenzy broke out shoreward, a few muskets went off, and the wall was breached. Some of the ronin-samurai fell back and ferocious individual combat began again. This time the enemy spearhead was contained, and repelled.

"Tell him to swim, by God!"

"He won't, Anjin-san. He's preparing to die."

"If he wants to die, for Christ's sake, why doesn't he go there?" Blackthorne's finger stabbed toward the fight. "Why doesn't he help his men? If he wants to die, why doesn't he die fighting, like a *man?*"

Mariko did not take her eyes from the wharf, leaning against the young woman. "Because he might be captured, and if he swam he might also be captured, and then the enemy would put him on show before the common people, shame him, do terrible things. A samurai cannot be captured and remain samurai. That's the worst dishonor—to be captured by an enemy—so my husband is doing what a *man,* a samurai, must do. A samurai dies with dignity. For what is life to a samurai? Nothing at all. All life is suffering, *neh?* It is his right and *duty* to die with honor, before witnesses."

"What a stupid waste," Blackthorne said, through his teeth.

"Be patient with us, Anjin-san."

"Patient for what? For more lies? Why won't you trust me? Haven't I earned that? You lied, didn't you? You pretended to faint and that was the signal. Wasn't it? I asked you and you lied."

"I was ordered . . . it was an order to protect you. Of course I trust you."

"You lied," he said, knowing that he was being unreasonable, but he was beyond caring, abhorring the insane disregard for life and starved for sleep and peace, starved for his own food and his own drink and his own ship and his own kind. "You're all animals," he said in English, knowing they were not, and moved away.

"What was he saying, Mariko-san?" the young woman asked, hard put to hide her distaste. She was half a head taller than Mariko, bigger-boned and square-faced with little, needle-shaped teeth. She was Usagi Fujiko, Mariko's niece, and she was nineteen.

Mariko told her.

"What an awful man! What foul manners! Disgusting, *neh?* How can you bear to be near him?"

"Because he saved our Master's honor. Without his bravery I'm sure Lord Toranaga would have been captured—we'd all have been captured." Both women shuddered.

"The gods protect us from that shame!" Fujiko glanced at Blackthorne, who leaned against the gunwale up the deck, staring at the shore. She studied him a moment. "He looks like a golden ape with blue eyes—a creature to frighten children with. Horrid, *neh?*" Fujiko shivered and dismissed him and looked again at Buntaro. After a moment she said, "I envy your husband, Mariko-san."

"Yes," Mariko replied sadly. "But I wish he had a second to help him." By custom another samurai always assisted at a seppuku, standing slightly behind the kneeling man, to decapitate him with a single stroke before the agony became unbearable and uncontrollable and so shamed the man at the supreme moment of his life. Unseconded, few men could die without shame.

"*Karma,*" Fujiko said.

"Yes. I pity him. That's the one thing he feared—not to have a second."

"We're luckier than men, *neh?*" Samurai women committed seppuku by thrusting their knives into their throats and therefore needed no assistance.

"Yes," Mariko said.

Screams and battle cries came wafting on the wind, distracting them. The breakwater was breached again. A small company of fifty Toranaga *ronin*-samurai raced out of the north in support, a few horsemen among them. Again the breach was ferociously contained, no quarter sought or given, the attackers thrown back and a few more moments of time gained.

Time for what, Blackthorne was asking bitterly. Toranaga's safe now. He's out to sea. He's betrayed you all.

The drum began again.

Oars bit into the water, the prow dipped and began to cut through the waves, and aft a wake appeared. Signal fires still burned from the castle walls above. The whole city was almost awake.

The main body of Grays hit the breakwater. Blackthorne's eyes went to Buntaro. "You poor bastard!" he said in English. "You poor, stupid bastard!"

He turned on his heel and walked down the companionway along the main deck toward the bow to watch for shoals ahead. No one except Fujiko and the captain noticed him leaving the quarterdeck.

The oarsmen pulled with fine discipline and the ship was gaining way. The sea was fair, the wind friendly. Blackthorne tasted the salt and welcomed it. Then he detected the ships crowding the harbor mouth half a league ahead. Fishing vessels yes, but they were crammed with samurai.

"We're trapped," he said out loud, knowing somehow they were enemy.

A tremor went through the ship. All who watched the battle on shore had shifted in unison.

Blackthorne looked back. Grays were calmly mopping up the breakwater, while others were heading unhurried toward the jetty for Buntaro, but four horsemen—Browns—were galloping across the beaten earth from out of the north, a fifth horse, a spare horse, tethered to the leader. This man clattered up the wide stone steps of the wharf with the spare horse and raced its length while the other three slammed toward the encroaching Grays. Buntaro had also looked around but he remained kneeling and, when the man reined in behind him, he waved him away and picked up the knife in both hands, blade toward himself. Immediately Toranaga cupped his hands and shouted, "Buntaro-san! Go with them now—try to escape!"

The cry swept across the waves and was repeated and then Buntaro heard it clearly. He hesitated, shocked, the knife poised. Again the call, insistent and imperious.

With effort Buntaro drew himself back from death and icily contemplated life and the escape that was ordered. The risk was bad. Better to die here, he told himself. Doesn't Toranaga know that? Here is an honorable death. There, almost certain capture. Where do you run? Three hundred *ri,* all the way to Yedo? You're certain to be captured!

He felt the strength in his arm, saw the firm, unshaking, needle-pointed dagger hovering near his naked abdomen, and he craved for the releasing agony of death at long last. At long last a death to expiate all the shame: the shame of his father's kneeling to Toranaga's standard when they should have kept faith with Yaemon, the Taikō's heir, as they had sworn to do; the shame of killing so many men who honorably served the Taikō's cause against the usurper, Toranaga; the shame of the woman, Mariko, and of his only son, both forever tainted, the son because of the mother and she because of her father, the monstrous assassin, Akechi Jinsai. And the shame of knowing that because of them, his own name was befouled forever.

How many thousand agonies have I not endured because of her?

His soul cried out for oblivion. Now so near and easy and honorable. The next life will be better; how could it be worse?

Even so, he put down the knife and obeyed, and cast himself back into the abyss of life. His liege lord had ordered the ultimate suffering and had decided to cancel his attempt at peace. What else is there for a samurai but obedience?

He jumped up, hurled himself into the saddle, jammed his heels into the horse's sides, and, together with the other man, he fled. Other *ronin*-cavalry galloped out of the night to guard their retreat and cut down the leading Grays. Then they too vanished, a few Gray horsemen in pursuit.

Laughter erupted over the ship.

Toranaga was pounding the gunwale with his fist in glee, Yabu and the samurai were roaring. Even Mariko was laughing.

"One man got away, but what about all the dead?" Blackthorne cried out, enraged. "Look ashore—there must be three, four hundred bodies there. *Look at them, for Christ's sake!*"

But his shout did not come through the laughter.

Then a cry of alarm from the bow lookout. And the laughter died.

CHAPTER 26

Toranaga said calmly, "Can we break through them, Captain?" He was watching the grouped fishing boats five hundred yards ahead, and the tempting passage they had left between them.

"No, Sire."

"We've no alternative," Yabu said. "There's nothing else we can do." He glared aft at the massed Grays who waited on the shore and the jetty, their faint, jeering insults riding on the wind.

Toranaga and Yabu were on the forepoop now. The drum had been silenced and the galley wallowed in a light sea. All aboard waited to see what would be decided. They knew that they were bottled tight. Ashore disaster, ahead disaster, to wait disaster. The net would come closer and closer and then they would be captured. If need be, Ishido could wait days.

Yabu was seething. If we'd rushed for the harbor mouth directly we'd boarded instead of wasting useless time over Buntaro, we'd be safely out to sea by now, he told himself. Toranaga's losing his wits. Ishido will believe I betrayed him. There's nothing I can do—unless we can fight our way out, and even then I'm committed to fight for Toranaga against Ishido. Nothing I can do. Except give Ishido Toranaga's head. *Neh?* That would make you a Regent and bring you the Kwanto, *neh?* And then with six months of time and the musket samurai, why not even President of the Council of Regents? Or why not the big prize! Eliminate Ishido and become Chief General of the Heir, Lord Protector and Governor of Osaka Castle, the controlling general of all the legendary wealth in the donjon, with power over the Empire during Yaemon's minority, and afterwards power second only to Yaemon. Why not?

Or even the biggest prize of all. Shōgun. Eliminate Yaemon, then you'll be Shōgun.

All for a single head and some benevolent gods!

Yabu's knees felt weak as his longing soared. So easy to do, he thought, but no way to take the head and escape—yet.

"Order attack stations!" Toranaga commanded at last.

As Yabu gave the orders and samurai began to prepare, Toranaga turned his attention to the barbarian who was still near the forepoop where he had stopped when the alarm was given, leaning against the short mainmast.

I wish I could understand him, Toranaga thought. One moment so brave, the next so weak. One moment so valuable, the next so useless. One moment killer, the next coward. One moment docile, the next dangerous. He's man and woman, *Yang* and *Yin*. He's nothing but opposites, and unpredictable.

Toranaga had studied him carefully during the escape from the castle, during the ambush and after it. He had heard from Mariko and the captain and others what had happened during the fight aboard. He had witnessed the astonishing anger a few moments ago and then, when Buntaro had been sent off, he had heard the shout and had seen through veiled eyes the stretched ugliness on the man's face, and then, when there should have been laughter, only anger.

Why not laughter when an enemy's outsmarted? Why not laughter to empty the tragedy from you when *karma* interrupts the beautiful death of a true samurai, when *karma* causes the useless death of a pretty girl? Isn't it only through laughter that we become one with the gods and thus can endure life and can overcome all the horror and waste and suffering here on earth? Like tonight, watching all those brave men meet their fate here, on this shore, on this gentle night, through a *karma* ordained a thousand lifetimes ago, or perhaps even one.

Isn't it only through laughter we can stay human?

Why doesn't the pilot realize he's governed by *karma* too, as I am, as we all are, as even this Jesus the Christ was, for, if the truth were known, it was only his *karma* that made him die dishonored like a common criminal with other common criminals, on the hill the barbarian priests tell about.

All *karma*.

How barbaric to nail a man to a piece of wood and wait for him to die. They're worse than the Chinese, who are pleasured by torture.

"Ask him, Yabu-san!" Toranaga said.

"Sire?"

"Ask him what to do. The pilot. Isn't this a sea battle? Haven't you told me the pilot's a genius at sea? Good, let's see if you're right. Let him prove it."

Yabu's mouth was a tight cruel line and Toranaga could feel the man's fear and it delighted him.

"Mariko-san," Yabu barked. "Ask the pilot how to get out—how to break through those ships."

Obediently Mariko moved away from the gunwale, the girl still sup-

porting her. "No, I'm all right now, Fujiko-san," she said. "Thank you."
Fujiko let her go and watched Blackthorne distastefully.

Blackthorne's answer was short.

"He says 'with cannon,' Yabu-san," Mariko said.

"Tell him he'll have to do better than that if he wants to retain his
head!"

"We must be patient with him, Yabu-san," Toranaga interrupted.
"Mariko-san, tell him politely, 'Regrettably we have no cannon. Isn't
there another way to break out? It's impossible by land.' Translate
exactly what he replies. Exactly."

Mariko did so. "I'm sorry, Lord, but he says, no. Just like that. 'No.'
Not politely."

Toranaga moved his sash and scratched an itch under his armor.
"Well then," he said genially, "the Anjin-san says cannon and he's the
expert, so cannon it is. Captain, go there!" His blunt, calloused finger
pointed viciously at the Portuguese frigate. "Get the men ready, Yabu-
san. If the Southern Barbarians won't lend me their cannon, then you
will have to take them. Won't you?"

"With very great pleasure," Yabu said softly.

"You were right, he is a genius."

"But you found the solution, Toranaga-san."

"It's easy to find solutions given the answer, neh? What's the solution to Osaka Castle, Ally?"

"There isn't one. In that the Taikō was perfect."

"Yes. What's the solution to treachery?"

"Of course, ignominious death. But I don't understand why you
should ask me that."

"A passing thought—Ally." Toranaga glanced at Blackthorne. "Yes,
he's a clever man. I have great need of clever men. Mariko-san, will the
barbarians give me their cannon?"

"Of course. Why shouldn't they?" It had never occurred to her that
they would not. She was still filled with anxiety over Buntaro. It would
have been so much better to allow him to die back there. Why risk his
honor? She wondered why Toranaga had ordered Buntaro away by land
at the very last moment. Toranaga could just as easily have ordered him
to swim to the boat. It would have been much safer and there was
plenty of time. He could even have ordered it when Buntaro had first
reached the end of the jetty. Why wait? Her most secret self answered
that their lord must have had a very good reason to have waited and to
have so ordered.

"And if they don't? Are you prepared to kill Christians, Mariko-san?"

Toranaga asked. "Isn't that their most impossible law? Thou shalt not kill?"

"Yes, it is. But for you, Lord, we will go gladly into hell, my husband and my son and I."

"Yes. You're true samurai and I won't forget that you took up a sword to defend me."

"Please do not thank me. If I helped, in any minor way, it was my duty. If anyone is to be remembered, please let it be my husband or my son. They are more valuable to you."

"At the moment you're more valuable to me. You could be even more valuable."

"Tell me how, Sire. And it will be done."

"Put this foreign God away."

"Sire?" Her face froze.

"Put your God away. You have one too many loyalties."

"You mean become apostate, Sire? Give up Christianity?"

"Yes, unless you can put this God where He belongs—in the back of your spirit, not in the front."

"Please excuse me, Sire," she said shakily, "but my religion has never interfered with my loyalty to you. I've always kept my religion a private matter, all the time. How have I failed you?"

"You haven't yet. But you will."

"Tell me what I must do to please you."

"The Christians may become my enemies, *neh?*"

"Your enemies are mine, Lord."

"The priests oppose me now. They may order all Christians to war on me."

"They can't, Sire. They're men of peace."

"And if they continue to oppose me? If Christians war on me?"

"You will never have to fear my loyalty. Never."

"This Anjin-san may speak the truth and your priests with false tongues."

"There are good priests and bad priests, Sire. But you are my liege lord."

"Very well, Mariko-san," Toranaga said. "I'll accept that. You're ordered to become friends with this barbarian, to learn all he knows, to report everything he says, to learn to think like him, to 'confess' nothing about what you're doing, to treat all priests with suspicion, to report everything the priests ask you or say to you. Your God must fit in between, elsewhere—or not at all."

Mariko pushed a thread of hair out of her eyes. "I can do all that, Sire, and still remain Christian. I swear it."

"Good. Swear it by this Christian God."

"Before God I swear it."

"Good." Toranaga turned and called out, "Fujiko-san!"

"Yes, Sire?"

"Did you bring maids with you?"

"Yes, Sire. Two."

"Give one to Mariko-san. Send the other for cha."

"There's saké if you wish."

"Cha. Yabu-san, would you like cha or saké?"

"Cha, please."

"Bring saké for the Anjin-san."

Light caught the little golden crucifix that hung from Mariko's neck. She saw Toranaga stare at it. "You . . . you wish me not to wear it, Sire? To throw it away?"

"No," he said. "Wear it as a reminder of your oath."

They all watched the frigate. Toranaga felt someone looking at him and glanced around. He saw the hard face and cold blue eyes and felt the hate—no, not hate, the suspicion. How dare the barbarian be suspicious of me, he thought.

"Ask the Anjin-san why didn't he just say there're plenty of cannon on the barbarian ship? Get them to escort us out of the trap?"

Mariko translated. Blackthorne answered.

"He says . . ." Mariko hesitated, then continued in a rush, "Please excuse me, he said, 'It's good for him to use his own head.'"

Toranaga laughed. "Thank him for his. It's been most useful. I hope it stays on his shoulders. Tell him that now we're equal."

"He says, 'No, we're not equal, Toranaga-sama. But give me my ship and a crew and I'll wipe the seas clean. Of any enemy.'"

"Mariko-san, do you think he meant me as well as the others— the Spanish and the Southern Barbarians?" The question was put lightly.

The breeze wafted strands of hair into her eyes. She pushed them away tiredly. "I don't know, so sorry. Perhaps, perhaps not. Do you want me to ask him? I'm sorry, but he's a . . . he's very strange. I'm afraid I don't understand him. Not at all."

"We've plenty of time. Yes. In time he'll explain himself to us."

Blackthorne had seen the frigate quietly slip her moorings the moment her escort of Grays had hurried away, had watched her launch her longboat, which had quickly warped the ship away from her berth at the jetty, well out into the stream. Now she lay a few cables offshore in deep water, safe, a light bow anchor holding her gently, broadside to the shore.

This was the normal maneuver of all European ships in alien or hostile harbors when a shore danger threatened. He knew, too, that though there was—and had been—no untoward movement on deck, by now all cannon would be primed, muskets issued, grape, cannonball, and chain-shot ready in abundance, cutlasses waiting in their racks—and armed men aloft in the shrouds. Eyes would be searching all points of the compass. The galley would have been marked the moment it had changed course. The two stern chasers, thirty pounders, which were pointing directly at them, would be trained on them. Portuguese gunners were the best in the world, after the English.

And they'll know about Toranaga, he told himself with great bitterness, because they're clever and they'd have asked their porters or the Grays what all the trouble was about. Or by now the God-cursed Jesuits who know everything would have sent word about Toranaga's escape, and about me.

He could feel his short hairs curling. Any one of those guns can blow us to hell. Yes, but we're safe because Toranaga's aboard. Thank God for Toranaga.

Mariko was saying, "My Master asks what is your custom when you want to approach a warship?"

"If you had cannon you'd fire a salute. Or you can signal with flags, asking permission to come alongside."

"My Master says, and if you have no flags?"

Though they were still outside cannon range it was almost, to Blackthorne, as if he were already climbing down one of the barrels, though the gunports were still closed. The ship carried eight cannon a side on her main deck, two at the stern and two at the bow. *Erasmus* could take her, he told himself, without a doubt, providing the crew was right. I'd like to take her. Wake up, stop daydreaming, we're not aboard *Erasmus* but this sow-gutted galley and that Portuguese ship's the only hope we have. Under her guns we're safe. Bless your luck for Toranaga.

"Tell the captain to break out Toranaga's flag at the masthead. That'll be enough, senhora. That'll make it formal and tell them who's aboard, but I'd bet they know already."

This was done quickly. Everyone in the galley seemed to be more confident now. Blackthorne marked the change. Even he felt better under the flag.

"My Master says, but how do we tell them we wish to go alongside?"

"Tell him without signal flags he has two choices: he waits outside cannon range and sends a deputation aboard her in a small boat, or we go directly within hailing distance."

"My Master says, which do you advise?"

"Go straight alongside. There's no reason for caution. Lord Toranaga's aboard. He's the most important *daimyo* in the Empire. Of course she'll help us and— Oh Jesu God!"

"Senhor?"

But he did not reply, so she quickly translated what had been said and listened to Toranaga's next question. "My Master asks, the frigate will what? Please explain your thought and the reason you stopped."

"I suddenly realized, he's at war with Ishido now. Isn't he? So the frigate may not be inclined to help him."

"Of course they'll help him."

"No. Which side benefits the Portuguese more, Lord Toranaga or Ishido? If they believe Ishido will, they'll blow us to hell out of the water."

"It's unthinkable that the Portuguese would fire on any Japanese ship," Mariko said at once.

"Believe me, they will, senhora. And I'll bet that frigate won't let us alongside. I wouldn't if I were her pilot. Christ Jesus!" Blackthorne stared ashore.

The taunting Grays had left the jetty now and were spreading out parallel to the shore. No chance there, he thought. The fishing boats still lay malevolently clogging the harbor's neck. No chance there either. "Tell Toranaga there's only one other way to get out of the harbor. That's to hope for a storm. Maybe we could ride it out, where the fishing boats can't. Then we could slip past the net."

Toranaga questioned the captain, who answered at length, then Mariko said to Blackthorne, "My Master asks, do you think there'll be a storm?"

"My nose says yes. But not for days. Two or three. Can we wait that long?"

"Your nose tells you? There is a smell to a storm?"

"No, senhora. It's just an expression."

Toranaga pondered. Then he gave an order.

"We are going to within hailing distance, Anjin-san."

"Then tell him to go directly astern of her. That way we're the smallest target. Tell him they're treacherous—I know how seriously treacherous they are when their interests are threatened. They're worse than the Dutch! If that ship helps Toranaga escape, Ishido will take it out on all Portuguese and they won't risk that."

"My Master says we'll soon have that answer."

"We're naked, senhora. We've no chance against those cannon. If the ship's hostile—even if it's simply neutral—we're sunk."

"My Master says, yes, but it will be your duty to persuade them to be benevolent."

"How can I do that? I'm their enemy."

"My Master says, in war and in peace, a good enemy can be more valuable than a good ally. He says you will know their minds—you will think of a way to persuade them."

"The only sure way's by force."

"Good. I agree, my Master says. Please tell me how you would pirate that ship."

"What?"

"He said, good, I agree. How would you pirate the ship, how would you conquer it? I require the use of their cannon. So sorry, isn't that clear, Anjin-san?"

"And again I say I'm going to blow her out of the water," Ferriera, the Captain-General, declared.

"No," dell'Aqua replied, watching the galley from the quarterdeck. "Gunner, is she in range yet?"

"No, Don Ferriera," the chief gunner replied. "Not yet."

"Why else is she coming at us if not for hostile reasons, Eminence? Why doesn't she just escape? The way's clear." The frigate was too far from the harbor mouth for anyone aboard to see the encroaching fishing boats crowding in ambush.

"We risk nothing, Eminence, and gain everything," Ferriera said. "We pretend we didn't know Toranaga was aboard. We thought the bandits —bandits led by the pirate heretic—were going to attack us. Don't worry, it will be easy to provoke them once they're in range."

"No," dell'Aqua ordered.

Father Alvito turned back from the gunwale. "The galley's flying Toranaga's flag, Captain-General."

"False colors!" Ferriera added sardonically, "That's the oldest sea trick in the world. We haven't seen Toranaga. Perhaps he isn't aboard."

"No."

"God's death, war would be a catastrophe! It'll hurt, if not ruin, the Black Ship's voyage this year. I can't afford that! I won't have anything interfere with that!"

"Our finances are in a worse position than yours, Captain-General," dell'Aqua rapped. "If we don't trade this year, the Church is bankrupt, is that clear? We've had no funds from Goa or Lisbon for three years and the loss of last year's profit. . . . God give me patience! I know better than you what's at stake. The answer is no!"

Rodrigues was sitting painfully in his seachair, his leg in a splint resting on a padded stool that was lashed safe near the binnacle. "The Captain-General's right, Eminence. Why should she come at us, if not to try something? Why not escape, eh? Eminence, we've a piss-cutting opportunity here."

"Yes, and it is a military decision," Ferriera said.

Alvito turned on him sharply. "No, his Eminence is arbiter in this, Captain-General. We must not hurt Toranaga. We must help him."

Rodrigues said, "You've told me a dozen times that once war starts it'll go on forever. War's started, hasn't it? We've seen it start. That's got to hurt trade. With Toranaga dead the war's over and all our interests are safe. I say blow the ship to hell."

"We even get rid of the heretic," Ferriera added, watching Rodrigues. "You prevent a war for the glory of God, and another heretic goes to torment."

"It would be unwarranted interference in their politics," dell'Aqua replied, avoiding the real reason.

"We interfere all the time. The Society of Jesus is famous for it. We're not simple, thick-headed peasants!"

"I'm not suggesting you are. But while I'm aboard you will not sink that ship."

"Then kindly go ashore."

"The sooner the archmurderer is dead, the better, Eminence," Rodrigues suggested. "Him or Ishido, what's the difference? They're both heathen, and you can't trust either of them. The Captain-General's right, we'll never get an opportunity like this again. And what about our Black Ship?" Rodrigues was pilot with a fifteenth part of all the profit. The real pilot of the Black Ship had died of the pox in Macao three months ago and Rodrigues had been taken off his own ship, the *Santa Theresa,* and given the new post, to his everlasting joy. Pox was the official reason, Rodrigues reminded himself grimly, though many said the other pilot was knifed in the back by a *ronin* in a whorehouse brawl. By God, this is my great chance. Nothing's going to interfere with that!

"I will accept full responsibility," Ferriera was saying. "It's a military decision. We're involved in a native war. My ship's in danger." He turned again to the chief gunner. "Are they in range yet?"

"Well, Don Ferriera, that depends what you wish." The chief gunner blew on the end of the taper which made it glow and spark. "I could take off her bow now, or her stern, or hit her amidships, whichever you prefer. But if you want a man dead, a particular man, then a moment or two would bring them into killing range."

"I want Toranaga dead. And the heretic."

"You mean the Ingeles, the pilot?"

"Yes."

"Someone will have to point the Jappo out. The pilot I'll recognize, doubtless."

Rodrigues said, "If the pilot's got to die to kill Toranaga and stop the war then I'm for it, Captain-General. Otherwise he should be spared."

"He's a heretic, an enemy of our country, an abomination, and he's already caused us more trouble than a nest of vipers."

"I've already pointed out that first the Ingeles is a pilot and last he's a pilot, one of the best in the world."

"Pilots should have special privileges? Even heretics?"

"Yes, by God. We should use him like they use us. It'd be a God-cursed waste to kill such experience. Without pilots there's no piss-cutting Empire and no trade and no nothing. Without me, by God, there's no Black Ship and no profit and no way home, so my opinion's God-cursed important."

There was a cry from the masthead, "Ho on the quarterdeck, the galley's changing her course!" The galley had been heading straight for them but now she had swung a few points to port, out into the harbor.

Immediately Rodrigues shouted, "Action stations! Starboard watch aloft—all sails ho! Up anchor!" At once men rushed to obey.

"What's amiss, Rodrigues?"

"I don't know, Captain-General, but we're getting out into open sea. That fat-gutted whore's going to windward."

"What does that matter? We can sink them at any time," Ferriera said. "We've stores still to bring aboard and the Fathers have to go back to Osaka."

"Aye. But no hostile's getting to windward of my ship. That whore doesn't depend on the wind, she can go against it. She might be coming round to hack at us from our bow where we've only one cannon and board us!"

Ferriera laughed contemptuously. "We've twenty cannon aboard! They've none! You think that filthy heathen pig boat would dare to try to attack us? You're simple in the head!"

"Yes, Captain-General, that's why I've still got one. The *Santa Theresa*'s ordered to sea!"

The sails were crackling out of their ropes and the wind took them, the spars grinding. Both watches were on deck at battle stations. The frigate began to make way but her going was slow. "Come on, you bitch," Rodrigues urged.

"We're ready, Don Ferriera," the chief gunner said. "I've got her in my sights. I can't hold her for long. Which is this Toranaga? Point him out!"

There were no flares aboard the galley; the only illumination came from the moonlight. The galley was still astern, a hundred yards off, but turned to port now and headed for the far shore, the oars dipping and falling in unbroken rhythm. "Is that the pilot? The tall man on the quarterdeck?"

"Yes," Rodrigues said.

"Manuel and Perdito! Take him and the quarterdeck!" The cannon nearest made slight adjustments. "Which is this Toranaga? Quickly! Helmsmen, two points to starboard!"

"Two points to starboard it is, Gunner!"

Conscious of the sanding bottom and the shoals nearby, Rodrigues was watching the shrouds, ready at any second to override the chief gunner, who by custom had the con on a stern cannonade. "Ho, port maindeck cannon!" the gunner shouted. "Once we've fired we'll let her fall off the wind. Drop all gun ports, prepare for a broadside!" The gun crews obeyed, their eyes going to the officers on the quarterdeck. And the priests. "For the love of God, Don Ferriera, which is this Toranaga?"

"Which is he, Father?" Ferriera had never seen him before.

Rodrigues had recognized Toranaga clearly on the foredeck in a ring of samurai, but he did not want to be the one to put the mark on him. Let the priests do that, he thought. Go on, Father, play the Judas. Why should we always do all the pox-foul work, not that I care a chipped doubloon for that heathen son of a whore.

Both priests were silent.

"Quick, which would Toranaga be?" the gunner asked again.

Impatiently Rodrigues pointed him out. "There, on the poop. The short, thickset bastard in the middle of those other heathen bastards."

"I see him, Senhor Pilot."

The gun crews made last slight adjustments.

Ferriera took the taper out of the gunner's mate's hand.

"Are you trained on the heretic?"

"Yes, Captain-General, are you ready? I'll drop my hand. That's the signal!"

"Good."

"Thou shalt not kill!" It was dell'Aqua.

Ferriera whirled on him. "They're heathens and heretics!"

"There are Christians among them and even if there weren't—"

"Pay no attention to him, Gunner!" the Captain-General snarled. "We fire when you're ready!"

Dell'Aqua went forward to the muzzle of the cannon and stood in the way. His bulk dominated the quarterdeck and the armed sailors that lay in ambush. His hand was on the crucifix. "I say, *Thou shalt not kill!*"

"We kill all the time, Father," Ferriera said.

"I know, and I'm ashamed of it and I beg God's forgiveness for it." Dell'Aqua had never before been on the quarterdeck of a fighting ship with primed guns, and muskets, and fingers on triggers, readying for death. "While I'm here there'll be no killing and I'll not condone killing from ambush!"

"And if they attack us? Try to take the ship?"

"I will beg God to assist us against them!"

"What's the difference, now or later?"

Dell'Aqua did not answer. Thou shalt not kill, he thought, and Toranaga has promised everything, Ishido nothing.

"What's it to be, Captain-General? Now's the time!" the master gunner cried. "Now!"

Ferriera bitterly turned his back on the priests, threw down the taper and went to the rail. "Get ready to repel an attack," he shouted. "If she comes within fifty yards uninvited, you're all ordered to blow her to hell whatever the priests say!"

Rodrigues was equally enraged but he knew that he was as helpless as the Captain-General against the priest. Thou shalt not kill? By the blessed Lord Jesus, what about you? he wanted to shout. What about the auto da fé? What about the Inquisition? What about you priests who pronounce the sentence "guilty" or "witch" or "satanist" or "heretic"? Remember the two thousand witches burned in Portugal alone, the year I sailed for Asia? What about almost every village and town in Portugal and Spain, and the dominions visited and investigated by the Scourges of God, as the cowled Inquisitors proudly called themselves, the smell of burning flesh in their wake? Oh, Lord Jesus Christ, protect us!

He pushed his fear and loathing away and concentrated on the galley. He could just see Blackthorne and he thought, ah Ingeles, it's good to see you, standing there holding the con, so tall and cocky. I was afraid you'd gone to the execution ground. I'm glad you escaped, but even so it's lucky you don't have a single little cannon aboard, for then I'd blow you out of the water, and to hell with what the priests would say.

Oh, Madonna, protect me from a bad priest.

"Ahoy, *Santa Theresa!*"

"Ahoy, Ingeles!"

"Is that you, Rodrigues?"

"Aye!"

"Thy leg?"

"Thy mother!"

Rodrigues was greatly pleased by the bantering laugh that came across the sea that separated them.

For half an hour the two ships had maneuvered for position, chasing, tacking, and falling away, the galley trying to get windward and bottle the frigate on a lee shore, the frigate to gain sea room to sail out of harbor if she desired. But neither had been able to gain an advantage, and it was during this chase that those aboard the frigate had seen the fishing boats crowding the mouth of the harbor for the first time and realized their significance.

"That's why he's coming at us! For protection!"

"Even more reason for us to sink him now he's trapped. Ishido will thank us forever," Ferriera had said.

Dell'Aqua had remained obdurate. "Toranaga's much too important. I insist first we must talk to Toranaga. You can always sink him. He doesn't have cannon. Even I know that only cannon can fight cannon."

So Rodrigues had allowed a stalemate to develop to give them breathing time. Both ships were in the center of the harbor, safe from fishing ships and safe from each other, the frigate trembling into the wind, ready to fall off instantly, and the galley, oars shipped, drifting broadside to just within calling distance. It was only when Rodrigues had seen the galley ship all oars and turn broadside to his guns that he had turned into the wind to allow her to approach within shouting range and had prepared for the next series of moves. Thank God, the blessed Jesus, Mary, and Joseph, we've cannon and that bastard has none, Rodrigues thought again. The Ingeles is too smart.

But it's good to be opposed by a professional, he told himself. Much safer. Then no one makes a foolhardy mistake and no one gets hurt unnecessarily.

"Permission to come aboard?"

"Who, Ingeles?"

"Lord Toranaga, his interpreter, and guards."

Ferriera said quietly, "No guards."

Alvito said, "He must bring some. It's a matter of face."

"The pox on face. No guards."

"I don't want samurai aboard," Rodrigues agreed.

"Would you agree to five?" Alvito asked. "Just his personal guards? You understand the problem, Rodrigues."

Rodrigues thought a moment, then nodded. "Five are all right, Captain-General. We'll detail five men as your 'personal bodyguards' with a brace of pistols apiece. Father, you fix the details now. Better the Father to arrange the details, Captain-General, he knows how. Go on, Father, but tell us what's being said."

Alvito went to the gunwale and shouted, "You gain nothing by your lies! Prepare your souls for hell—you and your bandits. You've ten minutes, then the Captain-General's going to blow you to eternal torment!"

"We're flying Lord Toranaga's flag, by God!"

"False colors, pirate!"

Ferriera took a step forward. "What are you playing at, Father?"

"Please be patient, Captain-General," Alvito said. "This is only a matter of form. Otherwise Toranaga has to be permanently offended that we've insulted his flag—which we have. That's Toranaga—that's no simple *daimyo!* Perhaps you'd better remember that he personally has more troops under arms than the King of Spain!"

The wind was sighing in the rigging, the spars clattering nervously. Then flares were lit on the quarterdeck and now they could see Toranaga clearly. His voice came across the waves.

"Tsukku-san! How dare you avoid my galley! There are no pirates here—only in those fishing ships at the harbor mouth. I wish to come alongside instantly!"

Alvito shouted back in Japanese, feigning astonishment, "But Lord Toranaga, so sorry, we had no idea! We thought it was just a trick. The Grays said bandit-*ronin* had taken the galley by force! We thought bandits, under the English pirate, were sailing under false colors. I will come immediately."

"No. I will come alongside at once."

"I beg you, Lord Toranaga, allow me to come to escort you. My Master, the Father-Visitor, is here and also the Captain-General. They insist we make amends. Please accept our apologies!" Alvito changed to Portuguese again and shouted loudly to the bosun, "Launch a longboat," and back again to Toranaga in Japanese, "The boat is being launched at once, my Lord."

Rodrigues listened to the cloying humility in Alvito's voice and he thought how much more difficult it was to deal with Japanese than with Chinese. The Chinese understood the art of negotiation, of compromise and concession and reward. But the Japanese were pride-filled and when a man's pride was injured—any Japanese, not necessarily just samurai—then death was a small price to repay the insult. Come on, get it over with, he wanted to shout.

"Captain-General, I'll go at once," Father Alvito was saying. "Eminence, if you come as well that compliment will do much to appease him."

"I agree."

"Isn't that dangerous?" Ferriera said. "You two could be used as hostages."

Dell'Aqua said, "The moment there's a sign of treachery, I order you, in God's name, to obliterate that ship and all who sail in her, whether we're aboard or not." He strode off the quarterdeck, down onto the main deck, past the guns, the skirts of his robe swinging majestically. At the head of the gangway he turned and made the sign of the cross. Then he clattered down the gangway into the boat.

The bosun cast off. All the sailors were armed with pistols, and a fused keg of powder was under the bosun's seat.

Ferriera leaned over the gunwale and called down quietly, "Eminence, bring the heretic back with you."

"What? What did you say?" It amused dell'Aqua to toy with the Captain-General, whose continual insolence had mortally offended him, for of course he had decided long since to acquire Blackthorne, and he could hear perfectly well. *Che stupido,* he was thinking.

"Bring the heretic back with you, eh?" Ferriera called again.

On the quarterdeck Rodrigues heard the muffled, "Yes, Captain-General," and he thought, what treachery are you about, Ferriera?

He shifted in the chair with difficulty, his face bloodless. The pain in his leg was grinding and it took much of his strength to contain it. The bones were knitting well and, Madonna be praised, the wound was clean. But the fracture was still a fracture and even the slight dip of the ship at rest was troublesome. He took a swallow of grog from the well-used seabag that hung from a peg on the binnacle.

Ferriera was watching him. "Your leg's bad?"

"It's all right." The grog deadened the hurt.

"Will it be all right enough to voyage from here to Macao?"

"Yes. And to fight a sea battle all the way. And to come back in the summer, if that's what you mean."

"Yes, that's what I mean, Pilot." The lips were thin again, drawn into that tight mocking smile. "I need a fit pilot."

"I'm fit. My leg's mending well." Rodrigues shook off the pain. "The Ingeles won't come aboard us willingly. I wouldn't't."

"A hundred guineas says you're wrong."

"That's more than I make in a year."

"Payable after we reach Lisbon, from the profits from the Black Ship."

"Done. Nothing'll make him come aboard, not willingly. I'm a hundred guineas richer, by God!"

"Poorer! You forget the Jesuits want him here more than I do."

"Why should they want that?"

Ferriera looked at him levelly and did not answer, wearing the same twisted smile. Then, baiting him, he said, "I'd escort Toranaga out, for possession of the heretic."

"I'm glad I'm your comrade and necessary to you and the Black Ship," Rodrigues said. "I wouldn't want to be your enemy."

"I'm glad we understand one another, Pilot. At long last."

"I require escort out of the harbor. I need it quickly," Toranaga told dell'Aqua through the interpreter Alvito, Mariko nearby, also listening, with Yabu. He stood on the galley's poopdeck, dell'Aqua below on the main deck, Alvito beside him, but even so their eyes were almost level. "Or, if you wish, your warship can remove the fishing boats from out of my way."

"Forgive me, but that would be an unwarranted hostile act that you would not—could not recommend to the frigate, Lord Toranaga," dell'Aqua said, talking directly to him, finding Alvito's simultaneous translation eerie, as always. "That would be impossible—an open act of war."

"Then what do you suggest?"

"Please come back to the frigate. Let us ask the Captain-General. He will have a solution, now that we know what your problem is. He's the military man, we are not."

"Bring him here."

"It would be quicker for you to go there, Sire. Apart, of course, from the honor you would do us."

Toranaga knew the truth of this. Only moments before they had seen more fishing boats loaded with archers launched from the southern shore and, though they were safe at the moment, it was clear that within the hour the neck of the harbor would be choked with hostiles.

And he knew he had no choice.

"Sorry, Sire," the Anjin-san had explained earlier, during the abortive chase, "I can't get near the frigate. Rodrigues is too clever. I can stop him escaping if the wind holds but I can't trap him, unless he makes a mistake. We'll have to parley."

"Will he make a mistake and will the wind hold?" he had asked through Mariko.

She had replied, "The Anjin-san says, a wise man never bets on the wind, unless it's a trade wind and you're out to sea. Here we're in a harbor where the mountains cause the wind to eddy and flow. The pilot, Rodrigues, won't make a mistake."

Toranaga had watched the two pilots pit their wits against each other and he knew, beyond doubt, that both were masters. And he had come to realize also that neither he nor his lands nor the Empire would ever be safe without possessing modern barbarian ships, and through these ships, control of their own seas. The thought had shattered him.

"But how can I negotiate with them? What possible excuse could they use for such open hostility against me? Now it's my duty to bury them for their insults to my honor."

Then the Anjin-san had explained the ploy of false colors: how all ships used the device to get close to the enemy, or to attempt to avoid an enemy, and Toranaga had been greatly relieved that there might be an acceptable face-saving solution to that problem.

Now Alvito was saying, "I think we should go at once, Sire."

"Very well," Toranaga agreed. "Yabu-san, take command of the ship. Mariko-san, tell the Anjin-san he is to stay on the quarterdeck and to keep the helm, then you come with me."

"Yes, Lord."

It had been clear to Toranaga from the size of the longboat that he could take only five guards with him. But this, too, had been anticipated and the final plan was simple: if he could not persuade the frigate to help, then he and his guards would kill the Captain-General, their pilot, and the priests and barricade themselves in one of the cabins. Simultaneously the galley would be flung at the frigate from her bow as the Anjin-san had suggested and, together, they would try to take the frigate by storm. They would take her or they would not take her, but either way there would be a quick solution.

"It is a good plan, Yabu-san," he had said.

"Please allow me to go in your place to negotiate."

"They would not agree."

"Very well, but once we're out of the trap expel all barbarians from our realm. If you do, you'll gain more *daimyos* than you lose."

"I'll consider it," Toranaga had said, knowing it was nonsense, that he must have the Christian *daimyos* Onoshi and Kiyama on his side, and therefore the other Christian *daimyos,* or by default he would be eaten up. Why would Yabu wish to go to the frigate? What treachery did he plan if there was no help?

"Sire," Alvito was saying for dell'Aqua, "may I invite the Anjin-san to accompany us?"

"Why?"

"It occurred to me that he might like to greet his colleague the anjin Rodrigues. The man has a broken leg and cannot come here. Rodrigues would like to see him again, thank him for saving his life, if you don't mind."

Toranaga could not think of any reason why the Anjin-san should not go. The man was under his protection, therefore inviolate. "If he wishes to do so, very well. Mariko-san, accompany Tsukku-san."

Mariko bowed. She knew her job was to listen and to report and to ensure that everything that was said was reported correctly, without omission. She felt better now, her coiffure and face once more perfect, a fresh kimono borrowed from Lady Fujiko, her left arm in a neat sling. One of the mates, an apprentice doctor, had dressed her wound. The slice into her upper arm had not cut a tendon and the wound itself was clean. A bath would have made her whole, but there were no facilities on the galley.

Together she and Alvito walked back to the quarterdeck. He saw the knife in Blackthorne's sash and the way the soiled kimono seemed to fit. How far has he leeched his way into Toranaga's confidence, he asked himself. "Well met, Captain-Pilot Blackthorne."

"Rot in hell, Father!" Blackthorne replied affably.

"Perhaps we'll meet there, Anjin-san. Perhaps we will. Toranaga said you can come aboard the frigate."

"His orders?"

"'If you wish,' he said."

"I don't wish."

"Rodrigues would like to thank you again and to see you."

"Give him my respects and say I'll see him in hell. Or here."

"His leg prevents that."

"How is his leg?"

"Healing. Through your help and the grace of God, in a few weeks, God willing, he will walk, though he will limp forever."

"Tell him I wish him well. You'd better be going, Father, time's a-wasting."

"Rodrigues would like to see you. There's grog on the table and a fine roast capon with fresh greens and gravy and new fresh bread, butter hot. It'd be sad, Pilot, to waste such food."

"What?"

"There's new golden bread, Captain-Pilot, fresh hardtack, butter, and a side of beef. Fresh oranges from Goa and even a gallon of Madeira wine to wash it down with, or brandy if you'd prefer. There's beer, too. Then there's Macao capon, hot and juicy. The Captain-General's an epicure."

"God damn you to hell!"

"He will, when it pleases Him. I only tell you what exists."

"What does 'epicure' mean?" Mariko asked.

"It's one who enjoys food and sets a fine table, Senhora Maria," Alvito said, using her baptismal name. He had marked the sudden change on Blackthorne's face. He could almost see the saliva glands working and feel the stomach-churning agony. Tonight when he had seen the repast set out in the great cabin, the gleaming silver and white tablecloth and chairs, real leather-cushioned chairs, and smelt the new breads and butter and rich meats, he himself had been weak with hunger, and he wasn't starved for food or unaccustomed to Japanese cuisine.

It is so simple to catch a man, he told himself. All you need to know is the right bait. "Good-by, Captain-Pilot!" Alvito turned and walked for the gangway. Blackthorne followed.

"What's amiss, Ingeles?" Rodrigues asked.

"Where's the food? Then we can talk. First the food you promised." Blackthorne stood shakily on the main deck.

"Please follow me," Alvito said.

"Where are you taking him, Father?"

"Of course to the great cabin. Blackthorne can eat while Lord Toranaga and the Captain-General talk."

"No. He can eat in my cabin."

"It's easier, surely, to go where the food is."

"Bosun! See that the pilot's fed at once—all that he needs, in my cabin, anything from the table. Ingeles, do you want grog, or wine or beer?"

"Beer first, then grog."

"Bosun, see to it, take him below. And listen, Pesaro, give him some clothes out of my locker, and boots, everything. And stay with him till I call you."

Wordlessly Blackthorne followed Pesaro the bosun, a large burly man, down the companionway. Alvito began to go back to dell'Aqua and Toranaga, who were talking through Mariko near the companionway, but Rodrigues stopped him.

"Father! Just a moment. What did you say to him?"

"Only that you would like to see him and that we had food aboard."

"But I was offering him the food?"

"No, Rodrigues, I didn't say that. But wouldn't you want to offer food to a fellow pilot who was hungry?"

"That poor bastard's not hungry, he's starving. If he eats in that state he'll gorge like a ravenous wolf, then he'll vomit it up as fast as a drunkgluttoned whore. Now, we wouldn't want one of us, even a heretic, to eat like an animal and vomit like an animal in front of Toranaga, would we, Father? Not in front of a piss-cutting sonofabitch—particularly one as clean-minded as a pox-mucked whore's cleft!"

"You must learn to control the filth of your tongue, my son," Alvito said. "It will send you to hell. You'd better say a thousand Ave Marias and go without food for two days. Bread and water only. A penance to God's Grace to remind you of His Mercy."

"Thank you, Father, I will. Gladly. And if I could kneel I would, and I'd kiss your cross. Yes, Father, this poor sinner thanks you for your God-given patience. I must guard my tongue."

Ferriera called out from the companionway, "Rodrigues, are you coming below?"

"I'll stay on deck while that bitch galley's there, Captain-General. If you need me I'm here." Alvito began to leave. Rodrigues noticed Mariko. "Just a minute, Father. Who's the woman?"

"Donna Maria Toda. One of Toranaga's interpreters."

Rodrigues whistled tonelessly. "Is she good?"

"Very good."

"Stupid to allow her aboard. Why did you say 'Toda'? She's one of old Toda Hiro-matsu's consorts?"

"No. She's the wife of his son."

"Stupid to bring her aboard." Rodrigues beckoned one of the seamen. "Spread the word the woman speaks Portuguese."

"Yes, senhor." The man hurried away and Rodrigues turned back to Father Alvito.

The priest was not in the least intimidated by the obvious anger. "The Lady Maria speaks Latin too—and just as perfectly. Was there anything else, Pilot?"

"No, thank you. Perhaps I'd better get on with my Hail Marys."

"Yes, you should." The priest made the sign of the cross and left. Rodrigues spat into the scuppers and one of the helmsmen winced and crossed himself.

"Go nail yourself to the mast by your green-addled foreskin!" Rodrigues hissed.

"Yes, Captain-Pilot, sorry, senhor. But I get nervous near the good Father. I meant no harm." The youth saw the last grains of sand fall through the neck of the hourglass and he turned it.

"At the half, go below, and take a God-cursed pail and water and a scrubbing brush with you, and clean up the mess in my cabin. Tell the bosun to bring the Ingeles aloft and you make my cabin clean. And it'd better be very clean, or I'll have your guts for garters. And while you're doing it, say Ave Marias for your God-cursed soul."

"Yes, Senhor Pilot," the youth said weakly. Rodrigues was a fanatic, a madman, about cleanliness, and his own cabin was like the ship's Holy Grail. Everything had to be spotless, no matter what the weather.

CHAPTER 27

"THERE must be a solution, Captain-General," dell'Aqua said patiently.

"Do you want an overt act of war against a friendly nation?"

"Of course not."

Everyone in the great cabin knew that they were all in the same trap. Any overt act put them squarely with Toranaga against Ishido, which they should absolutely avoid in case Ishido was the eventual victor. Presently Ishido controlled Osaka, and the capital Kyoto, and the majority of the Regents. And now, through the *daimyos* Onoshi and Kiyama, Ishido controlled most of the southern island of Kyushu, and with Kyushu, the port of Nagasaki, the main center of all trading, and thus all trade and the Black Ship this year.

Toranaga said through Father Alvito, "What's so difficult? I just want you to blow the pirates out of the harbor mouth. *Neh.*"

Toranaga sat uncomfortably in the place of honor, in the high-backed chair at the great table. Alvito sat next to him, the Captain-General opposite, dell'Aqua beside the Captain-General. Mariko stood behind Toranaga and the samurai guards waited near the door, facing the armed seamen. And all the Europeans were conscious that though Alvito translated for Toranaga everything that was said in the room, Mariko was there to ensure that nothing was said openly between them against her Master's interests and that the translation was complete and accurate.

Dell'Aqua leaned forward. "Perhaps, Sire, you could send messengers ashore to Lord Ishido. Perhaps the solution lies in negotiation. We could offer this ship as a neutral place for the negotiations. Perhaps in this way you could settle the war."

Toranaga laughed scornfully. "What war? We're not at war, Ishido and I."

"But, Sire, we saw the battle on the shore."

"Don't be naïve! Who were killed? A few worthless *ronin*. Who attacked whom? Only *ronin*, bandits or mistaken zealots."

"And at the ambush? We understand that Browns fought Grays."

"Bandits were attacking all of us, Browns and Grays. My men merely fought to protect me. In night skirmishes mistakes often happen. If Browns killed Grays or Grays Browns that's a regrettable error. What are a few men to either of us? Nothing. We're not at war."

Toranaga read their disbelief so he added, "Tell them, Tsukku-san, that armies fight wars in Japan. These ridiculous skirmishes and assassination attempts are mere probes, to be dismissed when they fail. War didn't begin tonight. It began when the Taikō died. Even before that, when he died without leaving a grown son to follow him. Perhaps even before that, when Goroda, the Lord Protector, was murdered. Tonight has no lasting significance. None of you understands our realm, or our politics. How could you? Of course Ishido's trying to kill me. So are many other *daimyos*. They've done so in the past and they'll do so in the future. Kiyama and Onoshi have been both friend and enemy. Listen, if I'm killed that would simplify things for Ishido, the real enemy, but only for a moment. I'm in his trap now and if his trap's successful he merely has a momentary advantage. If I escape, there never was a trap. But understand clearly, all of you, that my death will not remove the cause of war nor will it prevent further conflict. Only if Ishido dies will there be no conflict. So there's no open war now. None." He shifted in the chair, detesting the odor in the cabin from the oily foods and unwashed bodies. "But we do have an immediate problem. I want your cannon. I want them now. Pirates beset me at the harbor mouth. I said earlier, Tsukku-san, that soon everyone must choose sides. Now, where do you and your leader and the whole Christian Church stand? And are my Portuguese friends with me or against me?"

Dell'Aqua said, "You may be assured, Lord Toranaga, we all support your interests."

"Good. Then remove the pirates at once."

"That'd be an act of war and there's no profit in it. Perhaps we can make a trade, eh?" Ferriera said.

Alvito did not translate this but said instead, "The Captain-General says, we're only trying to avoid meddling in your politics, Lord Toranaga. We're traders."

Mariko said in Japanese to Toranaga, "So sorry, Sire, that's not correct. That's not what was said."

Alvito sighed. "I merely transposed some of his words, Sire. The Captain-General is not aware of certain politenesses as he is a stranger. He has no understanding of Japan."

"But you do have, Tsukku-san?" Toranaga asked.

"I try, Sire."

"What did he actually say?"

Alvito told him.

After a pause Toranaga said, "The Anjin-san told me the Portuguese were very interested in trade, and in trade they have no manners, or humor. I understand and will accept your explanation, Tsukku-san. But from now on please translate everything exactly as it is said."

"Yes, Lord."

"Tell the Captain-General this: When the conflict is resolved I will expand trade. I am in favor of trade. Ishido is not."

Dell'Aqua had marked the exchange and hoped that Alvito had covered Ferriera's stupidity. "We're not politicians, Sire, we're religious and we represent the Faith and the Faithful. We do support your interests. Yes."

"I agree. I was considering—" Alvito stopped interpreting and his face lit up and he let Toranaga's Japanese get away from him for a moment. "I'm sorry, Eminence, but Lord Toranaga said, 'I was considering asking you to build a temple, a large temple in Yedo, as a measure of my confidence in your interests.'"

For years, ever since Toranaga had become Lord of the Eight Provinces, dell'Aqua had been maneuvering for that concession. And to get it from him now, in the third greatest city in the Empire, was a priceless concession. The Visitor knew the time had come to resolve the problem of the cannon. "Thank him, Martin Tsukku-san," he said, using the code phrase that he had previously agreed upon with Alvito, committing their course of action, with Alvito the standard-bearer, "and say we will try always to be at his service. Oh yes, and ask him what he had in mind about the cathedral," he added for the Captain-General's benefit.

"Perhaps I may speak directly, Sire, for a moment," Alvito began to Toranaga. "My Master thanks you and says what you previously asked is perhaps possible. He will endeavor always to assist you."

"Endeavor is an abstract word, and unsatisfactory."

"Yes, Sire." Alvito glanced at the guards who, of course, listened without appearing to. "But I remember you saying earlier that it is sometimes wise to be abstract."

Toranaga understood at once. He waved his hand in dismissal to his men. "Wait outside, all of you."

Uneasily they obeyed. Alvito turned to Ferriera. "We don't need your guards now, Captain-General."

When the samurai had gone Ferriera dismissed his men and glanced at Mariko. He wore pistols in his belt and had another in his boot.

Alvito said to Toranaga, "Perhaps, Sire, you would like the Lady Mariko to sit?"

Again Toranaga understood. He thought for a moment, then half nodded and said, without turning around, "Mariko-san, take one of my guards and find the Anjin-san. Stay with him until I send for you."

"Yes, Lord."

The door closed behind her.

Now they were alone. The four of them.

Ferriera said, "What's the offer? What's he offering?"

"Be patient, Captain-General," dell'Aqua replied, his fingers drumming on his cross, praying for success.

"Sire," Alvito began to Toranaga, "the Lord my Master says that everything you asked he will try to do. Within the forty days. He will send you word privately about progress. I will be the courier, with your permission."

"And if he's not successful?"

"It will not be through want of trying, or persuasion, or through want of thought. He gives you his word."

"Before the Christian God?"

"Yes. Before God."

"Good. I will have it in writing. Under his seal."

"Sometimes full agreements, delicate agreements, should not be reduced to writing, Sire."

"You're saying unless I put my agreement in writing, you won't?"

"I merely remembered one of your own sayings that a samurai's honor is certainly more important than a piece of paper. The Visitor gives you his word before God, his word of honor, as a samurai would. Your honor is totally sufficient for the Visitor. I just thought he would be saddened to be so untrusted. Do you wish me to ask for a signature?"

At length Toranaga said, "Very well. His word before the God Jesus, *neh*? His word before his God?"

"I give it on his behalf. He has sworn by the Blessed Cross to try."

"You as well, Tsukku-san?"

"You have equally my word, before my God, by the Blessed Cross, that I will do everything I can to help him persuade the Lords Onoshi and Kiyama to be your allies."

"In return I will do what I previously promised. On the forty-first day you may lay the foundation stone for the biggest Christian temple in the Empire."

"Could that land, Sire, be put aside at once?"

"As soon as I arrive at Yedo. Now. What about the pirates? The pirates in the fishing boats? You will remove them at once?"

"If you had cannon, would you have done that yourself, Sire?"

"Of course, Tsukku-san."

"I apologize for being so devious, Sire, but we have had to formulate a plan. The cannon do not belong to us. Please give me one moment." Alvito turned to dell'Aqua. "Everything is arranged about the cathedral, Eminence." Then to Ferriera he added, beginning their agreed plan:

"You will be glad you did not sink him, Captain-General. Lord Tora-naga asks if you would carry ten thousand ducats of gold for him when you leave with the Black Ship for Goa, to invest in the gold market in India. We would be delighted to help in the transaction through our usual sources there, placing the gold for you. Lord Toranaga says half the profit is yours." Both Alvito and dell'Aqua had decided that by the time the Black Ship had turned about, in six months, Toranaga either would be reinstated as President of the Regents and therefore more than pleased to permit this most profitable transaction, or he would be dead. "You should easily clear four thousand ducats profit. At no risk."

"In return for what concession? That's more than your annual sub-sidy from the King of Spain for your whole Society of Jesus in Asia. In return for what?"

"Lord Toranaga says pirates prevent him leaving the harbor. He would know better than you if they're pirates."

Ferriera replied in the same matter-of-fact voice that both knew was only for Toranaga's benefit, "It's ill-advised to put your faith in this man. His enemy holds all the royal cards. All the Christian kings are against him. Certainly the main two, I heard them with my own ears. They said this Jappo's the real enemy. I believe them and not this motherless cretin."

"I'm sure Lord Toranaga knows better than us who are pirates and who are not," dell'Aqua told him unperturbed, knowing the solution as Alvito knew the solution. "I suppose you've no objection to Lord Tora-naga's dealing with the pirates himself?"

"Of course not."

"You have plenty of spare cannon aboard," the Visitor said. "Why not give him some privately. Sell him some, in effect. You sell arms all the time. He's buying arms. Four cannon should be more than enough. It would be easy to transship them in the longboat, with enough powder and shot, again privately. Then the matter is solved."

Ferriera sighed. "Cannon, my dear Eminence, are useless aboard the galley. There are no gun ports, no gun ropes, no gun stanchions. They can't use cannon, even if they had the gunners, which they don't."

Both priests were flabbergasted. "Useless?"

"Totally."

"But surely, Don Ferriera, they can adapt . . ."

"That galley's incapable of using cannon without a refit. It would take at least a week."

"Nan ja?" Toranaga said suspiciously, aware that something was amiss however much they had tried to hide it.

"What is it, Toranaga asks," Alvito said.

Dell'Aqua knew the sand had run out on them. "Captain-General, please help us. Please. I ask you openly. We've gained enormous concessions for the Faith. You must believe me and yes, you must trust us. You must help Lord Toranaga out of the harbor somehow. I beg you on behalf of the Church. The cathedral alone is an enormous concession. Please."

Ferriera allowed none of the ecstasy of victory to show. He even added a token gravity to his voice. "Since you ask help in the Church's name, Eminence, of course I'll do what you ask. I'll get him out of this trap. But in return I want the Captain-Generalship of next year's Black Ship whether this year's is successful or not."

"That's the personal gift of the King of Spain, his alone. That's not mine to bestow."

"Next: I accept the offer of his gold, but I want your guarantee that I'll have no trouble from the Viceroy at Goa, or here, about the gold or about either of the Black Ships."

"You dare to hold me and the Church to ransom?"

"This is merely a business arrangement between you, me, and this monkey."

"He's no monkey, Captain-General. You'd better remember it."

"Next: Fifteen percent of this year's cargo instead of ten."

"Impossible."

"Next: To keep everything tidy, Eminence, your word before God —now—that neither you nor any of the priests under your jurisdiction will ever threaten me with excommunication unless I commit a future act of sacrilege, which none of this is. And further, your word that you and the Holy Fathers will actively support me and help these two Black Ships—also before God."

"And next, Captain-General? Surely that's not all? Surely there's something else?"

"Last: I want the heretic."

Mariko stared down at Blackthorne from the cabin doorway. He lay in a semicoma on the floor, retching his innards out. The bosun was leaning against the bunk leering at her, the stumps of his yellow teeth showing.

"Is he poisoned, or is he drunk?" she asked Totomi Kana, the samurai beside her, trying without success to close her nostrils to the stench of the food and the vomit, to the stench of the ugly seaman in front of her, and to the ever present stench from the bilges that pervaded the whole ship. "It almost looks as though he's been poisoned, *neh?*"

"Perhaps he has, Mariko-san. Look at that filth!" The samurai waved distastefully at the table. It was strewn with wooden platters containing the remains of a mutilated haunch of roast beef, blood rare, half the carcass of a spitted chicken, torn bread and cheese and spilled beer, butter and a dish of cold bacon-fat gravy, and a half emptied bottle of brandy.

Neither of them had ever seen meat on a table before.

"What d'you want?" the bosun asked. "No monkeys in here, *waka-rimasu*? No monkey-sans this-u room-u!" He looked at the samurai and waved him away. "Out! Piss off!" His eyes flowed back over Mariko. "What's your name? *Namu,* eh?"

"What's he saying, Mariko-san?" the samurai asked.

The bosun glanced at the samurai for a moment then back to Mariko again.

"What's the barbarian saying, Mariko-san?"

Mariko took her mesmerized eyes off the table and concentrated on the bosun. "I'm sorry, senhor, I didn't understand you. What did you say?"

"Eh?" The bosun's mouth dropped further open. He was a big fat man with eyes too close together and large ears, his hair in a ratty tarred pigtail. A crucifix hung from the rolls of his neck and pistols were loose in his belt. "Eh? You can talk Portuguese? A Jappo who can talk good Portuguese? Where'd you learn to talk civilized?"

"The—the Christian Father taught me."

"I'll be a God-cursed son of a whore! Madonna, a flower-san who can talk civilized!"

Blackthorne retched again and tried feebly to get off the deck.

"Can you—please can you put the pilot there?" She pointed at the bunk.

"Aye. If this monkey'll help."

"Who? I'm sorry, what did you say? Who?"

"Him! The Jappo. Him."

The words rocked through her and it took all of her will to remain calm. She motioned to the samurai. "Kana-san, will you please help this barbarian. The Anjin-san should be put there."

"With pleasure, Lady."

Together the two men lifted Blackthorne and he flopped back in the bunk, his head too heavy, mouthing stupidly.

"He should be washed," Mariko said in Japanese, still half stunned by what the bosun had called Kana.

"Yes, Mariko-san. Order the barbarian to send for servants."

"Yes." Her disbelieving eyes went inexorably to the table again. "Do they really eat that?"

The bosun followed her glance. At once he leaned over and tore off a chicken leg and offered it to her. "You hungry? Here, little Flower-san, it's good. It's fresh today—real Macao capon."

She shook her head.

The bosun's grizzled face split into a grin and he helpfully dipped the chicken leg into the heavy gravy and held it under her nose. "Gravy makes it even better. Hey, it's good to be able to talk proper, eh? Never did that before. Go on, it'll give you strength—where it counts! It's Macao capon I tell you."

"No—no, thank you. To eat meat—to eat meat is forbidden. It's against the law, and against Buddhism and Shintoism."

"Not in Nagasaki it isn't!" The bosun laughed. "Lots of Jappos eat meat all the time. They all do when they can get it, and swill our grog as well. You're Christian, eh? Go on, try, little Donna. How d'you know till you try?"

"No, no, thank you."

"A man can't live without meat. That's real food. Makes you strong so you can jiggle like a stoat. Here—" He offered the chicken leg to Kana. "You want?"

Kana shook his head, equally nauseated. "*Iyé!*"

The bosun shrugged and threw it carelessly back onto the table. "*Iyé* it is. What've you done to your arm? You hurt in the fight?"

"Yes. But not badly." Mariko moved it a little to show him and swallowed the pain.

"Poor little thing! What d'you want here, Donna Senhorita, eh?"

"To see the An— to see the pilot. Lord Toranaga sent me. The pilot's drunk?"

"Yes, that and the food. Poor bastard ate too fast 'n drank too fast. Took half the bottle in a gulp. Ingeles're all the same. Can't hold their grog and they've no *cojones*." His eyes went all over her. "I've never seen a flower as small as you before. And never talked to a Jappo who could talk civilized before."

"Do you call all Japanese ladies and samurai Jappos and monkeys?"

The seaman laughed shortly. "Hey, senhorita, that was a slip of the tongue. That's for usuals, you know, the pimps and whores in Nagasaki. No offense meant. I never did talk to a civilized senhorita before, never knowed there was any, by God."

"Neither have I, senhor. I've never talked to a civilized Portuguese before, other than a Holy Father. We're Japanese, not Jappos, *neh*? And monkeys are animals, aren't they?"

"Sure." The bosun showed the broken teeth. "You speak like a Donna. Yes. No offense, Donna Senhorita."

Blackthorne began mumbling. She went to the bunk and shook him gently. "Anjin-san! Anjin-san!"

"Yes—yes?" Blackthorne opened his eyes. "Oh—hello—I'm sor—I . . ." But the weight of his pain and the spinning of the room forced him to lie back.

"Please send for a servant, senhor. He should be washed."

"There's slaves—but not for that, Donna Senhorita. Leave the Ingeles —what's a little vomit to a heretic?"

"No servants?" she asked, flabbergasted.

"We have slaves—black bastards, but they're lazy—wouldn't trust one to wash him myself," he added with a twisted grin.

Mariko knew she had no alternative. Lord Toranaga might have need of the Anjin-san at once and it was her duty. "Then I need some water," she said. "To wash him with."

"There's a barrel in the stairwell. In the deck below."

"Please fetch some for me, senhor."

"Send him." The bosun jerked a finger at Kana.

"No. You will please fetch it. Now."

The bosun looked back at Blackthorne. "You his doxie?"

"What?"

"The Ingeles's doxie?"

"What's a doxie, senhor?"

"His woman. His mate, you know, senhorita, this pilot's sweetheart, his jigajig. Doxie."

"No. No, senhor, I'm not his doxie."

"His, then? This mon— this samurai's? Or the king's maybe, him that's just come aboard? Tora-something? You one of his?"

"No."

"Nor any aboard's?"

She shook her head. "Please, would you get some water?"

The bosun nodded and went out.

"That's the ugliest, foulest-smelling man I've ever been near," the samurai said. "What was he saying?"

"He—the man asked if—if I was one of the pilot's consorts."

The samurai went for the door.

"Kana-san!"

"I demand the right on your husband's behalf to avenge that insult. At once! As though you'd cohabit with any barbarian!"

"Kana-san! Please close the door."

"You're Toda Mariko-san! How dare he insult you? The insult must be avenged!"

"It will be, Kana-san, and I thank you. Yes. I give you the right. But we are here at Lord Toranaga's order. Until he gives his approval it would not be correct for you to do this."

Kana closed the door reluctantly. "I agree. But I formally ask that you petition Lord Toranaga before we leave."

"Yes. Thank you for your concern over my honor." What would Kana do if he knew all that had been said, she asked herself appalled. What would Lord Toranaga do? Or Hiro-matsu? Or my husband? Monkeys? Oh, Madonna, give me thy help to hold myself still and keep my mind working. To ease Kana's wrath, she quickly changed the subject. "The Anjin-san looks so helpless. Just like a baby. It seems barbarians can't stomach wine. Just like some of our men."

"Yes. But it's not the wine. Can't be. It's what he's eaten."

Blackthorne moved uneasily, groping for consciousness.

"They've no servants on the ship, Kana-san, so I'll have to substitute for one of the Anjin-san's ladies." She began to undress Blackthorne, awkwardly because of her arm.

"Here, let me help you." Kana was very deft. "I used to do this for my father when the saké took him."

"It's good for a man to get drunk once in a while. It releases all the evil spirits."

"Yes. But my father used to suffer badly the next day."

"My husband suffers very badly. For days."

After a moment, Kana said, "May Buddha grant that Lord Buntaro escapes."

"Yes." Mariko looked around the cabin. "I don't understand how they can live in such squalor. It's worse than the poorest of our people. I was almost fainting in the other cabin from the stench."

"It's revolting. I've never been aboard a barbarian ship before."

"I've never been on the sea before."

The door opened and the bosun set down the pail. He was shocked at Blackthorne's nudity and jerked out a blanket from under the bunk and covered him. "He'll catch his death. Apart from that—shameful to do that to a man, even him."

"What?"

"Nothing. What's your name, Donna Senhorita?" His eyes glittered.

She did not answer. She pushed the blanket aside and washed Blackthorne clean, glad for something to do, hating the cabin and the foul presence of the bosun, wondering what they were talking about in the other cabin. Is our Master safe?

When she had finished she bundled the kimono and soiled loincloth. "Can this be laundered, senhor?"

"Eh?"

"These should be cleaned at once. Could you send for a slave, please?"

"They're a lazy bunch of black bastards, I told you. That'd take a week or more. Throw 'em away, Donna Senhorita, they're not worth breath. Our Pilot-Captain Rodrigues said to give him proper clothes. Here." He opened a sea locker. "He said to give him any from here."

"I don't know how to dress a man in those."

"He needs a shirt 'n trousers 'n codpiece 'n socks and boots 'n sea jacket." The bosun took them out and showed her. Then, together, she and the samurai began to dress Blackthorne, still in his half-conscious stupor.

"How does he wear this?" She held up the triangular, baglike codpiece with its attached strings.

"Madonna, he wears it in front, like this," the bosun said embarrassed, fingering his own. "You tie it in place over his trousers, like I told. Over his cod."

She looked at the bosun's, studying it. He felt her look and stirred.

She put the codpiece on Blackthorne and settled him carefully in place, and together she and the samurai put the back strings between his legs and tied the strings around his waist. To the samurai she said quietly, "This is the most ridiculous way of dressing I've ever seen."

"It must be very uncomfortable," Kana replied. "Do priests wear them, Mariko-san? Under their robes?"

"I don't know."

She brushed a strand of hair out of her eyes. "Senhor. Is the Anjin-san dressed correctly now?"

"Aye. Except for his boots. They're there. They can wait." The bosun came over to her and her nostrils clogged. He dropped his voice, keeping his back to the samurai. "You want a quickie?"

"What?"

"I fancy you, senhorita, eh? What'd you say? There's a bunk in the next cabin. Send your friend aloft. The Ingeles's out for an hour yet. I'll pay the usual."

"What?"

"You'll earn a piece of copper—even three if you're like a stoat, and you'll straddle the best cock between here and Lisbon, eh? What d'you say?"

The samurai saw her horror. "What is it, Mariko-san?"

Mariko pushed past the bosun, away from the bunk. Her words stumbled. "He . . . he said . . ."

Kana drew out his sword instantly but found himself staring into the barrels of two cocked pistols. Nevertheless he began to lunge.

"Stop, Kana-san!" Mariko gasped. "Lord Toranaga forbade any attack until he ordered it!"

"Go on, monkey, come at me, you stink-pissed shithead! You! Tell this monkey to put up his sword or he'll be a headless sonofabitch before he can fart!"

Mariko was standing within a foot of the bosun. Her right hand was still in her obi, the haft of the stiletto knife still in her palm. But she remembered her duty and took her hand away. "Kana-san, replace your sword. Please. We must obey Lord Toranaga. We must obey him."

With a supreme effort, Kana did as he was told.

"I've a mind to send you to hell, Jappo!"

"Please excuse him, senhor, and me," Mariko said, trying to sound polite. "There was a mistake, a mis—"

"That monkey-faced bastard pulled a sword. That wasn't a mistake, by Jesus!"

"Please excuse it, senhor, so sorry."

The bosun wet his lips. "I'll forget it if you're friendly, Little Flower. Into the next cabin with you, and tell this monk—tell him to stay here and I'll forget about it."

"What—what's your name, senhor?"

"Pesaro. Manuel Pesaro, why?"

"Nothing. Please excuse the misunderstanding, Senhor Pesaro."

"Get in the next cabin. Now."

"What's going on? What's . . ." Blackthorne did not know if he was awake or still in a nightmare, but he felt the danger. "What's going on, by God!"

"This stinking Jappo drew on me!"

"It was a—a mistake, Anjin-san," Mariko said. "I—I've apologized to the Senhor Pesaro."

"Mariko? Is that you—Mariko-san?"

"*Hai*, Anjin-san. *Honto. Honto.*"

She came nearer. The bosun's pistols never wavered off Kana. She had to brush past him and it took her an even greater effort not to take out her knife and gut him. At that moment the door opened. The youthful helmsman came into the cabin with a pail of water. He gawked at the pistols and fled.

"Where's Rodrigues?" Blackthorne said, attempting to get his mind working.

"Aloft, where a good pilot should be," the bosun said, his voice grating. "This Jappo drew on me, by God!"

"Help me up on deck." Blackthorne grasped the bunk sides. Mariko took his arm but she could not lift him.

The bosun waved a pistol at Kana. "Tell him to help. And tell him if there's a God in heaven he'll be swinging from the yardarm before the turn."

First Mate Santiago took his ear away from the secret knothole in the wall of the great cabin, the final "Well, that's all settled then" from dell'-Aqua ringing in his brain. Noiselessly he slipped across the darkened cabin, out into the corridor, and closed the door quietly. He was a tall, spare man with a lived-in face, and wore his hair in a tarred pigtail. His clothes were neat, and like most seamen, he was barefoot. In a hurry, he shinned up the companionway, ran across the main deck up on to the quarterdeck where Rodrigues was talking to Mariko. He excused himself and leaned down to put his mouth very close to Rodrigues' ear and began to pour out all that he had heard, and had been sent to hear, so that no one else on the quarterdeck could be party to it.

Blackthorne was sitting aft on the deck, leaning against the gunwale, his head resting on his bent knees. Mariko sat straight-backed facing Rodrigues, Japanese fashion, and Kana, the samurai, bleakly beside her. Armed seamen swarmed the decks and crow's nest aloft and two more were at the helm. The ship still pointed into the wind, the air and night clean, the nimbus stronger and rain not far off. A hundred yards away the galley lay broadside, at the mercy of their cannon, oars shipped, except for two each side which kept her in station, the slight tide taking her. The ambushing fishing ships with hostile samurai archers were closer but they were not encroaching as yet.

Mariko was watching Rodrigues and the mate. She could not hear what was being said, and even if she could, her training would have made her prefer to close her ears. Privacy in paper houses was impossible without politeness and consideration; without privacy civilized life could not exist, so all Japanese were trained to hear and not hear. For the good of all.

When she had come on deck with Blackthorne, Rodrigues had listened to the bosun's explanation and to her halting explanation that it was her fault, that she had mistaken what the bosun had said, and that this had caused Kana to pull out his sword to protect her honor. The bosun had listened, grinning, his pistols still leveled at the samurai's back.

"I only asked if she was the Ingeles's doxie, by God, she being so free with washing him and sticking his privates into the cod."

"Put up your pistols, bosun."

"He's dangerous, I tell you. String him up!"

"I'll watch him. Go for'ard!"

"This monkey'd've killed me if I wasn't faster. Put him on the yard-arm. That's what we'd do in Nagasaki!"

"We're not in Nagasaki—go for'ard! Now!"

And when the bosun had gone Rodrigues had asked, "What did he say to you, senhora? Actually say?"

"It—nothing, senhor. Please."

"I apologize for that man's insolence to you and to the samurai. Please apologize to the samurai for me, ask his pardon. And I ask you both formally to forget the bosun's insults. It will not help your liege lord or mine to have trouble aboard. I promise you I will deal with him in my own way in my own time."

She had spoken to Kana and, under her persuasion, at length he had agreed.

"Kana-san says, very well, but if he ever sees the bosun Pesaro on shore he will take his head."

"That's fair, by God. Yes. *Domo arigato,* Kana-san," Rodrigues said with a smile, "and *domo arigato goziemashita,* Mariko-san."

"You speak Japanese?"

"Oh no, just a word or two. I've a wife in Nagasaki."

"Oh! You have been long in Japan?"

"This is my second tour from Lisbon. I've spent seven years in these waters all told—here, and back and forth to Macao and to Goa." Rodrigues added, "Pay no attention to him—he's *eta.* But Buddha said even *eta* have a right to life. *Neh?*"

"Of course," Mariko said, the name and face branded forever into her mind.

"My wife speaks some Portuguese, nowhere near as perfectly as you. You're Christian, of course?"

"Yes."

"My wife's a convert. Her father's samurai, though a minor one. His liege lord is Lord Kiyama."

"She is lucky to have such a husband," Mariko said politely, but she asked herself, staggered, how could one marry and live with a barbarian? In spite of her inherent manners, she asked, "Does the lady, your wife, eat meat, like—like that in the cabin?"

"No," Rodrigues replied with a laugh, his teeth white and fine and strong. "And in my house at Nagasaki I don't eat meat either. At sea I do and in Europe. It's our custom. A thousand years ago before the Buddha came it was your custom too, *neh?* Before Buddha lived to point the *Tao,* the Way, all people ate meat. Even here, senhora. Even here. Now of course, we know better, some of us, *neh?*"

Mariko thought about that. Then she said, "Do all Portuguese call us monkeys? And Jappos? Behind our backs?"

Rodrigues pulled at the earring he wore. "Don't you call us barbarians? Even to our face? We're civilized, at least we think so, senhora. In India, the land of Buddha, they call Japanese 'Eastern Devils' and won't allow any to land if they're armed. You call Indians 'Blacks' and nonhuman. What do the Chinese call Japanese? What do you call the Chinese? What do you call the Koreans? Garlic Eaters, *neh?*"

"I don't think Lord Toranaga would be pleased. Or Lord Hiro-matsu, or even the father of your wife."

"The Blessed Jesus said, 'First cast the mote out of your own eye before you cast the beam out of mine.'"

She thought about that again now as she watched the first mate whispering urgently to the Portuguese pilot. It's true: we sneer at other people. But then, we're citizens of the Land of the Gods, and therefore especially chosen by the gods. We alone, of all peoples, are protected by a divine Emperor. Aren't we, therefore, completely unique and superior to all others? And if you are Japanese *and* Christian? I don't know. Oh, Madonna, give me thy understanding. This Rodrigues pilot is as strange as the English pilot. Why are they very special? Is it their training? It's unbelievable what they do, *neh?* How can they sail around the earth and walk the sea as easily as we do the land? Would Rodrigues' wife know the answer? I'd like to meet her, and talk to her.

The mate lowered his voice even more.

"He said what?" Rodrigues exclaimed with an involuntary curse and in spite of herself Mariko tried to listen. But she could not hear what the mate repeated. Then she saw them both look at Blackthorne and she followed their glance, perturbed by their concern.

"What else happened, Santiago?" Rodrigues asked guardedly, conscious of Mariko.

The mate told him in a whisper behind a cupped mouth. "How long'll they stay below?"

"They were toasting each other. And the bargain."

"Bastards!" Rodrigues caught the mate's shirt. "No word of this, by God. On your life!"

"No need to say that, Pilot."

"There's always a need to say it." Rodrigues glanced across at Blackthorne. "Wake him up!"

The mate went over and shook him roughly.

"Whatsamatter, eh?"

"Hit him!"

Santiago slapped him.

"Jesus Christ, I'll . . ." Blackthorne was on his feet, his face on fire, but he swayed and fell.

"God damn you, wake up, Ingeles!" Furiously Rodrigues stabbed a finger at the two helmsmen. "Throw him overboard!"

"Eh?"

"Now, by God!"

As the two men hurriedly picked him up, Mariko said, "Pilot Rodrigues, you mustn't—" but before she or Kana could interfere the two men had hurled Blackthorne over the side. He fell the twenty feet and belly-flopped in a cloud of spray and disappeared. In a moment he surfaced, choking and spluttering, flailing at the water, the ice-cold clearing his head.

Rodrigues was struggling out of his seachair. "Madonna, give me a hand!"

One of the helmsmen ran to help as the first mate got a hand under his armpit. "Christ Jesus, be careful, mind my foot, you clumsy dung-head!"

They helped him to the side. Blackthorne was still coughing and sputtering, but now as he swam for the side of the ship he was shouting curses at those who had cast him overboard.

"Two points starboard!" Rodrigues ordered. The ship fell off the wind slightly and eased away from Blackthorne. He shouted down, "Stay to hell off my ship!" Then urgently to his first mate, "Take the longboat, pick up the Ingeles, and put him aboard the galley. Fast. Tell him . . ." He dropped his voice.

Mariko was grateful that Blackthorne was not drowning. "Pilot! The Anjin-san's under Lord Toranaga's protection. I demand he be picked up at once!"

"Just a moment, Mariko-san!" Rodrigues continued to whisper to Santiago, who nodded, then scampered away. "I'm sorry, Mariko-san, *gomen kudasai,* but it was urgent. The Ingeles had to be woken up. I knew he could swim. He has to be alert and fast!"

"Why?"

"I'm his friend. Did he ever tell you that?"

"Yes. But England and Portugal are at war. Also Spain."

"Yes. But pilots should be above war."

"Then to whom do you owe duty?"

"To the flag."

"Isn't that to your king?"

"Yes and no, senhora. I owed the Ingeles a life." Rodrigues was watching the longboat. "Steady as she goes—now put her into the wind," he ordered the helmsman.

"Yes, senhor."

He waited, checking and rechecking the wind and the shoals and the far shore. The leadsman called out the fathoms. "Sorry, senhora, you were saying?" Rodrigues looked at her momentarily, then went back once more to check the lie of his ship and the longboat. She watched the longboat too. The men had hauled Blackthorne out of the sea and were pulling hard for the galley, sitting instead of standing and pushing the oars. She could no longer see their faces clearly. Now the Anjin-san was blurred with the other man close beside him, the man that Rodrigues had whispered to. "What did you say to him, senhor?"

"Who?"

"Him. The senhor you sent after the Anjin-san."

"Just to wish the Ingeles well and Godspeed." The reply was flat and noncommittal.

She translated to Kana what had been said.

When Rodrigues saw the longboat alongside the galley he began to breathe again. "Hail Mary, Mother of God . . ."

The Captain-General and the Jesuits came up from below. Toranaga and his guards followed.

"Rodrigues! Launch the longboat! The Fathers are going ashore," Ferriera said.

"And then?"

"And then we put to sea. For Yedo."

"Why there? We were sailing for Macao," Rodrigues replied, the picture of innocence.

"We're taking Toranaga home to Yedo. First."

"We're what? But what about the galley?"

"She stays or she fights her way out."

Rodrigues seemed to be even more surprised and looked at the galley, then at Mariko. He saw the accusation written in her eyes.

"*Matsu*," the pilot told her quietly.

"What?" Father Alvito asked. "Patience? Why patience, Rodrigues?"

"Saying Hail Marys, Father. I was saying to the lady it teaches you patience."

Ferriera was staring at the galley. "What's our longboat doing there?"

"I sent the heretic back aboard."

"You what?"

"I sent the Ingeles back aboard. What's the problem, Captain-General? The Ingeles offended me so I threw the bugger overboard. I'd have let him drown but he could swim so I sent the mate to pick him up and put him back aboard his ship as he seemed to be in Lord Toranaga's favor. What's wrong?"

"Fetch him back aboard."

"I'll have to send an armed boarding party, Captain-General. Is that what you want? He was cursing and heaping hellfire on us. He won't come back willingly this time."

"I want him back aboard."

"What's the problem? Didn't you say the galley's to stay and fight or whatever? So what? So the Ingeles is hip-deep in shit. Good. Who needs the bugger, anyway? Surely the Fathers'd prefer him out of their sight. Eh, Father?"

Dell'Aqua did not reply. Nor did Alvito. This disrupted the plan that Ferriera had formulated and had been accepted by them and by Toranaga: that the priests would go ashore at once to smooth over Ishido, Kiyama, and Onoshi, professing that they had believed Toranaga's story about the pirates and did not know that he had "escaped" from the castle. Meanwhile the frigate would charge for the harbor mouth, leaving the galley to draw off the fishing boats. If there was an overt attack on the frigate, it would be beaten off with cannon, and the die cast.

"But the boats shouldn't attack us," Ferriera had reasoned. "They have the galley to catch. It will be your responsibility, Eminence, to persuade Ishido that we had no other choice. After all, Toranaga is President of the Regents. Finally, the heretic stays aboard."

Neither of the priests had asked why. Nor had Ferriera volunteered his reason.

The Visitor put a gentle hand on the Captain-General and turned his back on the galley. "Perhaps it's just as well the heretic's there," he said, and he thought, how strange are the ways of God.

No, Ferriera wanted to scream. I wanted to see him drown. A man overboard in the early dawn at sea—no trace, no witnesses, so easy. Toranaga would never be the wiser; a tragic accident, as far as he was concerned. And it was the fate Blackthorne deserved. The Captain-General also knew the horror of sea death to a pilot.

"Nan ja?" Toranaga asked.

Father Alvito explained that the pilot was on the galley and why. Toranaga turned to Mariko, who nodded and added what Rodrigues had said previously.

Toranaga went to the side of the ship and gazed into the darkness. More fishing boats were being launched from the north shore and the others would soon be in place. He knew that the Anjin-san was a political embarrassment and this was a simple way the gods had given him if he desired to be rid of the Anjin-san. Do I want that? Certainly the Christian priests will be vastly happier if the Anjin-san vanishes, he thought.

And also Onoshi and Kiyama, who feared the man so much that either or both had mounted the assassination attempts. Why such fear?

It's *karma* that the Anjin-san is on the galley now and not safely here. *Neh?* So the Anjin-san will drown with the ship, along with Yabu and the others and the guns, and that is also *karma*. The guns I can lose, Yabu I can lose. But the Anjin-san?

Yes.

Because I still have eight more of these strange barbarians in reserve. Perhaps their collective knowledge will equal or exceed that of this single man. The important thing is to be back in Yedo as quickly as possible to prepare for the war which cannot be avoided. Kiyama and Onoshi? Who knows if they'll support me. Perhaps they will, perhaps not. But a plot of land and some promises are nothing in the balance if the Christian weight is on my side in forty days.

"It's *karma*, Tsukku-san. *Neh?*"

"Yes, Sire." Alvito glanced at the Captain-General, very satisfied. "Lord Toranaga suggests that nothing is done. It's the will of God."

"Is it?"

The drum on the galley began abruptly. The oars bit into the water with great strength.

"What, in the name of Christ, is he doing?" Ferriera bellowed.

And then, as they watched the galley pulling away from them, Toranaga's pennant came fluttering down from the masthead.

Rodrigues said, "Looks like they're telling every God-cursed fishing boat in the harbor that Lord Toranaga's no longer aboard."

"What's he going to do?"

"I don't know."

"Don't you?" Ferriera asked.

"No. But if I was him I'd head for sea and leave us in the cesspit—or try to. The Ingeles has put the finger on us now. What's it to be?"

"You're ordered to Yedo." The Captain-General wanted to add, if you ram the galley all the better, but he didn't. Because Mariko was listening.

The priests thankfully went ashore in the longboat.

"All sails ho!" Rodrigues shouted, his leg paining and throbbing. "Sou' by sou'west! All hands lay to!"

"Senhora, please tell Lord Toranaga he'd best go below. It'll be safer," Ferriera said.

"He thanks you and says he will stay here."

Ferriera shrugged, went to the edge of the quarterdeck. "Prime all cannon. Load grape! Action stations!"

CHAPTER 28

"Isogi!" Blackthorne shouted, urging the oarsmaster to increase the beat. He looked aft at the frigate that was bearing down on them, close-hauled now under full sail, then for'ard again, estimating the next tack that she must use. He wondered if he had judged right, for there was very little sea room here, near the cliffs, barely a few yards between disaster and success. Because of the wind, the frigate had to tack to make the harbor mouth, while the galley could maneuver at its whim. But the frigate had the advantage of speed. And on the last tack Rodrigues had made it clear that the galley had better stay out of the way when the Santa Theresa needed sea room.

Yabu was chattering at him again but he paid no heed. "Don't understand—wakarimasen, Yabu-san! Listen, Toranaga-sama said, me, Anjin-san, ichi-ban ima! I'm chief Captain-san now! Wakarimasu ka, Yabu-san?" He pointed the course on the compass to the Japanese captain who gesticulated at the frigate barely fifty yards aft now, overtaking them rapidly on another collision path.

"Hold your course, by God!" Blackthorne said, the breeze cooling his sea-sodden clothes, which chilled him but helped to clear his head. He checked the sky. No clouds were near the bright moon and the wind was fair. No danger there, he thought. God keep the moon bright till we're through.

"Hey, Captain!" he called out in English, knowing it made no difference if he spoke English or Portuguese or Dutch or Latin because he was alone. "Send someone for saké! Saké! Wakarimasu ka?"

"Hai, Anjin-san."

A seaman was sent scurrying. As the man ran he looked over his shoulder, frightened by the size of the approaching frigate and her speed. Blackthorne held their course, trying to force the frigate to turn before she had gained all space to windward. But she never wavered and came directly at him. At the last second he swung out of her way and then, when her bowsprit was almost over their aft deck, he heard Rodrigues' order, "Bear on the larboard tack! Let go stays'ls, and steady as she goes!" Then a shout at him in Spanish, "Thy mouth in the devil's arse, Ingeles!"

"Thy mother was there first, Rodrigues!"

Then the frigate peeled off the wind to scud now for the far shore, where she would have to turn again to reach into the wind and tack for this side once more before she could turn a last time again and make for the harbor mouth.

For an instant the ships were so close that he could almost touch her, Rodrigues, Toranaga, Mariko, and the Captain-General swaying on the quarterdeck. Then the frigate was away and they were twisting in her wash.

"*Isogi, isogi,* by God!"

The rowers redoubled their efforts and with signs Blackthorne ordered more men on the oars until there were no reserves. He had to get to the mouth before the frigate or they were lost.

The galley was eating up the distance. But so was the frigate. At the far side of the harbor she spun like a dancer and he saw that Rodrigues had added tops'ls and topgallants.

"He's as canny a bastard as any Portuguese born!"

The saké arrived but it was taken out of the seaman's hands by the young woman who had helped Mariko and offered precariously to him. She had stayed gamely on deck, even though clearly out of her element. Her hands were strong, her hair well groomed, and her kimono rich, in good taste and neat. The galley lurched in the chop. The girl reeled and dropped the cup. Her face did not change but he saw the flush of shame.

"*Por nada,*" he said as she groped for it. "It doesn't matter. *Namae ka?*"

"Usagi Fujiko, Anjin-san."

"Fujiko-san. Here, give it to me. *Dozo.*" He held out his hand and took the flask and drank directly from it, gulping the wine, eager to have its heat inside his body. He concentrated on the new course, skirting the shoals that Santiago, on Rodrigues' orders, had told him about. He rechecked the bearing from the headland that gave them a clean, hazardless run to the mouth while he finished the warmed wine, wondering in passing how it had been warmed, and why they always served it warm and in small quantities.

His head was clear now, and he felt strong enough, if he was careful. But he knew he had no reserves to draw upon, just as the ship had no reserves.

"Saké, *dozo,* Fujiko-san." He handed her the flask and forgot her.

On the windward tack the frigate made way too well and she passed a hundred yards ahead of them, bearing for the shore. He heard obscenities coming down on the wind and did not bother to reply, conserving his energy.

"*Isogi,* by God! We're losing!"

The excitement of the race and of being alone again and in command —more by the strength of his will than by position—added to the rare privilege of having Yabu in his power, filled him with unholy glee. "If it wasn't that the ship'd go down and me with her, I'd put her on the rocks just to see you drown, shit-face Yabu! For old Pieterzoon!"

But didn't Yabu save Rodrigues when you couldn't? Didn't he charge the bandits when you were ambushed? And he was brave tonight. Yes, he's a shit-face, but even so he's a brave shit-face and that's the truth.

The flask of saké was offered again. *"Domo,"* he said.

The frigate was keeled over, close-hauled and greatly pleasing to him. "I couldn't do better," he said aloud to the wind. "But if I had her, I'd go through the boats and out to sea and never come back. I'd sail her home, somehow, and leave the Japans to the Japanese and to the pestilential Portuguese." He saw Yabu and the captain staring at him. "I wouldn't really, not yet. There's a Black Ship to catch and plunder to be had. And revenge, eh, Yabu-san?"

"Nan desu ka, Anjin-san? *Nan ja?"*

"Ichi-ban! Number one!" he replied, waving at the frigate. He drained the flask. Fujiko took it from him.

"Saké, Anjin-san?"

"Domo, iyé!"

The two ships were very near the massed fishing boats now, the galley heading straight for the pass that had been deliberately left between them, the frigate on the last reach and turning for the harbor mouth. Here the wind freshened as the protecting headlands fell away, open sea half a mile ahead. Gusts billowed the frigate's sails, the shrouds crackling like pistol shots, froth now at her bow and in her wake.

The rowers were bathed with sweat and flagging. One man dropped. And another. The fifty-odd *ronin*-samurai were already in position. Ahead, archers in the fishing boats either side of the narrow channel were arming their bows. Blackthorne saw small braziers in many of the boats and he knew that the arrows would be fire arrows when they came.

He had prepared for battle as best he could. Yabu had understood that they would have to fight, and had understood fire arrows immediately. Blackthorne had erected protective wooden bulkheads around the helm. He had broken open some of the crates of muskets and had set those who could to arming them with powder and with shot. And he had brought several small kegs of powder up onto the quarterdeck and fused them.

When Santiago, the first mate, had helped him aboard the longboat, he had told him that Rodrigues was going to help, with God's good grace.

"Why?" he had asked.

"My Pilot says to tell you that he had you thrown overboard to sober you up, senhor."

"Why?"

"Because, he said to tell you, Senhor Pilot, because there was danger aboard the *Santa Theresa,* danger for you."

"What danger?"

"You are to fight your own way out, he tells you, if you can. But he will help."

"Why?"

"For the Madonna's sweet sake, hold your heretic tongue and listen, I've little time."

Then the mate had told him the shoals and the bearings and the way of the channel and the plan. And given him two pistols. "How good a shot are you, my Pilot asks."

"Poor," he had lied.

"Go with God, my Pilot said to tell you finally."

"And him—and you."

"For me I assign thee to hell!"

"Thy sister!"

Blackthorne had fused the kegs in case the cannon began and there was no plan, or if the plan proved false, and also against encroaching hostiles. Even such a little keg, the fuse alight, floated against the side of the frigate would sink her as surely as a seventy-gun broadside. It doesn't matter how small the keg, he thought, providing it guts her.

"*Isogi* for your lives!" he called out and took the helm, thanking God for Rodrigues and the brightness of the moon.

Here at the mouth the harbor narrowed to four hundred yards. Deep water was almost shore to shore, the rock headlands rising sharp from the sea.

The space between the ambushing fishing boats was a hundred yards.

The *Santa Theresa* had the bit between her teeth now, the wind abaft the beam to starboard, strong wake aft, and she was gaining on them fast. Blackthorne held the center of channel and signed to Yabu to be ready. All their *ronin*-samurai had been ordered to squat below the gunwales, unseen, until Blackthorne gave the signal, when it was every man —with musket or sword—to port or to starboard, wherever they were needed, Yabu commanding the fight. The Japanese captain knew that his oarsmen were to follow the drum and the drum master knew that he had to obey the Anjin-san. And the Anjin-san alone was to guide the ship.

The frigate was fifty yards astern, in mid-channel, heading directly for them, and making it obvious that she required the mid-channel path.

Aboard the frigate, Ferriera breathed softly to Rodrigues, "Ram him." His eyes were on Mariko who stood ten paces off, near the railings, with Toranaga.

"We daren't—not with Toranaga there and the girl."

"Senhora!" Ferriera called out. "Senhora—better to get below, you and your master. It'd be safer for him on the gundeck."

Mariko translated to Toranaga who thought a moment, then walked down the companionway onto the gundeck.

"God damn my eyes," the chief gunner said to no one in particular. "I'd like to fire a broadside and sink something. It's a God-cursed year since we sunk even a poxed pirate."

"Aye. The monkeys deserve a bath."

On the quarterdeck Ferriera repeated, "Ram the galley, Rodrigues!"

"Why kill your enemy when others're doing it for you?"

"Madonna! You're as bad as the priest! Thou hast no blood in thee!"

"Yes, I have none of the killing blood," Rodrigues replied also in Spanish. "But thou? Thou hast it. Eh? And Spanish blood perhaps?"

"Are you going to ram him or not?" Ferriera asked in Portuguese, the nearness of the kill possessing him.

"If she stays where she is, yes."

"Then Madonna let her stay where she is."

"What had you in mind for the Ingeles? Why were you so angry he wasn't aboard us?"

"I do not like you or trust you now, Rodrigues. Twice you've sided, or seemed to side, with the heretic against me, or us. If there was another acceptable pilot in all Asia, I would beach you, Rodrigues, and I would sail off with my Black Ship."

"Then you will drown. There's a smell of death over you and only I can protect you."

Ferriera crossed himself superstitiously. "Madonna, thou and thy filthy tongue! What right hast thou to say that?"

"My mother was a gypsy and she the seventh child of a seventh child, as I am."

"Liar!"

Rodrigues smiled. "Ah, my Lord Captain-General, perhaps I am." He cupped his hands and shouted, "Action stations!" and then to the helmsman, "Steady as she goes, and if that belly-gutter whore doesn't move, sink her!"

Blackthorne held the wheel firmly, arms aching, legs aching. The oarsmaster was pounding the drum, the oarsmen making a final effort.

Now the frigate was twenty yards astern, now fifteen, now ten. Then Blackthorne swung hard to port. The frigate almost brushed them, heeled over toward them, and then she was alongside. Blackthorne swung hard astarboard to come parallel to the frigate, ten yards from her. Then, together—side by side—they were ready to run the gauntlet between the hostiles.

"Puuuull, pull, you bastards!" Blackthorne shouted, wanting to stay exactly alongside, because only here were they guarded by the frigate's bulk and by her sails. Some musket shots, then a salvo of burning arrows slashed at them, doing no real damage, but several by mistake struck the frigate's lower sails and fire broke out.

All the commanding samurai in the boats stopped their archers in horror. No one had ever attacked a Southern Barbarian ship before. Don't they alone bring the silks which make every summer's humid heat bearable, and every winter's cold bearable, and every spring and fall a joy? Aren't the Southern Barbarians protected by Imperial decrees? Wouldn't burning one of their ships infuriate them so much that they would, rightly, never come back again?

So the commanders held their men in check while Toranaga's galley was under the frigate's wing, not daring to risk the merest chance that one of them would be the cause of the cessation of the Black Ships without General Ishido's direct approval. And only when seamen on the frigate had doused the flames did they breathe easier.

When the arrows stopped, Blackthorne also began to relax. And Rodrigues. The plan was working. Rodrigues had surmised that under his lee the galley had a chance, its only chance. 'But my Pilot says you must prepare for the unexpected, Ingeles,' Santiago had reported.

"Shove that bastard aside," Ferriera said. "God damn it, I ordered you to shove him into the monkeys!"

"Five points to port!" Rodrigues ordered obligingly.

"Five points aport it is!" the helmsman echoed.

Blackthorne heard the command. Instantly he steered port five degrees and prayed. If Rodrigues held the course too long they would smash into the fishing boats and be lost. If he slackened the beat and fell behind, he knew the enemy boats would swamp him whether they believed Toranaga was aboard or not. He must stay alongside.

"Five points starboard!" Rodrigues ordered, just in time. He wanted no more fire arrows either; there was too much powder on deck. "Come on, you pimp," he muttered to the wind. "Put your *cojones* in my sails and get us to hell out of here."

Again Blackthorne had swung five points starboard to maintain station with the frigate and the two ships raced side by side, the galley's starboard oars almost touching the frigate, the port oars almost swamping the fishing boats. Now the captain understood, and so did the oarsmaster and the rowers. They put their final strength into the oars. Yabu shouted a command and the *ronin*-samurai put down their bows and rushed to help and Yabu pitched in also.

Neck and neck. Only a few hundred yards to go.

Then Grays on some of the fishing boats, more intrepid than the others, sculled forward into their path and threw grappling hooks. The prow of the galley swamped the boats. The grappling hooks were cast overboard before they caught. The samurai holding them were drowned. And the stroke did not falter.

"Go more to port!"

"I daren't, Captain-General. Toranaga's no fool and look, there's a reef ahead!"

Ferriera saw the spines near the last of the fishing boats. "Madonna, drive him onto it!"

"Two points port!"

Again the frigate swung over and so did Blackthorne. Both ships aimed for the massed fishing boats. Blackthorne had also seen the rocks. Another boat was swamped and a salvo of arrows came aboard. He held his course as long as he dared, then shouted, "Five points starboard!" to warn Rodrigues, and swung the helm over.

Rodrigues took evasive action and fell away. But this time he held a slight collision course which was not part of the plan.

"Go on, you bastard," Rodrigues said, whipped by the chase and by dread. "Let's weigh your *cojones*."

Blackthorne had to choose instantly between the spines and the frigate. He blessed the rowers who still stayed at their oars, and the crew and all aboard who, through their discipline, gave him the privilege of choice. And he chose.

He swung further to starboard, pulled out his pistol and aimed it. "Make way, by God!" he shouted and pulled the trigger. The ball whined over the frigate's quarterdeck just between the Captain-General and Rodrigues.

As the Captain-General ducked, Rodrigues winced. Thou Ingeles son

of a milkless whore! Was that luck or good shooting or did you aim to
kill?

He saw the second pistol in Blackthorne's hand, and Toranaga staring at him. He dismissed Toranaga as unimportant.

Blessed Mother of God, what should I do? Stick with the plan or
change it? Isn't it better to kill this Ingeles? For the good of all? Tell me,
yes or no!

Answer thyself, Rodrigues, on thy eternal soul! Art thou not a man?

Listen then: Other heretics will follow this Ingeles now, like lice,
whether this one is killed or not killed. I owe him a life and I swear I do
not have the killing blood in me—not to kill a pilot.

"Starboard your helm," he ordered and gave way.

"My Master asks why did you almost smash into the galley?"

"It was just a game, senhora, a game pilots play. To test the other's
nerves."

"And the pistol shot?"

"Equally a game—to test my nerve. The rocks were too close and perhaps I was pushing the Ingeles too much. We are friends, no?"

"My Master says it is foolish to play such games."

"Please give him my apologies. The important thing is that he is safe
and now the galley is safe and therefore I am glad. *Honto.*"

"You arranged this escape, this ruse, with the Anjin-san?"

"It happened that he is very clever and was perfect in his timing.
The moon lit his way, the sea favored him, and no one made a mistake.
But why the hostiles didn't swamp him, I don't know. It was the will of
God."

"Was it?" Ferriera said. He was staring at the galley astern of them
and he did not turn around.

They were well beyond the harbor mouth now, safely out into the
Osaka Roads, the galley a few cables aft, neither ship hurrying. Most of
the galley's oars had been shipped temporarily, leaving only enough to
make way calmly while the majority of the oarsmen recuperated.

Rodrigues paid Captain-General Ferriera no heed. He was absorbed
instead with Toranaga. I'm glad we're on Toranaga's side, Rodrigues
told himself. During the race, he had studied him carefully, glad for the
rare opportunity. The man's eyes had been everywhere, watching gunners and guns and the sails and the fire party with an insatiable curiosity,
asking questions, through Mariko, of the seamen or the mate: What's
this for? How do you load a cannon? How much powder? How do you
fire them? What are these ropes for?

"My Master says, perhaps it was just *karma*. You understand *karma*, Captain-Pilot?"

"Yes."

"He thanks you for the use of your ship. Now he will go back to his own."

"What?" Ferriera turned around at once. "We'll be in Yedo long before the galley. Lord Toranaga's welcome to stay aboard."

"My Master says, there's no need to trouble you anymore. He will go onto his own ship."

"Please ask him to stay. I would enjoy his company."

"Lord Toranaga thanks you but he wishes to go at once to his own ship."

"Very well. Do as he says, Rodrigues. Signal her and lower the longboat." Ferriera was disappointed. He had wanted to see Yedo and wanted to get to know Toranaga better now that so much of their future was tied to him. He did not believe what Toranaga had said about the means of avoiding war. We're at war on this monkey's side against Ishido whether we like it or not. And I don't like it. "I'll be sorry not to have Lord Toranaga's company." He bowed politely.

Toranaga bowed back, and spoke briefly.

"My Master thanks you." To Rodrigues, she added, "My Master says he will reward you for the galley when you return with the Black Ship."

"I did nothing. It was merely a duty. Please excuse me for not getting up from my chair—my leg, *neh?*" Rodrigues replied, bowing. "Go with God, senhora."

"Thank you, Captain-Pilot. Do thou likewise."

As she groped wearily down the companionway behind Toranaga, she noticed that the bosun Pesaro was commanding the longboat. Her skin crawled and she almost heaved. She willed the spasm away, thankful that Toranaga had ordered them all off this malodorous vessel.

"A fair wind and safe voyage," Ferriera called down to them. He waved once and the salutation was returned and then the longboat cast off.

"Stand down when the longboat's back and that bitch galley's out of sight," he ordered the chief gunner.

On the quarterdeck he stopped in front of Rodrigues. He pointed at the galley. "You'll live to regret keeping him alive."

"That's in the hands of God. The Ingeles is an 'acceptable' pilot, if you could pass over his religion, my Captain-General."

"I've considered that."

"And?"

"The sooner we're in Macao the better. Make record time, Rodrigues." Ferriera went below.

Rodrigues' leg was throbbing badly. He took a swig from the grog sack. May Ferriera go to hell, he told himself. But, please God, not until we reach Lisbon.

The wind veered slightly and a cloud reached for the nimbus of the moon, rain not far off and dawn streaking the sky. He put his full attention on his ship and her sails and the lie of her. When he was completely satisfied, he watched the longboat. And finally the galley.

He sipped more rum, content that his plan had worked so neatly. Even the pistol shot that had closed the issue. And content with his decision.

It was mine to make and I made it.

"Even so, Ingeles," he said with a great sadness, "the Captain-General's right. With thee, heresy has come to Eden."

CHAPTER 29

A NJIN-SAN?"

"*Hai?*" Blackthorne swooped out of a deep sleep.

"Here's some food. And cha."

For a moment he could not remember who he was or where he was. Then he recognized his cabin aboard the galley. A shaft of sunlight was piercing the darkness. He felt greatly rested. There was no drumbeat now and even in his deepest sleep, his senses had told him that the anchor was being lowered and his ship was safe, near shore, the sea gentle.

He saw a maid carrying a tray, Mariko beside her—her arm no longer in a sling—and he was lying in the pilot's bunk, the same that he had used during the Rodrigues voyage from Anjiro village to Osaka and that was now, in a way, almost as familiar as his own bunk and cabin aboard *Erasmus*. *Erasmus!* It'll be grand to be back aboard and to see the lads again.

He stretched luxuriously, then took the cup of cha Mariko offered.

"Thank you. That's delicious. How's your arm?"

"Much better, thank you." Mariko flexed it to show him. "It was just a flesh wound."

"You're looking better, Mariko-san."

"Yes, I'm better now."

When she had come back aboard at dawn with Toranaga she had been near fainting. "Better to stay aloft," he had told her. "The sickness will leave you faster."

"My Master asks—asks why the pistol shot?"

"It was just a game pilots play," he had told her.

"My Master compliments you on your seamanship."

"We were lucky. The moon helped. And the crew were marvelous. Mariko-san, would you ask the Captain-san if he knows these waters? Sorry, but tell Toranaga-sama I can't keep awake much longer. Or can we hove to for an hour or so out to sea? I've got to sleep."

He vaguely remembered her telling him that Toranaga said he could go below, that the Captain-san was quite capable as they would be staying in coastal waters and not going out to sea.

Blackthorne stretched again and opened a cabin porthole. A rocky shore was two hundred-odd yards away. "Where are we?"

"Off the coast of Totomi Province, Anjin-san. Lord Toranaga wanted to swim and to rest the oarsmen for a few hours. We'll be at Anjiro to-morrow."

"The fishing village? That's impossible. It's near noon and at dawn we were off Osaka. It's impossible!"

"Ah, that was yesterday, Anjin-san. You've slept a day and a night and half another day," she replied. "Lord Toranaga said to let you sleep. Now he thinks a swim would be good to wake you up. After food."

Food was two bowls of rice and charcoal-roasted fish with the dark, salt-bitter, vinegar-sweet sauce that she had told him was made from fermented beans.

"Thank you—yes, I'd like a swim. Almost thirty-six hours? No wonder I feel fine." He took the tray from the maid, ravenous. But he did not eat at once. "Why is she afraid?" he asked.

"She's not, Anjin-san. Just a little nervous. Please excuse her. She's never seen a foreigner close to before."

"Tell her when the moon's full, barbarians sprout horns and fire comes out of our mouths like dragons."

Mariko laughed. "I certainly will not." She pointed to the sea table. "There is tooth powder and a brush and water and fresh towels." Then said in Latin, "It pleasures me to see thou art well. It is as was related on the march, thou hast great bravery."

Their eyes locked and then the moment was allowed to pass. She bowed politely. The maid bowed. The door closed behind them.

Don't think about her, he ordered himself. Think about Toranaga or Anjiro. Why do we stop at Anjiro tomorrow? To off-load Yabu? Good riddance!

Omi will be at Anjiro. What about Omi?

Why not ask Toranaga for Omi's head? He owes you a favor or two. Or why not ask to fight Omi-san. How? With pistols or with swords? You'd have no chance with a sword and it'd be murder if you had a gun. Better to do nothing and wait. You'll have a chance soon and then you'll be revenged on both of them. You bask in Toranaga's favor now. Be patient. Ask yourself what you need from him. Soon we'll be in Yedo, so you've not much time. What about Toranaga?

Blackthorne was using the chopsticks as he had seen the men in the prison use them, lifting the bowl of rice to his lips and pushing the tacky rice from the lip of the bowl into his mouth with the sticks. The pieces of fish were more difficult. He was still not deft enough, so he used his fingers, glad to eat alone, knowing that to eat with your fingers would be very impolite in front of Mariko or Toranaga or any Japanese.

When every morsel had gone he was still famished.

"Got to get more food," he said aloud. "Jesus God in heaven, I'd like some fresh bread and fried eggs and butter and cheese. . . ."

He came on deck. Almost everyone was naked. Some of the men were drying themselves, others sunbathing, and a few were leaping overboard. In the sea alongside the ship, samurai and seamen were swimming or splashing as children would.

"*Konnichi wa,* Anjin-san."

"*Konnichi wa,* Toranaga-sama," he said.

Toranaga, quite naked, was coming up the gangway that had been let down to the sea. "*Sonata wa oyogitamo ka?*" he said, motioning at the sea, slapping the water off his belly and his shoulders, warm under the bright sun.

"*Hai,* Toranaga-sama, *domo,*" Blackthorne said, presuming that he was being asked if he wanted to swim.

Again Toranaga pointed at the sea and spoke shortly, then called Mariko to interpret. Mariko walked down from the poopdeck, shielding her head with a crimson sunshade, her informal white cotton kimono casually belted.

"Toranaga-sama says you look very rested, Anjin-san. The water's invigoration."

"Invigorating," he said, correcting her politely. "Yes."

"Ah, thank you—invigorating. He says please swim then."

Toranaga was leaning carelessly against the gunwale, wiping the water out of his ears with a small towel, and when his left ear would not clear, he hung his head over and hopped on his left heel until it did. Blackthorne saw that Toranaga was very muscular and very taut, apart from his belly. Ill at ease, very conscious of Mariko, he stripped off his shirt and his codpiece and trousers until he was equally naked.

"Lord Toranaga asks if all Englishmen are as hairy as you? The hair so fair?"

"Some are," he said.

"We—our men don't have hair on their chests or arms like you do. Not very much. He says you've a very good build."

"So has he. Please thank him." Blackthorne walked away from her to the head of the gangplank, aware of her and the young woman, Fujiko, who was kneeling on the poop under a yellow parasol, a maid beside her, also watching him. Then, unable to contain his dignity enough to walk naked all the way down to the sea, he dived over the side into the pale blue water. It was a fine dive and the sea chill reached into him exhilaratingly. The sanding bottom was three fathoms down, seaweed waving, multitudes of fish unfrightened by the swimmers. Near the seabed his plummeting stopped and he twisted and played with the fish, then surfaced and began a seemingly lazy, easy, but very fast overarm stroke for the shore that Alban Caradoc had taught him.

The small bay was desolate: many rocks, a tiny pebbled shore, and no sign of life. Mountains climbed a thousand feet to a blue, measureless sky.

He lay on a rock sunning himself. Four samurai had swum with him and were not far away. They smiled and waved. Later he swam back, and they followed. Toranaga was still watching him.

He came up on deck. His clothes were gone. Fujiko and Mariko and two maids were still there. One of the maids bowed and offered him a ridiculously small towel which he took and began to dry himself with, turning uneasily into the gunwale.

I order you to be at ease, he told himself. You're at ease naked in a locked room with Felicity, aren't you? It's only in public when women are around—when she's around—that you're embarrassed. Why? They don't notice nakedness and that's totally sensible. You're in Japan. You're to do as they do. You will be like them and act like a king.

"Lord Toranaga says you swim very well. Would you teach him that stroke?" Mariko was saying.

"I'd be glad to," he said and forced himself to turn around and lean as Toranaga was leaning. Mariko was smiling up at him—looking so pretty, he thought.

"The way you dived into the sea. We've—we've never seen that before. We always jump. He wants to learn how to do that."

"Now?"

"Yes, please."

"I can teach him—at least, I can try."

A maid was holding a cotton kimono for Blackthorne so, gratefully, he slipped it on, tying it with the belt. Now, completely relaxed, he explained how to dive, how to tuck your head between your arms and spring up and out but to beware of belly flopping.

"It's best to start from the foot of the gangway and sort of fall in head first to begin with, without jumping or running. That's the way we teach children."

Toranaga listened and asked questions and then, when he was satisfied, he said through Mariko, "Good. I think I understand." He walked to the head of the gangway. Before Blackthorne could stop him, Toranaga had launched himself toward the water, fifteen feet below. The belly flop was vicious. No one laughed. Toranaga spluttered back to the deck and tried again. Again he landed flat. Other samurai were equally unsuccessful.

"It's not easy," Blackthorne said. "It took me a long time to learn. Give it a rest and we'll try again tomorrow."

"Lord Toranaga says, 'Tomorrow is tomorrow. Today I will learn how to dive.' "

Blackthorne put his kimono aside and demonstrated again. Samurai aped him. Again they failed. So did Toranaga. Six times.

After another demonstration dive Blackthorne scrambled onto the foot of the gangplank and saw Mariko among them, nude, readying to launch herself into space. Her body was exquisite, the bandage on her upper arm fresh. "Wait, Mariko-san! Better to try from here. The first time."

"Very well, Anjin-san."

She walked down to him, the tiny crucifix enhancing her nudity. He showed her how to bend and to fall forward into the sea, catching her by the waist to turn her over so that her head went in first.

Then Toranaga tried near the waterline and was moderately successful. Mariko tried again and the touch of her skin warmed Blackthorne and he clowned momentarily and fell into the water, directing them from there until he had cooled off. Then he ran up to the deck and stood on the gunwale and showed them a deadman's dive, which he thought might be easier, knowing that it was vital for Toranaga to succeed. "But you've got to keep rigid, *hai*? Like a sword. Then you cannot fail." He fell outward. The dive was clean and he trod water and waited.

Several samurai came forward but Toranaga waved them aside. He held up his arms stiffly, his backbone straight. His chest and loins were scarlet from the belly flops. Then he let himself fall forward as Blackthorne had shown. His head went into the water first and his legs tumbled over him, but it was a dive and the first successful dive of any of them and a roar of approval greeted him when he surfaced. He did it again, this time better. Other men followed, some successful, others not. Then Mariko tried.

Blackthorne saw the taut little breasts and tiny waist, flat stomach and curving legs. A flicker of pain went across her face as she lifted her arms above her head. But she held herself like an arrow and fell bravely outward. She speared the water cleanly. Almost no one except him noticed.

"That was a fine dive. Really fine," he said, giving her a hand to lift her easily out of the water onto the gangway platform. "You should stop now. You might open up the cut on your arm."

"Yes, thank you, Anjin-san." She stood beside him, barely reaching his shoulder, very pleased with herself. "That's a rare sensation, the falling outward and the having to stay stiff, and most of all, the having to dominate your fear. Yes, that was a very rare sensation indeed." She walked up the companionway and put on the kimono that the maid held out for her. Then, drying her face delicately, she went below.

Christ Jesus, that's much woman, he thought.

That sunset Toranaga sent for Blackthorne. He was sitting on the poopdeck on clean futons near a small charcoal brazier upon which small pieces of aromatic wood were smoking. They were used to perfume the air and keep away the dusk gnats and mosquitoes. His kimono was pressed and neat, and the huge, winglike shoulders of the starched overmantle gave him a formidable presence. Yabu, too, was formally dressed, and Mariko. Fujiko was also there. Twenty samurai sat silently on guard. Flares were set into stands and the galley still swung calmly at anchor in the bay.

"Saké, Anjin-san?"

"*Domo,* Toranaga-sama." Blackthorne bowed and accepted the small cup from Fujiko, lifted it in toast to Toranaga and drained it. The cup was immediately refilled. Blackthorne was wearing a Brown uniform kimono and it felt easier and freer than his own clothes.

"Lord Toranaga says we're staying here tonight. Tomorrow we arrive at Anjiro. He would like to hear more about your country and the world outside."

"Of course. What would he like to know? It's a lovely night, isn't it?" Blackthorne settled himself comfortably, aware of her femininity. Too aware. Strange, I'm more conscious of her now that she's clothed than when she wore nothing.

"Yes, very. Soon it will be humid, Anjin-san. Summer is not a good time." She told Toranaga what she had said. "My Master says to tell you that Yedo is marshy. The mosquitoes are bad in summer, but spring and autumn are beautiful—yes, truly the birth and the dying seasons of the year are beautiful."

"England's temperate. The winter's bad perhaps one winter in seven. And the summer also. Famine about once in six years, though sometimes we get two bad years in a row."

"We have famine too. All famine is bad. How is it in your country now?"

"We've had bad harvests three times in the last ten years and no sun to ripen the corn. But that's the Hand of the Almighty. Now England's very strong. We're prosperous. Our people work hard. We make all our own cloth, all arms—most of the woolen cloth of Europe. A few silks come from France but the quality's poor and they're only for the very rich."

Blackthorne decided not to tell them about plague or the riots or insurrections caused by enclosing the common lands, and the drift of peasants to towns and to cities. Instead he told them about the good kings and queens, sound leaders and wise parliaments and successful wars.

"Lord Toranaga wants to be quite clear. You claim only sea power protects you from Spain and Portugal?"

"Yes. That alone. Command of our seas keeps us free. You're an island nation too, just like us. Without command of your seas, aren't you also defenseless against an outside enemy?"

"My Master agrees with you."

"Ah, you've been invaded too?" Blackthorne saw a slight frown as she turned to Toranaga and he reminded himself to confine himself to answers and not questions.

When she spoke to him again she was more grave. "Lord Toranaga says I should answer your question, Anjin-san. Yes, we've been invaded twice. More than three hundred years ago—it would be 1274 of your counting—the Mongols of Kublai Khan, who had just conquered China and Korea, came against us when we refused to submit to his authority. A few thousand men landed in Kyushu but our samurai managed to contain them, and after a while the enemy withdrew. But seven years later they came again. This time the invasion consisted of almost a thousand Chinese and Korean ships with two hundred thousand enemy troops—Mongols, Chinese, and Korean—mostly cavalry. In all Chinese history, this was the greatest invasion force ever assembled. We were helpless against such an overwhelming force, Anjin-san. Again they began to land at Hakata Bay in Kyushu but before they could deploy all their armies a Great Wind, a *tai-fun*, came out of the south and destroyed the fleet and all it contained. Those left ashore were quickly killed. It was a *kamikazi*, a Divine Wind, Anjin-san," she said with complete belief, "a *kamikazi* sent by the gods to protect this Land of the Gods from the foreign invader. The Mongols never came back and after eighty years or so their dynasty, the Chin, was thrown out of China," Mariko added with great satisfaction. "The gods protected us against them. The gods will always protect us against invasion. After all, this is *their* land, *neh?*"

Blackthorne thought about the huge numbers of ships and men in the invasion; it made the Spanish Armada against England seem insignificant. "We were helped by a storm too, senhora," he said with equal seriousness. "Many believe it was also sent by God—certainly it was a miracle—and who knows, perhaps it was." He glanced at the brazier as a coal spluttered and flames danced. Then he said, "The Mongols nearly engulfed us in Europe, too." He told her how the hordes of Genghis Khan,

Kublai Khan's grandfather, had come almost to the gates of Vienna before his onslaught was stopped and then turned back, mountains of skulls in his wake. "People in those days believed Genghis Khan and his soldiers were sent by God to punish the world for its sins."

"Lord Toranaga says he was just a barbarian who was immensely good at war."

"Yes. Even so, in England we bless our luck we're an island. We thank God for that and the Channel. And our navy. With China so close and so powerful—and with you and China at war—I'm surprised you don't have a big navy. Aren't you afraid of another attack?" Mariko did not answer but translated for Toranaga what had been said. When she had finished, Toranaga spoke to Yabu, who nodded and answered, equally serious. The two men conversed for a while. Mariko answered another question from Toranaga, then spoke to Blackthorne once more.

"To control your seas, Anjin-san, how many ships do you need?"

"I don't know exactly, but now the Queen's got perhaps a hundred and fifty ships-of-the-line. Those are ships built only for war."

"My Master asks how many ships a year does your queen build?"

"Twenty to thirty warships, the best and fleetest in the world. But the ships are usually built by private groups of merchants and then sold to the Crown."

"For a profit?"

Blackthorne remembered samurai opinion of profit and money. "The Queen generously gives more than the actual cost to encourage research and new styles of building. Without royal favor this would hardly be possible. For example, *Erasmus*, my ship, is a new class, an English design built under license in Holland."

"Could you build such a ship here?"

"Yes. If I had carpenters, interpreters, and all the materials and time. First I'd have to build a smaller vessel. I've never built one entirely by myself before so I'd have to experiment. . . . Of course," he added, attempting to contain his excitement as the idea developed, "of course, if Lord Toranaga wanted a ship, or ships, perhaps a trade could be arranged. Perhaps he could order a number of warships to be built in England. We could sail them out here for him—rigged as he'd want and armed as he'd want."

Mariko translated. Toranaga's interest heightened. So did Yabu's. "He asks, can our sailors be trained to sail such ships?"

"Certainly, given time. We could arrange for the sailing masters—or one of them—to stay in your waters for a year. Then he could set up a training program for you. In a few years you'd have your own navy. A modern navy. Second to none."

Mariko spoke for a time. Toranaga questioned her again searchingly and so did Yabu.

"Yabu-san asks, second to none?"

"Yes. Better than anything the Spaniards would have. Or the Portuguese."

A silence gathered. Toranaga was evidently swept by the idea though he tried to hide it.

"My Master asks, are you sure this could be arranged?"

"Yes."

"How long would it take?"

"Two years for me to sail home. Two years to build a ship or ships. Two to sail back. Half the cost would have to be paid in advance, the remainder on delivery."

Toranaga thoughtfully leaned forward and put some more aromatic wood on the brazier. They all watched him and waited. Then he talked with Yabu at length. Mariko did not translate what was being said and Blackthorne knew better than to ask, as much as he would dearly have liked to be party to the conversation. He studied them all, even the girl Fujiko, who also listened attentively, but he could gather nothing from any of them. He knew this was a brilliant idea that could bring immense profit and guarantee his safe passage back to England.

"Anjin-san, how many ships could you sail out?"

"A flotilla of five ships at a time would be best. You could expect to lose at least one ship through storm, tempest, or Spanish-Portuguese interference—I'm sure they'd try very hard to prevent your having warships. In ten years Lord Toranaga could have a navy of fifteen to twenty ships." He let her translate that, then he continued, slowly. "The first flotilla could bring you master carpenters, shipwrights, gunners, seamen, and masters. In ten to fifteen years, England could supply Lord Toranaga with thirty modern warships, more than enough to dominate your home waters. And, by that time, if you wanted, you could possibly be building your own replacements here. We'll—" He was going to say "sell" but changed the word. "My Queen would be honored to help you form your own navy, and yes, if you wish, we'll train it and provision it."

Oh yes, he thought exultantly, as the final embellishment to the plan dropped into place, and we'll officer it and provide the Admiral and the Queen'll offer you a binding alliance—good for you and good for us—which will be part of the trade, and then together, friend Toranaga, we will harry the Spaniard and Portuguese dog out of these seas and own them forever. This could be the greatest single trading pact any nation has ever made, he thought gleefully. And with an Anglo-Japanese fleet clearing these seas, we English will dominate the Japan-China silk trade. Then it'll be millions every year!

If I can pull this off I'll turn the course of history. I'll have riches and honors beyond my dream. I'll become an ancestor. And to become an ancestor is just about the best thing a man can try to do, even though he fails in the trying.

"My Master says, it's a pity you don't speak our language."

"Yes, but I'm sure you're interpreting perfectly."

"He says that not as a criticism of me, Anjin-san, but as an observation. It's true. It would be much better for my Lord to talk direct, as I can talk to you."

"Do you have any dictionaries, Mariko-san? And grammars—Portuguese-Japanese or Latin-Japanese grammars? If Lord Toranaga could help me with books and teachers I'd try to learn your tongue."

"We have no such books."

"But the Jesuits have. You said so yourself."

"Ah!" She spoke to Toranaga, and Blackthorne saw both Yabu's and Toranaga's eyes light up, and smiles spread over their faces.

"My Master says you will be helped, Anjin-san."

At Toranaga's orders Fujiko gave Blackthorne and Yabu more saké. Toranaga drank only cha, as did Mariko. Unable to contain himself Blackthorne said, "What does he say to my suggestion? What's his answer?"

"Anjin-san, it would be better to be patient. He will answer in his own time."

"Please ask him now."

Reluctantly Mariko turned to Toranaga. "Please excuse me, Sire, but the Anjin-san asks with great deference, what do you think of his plan? He very humbly and most politely requests an answer."

"He'll have my answer in good time."

Mariko said to Blackthorne, "My Master says he will consider your plan and think carefully about what you have said. He asks you to be patient."

"*Domo,* Toranaga-sama."

"I'm going to bed now. We'll leave at dawn." Toranaga got up. Everyone followed him below, except Blackthorne. Blackthorne was left with the night.

At first promise of dawn Toranaga released four of the carrier pigeons that had been sent to the ship with the main baggage when the ship was being prepared. The birds circled twice, then broke off, two homing for

Osaka, two for Yedo. The cipher message to Kiritsubo was an order to be passed on to Hiro-matsu that they should all attempt to leave peacefully at once. Should they be prevented, they were to lock themselves in. The moment the door was forced they were to set fire to that part of the castle and to commit seppuku.

The cipher to his son Sudara, in Yedo, told that he had escaped, was safe, and ordered him to continue secret preparations for war.

"Get to sea, Captain."

"Yes, Lord."

By noon they had crossed the bight between Totomi and Izu provinces and were off Cape Ito, the southernmost point of the Izu peninsula. The wind was fair, the swell modest, and the single mainsail helped their passage.

Then, close by shore in a deep channel between the mainland and some small rock islands, when they had turned north, there was an ominous rumbling ashore.

All oars ceased.

"What in the name of Christ . . ." Blackthorne's eyes were riveted shoreward.

Suddenly a huge fissure snaked up the cliffs and a million tons of rock avalanched into the sea. The waters seemed to boil for a moment. A small wave came out to the galley, then passed by. The avalanche ceased. Again the rumbling, deeper now and more growling, but farther off. Rocks dribbled from the cliffs. Everyone listened intently and waited, watching the cliff face. Sounds of gulls, of surf and wind. Then Toranaga motioned to the drum master, who picked up the beat once more. The oars began. Life on the ship became normal.

"What was that?" Blackthorne said.

"Just an earthquake." Mariko was perplexed. "You don't have earthquakes?"

"No. Never. I've never seen one before."

"Oh, we have them frequently, Anjin-san. That was nothing, just a small one. The main shock center would be somewhere else, even out to sea. Or perhaps this one was just a little one here, all by itself. You were lucky to witness a small one."

"It was as though the whole earth was shaking. I could have sworn I saw . . . I've heard about tremors. In the Holy Land and the Ottomans, they have them sometimes. Jesus!" He exhaled, his heart still thumping roughly. "I could have sworn I saw that whole cliff shake."

"Oh, it did, Anjin-san. When you're on land, it's the most terrible feeling in the whole world. There's no warning, Anjin-san. The tremors come in waves, sometimes sideways, sometimes up and down, sometimes three or four shakes quickly. Sometimes a small one followed by a greater one a day later. There's no pattern. The worst that I was in was at night, six years ago near Osaka, the third day of the Month of the Falling Leaves. Our house collapsed on us, Anjin-san. We weren't hurt, my son and I. We dug ourselves out. The shocks went on for a week or more, some bad, some very bad. The Taikō's great new castle at Fujimi was totally destroyed. Hundreds of thousands of people were lost in that earthquake and in the fires that followed. That's the greatest danger, Anjin-san—the fires that always follow. Our towns and cities and villages die so easily. Sometimes there is a bad earthquake far out to sea and legend has it that this causes the birth of the Great Waves. They are ten or twenty feet high. There is never a warning and they have no season. A Great Wave just comes out of the sea to our shores and sweeps inland. Cities can vanish. Yedo was half destroyed some years ago by such a wave."

"This is normal for you? Every year?"

"Oh, yes. Every year in this Land of the Gods we have earth tremors. And fires and flood and Great Waves, and the monster storms—the *taifuns*. Nature is very strong with us." Tears gathered at the corners of her eyes. "Perhaps that is why we love life so much, Anjin-san. You see, we have to. Death is part of our air and sea and earth. You should know, Anjin-san, in this Land of Tears, death is our heritage."

BOOK THREE

BOOK THREE

CHAPTER 30

Y OU'RE certain everything's ready, Mura?"
"Yes, Omi-san, yes, I think so. We've followed your orders
exactly—and Igurashi-san's."
"Nothing had better go wrong or there'll be another headman by sunset," Igurashi, Yabu's chief lieutenant, told him with great sourness, his
one eye bloodshot from lack of sleep. He had arrived yesterday from
Yedo with the first contingent of samurai and with specific instructions.

Mura did not reply, just nodded deferentially and kept his eyes on the
ground.

They were standing on the foreshore, near the jetty, in front of the
kneeling rows of silent, overawed, and equally exhausted villagers—every
man, woman, and child, except for the bed-ridden—waiting for the galley
to arrive. All wore their best clothes. Faces were scrubbed, the whole
village swept and sparkling and made wholesome as though this were
the day before New Year when, by ancient custom, all the Empire was
cleaned. Fishing boats were meticulously marshaled, nets tidy, ropes
coiled. Even the beach along the bay had been raked.

"Nothing will go wrong, Igurashi-san," Omi said. He had had little
sleep this last week, ever since Yabu's orders had come from Osaka via
one of Toranaga's carrier pigeons. At once he had mobilized the village
and every able-bodied man within twenty *ri* to prepare Anjiro for the
arrival of the samurai and Yabu. And now that Igurashi had whispered
the very private secret, for his ears only, that the great *daimyo* Toranaga
was accompanying his uncle and had successfully escaped Ishido's trap,
he was more than pleased he had expended so much money. "There's no
need for you to worry, Igurashi-san. This is my fief and my responsibility."

"I agree. Yes, it is." Igurashi waved Mura contemptuously away. And
then he added quietly, "You're responsible. But without offense, I tell
you you've never seen our Master when something goes wrong. If we've
forgotten anything, or these dung eaters haven't done what they're supposed to, our Master will make your whole fief and those to the north
and south into manure heaps before sunset tomorrow." He strode back
to the head of his men.

This morning the final companies of samurai had ridden in from
Mishima, Yabu's capital city to the north. Now they, too, with all the

others, were drawn up in packed military formation on the foreshore, in the square, and on the hillside, their banners waving with the slight breeze, upright spears glinting in the sun. Three thousand samurai, the elite of Yabu's army. Five hundred cavalry.

Omi was not afraid. He had done everything it was possible to do and had personally checked everything that could be checked. If something went wrong then that was just *karma*. But nothing is going to go wrong, he thought excitedly. Five hundred koku had been spent or was committed on the preparations—more than his entire year's income before Yabu had increased his fief. He had been staggered by the amount but Midori, his wife, had said they should spend lavishly, that the cost was minuscule compared to the honor that Lord Yabu was doing him. "And with Lord Toranaga here—who knows what great opportunities you'll have?" she had whispered.

She's so right, Omi thought proudly.

He rechecked the shore and the village square. Everything seemed perfect. Midori and his mother were waiting under the awning that had been prepared to receive Yabu and his guest, Toranaga. Omi noticed that his mother's tongue was wagging and he wished that Midori could be spared its constant lash. He straightened a fold in his already impeccable kimono and adjusted his swords and looked seaward.

"Listen, Mura-san," Uo, the fisherman, was whispering cautiously. He was one of the five village elders and they were kneeling with Mura in front of the rest. "You know, I'm so frightened, if I pissed I'd piss dust."

"Then don't, old friend." Mura suppressed his smile.

Uo was a broad-shouldered, rocklike man with vast hands and broken nose, and he wore a pained expression. "I won't. But I think I'm going to fart." Uo was famous for his humor and for his courage and for the quantity of his wind. Last year when they had had the wind-breaking contest with the village to the north he had been champion of champions and had brought great honor to Anjiro.

"Eeeeee, perhaps you'd better not," Haru, a short, wizened fisherman, chortled. "One of the shitheads might get jealous."

Mura hissed, "You're ordered not to call samurai that while even one's near the village." *Oh ko,* he was thinking wearily, I hope we've not forgotten anything. He glanced up at the mountainside, at the bamboo stockade surrounding the temporary fortress they had constructed with such speed and sweat. Three hundred men, digging and building and carrying. The other new house had been easier. It was on the knoll, just below Omi's house, and he could see it, smaller than Omi's but with a tiled roof, a makeshift garden, and a small bath house. I suppose Omi will move there and give Lord Yabu his, Mura thought.

He looked back at the headland where the galley would appear any moment now. Soon Yabu would step ashore and then they were all in the hands of the gods, all *kami,* God the Father, His Blessed Son, and the Blessed Madonna, *oh ko!*

Blessed Madonna, protect us! Would it be too much to ask to put Thy great eye on this special village of Anjiro? Just for the next few days? We need special favor to protect us from our Lord and Master, oh yes! I will light fifty candles and my sons will definitely be brought up in the True Faith, Mura promised.

Today Mura was very glad to be a Christian; he could intercede with the One God and that was an added protection for his village. He had become a Christian in his youth because his own liege lord had been converted and had at once ordered all his followers to become Christians. And when, twenty years ago, this lord was killed fighting for Toranaga against the Taikō, Mura had remained Christian to honor his memory. A good soldier has but one master, he thought. One real master.

Ninjin, a round-faced man with very buck teeth, was especially agitated by the presence of so many samurai. "Mura-san, so sorry, but it's dangerous what you've done—terrible, *neh?* That little earthquake this morning, it was a sign from the gods, an omen. You've made a terrible mistake, Mura-san."

"What is done is done, Ninjin. Forget about it."

"How can I? It's in my cellar and—"

"Some of it's in your cellar. I've plenty myself," Uo said, no longer smiling.

"Nothing's anywhere. Nothing, old friends," Mura said cautiously. "Nothing exists." On his orders, thirty koku of rice had been stolen over the last few days from the samurai commissariat and was now secreted around the village, along with other stores and equipment—and weapons.

"Not weapons," Uo had protested. "Rice yes, but not weapons!"

"War is coming."

"It's against the law to have weapons," Ninjin had wailed.

Mura snorted. "That's a new law, barely twelve years old. Before that we could have any weapons we wanted and we weren't tied to the village. We could go where we wanted, be what we wanted. We could be peasant-soldier, fisherman, merchant, even samurai—some could, you know it's the truth."

"Yes, but now it's different, Mura-san, different. The Taikō ordered it to be different!"

"Soon it'll be as it's always been. We'll be soldiering again."

"Then let's wait," Ninjin had pleaded. "Please. Now it's against the law. If the law changes that's *karma*. The Taikō made the law: no weapons. None. On pain of instant death."

"Open your eyes, all of you! The Taikō's dead! And I tell you, soon Omi-san'll need trained men and most of us have warred, *neh?* We've fished and warred, all in their season. Isn't that true?"

"Yes, Mura-san," Uo had agreed through his fear. "Before the Taikō we weren't tied."

"They'll catch us, they have to catch us," Ninjin had wept. "They'll have no mercy. They'll boil us like they boiled the barbarian."

"Shut up about the barbarian!"

"Listen, friends," Mura had said. "We'll never get such a chance again. It's sent by God. Or by the gods. We must take every knife, arrow, spear, sword, musket, shield, bow we can. The samurai'll think other samurai've stolen them—haven't the shitheads come from all over Izu? And what samurai really trusts another? We must take back our right to war, *neh?* My father was killed in battle—so was his and his! Ninjin, how many battles have you been in—dozens, *neh?* Uo—what about you? Twenty? Thirty?"

"More. Didn't I serve with the Taikō, curse his memory? Ah, before he became Taikō, he was a man. That's the truth! Then something changed him, *neh?* Ninjin, don't forget that Mura-san is headman! And we shouldn't forget his father was headman too! If the headman says weapons, then weapons it has to be."

Now, kneeling in the sun, Mura was convinced that he had done correctly, that this new war would last forever and their world would be again as it had always been. The village would be here, and the boats and some villagers. Because all men—peasant, *daimyo,* samurai, even the *eta*—all men had to eat and the fish were waiting in the sea. So the soldier-villagers would take time out from war from time to time, as always, and they would launch their boats. . . .

"Look!" Uo said and pointed involuntarily in the sudden hush.

The galley was rounding the headland.

Fujiko was kneeling abjectly in front of Toranaga in the main cabin that he had used during the voyage, and they were alone.

"I beg you, Sire," she pleaded. "Take this sentence off my head."

"It's not a sentence, it's an order."

"I will obey, of course. But I cannot do—"

"Cannot?" Toranaga flared. "How dare you argue! I tell you you're to be the pilot's consort and you have the impertinence to argue?"

"I apologize, Sire, with all my heart," Fujiko said quickly, the words gushing. "That was not meant as an argument. I only wanted to say that I cannot do this in the way that you wished. I beg you to understand. Forgive me, Sire, but it's not possible to be happy—or to pretend happiness." She bowed her head to the futon. "I humbly beseech you to allow me to commit seppuku."

"I've said before I do not approve of senseless death. I have a use for you."

"Please, Sire, I wish to die. I humbly beg you. I wish to join my husband and my son."

Toranaga's voice slashed at her, drowning the sounds of the galley. "I've already refused you that honor. You don't merit it, yet. And it's only because of your grandfather, because Lord Hiro-matsu's my oldest friend, that I've listened patiently to your ill-mannered mouthings so far. Enough of this nonsense, woman. Stop acting like a dung-headed peasant!"

"I humbly beg permission to cut off my hair and become a nun. Buddha will—"

"No. I've given you an order. Obey it!"

"Obey?" she said, not looking up, her face stark. Then, half to herself, "I thought I was ordered to Yedo."

"You were ordered to this vessel! You forget your position, you forget your heritage, you forget your duty. You forget your duty! I'm disgusted with you. Go and get ready."

"I want to die, please let me join them, Sire."

"Your husband was born samurai by mistake. He was malformed, so his offspring would be equally malformed. That fool almost ruined me! Join them? What nonsense! You're forbidden to commit seppuku! Now, get out!"

But she did not move.

"Perhaps I'd better send you to the *eta*. To one of their houses. Perhaps that'd remind you of your manners and your duty."

A shudder racked her, but she hissed back defiantly, "At least they'd be Japanese!"

"*I am your liege lord.* You-will-do-as-I-order."

Fujiko hesitated. Then she shrugged. "Yes, Lord. I apologize for my ill manners." She placed her hands flat on the futon and bowed her head low, her voice penitent. But in her heart she was not persuaded and he knew and she knew what she intended to do. "Sire, I sincerely apologize for disturbing you, for destroying your *wa,* your harmony, and for my bad manners. You were right. I was wrong." She got up and went quietly to the door of the cabin.

"If I grant you what you wish," Toranaga said, "will you, in return, do what I want, with all your heart?"

Slowly she looked back. "For how long, Sire? I beg to ask for how long must I be consort to the barbarian?"

"A year."

She turned away and reached for the door handle.

Toranaga said, "Half a year."

Fujiko's hand stopped. Trembling, she leaned her head against the door. "Yes. Thank you, Sire. Thank you."

Toranaga got to his feet and went to the door. She opened it for him and bowed him through and closed it after him. Then the tears came silently.

She was samurai.

Toranaga came on deck feeling very pleased with himself. He had achieved what he wanted with the minimum of trouble. If the girl had been pressed too far she would have disobeyed and taken her own life without permission. But now she would try hard to please and it was important that she become the pilot's consort happily, at least outwardly so, and six months would be more than enough time. Women are much easier to deal with than men, he thought contentedly. So much easier, in certain things.

Then he saw Yabu's samurai massed around the bay and his sense of well-being vanished.

"Welcome to Izu, Lord Toranaga," Yabu said. "I ordered a few men here to act as escort for you."

"Good."

The galley was still two hundred yards from the dock, approaching neatly, and they could see Omi and Igurashi and the futons and the awning.

"Everything's been done as we discussed in Osaka," Yabu was saying. "But why not stay with me for a few days? I'd be honored and it would prove very useful. You could approve the choice of the two hundred and fifty men for the Musket Regiment, and meet their commander."

"Nothing would please me more but I must get to Yedo as quickly as possible, Yabu-san."

"Two or three days? Please. A few days free from worry would be good for you, *neh*? Your health is important to me—to all your allies. Some rest, good food, and hunting."

Toranaga was desperately seeking a solution. To stay here with only fifty guards was unthinkable. He would be totally in Yabu's power, and that would be worse than his situation at Osaka. At least Ishido was predictable and bound by certain rules. But Yabu? Yabu's as treacherous as a shark and you don't tempt sharks, he told himself. And never in their home waters. And never with your own life. He knew that the bargain he had made with Yabu at Osaka had as much substance as the weight of their urine when it had reached the ground, once Yabu believed he could get better concessions from Ishido. And Yabu's presenting Toranaga's head on a wooden platter to Ishido would get Yabu immediately far more than Toranaga was prepared to offer.

Kill him or go ashore? Those were the choices.

"You're too kind," he said. "But I must get to Yedo." I never thought Yabu would have time to gather so many men here. Has he broken our code?

"Please allow me to insist, Toranaga-sama. The hunting's very good nearby. I've falcons with my men. A little hunting after being confined at Osaka would be good, *neh?*"

"Yes, it would be good to hunt today. I regret losing my falcons there."

"But they're not lost. Surely Hiro-matsu will bring them with him to Yedo?"

"I ordered him to release them once we were safely away. By the time they'd have reached Yedo they would have been out of training and tainted. It's one of my few rules: only to fly the falcons that I've trained, and to allow them no other master. That way they make only my mistakes."

"It's a good rule. I'd like to hear the others. Perhaps over food, tonight?"

I need this shark, Toranaga thought bitterly. To kill him now is premature.

Two ropes sailed ashore to be caught and secured. The ropes tightened and screeched under the strain and the galley swung alongside deftly. Oars were shipped. The gangway slid into place and then Yabu stood at its head.

At once the massed samurai shouted their battle cry in unison. "*Kasigi! Kasigi!*" and the roar that they made sent the gulls cawing and mewing into the sky. As one man, the samurai bowed.

Yabu bowed back, then turned to Toranaga and beckoned him expansively. "Let's go ashore."

Toranaga looked out over the massed samurai, over the villagers prostrate in the dust, and he asked himself, Is this where I die by the sword as the astrologer has foretold? Certainly the first part has come to pass: my name is now written on Osaka walls.

He put that thought aside. At the head of the gangway he called out loudly and imperiously to his fifty samurai, who now wore Brown uniform kimonos as he did, "All of you, stay here! You, Captain, you will prepare for instant departure! Mariko-san, you will be staying in Anjiro for three days. Take the pilot and Fujiko-san ashore at once and wait for me in the square." Then he faced the shore and to Yabu's amazement increased the force of his voice. "Now, Yabu-san, I will inspect your regiments!" At once he walked past him and stomped down the gangplank with all the easy confident arrogance of the fighting general he was.

No general had ever won more battles and no one was more cunning except the Taikō, and he was dead. No general had fought more battles, or was ever more patient or had lost so few men. And he had never been defeated.

A rustle of astonishment sped throughout the shore as he was recognized. This inspection was completely unexpected. His name was passed from mouth to mouth and the strength of the whispering, the awe that it generated, gratified him. He felt Yabu following but did not look back.

"Ah, Igurashi-san," he said with a geniality he did not feel. "It's good to see you. Come along, we'll inspect your men together."

"Yes, Lord."

"And you must be Kasigi Omi-san. Your father's an old comrade in arms of mine. You follow, too."

"Yes, Lord," Omi replied, his size increasing with the honor being done to him. "Thank you."

Toranaga set a brisk pace. He had taken them with him to prevent them from talking privately with Yabu for the moment, knowing that his life depended on keeping the initiative.

"Didn't you fight with us at Odawara, Igurashi-san?" he was asking, already knowing that this was where the samurai had lost his eye.

"Yes, Sire. I had the honor. I was with Lord Yabu and we served on the Taikō right wing."

"Then you had the place of honor—where fighting was the thickest. I have much to thank you and your master for."

"We smashed the enemy, Lord. We were only doing our duty." Even though Igurashi hated Toranaga, he was proud that the action was remembered and that he was being thanked.

Now they had come to the front of the first regiment. Toranaga's voice carried loudly. "Yes, you and the men of Izu helped us greatly. Perhaps, if it weren't for you, I would not have gained the Kwanto! Eh, Yabu-sama?" he added, stopping suddenly, giving Yabu publicly the added title, and thus the added honor.

Again Yabu was thrown off balance by the flattery. He felt it was no more than his due, but he had not expected it from Toranaga, and it had never been his intention to allow a formal inspection. "Perhaps, but I doubt it. The Taikō ordered the Beppu clan obliterated. So it was obliterated."

That had been ten years ago, when only the enormously powerful and ancient Beppu clan, led by Beppu Genzaemon, opposed the combined forces of General Nakamura, the Taikō-to-be, and Toranaga—the last major obstacle to Nakamura's complete domination of the Empire. For centuries the Beppu had owned the Eight Provinces, the Kwanto. A hundred and fifty thousand men had ringed their castle-city of Odawara that guarded the pass that led through the mountains into the incredibly rich rice plains beyond. The siege lasted eleven months. Nakamura's new consort, the patrician Lady Ochiba, radiant and barely eighteen, had come to her lord's household outside the battlements, her infant son in her arms, Nakamura doting on his firstborn child. And with Lady Ochiba had come her younger sister, Genjiko, whom Nakamura proposed giving in marriage to Toranaga.

"Sire," Toranaga had said, "I'd certainly be honored to lock our houses closer together, but instead of me marrying the Lady Genjiko as you suggest, let her marry my son and heir, Sudara."

It had taken Toranaga many days to persuade Nakamura but he had agreed. Then when the decision was announced to the Lady Ochiba, she had replied at once, "With humility, Sire, I oppose the marriage."

Nakamura had laughed. "So do I! Sudara's only ten and Genjiko thirteen. Even so, they're now betrothed and on his fifteenth birthday they'll marry."

"But, Sire, Lord Toranaga's already your brother-in-law, *neh*? Surely that's enough of a connection? You need closer ties with the Fujimoto and the Takashima—even at the Imperial Court."

"They're dungheads at Court, and all in pawn," Nakamura had said in his rough, peasant voice. 'Listen, O-chan: Toranaga's got seventy thousand samurai. When we've smashed the Beppu he'll have the Kwanto and more men. My son will need leaders like Yoshi Toranaga, like I need them. Yes, and one day my son will need Yoshi Sudara. Better Sudara should be my son's uncle. Your sister's betrothed to Sudara, but Sudara will live with us for a few years, *neh?*'

"Of course, Sire," Toranaga had agreed instantly, giving up his son and heir as a hostage.

"Good. But listen, first you and Sudara will swear eternal loyalty to my son."

And so it had happened. Then during the tenth month of siege this first child of Nakamura had died, from fever or bad blood or malevolent *kami*.

"May all gods curse Odawara and Toranaga," Ochiba had raved. "It's Toranaga's fault that we're here—he wants the Kwanto. It's his fault our son's dead. He's your real enemy. He wants you to die and me to die! Put him to death—or put him to work. Let him lead the attack, let him pay with his life for the life of our son! I demand vengeance. . . ."

So Toranaga had led the attack. He had taken Odawara Castle by mining the walls and by frontal attack. Then the grief-stricken Nakamura had stamped the city into dust. With its fall and the hunting down of all the Beppu, the Empire was subdued and Nakamura became first Kwampaku and then Taikō. But many had died at Odawara.

Too many, Toranaga thought, here on the Anjiro shore. He watched Yabu. "It's a pity the Taikō's dead, *neh?*"

"Yes."

"My brother-in-law was a great leader. And a great teacher too. Like him, I never forget a friend. Or an enemy."

"Soon Lord Yaemon will be of age. His spirit is the Taikō's spirit. Lord Tora—" But before Yabu could stop the inspection Toranaga had already gone on again and there was little he could do but follow.

Toranaga walked down the ranks, exuding geniality, picking out a man here, another there, recognizing some, his eyes never still as he reached into his memory for faces and names. He had that very rare quality of special generals who inspect so that every man feels, at least for a moment, that the general has looked at him alone, perhaps even talked with him alone among his comrades. Toranaga was doing what he was born to do, what he had done a thousand times: controlling men with his will.

By the time the last samurai was passed, Yabu, Igurashi, and Omi were exhausted. But Toranaga was not, and again, before Yabu could stop him, he had walked rapidly to a vantage point and stood high and alone.

"Samurai of Izu, vassals of my friend and ally, Kasigi Yabu-sama!" he called out in that vast sonorous voice. "I'm honored to be here. I'm honored to see part of the strength of Izu, part of the forces of my great ally. Listen, samurai, dark clouds are gathering over the Empire and threaten the Taikō's peace. We must protect the Taikō's gifts to us against treachery in high places! Let every samurai be prepared! Let every weapon be sharp! Together we will defend his will! And we will prevail! May the gods of Japan both great and small pay attention! May they blast without pity all those who oppose the Taikō's orders!" Then he raised both his arms and uttered their battle cry, *"Kasigi,"* and, incredibly, he bowed to the legions and held the bow.

They all stared at him. Then, *"Toranaga!"* came roaring back at him from the regiments again and again. And the samurai bowed in return.

Even Yabu bowed, overcome by the strength of the moment.

Before Yabu could straighten, Toranaga had set off down the hill once more at a fast pace. "Go with him, Omi-san," Yabu ordered. It would have been unseemly for him to run after Toranaga himself.

"Yes, Lord."

When Omi had gone, Yabu said to Igurashi, "What's the news from Yedo?"

"The Lady Yuriko, your wife, said first to tell you there's a tremendous amount of mobilization over the whole Kwanto. Nothing much on the surface but underneath everything's boiling. She believes Toranaga's preparing for war—a sudden attack, perhaps against Osaka itself."

"What about Ishido?"

"Nothing before we left. That was five days ago. Nor anything about Toranaga's escape. I only heard about that yesterday when your Lady sent a carrier pigeon from Yedo."

"Ah, Zukimoto's already set up that courier service?"

"Yes, Sire."

"Good."

"Her message read: 'Toranaga has successfully escaped from Osaka with our Master in a galley. Make preparations to welcome them at Anjiro.' I thought it best to keep this secret except from Omi-san, but we're all prepared."

"How?"

"I've ordered a war 'exercise,' Sire, throughout Izu. Within three days every road and pass into Izu will be blocked, if that's what you want. There's a mock pirate fleet to the north that could swamp any unescorted ship by day or by night, if that's what you want. And there's space here for you and a guest, however important, if that's what you want."

"Good. Anything else? Any other news?"

Igurashi was reluctant to pass along news the implications of which he did not understand. "We're prepared for anything here. But this morning a cipher came from Osaka: 'Toranaga has resigned from the Council of Regents.'"

"Impossible! Why should he do that?"

"I don't know. I can't think this one out. But it must be true, Sire. We've never had wrong information from this source before."

"The Lady Sazuko?" Yabu asked cautiously, naming Toranaga's youngest consort, whose maid was a spy in his employ.

Igurashi nodded. "Yes. But I don't understand it at all. Now the Regents will impeach him, won't they? They'll order his death. It'd be madness to resign, *neh?*"

"Ishido must have forced him to do it. But how? There wasn't a breath of rumor. Toranaga would never resign on his own! You're right, that'd be the act of a madman. He's lost if he has. It must be false."

Yabu walked down the hill in turmoil and watched Toranaga cross the square toward Mariko and the barbarian, with Fujiko nearby. Now Mariko was walking beside Toranaga, the others waiting in the square. Toranaga was talking quickly and urgently. And then Yabu saw him give her a small parchment scroll and he wondered what it contained and what was being said. What new trickery is Toranaga planning, he asked himself, wishing he had his wife Yuriko here to help him with her wise counsel.

At the dock Toranaga stopped. He did not go onto the ship and into the protection of his men. He knew that it was on the shore that the final decision would be made. He could not escape. Nothing was yet resolved. He watched Yabu and Igurashi approaching. Yabu's untoward impassivity told him very much.

"So, Yabu-san?"

"You will stay for a few days, Lord Toranaga?"

"It would be better for me to leave at once."

Yabu ordered everyone out of hearing. In a moment the two men were alone on the shore.

"I've had disquieting news from Osaka. You've resigned from the Council of Regents?"

"Yes. I've resigned."

"Then you've killed yourself, destroyed your cause, all your vassals, all your allies, all your friends! You've buried Izu and you've murdered me!"

"The Council of Regents can certainly take away your fief, and your life if they want. Yes."

"By all gods, living and dead and yet to be born . . ." Yabu fought to dominate his temper. "I apologize for my bad manners but your—your incredible attitude . . . yes, I apologize." There was no real purpose to be gained in a show of emotion which all knew was unseemly and defacing. "Yes, it is better for you to stay here then, Lord Toranaga."

"I think I would prefer to leave at once."

"Here or Yedo, what's the difference? The Regents' order will come immediately. I imagine you'd want to commit seppuku at once. With dignity. In peace. I would be honored to act as your second."

"Thank you. But no legal order's yet arrived so my head will stay where it is."

"What does a day or two matter? It's inevitable that the order will come. I will make all arrangements, yes, and they will be perfect. You may rely on me."

"Thank you. Yes, I can understand why you would want my head."

"My own head will be forfeit too. If I send yours to Ishido, or take it and ask his pardon, that might persuade him, but I doubt it, *neh?*"

"If I were in your position I might ask for your head. Unfortunately my head will help you not at all."

"I'm inclined to agree. But it's worth trying." Yabu spat violently in the dust. "I deserve to die for being so stupid as to put myself in that dunghead's power."

"Ishido will never hesitate to take your head. But first he'll take Izu. Oh yes, Izu's lost with him in power."

"Don't bait me! I know that's going to happen!"

"I'm not baiting you, my friend," Toranaga told him, enjoying Yabu's loss of face. "I merely said, with Ishido in power you're lost and Izu's lost, because his kinsman Ikawa Jikkyu covets Izu, *neh?* But, Yabu-san, Ishido doesn't have the power. Yet." And he told him, friend to friend, why he had resigned.

"The Council's hamstrung!" Yabu couldn't believe it.

"*There isn't any Council.* There won't be until there are five members again." Toranaga smiled. "Think about it, Yabu-san. Now I'm stronger than ever, *neh?* Ishido's neutralized—so is Jikkyu. Now you've got all the time you need to train your guns. Now you own Suruga and Totomi. Now you own Jikkyu's head. In a few months you'll see his head on a spike and the heads of all his kin, and you'll ride in state into your new domains." Abruptly he spun and shouted, "Igurashi-san!" and five hundred men heard the command.

Igurashi came running but before the samurai had gone three paces, Toranaga called out, "Bring an honor guard with you. Fifty men! At once!" He did not dare to give Yabu a moment's respite to detect the enormous flaw in his argument: that if Ishido was hamstrung now and did not have power, then Toranaga's head on a wooden platter would be of enormous value to Ishido and thus to Yabu. Or even better, Toranaga bound like a common felon and delivered alive at the gates of Osaka Castle would bring Yabu immortality and the keys to the Kwanto.

While the honor guard was forming in front of him, Toranaga said loudly, "In honor of this occasion, Yabu-sama, perhaps you would accept this as a token of friendship." Then he took out his long sword, held it flat on both hands, and offered it.

Yabu took the sword as though in a dream. It was priceless. It was a Minowara heirloom and famous throughout the land. Toranaga had possessed this sword for fifteen years. It had been presented to him by Nakamura in front of the assembled majesty of all the important *daimyos* in the Empire, except Beppu Genzaemon, as part payment for a secret agreement.

This had happened shortly after the battle of Nagakudé long before the Lady Ochiba. Toranaga had just defeated General Nakamura, the Taikō-to-be, when Nakamura was still just an upstart without mandate or formal power or formal title and his reach for absolute power still in the balance. Instead of gathering an overwhelming host and burying Toranaga, which was his usual policy, Nakamura had decided to be conciliatory. He had offered Toranaga a treaty of friendship and a binding alliance, and to cement them, his half sister as wife. That the woman was already married and middle-aged bothered neither Nakamura nor Toranaga at all. Toranaga agreed to the pact. At once the woman's husband, one of Nakamura's vassals—thanking the gods that the invitation to divorce her had not been accompanied by an invitation to commit seppuku—had gratefully sent her back to her half brother. Immediately Toranaga married her with all the pomp and ceremony he could muster, and the same day concluded a secret friendship pact with the immensely powerful Beppu clan, the open enemies of Nakamura, who, at this time, still sat disdainfully in the Kwanto on Toranaga's very unprotected back door.

Then Toranaga had flown his falcons and waited for Nakamura's inevitable attack. But none had come. Instead, astoundingly, Nakamura had sent his revered and beloved mother into Toranaga's camp as a hostage, ostensibly to visit her stepdaughter, Toranaga's new wife, but still hostage nonetheless, and had, in return, invited Toranaga to the vast meeting of all the *daimyos* that he had arranged at Osaka. Toranaga had thought hard and long. Then he had accepted the invitation, suggesting to his ally, Beppu Genzaemon, that it would be unwise for them both to go. Next, he had set sixty thousand samurai secretly into motion toward Osaka against Nakamura's expected treachery, and had left his eldest son Noboru in charge of his new wife and her mother. Noboru had at once piled tinder-dry brushwood to the eaves of their residence and had told them bluntly he would fire it if anything happened to his father.

Toranaga smiled, remembering. The night before he was due to enter Osaka, Nakamura, unconventional as ever, had paid him a secret visit, alone and unarmed.

"Well met, Tora-san."

"Well met, Lord Nakamura."

"Listen: We've fought too many battles together, we know too many secrets, we've shit too many times in the same pot to want to piss on our own feet or on each other's."

"I agree," Toranaga had said cautiously.

"Listen then: I'm within a sword's edge of winning the realm. To get total power I've got to have the respect of the ancient clans, the hereditary fief holders, the present heirs of the Fujimoto, the Takashima, and Minowara. Once I've got power, any *daimyo* or any three together can piss blood for all I care."

"You have my respect—you've always had it."

The little monkey-faced man had laughed richly. "You won at Nagakudé fairly. You're the best general I've ever known, the greatest *daimyo* in the realm. But now we're going to stop playing games, you and I. Listen: tomorrow I want you to bow to me before all the *daimyos, as a vassal.* I want you, Yoshi Toranaga-noh-Minowara a willing vassal. Publicly. Not to tongue my hole, but polite, humble, and respectful. If you're my vassal, the rest'll fart in their haste to put their heads in the dust and their tails in the air. And the few that don't—well, let them beware."

"That will make you Lord of all Japan. *Neh?*"

"Yes. The first in history. And you'll have given it to me. I admit I can't do it without you. But listen: If you do that for me you'll have first place after me. Every honor you want. Anything. There's enough for both of us."

"Is there?"

"Yes. First I take Japan. Then Korea. Then China. I told Goroda I wanted that and that's what I'll have. Then you can have Japan—a province of my China!"

"But now, Lord Nakamura? Now I have to submit, *neh?* I'm in your power, *neh?* You're in overwhelming strength in front of me—and the Beppu threaten my back."

"I'll deal with them soon enough," the peasant warlord had said. "Those sneering carrion refused my invitation to come here tomorrow— they sent my scroll back covered in bird's shit. You want their lands? The whole Kwanto?"

"I want nothing from them or from anyone," he had said.

"Liar," Nakamura had said genially. "Listen, Tora-san: I'm almost fifty. None of my women has ever birthed. I've juice in plenty, always have had, and in my life I must have pillowed a hundred, two hundred women, of all types, of all ages, in every way, but none has ever birthed a child, not even stillborn. I've everything but I've no sons and never will. That's my *karma*. You've four sons living and who knows how many daughters. You're forty-three so you can pillow your way to a dozen more sons as easy as horses shit and that's your *karma*. Also you're Minowara and that's *karma*. Say I adopt one of your sons and make him my heir?"

"Now?"

"Soon. Say in three years. It was never important to have an heir before but now things're different. Our late Master Goroda had the stupidity to get himself murdered. Now the land's mine—could be mine. Well?"

"You'll make the agreements formal, publicly formal, in two years?"

"Yes. In two years. You can trust me—our interests are the same. Listen: In two years, in public; and we agree, you and I, which son. This way we share everything, eh? Our joint dynasty's settled into the future, so no problems there and that's good for you and good for me. The pickings'll be huge. First the Kwanto. Eh?"

"Perhaps Beppu Genzaemon will submit—*if* I submit."

"I can't allow them to, Tora-san. You covet their lands."

"I covet nothing."

Nakamura's laugh had been merry. "Yes. But you should. The Kwanto's worthy of you. It's safe behind mountain walls, easy to defend. With the delta you'll control the richest rice lands in the Empire. You'll have your back to the sea and an income of two million koku. But don't make Kamakura your capital. Or Odawara."

"Kamakura's always been capital of the Kwanto."

"Why shouldn't you covet Kamakura, Tora-san? Hasn't it contained the holy shrine of your family's guardian *kami* for six hundred years? Isn't Hachiman, the *kami* of war, the Minowara deity? Your ancestor was wise to choose the *kami* of war to worship."

"I covet nothing, worship nothing. A shrine is just a shrine and the *kami* of war's never been known to stay in any shrine."

"I'm glad you covet nothing, Tora-san, then nothing will disappoint you. You're like me in that. But Kamakura's no capital for you. There are seven passes into it, too many to defend. And it's not on the sea. No, I wouldn't advise Kamakura. Listen: You'd be better and safer to go farther over the mountains. You need a seaport. There's one I saw once—Yedo—a fishing village now, but you'll make it into a great city. Easy to defend, perfect for trade. You favor trade. I favor trade. Good. So you must have a seaport. As to Odawara, we're going to stamp it out, as a lesson to all the others."

"That will be very difficult."

"Yes. But it'd be a good lesson for all the other *daimyos, neh?*"

"To take that city by storm would be costly."

Again the taunting laugh. "It could be, to you, if you don't join me. I've got to go through your present lands to get at it—did you know you're the Beppu front line? The Beppu pawn? Together you and them could keep me off for a year or two, even three. But I'll get there in the end. Oh, yes. Eeeee, why waste more time on them? They're all dead—except your son-in-law if you want—ah, I know you've an alliance with them, but it's not worth a bowl of horseshit. So what's your answer? The pickings are going to be vast. First the Kwanto—that's yours—then I've all Japan. Then Korea—easy. Then China—hard but not impossible. I know a peasant can't become Shōgun, but 'our' son *will* be Shōgun, and he could straddle the Dragon Throne of China too, or his son. Now that's the end of talk. What's your answer, Yoshi Toranaga-noh-Minowara, vassal or not? Nothing else is of value to me."

"Let's piss on the bargain," Toranaga had said, having gained everything that he had wanted and planned for. And the next day, before the bewildered majesty of the truculent *daimyos,* he had humbly offered up his sword and his lands and his honor and his heritage to the upstart peasant warlord. He had begged to be allowed to serve Nakamura and his house forever. And he, Yoshi Toranaga-noh-Minowara, had bowed his head abjectly into the dust. The Taikō-to-be now had been magnanimous and had taken his lands and had at once gifted him the Kwanto as a fief once it was conquered, ordering total war on the Beppu for their insults to the Emperor. And he had also given Toranaga this sword that he had recently acquired from one of the Imperial treasuries. The sword had been made by the master swordsmith, Miyoshi-Go, centuries before, and had once belonged to the most famous warrior in history, Minowara Yoshitomo, the first of the Minowara Shōguns.

Toranaga remembered that day. And he recalled other days: a few years later when the Lady Ochiba gave birth to a boy; and another when, incredibly, after the Taikō's first son had conveniently died, Yaemon, the second son, was born. So was the whole plan ruined. *Karma.*

He saw Yabu holding the sword of his ancestor with reverence.

"Is it as sharp as they say?" Yabu asked.

"Yes."

"You do me great honor. I will treasure your gift." Yabu bowed, conscious that, because of the gift, he would be the first in the land after Toranaga.

Toranaga bowed back, and then, unarmed, he walked for the gangway. It took all his will to hide his fury and not to let his feet falter, and he prayed that Yabu's avariciousness would keep him mesmerized for just a few moments more.

"Cast off!" he ordered, coming onto the deck, and then turned shoreward and waved cheerfully.

Someone broke the silence and shouted his name, then others took up the shout. There was a general roar of approval at the honor done to their lord. Willing hands shoved the ship out to sea. The oarsmen pulled briskly. The galley made way.

"Captain, get to Yedo quickly!"

"Yes, Sire."

Toranaga looked aft, his eyes ranging the shore, expecting danger any instant. Yabu stood near the jetty, still bemused by the sword. Mariko and Fujiko were waiting beside the awning with the other women. The Anjin-san was on the edge of the square where he had been told to wait —rigid, towering, and unmistakably furious. Their eyes met. Toranaga smiled and waved.

The wave was returned, but coldly, and this amused Toranaga very much.

Blackthorne walked cheerlessly up to the jetty.

"When's he coming back, Mariko-san?"

"I don't know, Anjin-san."

"How do we get to Yedo?"

"We stay here. At least, I stay for three days. Then I'm ordered there."

"By sea?"

"By land."

"And me?"

"You are to stay here."

"Why?"

"You expressed an interest in learning our language. And there's work for you to do here."

"What work?"

"I don't know, I'm sorry. Lord Yabu will tell you. My Master left me here to interpret, for three days."

Blackthorne was filled with foreboding. His pistols were in his belt but he had no knives and no more powder and no more shot. That was all in the cabin aboard the galley.

"Why didn't you tell me we were staying here?" he asked. "You just said to come ashore."

"I didn't know you were to remain here also," she replied. "Lord Toranaga told me only a moment ago, in the square."

"Why didn't he tell me then? Tell me himself?"

"I don't know."

"I was supposed to be going to Yedo. That's where my crew is. That's where my ship is. What about them?"

"He just said you were to stay here."

"For how long?"

"He didn't tell me, Anjin-san. Perhaps Lord Yabu will know. Please be patient."

Blackthorne could see Toranaga standing on the quarterdeck, watching shoreward. "I think he knew all along I was to stay here, didn't he?"

She did not answer. How childish it is, she said to herself, to speak aloud what you think. And how extraordinarily clever Toranaga was to have escaped this trap.

Fujiko and the two maids stood beside her, waiting patiently in the shade with Omi's mother and wife whom she had met briefly, and she looked beyond them to the galley. It was picking up speed now. But it was still within easy arrow range. Any moment now she knew she must begin. Oh, Madonna, let me be strong, she prayed, all her attention centering on Yabu.

"Is it true? Is that true?" Blackthorne was asking.

"What? Oh, I'm sorry, I don't know, Anjin-san. I can only tell you Lord Toranaga is very wise. The wisest man. Whatever his reason, it was good." She studied the blue eyes and hard face, knowing that Blackthorne had no understanding of what had occurred here. "Please be patient, Anjin-san. There's nothing to be afraid of. You're his favored vassal and under his—"

"I'm not afraid, Mariko-san. I'm just tired of being shoved around the board like a pawn. And I'm no one's vassal."

"Is 'retainer' better? Or how would you describe a man who works for another or is retained by another for special . . ." Then she saw the blood soar into Yabu's face.

"The guns—the guns are still on the galley!" he cried out.

Mariko knew the time had come. She hurried over to him as he turned to shout orders at Igurashi.

"Your pardon, Lord Yabu," she said, overriding him, "there's no need to worry about your guns. Lord Toranaga said to ask your pardon for his haste but he has urgent things to do on your joint behalves at Yedo. He said he would return the galley instantly. With the guns. And with extra powder. And also with the two hundred and fifty men you require from him. They'll be here in five or six days."

"What?"

Mariko explained patiently and politely again as Toranaga had told her to do. Then, once Yabu understood, she took out a roll of parchment from her sleeve. "My Master begs you to read this. It concerns the Anjin-san." She formally offered it to him.

But Yabu did not take the scroll. His eyes went to the galley. It was well away now, going very fast. Out of range. But what does that matter, he thought contentedly, now over his anxiety. I'll get the guns back quickly and now I'm out of the Ishido trap and I've Toranaga's most famous sword and soon all the *daimyos* in the land will be aware of my new position in the armies of the East—second to Toranaga alone! Yabu could still see Toranaga and he waved once and the wave was returned. Then Toranaga vanished off the quarterdeck.

Yabu took the scroll and turned his mind to the present. And to the Anjin-san.

Blackthorne was watching thirty paces away and he felt his hackles rise under Yabu's piercing gaze. He heard Mariko speaking in her lilting voice but that did not reassure him. His hand tightened covertly on the pistol.

"Anjin-san!" Mariko called out. "Would you please come over here!"

As Blackthorne approached them, Yabu glanced up from the parchment, nodded in friendly fashion. When Yabu had finished reading he handed the paper back to Mariko and spoke briefly, partly to her, partly to him.

Reverently Mariko offered the paper to Blackthorne. He took it and examined the incomprehensible characters.

"Lord Yabu says you are welcome in this village. This paper is under Lord Toranaga's seal, Anjin-san. You are to keep it. He's given you a rare honor. Lord Toranaga has made you a hatamoto. This is the position of a special retainer of his personal staff. You have his absolute protection, Anjin-san. Lord Yabu, of course, acknowledges this. I will explain later the privileges, but Lord Toranaga has given you also a salary of twenty koku a month. That is about—"

Yabu interrupted her, expansively waving his hand at Blackthorne then at the village and spoke at length. Mariko translated. "Lord Yabu repeats that you are welcome here. He hopes you will be content, that everything will be done to make your stay comfortable. A house will be provided for you. And teachers. You will please learn Japanese as quickly as possible, he says. Tonight he will ask you some questions and tell you about some special work."

"Please ask him, what work?"

"May I advise just a little more patience, Anjin-san. Now is not the time, truly."

"All right."

"*Wakarimasu ka,* Anjin-san?" Yabu said. Do you understand?

"*Hai,* Yabu-san. *Domo.*"

Yabu gave orders to Igurashi to dismiss the regiment, then strode over to the villagers, who were still prostrate in the sand.

He stood in front of them in the warm fine spring afternoon, Toranaga's sword still in his hand. His words whipped over them. Yabu pointed the sword at Blackthorne and harangued them a few moments more and ended abruptly. A tremor went through the villagers. Mura bowed and said "*hai*" several times and turned and asked the villagers a question and all eyes went to Blackthorne.

"*Wakarimasu ka?*" Mura called out and they all answered "*Hai,*" their voices mixing with the sighing of the waves upon the beach.

"What's going on?" Blackthorne asked Mariko, but Mura shouted, "*Keirei!*" and the villagers bowed low again, once to Yabu and once to Blackthorne. Yabu strode off without looking back.

"What's going on, Mariko-san?"

"He—Lord Yabu told them you are his honored guest here. That you are also Lord Toranaga's very honored vas—retainer. That you are here mostly to learn our tongue. That he has given the village the honor and responsibility of teaching you. The village is responsible, Anjin-san. Everyone here is to help you. He told them that if you have not learned satisfactorily within six months, the village will be burnt, but before that, every man, woman, and child will be crucified."

CHAPTER 31

T^{HE} day was dying now, the shadows long, the sea red, and a kind
wind blowing.

Blackthorne was coming up the path from the village toward
the house that Mariko had earlier pointed out and told him was to be
his. She had expected to escort him there but he had thanked her and
refused and had walked past the kneeling villagers toward the promon-
tory to be alone and to think.

He had found the effort of thinking too great. Nothing seemed to fit.
He had doused salt water over his head to try to clear it but that had not
helped. At length he had given up and had walked back aimlessly along
the shore, past the jetty, across the square and through the village, up to
this house where he was to live now and where, he remembered, there
had not been a dwelling before. High up, dominating the opposite hillside was another sprawling dwelling, part thatch, part tile, within a tall
stockade, many guards at the fortified gateway.

Samurai were strutting through the village or standing talking in
groups. Most had already marched off behind their officers in disciplined
groups up the paths and over the hill to their bivouac encampment.
Those samurai that Blackthorne met, he absently greeted and they
greeted him in return. He saw no villagers.

Blackthorne stopped outside the gate that was set into the fence.
There were more of the peculiar characters painted over the lintel and
the door itself was cut out in ingenious patterns designed to hide and at
the same time to reveal the garden behind.

Before he could open the door it swung inward and a frightened old
man bowed him through.

"*Konbanwa,* Anjin-san." His voice quavered piteously—Good
evening.

"*Konbanwa,*" he replied. "Listen, old man, er—*o namae ka?*"

"*Namae watashi wa,* Anjin-sama? *Ah, watashi* Ueki-ya . . . Ueki-ya."
The old man was almost slavering with relief.

Blackthorne said the name several times to help remember it and
added "san" and the old man shook his head violently. "*Iyé, gomen
nasai! Iyé* 'san,' Anjin-sama. Ueki-ya! Ueki-ya!"

"All right, Ueki-ya." But Blackthorne thought, why not "san" like
everyone else?

Blackthorne waved his hand in dismissal. The old man hobbled away quickly. "I'll have to be more careful. I have to help them," he said aloud.

A maid came apprehensively onto the veranda through an opened shoji and bowed low.

"*Konbanwa,* Anjin-san."

"*Konbanwa,*" he replied, vaguely recognizing her from the ship. He waved her away too.

A rustle of silk. Fujiko came from within the house. Mariko was with her.

"Was your walk pleasant, Anjin-san?"

"Yes, pleasant, Mariko-san." He hardly noticed her or Fujiko or the house or garden.

"Would you like cha? Or perhaps saké? Or a bath perhaps? The water is hot." Mariko laughed nervously, perturbed by the look in his eyes. "The bath house is not completely finished, but we hope it will prove adequate."

"Saké, please. Yes, some saké first, Mariko-san."

Mariko spoke to Fujiko, who disappeared inside the house once more. A maid silently brought three cushions and went away. Mariko gracefully sat on one.

"Sit down, Anjin-san, you must be tired."

"Thank you."

He sat on the steps of the veranda and did not take off his thongs. Fujiko brought two flasks of saké and a teacup, as Mariko had told her, not the tiny porcelain cup that should have been used.

"Better to give him a lot of saké quickly," Mariko had said. "It would be better to make him quite drunk but Lord Yabu needs him tonight. A bath and saké will perhaps ease him."

Blackthorne drank the proffered cup of warmed wine without tasting it. And then a second. And a third.

They had watched him coming up the hill through the slit of barely opened shojis.

"What's the matter with him?" Fujiko had asked, alarmed.

"He's distressed by what Lord Yabu said—the promise to the village."

"Why should that bother him? He's not threatened. It's not his life that was threatened."

"Barbarians are very different from us, Fujiko-san. For instance, the Anjin-san believes villagers are people, like any other people, like samurai, some perhaps even better than samurai."

Fujiko had laughed nervously. "That's nonsense, *neh?* How can peasants equal samurai?"

Mariko had not answered. She had just continued watching the Anjin-san. "Poor man," she said.

"Poor village!" Fujiko's short upper lip curled disdainfully. "A stupid waste of peasants and fishermen! Kasigi Yabu-san's a fool! How can a barbarian learn our tongue in half a year? How long did the barbarian Tsukku-san take? More than twenty years, *neh?* And isn't he the only barbarian who's ever been able to talk even passable Japanese?"

"No, not the only one, though he's the best I've ever heard. Yes, it's difficult for them. But the Anjin-san's an intelligent man and Lord Toranaga said that in half a year, isolated from barbarians, eating our food, living as we do, drinking cha, bathing every day, the Anjin-san will soon be like one of us."

Fujiko's face had been set. "Look at him, Mariko-san . . . so ugly. So monstrous and alien. Curious to think that as much as I detest barbarians, once he steps through the gate I'm committed and he becomes my lord and master."

"He's brave, very brave, Fujiko. And he saved Lord Toranaga's life and is very valuable to him."

"Yes, I know, and that should make me dislike him less but, so sorry, it doesn't. Even so, I'll try with all my strength to change him into one of us. I pray Lord Buddha will help me."

Mariko had wanted to ask her niece, why the sudden change? Why are you now prepared to serve the Anjin-san and obey Lord Toranaga so absolutely, when only this morning you refused to obey, you swore to kill yourself without permission or to kill the barbarian the moment he slept? What did Lord Toranaga say to change you, Fujiko?

But Mariko had known better than to ask. Toranaga had not taken her into this confidence. Fujiko would not tell her. The girl had been too well trained by her mother, Buntaro's sister, who had been trained by her father, Hiro-matsu.

I wonder if Lord Hiro-matsu will escape from Osaka Castle, she asked herself, very fond of the old general, her father-in-law. And what about Kiri-san and the Lady Sazuko? Where is Buntaro, my husband? Where was he captured? Or did he have time to die?

Mariko watched Fujiko pour the last of the saké. This cup too was consumed like the others, without expression.

"*Dozo.* Saké," Blackthorne said.

More saké was brought. And finished. "*Dozo,* saké."

"Mariko-san," Fujiko said, "the Master shouldn't have any more, *neh?* He'll get drunk. Please ask him if he'd like his bath now. I will send for Suwo."

Mariko asked him. "Sorry, he says he'll bathe later."

Patiently Fujiko ordered more saké and Mariko added quietly to the maid, "Bring some charcoaled fish."

The new flask was emptied with the same silent determination. The food did not tempt him but he took a piece at Mariko's gracious persuasion. He did not eat it.

More wine was brought, and two more flasks were consumed.

"Please give the Anjin-san my apologies," Fujiko said. "So sorry, but there isn't any more saké in his house. Tell him I apologize for this lack. I've sent the maid to fetch some more from the village."

"Good. He's had more than enough, though it doesn't seem to have touched him at all. Why not leave us now, Fujiko? Now would be a good time to make the formal offer on your behalf."

Fujiko bowed to Blackthorne and went away, glad that custom decreed that important matters were always to be handled by a third party in private. Thus dignity could always be maintained on both sides.

Mariko explained to Blackthorne about the wine.

"How long will it take to get more?"

"Not long. Perhaps you'd like to bathe now. I'll see that saké's sent the instant it arrives."

"Did Toranaga say anything about my plan before he left? About the navy?"

"No. I'm sorry, he said nothing about that." Mariko had been watching for the telltale signs of drunkenness. But to her surprise none had appeared, not even a slight flush, or a slurring of words. With this amount of wine consumed so fast, any Japanese would be drunk. "The wine is not to your taste, Anjin-san?"

"Not really. It's too weak. It gives me nothing."

"You seek oblivion?"

"No—a solution."

"Anything that can be done to help, will be done."

"I must have books and paper and pens."

"Tomorrow I will begin to collect them for you."

"No, tonight, Mariko-san. I must start now."

"Lord Toranaga said he will send you a book—what did you call it?—the grammar books and word books of the Holy Fathers."

"How long will that take?"

"I don't know. But I'm here for three days. Perhaps this may be a help to you. And Fujiko-san is here to help also." She smiled, happy for him. "I'm honored to tell you she is given to you as consort and she—"

"*What?*"

"Lord Toranaga asked her if she would be your consort and she said she would be honored and agreed. She will—"

"But I haven't agreed."

"Please? I'm sorry, I don't understand."

"I don't want her. Either as consort or around me. I find her ugly."

Mariko gaped at him. "But what's that got to do with consort?"

"Tell her to leave."

"But Anjin-san, you can't refuse! That would be a terrible insult to Lord Toranaga, to her, to everyone! What harm has she done you? None at all! Usagi Fujiko's consen—"

"You listen to me!" Blackthorne's words ricocheted around the veranda and the house. "Tell her to leave!"

Mariko said at once, "So sorry, Anjin-san, yes you're right to be angry. But—"

"I'm not angry," Blackthorne said icily. "Can't you . . . *can't* you people get it through your heads I'm tired of being a puppet? I don't want that woman around, I want my ship back and my crew back and that's the end of it! I'm not staying here six months and I detest your customs. It's God-cursed terrible that one man can threaten to bury a whole village just to teach me Japanese, and as to consorts—that's worse than slavery—and it's a goddamned insult to arrange that without asking me in advance!"

What's the matter now? Mariko was asking herself helplessly. What has ugliness to do with consort? And anyway Fujiko's not ugly. How can he be so incomprehensible? Then she remembered Toranaga's admonition: 'Mariko-san, you're personally responsible, firstly that Yabu-san doesn't interfere with my departure after I've given him my sword, and secondly, you're totally responsible for settling the Anjin-san docilely in Anjiro.'

'I'll do my best, Sire. But I'm afraid the Anjin-san baffles me.'

'Treat him like a hawk. That's the key to him. I tame a hawk in two days. You've three.'

She looked away from Blackthorne and put her wits to work. He does seem like a hawk when he's in a rage, she thought. He has the same screeching, senseless ferocity, and when not in rage the same haughty, unblinking stare, the same total selfcenteredness, with exploding viciousness never far away.

"I agree. You're completely right. You've been imposed upon terribly, and you're quite right to be angry," she said soothingly. "Yes, and certainly Lord Toranaga should have asked even though he doesn't understand your customs. But it never occurred to him that you would object. He only tried to honor you as he would a most favored samurai. He made you a hatamoto, that's almost like a kinsman, Anjin-san. There are only about a thousand hatamoto in all the Kwanto. And as to the

Lady Fujiko, he was only trying to help you. The Lady Usagi Fujiko would be considered . . . among us, Anjin-san, this would be considered a great honor."

"Why?"

"Because her lineage is ancient and she's very accomplished. Her father and grandfather are *daimyos*. Of course she's samurai, and of course," Mariko added delicately, "you would honor her by accepting her. And she does need a home and a new life."

"Why?"

"She is recently widowed. She's only nineteen, Anjin-san, poor girl, but she lost a husband and a son and is filled with remorse. To be formal consort to you would give her a new life."

"What happened to her husband and son?"

Mariko hesitated, distressed at Blackthorne's impolite directness. But she knew enough about him by now to understand that this was *his* custom and not meant as lack of manners. "They were put to death, Anjin-san. While you're here you will need someone to look after your house. The Lady Fujiko will be—"

"Why were they put to death?"

"Her husband almost caused the death of Lord Toranaga. Please con—"

"Toranaga ordered their deaths?"

"Yes. But he was correct. Ask her—she will agree, Anjin-san."

"How old was the child?"

"A few months, Anjin-san."

"Toranaga had an infant put to death for something the father did?"

"Yes. It's our custom. Please be patient with us. In some things we are not free. Our customs are different from yours. You see, by law, we belong to our liege lord. By law a father possesses the lives of his children and wife and consorts and servants. By law his life is possessed by his liege lord. This is our custom."

"So a father can kill anyone in his house?"

"Yes."

"Then you're a nation of murderers."

"No."

"But your custom condones murder. I thought you were Christian."

"I am, Anjin-san."

"What about the Commandments?"

"I cannot explain, truly. But I am Christian and samurai and Japanese, and these are not hostile to one another. To me, they're not. Please be patient with me and with us. Please."

"You'd put your own children to death if Toranaga ordered it?"

"Yes. I only have one son but yes, I believe I would. Certainly it would be my duty to do so. That's the law—if my husband agreed."

"I hope God can forgive you. All of you."

"God understands, Anjin-san. Oh, He will understand. Perhaps He will open your mind so you can understand. I'm sorry, I cannot explain very well, *neh?* I apologize for my lack." She watched him in the silence, unsettled by him. "I don't understand you either, Anjin-san. You baffle me. Your customs baffle me. Perhaps if we're both patient we can both learn. The Lady Fujiko, for instance. As consort she will look after your house and your servants. And your needs—any of your needs. You must have someone to do that. She will see to the running of your house, everything. You do not need to pillow her, if that concerns you—if you do not find her pleasing. You do not even need to be polite to her, though she merits politeness. She will serve you, as you wish, in any way you wish."

"I can treat her any way I want?"

"Yes."

"I can pillow her or not pillow her?"

"Of course. She will find someone that pleases you, to satisfy your body needs, if you wish, or she will not interfere."

"I can treat her like a servant? A slave?"

"Yes. But she merits better."

"Can I throw her out? Order her out?"

"If she offends you, yes."

"What would happen to her?"

"Normally she would go back to her parents' house in disgrace, who may or may not accept her back. Someone like Lady Fujiko would prefer to kill herself before enduring that shame. But she . . . you should know true samurai are not permitted to kill themselves without their lord's permission. Some do, of course, but they've failed in their duty and aren't worthy to be considered samurai. I would not kill myself, whatever the shame, not without Lord Toranaga's permission or my husband's permission. Lord Toranaga has forbidden her to end her life. If you send her away, she'll become an outcast."

"Why? Why won't her family accept her back?"

Mariko sighed. "So sorry, Anjin-san, but if you send her away, her disgrace will be such that no one will accept her."

"Because she's contaminated? From being near a barbarian?"

"Oh no, Anjin-san, only because she had failed in her duty to you," Mariko said at once. "She is your consort now—Lord Toranaga ordered it and she agreed. You're master of a house now."

"Am I?"

"Oh, yes, believe me, Anjin-san, you have privileges. And as a hata-moto you're blessed. And well off. Lord Toranaga's given you a salary of twenty koku a month. For that amount of money a samurai would normally have to provide his lord with himself and two other samurai, armed, fed, and mounted for the whole year, and of course pay for their families as well. But you don't have to do that. I beg you, consider Fujiko as a person, Anjin-san. I beg you to be filled with Christian charity. She's a good woman. Forgive her her ugliness. She'll be a worthy consort."

"She hasn't a home?"

"Yes. This is her home." Mariko took hold of herself. "I beg you to accept her formally. She can help you greatly, teach you if you wish to learn. If you prefer, think of her as nothing—as this wooden post or the shoji screen, or as a rock in your garden—anything you wish, but allow her to stay. If you won't have her as consort, be merciful. Accept her and then, as head of the house, according to our law, kill her."

"That's the only answer you have, isn't it? Kill!"

"No, Anjin-san. But life and death are the same thing. Who knows, perhaps you'll do Fujiko a greater service by taking her life. It's your right now before all the law. *Your* right. If you prefer to make her outcast, that too is your right."

"So I'm trapped again," Blackthorne said. "Either way she's killed. If I don't learn your language then a whole village is butchered. If I don't do whatever you want, some innocent is always killed. There's no way out."

"There's a very easy solution, Anjin-san. Die. You do not have to endure the unendurable."

"Suicide's crazy—and a mortal sin. I thought you were Christian."

"I've said I am. But for you, Anjin-san, for you there are many ways of dying honorably without suicide. You sneered at my husband for not wanting to die fighting, *neh?* That's not our custom, but apparently it's yours. So why don't you do that? You have a pistol. Kill Lord Yabu. You believe he's a monster, *neh?* Even attempt to kill him and today you'll be in heaven or hell."

He looked at her, hating her serene features, seeing her loveliness through his hate. "It's weak to die like that for no reason. Stupid's a better word."

"You say you're Christian. So you believe in the Jesus child—in God —and in heaven. Death shouldn't frighten you. As to 'no reason,' it is up to you to judge the value or nonvalue. You may have reason enough to die."

"I'm in your power. You know it. So do I."

Mariko leaned over and touched him compassionately. "Anjin-san, forget the village. A thousand million things can happen before those six months occur. A tidal wave or earthquake, or you get your ship and sail away, or Yabu dies, or we all die, or who knows? Leave the problems of God to God and *karma* to *karma*. Today you're here and nothing you can do will change that. Today you're alive and here and honored, and blessed with good fortune. Look at this sunset, it's beautiful, *neh?* This sunset exists. Tomorrow does not exist. There is only *now*. Please look. It is so beautiful and it will never happen ever again, never, not *this* sunset, never in all infinity. Lose yourself in it, make yourself one with nature and do not worry about *karma,* yours, mine, or that of the village."

He found himself beguiled by her serenity, and by her words. He looked westward. Great splashes of purple-red and black were spreading across the sky.

He watched the sun until it vanished.

"I wish you were to be consort," he said.

"I belong to Lord Buntaro and until he is dead I cannot think or say what might be thought or said."

Karma, thought Blackthorne.

Do I accept *karma?* Mine? Hers? Theirs?

The night's beautiful.

And so is she and she belongs to another.

Yes, she's beautiful. And very wise: Leave the problems of God to God and *karma* to *karma*. You did come here uninvited. You are here. You are in their power.

But what's the answer?

The answer will come, he told himself. Because there's a God in heaven, a God somewhere.

He heard the tread of feet. Some flares were approaching up the hill. Twenty samurai, Omi at their head.

"I'm sorry, Anjin-san, but Omi-san orders you to give him your pistols."

"Tell him to go to hell!"

"I can't, Anjin-san. I dare not."

Blackthorne kept one hand loosely on the pistol hilt, his eyes on Omi. He had deliberately remained seated on the veranda steps. Ten samurai were within the garden behind Omi, the rest near the waiting palanquin. As soon as Omi had entered uninvited, Fujiko had come from the interior of the house and now stood on the veranda, white-faced, behind

Blackthorne. "Lord Toranaga never objected and for days I've been armed around him and Yabu-san."

Mariko said nervously, "Yes, Anjin-san, but please understand, what Omi-san says is true. It's our custom that you cannot go into a *daimyo's* presence with arms. There's nothing to be af—nothing to concern you. Yabu-san's your friend. You're his guest here."

"Tell Omi-san I won't give him my guns." Then, when she remained silent, Blackthorne's temper snapped and he shook his head. "*Iyé*, Omi-san! *Wakarimasu ka? Iyé!*"

Omi's face tightened. He snarled an order. Two samurai moved forward. Blackthorne whipped out the guns. The samurai stopped. Both guns were pointed directly into Omi's face.

"*Iyé!*" Blackthorne said. And then, to Mariko, "Tell him to call them off or I'll pull the triggers."

She did so. No one moved. Blackthorne got slowly to his feet, the pistols never wavering from their target. Omi was absolutely still, fearless, his eyes following Blackthorne's catlike movements.

"Please, Anjin-san. This is very dangerous. You must see Lord Yabu. You may not go with pistols. You're hatamoto, you're protected and you're also Lord Yabu's guest."

"Tell Omi-san if he or any of his men come within ten feet of me I'll blow his head off."

"Omi-san says politely, 'For the last time you are ordered to give me the guns. Now.'"

"*Iyé.*"

"Why not leave them here, Anjin-san? There's nothing to fear. No one will touch—"

"You think I'm a fool?"

"Then give them to Fujiko-san!"

"What can she do? He'll take them from her—anyone'll take them—then I'm defenseless."

Mariko's voice sharpened. "Why don't you listen, Anjin-san? Fujiko-san is your consort. If you order it she'll protect the guns with her life. That's her duty. I'll never tell you again, but Toda-noh-Usagi Fujiko is samurai."

Blackthorne was concentrating on Omi, hardly listening to her. "Tell Omi-san I don't like orders. I'm Lord Toranaga's guest. I'm Lord Yabu's guest. You 'ask' guests to do things. You don't order them, and you don't march into a man's house uninvited."

Mariko translated this. Omi listened expressionlessly, then replied shortly, watching the unwavering barrels.

"He says, 'I, Kasigi Omi, I would ask for your pistols, and ask you to come with me because Kasigi Yabu-sama orders you into his presence. But Kasigi Yabu-sama orders me to order you to give me your weapons. So sorry, Anjin-san, for the last time I order you to give them to me.'"

Blackthorne's chest was constricted. He knew he was going to be attacked and he was furious at his own stupidity. But there comes a time when you can't take any more and you pull a gun or a knife and then blood is spilled through stupid pride. Most times stupid. If I'm to die Omi will die first, by God!

He felt very strong though somewhat light-headed. Then what Mariko said began to ring in his ears: 'Fujiko's samurai, she is your consort!' And his brain began to function. "Just a moment! Mariko-san, please say this to Fujiko-san. Exactly: 'I'm going to give you my pistols. You are to guard them. No one except me is to touch them.'"

Mariko did as he asked, and behind him, he heard Fujiko say, *"Hai."*

"Wakarimasu ka, Fujiko-san?" he asked her.

"Wakarimasu, Anjin-san," she replied in a thin, nervous voice.

"Mariko-san, please tell Omi-san I'll go with him now. I'm sorry there's been a misunderstanding. Yes, I'm sorry there was a misunderstanding."

Blackthorne backed away, then turned. Fujiko accepted the guns, perspiration beading her forehead. He faced Omi and prayed he was right. "Shall we go now?"

Omi spoke to Fujiko and held out his hand. She shook her head. He gave a short order. The two samurai started toward her. Immediately she shoved one pistol into the sash of her obi, held the other with both hands at arm's length and leveled it at Omi. The trigger came back slightly and the striking lever moved. *"Ugoku na!"* she said. *"Dozo!"*

The samurai obeyed. They stopped.

Omi spoke rapidly and angrily and she listened and when she replied her voice was soft and polite but the pistol never moved from his face, the lever half-cocked now, and she ended, *"Iyé, gomen nasai,* Omi-san!" No, I'm sorry, Omi-san.

Blackthorne waited.

A samurai moved a fraction. The lever came back dangerously, almost to the top of its arc. But her arm remained steady.

"Ugoku na!" she ordered.

No one doubted that she would pull the trigger. Not even Blackthorne. Omi said something curtly to her and to his men. They came back. She lowered the pistol but it was still ready.

"What did he say?" Blackthorne asked.

"Only that he would report this incident to Yabu-san."

"Good. Tell him I will do the same." Blackthorne turned to her. "*Domo,* Fujiko-san." Then, remembering the way Toranaga and Yabu talked to women, he grunted imperiously at Mariko. "Come on, Mariko-san . . . *ikamasho!*" He started for the gate.

"Anjin-san!" Fujiko called out.

"*Hai?*" Blackthorne stopped. Fujiko was bowing to him and spoke quickly to Mariko.

Mariko's eyes widened, then she nodded and replied, and spoke to Omi, who also nodded, clearly enraged but restraining himself.

"What's going on?"

"Please be patient, Anjin-san."

Fujiko called out, and there was an answer from within the house. A maid came onto the veranda. In her hands were two swords. Samurai swords.

Fujiko took them reverently, offered them to Blackthorne with a bow, speaking softly.

Mariko said, "Your consort rightly points out that a hatamoto is, of course, obliged to wear the two swords of the samurai. More than that, it's his duty to do so. She believes it would not be correct for you to go to Lord Yabu without swords—that it would be impolite. By our law it's *duty* to carry swords. She asks if you would consider using these, unworthy though they are, until you buy your own."

Blackthorne stared at her, then at Fujiko and back to her again. "Does that mean I'm samurai? That Lord Toranaga made me samurai?"

"I don't know, Anjin-san. But there's never been a hatamoto who wasn't samurai. Never." Mariko turned and questioned Omi. Impatiently he shook his head and answered. "Omi-san doesn't know either. Certainly it's the special privilege of a hatamoto to wear swords at all times, even in the presence of Lord Toranaga. It is his duty because he's a completely trustworthy bodyguard. Also only a hatamoto has the right of immediate audience with a lord."

Blackthorne took the short sword and stuck it in his belt, then the other, the long one, the killing one, exactly as Omi was wearing his. Armed, he did feel better. "*Arigato goziemashita,* Fujiko-san," he said quietly.

She lowered her eyes and replied softly. Mariko translated.

"Fujiko-san says, with permission, Lord, because you must learn our language correctly and quickly, she humbly wishes to point out that '*domo*' is more than sufficient for a man to say. '*Arigato,*' with or without '*goziemashita,*' is an unnecessary politeness, an expression that only women use."

"*Hai. Domo. Wakarimasu,* Fujiko-san." Blackthorne looked at her clearly for the first time with his newfound knowledge. He saw the sweat on her forehead and the sheen on her hands. The narrow eyes and square face and ferret teeth. "Please tell my consort, in this one case I do not consider '*arigato goziemashita*' an unnecessary politeness to her."

Yabu glanced at the swords again. Blackthorne was sitting cross-legged on a cushion in front of him in the place of honor, Mariko to one side, Igurashi beside him. They were in the main room of the fortress.

Omi finished talking.

Yabu shrugged. "You handled it badly, nephew. Of course it's the consort's duty to protect the Anjin-san and his property. Of course he has the right to wear swords now. Yes, you handled it badly. I made it clear the Anjin-san's my honored guest here. Apologize to him."

Immediately Omi got up and knelt in front of Blackthorne and bowed. "I apologize for my error, Anjin-san." He heard Mariko say that the barbarian accepted the apology. He bowed again and calmly went back to his place and sat down again. But he was not calm inside. He was now totally consumed by one idea: the killing of Yabu.

He had decided to do the unthinkable: kill his liege Lord and the head of his clan.

But not because he had been made to apologize publicly to the barbarian. In this Yabu had been right. Omi knew he had been unnecessarily inept, for although Yabu had stupidly ordered him to take the pistols away at once tonight, he knew they should have been manipulated away and left in the house, to be stolen later or broken later.

And the Anjin-san had been perfectly correct to give the pistols to his consort, he told himself, just as she was equally correct to do what she did. And she would certainly have pulled the trigger, her aim true. It was no secret that Usagi Fujiko sought death, or why. Omi knew, too, that if it hadn't been for his earlier decision this morning to kill Yabu, he would have stepped forward into death and then his men would have taken the pistols away from her. He would have died nobly as she would be ordered into death nobly and men and women would have told the tragic tale for generations. Songs and poems and even a Nōh play, all so inspiring and tragic and brave, about the three of them: the faithful consort and faithful samurai who both died dutifully because of the incredible barbarian who came from the eastern sea.

No, Omi's decision had nothing to do with this public apology, although the unfairness added to the hatred that now obsessed him. The main reason was that today Yabu had publicly insulted Omi's mother and wife in front of peasants by keeping them waiting for hours in the sun like peasants, and had then dismissed them without acknowledgment like peasants.

"It doesn't matter, my son," his mother had said. "It's his privilege."

"He's our liege Lord," Midori, his wife, had said, the tears of shame running down her cheeks. "Please excuse him."

"And he didn't invite either of you to greet him and his officers at the fortress," Omi had continued. "At the meal you arranged! The food and saké alone cost one koku!"

"It's our duty, my son. It's our duty to do whatever Lord Yabu wants."

"And the order about Father?"

"It's not an order yet. It's a rumor."

"The message from Father said he'd heard that Yabu's going to order him to shave his head and become a priest, or slit his belly open. Yabu's wife privately boasts it!"

"That was whispered to your father by a spy. You cannot always trust spies. So sorry, but your father, my son, isn't always wise."

"What happens to you, Mother, if it isn't a rumor?"

"Whatever happens is *karma*. You must accept *karma*."

"No, these insults are unendurable."

"Please, my son, accept them."

"I gave Yabu the key to the ship, the key to the Anjin-san and the new barbarians, and the way out of Toranaga's trap. My help has brought him immense prestige. With the symbolic gift of the sword he's now second to Toranaga in the armies of the East. And what have we got in return? Filthy insults."

"Accept your *karma*."

"You must, husband, I beg you, listen to the Lady, your mother."

"I can't live with this shame. I will have vengeance and then I will kill myself and these shames will pass from me."

"For the last time, my son, accept your *karma*, I beg you."

"My *karma* is to destroy Yabu."

The old lady had sighed. "Very well. You're a man. You have the right to decide. What is to be is to be. But the killing of Yabu by itself is nothing. We must plan. His son must also be removed, and also Igurashi. Particularly Igurashi. Then your father will lead the clan as is his right."

"How do we do that, Mother?"

"We will plan, you and I. And be patient, *neh?* Then we must consult with your father. Midori, even you may give counsel, but try not to make it valueless, *neh?*"

"What about Lord Toranaga? He gave Yabu his sword."

"I think Lord Toranaga only wants Izu strong and a *vassal* state. Not as an ally. He doesn't want allies any more than the Taikō did. Yabu thinks he's an ally. I think Toranaga detests allies. Our clan will prosper as Toranaga vassals. *Or as Ishido vassals!* Who to choose, eh? And how to do the killing?"

Omi remembered the surge of joy that had possessed him once the decision had been made final.

He felt it now. But none of it showed on his face as cha and wine were offered by carefully selected maids imported from Mishima for Yabu. He watched Yabu and the Anjin-san and Mariko and Igurashi. They were all waiting for Yabu to begin.

The room was large and airy, big enough for thirty officers to dine and wine and talk. There were many other rooms and kitchens for bodyguards and servants, and a skirting garden, and though all were makeshift and temporary, they had been excellently constructed in the time at his disposal and easily defendable. That the cost had come out of Omi's increased fief bothered him not at all. This had been his duty.

He looked through the open shoji. Many sentries in the forecourt. A stable. The fortress was guarded by a ditch. The stockade was constructed of giant bamboos lashed tightly. Big central pillars supported the tiled roof. Walls were light sliding shoji screens, some shuttered, most of them covered with oiled paper as was usual. Good planks for the flooring were set on pilings raised off beaten earth below and these were covered with tatamis.

At Yabu's command, Omi had ransacked four villages for materials to construct this and the other house and Igurashi had brought quality tatamis and futons and things unobtainable in the village.

Omi was proud of his work, and the bivouac camp for three thousand samurai had been made ready on the plateau over the hill that guarded the roads that led to the village and to the shore. Now the village was locked tight and safe by land. From the sea there would always be plenty of warning for a liege lord to escape.

But I have no liege lord. Whom shall I serve now, Omi was asking himself. Ikawa Jukkyu? Or Toranaga directly? Would Toranaga give me what I want in return? Or Ishido? Ishido's so difficult to get to, *neh?* But much to tell him now. . . .

This afternoon Yabu had summoned Igurashi, Omi, and the four chief captains and had set into motion his clandestine training plan for the five hundred gun-samurai. Igurashi was to be commander, Omi was to lead one of the hundreds. They had arranged how to induct Toranaga's men into the units when they arrived, and how these outlanders were to be neutralized if they proved treacherous.

Omi had suggested that another highly secret cadre of three more units of one hundred samurai each should be trained surreptitiously on the other side of the peninsula as replacements, as a reserve, and as a precaution against a treacherous move by Toranaga.

"Who'll command Toranaga's men? Who'll he send as second in command?" Igurashi had asked.

"It makes no difference," Yabu had said. "I'll appoint his five assistant officers who'll be given the responsibility of slitting his throat, should it be necessary. The code for killing him and all the outlanders will be 'Plum Tree.' Tomorrow, Igurashi-san, you will choose the men. I will approve each personally and none of them is to know, yet, my overall strategy of the musket regiment."

Now as Omi was watching Yabu, he savored the newfound ecstasy of vengeance. To kill Yabu would be easy, but the killing must be coordinated. Only then would his father or his elder brother be able to assume control of the clan, and Izu.

Yabu came to the point. "Mariko-san, please tell the Anjin-san, tomorrow I want him to start training my men to shoot like barbarians and I want to learn everything there is to know about the way that barbarians war."

"But, so sorry, the guns won't arrive for six days, Yabu-san," Mariko reminded him.

"I've enough among my men to begin with," Yabu replied. "I want him to start tomorrow."

Mariko spoke to Blackthorne.

"What does he want to know about war?" he asked.

"He said everything."

"What particularly?"

Mariko asked Yabu.

"Yabu-san says, have you been part of any battles on land?"

"Yes. In the Netherlands. One in France."

"Yabu-san says, excellent. He wants to know European strategy. He wants to know how battles are fought in your lands. In detail."

Blackthorne thought a moment. Then he said, "Tell Yabu-san I can train any number of men for him and I know exactly what he wants to know." He had learned a great deal about the way the Japanese warred from Friar Domingo. The friar had been an expert and vitally concerned. 'After all, señor,' the old man had said, 'that knowledge is essential, isn't it—to know how the heathen war? Every Father must protect his flock.

And are not our glorious conquistadores the blessed spearhead of Mother Church? And haven't I been with them in the front of the fighting in the New World and the Philippines and studied them for more than twenty years? I know war, señor, I *know* war. It has been my duty —God's will to know war. Perhaps God has sent you to me to teach you, in case I die. Listen, my flock here in this jail have been my teachers about Japan warfare, señor. So now I know how their armies fight and how to beat them. How they could beat us. Remember, señor, I tell thee a secret on thy soul: Never join Japanese ferocity with modern weapons and modern methods. Or on land they will destroy us.'

Blackthorne committed himself to God. And began. "Tell Lord Yabu I can help him very much. And Lord Toranaga. I can make their armies unbeatable."

"Lord Yabu says, if your information proves useful, Anjin-san, he will increase your salary from Lord Toranaga's two hundred and forty koku to five hundred koku after one month."

"Thank him. But say, if I do all that for him, I request a favor in return: I want him to rescind his decree about the village and I want my ship and crew back in five months."

Mariko said, "Anjin-san, you cannot bargain with him, like a trader."

"Please ask him. As a humble favor. From an honored guest and grateful vassal-to-be."

Yabu frowned and replied at length.

"Yabu-san says that the village is unimportant. The villagers need a fire under their rumps to make them do anything. You are not to concern yourself with them. As to the ship, it's in Lord Toranaga's care. He's sure you'll get it back soon. He asked me to put your request to Lord Toranaga the moment I arrive in Yedo. I'll do this, Anjin-san."

"Please apologize to Lord Yabu, but I must ask him to rescind the decree. Tonight."

"He's just said no, Anjin-san. It would not be good manners."

"Yes, I understand. But please ask him again. It's very important to me . . . a petition."

"He says you must be patient. Don't concern yourself with villagers."

Blackthorne nodded. Then he decided. "Thank you. I understand. Yes. Please thank Yabu-san but tell him I cannot live with this shame."

Mariko blanched. "What?"

"I cannot live with the shame of having the village on my conscience. I'm dishonored. I cannot endure this. It's against my Christian belief. I will have to commit suicide at once."

"Suicide?"

"Yes. That's what I've decided to do."

Yabu interrupted. *"Nan ja,* Mariko-san?"

Haltingly she translated what Blackthorne had said. Yabu questioned her and she answered. Then Yabu said, "If it wasn't for your reaction this would be a joke, Mariko-san. Why are you so concerned? Why do you think he means it?"

"I don't know, Sire. He seems . . . I don't know. . . ." Her voice trailed off.

"Omi-san?"

"Suicide's against all Christian beliefs, Sire. They never suicide as we do. As a samurai would."

"Mariko-san, you're Christian. Is that true?"

"Yes, Sire. Suicide's a mortal sin, against the word of God."

"Igurashi-san? What do you think?"

"It's a bluff. He's no Christian. Remember the first day, Sire? Remember what he did to the priest? And what he allowed Omi-san to do to him to save the boy?"

Yabu smiled, recollecting that day and the night that had followed. "Yes. I agree. He's no Christian, Mariko-san."

"So sorry, but I don't understand, Sire. What about the priest?"

Yabu told her what had happened the first day between Blackthorne and the priest.

"He desecrated a cross?" she said, openly shocked.

"And threw the pieces into the dust," Igurashi added. "It's all a bluff, Sire. If this thing with the village dishonors him, how can he stay here when Omi-san so dishonored him by pissing on him?"

"What? I'm sorry, Sire," Mariko said, "but again I don't understand."

Yabu said to Omi, "Explain that to her."

Omi obeyed. She was disgusted by what he told her but kept it off her face.

"Afterwards the Anjin-san was completely cowed, Mariko-san." Omi finished, "Without weapons he'll always be cowed."

Yabu sipped some saké. "Say this to him, Mariko-san: suicide's not a barbarian custom. It's against his Christian God. So how can he suicide?"

Mariko translated. Yabu was watching carefully as Blackthorne replied.

"The Anjin-san apologizes with great humility, but he says, custom or not, God or not, this shame of the village is too great to bear. He says that . . . that he's in Japan, he's hatamoto and has the right to live according to our laws." Her hands were trembling. "That's what he said, Yabu-san. The right to live according to our customs—our law."

"Barbarians have no rights."

She said, "Lord Toranaga made him hatamoto. That gives him the right, *neh?*"

A breeze touched the shoji, rattling them.

"How could he commit suicide? Eh? Ask him."

Blackthorne took out the short, needle-sharp sword and placed it gently on the tatami, point facing him.

Igurashi said simply, "It's a bluff! Who ever heard of a barbarian acting like a civilized person?"

Yabu frowned, his heartbeat slowed by the excitement. "He's a brave man, Igurashi-san. No doubt about that. And strange. But this?" Yabu wanted to see the act, to witness the barbarian's measure, to see how he went into death, to experience with him the ecstasy of the going. With an effort he stopped the rising tide of his own pleasure. "What's your counsel, Omi-san?" he asked throatily.

"You said to the village, Sire, 'If the Anjin-san did not learn *satisfactorily.*' I counsel you to make a slight concession. Say to him that whatever he learns within the five months will be 'satisfactory,' but he must, in return, swear by his God never to reveal this to the village."

"But he's not Christian. How will that oath bind him?"

"I believe he's a type of Christian, Sire. He's against the Black Robes and that's what is important. I believe swearing by his own God will be binding. And he should also swear, in this God's name, that he'll apply his mind totally to learning and totally to your service. Because he's clever he will have learned very much in five months. Thus, your honor is saved, his—if it exists or not—is also saved. You lose nothing, gain everything. Very important, you gain his allegiance of his own free will."

"You believe he'll kill himself?"

"Yes."

"Mariko-san?"

"I don't know, Yabu-san. I'm sorry, I cannot advise you. A few hours ago I would have said, no, he will not commit suicide. Now I don't know. He's . . . since Omi-san came for him tonight, he's been . . . different."

"Igurashi-san?"

"If you give in to him now and it's bluff he'll use the same trick all the time. He's cunning as a fox-*kami*—we've all seen how cunning, *neh?* You'll have to say 'no' one day, Sire. I counsel you to say it now—it's a bluff."

Omi leaned forward and shook his head. "Sire, please excuse me, but I must repeat, if you say no you risk a great loss. If it is a bluff—and it may well be—then as a proud man he will become hate-filled at his further humiliation and he won't help you to the limit of his being, which you need. He's asked for something as a hatamoto which he's entitled to, he says he wants to live according to our customs of his own free will. Isn't that an enormous step forward, Sire? That's marvelous for you, and for him. I counsel caution. Use him to your advantage."

"I intend to," Yabu said thickly.

Igurashi said, "Yes, he's valuable and yes, I want his knowledge. But he's got to be controlled—you've said that many times, Omi-san. He's barbarian. That's all he is. Oh, I know he's hatamoto today and yes, he can wear the two swords from today. But that doesn't make him samurai. He's not samurai and never will be."

Mariko knew that of all of them she should be able to read the Anjin-san the most clearly. But she could not. One moment she understood him, the next, he was incomprehensible again. One moment she liked him, the next she hated him. Why?

Blackthorne's haunted eyes looked into the distance. But now there were beads of sweat on his forehead. Is that from fear? thought Yabu. Fear that the bluff will be called? Is he bluffing?

"Mariko-san?"

"Yes, Lord?"

"Tell him . . ." Yabu's mouth was suddenly dry, his chest aching. "Tell the Anjin-san the sentence stays."

"Sire, please excuse me, but I urge you to accept Omi-san's advice."

Yabu did not look at her, only at Blackthorne. The vein in his forehead pulsed. "The Anjin-san says he's decided. So be it. Let's see if he's barbarian—or hatamoto."

Mariko's voice was almost imperceptible. "Anjin-san, Yabu-san says the sentence stays. I'm sorry."

Blackthorne heard the words but they did not disturb him. He felt stronger and more at peace than he had ever been, with a greater awareness of life than he had ever had.

While he was waiting he had not been listening to them or watching them. The commitment had been made. The rest he had left to God. He had been locked in his own head, hearing the same words over and over, the same that had given him the clue to life here, the words that surely had been sent from God, through Mariko as medium: 'There is an easy solution—die. To survive here you must live according to our customs. . . .'

". . . the sentence stays."

So now I must die.

I should be afraid. But I'm not.

Why?

I don't know. I know only that once I truly decided that the sole way to live here as a man is to do so according to their customs, to risk death, to die—perhaps to die—that suddenly the fear of death was gone. 'Life and death are the same . . . Leave *karma* to *karma*.'

I am not afraid to die.

Beyond the shoji, a gentle rain had begun to fall. He looked down at the knife.

I've had a good life, he thought.

His eyes came back to Yabu. *"Wakarimasu,"* he said clearly and though he knew his lips had formed the word it was as though someone else had spoken.

No one moved.

He watched his right hand pick up the knife. Then his left also grasped the hilt, the blade steady and pointing at his heart. Now there was only the sound of his life, building and building, soaring louder and louder until he could listen no more. His soul cried out for eternal silence.

The cry triggered his reflexes. His hands drove the knife unerringly toward its target.

Omi had been ready to stop him but he was unprepared for the suddenness and ferocity of Blackthorne's thrust, and as Omi's left hand caught the blade and his right the haft, pain bit into him and blood spilled from his left hand. He fought the power of the thrust with all his strength. He was losing. Then Igurashi helped. Together they halted the blow. The knife was taken away. A thin trickle of blood ran from the skin over Blackthorne's heart where the point of the knife had entered.

Mariko and Yabu had not moved.

Yabu said, "Say to him, say to him whatever he learns is enough, Mariko-san. Order him—no, ask him, ask the Anjin-san to swear as Omi-san said. Everything as Omi-san said."

Blackthorne came back from death slowly. He stared at them and the knife from an immense distance, without understanding. Then the torrent of his life rushed back but he could not grasp its significance, believing himself dead and not alive.

"Anjin-san? Anjin-san?"

He saw her lips move and heard her words but all his senses were concentrated on the rain and the breeze.

"Yes?" His own voice was still far off but he smelt the rain and heard the droplets and tasted the sea salt upon the air.

I'm alive, he told himself in wonder. I'm alive and that's real rain outside and the wind's real and from the north. There's a real brazier with real coals and if I pick up the cup it will have real liquid in it and it will have taste. I'm not dead. I'm alive!

The others sat in silence, waiting patiently, gentle with him to honor his bravery. No man in Japan had ever seen what they had seen. Each was asking silently, what's the Anjin-san going to do now? Will he be able to stand by himself and walk away or will his spirit leave him? How would I act if I were he?

Silently a servant brought a bandage and bound Omi's hand where the blade had cut deeply, staunching the flow of blood. Everything was very still. From time to time Mariko would say his name quietly as they sipped cha or saké, but very sparingly, savoring the waiting, the watching, and the remembering.

For Blackthorne this no life seemed to last forever. Then his eyes saw. His ears heard.

"Anjin-san?"

"*Hai?*" he answered through the greatest weariness he had ever known.

Mariko repeated what Omi had said as though it came from Yabu. She had to say it several times before she was sure that he understood clearly.

Blackthorne collected the last of his strength, victory sweet to him. "My word is enough, as his is enough. Even so, I'll swear by God as he wants. Yes. As Yabu-san will swear by his god in equal honor to keep his side of the bargain."

"Lord Yabu says yes, he swears the Lord Buddha."

So Blackthorne swore as Yabu wished him to swear. He accepted some cha. Never had it tasted so good. The cup seemed very heavy and he could not hold it for long.

"The rain is fine, isn't it?" he said, watching the raindrops breaking and vanishing, astonished by the untoward clarity of his vision.

"Yes," she told him gently, knowing that his senses were on a plane never to be reached by one who had not gone freely out to meet death, and, through an unknowing *karma,* miraculously come back again.

"Why not rest now, Anjin-san? Lord Yabu thanks you and says he will talk more with you tomorrow. You should rest now."

"Yes. Thank you. That would be fine."

"Do you think you can stand?"

"Yes. I think so."

"Yabu-san asks if you would like a palanquin?"

Blackthorne thought about that. At length he decided that a samurai would walk—would try to walk.

"No, thank you," he said, as much as he would have liked to lie down, to be carried back, to close his eyes and to sleep instantly. At the same time he knew he would be afraid to sleep yet, in case this was the dream of after-death and the knife not there on the futon but still buried in the real him, and this hell, or the beginning of hell.

Slowly he took up the knife and studied it, glorying in the *real* feel. Then he put it in its scabbard, everything taking so much time.

"Sorry I'm so slow," he murmured.

"You mustn't be sorry, Anjin-san. Tonight you're reborn. This is another life, a new life," Mariko said proudly, filled with honor for him. "It's given to few to return. Do not be sorry. We know it takes great fortitude. Most men do not have enough strength left afterwards even to stand. May I help you?"

"No. No, thank you."

"It is no dishonor to be helped. I would be honored to be allowed to help you."

"Thank you. But I—I wish to try. First."

But he could not stand at once. He had to use his hands to get to his knees and then he had to pause to get more strength. Later he lurched up and almost fell. He swayed but did not fall.

Yabu bowed. And Mariko, Omi, and Igurashi.

Blackthorne walked like a drunk for the first few paces. He clutched a pillar and held on for a moment. Then he began again. He faltered, but he was walking away, alone. As a man. He kept one hand on the long sword in his belt and his head was high.

Yabu exhaled and drank deeply of the saké. When he could speak he said to Mariko, "Please follow him. See that he gets home safely."

"Yes, Sire."

When she had gone, Yabu turned on Igurashi. "You—manure-pile-fool!"

Instantly Igurashi bowed his head to the mat in penitence.

"Bluff you said, *neh*? Your stupidity almost cost me a priceless treasure."

"Yes, Sire, you're right, Sire. I beg leave to end my life at once."

"That would be too good for you! Go and live in the stables until I send for you! Sleep with the stupid horses. You're a horse-headed fool!"

"Yes, Sire. I apologize, Sire."

"Get out! Omi-san will command the guns now. Get out!"

The candles flickered and spluttered. One of the maids spilled the tiniest drop of saké on the small lacquered table in front of Yabu and he cursed her eloquently. The others apologized at once. He allowed them to placate him, and accepted more wine. "Bluff? Bluff, he said. Fool! Why do I have fools around me?"

Omi said nothing, screaming with laughter inside.

"But you're no fool, Omi-san. Your counsel's valuable. Your fief's doubled from today. Six thousand koku. For next year. Take thirty *ri* around Anjiro as your fief."

Omi bowed to the futon. Yabu deserves to die, he thought scornfully, he's so easy to manipulate. "I deserve nothing, Sire. I was just doing my duty."

"Yes. But a liege lord should reward faithfulness and duty." Yabu was wearing the Yoshitomo sword tonight. It gave him great pleasure to touch it. "Suzu," he called to one of the maids. "Send Zukimoto here!"

"How soon will war begin?" Omi asked.

"This year. Maybe you have six months, perhaps not. Why?"

"Perhaps the Lady Mariko should stay more than three days. To protect you."

"Eh? Why?"

"She's the mouth of the Anjin-san. In half a month—with her—he can train twenty men who can train a hundred who can train the rest. Then whether he lives or dies doesn't matter."

"Why should he die?"

"You're going to call the Anjin-san again, his next challenge or the one after, Sire. The result may be different next time, who knows? You may want him to die." Both men knew, as Mariko and Igurashi had known, that for Yabu to swear by any god was meaningless and, of course, he had no intention of keeping any promise. "You may want to put pressure on him. Once you have the information, what good is the carcass?"

"None."

"You need to learn barbarian war strategy but you must do it very quickly. Lord Toranaga may send for him, so you must have the woman as long as you can. Half a month should be enough to squeeze his head dry of what he knows, now that you have his complete attention. You'll have to experiment, to adapt their methods to our ways. Yes, it would take at least half a month. *Neh?*"

"And Toranaga-san?"

"He will agree, if it's put correctly to him, Sire. He must. The guns are his as well as yours. And her continuing presence here is valuable in other ways."

"Yes," Yabu said with satisfaction, for the thought of holding her as hostage had also entered his mind on the ship when he had planned to offer Toranaga as a sacrifice to Ishido. "Toda Mariko should be protected, certainly. It would be bad if she fell into evil hands."

"Yes. And perhaps she could be the means of controlling Hiro-matsu, Buntaro, and all their clan, even Toranaga."

"You draft the message about her."

Omi said, offhand, "My mother heard from Yedo today, Sire. She asked me to tell you that the Lady Genjiko has presented Toranaga with his first grandson."

Yabu was at once attentive. Toranaga's grandson! Could Toranaga be controlled through this infant? The grandson assures Toranaga's dynasty, *neh*? How can I get the infant as hostage? "And Ochiba, the Lady Ochiba?" he asked.

"She's left Yedo with all her entourage. Three days ago. By now she's safe in Lord Ishido's territory."

Yabu thought about Ochiba and her sister, Genjiko. So different! Ochiba, vital, beautiful, cunning, relentless, the most desirable woman in the Empire and mother of the Heir. Genjiko, her younger sister, quiet, brooding, flat-faced and plain, with a pitilessness that was legend, even now, that had come down to her from their mother, who was one of Goroda's sisters. The two sisters loved each other, but Ochiba hated Toranaga and his brood, as Genjiko detested the Taikō and Yaemon, his son. Did the Taikō really father Ochiba's son, Yabu asked himself again, as all *daimyos* had done secretly for years. What wouldn't I give to know the answer to that. What wouldn't I give to possess that woman.

"Now that Lady Ochiba's no longer hostage in Yedo . . . that could be good and bad," Yabu said tentatively. "*Neh?*"

"Good, only good. Now Ishido and Toranaga must begin very soon." Omi deliberately omitted the "sama" from those two names. "The Lady Mariko should stay, for your protection."

"See to it. Draft the message to send to Toranaga."

Suzu, the maid, knocked discreetly and opened the door. Zukimoto came into the room. "Sire?"

"Where are all the gifts I ordered brought from Mishima for Omi-san?"

"They're all in the storehouse, Lord. Here's the list. The two horses can be selected from the stables. Do you want me to do that now?"

"No. Omi-san will choose them tomorrow." Yabu glanced at the carefully written list: "Twenty kimonos (second quality); two swords; one suit of armor (repaired but in good condition); two horses; arms for one hundred samurai—one sword, helmet, breastplate, bow, twenty arrows and spear for each man (best quality). Total value: four hun-

dred and twenty-six koku. Also the rock called 'The Waiting Stone'—
value: priceless."

"Ah yes," he said in better humor, remembering that night. "The rock
I found in Kyushu. You were going to rename it 'The Waiting Barbarian,'
weren't you?"

"Yes, Sire, if it still pleases you," Omi said. "But would you honor
me tomorrow by deciding where it should go in the garden? I don't think
there's a place good enough."

"Tomorrow I'll decide. Yes." Yabu let his mind rest on the rock, and
on those far-off days with his revered master, the Taikō, and last on the
Night of the Screams. Melancholy seeped into him. Life is so short and
sad and cruel, he thought. He eyed Suzu. The maid smiled back hesi-
tantly, oval-faced, slender, and very delicate like the other two. The
three had been brought by palanquin from his household in Mishima.
Tonight they were all barefoot, their kimonos the very best silk, their
skins very white. Curious that boys can be so graceful, he pondered,
in many ways more feminine, more sensuous than girls are. Then he
noticed Zukimoto. "What're you waiting for? Eh? Get out!"

"Yes, Sire. You asked me to remind you about taxes, Sire." Zukimoto
heaved up his sweating bulk and gratefully hurried away.

"Omi-san, you will double all taxes at once," Yabu said.

"Yes, Sire."

"Filthy peasants! They don't work hard enough. They're lazy—all of
them! I keep the roads safe from bandits, the seas safe, give them good
government, and what do they do? They spend the days drinking cha
and saké and eating rice. It's time my peasants lived up to their respon-
siblity!"

"Yes, Sire," Omi said.

Next, Yabu turned to the subject that possessed his mind. "The
Anjin-san astonished me tonight. But not you?"

"Oh yes he did, Sire. More than you. But you were wise to make him
commit himself."

"You say Igurashi was right?"

"I merely admired your wisdom, Sire. You would have had to say
'no' to him some time. I think you were very wise to say it now, tonight."

"I thought he'd killed himself. Yes. I'm glad you were ready. I
planned on you being ready. The Anjin-san's an extraordinary man, for
a barbarian, neh? A pity he's barbarian and so naïve."

"Yes."

Yabu yawned. He accepted saké from Suzu. "Half a month, you say?
Mariko-san should stay at least that, Omi-san. Then I'll decide about

her, and about him. He'll need to be taught another lesson soon." He laughed, showing his bad teeth. "If the Anjin-san teaches us, we should teach him, *neh?* He should be taught how to commit seppuku correctly. That'd be something to watch, *neh?* See to it! Yes, I agree the barbarian's days are numbered."

CHAPTER 32

TWELVE days later, in the afternoon, the courier from Osaka arrived. An escort of ten samurai rode in with him. Their horses were lathered and near death. The flags at their spearheads carried the cipher of the all-powerful Council of Regents. It was hot, overcast, and humid.

The courier was a lean, hard samurai of senior rank, one of Ishido's chief lieutenants. His name was Nebara Jozen and he was known for his ruthlessness. His Gray uniform kimono was tattered and mud-stained, his eyes red with fatigue. He refused food or drink and impolitely demanded an immediate audience with Yabu.

"Forgive my appearance, Yabu-san, but my business is urgent," he said. "Yes, I ask your pardon. My Master says first, why do you train Toranaga's soldiers along with your own and, second, why do they drill with so many guns?"

Yabu had flushed at the rudeness but he kept his temper, knowing that Jozen would have had specific instructions and that such lack of manners bespoke an untoward position of power. And too, he was greatly unsettled that there had been another leak in his security.

"You're very welcome, Jozen-san. You may assure your master that I always have his interests at heart," he said with a courteousness that fooled no one present.

They were on the veranda of the fortress. Omi sat just behind Yabu. Igurashi, who had been forgiven a few days before, was nearer to Jozen and surrounding them were intimate guards. "What else does your master say?"

Jozen replied, "My Master will be glad that your interests are his. Now, about the guns and the training: my Master would like to know why Toranaga's son, Naga, is second-in-command. Second-in-command of what? What's so important that a Toranaga son should be here, the Lord General Ishido asks with politeness. That's of interest to him. Yes. Everything his allies do interests him. Why is it, for instance, the barbarian seems to be in charge of training? Training of what? Yes, Yabu-sama, that's very interesting also." Jozen shifted his swords more comfortably, glad that his back was protected by his own men. "Next: The Council of Regents meets again on the first day of the new moon.

In twenty days. You are formally invited to Osaka to renew your oath of fidelity."

Yabu's stomach twisted. "I understood Toranaga-sama had resigned?"

"He has, Yabu-san, indeed he has. But Lord Ito Teruzumi's taking his place. My Master will be the new President of the Regents."

Yabu was panic-stricken. Toranaga had said that the four Regents could never agree on a fifth. Ito Teruzumi was a minor *daimyo* of Negato Province in western Honshu but his family was ancient, descended from Fujimoto lineage, so he would be acceptable as a Regent, though he was an ineffectual man, effeminate and a puppet. "I would be honored to receive their invitation," Yabu said defensively, trying to buy time to think.

"My Master thought you might wish to leave at once. Then you would be in Osaka for the formal meeting. He orders me to tell you all the *daimyos* are getting the same invitation. Now. So *all* will have an opportunity to be there in good time on the twenty-first day. A Flower-Viewing Ceremony has been authorized by His Imperial Highness, Emperor Go-Nijo, to honor the occasion." Jozen offered an official scroll.

"This isn't under the seal of the Council of Regents."

"My Master has issued the invitation now, knowing that, as a loyal vassal of the late Taikō, as a loyal vassal of Yaemon, his son and heir and the rightful ruler of the Empire when he becomes of age, you will understand that the new Council will, of course, approve his action. *Neh?*"

"It would certainly be a privilege to witness the formal meeting." Yabu struggled to control his face.

"Good," Jozen said. He pulled out another scroll, opened it, and held it up. "This is a copy of Lord Ito's letter of appointment, accepted and signed and authorized by the other Regents, Lords Ishido, Kiyama, Onoshi, and the Lord Sugiyama." Jozen did not bother to conceal a triumphant look, knowing that this totally closed the trap on Toranaga and any of his allies, and that equally the scroll made him and his men invulnerable.

Yabu took the scroll. His fingers trembled. There was no doubt of its authenticity. It had been countersigned by the Lady Yodoko, the wife of the Taikō, who affirmed that the document was true and signed in her presence, one of six copies that were being sent throughout the Empire, and that this particular copy was for the Lords of Iwari, Mikawa, Totomi, Suruga, Izu, and the Kwanto. It was dated eleven days ago.

"The Lords of Iwari, Mikawa, Suruga and Totomi have already accepted. Here are their seals. You're the last but one on my list. Last is the Lord Toranaga."

"Please thank your master and tell him I look forward to greeting him and congratulating him," Yabu said.

"Good. I'll require it in writing. Now would be satisfactory."

"This evening, Jozen-san. After the evening meal."

"Very well. And now we can go and see the training."

"There is none today. All my men are on forced marches," Yabu said. The moment Jozen and his men had entered Izu, word had been rushed to Yabu, who had at once ordered his men to cease all firing and to continue only silent weapon training well away from Anjiro. "Tomorrow you can come with me—at noon, if you wish."

Jozen looked at the sky. It was late afternoon now. "Good. I could use a little sleep. But I'll come back at dusk, with your permission. Then you and your commander, Omi-san, and the second commander, Naga-san, will tell me, for my Master's interest, about the training, the guns, and everything. And about the barbarian."

"He's—yes. Of course." Yabu motioned to Igurashi. "Arrange quarters for our honored guest and his men."

"Thank you, but that's not necessary," Jozen said at once. "The ground's futon enough for a samurai, my saddle's pillow enough. Just a bath, if you please . . . this humidity, *neh?* I'll camp on the crest—of course, with your permission."

"As you wish."

Jozen bowed stiffly and walked away, surrounded by his men. All were heavily armed. Two bowmen had been left holding their horses.

Once they were well away, Yabu's face contorted with rage. "Who betrayed me? Who? Where's the spy?"

Equally ashen, Igurashi waved the guards out of earshot. "Yedo, Sire," he said. "Must be. Security's perfect here."

"*Oh ko!*" Yabu said, almost rending his clothes. "I'm betrayed. We're isolated. Izu and the Kwanto are isolated. Ishido's won. He's won."

Omi said quickly, "Not for twenty days, Sire. Send a message at once to Lord Toranaga. Inform him that—"

"Fool!" Yabu hissed. "Of course Toranaga already knows. Where I've one spy he has fifty. He's left me in the trap."

"I don't think so, Sire," Omi said, unafraid. "Iwari, Mikawa, Totomi, and Suruga are all hostile to him, *neh?* And to anyone who's allied to him. They'd never warn him, so perhaps he doesn't know yet. Inform him and suggest—"

"Didn't you hear?" Yabu shouted. "All four Regents agree to Ito's appointment, so the Council's legal again and the Council meets in twenty days!"

"The answer to that is simple, Sire. Suggest to Toranaga that he have Ito Teruzumi or one of the other Regents assassinated at once."

Yabu's mouth dropped open. "What?"

"If you don't wish to do that, send me, let me try. Or Igurashi-san. With Lord Ito dead, Ishido's helpless again."

"I don't know whether you've gone mad, or what," Yabu said helplessly. "Do you understand what you've just said?"

"Sire, I beg you, please, to be patient with me. The Anjin-san's given you priceless knowledge, *neh?* More than we ever dreamed possible. Now Toranaga knows this also, through your reports, and probably from Naga-san's private reports. If we can win enough time, our five hundred guns and the other three hundred will give you absolute battle power, but only once. When the enemy, whoever he is, sees the way you use men and firepower they'll learn quickly. But they'll have lost that first battle. One battle—if it's the right battle—will give Toranaga total victory."

"Ishido doesn't need any battle. In twenty days he has the Emperor's mandate."

"Ishido's a peasant. He's the son of a peasant, a liar, and he runs away from his comrades in battle."

Yabu stared at Omi, his face mottled. "You—do you know what you're saying?"

"That's what he did in Korea. I was there. I saw it, my father saw it. Ishido *did* leave Buntaro-san and us to fight our own way out. He's just a treacherous peasant—the Taikō's dog, certainly. You can't trust peasants. But Toranaga's Minowara. You can trust him. I advise you to consider only Toranaga's interests."

Yabu shook his head in disbelief. "Are you deaf? Didn't you hear Nebara Jozen? Ishido's won. The Council is in power in twenty days."

"*May be* in power."

"Even if Ito. . . . How could you? It's not possible."

"Certainly I could try but I could never do it in time. None of us could, not in twenty days. But Toranaga could." Omi knew he had put himself into the jaws of the dragon. "I beg you to consider it."

Yabu wiped his face with his hands, his body wet. "After this summons, if the Council is convened and I'm not present, I and all my clan are dead, you included. I need two months, at least, to train the regiment. Even if we had them trained now, Toranaga and I could never win against all the others. No, you're wrong, I have to support Ishido."

Omi said, "You don't have to leave for Osaka for ten days—fourteen, if you go by forced march. Tell Toranaga about Nebara Jozen at once. You'll save Izu and the Kasigi house. I beg you. Ishido will betray you and eat you up. Ikawa Jikkyu is his kinsman, *neh?*"

"But what about Jozen?" Igurashi exclaimed. "Eh? And the guns? The grand strategy? He wants to know about everything tonight."

"Tell him. In detail. What is he but a lackey," Omi said, beginning to maneuver them. He knew he was risking everything, but he had to try to protect Yabu from siding with Ishido and ruining any chance they had. "Open your plans to him."

Igurashi disagreed heatedly. "The moment Jozen learns what we're doing, he'll send a message back to Lord Ishido. It's too important not to. Ishido'll steal the plans, then we're finished."

"We trail the messenger and kill him at our convenience."

Yabu flushed. "That scroll was signed by the highest authority in the land! They all travel under the Regents' protection! You must be mad to suggest such a thing! That would make me an outlaw!"

Omi shook his head, keeping confidence on his face. "I believe Yodoko-sama and the others have been duped, as His Imperial Highness has been duped, by the traitor Ishido. We must protect the guns, Sire. We must stop any messenger—"

"Silence! Your advice is madness!"

Omi bowed under the tongue-lash. But he looked up and said calmly, "Then please allow me to commit seppuku, Sire. But first, please allow me to finish. I would fail in my duty if I didn't try to protect you. I beg this last favor as a faithful vassal."

"Finish!"

"There's no Council of Regents *now,* so there is no legal protection now for that insulting, foul-mannered Jozen and his men, unless you honor an illegal document through—" Omi was going to say "weakness" but he changed the word and kept his voice quietly authoritative, "through being duped like the others, Sire. *There is no Council.* They cannot 'order' you to do anything, or anyone. Once it's convened, yes, they can, and then you will have to obey. But now, how many *daimyos* will obey before *legal* orders can be issued? Only Ishido's allies, *neh?* Aren't Iwari, Mikawa, Totomi, and Suruga all ruled by his kinsmen and allied to him openly? That document absolutely means war, yes, but I beg you to wage it on your terms and not Ishido's. Treat this threat with the contempt it deserves! Toranaga's never been beaten in battle. Ishido has. Toranaga avoided being part of the Taikō's ruinous attack on Korea. Ishido didn't. Toranaga's in favor of ships and trade. Ishido isn't. Toranaga will want the barbarian's navy—didn't you advocate it to him? Ishido won't. Ishido will close the Empire. Toranaga will keep it open. Ishido will give Ikawa Jikkyu your hereditary fief of Izu if he wins. Toranaga will give you all Jikkyu's province. You're Toranaga's chief ally. Didn't he give you his sword? Hasn't he given you control of the guns? Don't the guns guarantee one victory, *with surprise?* What does the peasant Ishido give in return? He sends a *ronin*-samurai with no manners, with deliberate orders to shame you in your own province! I say Toranaga Minowara is your only choice. You must go with him." He bowed and waited in silence.

Yabu glanced at Igurashi. "Well?"

"I agree with Omi-san, Sire." Igurashi's face mirrored his worry. "As to killing a messenger—that would be dangerous, no turning back then, Sire. Jozen will certainly send one or two tomorrow. Perhaps they could vanish, killed by bandits—" He stopped in mid-sentence. "Carrier pigeons! There were two panniers of them on Jozen's pack horses!"

"We'll have to poison them tonight," Omi said.

"How? They'll be guarded."

"I don't know. But they've got to be removed or maimed before dawn."

Yabu said, "Igurashi, send men to watch Jozen at once. See if he sends one of his pigeons now—today."

"I suggest you send all our falcons and falconers to the east, also at once," Omi added quickly.

Igurashi said, "He'll suspect treachery if he sees his bird downed, or his birds tampered with."

Omi shrugged. "It must be stopped."

Igurashi looked at Yabu.

Yabu nodded resignedly. "Do it."

When Igurashi came back he said, "Omi-san, one thing occurred to me. A lot of what you said was right, about Jikkyu and Lord Ishido. But if you advise making the messengers 'vanish,' why toy with Jozen at all? Why tell him anything? Why not just kill them all at once?"

"Why not indeed? Unless it might amuse Yabu-sama. I agree your plan's better, Igurashi-san," Omi said.

Both men were looking at Yabu now. "How can I keep the guns secret?" he asked them.

"Kill Jozen and his men," Omi replied.

"No other way?"

Omi shook his head. Igurashi shook his head.

"Maybe I could barter with Ishido," Yabu said, shaken, trying to think of a way out of the trap. "You're correct about the time. I've ten days, fourteen at the most. How to deal with Jozen and still leave time to maneuver?"

"It would be wise to pretend that you're going to Osaka," Omi said. "But there's no harm in informing Toranaga at once, *neh?* One of our pigeons could get to Yedo before dusk. Perhaps. No harm in that."

Igurashi said, "You could tell Lord Toranaga about Jozen arriving, and about the Council meeting in twenty days, yes. But the other, about assassinating Lord Ito, that's too dangerous to put in writing even if . . . Much too dangerous, *neh?*"

"I agree. Nothing about Ito. Toranaga should think of that himself. It's obvious, *neh?*"

"Yes, Sire. Unthinkable but obvious."

Omi waited in the silence, his mind frantically seeking a solution. Yabu's eyes were on him but he was not afraid. His advice had been sound and offered only for the protection of the clan and the family and Yabu, the present leader of the clan. That Omi had decided to remove Yabu and change the leadership had not prevented him from counseling Yabu sagaciously. And he was prepared to die now. If Yabu was so stupid as not to accept the obvious truth of his ideas, then there soon would be no clan to lead anyway. *Karma.*

Yabu leaned forward, still undecided. "Is there any way to remove Jozen and his men without danger to me, and stay uncommitted for ten days?"

"Naga. Somehow bait a trap with Naga," Omi said simply.

At dusk, Blackthorne and Mariko rode up to the gate of his house, outriders following. Both were tired. She rode as a man would ride, wearing loose trousers and over them a belted mantle. She had on a wide-brimmed hat and gloves to protect her from the sun. Even peasant women tried to protect their faces and their hands from the rays of the sun. From time immemorial, the darker the skin the more common the person; the whiter, the more prized.

Male servants took the halters and led the horses away. Blackthorne dismissed his outriders in tolerable Japanese and greeted Fujiko, who waited proudly on the veranda as usual.

"May I serve you cha, Anjin-san," she said ceremoniously, as usual, and "No," he said as usual. "First I will bathe. Then saké and some food." And, as usual, he returned her bow and went through the corridor to the back of the house, out into the garden, along the circling path to the mud-wattled bath house. A servant took his clothes and he went in and sat down naked. Another servant scrubbed him and soaped him and shampooed him and poured water over him to wash away the lather and the dirt. Then, completely clean, gradually—because the water was so hot—he stepped into the huge iron-sided bath and lay down.

"Christ Jesus, that's grand," he exulted, and let the heat seep into his muscles, his eyes closed, the sweat running down his forehead.

He heard the door open and Suwo's voice and "Good evening, Master," followed by many words of Japanese which he did not understand. But tonight he was too tired to try to converse with Suwo. And the bath, as Mariko had explained many times, 'is not merely for cleaning the skin. The bath is a gift to us from God or the gods, a god-bequeathed pleasure to be enjoyed and treated as such.'

"No talk, Suwo," he said. "Tonight wish think."

"Yes, Master. Your pardon, but you should say, 'Tonight I wish to think.'"

"Tonight I wish to think." Blackthorne repeated the correct Japanese, trying to get the almost incomprehensible sounds into his head, glad to be corrected but very weary of it.

"Where's the dictionary-grammar book?" he had asked Mariko first thing this morning. "Has Yabu-sama sent another request for it?"

"Yes. Please be patient, Anjin-san. It will arrive soon."

"It was promised with the galley and the troops. It didn't arrive. Troops and guns but no books. I'm lucky you're here. It'd be impossible without you."

"Difficult, but not impossible, Anjin-san."

"How do I say? 'No, you're doing it wrong! You must all run as a team, stop as a team, aim and fire as a team.'?"

"To whom are you talking, Anjin-san?" she had asked.

And then again he had felt his frustration rising. "It's all very difficult, Mariko-san."

"Oh, no, Anjin-san. Japanese is very simple to speak compared with other languages. There are no articles, no 'the' 'a' or 'an.' No verb conjugations or infinitives. All verbs are regular, ending in *masu,* and you can say almost everything by using the present tense only, if you want. For a question just add *ka* after the verb. For a negative just change *masu* to *masen.* What could be easier? *Yukimasu* means I go, but equally you he she it we they go, or will go, or even could have gone. Even plural and singular nouns are the same. *Tsuma* means wife, or wives. Very simple."

"Well, how do you tell the difference between I go, *yukimasu,* and they went, *yukimasu?*"

"By inflection, Anjin-san, and tone. Listen: *yukimasu—yukimasu.*"

"But these both sounded exactly the same."

"Ah, Anjin-san, that's because you're thinking in your own language. To understand Japanese you have to think Japanese. Don't forget our language is the language of the infinite. It's all so simple, Anjin-san. Just change your concept of the world. Japanese is just learning a new art, detached from the world. . . . It's all so simple."

"It's all shit," he had muttered in English, and felt better.

"What? What did you say?"

"Nothing. But what you say doesn't make sense."

"Learn the written characters," Mariko had said.

"I can't. It'll take too long. They're meaningless."

"Look, they're really simple pictures, Anjin-san. The Chinese are very clever. We borrowed their writing a thousand years ago. Look, take this character, or symbol, for a pig."

"It doesn't look like a pig."

"Once it did, Anjin-san. Let me show you. Here. Add a 'roof' symbol over a 'pig' symbol and what do you have?"

"A pig and a roof."

"But what does that mean? The new character?"

"I don't know."

" 'Home.' In the olden days the Chinese thought a pig under a roof was home. They're not Buddhists, they're meat eaters, so a pig to them, to peasants, represented wealth, hence a good home. Hence the character."

"But how do you say it?"

"That depends if you're Chinese or Japanese."

"*Oh ko!*"

"*Oh ko,* indeed," she had laughed. "Here's another character. A 'roof' symbol and a 'pig' symbol and a 'woman' symbol. A 'roof' with two 'pigs' under it means 'contentment.' A 'roof' with two 'women' under it equals 'discord.' *Neh?*"

"Absolutely!"

"Of course, the Chinese are very stupid in many things and their women are not trained as women are here. There's no discord in your home, is there?"

Blackthorne thought about that now, on the twelfth day of his rebirth. No. There was no discord. But neither was it a home. Fujiko was only like a trustworthy housekeeper and tonight when he went to his bed to sleep, the futons would be turned back and she would be kneeling beside them patiently, expressionlessly. She would be dressed in her sleeping kimono, which was similar to a day kimono but softer and with only a loose sash instead of a stiff obi at the waist.

"Thank you, Lady," he would say. "Good night."

She would bow and go silently to the room across the corridor, next to the one Mariko slept in. Then he would get under the fine silk mosquito net. He had never known such nets before. Then he would lie back happily, and in the night, hearing the few insects buzzing outside, he would dwell on the Black Ship, how important the Black Ship was to Japan.

Without the Portuguese, no trade with China. And no silks for clothes or for nets. Even now with the humidity only just beginning he knew their value.

If he stirred in the night a maid would open the door almost instantly to ask if there was anything he wanted. Once he had not understood. He motioned the maid away and went to the garden and sat on the steps, looking at the moon. Within a few minutes Fujiko, tousled and bleary, came and sat silently behind him.

"Can I get you anything, Lord?"

"No, thank you. Please go to bed."

She had said something he did not understand. Again he had motioned her away so she spoke sharply to the maid, who attended her like a shadow. Soon Mariko came.

"Are you all right, Anjin-san?"

"Yes. I don't know why you were disturbed. Christ Jesus—I'm just looking at the moon. I couldn't sleep. I just wanted some air."

Fujiko spoke to her haltingly, ill at ease, hurt by the irritation in his voice. "She says you told her to go back to sleep. She just wanted you to know that it's not our custom for a wife or consort to sleep while her master's awake, that's all, Anjin-san."

"Then she'll have to change her custom. I'm often up at night. By myself. It's a habit from being at sea—I sleep very lightly ashore."

"Yes, Anjin-san."

Mariko had explained and the two women had gone away. But Blackthorne knew that Fujiko had not gone back to sleep and would not, until he slept. She was always up and waiting whatever time he came back to the house. Some nights he walked the shore alone. Even though he insisted on being alone, he knew that he was followed and watched. Not because they were afraid he was trying to escape. Only because it was their custom for important people always to be attended. In Anjiro he was important.

In time he accepted her presence. It was as Mariko had first said, 'Think of her as a rock or a shoji or a wall. It is her duty to serve you.'

It was different with Mariko.

He was glad that she had stayed. Without her presence he could never have begun the training, let alone explained the intricacies of strategy.

He blessed her and Father Domingo and Alban Caradoc and his other teachers.

I never thought the battles would ever be put to good use, he thought again. Once when his ship was carrying a cargo of English wools to Antwerp, a Spanish army had swooped down upon the city and every man had gone to the barricades and to the dikes. The sneak attack had been beaten off and the Spanish infantry outgunned and outmaneuvered. That was the first time he had seen William, Duke of Orange, using regiments like chess pieces. Advancing, retreating in pretended panic to regroup again, charging back again, guns blazing in packed, gut-hurting, ear-pounding salvos, breaking through the Invincibles to leave them dying and screaming, to stench of blood and powder and urine and horses and dung filling you, and a wild frantic joy of killing possessing you and the strength of twenty in your arms.

"Christ Jesus, it's grand to be victorious," he said aloud in the tub.

"Master?" Suwo said.

"Nothing," he replied in Japanese. "I talking—I was just think—just thinking aloud."

"I understand, Master. Yes. Your pardon."

Blackthorne let himself drift away.

Mariko. Yes, she's been invaluable.

After that first night of his almost suicide, nothing had ever been said again. What was there to say?

I'm glad there's so much to do, he thought. No time to think except here in the bath for these few minutes. Never enough time to do everything. Ordered to concentrate on training and teaching and not on learning, but wanting to learn, trying to learn, needing to learn to fulfill the promise to Yabu. Never enough hours. Always exhausted and drained by bedtime, sleeping instantly, to be up at dawn and riding fast to the plateau. Training all morning, then a sparse meal, never satisfying and never meat. Then every afternoon until nightfall—sometimes till very late at night—with Yabu and Omi and Igurashi and Naga and Zukimoto and a few of the other officers, talking about war, answering questions about war. How to wage war. How barbarians war and how Japanese war. On land and at sea. Scribes always taking notes. Many, many notes.

Sometimes with Yabu alone.

But always Mariko there—part of him—talking for him. And for Yabu. Mariko different now toward him, he no longer a stranger.

Other days the scribes reading back the notes, always checking, being meticulous, revising and checking again until now, after twelve days and a hundred hours or so of detailed exhaustive explanation, a war manual was forming. Exact. And lethal.

Lethal to whom? Not to us English or Hollanders, who will come here peacefully and only as traders. Lethal to Yabu's enemies and to Toranaga's enemies, and to our Portuguese and Spanish enemies when they try to conquer Japan. Like they've done everywhere else. In every newly discovered territory. First the priests arrive. Then the conquistadores.

But not here, he thought with great contentment. Never here—now. The manual's lethal and proof against that. No conquest here, given a few years for the knowledge to spread.

"Anjin-san?"

"*Hai,* Mariko-san?"

She was bowing to him. "Yabu-*ko wa kiden no goshusseki o kon-ya wa hitsuyo to senu to oserareru,* Anjin-san."

The words formed slowly in his head: 'Lord Yabu does not require to see you tonight.'

"*Ichi-ban,*" he said blissfully. "*Domo.*"

"*Gomen nasai,* Anjin-san. *Anatawa—*"

"Yes, Mariko-san," he interrupted her, the heat of the water sapping his energy. "I know I should have said it differently but I don't want to speak any more Japanese now. Not tonight. Now I feel like a schoolboy who's been let out of school for the Christmas holiday. Do you realize these'll be the first free hours I've had since I arrived?"

"Yes, yes I do." She smiled wryly. "And do you realize, Senhor Captain-Pilot B'rack'fon, these will be the first free hours I've had since I arrived?"

He laughed. She was wearing a thick cotton bathing robe tied loosely, and a towel around her head to protect her hair. Every evening as soon as his massage began, she would take the bath, sometimes alone, sometimes with Fujiko.

"Here, you have it now," he said, beginning to get out.

"Oh, please, no, I don't wish to disturb you."

"Then share it. It's wonderful."

"Thank you. I can hardly wait to soak the sweat and dust away." She took off her robe and sat on the tiny seat. A servant began to lather her, Suwo waiting patiently near the massage table.

"It *is* rather like a school holiday," she said, as happily.

The first time Blackthorne had seen her naked on the day that they swam he had been greatly affected. Now her nakedness, of itself, did not touch him physically. Living closely in Japanese style in a Japanese house where the walls were paper and the rooms multipurpose, he had seen her unclothed and partially clothed many times. He had even seen her relieving herself.

"What's more normal, Anjin-san? Bodies are normal, and differences between men and women are normal, *neh?*"

"Yes, but it's, er, just that we're trained differently."

"But now you're here and our customs are your customs and normal is normal. *Neh?*"

Normal was urinating or defecating in the open if there were no latrines or buckets, just lifting your kimono or parting it and squatting or standing, everyone else politely waiting and not watching, rarely screens for privacy. Why should one require privacy? And soon one of the peasants would gather the feces and mix it with water to fertilize crops. Human manure and urine were the only substantial source of fertilizer in the Empire. There were few horses and bullocks, and no other animal sources at all. So every human particle was harbored and sold to the farmers throughout the land.

And after you've seen the highborn or the lowborn parting or lifting and standing or squatting, there's not much left to be embarrassed about.

"Is there, Anjin-san?"

"No."

"Good," she had said, very satisfied. "Soon you will like raw fish and fresh seaweed and then you'll really be hatamoto."

The maid poured water over her. Then, cleansed, Mariko stepped into the bath and lay down opposite him with a long-drawn sigh of ecstasy, the little crucifix dangling between her breasts.

"How do you do that?" he said.

"What?"

"Get in so quickly. It's so hot."

"I don't know, Anjin-san, but I asked them to put more firewood on and to heat up the water. For you, Fujiko always makes sure it's—we would call it tepid."

"If this is tepid, then I'm a Dutchman's uncle!"

"What?"

"Nothing."

The water's heat made them drowsy and they lolled a while, not saying a word.

Later she said, "What would you like to do this evening, Anjin-san?"

"If we were up in London we'd—" Blackthorne stopped. I won't think about them, he told himself. Or London. That's gone. That doesn't exist. Only here exists.

"If?" She was watching him, aware of the change.

"We'd go to a theater and see a play," he said, dominating himself. "Do you have plays here?"

"Oh, yes, Anjin-san. Plays are very popular with us. The Taikō liked to perform in them for the entertainment of his guests, even Lord Toranaga likes to. And of course there are many touring companies for the common people. But our plays are not quite like yours, so I believe. Here our actors and actresses wear masks. We call the plays 'Nōh.' They're part music, partially danced and mostly very sad, very tragic, historical plays. Some are comedies. Would we see a comedy, or perhaps a religious play?"

"No, we'd go to the Globe Theater and see something by a playwright called Shakespeare. I like him better than Ben Jonson or Marlowe. Perhaps we'd see *The Taming of the Shrew* or *A Midsummer Night's Dream* or *Romeo and Juliet.* I took my wife to *Romeo and Juliet* and she liked it very much." He explained the plots to her.

Mostly Mariko found them incomprehensible. "It would be unthinkable here for a girl to disobey her father like that. But so sad, *neh?* Sad for a young girl and sad for the boy. She was only thirteen? Do all your ladies marry so young?"

"No. Fifteen or sixteen's usual. My wife was seventeen when we were married. How old were you?"

"Just fifteen, Anjin-san." A shadow crossed her brow which he did not notice. "And after the play, what would we do?"

"I would take you to eat. We'd go to Stone's Chop House in Fetter Lane, or the Cheshire Cheese in Fleet Street. They are inns where the food's special."

"What would you eat?"

"I'd rather not remember," he said with a lazy smile, turning his mind back to the present. "I can't remember. Here is where we are and here is where we'll eat, and I enjoy raw fish and *karma* is *karma.*" He sank deeper into the tub. "A great word '*karma.*' And a great idea. Your help's been enormous to me, Mariko-san."

"It's my pleasure to be of a little service to you." Mariko relaxed into the warmth. "Fujiko has some special food for you tonight."

"Oh?"

"She bought a—I think you call it a pheasant. It's a large bird. One of the falconers caught it for her."

"A pheasant? You really mean it? *Honto?*"

"*Honto,*" she replied. "Fujiko asked them to hunt for you. She asked me to tell you."

"How is it being cooked?"

"One of the soldiers had seen the Portuguese preparing them and he told Fujiko-san. She asks you to be patient if it's not cooked properly."

"But how is she doing it—how're the cooks doing it?" He corrected himself, for servants alone did the cooking and cleaning.

"She was told that first someone pulls out all the feathers, then—then takes out the entrails." Mariko controlled her squeamishness. "Then the bird's either cut into small pieces and fried with oil, or boiled with salt and spices." Her nose wrinkled. "Sometimes they cover it with mud and put it into the coals of a fire and bake it. We have no ovens, Anjin-san. So it will be fried. I hope that's all right."

"I'm sure it'll be perfect," he said, certain it would be inedible.

She laughed. "You're so transparent, Anjin-san, sometimes."

"You don't understand how important food is!" In spite of himself he smiled. "You're right. I shouldn't be interested in food. But I can't control hunger."

"You'll soon be able to do that. You'll even learn how to drink cha from an empty cup."

"What?"

"This is not the place to explain that, Anjin-san, or the time. For that you must be very awake and very alert. A quiet sunset, or dawning, is necessary. I will show you how, one day, because of what you did. Oh, it is so good to lie here, isn't it? A bath is truly the gift of God."

He heard the servants outside the wall, stoking the fire. He bore the intensifying heat as long as he could, then emerged from the water, half helped by Suwo, and lay back gasping on the thick towel cloth. The old man's fingers probed. Blackthorne could have cried out with pleasure. "That's so good."

"You've changed so much in the last few days, Anjin-san."

"Have I?"

"Oh yes, since your rebirth—yes, very much."

He tried to recall the first night but could remember little. Somehow he had made it back on his own legs. Fujiko and the servants had helped him to bed. After a dreamless sleep, he woke at dawn and went for a swim. Then, drying in the sun, he had thanked God for the strength and the clue that Mariko had given him. Later, walking home, he greeted the villagers, knowing secretly that they were freed of Yabu's curse, as he was freed.

Then, when Mariko had arrived, he had sent for Mura.

"Mariko-san, please tell Mura this: 'We have a problem, you and I. We will solve it together. I want to join the village school. To learn to speak with children.'"

"They haven't a school, Anjin-san."

"None?"

"No. Mura says there's a monastery a few ri to the west and the monks could teach you reading and writing if you wish. But this is a village, Anjin-san. The children here need to learn the ways of fish, the sea, making nets, planting and growing rice and crops. There's little time for anything else, except reading and writing. And, too, parents and grandparents teach their own, as always."

"Then how can I learn when you've gone?"

"Lord Toranaga will send the books."

"I'll need more than books."

"Everything will be satisfactory, Anjin-san."

"Yes. Perhaps. But tell the headman that whenever I make a mistake, everyone—everyone, even a child—is to correct me. At once. I order it."

"He says thank you, Anjin-san."

"Does anyone here speak Portuguese?"

"He says no."

"Anyone nearby?"

"*Iyé*, Anjin-san."

"Mariko-san. I've got to have someone when you leave."

"I'll tell Yabu-san what you've said."

"Mura-san, you—"

"He says you must not use 'san' to him or to any villagers. They are beneath you. It's not correct for you to say 'san' to them or anyone beneath you."

Fujiko had also bowed to the ground that first day. "Fujiko-san welcomes you home, Anjin-san. She says you have done her great honor and she begs your forgiveness for being rude on the ship. She is honored to be consort and head of your house. She asks if you will keep the swords as it would please her greatly. They belonged to her father who is dead. She had not given them to her husband because he had swords of his own."

"Thank her and say I'm honored she's consort," he had said.

Mariko had bowed too. Formally. "You are in a new life now, Anjin-san. We look at you with new eyes. It is our custom to be formal sometimes, with great seriousness. You have opened my eyes. Very much. Once you were just a barbarian to me. Please excuse my stupidity. What you did proves you're samurai. Now you *are* samurai. Please forgive my previous bad manners."

He had felt very tall that day. But his self-inflicted near-death had changed him more than he realized and scarred him forever, more than the sum of all his other near-deaths.

Did you rely on Omi? he asked himself. That Omi would catch the blow? Didn't you give him plenty of warning?

I don't know. I only know I'm glad he *was* ready, Blackthorne answered himself truthfully. That's another life gone!

"That's my ninth life. The last!" he said aloud. Suwo's fingers ceased at once.

"What?" Mariko asked. "What did you say, Anjin-san?"

"Nothing. It was nothing," he replied, ill at ease.

"I hurt you, Master?" Suwo said.

"No."

Suwo said something more that he did not understand.

"*Dozo?*"

Mariko said distantly, "He wants to massage your back now."

Blackthorne turned on his stomach and repeated the Japanese and forgot it at once. He could see her through the steam. She was breathing deeply, her head tilted back slightly, her skin pink.

How does she stand the heat, he asked himself. Training I suppose, from childhood.

Suwo's fingers pleasured him, and he drowsed momentarily.

What was I thinking about?

You were thinking about your ninth life, your last life, and you were frightened, remembering the superstition. But it is foolish here in this Land of the Gods to be superstitious. Things are different here and this is forever. Today is forever.

Tomorrow many things can happen.

Today I'll abide by their rules.

I will.

The maid brought in the covered dish. She held it high above her head as was custom, so that her breath would not defile the food. Anxiously she knelt and placed it carefully on the tray table in front of Blackthorne. On each little table were bowls and chopsticks, saké cups and napkins, and a tiny flower arrangement. Fujiko and Mariko were sitting opposite him. They wore flowers and silver combs in their hair. Fujiko's kimono was a pale green pattern of fish on a white background, her obi gold. Mariko wore black and red with a thin silver overlay of chrysanthemums and a red and silver check obi. Both wore perfume, as always. Incense burned to keep the night bugs away.

Blackthorne had long since composed himself. He knew that any displeasure from him would destroy their evening. If pheasants could be caught there would be other game, he thought. He had a horse and guns and he could hunt himself, if only he could get the time.

Fujiko leaned over and took the lid off the dish. The small pieces of fried meat were browned and seemed perfect. He began to salivate at the aroma.

Slowly he took a piece of meat in his chopsticks, willing it not to fall, and chewed the flesh. It was tough and dry, but he had been meatless for so long it was delicious. Another piece. He sighed with pleasure. "*Ichi-ban, ichi-ban,* by God!"

Fujiko blushed and poured him saké to hide her face. Mariko fanned herself, the crimson fan a dragonfly. Blackthorne quaffed the wine and ate another piece and poured more wine and ritualistically offered his brimming cup to Fujiko. She refused, as was custom, but tonight he insisted, so she drained the cup, choking slightly. Mariko also refused and was also made to drink. Then he attacked the pheasant with as little gusto as he could manage. The women hardly touched their small portions of vegetables and fish. This didn't bother him because it was a female custom to eat before or afterward so that all their attention could be devoted to the master.

He ate all the pheasant and three bowls of rice and slurped his saké, which was also good manners. He felt replete for the first time in months. During the meal he had finished six flasks of the hot wine, Mariko and Fujiko two between them. Now they were flushed and giggling and at the silly stage.

Mariko chuckled and put her hand in front of her mouth. "I wish I could drink saké like you, Anjin-san. You drink saké better than any man I've ever known. I wager you'd be the best in Izu! I could win a lot of money on you!"

"I thought samurai disapproved of gambling."

"Oh they do, absolutely they do, they're not merchants and peasants. But not all samurai are as strong as others and many—how do you say —many'll bet like the Southern Bar—like the Portuguese bet."

"Do women bet?"

"Oh, yes. Very much. But only with other ladies and in careful amounts and always so their husbands never find out!" She gaily translated for Fujiko, who was more flushed than she.

"Your consort asks do Englishmen bet? Do you like to wager?"

"It's our national pastime." And he told them about horse racing and skittles and bull baiting and coursing and whippets and hawking and bowls and the new stock companies and letters of marque and shooting and darts and lotteries and boxing and cards and wrestling and dice and checkers and dominoes and the time at the fairs when you put farthings on numbers and bet against the wheels of chance.

"But how do you find time to live, to war, and to pillow, Fujiko asks?"

"There's always time for those." Their eyes met for a moment but he could not read anything in hers, only happiness and maybe too much wine.

Mariko begged him to sing the hornpipe song for Fujiko, and he did and they congratulated him and said it was the best they had ever heard.

"Have some more saké!"

"Oh, *you* mustn't pour, Anjin-san, that's woman's duty. Didn't I tell you?"

"Yes. Have some more, *dozo*."

"I'd better not. I think I'll fall over." Mariko fluttered her fan furiously and the draft stirred the threads of hair that had escaped from her immaculate coiffure.

"You have nice ears," he said.

"So have you. We, Fujiko-san and I, we think your nose is perfect too, worthy of a *daimyo*."

He grinned and bowed elaborately to them. They bowed back. The folds of Mariko's kimono fell away from her neck slightly, revealing the edge of her scarlet under-kimono and the swell of her breasts, and it stirred him considerably.

"Saké, Anjin-san?"

He held out the cup, his fingers steady. She poured, watching the cup, the tip of her tongue touching her lips as she concentrated.

Fujiko reluctantly accepted some too, though she said that she couldn't feel her legs anymore. Her quiet melancholia had gone tonight and she seemed young again. Blackthorne noticed that she was not as ugly as he had once thought.

Jozen's head was buzzing. Not from saké but from the incredible war strategy that Yabu, Omi, and Igurashi had described so openly. Only Naga, the second-in-command, son of the arch-enemy, had said nothing, and had remained throughout the evening cold, arrogant, stiff-backed, with the characteristic large Toranaga nose on a taut face.

"Astonishing, Yabu-sama," Jozen said. "Now I can understand the reason for secrecy. My Master will understand it also. Wise, very wise. And you, Naga-san, you've been silent all evening. I'd like your opinion. How do you like this new mobility—this new strategy?"

"My father believes that all war possibilities should be considered, Jozen-san," the young man replied.

"But you, what's your opinion?"

"I was sent here only to obey, to observe, to listen, to learn, and to test. Not to give opinions."

"Of course. But as second-in-command—I should say, as an illustrious second-in-command—do you consider the experiment a success?"

"Yabu-sama or Omi-san should answer that. Or my father."

"But Yabu-sama said that everyone tonight was to talk freely. What's there to hide? We are all friends, *neh?* So famous a son of so famous a father must have an opinion. *Neh?*"

Naga's eyes narrowed under the taunt but he did not reply.

"Everyone can speak freely, Naga-san," Yabu said. "What do you think?"

"I think that, with surprise, this idea would win one skirmish or possibly one battle. With surprise, yes. But then?" Naga's voice swept on icily. "Then all sides would use the same plan and vast numbers of men would die unnecessarily, slain without honor by an assailant who won't even know who he has killed. I doubt if my father will actually authorize its use in a real battle."

"He's said that?" Yabu put the question incisively, careless of Jozen.

"No, Yabu-sama. I'm giving my own opinion. Of course."

"But the Musket Regiment—you don't approve of it? It disgusts you?" Yabu asked darkly.

Naga looked at him with flat, reptilian eyes. "With great deference, since you ask my opinion, yes, I find it disgusting. Our forefathers have always known whom they killed or who defeated them. That's *bushido,* our way, the Way of the Warrior, the way of a true samurai. The better man victorious, *neh?* But now this? How do you prove your valor to your lord? How can he reward courage? To charge bullets is brave, yes, but also stupid. Where's the valor in that? Guns are against our samurai code. Barbarians fight this way, peasants fight this way. Do you realize filthy merchants and peasants, even *eta,* could fight this way?" Jozen laughed and Naga continued even more menacingly. "A few fanatic peasants could easily kill any number of samurai with enough guns! Yes, peasants could kill any one of us, even the Lord Ishido who wants to sit in my father's place."

Jozen bridled. "Lord Ishido doesn't covet your father's lands. He only seeks to protect the Empire for its rightful heir."

"My father's no threat to the Lord Yaemon, or to the Realm."

"Of course, but you were talking about peasants. The Lord Taikō was once a peasant. My Lord Ishido was once a peasant. I was once a peasant. And a *ronin!*"

Naga wanted no quarrel. He knew he was no match for Jozen, whose prowess with sword and ax was renowned. "I wasn't trying to insult your master or you or anyone, Jozen-san. I was merely saying that we samurai must all make very certain that peasants never have guns or none of us will be safe."

"Merchants and peasants'll never worry us," Jozen said.

"I agree," Yabu added, "and Naga-san, I agree with part of what you say. Yes. But guns are modern. Soon all battles will be fought with guns. I agree it's distasteful. But it's the way of modern war. And then it'll be as it always was—the bravest samurai will always conquer."

"No, so sorry, but you're wrong, Yabu-sama! What did this cursed barbarian tell us—the essence of their war strategy? He freely admits that all their armies are conscript and mercenary. *Neh?* Mercenary! No sense of duty to their lords. The soldiers only fight for pay and loot, to rape and to gorge. Didn't he say their armies are *peasant armies?* That's what guns have brought to their world and that's what guns will bring to ours. If I had power, I'd take this barbarian's head tonight and outlaw all guns permanently."

"Is that what your father thinks?" Jozen asked too quickly.

"My father doesn't tell me or anyone what he thinks, as you surely know. I don't speak for my father, no one speaks for him," Naga replied, angry at allowing himself to be trapped into talking at all. "I was sent here to obey, to listen and not to talk. I apologize for talking. I would not have spoken unless you asked me. If I have offended you, or you, Yabu-sama, or you, Omi-san, I apologize."

"There's no need to apologize. I asked your views," Yabu said. "Why should anyone be offended? This is a discussion, *neh?* Among leaders. You'd outlaw guns?"

"Yes. I think you'd be wise to keep a very close check on every gun in your domain."

"All peasants are forbidden weapons of any kind. My peasants and my people are very well controlled."

Jozen smirked at the slim youth, loathing him. "Interesting ideas you have, Naga-san. But you're mistaken about the peasants. They're nothing to samurai but providers. They're no more threat than a pile of dung."

"At the moment!" Naga said, his pride commanding him. "That's why I'd outlaw guns now. You're right, Yabu-san, that a new era requires new methods. But because of what this Anjin-san, this one barbarian, has said, I'd go much further than our present laws. I would issue Edicts that anyone other than a samurai found with a gun or caught trading in guns would immediately forfeit his life and that of every member of his family of every generation. Further, I would prohibit the making or importing of guns. I'd prohibit barbarians from wearing them or from bringing them to our shores. Yes, if I had power—which I do not seek and never will—I'd keep barbarians out of our country totally, except for a few priests and one port for trade, which I'd surround with a high fence and trusted warriors. Last, I'd put this foul-minded barbarian, the Anjin-san, to death at once so that his filthy knowledge will not spread. He's a disease."

Jozen said, "Ah, Naga-san, it must be good to be so young. You know, my Master agrees with much of what you said about the barbarians. I've heard him say many times, 'Keep them out—kick them out—kick their arses away to Nagasaki and keep them bottled there!' You'd kill the Anjin-san, eh? Interesting. My Master doesn't like the Anjin-san either. But for him—" He stopped. "Ah, yes, you've a good thought about guns. I can see that clearly. May I tell that to my Master? Your idea about new laws?"

"Of course." Naga was mollified, and calmer now that he had spoken what had been bottled up from the first day.

"You've given this opinion to Lord Toranaga?" Yabu asked.

"Lord Toranaga has not asked my opinion. I hope one day he will honor me by asking as you have done," Naga replied at once with sincerity, and wondered if any of them detected the lie.

Omi said, "As this is a free discussion, Sire, I say this barbarian is a treasure. I believe we must learn from the barbarian. We must know about guns and fighting ships because they know about them. We must know everything they know as soon as they know it, and even now, some of us must begin to learn to think like they do so that soon we can surpass them."

Naga said confidently, "What could they possibly know, Omi-san? Yes, guns and ships. But what else? How could they destroy us? There's not a samurai among them. Doesn't this Anjin admit openly that even their kings are murderers and religious fanatics? We're millions, they're a handful. We could swamp them with our hands alone."

"This Anjin-san opened my eyes, Naga-san. I've discovered that our land, and China, isn't the whole world, it's only a very small part. At first I thought the barbarian was just a curiosity. Now I don't. I thank the gods for him. I think he's saved us and I know we can learn from him. Already he's given us power over the Southern Barbarians—and over China."

"What?"

"The Taikō failed because their numbers are too great for us, man to man, arrow to arrow, neh? With guns and barbarian skill we could take Peking."

"With barbarian treachery, Omi-san!"

"With barbarian knowledge, Naga-san, we could take Peking. Whoever takes Peking eventually controls China. And whoever controls China can control the world. We must learn not to be ashamed of taking knowledge from wherever it comes."

"I say we need nothing from outside."

"Without offense, Naga-san, I say we must protect this land of the Gods by any means. It's our prime duty to protect the unique, divine position we have on earth. Only this is the Land of the Gods, *neh?* Only our Emperor is divine. I agree this barbarian should be gagged. But not by death. By permanent isolation here in Anjiro, until we have learned everything he knows."

Jozen scratched thoughtfully. "My Master will be told of your views. I agree the barbarian should be isolated. Also that training should cease at once."

Yabu took a scroll from his sleeve. "Here is a full report on the experiment for Lord Ishido. When Lord Ishido wishes the training to cease, of course, the training will cease."

Jozen accepted the scroll. "And Lord Toranaga? What about him?" His eyes went to Naga. Naga said nothing but stared at the scroll.

Yabu said, "You will be able to ask his opinion directly. He has a similar report. I presume you'll be leaving for Yedo tomorrow? Or would you like to witness the training? I hardly need tell you the men are not yet proficient."

"I would like to see one 'attack.'"

"Omi-san, arrange it. You lead it."

"Yes, Sire."

Jozen turned to his second-in-command and gave him the scroll. "Masumoto, take this to Lord Ishido. You will leave at once."

"Yes, Jozen-san."

Yabu said to Igurashi, "Provide him with guides to the border and fresh horses."

Igurashi left with the samurai immediately.

Jozen stretched and yawned. "Please excuse me," he said, "but it's all the riding I've done in the last few days. I must thank you for an extraordinary evening, Yabu-sama. Your ideas are far-reaching. And yours, Omi-san. And yours, Naga-san. I'll compliment you to the Lord Toranaga and to my Master. Now if you'll excuse me, I'm very tired and Osaka is a long way off."

"Of course," Yabu said. "How was Osaka?"

"Very good. Remember those bandits, the ones that attacked you by land and sea?"

"Of course."

"We took four hundred and fifty heads that night. Many were wearing Toranaga uniforms."

"*Ronin* have no honor. None."

"Some *ronin* have," Jozen said, smarting from the insult. He lived always with the shame of having once been *ronin.* "Some were even wearing our Grays. Not one escaped. They all died."

"And Buntaro-san?"

"No. He—" Jozen stopped. The "no" had slipped out but now that he had said it he did not mind. "No. We don't know for certain—no one collected his head. You've heard nothing about him?"

"No," Naga said.

"Perhaps he was captured. Perhaps they just cut him into pieces and scattered him. My Master would like to know when you have news. All's very good now at Osaka. Preparations for the meeting go forward. There'll be lavish entertainments to celebrate the new era, and of course, to honor *all* the daimyos."

"And Lord Toda Hiro-matsu?" Naga asked politely.

"Old Iron Fist's as strong and gruff as ever."

"He's still there?"

"No. He left with all your father's men a few days before I did."

"And my father's household?"

"I heard that the Lady Kiritsubo and the Lady Sazuko asked to stay with my Master. A doctor advised the Lady to rest for a month—her health, you know. He thought the journey would not be good for the expected child." To Yabu he added, "She fell down the night you left, didn't she?"

"Yes."

"There's nothing serious, I hope," Naga asked, very concerned.

"No, Naga-san, nothing serious," Jozen said, then again to Yabu, "You've informed Lord Toranaga of my arrival?"

"Of course."

"Good."

"The news you brought us would interest him greatly."

"Yes. I saw a carrier pigeon circle and fly north."

"I have that service now." Yabu did not add that Jozen's pigeon had also been observed, or that falcons had intercepted it near the mountains, or that the message had been decoded: "At Anjiro. All true as reported. Yabu, Naga, Omi, and barbarian here."

"I will leave tomorrow, with your permission, after the 'attack.' You'll give me fresh horses? I must not keep Lord Toranaga waiting. I look forward to seeing him. So does my Master. At Osaka. I hope you'll accompany him, Naga-san."

"If I'm ordered there, I will be there." Naga kept his eyes lowered but he was burning with suppressed fury.

Jozen left and walked with his guards up the hill to his camp. He re-arranged the sentries and ordered his men to sleep and got into his small brush lean-to that they had constructed against the coming rain. By candlelight, under a mosquito net, he rewrote the previous message on a thin piece of rice paper and added: "The 500 guns are lethal. Massed surprise gun attacks planned—full report already sent with Masumoto." Then he dated it and doused the candle. In the darkness he slipped out of his net, removed one of the pigeons from the panniers and placed the message in the tiny container on its foot. Then he stealthily made his way to one of his men and handed him the bird.

"Take it out into the brush," he whispered. "Hide it somewhere where it can roost safely until dawn. As far away as you can. But be careful, there are eyes all around. If you're intercepted say I told you to patrol, but hide the pigeon first."

The man slid away as silently as a cockroach.

Pleased with himself, Jozen looked toward the village below. There were lights on in the fortress and on the opposite slope, in the house that he knew to be Omi's. There were a few also in the house just below, the one presently occupied by the barbarian.

That whelp Naga's right, Jozen thought, waving his hand at a mosquito. The barbarian's a filthy plague.

"Good night, Fujiko-san."

"Good night, Anjin-san."

The shoji closed behind her. Blackthorne took off his kimono and loincloth and put on the lighter sleeping kimono, got under the mosquito net, and lay down.

He blew out the candle. Deep darkness enveloped him. The house was quiet now. The small shutters were closed and he could hear the surf. Clouds obscured the moon.

The wine and laughter had made him drowsy and euphoric and he listened to the surf and felt himself drifting with it, his mind fogged. Occasionally, a dog barked in the village below. I should get a dog, he thought, remembering his own bull terrier at home. Wonder if he's still alive? Grog was his name but Tudor, his son, always called him "Og-Og."

Ah, Tudor, laddie. It's been such a long time.

Wish I could see you all—even write a letter and send it home. Let's see, he thought. How would I begin?

"My darlings: This is the first letter I've been able to send home since we made landfall in Japan. Things are well now that I know how to live according to their ways. The food is terrible but tonight I had pheasant and soon I'll get my ship back again. Where to start my story? Today

I'm like a feudal lord in this strange country. I have a house, a horse, eight servants, a housekeeper, my own barber, and my own interpreter. I'm clean-shaven now and shave every day—the steel razors they have here must certainly be the best in the world. My salary's huge—enough to feed two hundred and fifty Japan families for one year. In England that'd be the equivalent of almost a thousand golden guineas a year! Ten times my salary from the Dutch company. . . ."

The shoji began to open. His hand sought his pistol under the pillow and he readied, dragging himself back. Then he caught the almost imperceptible rustle of silk and a waft of perfume.

"Anjin-san?" A thread of whisper, filled with promise.

"*Hai?*" he asked as softly, peering into the darkness, unable to see clearly.

Footsteps came closer. There was the sound of her kneeling and the net was pulled aside and she joined him inside the enclosing net. She took his hand and lifted it to her breast, then to her lips.

"Mariko-san?"

At once fingers reached up in the darkness and touched his lips, cautioning silence. He nodded, understanding the awful risk they were taking. He held her tiny wrist and brushed it with his lips. In the pitch black his other hand sought and caressed her face. She kissed his fingers one by one. Her hair was loose and waist length now. His hands traveled her. The lovely feel of silk, nothing beneath.

Her taste was sweet. His tongue touched her teeth, then rimmed her ears, discovering her. She loosed his robe and let hers fall aside, her breathing more languorous now. She pushed closer, nestling, and pulled the covering over their heads. Then she began to love him, with hands and with lips. With more tenderness and seeking and knowledge than he had ever known.

CHAPTER 33

BLACKTHORNE awoke at dawn. Alone. At first he was sure he had been dreaming, but her perfume still lingered and he knew that it had not been a dream.

A discreet knock.

"*Hai?*"

"*Ohayo, Anjin-san, gomen nasai.*" A maid opened the shoji for Fujiko, then carried in the tray with cha and a bowl of rice gruel and sweet rice cakes.

"*Ohayo, Fujiko-san, domo,*" he said, thanking her. She always came with his first meal personally, opened the net and waited while he ate, and the maid laid out a fresh kimono and tabi and loincloth.

He sipped the cha, wondering if Fujiko knew about last night. Her face gave nothing away.

"*Ikaga desu ka?*" How are you, Blackthorne asked.

"*Okagasama de genki desu,* Anjin-san. *Anata wa?*" Very well, thank you. And you?

The maid took out his fresh clothes from the concealed cupboard that melted neatly into the rest of the paper-latticed room, then left them alone.

"*Anata wa yoku nemutta ka?*" Did you sleep well?

"*Hai,* Anjin-san, *arigato goziemashita!*" She smiled, put her hand to her head pretending pain, mimed being drunk and sleeping like a stone. "*Anata wa?*"

"*Watashi wa yoku nemuru.*" I slept very well.

She corrected him, "*Watashi wa yoku nemutta.*"

"*Domo. Watashi wa yoku nemutta.*"

"*Yoi! Taihenyoi!*" Good. Very good.

Then from the corridor he heard Mariko call out, "Fujiko-san?"

"*Hai,* Mariko-san?" Fujiko went to the shoji and opened it a crack. He could not see Mariko. And he did not understand what they were saying.

I hope no one knows, he thought. I pray it is secret, just between us. Perhaps it would be better if it had been a dream.

He began to dress. Fujiko came back and knelt to do up the catches on the tabi.

"Mariko-san? *Nan ja?*"

"Nane mo, Anjin-san," she replied. It was nothing important.

She went to the *takonama,* the alcove with its hanging scroll and flower arrangement, where his swords were always put. She gave them to him. He stuck them in his belt. The swords no longer felt ridiculous to him, though he wished that he could wear them less self-consciously.

She had told him that her father had been granted the swords for bravery after a particularly bloody battle in the far north of Korea, seven years ago during the first invasion. The Japanese armies had ripped through the kingdom, victorious, slashing north. Then, when they were near the Yalu River, the Chinese hordes had abruptly poured across the border to join battle with the Japanese armies and, through the weight of their incredible numbers, had routed them. Fujiko's father had been part of the rearguard that had covered the retreat back to the mountains north of Seoul, where they had turned and fought the battle to a stalemate. This and the second campaign had been the costliest military expedition ever undertaken. When the Taikō had died last year, Toranaga, on behalf of the Council of Regents, had at once ordered the remnants of their armies home, to the great relief of the vast majority of *daimyos,* who detested the Korean campaign.

Blackthorne walked out to the veranda. He stepped into his thongs and nodded to his servants, who had been assembled in a neat line to bow him off, as was custom.

It was a drab day. The sky was overcast and a warm wet wind came off the sea. The steppingstones that were set into the gravel of the path were wet with the rain that had fallen in the night.

Beyond the gate were the horses and his ten samurai outriders. And Mariko.

She was already mounted and wore a pale yellow mantle over pale green silk trousers, a wide-brimmed hat and veil held with yellow ribbons, and gloves. A rain parasol was ready in its saddle-sheath.

"Ohayo," he said formally. *"Ohayo,* Mariko-san."

"Ohayo, Anjin-san. *Ikaga desu ka?"*

"Okagesama de genki desu. Anata wa?"

She smiled. *"Yoi, arigato goziemashita."*

She gave not the faintest hint that anything was different between them. But he expected none, not in public, knowing how dangerous the situation was. Her perfume came over him and he would have liked to kiss her here, in front of everyone.

"Ikimasho!" he said and swung into the saddle, motioning the samurai to ride off ahead. He walked his horse leisurely and Mariko fell into place beside him. When they were alone, he relaxed.

"Mariko."

"*Hai?*"

Then he said in Latin, "Thou art beautiful and I love thee."

"I thank thee, but so much wine last night makes my head to feel not beautiful today, not in truth, and love is a Christian word."

"Thou art beautiful and Christian, and wine could not touch thee."

"Thank thee for the lie, Anjin-san, yes, thank thee."

"No. I should thank thee."

"Oh? Why?"

"Never 'why,' no 'why.' I thank thee sincerely."

"If wine and meat make thee so warm and fine and gallant," she said, "then I must tell thy consort to move the heaven and the earth to obtain them for thee every evening."

"Yes. I would have everything the same, always."

"Thou art untoward happy today," she said. "Good, very good. But why? Why truly?"

"Because of thee. Thou knowest why."

"I know nothing, Anjin-san."

"Nothing?" he teased.

"Nothing."

He was taken aback. They were quite alone, and safe.

"Why doth 'nothing' take the heart out of thy smile?" she asked.

"Stupidity! Absolute stupidity! I forgot that it is most wise to be cautious. It was only that we were alone and I wanted to speak of it. And, in truth, to say more."

"Thou speakest in riddles. I do not understand thee."

He was nonplussed again. "Thou dost not wish to talk about it? At all?"

"About what, Anjin-san?"

"What passed in the night then?"

"I passed thy door in the night when my maid, Koi, was with thee."

"What!"

"We, your consort and I, we thought she would be a pleasing gift for thee. She pleased thee, did she not?"

Blackthorne was trying to recover. Mariko's maid was her size but younger and never so fair and never so pretty, and yes, it was pitch dark and yes, his head was fogged with wine but no, it was not the maid.

"That's not possible," he said in Portuguese.

"What's not possible, senhor?" she asked in the same language.

He reverted to Latin again, as the outriders were not far away, the wind blowing in their direction. "Please do not joke with me. No one can hear. I know a presence and a perfume."

"Thou thinkest it was me? Oh, it was not, Anjin-san. I would be honored but I could never possibly . . . however much I might want—oh no, Anjin-san. It was not me but Koi, my maid. I would be honored, but I belong to another even though he's dead."

"Yes, but it wasn't your maid." He bit back his anger. "But leave it as thou desirest."

"It was my maid, Anjin-san," she said placatingly. "We anointed her with my perfume and instructed her: no words, only touch. We never thought for a moment thou wouldst consider her to be me! This was not to trick thee but for thine ease, knowing that discussing things of the pillow still embarrasses thee." She was looking at him with wide, innocent eyes. "She pleasured thee, Anjin-san? Thou pleasured her."

"A joke concerning things of great importance is sometimes without humor."

"Things of great import will always be treated with great import. But a maid in the night with a man is without import."

"I do not consider thee without import."

"I thank thee. I say that equally. But a maid in the night with a man is private and without import. It is a gift from her to him and, sometimes, from him to her. Nothing more."

"Never?"

"Sometimes. But this private pillow matter does not have this vast seriousness of thine."

"Never?"

"Only when the woman and man join together against the law. In *this* land."

He reined in, finally comprehending the reason for her denial. "I apologize," he said. "Yes, thou art right and I most very wrong. I should never have spoken. I apologize."

"Why apologize? For what? Tell me, Anjin-san, was this girl wearing a crucifix?"

"No."

"I always wear it. Always."

"A crucifix can be taken off," he said automatically in Portuguese. "That proves nothing. It could be loaned, like a perfume."

"Tell me a last truth: Did you really see the girl? Really *see* her?"

"Of course. Please let us forget I ever—"

"The night was very dark, the moon overcast. Please, the truth, Anjin-san. Think! Did you really see the girl?"

Of course I saw her, he thought indignantly.

God damn it, think truly. You didn't *see* her. Your head *was* fogged. She could have been the maid but you knew it was Mariko because you wanted Mariko and saw only Mariko in your head, believing that Mariko would want you equally. You're a fool. A God damned fool.

"In truth, no. In truth I should really apologize," he said. "How do I apologize?"

"There's no need to apologize, Anjin-san," she replied calmly. "I've told you many times a man never apologizes, even when he's wrong. You were not wrong." Her eyes teased him now. "My maid needs no apology."

"Thank you," he said, laughing. "You make me feel less of a fool."

"The years flee from you when you laugh. The so-serious Anjin-san becomes a boy again."

"My father told me I was born old."

"Were you?"

"He thought so."

"What's he like?"

"He was a fine man. A shipowner, a captain. The Spanish killed him at a place called Antwerp when they put that city to the sword. They burned his ship. I was six, but I remember him as a big, tall, good-natured man with golden hair. My older brother, Arthur, he was just eight. . . . We had bad times then, Mariko-san."

"Why? Please tell me. Please!"

"It's all very ordinary. Every penny of money was tied into the ship and that was lost . . . and, well, not long after that, my sister died. She starved to death really. There was famine in '71 and plague again."

"We have plague sometimes. The smallpox. You were many in your family?"

"Three of us," he said, glad to talk to take away the other hurt. "Willia, my sister, she was nine when she died. Arthur, he was next—he wanted to be an artist, a sculptor, but he had to become an apprentice stonemason to help support us. He was killed in the Armada. He was twenty-five, poor fool, he just joined a ship, untrained, such a waste. I'm the last of the Blackthornes. Arthur's wife and daughter live with my wife and kids now. My mother's still alive and so's old Granny Jacoba—she's seventy-five and hard as a piece of English oak though she was Irish. At least they were alive when I left more than two years ago."

The ache was coming back. I'll think about them when I start for home, he promised himself, but not until then.

"There'll be a storm tomorrow," he said, watching the sea. "A strong one, Mariko-san. Then in three days we'll have fair weather."

"This is the season of squalls. Mostly it's overcast and rain-filled. When the rains stop it becomes very humid. Then begin the *tai-funs*."

I wish I were at sea again, he was thinking. Was I ever at sea? Was the ship real? What's reality? Mariko or the maid?

"You don't laugh very much, do you, Anjin-san?"

"I've been seafaring too long. Seamen're always serious. We've learned to watch the sea. We're always watching and waiting for disaster. Take your eyes off the sea for a second and she'll grasp your ship and make her matchwood."

"I'm afraid of the sea," she said.

"So am I. An old fisherman told me once, 'The man who's not afraid of the sea'll soon be drownded for he'll go out on a day he shouldn't. But we be afraid of the sea so we be only drownded now and again.'" He looked at her. "Mariko-san . . ."

"Yes?"

"A few minutes ago you'd convinced me that—well, let's say I was convinced. Now I'm not. What's the truth? The *honto*. I must know."

"Ears are to hear with. Of course it was the maid."

"This maid. Can I ask for her whenever I want?"

"Of course. A wise man would not."

"Because I might be disappointed? Next time?"

"Possibly."

"I find it difficult to possess a maid and lose a maid, difficult to say nothing. . . ."

"Pillowing is a pleasure. Of the body. Nothing has to be said."

"But how do I tell a maid that she is beautiful? That I love her? That she filled me with ecstasy?"

"It isn't seemly to 'love' a maid this way. Not here, Anjin-san. That passion's not even for a wife or a consort." Her eyes crinkled suddenly. "But only toward someone like Kiku-san, the courtesan, who is so beautiful and merits this."

"Where can I find this girl?"

"In the village. It would be my honor to act as your go-between."

"By Christ, I think you mean it."

"Of course. A man needs passions of all kinds. This Lady is worthy of romance—if you can afford her."

"What does that mean?"

"She would be very expensive."

"You don't buy love. That type's worth nothing. 'Love' is without price."

She smiled. "Pillowing always has its price. Always. Not necessarily money, Anjin-san. But a man pays, always, for pillowing in one way, or in another. True love, we call it duty, is of soul to soul and needs no such expression—no physical expression, except perhaps the gift of death."

"You're wrong. I wish I could show you the world as it is."

"I know the world as it is, and as it will be forever. You want this contemptible maid again?"

"Yes. You know I want . . ."

Mariko laughed gaily. "Then she will be sent to you. At sunset. We will escort her, Fujiko and I!"

"Goddamn it—I think you would too!" He laughed with her.

"Ah, Anjin-san, it is good to see you laugh. Since you came back to Anjiro you have gone through a great change. A very great change."

"No. Not so much. But last night I dreamed a dream. That dream was perfection."

"God is perfection. And sometimes so is a sunset or moonrise or the first crocus of the year."

"I don't understand you at all."

She turned back the veil on her hat and looked directly at him. "Once another man said to me, 'I don't understand you at all,' and my husband said, 'Your pardon, Lord, but no man can understand her. Her father doesn't understand her, neither do the gods, nor her barbarian God, not even her mother understands her.'"

"That was Toranaga? Lord Toranaga?"

"Oh, no, Anjin-san. That was the Taikō. Lord Toranaga understands me. He understands everything."

"Even me?"

"Very much you."

"You're sure of that, aren't you?"

"Yes. Oh, very yes."

"Will he win the war?"

"Yes."

"I'm his favored vassal?"

"Yes."

"Will he take my navy?"

"Yes."

"When will I get my ship back?"

"You won't."

"Why?"

Her gravity vanished. "Because you'll have your 'maid' in Anjiro and you'll be pillowing so much you'll have no energy to leave, even on your hands and knees, when she begs you to go aboard your ship, and when Lord Toranaga asks you to go aboard and to leave us all!"

"There you go again! One moment so serious, the next not!"

"That's only to answer you, Anjin-san, and to put certain things in a correct place. Ah, but before you leave us you should see the Lady Kiku. She's worthy of a great passion. She's so beautiful and talented. For her you would have to be extraordinary!"

"I'm tempted to accept that challenge."

"I challenge no one. But if you're prepared to be samurai and not—not foreigner—if you're prepared to treat pillowing for what it is, then I would be honored to act as go-between."

"What does that mean?"

"When you're in good humor, when you're ready for very special amusement, ask your consort to ask me."

"Why Fujiko-san?"

"Because it's your consort's duty to see that you are pleasured. It is our custom to make life simple. We admire simplicity, so *men* and *women* can take pillowing for what it is: an important part of life, certainly, but between a man and a woman there are more vital things. Humility, for one. Respect. Duty. Even this 'love' of yours. Fujiko 'loves' you."

"No she doesn't!"

"She will give you her life. What more is there to give?"

At length he took his eyes off her and looked at the sea. The waves were cresting the shore as the wind freshened. He turned back to her. "Then nothing is to be said?" he asked. "Between us?"

"Nothing. That is wise."

"And if I don't agree?"

"You must agree. You are here. This is your home."

The attacking five hundred galloped over the lip of the hill in a haphazard pack, down onto the rock-strewn valley floor where the two thousand "defenders" were drawn up in a battle array. Each rider wore a musket slung on his back and a belt with pouches for bullets, flints, and a powder horn. Like most samurai, their clothes were a motley collection of kimonos and rags, but their weapons always the best that each could afford. Only Toranaga and Ishido, copying him, insisted that their troops be uniformed and punctilious in their dress. All other *daimyos* considered such outward extravagance a foolish squandering of money, an unnecessary innovation. Even Blackthorne had agreed. The armies of Europe were never uniformed—what king could afford that, except for a personal guard?

He was standing on a rise with Yabu and his aides, Jozen and all his men, and Mariko. This was the first full-scale rehearsal of an attack.

He waited uneasily. Yabu was uncommonly tense, and Omi and Naga both had been touchy almost to the point of belligerence. Particularly Naga.

"What's the matter with everyone?" he had asked Mariko.

"Perhaps they wish to do well in front of their lord and his guest."

"Is he a *daimyo* too?"

"No. But important, one of Lord Ishido's generals. It would be good if everything were perfect today."

"I wish I'd been told there was to be a rehearsal."

"What would that have accomplished? Everything you could do, you have done."

Yes, Blackthorne thought, as he watched the five hundred. But they're nowhere near ready yet. Surely Yabu knows that too, everyone does. So if there is a disaster, well, that's *karma,* he told himself with more confidence, and found consolation in that thought.

The attackers gathered speed and the defenders stood waiting under the banners of their captains, jeering at the "enemy" as they would normally do, strung out in loose formation, three or four men deep. Soon the attackers would dismount out of arrow range. Then the most valiant warriors on both sides would truculently strut to the fore to throw down the gauntlet, proclaiming their own lineage and superiority with the most obvious of insults. Single armed conflicts would begin, gradually increasing in numbers, until one commander would order a general attack and then it was every man for himself. Usually the greater number defeated the smaller, then the reserves would be brought up and committed, and again the melee until the morale of one side broke, and the few cowards that retreated would soon be joined by the many and a rout would ensue. Treachery was not unusual. Sometimes whole regiments, following their master's orders, would switch sides, to be welcomed as allies—always welcomed but never trusted. Sometimes the defeated commanders would flee to regroup to fight again. Sometimes they would stay and fight to the death, sometimes they would commit seppuku with ceremony. Rarely were they captured. Some offered their services to the victors. Sometimes this was accepted but most times refused. Death was the lot of the vanquished, quick for the brave and shame-filled for the cowardly. And this was the historic pattern of all skirmishes in this land, even at great battles, soldiers here the same as everywhere, except that here they were more ferocious and many, many more were prepared to die for their masters than anywhere else on earth.

The thunder of the hoofs echoed in the valley.

"Where's the attack commander? Where's Omi-san?" Jozen asked.

"Among the men, be patient," Yabu replied.

"But where's his standard? And why isn't he wearing battle armor and plumes? Where's the commander's standard? They're just like a bunch of filthy no-good bandits!"

"Be patient! All officers are ordered to remain nondescript. I told you. And please don't forget we're pretending a battle is raging, that this is part of a big battle, with reserves and arm—"

Jozen burst out, "Where are their swords? None of them are wearing swords! Samurai without swords? They'd be massacred!"

"Be patient!"

Now the attackers were dismounting. The first warriors strode out from the defending ranks to show their valor. An equal number began to measure up against them. Then, suddenly, the ungainly mass of attackers rushed into five tight-disciplined phalanxes, each with four ranks of twenty-five men, three phalanxes ahead and two in reserve, forty paces back. As one, they charged the enemy. In range they shuddered to a stop on command and the front ranks fired an ear-shattering salvo in unison. Screams and men dying. Jozen and his men ducked reflexively, then watched appalled as the front ranks knelt and began to reload and the second ranks fired over them, with the third and fourth ranks following the same pattern. At each salvo more defenders fell, and the valley was filled with shouts and screams and confusion.

"You're killing your own men!" Jozen shouted above the uproar.

"It's blank ammunition, not real. They're all acting, but imagine it's a real attack with real bullets! Watch!"

Now the defenders "recovered" from the initial shock. They regrouped and whirled back to a frontal attack. But by this time the front ranks had reloaded and, on command, fired another salvo from a kneeling position, then the second rank fired standing, immediately kneeling to reload, then the third and the fourth, as before, and though many musketeers were slow and the ranks ragged, it was easy to imagine the awful decimation trained men would cause. The counterattack faltered, then broke apart, and the defenders retreated in pretended confusion, back up the rise to stop just below the observers. Many "dead" littered the ground.

Jozen and his men were shaken. "Those guns would break any line!"

"Wait. The battle's not over!"

Again the defenders re-formed and now their commanders exhorted them to victory, committed the reserves, and ordered the final general attack. The samurai rushed down the hill, emitting their terrible battle cries, to fall on the enemy.

"Now they'll be stamped into the ground," Jozen said, caught up like all of them in the realism of this mock battle.

And he was right. The phalanxes did not hold their ground. They broke and fled before the battle cries of the true samurai with their swords and spears, and Jozen and his men added their shouts of scorn as the regiments hurtled to the kill. The musketeers were fleeing like the Garlic Eaters, a hundred paces, two hundred paces, three hundred, then suddenly, on command, the phalanxes regrouped, this time in a V formation. Again the shattering salvos began. The attack faltered. Then stopped. But the guns continued. Then they, too, stopped. The game ceased. But all on the rise knew that under actual conditions the two thousand would have been slaughtered.

Now, in the silence, defenders and attackers began to sort themselves out. The "bodies" got up, weapons were collected. There was laughter and groaning. Many men limped and a few were badly hurt.

"I congratulate you, Yabu-sama," Jozen said with great sincerity. "Now I understand what all of you meant."

"The firing was ragged," Yabu said, inwardly delighted. "It will take months to train them."

Jozen shook his head. "I wouldn't like to attack them now. Not if they had real ammunition. No army could withstand that punch—no line. The ranks could never stay closed. And then you'd pour ordinary troops and cavalry through the gap and roll up the sides like an old scroll." He thanked all *kami* that he'd had the sense to see one attack. "It was terrible to watch. For a moment I thought the battle was real."

"They were ordered to make it look real. And now you may review my musketeers, if you wish."

"Thank you. That would be an honor."

The defenders were streaming off to their camps that sat on the far hillside. The five hundred musketeers waited below, near the path that went over the rise and slid down to the village. They were forming into their companies, Omi and Naga in front of them, both wearing swords again.

"Yabu-sama?"

"Yes, Anjin-san?"

"Good, no?"

"Yes, good."

"Thank you, Yabu-sama. I please."

Mariko corrected him automatically. "I am pleased."

"Ah, so sorry. I am pleased."

Jozen took Yabu aside. "This is all out of the Anjin-san's head?"

"No," Yabu lied. "But it's the way barbarians fight. He's just training the men to load and to fire."

"Why not do as Naga-san advised? You've the barbarian's knowledge now. Why risk its spreading? He is a plague. Very dangerous, Yabu-sama. Naga-san was right. It's true—peasants *could* fight this way. Easily. Get rid of the barbarian now."

"If Lord Ishido wants his head, he has only to ask."

"I ask it. Now." Again the truculence. "I speak with his voice."

"I'll consider it, Jozen-san."

"And also, in his name, I *ask* that all guns be withdrawn from those troops at once."

Yabu frowned, then turned his attention to the companies. They were approaching up the hill, their straight, disciplined ranks faintly ludicrous as always, only because such order was unusual. Fifty paces away they halted. Omi and Naga came on alone and saluted.

"It was all right for a first exercise," Yabu said.

"Thank you, Sire," Omi replied. He was limping slightly and his face was dirty, bruised, and powder marked.

Jozen said, "Your troops would have to carry swords in a real battle, Yabu-sama, *neh?* A samurai must carry swords—eventually they'd run out of ammunition, *neh?*"

"Swords will be in their way, in charge and retreat. Oh, they'll wear them as usual to maintain surprise, but just before the first charge they'll get rid of them."

"Samurai will always need swords. In a real battle. Even so, I'm glad you'll never have to use this attack force, or—" Jozen was going to add, "or this filthy treacherous method of war." Instead he said, "Or we'll all have to give our swords away."

"Perhaps we will, Jozen-san, when we go to war."

"You'd give up your Murasama blade? Or even Toranaga's gift?"

"To win a battle, yes. Otherwise no."

"Then you might have to run very fast to save your fruit when your musket jammed or your powder got wet." Jozen laughed at his own sally. Yabu did not.

"Omi-san! Show him!" he ordered.

At once Omi gave an order. His men slipped out the short sheathed bayonet sword that hung almost unnoticed from the back of their belts and snapped it into a socket on the muzzle of their muskets.

"*Charge!*"

Instantly the samurai charged with their battle cry, "*Kasigiiiiii!*"

The forest of naked steel stopped a pace away from them. Jozen and his men were laughing nervously from the sudden, unexpected ferocity. "Good, very good," Jozen said. He reached out and touched one of the bayonets. It was extremely sharp. "Perhaps you're right, Yabu-sama. Let's hope it's never put to the test."

"Omi-san!" Yabu called. "Form them up. Jozen-san's going to review them. Then go back to camp. Mariko-san, Anjin-san, you follow me!" He strode down the rise through the ranks, his aides, Blackthorne, and Mariko following.

"Form up at the path. Replace bayonets!"

Half the men obeyed at once, turned about, and walked down the slope again. Naga and his two hundred and fifty samurai remained where they were, bayonets still threatening.

Jozen bristled. "What's going on?"

"I consider your insults intolerable," Naga said venomously.

"That's nonsense. I haven't insulted you, or anyone! Your bayonets insult my position! Yabu-sama!"

Yabu turned back. Now he was on the other side of the Toranaga contingent. "Naga-san," he called out coldly. "What's the meaning of this?"

"I cannot forgive this man's insults to my father—or to me."

"He's protected. You cannot touch him now! He's under the cipher of the Regents!"

"Your pardon, Yabu-sama, but this is between Jozen-san and myself."

"No. You are under my orders. I order you to tell your men to return to camp."

Not a man moved. The rain began.

"Your pardon, Yabu-san, please forgive me, but this is between him and me and whatever happens I absolve you of responsibility of my action and those of my men."

Behind Naga, one of Jozen's men drew his sword and lunged for Naga's unprotected back. A volley of twenty muskets blew off his head at once. These twenty men knelt and began to reload. The second rank readied.

"Who ordered live ammunition?" Yabu demanded.

"I did. I, Yoshi Naga-noh-Toranaga!"

"Naga-san! I order you to let Nebara Jozen and his men go free. You are ordered to your quarters until I can consult Lord Toranaga about your insubordination!"

"Of course you will inform Lord Toranaga and karma is karma. But I regret, Lord Yabu, that first this man must die. All of them must die. Today!"

Jozen shrieked, "I'm protected by the Regents! You'll gain nothing by killing me."

"I regain my honor, *neh?*" Naga said. "I repay your sneers at my father and your insults to me. But you would have had to die anyway. *Neh?* I could not have been more clear last night. Now you've seen an attack. I cannot risk Ishido learning all this"—his hand waved at the battlefield—"this horror!"

"He already knows!" Jozen blurted out, blessing his foresight of the previous evening. "He knows already! I sent a message by pigeon secretly at dawn! You gain nothing by killing me, Naga-san!"

Naga motioned to one of his men, an old samurai, who came forward and threw the strangled pigeon at Jozen's feet. Then a man's severed head was also cast upon the ground—the head of the samurai, Masumoto, sent yesterday by Jozen with the scroll. The eyes were still open, the lips drawn back in a hate-filled grimace. The head began to roll. It tumbled through the ranks until it came to rest against a rock.

A moan broke from Jozen's lips. Naga and all his men laughed. Even Yabu smiled. Another of Jozen's samurai leaped for Naga. Twenty muskets blasted him, and the man next to him, who had not moved, also fell in agony, mortally wounded.

The laughter ceased.

Omi said, "Shall I order my men to attack, Sire?" It had been so easy to maneuver Naga.

Yabu wiped the rain off his face. "No, that would achieve nothing. Jozen-san and his men are already dead, whatever I do. That's his *karma*, as Naga-san has his. Naga-san!" he called out. "For the last time, I order you to let them all go!"

"Please excuse me but I must refuse."

"Very well. When it is finished, report to me."

"Yes. There should be an official witness, Yabu-sama. For Lord Toranaga and for Lord Ishido."

"Omi-san, you will stay. You will sign the death certification and make out the dispatch. Naga-san and I will countersign it."

Naga pointed at Blackthorne. "Let him stay too. Also as witness. He's responsible for their deaths. He should witness them."

"Anjin-san, go up there! To Naga-san! Do you understand?"

"Yes, Yabu-san. I understand, but why, please?"

"To be a witness."

"Sorry, don't understand."

"Mariko-san, explain 'witness' to him, that he's to witness what's going to happen—then you follow me." Hiding his vast satisfaction, Yabu turned and left.

Jozen shrieked, "Yabu-sama! Please! Yabuuuuu-samaaaa!"

* * *

Blackthorne watched. When it was finished he went home. There was silence in his house and a pall over the village. A bath did not make him feel clean. Saké did not take away the foulness from his mouth. Incense did not unclog the stench from his nostrils.

Later Yabu sent for him. The attack was dissected, moment by moment. Omi and Naga were there with Mariko—Naga as always cold, listening, rarely commenting, still second-in-command. None of them seemed touched by what had happened.

They worked till after sunset. Yabu ordered the tempo of training stepped up. A second five hundred was to be formed at once. In one week another.

Blackthorne walked home alone, and ate alone, beset by his ghastly discovery: *that they had no sense of sin, they were all conscienceless—even Mariko.*

That night he couldn't sleep. He left the house, the wind tugging at him. Gusts were frothing the waves. A stronger squall sent debris clattering against a village hovel. Dogs howled at the sky and foraged. The rice-thatched roofs moved like living things. Shutters were banging and men and women, silent wraiths, fought them closed and barred them. The tide came in heavily. All the fishing boats had been hauled to safety much farther up the beach than usual. Everything was battened down.

He walked the shore then returned to his house, leaning against the press of the wind. He had met no one. Rain squalled and he was soon drenched.

Fujiko waited for him on the veranda, the wind ripping at her, guttering the shielded oil lamp. Everyone was awake. Servants carried valuables to the squat adobe and stone storage building in the back of the garden.

The gale was not menacing yet.

A roof tile twisted loose as the wind squeezed under an eave and the whole roof shuddered. The tile fell and shattered loudly. Servants hurried about, some readying buckets of water, others trying to repair the roof. The old gardener, Ueki-ya, helped by children, was lashing the tender bushes and trees to bamboo stakes.

Another gust rocked the house.

"It's going to blow down, Mariko-san."

She said nothing, the wind clawing at her and Fujiko, wind tears in the corners of their eyes. He looked at the village. Now debris was blowing everywhere. Then the wind poured through a rip in the paper shoji of one dwelling and the whole wall vanished, leaving only a latticed skeleton. The opposite wall crumbled and the roof collapsed.

Blackthorne turned helplessly as the shoji of his room blew out. That wall vanished and so did the opposite one. Soon all the walls were in shreds. He could see throughout the house. But the roof supports held and the tiled roof did not shift. Bedding and lanterns and mats skittered away, servants chasing them.

The storm demolished the walls of all the houses in the village. And some dwellings were obliterated completely. No one was badly hurt. At dawn the wind subsided and men and women began to rebuild their homes.

By noon the walls of Blackthorne's house were remade and half the village was back to normal. The light lattice walls required little work to put up once more, only wooden pegs and lashings for joints that were always morticed and carpentered with great skill. Tiled and thatched roofs were more difficult but he saw that people helped each other, smiling and quick and very practiced. Mura hurried through the village, advising, guiding, chivying, and supervising. He came up the hill to inspect progress.

"Mura, you made . . ." Blackthorne sought the words. "You make it look easy."

"Ah, thank you, Anjin-san. Yes, thank you, but we were fortunate there were no fires."

"You fires oftens?"

"So sorry, 'Do you have fires often?' "

"Do you have fires often?" Blackthorne repeated.

"Yes. But I'd ordered the village prepared. *Prepared,* you understand?"

"Yes."

"When these storms come—" Mura stiffened and glanced over Blackthorne's shoulder. His bow was low.

Omi was approaching in his bouncing easy stride, his friendly eyes only on Blackthorne, as though Mura did not exist. "Morning, Anjin-san," he said.

"Morning, Omi-san. Your house is good?"

"All right. Thank you." Omi looked at Mura and said brusquely, "The men should be fishing, or working the fields. The women too. Yabu-sama wants his taxes. Are you trying to shame me in front of him with laziness?"

"No, Omi-sama. Please excuse me. I will see to it at once."

"It shouldn't be necessary to tell you. I won't tell you next time."

"I apologize for my stupidity." Mura hurried away.

"You're all right today," Omi said to Blackthorne. "No troubles in the night?"

"Good today, thank you. And you?"

Omi spoke at length. Blackthorne did not catch all of it, as he had not understood all of what Omi had said to Mura, only a few words here, a few there.

"So sorry. I don't understand."

"Enjoy? How did you like yesterday? The attack? The 'pretend' battle?"

"Ah, I understand. Yes, I think good."

"And the witnessing?"

"Please?"

"Witnessing! The *ronin* Nebara Jozen and his men?" Omi imitated the bayonet lunge with a laugh. "You witnessed their deaths. Deaths! You understand?"

"Ah, yes. The truth, Omi-san, not like killings."

"*Karma,* Anjin-san."

"*Karma.* Today trainings?"

"Yes. But Yabu-sama wants to talk only. Later. Understand, Anjin-san? Talk only, later," Omi repeated patiently.

"Talk only. Understand."

"You're beginning to speak our language very well. Yes. Very well."

"Thank you. Difficult. Small time."

"Yes. But you're a good man and you try very hard. That's important. We'll get you time, Anjin-san, don't worry—I'll help you." Omi could see that most of what he was saying was lost, but he didn't mind, so long as the Anjin-san got the gist. "I want to be your friend," he said, then repeated it very clearly. "Do you understand?"

"Friend? I understand 'friend.'"

Omi pointed at himself, then at Blackthorne. "I want to be your friend."

"Ah! Thank you. Honored."

Omi smiled again and bowed, equal to equal, and walked away.

"Friends with him?" Blackthorne muttered. "Has he forgotten? I haven't."

"Ah, Anjin-san," Fujiko said, hurrying up to him. "Would you like to eat? Yabu-sama is going to send for you soon."

"Yes, thank you. Many breakings?" he asked, pointing at the house.

"Excuse me, so sorry, but you should say, 'Was there much breakage?'"

"Was there much breakage?"

"No real damage, Anjin-san."

"Good. No hurtings?"

"Excuse me, so sorry, you should say, 'No one was hurt?'"

"Thank you. No one was hurt?"

"No, Anjin-san. No one was hurt."

Suddenly Blackthorne was sick of being continually corrected, so he terminated the conversation with an order. "I'm hunger. Food!"

"Yes, immediately. So sorry, but you should say, 'I'm *hungry.*' A person has hunger, but is hungry." She waited until he had said it correctly, then went away.

He sat on the veranda and watched Ueki-ya, the old gardener, tidying up the damage and the scattered leaves. He could see women and children repairing the village, and boats going to sea through the chop. Other villagers trudged off to the fields, the wind abating now. I wonder what taxes they have to pay, he asked himself. I'd hate to be a peasant here. Not only here—anywhere.

At first light he had been distressed by the apparent devastation of the village. "That storm'd hardly touch an English house," he had said to Mariko. "Oh, it was a gale all right, but not a bad one. Why don't you build out of stone or bricks?"

"Because of the earthquakes, Anjin-san. Any stone building would, of course, split and collapse and probably hurt or kill the inhabitants. With our style of building there's little damage. You'll see how quickly everything's put back together."

"Yes, but you've fire hazards. And what happens when the Great Winds come? The *tai-funs?*"

"It is very bad then."

She had explained about the *tai-funs* and their seasons—from June until September, sometimes earlier, sometimes later. And about the other natural catastrophes.

A few days ago there had been another tremor. It was slight. A kettle had fallen off the brazier and overturned it. Fortunately the coals had been smothered. One house in the village had caught fire but the fire did not spread. Blackthorne had never seen such efficient fire fighting. Apart from that, no one in the village had paid much attention. They had merely laughed and gone on with their lives.

"Why do people laugh?"

"We consider it very shameful and impolite to show strong feelings, particularly fear, so we hide them with a laugh or a smile. Of course we're all afraid, though we must never show it."

Some of you show it, Blackthorne thought.

Nebara Jozen had shown it. He had died badly, weeping with fear, begging for mercy, the killing slow and cruel. He had been allowed to run, then bayoneted carefully amidst laughter, then forced to run again, and hamstrung. Then he had been allowed to crawl away, then gutted slowly while he screamed, his blood dribbling with the phlegm, then left to die.

Next Naga had turned his attention to the other samurai. At once three of Jozen's men knelt and bared their bellies and put their short knives in front of them to commit ritual seppuku. Three of their comrades stood behind them as their seconds, long swords out and raised, two-handed, all of them now unmolested by Naga and his men. As the samurai who knelt reached out for their knives, they stretched their necks and the three swords flashed down and decapitated them with the single blow. Teeth chattered in the fallen heads, then were still. Flies swarmed.

Then two samurai knelt, the last man standing ready as second. The first of those kneeling was decapitated in the manner of his comrades as he reached for the knife. The other said, "No. I, Hirasaki Kenko, I know how to die—how a samurai should die."

Kenko was a lithe young man, perfumed and almost pretty, pale-skinned, his hair well oiled and very neat. He picked up his knife reverently and partially wrapped the blade with his sash to improve his grip.

"I protest Nebara Jozen-san's death and those of his men," he said firmly, bowing to Naga. He took a last look at the sky and gave his second a last reassuring smile. "Sayonara, Tadeo." Then he slid the knife deep into the left side of his stomach. He ripped it full across with both hands and took it out and plunged it deep again, just above his groin, and jerked it up in silence. His lacerated bowels spilled into his lap and as his hideously contorted, agonized face pitched forward, his second brought the sword down in a single slashing arc.

Naga personally picked up this head by the hair knot and wiped off the dirt and closed the eyes. Then he told his men to see that the head was washed, wrapped, and sent to Ishido with full honors, with a complete report on Hirasaki Kenko's bravery.

The last samurai knelt. There was no one left to second him. He too was young. His fingers trembled and fear consumed him. Twice he had done his duty to his comrades, twice cut cleanly, honorably, saving them the trial of pain and the shame of fear. And once he had waited for his dearest friend to die as a samurai should die, self-immolated in pride-filled silence, then again cut cleanly with perfect skill. He had never killed before.

His eyes focused on his own knife. He bared his stomach and prayed for his lover's courage. Tears were gathering but he willed his face into a frozen, smiling mask. He unwound his sash and partially wrapped the blade. Then, because the youth had done his duty well, Naga signaled to his lieutenant.

This samurai came forward and bowed, introducing himself formally. "Osaragi Nampo, Captain of Lord Toranaga's Ninth Legion. I would be honored to act as your second."

"Ikomo Tadeo, First Officer, vassal of Lord Ishido," the youth replied. "Thank you. I would be honored to accept you as my second."

His death was quick, painless, and honorable.

The heads were collected. Later Jozen shrieked into life again. His frantic hands tried helplessly to remake his belly.

They left him to the dogs that had come up from the village.

CHAPTER 34

A T the Hour of the Horse, eleven o'clock in the morning, ten days
after the death of Jozen and all his men, a convoy of three
galleys rounded the headland at Anjiro. They were crammed
with troops. Toranaga came ashore. Beside him was Buntaro.

"First I wish to see an attack exercise, Yabu-san, with the original
five hundred," Toranaga said. "At once."

"Could it be tomorrow? That would give me time to prepare," Yabu
said affably, but inwardly he was furious at the suddenness of Toranaga's
arrival and incensed with his spies for not forewarning him. He had
had barely enough time to hurry to the shore with a guard of honor.
"You must be tired—"

"I'm not tired, thank you," Toranaga said, intentionally brusque. "I
don't need 'defenders' or an elaborate setting or screams or pretended
deaths. You forget, old friend, I've acted in enough Nōh plays and
staged enough to be able to use my imagination. I'm not a *ronin*-peasant!
Please order it mounted at once."

They were on the beach beside the wharf. Toranaga was surrounded
by elite guards, and more were pouring off the moored galley. Another
thousand heavily armed samurai were crammed into the two galleys
that waited just offshore. It was a warm day, the sky cloudless, with a
light surf and heat haze on the horizon.

"Igurashi, see to it!" Yabu bottled his rage. Since the first message
he had sent concerning Jozen's arrival eleven days ago, there had been
the merest trickle of noncommittal reports from Yedo from his own
espionage network, and nothing but sporadic and infuriatingly incon-
clusive replies from Toranaga to his ever more urgent signals: "Your
message received and under serious study." "Shocked by your news
about my son. Please wait for further instructions." Then, four days
ago: "Those responsible for Jozen's death will be punished. They are
to remain at their posts but to continue under arrest until I can consult
with Lord Ishido." And yesterday, the bombshell: "Today I received
the new Council of Regents' formal invitation to the Osaka Flower-
Viewing Ceremony. When do you plan to leave? Advise immediately."

"Surely that doesn't mean Toranaga's actually going?" Yabu had
asked, baffled.

"He's forcing you to commit yourself," Igurashi had replied. "Whatever you say traps you."

"I agree," Omi had said.

"Why aren't we getting news from Yedo? What's happened to our spies?"

"It's almost as though Toranaga's put a blanket over the whole Kwanto," Omi had told him. "Perhaps he knows who your spies are!"

"Today's the tenth day, Sire," Igurashi had reminded Yabu. "Everything's ready for your departure to Osaka. Do you want to leave or not?"

Now, here on the beach, Yabu blessed his guardian *kami* who had persuaded him to accept Omi's advice to stay until the last possible day, three days hence.

"About your final message, Toranaga-sama, the one that arrived yesterday," he said. "You're surely not going to Osaka?"

"Are you?"

"I acknowledge you as leader. Of course, I've been waiting for your decision."

"My decision is easy, Yabu-sama. But yours is hard. If you go, the Regents will certainly chop you for destroying Jozen and his men. And Ishido is really very angry—and rightly so. *Neh?*"

"I didn't do it, Lord Toranaga. Jozen's destruction—however merited —was against my orders."

"It was just as well Naga-san did it, *neh?* Otherwise you'd certainly have had to do it yourself. I'll discuss Naga-san later, but come along, we'll talk as we walk up to the training ground. No need to waste time." Toranaga set off at his brisk pace, his guards following closely. "Yes, you really are in a dilemma, old friend. If you go, you lose your head, you lose Izu, and of course your whole Kasigi family goes to the execution ground. If you stay, the Council will order the same thing." He looked across at him. "Perhaps you should do what you suggested I do the last time I was in Anjiro. I'll be happy to be your second. Perhaps your head will ease Ishido's ill humor when I meet him."

"My head's of no value to Ishido."

"I don't agree."

Buntaro intercepted them. "Excuse me, Sire. Where do you want the men billeted?"

"On the plateau. Make your permanent camp there. Two hundred guards will stay with me at the fortress. When you've made the arrangements join me. I'll want you to see the training exercise." Buntaro hurried off.

"Permanent camp? You're staying here?" Yabu asked.

"No, only my men. If the attack's as good as I hear, we'll be forming nine assault battalions of five hundred samurai each."

"What?"

"Yes. I've brought another thousand selected samurai for you now. You'll provide the other thousand."

"But there aren't enough guns and the train—"

"So sorry, you're wrong. I've brought a thousand muskets and plenty of powder and shot. The rest will arrive within a week with another thousand men."

"We'll have nine assault battalions?"

"Yes. They'll be one regiment. Buntaro will command."

"Perhaps it would be better if I did that. He'll be—"

"Oh, but you forget the Council meets in a few days. How can you command a regiment if you're going to Osaka? Haven't you prepared to leave?"

Yabu stopped. "We're allies. We agreed you're the leader and we pissed on the bargain. I've kept it, and I'm keeping it. Now I ask, what's your plan? Do we war or don't we?"

"No one's declared war on me. Yet."

Yabu craved to unsheath the Yoshitomo blade and splash Toranaga's blood on the dirt, once and for all, whatever the cost. He could feel the breath of the Toranaga guards all around him but he was beyond caring now. "Isn't the Council your death knell too? You said that yourself. Once they've met, you have to obey. *Neh?*"

"Of course." Toranaga waved his guards back, leaning easily on his sword, his stocky legs wide and firm.

"Then what's your decision? What do you propose?"

"First to see an attack."

"Then?"

"Then to go hunting."

"Are you going to Osaka?"

"Of course."

"When?"

"When it pleases me."

"You mean, *not* when it pleases Ishido."

"I mean when it pleases me."

"We'll be isolated," Yabu said. "We can't fight all Japan, even with an assault regiment, and we can't possibly train it in ten days."

"Yes."

"Then what's the plan?"

"What exactly happened with Jozen and Naga-san?"

Yabu told it truly, omitting only the fact that Naga had been manipulated by Omi.

"And my barbarian? How's the Anjin-san behaving?"

"Good. Very good." Yabu told him about the attempted seppuku on the first night, and how he had neatly bent the Anjin-san to their mutual advantage.

"That was clever," Toranaga said slowly. "I'd never have guessed he'd try seppuku. Interesting."

"It was fortunate I told Omi to be ready."

"Yes."

Impatiently Yabu waited for more but Toranaga remained silent. "This news I sent about Lord Ito becoming a Regent," Yabu said at last. "Did you know about it before I sent word?"

Toranaga did not answer for a moment. "I'd heard rumors. Lord Ito's a perfect choice for Ishido. The poor fool's always enjoyed being shafted while he has his nose up another man's anus. They'll make good bedfellows."

"His vote will destroy you, even so."

"Providing there's a Council."

"Ah, then you do have a plan?"

"I always have a plan—or plans—didn't you know? But you, what's your plan, Ally? If you want to leave, leave. If you want to stay, stay. Choose!" He walked on.

Mariko handed Toranaga a scroll of closely written characters.

"Is this everything?" he asked.

"Yes, Sire," she replied, not liking the stuffiness of the cabin or being aboard the galley again, even moored at the dock. "A lot of what's in the War Manual will be repeated, but I made notes every night and wrote down everything as it happened—or tried to. It's almost like a diary of what was said and happened since you left."

"Good. Has anyone else read it?"

"Not to my knowledge." She used her fan to cool herself. "The Anjin-san's consort and servants have seen me writing it, but I've kept it locked away."

"What are your conclusions?"

Mariko hesitated. She glanced at the cabin door and at the closed porthole.

Toranaga said, "Only my men are aboard and no one's below decks. Except us."

"Yes, Sire. I just remembered the Anjin-san saying there are no secrets aboard a ship. So sorry." She thought a moment, then said confidently, "The Musket Regiment will win one battle. Barbarians could destroy us if they landed in force with guns and cannon. You must have a barbarian navy. Thus far, the Anjin-san's knowledge has been enormously valuable to you, so much so it should be kept secret, only for your ears. In the wrong hands his knowledge would be lethal to you."

"Who shares his knowledge now?"

"Yabu-san knows much but Omi-san more—he's the most intuitive. Igurashi-san, Naga-san, and the troops—the troops of course understand the strategy, not the finer details and none of the Anjin-san's political and general knowledge. Me, more than any. I've written down everything he's said, asked, or commented on, Sire. As best I can. Of course he has only told us about certain things, but his range is vast and his memory near perfect. With patience he can provide you with an accurate picture of the world, its customs and dangers. *If* he's telling the truth."

"Is he?"

"I believe so."

"What's your opinion of Yabu?"

"Yabu-san's a violent man with no scruples whatsoever. He honors nothing but his own interests. Duty, loyalty, tradition, mean nothing to him. His mind has flashes of great cunning, even brilliance. He's equally dangerous as ally or enemy."

"All commendable virtues. What's to be said against him?"

"A bad administrator. His peasants would revolt if they had weapons."

"Why?"

"Extortionate taxes. Illegal taxes. He takes seventy-five parts from every hundred of all rice, fish, and produce. He's begun a head tax, land tax, boat tax—every sale, every barrel of saké, everything's taxed in Izu."

"Perhaps I should employ him or his quartermaster for the Kwanto. Well, what he does here's his own business, his peasants'll never get weapons so we've nothing to worry about. I could still use this as a base if need be."

"But Sire, sixty parts is the legal limit."

"It was the legal limit. The Taikō made it legal but he's dead. What else about Yabu?"

"He eats little, his health appears good, but Suwo, the masseur, thinks he has kidney trouble. He has some curious habits."

"What?"

She told him about the Night of the Screams.

"Who told you about that?"

"Suwo. Also Omi-san's wife and mother."

"Yabu's father used to boil his enemies too. Waste of time. But I can understand his need to do it occasionally. His nephew, Omi?"

"Very shrewd. Very wise. Completely loyal to his uncle. A very capable, impressive vassal."

"Omi's family?"

"His mother is—is suitably firm with Midori, his wife. The wife is samurai, gentle, strong, and very good. All are loyal vassals of Yabu-san. Presently Omi-san has no consorts though Kiku, the most famous courtesan in Izu, is almost like a consort. If he could buy her contract I think he'd bring her into his house."

"Would he help me against Yabu if I wanted him to?"

She pondered that. Then shook her head. "No, Sire. I don't think so. I think he's his uncle's vassal."

"Naga?"

"As good a samurai as a man could be. He saw at once the danger of Jozen-san and his men to you, and locked things up until you could be consulted. As much as he detests the Musket Battalion he trains the companies hard to make them perfect."

"I think he was very stupid—to be Yabu's puppet."

She adjusted a fold in her kimono, saying nothing.

Toranaga fanned himself. "Now the Anjin-san?"

She had been expecting this question and now that it had come, all the clever observations she was going to make vanished from her head.

"Well?"

"You must judge from the scroll, Sire. In certain areas he's impossible to explain. Of course, his training and heritage have nothing in common with ours. He's very complex and beyond our—beyond *my* understanding. He used to be very open. But since his attempted seppuku, he's changed. He's more secretive." She told him what Omi had said and had done on that first night. And about Yabu's promise.

"Ah, Omi stopped him—not Yabu-san?"

"Yes."

"And Yabu followed Omi's advice?"

"Exactly, Sire."

"So Omi's the adviser. Interesting. But surely the Anjin-san doesn't expect Yabu to keep the promise?"

"Yes, absolutely."

Toranaga laughed. "How childish!"

"Christian 'conscience' is deeply set in him, so sorry. He cannot avoid his *karma*, one part of which is that he's totally to be governed through this hatred of a death, or deaths, of what he calls 'innocents.' Even Jozen's death affected him deeply. For many nights his sleep was disturbed and for days he hardly talked to anyone."

"Would this 'conscience' apply to all barbarians?"

"No, though it should to all Christian barbarians."

"Will he lose this 'conscience'?"

"I don't think so. But he's as defenseless as a doll until he does."

"His consort?"

She told him everything.

"Good." He was pleased that his choice of Fujiko and his plan had worked so well. "Very good. She did very well over the guns. What about his habits?"

"Mostly normal, except for an astounding embarrassment over pillow matters and a curious reluctance to discuss the most normal functions." She also described his unusual need for solitude, and his abominable taste in food. "In most other things he's attentive, reasonable, sharp, an adept pupil, and very curious about us and our customs. It's all in my report, but briefly, I've explained something of our way of life, a little of us and our history, about the Taikō and the problems besetting our Realm now."

"Ah, about the Heir?"

"Yes, Sire. Was that wrong?"

"No. You were told to educate him. How's his Japanese?"

"Very good, considering. In time he'll speak our language quite well. He's a good pupil, Sire."

"Pillowing?"

"One of the maids," she said at once.

"He chose her?"

"His consort sent her to him."

"And?"

"It was mutually satisfactory, I understand."

"Ah! Then she had no difficulty."

"No, Sire."

"But he's in proportion?"

"The girl said, 'Oh very yes.' 'Lavish' was the word she used."

"Excellent. At least in that his *karma's* good. That's the trouble with a lot of men—Yabu for one, Kiyama for another. Small shafts. Unfortunate to be born with a small shaft. Very. Yes." He glanced at the scroll, then closed his fan with a snap. "And you, Mariko-san? What about you?"

"Good, thank you, Sire. I'm very pleased to see you looking so well. May I offer you congratulations on the birth of your grandson."

"Thank you, yes. Yes, I'm pleased. The boy's well formed and appears healthy."

"And the Lady Genjiko?"

Toranaga grunted. "She's as strong as always. Yes." He pursed his lips, brooding for a moment. "Perhaps you could recommend a foster mother for the child." It was custom for sons of important samurai to have foster mothers so that the natural mother could attend to her husband and to the running of his house, leaving the foster mother to concentrate on the child's upbringing, making him strong and a credit to the parents. "I'm afraid it won't be easy to find the right person. The Lady Genjiko's not the easiest mistress to work for, *neh?*"

"I'm sure you'll find the perfect person, Sire. I'll certainly give it some thought," Mariko replied, knowing that to offer such advice would be foolish, for no woman born could possibly satisfy both Toranaga and his daughter-in-law.

"Thank you. But you, Mariko-san, what about you?"

"Good, Sire, thank you."

"And your Christian conscience?"

"There's no conflict, Sire. None. I've done everything you would wish. Truly."

"Have any priests been here?"

"No, Sire."

"You have need of one?"

"It would be good to confess and take the Sacrament and be blessed. Yes, truthfully, I would like that—to confess the things permitted and to be blessed."

Toranaga studied her closely. Her eyes were guileless. "You've done well, Mariko-san. Please continue as before."

"Yes, Sire, thank you. One thing—the Anjin-san needs a grammar book and dictionary badly."

"I've sent to Tsukku-san for them." He noticed her frown. "You don't think he'll send them?"

"He would obey, of course. Perhaps not with the speed you'd like."

"I'll soon know that." Toranaga added ominously, "He has only thirteen days left."

Mariko was startled. "Sire?" she asked, not understanding.

"Thirteen? Ah," Toranaga said nonchalantly, covering his momentary lapse, "when we were aboard the Portuguese ship he asked permission to visit Yedo. I agreed, providing it was within forty days. There are thirteen left. Wasn't forty days the time this *bonze*, this prophet, this Moses spent on the mountain collecting the commands of 'God' that were etched in stone?"

"Yes, Sire."

"Do you believe that happened?"

"Yes. But I don't understand how or why."

"A waste of time discussing 'God-things.' *Neh?*"

"If you seek facts, yes, Sire."

"While you were waiting for this dictionary, have you tried to make one?"

"Yes, Toranaga-sama. I'm afraid it's not very good. Unfortunately there seems to be so little time, so many problems. Here—everywhere," she added pointedly.

He nodded agreement, knowing that she would dearly like to ask many things: about the new Council and Lord Ito's appointment and Naga's sentence and if war would be immediate. "We're fortunate to have your husband back with us, *neh?*"

Her fan stopped. "I never thought he'd escape alive. Never. I've said a prayer and burnt incense to his memory daily." Buntaro had told her this morning how another contingent of Toranaga samurai had covered his retreat from the beach and he had made the outskirts of Osaka without trouble. Then, with fifty picked men and spare horses, disguised as bandits, he hastily took to the hills and lesser paths in a headlong dash for Yedo. Twice his pursuers caught up with him but there were not enough of the enemy to contain him and he fought his way through. Once he was ambushed and lost all but four men, and escaped again and went deeper into the forest, traveling by night, sleeping during the day. Berries and spring water, a little rice snatched from lonely farmhouses, then galloping on again, hunters always at his heels. It had taken him twenty days to reach Yedo. Two men had survived with him.

"It was almost a miracle," she said. "I thought I was possessed by a *kami* when I saw him here beside you on the beach."

"He's clever. Very strong and very clever."

"May I ask what news of Lord Hiro-matsu, Sire? And Osaka? Lady Kiritsubo and the Lady Sazuko?"

Noncommittal, Toranaga informed her that Hiro-matsu had arrived back at Yedo the day before he had left, though his ladies had decided to stay at Osaka, the Lady Sazuko's health being the reason for their delay. There was no need to elaborate. Both he and Mariko knew that this was merely a face-saving formula and that General Ishido would never allow two such valuable hostages to leave now that Toranaga was out of his grasp.

"*Shigata ga nai*," he said. "*Karma, neh?*" There's nothing that can be done. That's *karma*, isn't it?

"Yes."

He picked up the scroll. "Now I must read this. Thank you, Mariko-san. You've done very well. Please bring the Anjin-san to the fortress at dawn."

"Sire, now that my Master is here, I will have—"

"Your husband has already agreed that while I'm here you're to remain where you are and act as interpreter, your prime duty being to the Anjin-san for the next few days."

"But Sire, I must set up house for my Lord. He'll need servants and a house."

"That will be a waste of money, time, and effort at the moment. He'll stay with the troops—or at the Anjin-san's house—whichever pleases him." He noticed a flash of irritation. *"Nan ja?"*

"My place should be with my Master. To serve him."

"Your place is where I want it to be. *Neh?"*

"Yes, please excuse me. Of course."

"Of course."

She left.

He read the scroll carefully. And the War Manual. Then he reread parts of the scroll. He put them both away safely and posted guards on the cabin and went aloft.

It was dawn. The day promised warmth and overcast. He canceled the meeting with the Anjin-san, as he had intended, and rode to the plateau with a hundred guards. There he collected his falconers and three hawks and hunted for twenty *ri.* By noon he had bagged three pheasants, two large woodcock, a hare, and a brace of quail. He sent one pheasant and the hare to the Anjin-san, the rest to the fortress. Some of his samurai were not Buddhists and he was tolerant of their eating habits. For himself he ate a little cold rice with fish paste, some pickled seaweed with slivers of ginger. Then he curled up on the ground and slept.

Now it was late afternoon and Blackthorne was in the kitchen, whistling merrily. Around him were the chief cook, assistant cook, the vegetable preparer, fish preparer, and their assistants, all smiling but inwardly mortified because their master was here in their kitchen with their mistress, also because she had told them he was going to honor them by showing them how to prepare and cook in his style. And last because of the hare.

He had already hung the pheasant under the eaves of an outhouse with careful instructions that no one, *no one* was to touch it but him.

"Do they understand, Fujiko-san? No touching but me?" he asked with mock gravity.

"Oh, yes, Anjin-san. They all understand. So sorry, excuse me, but you should say 'No one's to touch it except me.'"

"Now," he was saying to no one in particular, "the gentle art of cooking. Lesson One."

"*Dozo gomen nasai?*" Fujiko asked.

"*Miru!*" Watch.

Feeling young again—for one of his first chores had been to clean the game he and his brother poached at such huge risk from the estates around Chatham—he selected a long, curving knife. The *sushi* chef blanched. This was his favorite knife, with an especially honed edge to ensure that the slivers of raw fish were always sliced to perfection. All the staff knew this and they sucked in their breaths, smiling even more to hide their embarrassment for him, as he increased the size of his smile to hide his own shame.

Blackthorne slit the hare's belly and neatly turned out the stomach sack and entrails. One of the younger maids heaved and fled silently. Fujiko resolved to fine her a month's wages, wishing at the same time that she too could be a peasant and so flee with honor.

They watched, glazed, as he cut off the paws and feet, then pushed the forelegs back into the pelt, easing the skin off the legs. He did the same with the back legs and worked the pelt around to bring the naked back legs out through the belly slit, and then, with a deft jerk, he pulled the pelt over the head like a discarded winter coat. He lay the almost skinned animal on the chopping table and decapitated it, leaving the head with its staring, pathetic eyes still attached to the pelt. He turned the pelt right side out again, and put it aside. A sigh went through the kitchen. He did not hear it as he concentrated on slicing off the legs into joints and quartering the carcass. Another maid fled unnoticed.

"Now I want a pot," Blackthorne said with a hearty grin.

No one answered him. They just stared with the same fixed smiles. He saw a large iron cauldron. It was spotless. He picked it up with bloody hands and filled it with water from a wooden container, then hung the pot over the brazier, which was set into the earthen floor in a pit surrounded by stone. He added the pieces of meat.

"Now some vegetables and spices," he said.

"*Dozo?*" Fujiko asked throatily.

He did not know the Japanese words so he looked around. There were some carrots, and some roots that looked like turnips in a wooden basket. These he cleaned and cut up and added to the soup with salt and some of the dark soya sauce.

"We should have some onions and garlic and port wine."

"*Dozo?*" Fujiko asked again helplessly.

"*Kotaba shirimasen.*" I don't know the words.

She did not correct him, just picked up a spoon and offered it. He shook his head. "Saké," he ordered. The assistant cook jerked into life and gave him the small wooden barrel.

"*Domo.*" Blackthorne poured in a cupful, then added another for good measure. He would have drunk some from the barrel but he knew that it would be bad manners, to drink it cold and without ceremony, and certainly not here in the kitchen.

"Christ Jesus, I'd love a beer," he said.

"*Dozo goziemashita,* Anjin-san?"

"*Kotaba shirimasen*—but this stew's going to be great. *Ichi-ban, neh?*" He pointed at the hissing pot.

"*Hai,*" she said without conviction.

"*Okuru tsukai arigato* Toranaga-sama," Blackthorne said. Send a messenger to thank Lord Toranaga. No one corrected the bad Japanese.

"*Hai.*" Once outside Fujiko rushed for the privvy, the little hut that stood in solitary splendor near the front door in the garden. She was very sick.

"Are you all right, Mistress?" her maid, Nigatsu, said. She was middle-aged, roly-poly, and had looked after Fujiko all her life.

"Go away! But first bring me some cha. No—you'll have to go into the kitchen . . . oh oh oh!"

"I have cha here, Mistress. We thought you'd need some so we boiled the water on another brazier. Here!"

"Oh, you're so clever!" Fujiko pinched Nigatsu's round cheek affectionately as another maid came to fan her. She wiped her mouth on the paper towel and sat gratefully on cushions on the veranda. "Oh, that's better!" And it was better in the open air, in the shade, the good afternoon sun casting dark shadows and butterflies foraging, the sea far below, calm and iridescent.

"What's going on, Mistress? We didn't dare even to peek."

"Never mind. The Master's—the Master's—never mind. His customs are weird but that's our *karma.*"

She glanced away as her chief cook came unctuously through the garden and her heart sank a little more. He bowed formally, a taut, thin little man with large feet and very buck teeth. Before he could utter a word Fujiko said through a flat smile, "Order new knives from the village. A new rice-cooking pot. A new chopping board, new water containers—all utensils you think necessary. Those that the Master used are to be kept for his private purposes. You will set aside a special area, construct another kitchen if you wish, where the Master can cook if he so desires—until you are proficient."

"Thank you, Fujiko-sama," the cook said. "Excuse me for interrupting you, but, so sorry, please excuse me, I know a fine cook in the next village. He's not a Buddhist and he's even been with the army in Korea so he'd know all about the—how to—how to cook for the Master so much better than I."

"When I want another cook I will tell you. When I consider you inept or malingering I will tell you. Until that time you will be chief cook here. You accepted the post for six months," she said.

"Yes, Mistress," the cook said with outward dignity, though quaking inside, for Fujiko-noh-Anjin was no mistress to trifle with. "Please excuse me, but I was engaged to cook. I am proud to cook. But I never accepted to—to be butcher. *Eta* are butchers. Of course we can't have an *eta* here but this other cook isn't a Buddhist like me, my father, his father before him and his before him, Mistress, and they never, never. . . . Please, this new cook will—"

"You will cook here as you've always cooked. I find your cooking excellent, worthy of a master cook in Yedo. I even sent one of your recipes to the Lady Kiritsubo in Osaka."

"Oh? Thank you. You do me too much honor. Which one, Mistress?"

"The tiny, fresh eels and jellyfish and sliced oysters, with just the right touch of soya, that you make so well. Excellent! The best I've ever tasted."

"Oh, thank you, Mistress," he groveled.

"Of course your soups leave much to be desired."

"Oh, so sorry!"

"I'll discuss those with you later. Thank you, cook," she said, experimenting with a dismissal.

The little man stood his ground gamely. "Please excuse me, Mistress, but *oh ko,* with complete humbleness, if the Master—when the Master—"

"When the Master tells you to cook or to butcher or whatever, you will rush to do it. Instantly. As any loyal servant should. Meanwhile, it may take you a great deal of time to become proficient so perhaps you'd better make temporary arrangements with this other cook to visit you on the rare days the Master might wish to eat in his own fashion."

His honor satisfied, the cook smiled and bowed. "Thank you. Please excuse my asking for enlightenment."

"Of course you pay for the substitute cook from your own salary."

When they were alone again, Nigatsu chortled behind her hand. "Oh, Mistress-chan, may I compliment you on your total victory and your wisdom? Chief cook almost broke wind when you said that he was going to have to pay too!"

"Thank you, Nanny-san." Fujiko could smell the hare beginning to cook. What if he asks me to eat it with him, she was thinking, and almost wilted. Even if he doesn't I'll still have to serve it. How can I avoid being sick? You will not be sick, she ordered herself. It's your *karma*. You must have been completely dreadful in your previous life. Yes. But remember everything is fine now. Only five months and six days more. Don't think of that, just think about your Master, who is a brave, strong man, though one with ghastly eating habits . . .

Horses clattered up to the gate. Buntaro dismounted and waved the rest of his men away. Then, accompanied only by his personal guard, he strode through the garden, dusty and sweat-soiled. He carried his huge bow and on his back was his quiver. Fujiko and her maid bowed warmly, hating him. Her uncle was famous for his wild, uncontrollable rages which made him lash out without warning or pick a quarrel with almost anyone. Most of the time only his servants suffered, or his women. "Please come in, Uncle. How kind of you to visit us so soon," Fujiko said.

"Ah, Fujiko-san. Do— What's that stench?"

"My Master's cooking some game Lord Toranaga sent him—he's showing my miserable servants how to cook."

"If he wants to cook, I suppose he can, though . . ." Buntaro wrinkled his nose distastefully. "Yes, a master can do anything in his own house, within the law, unless it disturbs the neighbors."

Legally such a smell could be cause for complaint and it could be very bad to inconvenience neighbors. Inferiors never did anything to disturb their superiors. Otherwise heads would fall. That was why, throughout the land, samurai lived cautiously and courteously near samurai of equal rank if possible, peasants next to peasants, merchants in their own streets, and *eta* isolated outside. Omi was their immediate neighbor. He's superior, she thought. "I hope sincerely no one's disturbed," she told Buntaro uneasily, wondering what new evil he was concocting. "You wanted to see my Master?" She began to get up but he stopped her.

"No, please don't disturb him, I'll wait," he said formally and her heart sank. Buntaro was not known for his manners and politeness from him was very dangerous.

"I apologize for arriving like this without first sending a messenger to request an appointment," he was saying, "but Lord Toranaga told me I might perhaps be allowed to use the bath and have quarters here.

From time to time. Would you ask the Anjin-san later, if he would give his permission?"

"Of course," she said, continuing the usual pattern of etiquette, loathing the idea of having Buntaro in her house. "I'm sure he will be honored, Uncle. May I offer you cha or saké while you wait?"

"Saké, thank you."

Nigatsu hurriedly set a cushion on the veranda and fled for the saké, as much as she would have liked to stay.

Buntaro handed his bow and quiver to his guard, kicked off his dusty sandals, and stomped onto the veranda. He pulled his killing sword out of his sash, sat cross-legged, and laid the sword on his knees.

"Where's my wife? With the Anjin-san?"

"No, Buntaro-sama, so sorry, she was ordered to the fortress where—"

"*Ordered?* By whom? By Kasigi Yabu?"

"Oh, no, by Lord Toranaga, Sire, when he came back from hunting this afternoon."

"Oh, Lord Toranaga?" Buntaro simmered down and scowled across the bay at the fortress. Toranaga's standard flew beside Yabu's.

"Would you like me to send someone for her?"

He shook his head. "There's time enough for her." He exhaled, looked across at his niece, daughter of his youngest sister. "I'm fortunate to have such an accomplished wife, *neh?*"

"Yes, Sire. Yes you are. She's been enormously valuable to interpret the Anjin-san's knowledge."

Buntaro stared at the fortress, then sniffed the wind as the smell of the cooking wafted up again. "It's like being at Nagasaki, or back in Korea. They cook meat all the time there, boil it or roast it. Stink—you've never smelled anything like it. Koreans're animals, like cannibals. The garlic stench even gets into your clothes and hair."

"It must have been terrible."

"The war was good. We could have won easily. And smashed through to China. And civilized both countries." Buntaro flushed and his voice rasped. "But we didn't. We failed and had to come back with our shame because we were betrayed. Betrayed by filthy traitors in high places."

"Yes, that's so sad, but you're right. Very right, Buntaro-sama," she said soothingly, telling the lie easily, knowing no nation on earth could conquer China, and no one could civilize China, which had been civilized since ancient times.

The vein on Buntaro's forehead was throbbing and he was talking almost to himself. "They'll pay. All of them. The traitors. It's only a

matter of waiting beside a river long enough for the bodies of your enemies to float by, *neh?* I'll wait and I'll spit on their heads soon, very soon.
I've promised myself that." He looked at her. "I hate traitors and adul-
terers. And all liars!"

"Yes, I agree. You're so right, Buntaro-sama," she said, chilled,
knowing there was no limit to his ferocity. When Buntaro was sixteen
he had executed his own mother, one of Hiro-matsu's lesser consorts,
for her supposed infidelity while his father, Hiro-matsu, was at war
fighting for the Dictator, Lord Goroda. Then, years later, he had killed
his own eldest son by his first wife for supposed insults and sent her
back to her family where she died by her own hand, unable to bear
the shame. He had done terrible things to his consorts and to Mariko.
And he had quarreled violently with Fujiko's father and had accused
him of cowardice in Korea, discrediting him to the Taikō, who had at
once ordered him to shave his head and become a monk, to die de-
bauched, so soon, eaten up by his own shame.

It took all of Fujiko's will to appear tranquil. "We were so proud to
hear that you had escaped the enemy," she said.

The saké arrived. Buntaro began to drink heavily.

When there had been the correct amount of waiting, Fujiko got up.
"Please excuse me for a moment." She went to the kitchen to warn
Blackthorne, to ask his permission for Buntaro to be quartered in the
house, and to tell him and the servants what had to be done.

"Why here?" Blackthorne asked irritably. "Why to stay here? Is necessary?"

Fujiko apologized and tried to explain that, of course, Buntaro could
not be refused. Blackthorne returned moodily to his cooking and she
came back to Buntaro, her chest aching.

"My Master says he's honored to have you here. His house is your
house."

"What's it like being consort to a barbarian?"

"I would imagine horrible. But to the Anjin-san who is hatamoto and
therefore samurai? I suppose like to other men. This is the first time I've
been consort. I prefer to be a wife. The Anjin-san's like other men,
though yes, some of his ways are very strange."

"Who'd have thought one of our house would be consort to a barbarian—even a hatamoto."

"I had no choice. I merely obeyed Lord Toranaga, and grandfather,
the leader of our clan. It's a woman's place to obey."

"Yes." Buntaro finished his cup of saké and she refilled it. "Obedience's important for a woman. And Mariko-san's obedient, isn't she?"

"Yes, Lord." She looked into his ugly, apelike face. "She's brought

you nothing but honor, Sire. Without the Lady, your wife, Lord Toranaga could never have got the Anjin-san's knowledge."

He smiled crookedly. "I hear you stuck pistols in Omi-san's face."

"I was only doing my duty, Sire."

"Where did you learn to use guns?"

"I had never handled a gun until then. I didn't know if the pistols were
loaded. But I would have pulled the triggers."

Buntaro laughed. "Omi-san thought that too."

She refilled his cup. "I never understood why Omi-san didn't try to
take them away from me. His lord had ordered him to take them, but he
didn't."

"I would have."

"Yes, Uncle. I know. Please excuse me, I would still have pulled the
triggers."

"Yes. But you would have missed!"

"Yes, probably. Since then I've learned how to shoot."

"He taught you?"

"No. One of Lord Naga's officers."

"Why?"

"My father would never allow his daughters to learn sword or spear.
He thought, wisely I believe, we should devote our time to learning
gentler things. But sometimes a woman needs to protect her master and
his house. The pistol's a good weapon for a woman, very good. It requires no strength and little practice. So now I can perhaps be a little
more use to my Master, for I will surely blow any man's head off to protect him, and for the honor of our house."

Buntaro drained his cup. "I was proud when I heard you'd opposed
Omi-san as you did. You were correct. Lord Hiro-matsu will be proud
too."

"Thank you, Uncle. But I was only doing an ordinary duty." She
bowed formally. "My Master asks if you would allow him the honor
of talking with you now, if it pleases you."

He continued the ritual. "Please thank him but first may I bathe? If
it pleases him, I'll see him when my *wife* returns."